The mark of the mage . . .

"Show them your hand," "Wallis said. Mr, Flattery, they mean you no harm, but they will not brook insubordination. These men are powerful, here. You must answer to them. It will prove the easier course, believe me."

But still Tristam held his hand close to his body, the sleeve pulled down, as he always kept it.

"Mr. Flattery. . . ." Wallis said, the warning in his tone compelling.

Tristam leaned toward the flame, reaching out his clenched fist.

The Old Man swung his stick aside as though to be sure it did not touch Tristam, and then moved forward to stare. He nodded to another who took hold of Tristam's elbow, jerking it forward until the naturalist could feel the hot breath of the flames. His shirt was yanked up, revealing the scar. Tristam tried to pull back, but the man was immensely strong.

The others moved forward, their gazes fixed on Tristam's hand. Suddenly one barked a single syllable and they all began to mutter.

Tristam looked down and then closed his eyes, trying desperately to pull his hand back. *The tattoo had reappeared!* It seemed to writhe across his wrist in the inconstant firelight and it *burned,* like a hot lash.

"Sweet Farrelle preserve us," Wallis intoned.

D0180583

SEAN RUSSELL
has written

THE INITIATE BROTHER
GATHERER OF CLOUDS

Moontide and Magic Rise:

WORLD WITHOUT END
SEA WITHOUT A SHORE

Sean Russell

Sea Without a Shore

Book Two of
Moontide and Magic Rise

Owl's song on whispered shores
Where the silvered sea dies
Along the wake of a running moon,
Moontide and magic rise.

DAW BOOKS, INC.
DONALD A. WOLLHEIM, FOUNDER
375 Hudson Street, New York, NY 10014

ELIZABETH R. WOLLHEIM
SHEILA E. GILBERT
PUBLISHERS

Copyright © 1996 by Sean Russell.

All Rights Reserved.

Cover art by Braldt Bralds.

DAW Book Collectors No. 1013.

DAW Books are distributed by Penguin U.S.A.

All characters and events in this book are fictitious.
Any resemblance to persons living or dead is
strictly coincidental.

If you purchase this book without a cover you should be
aware that this book may have been stolen property and reported as "unsold and destroyed" to the publisher. In such
case neither the author nor the publisher has received any
payment for this "stripped book."

First Printing, February 1996
1 2 3 4 5 6 7 8 9

DAW TRADEMARK REGISTERED
U.S. PAT. OFF. AND FOREIGN COUNTRIES
—MARCA REGISTRADA,
HECHO EN U.S.A.

PRINTED IN THE U.S.A.

ACKNOWLEDGMENTS

Sean Stewart actually moved to Texas to avoid reading this one, but my usual readers were up to the task. Thanks to Karen, naturally; Jill, Walter, and Chris at White Dwarf Books. I also want to thank Rose and Brian Klinkenberg for answering all of my botanical and zoological questions not only graciously but promptly!

*For Michael Moravec, Don Deese, and
John Higgenbotham—through thick and thin.*

We will now discuss in a little more detail the Struggle for Existence.

—Charles Darwin
The Origin of Species (1859)

ONE

Tristam lay in his gently swinging hammock listening to the burble and pulse of the ocean passing over the *Swallow*'s hull—like the sounds of the womb, he was sure. He did not open his eyes, but lay sensing the now familiar movement of the ship and exploring his own capacity for health.

Llewellyn's *regis* had stemmed the spread of infection, but the body was slow to replace the blood of which it had been robbed. As a result, the naturalist suffered continual exhaustion, dizziness, and lack of strength and vigor. He also suffered from his desire for the physic: nausea, pain in all of his joints, trembling, and headaches so violent that they could not be described.

And then there were the dreams—nightmares, in fact. Tristam tried not to think of these. He remembered the King describing his own dreams as *devouring wolves,* but this did not begin to describe it. Repeatedly he dreamed of a great battle on a darkened field. It was so strewn with the corpses of the fallen that it filled Tristam with horror.

Tristam felt as though he had been tainted. That letting the *regis* into his blood had changed him irrevocably.

He opened his eyes for a second to find that the open port had let in a small lens of sunlight which swung wildly across his cabin and appeared to be searching with the same frantic desperation that Tristam's body yearned for the *regis* physic. It was worse than a hunger, worse than starving, Tristam was sure. The disk of light flowed across the surfaces of his cabin, back and forth with mad determination.

I would not take it now if it was freely offered, Tristam vowed. *I would not.* He shut his eyes and struggled against the images that tried to form in his mind. The *regis,* he knew, would stop these nightmares, stop the feelings of anxiety and melancholia, restore his vitality and usual optimism. It would do all of these things ... temporarily.

Time, he almost whispered. *Time will restore me, and I will not be in thrall to the seed. Like Llewellyn. ...*

The doctor may have convinced Stern that he needed only the smallest handful of *regis* seed, but Tristam knew better. Unless Llewellyn had a strength of will like no other, there was little chance that the doctor would ever give up the physic willingly. Not after so many months of servitude.

Who else had become enslaved by the physic, Tristam wondered? Benjamin Rawdon's wife, or was that story entirely fabricated? Trevelyan, Tristam was now sure, or at least the baron had once been enslaved. Now he might be free ... and quite mad. Not a comforting thought.

Tristam pressed his eyes closed, feeling ill and fragile. Two weeks he had lain in this state, improving so slowly that it was impossible for him to see a difference day to day. His mind had been affected as well, unable to focus, to follow a train of thought, to draw on his hitherto excellent memory.

And there were other changes that were equally disconcerting. *Of all people, I should never have taken the seed,* Tristam thought. He had begun to realize that he was aware of things that he could not possibly know—or at least there was an illusion of knowledge. Like Trevelyan's habituation to *regis*—it seemed perfectly obvious to him now (how could he have not seen before?). Or Llewellyn's inability to break free of the seed. He knew also that Llewellyn was something else altogether. Knew it as though the man had told him.

Tristam wondered, for the thousandth time, if he were going mad.

With his new insight he saw that even Beacham was not quite what he appeared, as astonishing as that seemed. Only the duchess eluded him. Only the duchess kept her secrets, though he was not sure how. She had some talent of her own, he thought, though she made efforts to hide it. That night at her home she had not let Bertillon suspect. Unlike Tristam who had blundered on like a fool . . . bringing an Entonne marauder after them.

Too much knowledge, Tristam thought. *I can barely hold a thought for two minutes. Can I trust these insights?* But somehow they were undeniable. *Perhaps the delusional always feel this.*

The most frightening realizations had to do with himself. Tristam realized now that to become a mage was not to learn a difficult art—though it was that, too—but more than anything, it was a transformation. A transformation that Tristam had begun; perhaps when he had first touched the leaf of a *regis* plant, but certainly when he drank from the fount at the Farrow Ruin, and then climbed up to look into the volcano. And then he had been led to the Lost City, and the remains of a people who still performed arcane rituals. . . . But for what purpose?

To regain lost power.

This thought seemed to come from no knowledge that Tristam possessed—as though it were spoken into his mind.

But what use had they made of him? That he did not know, nor did he want to. They had been after his blood, just as Trevelyan had warned; that much he knew, and that was enough.

He remembered the endless trek with the ghost boy, who was drawn to Tristam in the same way that Tristam was being drawn along his own particular course. Thoughts of the boy pushed Tristam toward the strange dream state that the *regis* physic engendered.

He opened his eyes quickly, relieved to see the disk of light still searching his cabin. He felt suddenly that he could trap it by opening a drawer in its path and then pushing it quickly closed. Trap it as he had been caught, on this voyage he could not escape.

The effects of the physic were wearing off—not all of them and not all together—but there was a noticeable change.

I may never be entirely free of it, Tristam thought, *but I will be as free as I can. I will regain as much of myself as is possible. I am Tristam. Tristam.*

ॐ ॐ ॐ

"He is recovering as I would expect, Your Grace. There is no reason for concern. The body cannot make so much blood overnight. In a month he will begin to seem himself, and then another few weeks to regain the strength he has lost. Tristam is young and hale. In two months there will be no signs that he was ever ill."

The duchess perched on the sill of the stern window looking at the doctor who sat, leaning on the table. Llewellyn was lying to her—oh, not about Tristam's medical condition; that was no doubt true—but he was lying about other things. It was a difficult situation.

"Tell me, Doctor, why do you think Tristam was treated in this way? You seemed quite certain that his attackers had wanted his blood."

Llewellyn worried the cuff of his shirt for a few seconds, then opened his mouth to speak, apparently thought better of what he was about to say, and finally nodded his head to some inner decision. "I said that only because it was clear from the nature of his injuries. The radial artery had been slit with surgical precision. Whoever did that wanted to take as much blood as possible—or so I assumed. Why? You know as much as I, Your Grace. Tristam . . ." he looked out the stern window, "is the focus for strange occurrences. There is no denying it."

"But why is he such a focus, do you think?"

Llewellyn shrugged. "I don't know. . . ."

The duchess fixed him with her most piercing look. "But I think you do, Doctor Llewellyn. In fact I'm quite sure of it. Roderick would never have sent you otherwise."

Llewellyn turned in his seat as though he would rise and leave—an action he did not quite dare to take. He was in the presence of the Duchess of Morland, who was also his employer. He turned to the duchess, meeting her gaze steadily, something he almost never managed.

"I will tell you this, Your Grace," a bit of resentment coming to the surface, "you will need me to sustain this young man. Perhaps you think that your own knowledge of *regis* and its effects will be enough—but it won't. Without me, Tristam Flattery will not survive what is to come. I beg you remember this when next you consider threatening me with your dear brother." Llewellyn did rise then, stiff with some long contained rage. "Your Grace will excuse me; I have a patient to see." He bowed quickly and went out, leaving the duchess alone with her surprise.

"Well," she said. That, at least, was the truth—or so the doctor believed—there was no doubt of that.

🕏 🕏 🕏

"Come in Doctor," Tristam called out.

Llewellyn pushed his bulk through the narrow door. "And how are you today, Tristam?" Llewellyn asked, his tone professionally solicitous.

"Well enough."

Llewellyn nodded and smiled as though to encourage improvement, but his attention was focused on taking Tristam's pulse as the hammock swung.

"Still dizzy when you rise? Headaches?"

Tristam nodded.

"It will take time." Llewellyn turned Tristam's hand over, as though examining the color, but it was the fading tattoo that was of real interest, Tristam knew. "And these terrible nightmares?"

"They have begun to abate a little. How go your own, Doctor Llewellyn?"

Llewellyn lowered Tristam's hand. "It is you I am concerned about, Tristam." The man hesitated. "And you feel no . . . *need* of the physic?" He wet his lips gently as he asked the question.

Tristam brought his hand close to him, almost hiding it. "I feel the need, Doctor, but it grows weaker. Weaker as I grow stronger."

Llewellyn said nothing.

"What did you imagine, Doctor? That I would fall into madness like poor Trevelyan?"

Llewellyn searched blindly behind him for the door handle, but Tristam tried to hold the man a little longer.

"I know that you lied to Stern, Doctor Llewellyn. The tiny quantity of seed you require to cure your 'disease' will not be enough. There will never be enough, will there? Stern can never grant you all that you need. Or has Sir Roderick already promised that? Perhaps you have so much already in your possession that it does not matter?"

Llewellyn turned the knob, but didn't open the door. "One of the sad effects of the physic, Tristam, is it can make you believe that you are persecuted, plotted against. You should guard against this. I am your physician. Your well-being is my paramount concern." He managed a tight-lipped smile, trying to make a dignified escape.

Tristam lay thinking for a moment, watching the lens of sunlight tear about his cabin, searching. He held up his right hand, turning it slowly. The snake seemed to be fading from its head toward its tail, as though it were retreating into the wound on his wrist. Slipping back into the vein.

Quickly he lowered the hand to his heart, feeling it beat softly but surely.

TWO

False springs were not unknown to Averil Kent. He strolled in his February garden, basking like a newly awakened flower in the warmth of an unseasonal sun. For a moment he stopped to survey the garden in its entirety, gazing down the south-facing slope toward the nearby river. A scene of tired winter greens and grays and browns, relieved in places by bright berries of red and a few plants that would flower in Farrland's mild winter.

Come spring all this would change, but spring had not yet arrived—not really.

He went on, prodding the earth here and there with his walking stick. He had come to his country house to think in peace, but this was not yielding the results he wanted.

The air was cool but calm, and the sun so uncommonly warm, that the day seemed positively balmy. *False spring. Spuriverna.*

Kent had too much on his mind. Count Massenet's overture had disturbed him more than he liked to admit. He had been so cautious! Too cautious, he had sometimes thought. It had been Varese approaching Valary that had set the wheels in motion: there could be no other explanation. Obviously, Kent had not been conscious enough of the Entonne. Unlike the Farrlanders they realized the seriousness of Valary's work.

Valary.

He continued down a path of crushed gravel, the soles of his boots making a harsh grinding sound at each step.

Massenet was careful, of course, and he was unbeliev-

7

ably social. Over the years Kent had spoken to him fairly often. It would hardly raise suspicion—unless Palle and his cabal began looking toward Valary themselves.... A real concern. It was fortunate, Kent thought, that he had been so circumspect, telling Valary no more than necessary. It had been his habit with everyone he involved. No one was aware of all the strands of the web—except for Kent ... and the Countess. And now he was keeping something from her: his contact with Massenet.

"May they never find their way to the countess," he whispered.

He moved on, his focus wandering as his anxiety returned.

I have come to live a life of anxiety, he thought. And it was beginning to show. It sapped his energies, whittled away at him, both waking and sleeping. He felt like a wounded hart, escaping into the underwood, fleet of foot to begin, but the slow loss of blood from the unstopped wound.... It sucked his life away, and Averil Kent knew he could ill afford that. Not at his age.

But he was not down yet. Massenet had caught him unawares, but there was still some strength in his aged legs—enough for one last run.

Kent looked out across his garden. Forty years of effort.

"You see how you have squandered your days, Averil," he chided himself. No wife, no children to carry on. Everything that was in his heart had gone onto canvas and here, into this garden—almost everything. He stepped down three steps beneath the pergola, the tangle of wisteria vine twisting like strange braid around the faded wood.

Forty years. Kent had spent so much time in this garden that he believed he knew its every stone, every branch on each tree. Yet it was a garden, and each season it came forth from the earth, like magic, almost mockingly familiar, but never twice the same. An ever-changing canvas, no single day ever to be repeated. One could plan a garden in infinite detail, but what blossomed forth from the earth was only an approximation of the vision. And in this way, too, it was like a painting, or like a man's life, for that matter. One could never predict what the magic of the earth would produce.

False spring.

If too many flowers blossomed now and there was frost. . . .

He shook his head and walked on.

Massenet, Massenet, Massenet. He was a damnably unfathomable man. Charming, brilliant, deceptively kind, deceptive, gifted with great strength of character, and not lacking courage. Not lacking anything that Kent could think of: certainly not lacking women.

The Duchess of Morland—that was whom Kent was reminded of when he thought of Massenet. Oh, their personalities were differently formed, certainly, but they were more alike than dissimilar. Like two species of rose—different in color and structure, but both beautiful, resulting from endless effort, both concealing a thorn.

In many things Kent would be glad—more than glad—to have Massenet as an ally, there was no doubt of that. But Massenet was, first and foremost, Entonne: an emissary of His Holy Entonne Majesty. Thwarting Palle and his supporters was Kent's desperate hope, but to do so and betray Farrland to the Entonne. . . . Better, perhaps, to take his chances with Palle.

But was that true? He thought back to his conversation with Massenet. Either the wily count had taken Kent's exact measure, or Massenet and Averil Kent were of one mind on many of life's essential truths. And the fragment . . . ! Valary assured him that it was authentic. Not in his wildest dreams. . . . The painter paused for a moment, as though he had forgotten where he was and where he was going.

Yes. . . . Massenet. Valary. He shook his head and walked on, a sudden dull throbbing in his hip forcing him to put weight on his cane—something he had carried only for reasons of fashion all these years.

At the edge of the pond Kent took a seat on a stone bench. He closed his eyes and felt the warmth of the sun on his face, the cool breath of the softest breeze. He thought of the countess. Her life of seclusion had become almost macabre. The thought caused him pain. How distant she was, and yet he knew she was not without a heart. He knew.

How fortunate Jaimas Flattery was to have found a young woman like Alissa Somers. Warm of nature, and sweet of spirit—and with such an intellect! Not driven to sacrifice a part of her life upon any altar.

Not like the Countess of Chilton, who had taken on her role like a consumptive artist driven to finish one great work before the end. Sacrificing everything to this passion.

Passion. A word that was becoming frail. A spell that lost its power with age—but never all of its power.

The bare branches of a willow swayed, the sound vaguely skeletal. Kent opened his eyes to see a tiny cat's paw ripple across the pond, disturbing the water lilies on their moorings.

The *Swallow* had not reached Queen Anne Station, not at last report anyway. Foolish to begin worrying about that as well; they had not been a month overdue when he had heard. Not entirely out of order.

The world is vast and its problems endless, Kent told himself. *I cannot worry about them all, especially those so entirely out of my control.*

Thinking this, he raised himself up on his cane and continued along the path that skirted the pond's border. Water iris would begin to blossom here by mid May, dabs of yellow on curving lines of green, their forms reflected among the clouds on the surface of the pond. Beside these, a rare blue daylily, would sway delicately in the breeze. A trellis of climbing roses, in coral and pink, brought back from Doorn. Peonies, and to the path's left, hydrangea—multicolored and oddly foreign looking. Arrowhead and sweet coltsfoot.

Come spring the garden would rush into blossom, wave after wave of flowers, color and texture. They would wash across the garden like a succession of floods: life in all of its exuberance and mad rush toward existence. And then winter. A brief rest for flowers and gardeners. A brief rest.

Kent turned down another path crossing over a stone footbridge that he had designed himself, decades ago now. It should be.... Yes. Here. A variety of cherry and, as he had been told, it was coming into blossom; the silver-pink flowers half-opening as though uncertain of their decision.

Kent pulled a branch down to eye level, admiring the cluster of small blossoms, the perfect petals and delicate yellow-headed stamens.

False spring. He feared that they would be disappointed in their endeavor. There would be no bees to carry pollen. This tree would be barren that season. As barren as the King's *regis.*

Kent made his way back through his treasured garden, wondering, as he often had these past years, if this would be the last season he would witness its miracle. He had been told that Halden, in his eightieth year, had ordered the removal of the cherry tree outside his study window. Everyone thought it odd for a man who so loved nature, but Kent understood perfectly. That spectacular blaze, the blossoming cherry, stripped bare by the first wind. Life was short enough, the old did not need such pointed reminders.

As he approached the house in the fading light of a short winter day, Kent heard music. Someone was playing his pianum, though who in the world would be so presumptuous he could not imagine.

Kent did not go into the hall but went straight to the doors opening into the drawing room. As he stepped over the threshold, he stopped in surprise. He hadn't recognized the sheer virtuosity of the playing. His old pianum had never known such mastery!

On the bench a slender man bent over the keys, his lank hair falling free and hiding his features. As he played, the man contorted continually, almost spasming, as though the music inside fought to escape by any means it could and only supreme effort channeled it into the hands.

The man looked up, registered Kent, and the music died away, like petals taken on the wind.

The man's lean face split into a sad smile.

"Mr. Kent. Charl Bertillon, at your service."

Ah, the famous Entonne.

"I do hope you don't mind," he nodded to the pianum as he stood. "Your man put me in here to wait, and, well . . . I could not help myself."

"When the muse calls, Mr. Bertillon, one must respond. Certainly my poor pianum has never had such a master at its keyboard. I'm sure it will never be satisfied with my poor efforts again."

The young man crossed the room and took Kent's hands warmly.

"I hope you have time for a visit, Mr. Bertillon. I'm sure supper cannot be too far off . . . ?" Kent, who saved all of his socializing for Avonel, wondered what this young musician could want with him? Was he an admirer? An art collector? Kent usually knew of such people—those of stature, at least. But then many were fired with a sudden need to acquire art, some for more genuine reasons than others.

"I do not want to interrupt your contemplations and your work, Mr. Kent. You see, I am really just a messenger for another."

Kent stopped. Perhaps his eyebrows lifted.

"My good friend, Count Massenet, asked me to look in on you."

"Ah. And how is the ambassador?" Kent pulled light gloves off his fingers, gratified to see how still they remained.

"Well. I have never known the count to be less than well." Bertillon smiled. "It is his diet, I think."

Kent did not smile at this sally.

"I dare say. Shall I let the servants know there will be another for dinner?"

Despite the day's hints of spring, the night was clear and cool and Kent was glad of the fire. The two gentlemen sat at the table, cleared now of most of its dinnerware. By the light of the fire and candles Kent thought his Entonne visitor had a wraithlike quality. The man obviously cultivated the appearance of a sensitive artist, something Kent had always avoided. But then Bertillon's fine bone structure and light complexion lent themselves to it.

Kent looked down at the letter the young man had carried with him. It was couched in the terms of a letter of introduction, though it did ask Kent if he would return the "book" with Bertillon, and also stated that Massenet trusted Bertillon completely. Its meaning was clear. Kent was certain it was no forgery.

"I must apologize, Mr. Bertillon. The book in question is in the hands of a scholar of my acquaintance."

"That would be the able Mr. Valary, I assume," Bertillon said quietly.

Kent did not respond.

"Not to worry. I was to return it only if convenient to you, Mr. Kent," Bertillon said in Entonne. He shifted in his chair and reached for his glass. Like many another man of slight stature that Kent had known, Bertillon seemed to have enormous capacity for liquor. He had not stinted, before, during, or after dinner, and he didn't show the slightest effect. It was a myth that only large men could hold their drink, that was certain.

"May I make a small suggestion, Mr. Kent?"

"By all means."

"We should speak candidly. We are both aware of how important this matter is and how little time we might have."

Kent nodded, glancing at the letter again. He held it loosely in his hand, as though he could hardly bear to touch it, but neither could he bring himself to set it down.

Bertillon did not look the type to be an agent of Count Massenet, which, of course, made sense. And certainly the man had entrance everywhere. He had probably played for the King. In fact, Kent seemed to remember that he had. Perhaps Sir Roderick had even attended!

"It is our hope that you have considered the count's proposal and will agree to mutual assistance?"

Kent reached forward and with some effort placed the letter on the table, and then hooked his thumb into a pocket in his waistcoat. The diamond remained there, awaiting the right moment to be returned. Kent was not about to take money, in any form, from the Entonne. He looked into the dancing flames in the fire for a moment, thinking of his meetings with the countess—one did not want to look directly into the flames. It left one blind in the darkness.

"I cannot remember, in all my years, being offered such a difficult choice," Kent said. He was glad they spoke Entonne, a language none of his servants knew well.

Bertillon nodded, saying nothing until certain Kent was not about to speak. He must have realized that the painter had not made a decision.

"Perhaps, Mr. Kent, you could tell me what you would require to feel more inclined toward such an alliance?"

"Require? Oh, that is easy, Mr. Bertillon. What is difficult is finding a way to arrange for my requirements." Again a silence while Kent considered. "It has often been the experience of those who, for reasons of conscience, cooperated with foreign governments, that they would then find themselves unable to withdraw their services. They had, after all, committed a terrible crime—treason, punishable by death—and were henceforth easily coerced." He thought of making his point by returning the diamond, but he hesitated and the moment passed.

"You might respond that Count Massenet is a man of honor, Mr. Bertillon. And that this matter is far too momentous to even weigh such paltry concerns. But, as you have said, we must be candid here. Count Massenet has dealt with men in just this manner in the past. Do not protest. I know more of what goes on in Avonel than most—perhaps even more than Count Massenet—or you would not be here this night. The suicide of Lord Kastler I have never thought to be such a great mystery."

He looked up at Bertillon. *This is not an old fool you see before you.*

Bertillon rubbed a finger along his cheek. He nodded but offered no other response.

Kent's eye was drawn back to the flame, and he reached into his pocket to retrieve the diamond.

"Would it be reassuring to know," Bertillon began, staying Kent's hand, "that, if somehow the worst did occur in Farrland, you would be made welcome in my country? You are already famous there—famous in a land that venerates artists."

"I will have to tell you, Mr. Bertillon, that it is small comfort, for if I am forced to accept this offer, it will mean that I am perceived as a betrayer in my own country. I am not prepared to accept that. Call it pride, but I will not be known to history as a traitor."

Bertillon raised his eyebrows, perhaps a little impatient. "If Palle and his group manage to accomplish this thing, Mr. Kent. . . . Well, they cannot be allowed to get so far." Bertillon leaned forward in his chair. "I do not say this as a threat, but you must realize what this could lead to. My government cannot allow Palle, of all people, to gain such power. You know the man, Mr. Kent, you must realize what he would do. Entonne . . . it is his obsession. And the matter is larger than that. Farrland would be in terrible danger as well."

Kent thought that Bertillon would reach out and grasp his arm for emphasis, but the man held himself in check, only gazing up at the painter with those intense eyes. *War.* He was speaking of war.

Kent wondered if he were making a mistake. Perhaps the matter *was* too large to worry about the judgment of history.

Bertillon sat back in his chair, not taking his eyes from the painter. He let out a long breath, almost a sigh. "What if you were privy to information that would almost certainly guarantee your safety from Palle and would at the same time ruin the count—at least make it impossible for him to be of further use to the Entonne government?"

Kent shifted his position, his shoulders aching—from tension, he realized. "I can't imagine what this could be, Mr. Bertillon." *What in this round world?*

Bertillon considered a moment longer and then, motioning with his hand, he leaned forward, not speaking until he was close to Kent's ear.

The painter almost rose out of his chair at what he heard. "That is not possible!" he protested. "I know her!"

"I'm afraid it is more than possible, Mr. Kent." Bertillon said quietly. He reached into his frock coat and removed an envelope which he passed to Kent. "We trust you will keep this safe. Much depends on it."

Kent took the letter reluctantly. Would he be allowed to keep no illusions? Was no one beyond corruption? He opened the letter and read, feeling warm suddenly, perhaps his face flushed. When finished, he shut his eyes for a moment.

"Is it true," Bertillon said softly, "that the *Swallow* has not reached the Queen Anne Station?"

Kent felt his head nod, though with great effort. He did not look up.

"And what, do you think, are the intentions of the Duchess of Morland?"

Kent took a long breath, forcing his gaze toward the fire, into the center of the dancing flames. "It is a great mystery, Mr. Bertillon. I am not sure. There are so many rumors in the palace—there is no lack of information; but what is true. . . ? I cannot say."

"She wishes to extend her youth?"

"At the very least."

"We assume you have someone reliable aboard the *Swallow?*"

Kent nodded. "I have someone, yes. How reliable remains to be seen."

Bertillon paused for a second, as though recalling the list of questions he had, no doubt, been given. "This man; Professor Dandish. We are not clear about what happened there. He was the advisor for the palace arboretum, we know, but. . . ."

"He was secretly growing *regis* for the Duchess of Morland," Kent said, and then rose and moved to the fire.

Bertillon released a breath, almost a whistle. Massenet, apparently, did not know everything.

"And the cabal, Mr. Kent. Are our lists the same? Palle, Wells, Beall, Rawdon, Noyes, Hawksmoor, of course."

"Sir Stedman Galton. Prince Kori."

Bertillon looked up, hesitating, then he looked away. "Yes, though we have hopes that His Highness will see the folly of this course." Bertillon caught Kent's eye. "Who is unraveling this mystery for them?"

"Wells, primarily. Galton, too. And now a young man named Egar Littel—a complete innocent. He has no idea of their intentions."

Bertillon nodded. "The innocent," he said quietly.

"And who do *you* have unraveling this mystery?" Kent said, a bit of resentment coming through in his tone. When Bertillon showed surprise, Kent went on. "An exchange of information was what I agreed to."

Bertillon nodded. "A woman—I should not say. . . ." The young musician looked up and perhaps read the look on Kent's face. "Miss Simoe Dewitt. She is the daughter of Dewitt, the linguist. And now Varese—you were witness to our folly there. We had hoped for Valary, but someone was too quick for us." He smiled.

Silence. The two men regarding each other, like duelists. Like brothers.

"What do you think they will do, Mr. Kent?" Bertillon asked at last.

Kent paced across the hearth and then back.

"It is not easy to say. Their intentions, I'm sure, you have guessed. They are too fascinated by knowledge to stop—believing themselves wiser than the mages." He looked up at the painting above the mantel. The Countess of Chilton. One of several Kent had done. "So much depends on the nature of the text," he said almost to himself and then glanced over at his guest, hoping.

Bertillon shook his head. "We know no more than you, there."

"Even if they manage the translation, there is more, or so Valary says. They need the *regis* seed. They need time to learn—perhaps a great deal of time, we don't know. And they need someone with talent. Without that they are lost."

"Flattery?"

"You tell me, Mr. Bertillon. Did you not test him yourself?"

Bertillon nodded, no longer showing surprise at what Kent knew. "There is no one else?"

"Well, I have a fear. . . ."

Bertillon raised his eyebrows.

"Tristam Flattery has a cousin. Lord Jaimas."

"Is he one of them?"

"No. No. Not at this time, at least. And unlikely that he would become so. His father, the duke, has always been wary of Palle, and Lord Jaimas is no fool. It is only a hunch, anyway. But I watch him, all the same." Kent stopped his pacing. "And you, Mr. Bertillon; how far along are you?"

"Not far. Not as far as Palle and his friends, that is certain."

"But you yourself—you have talent? You could not have performed the test otherwise."

Bertillon reached out and brushed a crumb from the table. "Yes, though I have it in small degree only, Mr. Kent. Nothing like your young friend Tristam Flattery. Just learning that single test . . . by comparison, learning to play the pianum was child's play."

"Worth it, though. Invaluable, I would say."

Bertillon nodded. "Perhaps I should meet this young lord. I could answer your question once and for all."

"I'm not sure how we would arrange such a thing, but I will consider it." A moment while both men thought.

"If Prince Kori cannot be swayed in his path, Mr. Kent. . . . Well, there is concern in Entonne about the succession."

Kent felt great alarm at Bertillon's words, and stopped himself from pacing in agitation. This was a foreign agent making such a statement. A foreign agent in Kent's house!

"It would be unwise to meddle in this matter, Mr. Bertillon."

The musician looked up. "Unwise?" He shook his head. "Many people are involved in matters that are unwise. It forces us to consider desperate measures, Mr. Kent. Unwise? I agree. But what else can we do? You know what is at stake here."

A log shifted in the fire, sending a spray of sparks up

the chimney. Kent felt nothing but discomfort now, regretting having said a word to this man. His gaze came to rest on the letter lying on the table and he motioned to it. "You realize that I could do great damage with this letter, and not just send the count back to Entonne."

"Perhaps." Bertillon flexed his fingers as though preparing to play. "Count Massenet is a man of honor, Mr. Kent, he would not endanger the lady. He trusts you will not use this information unless absolutely necessary."

Kent shook his head. "Strange conception of honor," he muttered.

"He has the lady's permission, Mr. Kent," Bertillon said evenly, showing no sign that his friend had just been insulted.

This brought Kent up short. "Really?"

Bertillon nodded.

"Blood and flames," the painter said.

Kent still stood before the fire—more out of habit than necessity. Bertillon had taken a candlestick from the table, increasing the shadows and darkening the colors in the room, and retreated to the drawing room, from which now emanated the most extraordinary music. A minor key, richly melancholic, darkly melodious. Kent did not recognize the piece, but it was a powerful composition. Bertillon must have been afraid he had not driven his message home with ever-unreliable words, and so resorted to his true medium of expression. The piece was unquestionably a requiem.

The painter patted his waistcoat pocket, realizing that he had forgotten the diamond, but he made no move, now, to return it.

Kent looked up at the portrait of the countess, those imperious blue eyes staring coolly down at him. "*Isollae*," he whispered.

THREE

The scent of flowers drifted in the open port and this perfume was so out of place that it roused Tristam from his sleep as surely as a touch or a sound—a bell to his olfactory senses. He inhaled the fragrance, the pungent cinnamon of sun-warmed soil blended with . . . with what? Sweet pollens, honey, lavender, lilac and plum: all of the sweetest fragrances he could conjure up did not compare. This perfume had even sweetened his dreams, for he had been dreaming . . . what? Something comforting and languorous, vaguely sensual. After weeks in the confines of the *Swallow* this smell was like a glimpse of light to an unsighted man.

Tristam realized that the ship was not moving forward through the seas, as he had come to expect, but was lying to, her motion eased. Rocked only by the whispered sigh of waves as they lifted the ship and passed beneath.

Varua, Tristam thought; *we are lying off Varua.* He rolled from his hammock and searched the darkness for his clothes.

By the time Tristam emerged onto the deck, a soft trade was blowing, sweeping the perfume of flowers back toward the island. Tristam paused at the top of the stairs and realized he wasn't alone. Not only was the entire watch on deck, but there were others as well. A quiet anticipation almost charged the air. *Land.* And not just land, but the fabled island of Varua. The voyage out was over.

Gregory had said that the Varuans were the most contented people in the known world, and he had called the

20

island group the Happy Isles. Even Tristam, who believed the reports of the islands were exaggerated, felt his imagination fire.

A party of Jacks sprawled on the forecastle, singing low—a sad song that was much loved by them. The words drifted back to Tristam:

> *"Bury me deep, fifty fathoms or more,*
> *Beyond all sight of land-o.*
> *And if I have a son,*
> *By the sea's tumble and run,*
> *May he stay upon the strand-o."*

Tristam moved away from the hatch, going to the rail. To the west he was sure the stars on the horizon were interrupted over a small area: the darkened peaks of the island. There might even be a sound of surf—the endless succession of waves that had crossed the Great Ocean before the trades to end weeks of travel by casting themselves upon the reef. It was like a doomed migration—salmon struggling up the river.

> *"My pay I cast upon the quay*
> *For it'd been six months or more-o.*
> *And an ancient whore with a heart of stone*
> *Took me for her boy-o.*
>
> *So bury me deep . . ."*

"I had begun to think we should never arrive." The duchess appeared at Tristam's side and for a second she pressed his hand on the rail, but then she seemed to remember his injury and pulled her hand away as though she had touched heat in the darkness.

Tristam turned to look at her. In the faint, cool light of the stars the duchess' face was a mask—planes of pale light and shadow—and Tristam immediately thought of the theater and wondered which character would wear this mask. Not the ingenue, certainly; the duchess was neither innocent nor naive. Not the dutiful wife, never the harridan. Elorin, Duchess of Morland was only herself; the beautiful widow, with more intelligence than Farr women were supposed to reveal; all the strength of a King's Minister; and somewhere behind the mask, a heart that truly longed for lost love—or so Tristam had come to believe. A heart the character only revealed by the pains she took never to let it be seen.

"I have often looked at the great globe of our world in Merton College," Tristam said, "and yet I never conceived of the size of the Ocean Beyond. There are things that cannot be comprehended with the intellect alone."

"I thought I should never hear such an admission pass your lips, Tristam Flattery." In the poor light he thought he saw the mask smile, teasing but not cruel.

A shooting star blazed briefly across the sky, and he found himself making a wish, not sure which embarrassed him more: the urge to wish or the wish itself—something to do with the woman standing beside him.

"I have a confession as well," she whispered.

There had been no opportunity on the voyage for them to spend a night together and Tristam found the intimacy suggested by Elorin's whisper was enough to set his blood coursing, though he was sure she meant to suggest no such thing.

"I cannot quite believe it, but I have some regrets that our voyage nears its conclusion," she said, her breath sweet as the scent of flowers. "How insular a ship is, and though one is cut off from many of the amusements one loves, all of the affairs that one detests are equally held at bay. No secretaries can reach you, there is no post, no unwanted guest, no intrigues, no plotting among courtiers, no gossip mongers, no surprises arriving at one's gate. We have been on a moving island, isolated, untouched by all the blather that goes with our positions in the world." She smiled in the darkness—Tristam saw the mask change. "Of course, the ship itself could bear some improvement, but it has carried us over the great ocean, and that has been an experience I shall not soon forget. I feel the entire pulse of my life has slowed. Most of my anxieties have fallen away—for what can a body do about them aboard a ship? Not a thing. The pulse of my own existence has begun to follow the rise and fall of the ship on the trade wind seas. A languid lifting and falling, regular in the extreme, and though strong, gentle in nature." She stopped, her speech tapering off like a ship's wake. "I have not the wit to tell what it is I mean."

"Nor has anyone, I think," Tristam said. "But I believe I understand all the same. The sailors call it an evolution—what happens after some time on the open ocean. A 'sea change,' they say."

The duchess might have nodded, shifting the light on the mask. Neither of them spoke, but they stared off toward the dark area on the horizon, the deep voices of the Jacks carrying off into the night.

> "There is no place for a sailor boy
> Where his heart can wonder free-o,
> So I left the land, with its heart of stone,
> And set once more to sea.
>
> Oh, bury me deep ..."

❦   ❦   ❦

It was the next afternoon before the survey vessel *Swallow* entered the pass into the lagoon, for navigation among the coral reefs must be done with the sun at one's back or the dangers in the water would be hidden by reflection on the surface.

Varua rose up out of the deep ocean, the peaks of her green mountains awash in cloud and cleansed by dark curtains of silken rain that wafted, skeinlike, over the high valleys and sheer cliffs. Tropical sun illuminated the swaying fronds and leaves that, Tristam thought, looked like cilia—the green slopes the flank of one great organism.

This contrast of light and dark—brilliant green and the shadows of cloud and falling rain—brought much drama to the scene, as did the slow powerful rhythm of the surf with its crests and foam of snow: the graveyard of the white-maned seas.

The sun did not appear to be the same star that illuminated the countries surrounding the Entide Sea. The light it cast infused colors with an astonishing vibrancy, and did not muddy the air but was at once clear and warm. For some reason Tristam thought this light was pure, unsullied by the deeds of men.

From his perch at the masthead, Tristam could see deep into the waters of the lagoon where the *Swallow*'s shadow swept across the bottom before them, like the passing of a great bird.

"Take a turn of this around your waist," Osler said, holding out the end of a line. "If we run onto a coral head, we would be thrown to the deck. A fate, perhaps, preferable to the rage of the captain."

Tristam took the salt-stiffened line and tied it loosely around his middle. A shoal of fish darted away from the approaching shadow, like bright autumn leaves plucked up by a sudden wind.

The two men were aloft, "conning" the ship through the intricacies of the lagoon, which, in places, was a maze of coral heads, some quite near to the surface. Fortunately, these dangers could be clearly seen on such a day, and the light colored waters, sandy brown and palest turquoise, were easily avoided, the ship staying to the darker blues and greens—Osler calling instructions down to the helmsman.

Below them, Tristam could see the duchess standing at the rail with Doctor Llewellyn and her maid. Her summer dress appeared from beneath a yellow parasol as she moved, talking to those around her, pointing excitedly. Occasionally she peeked out from under the arc of her parasol and, catching Tristam's eye, she grinned—as delighted as a child—the whiteness of her teeth bright against the coloring of the sun in her face.

Across the lagoon Tristam could see the gracefully curving trunks of palms along the shore, their shaggy heads swaying in the fall winds that swept down from the highlands above. There was no sign of habitation here.

No smoke from cooking fires. The islanders preferred to live on the eastern shores where the trade blew and kept at bay such insects as there were. Parties would occasionally come to the western side to harvest coconuts and other fruits and to fish and dive for shells in the lagoon, but otherwise this shore was left to the hermit or holy man who required solitude—a difficult thing to find among the social Varuans.

The clarity of the water seemed impossible to Tristam, as though it were merely air, and the *Swallow* had truly taken wing. As if to prove this true, a skate soared languidly through the air-clear waters, looking as though the lazy beat of its wings could carry it up through the invisible surface until it took its place among the birds. All around the ship, terns cried and dove, splashing into the lagoon, proving there was, after all, a boundary between sky and water—between the two worlds.

The ship was closer to the island now, and Tristam focused his glass there for a moment, picking out the trees and flowering bushes that he knew; though the small white flower he sought could not be seen—to his relief. The trees admired by the islanders grew in profusion, breadfruit and coconut palm, and banana: the trees that provided so much of their sustenance.

For the past week he had swung between great excitement and anticipation, and utter dread. Arrival in Varua would bring many things to the surface that had lain dormant aboard ship.

He glanced down and saw the doctor staring through his field glass. Llewellyn, who had spirited the seed aboard this ship. Llewellyn, who had rescued Tristam with the physic that he should never have taken, and then had told the duchess that only he could preserve Tristam in the days to come. The naturalist brushed his wrist against his leg, pulling down the shirt cuff to mask the scar.

Over the past weeks Tristam had spent much time trying to acquire a little of the islanders' language, and in this endeavor the doctor had been a great help, for Llewellyn had an astonishing grasp of the language for a man who had never been to Oceana. But it had become clear to Tristam that either there was a significant gap in Llewellyn's knowledge, or there was an area he was not ready to share, for Tristam could learn little about the language surrounding the islanders' religion—which all but governed their lives. The doctor would only shrug when questioned, that condescending smile appearing. "Perhaps, Tristam, you will be able to fill in that particular area of linguistic study. Llewellyn must admit ignorance there."

Unlikely, Tristam thought. There were things that Llewellyn was not telling. Why, Tristam did not know. His dislike of the man had intensified greatly. Even the pity he felt for the doctor's condition was disappearing. The man was hiding things from him.

Osler pointed suddenly, sighting along his hand as though it were an arrow. "Islanders!"

Tristam raised his glass and on a not-too-distant headland he saw a dozen figures, all women, scrambling easily out over the broken rock, their tanned sturdy legs flashing in the sunlight. Shining black hair wafted in the breeze, and Tristam could see dusky cinnamon skin barely covered by brightly patterned fabric wrapped about the waist. Flowers took the place of jewelry, and the women wore them in their hair and around their necks in chains. Tristam felt a stirring, remembering his dream from the first night in Avonel.

"I think the master would feel more confident if your attention was focused on the lagoon," Osler said quietly.

Tristam glanced down quickly and saw Hobbes looking up at him, hands on his hips. The naturalist went back to his duty—which was not his duty, really, for he was not a member of the ship's regular company.

Gusts of wind drove the ship in bursts and she seemed to lurch closer to the point until a glass was no longer needed to appreciate the beauty of the women. The officers prowled the deck and the sound of a knotted rope punctuated the soft sounds of the day and sent the love-starved sailors back to their tasks.

When the ship drew near enough, the women began to

sing, their song drifting over the lagoon, the surf beating out its pulsing rhythm. To this music they danced slowly and gracefully, motioning with their hands and arms. It was an enticing song, almost an enchantment, and Tristam could feel the bite of the rope around his middle as he leaned out to catch a last glimpse of the singers disappearing behind a sail. Several of the women stripped off their pareus and plunged into the lagoon, as at home there as seals.

"Well," Osler said, "it would seem that some things about Varua have not been exaggerated. I don't think one could mistake their meaning."

"Should we alter course to larboard?" Tristam asked suddenly.

"A point to larboard!" Osler shouted down to the deck.

In the lee of the island the mountains blocked the trade, and as the afternoon wore on to evening, the fallwinds coming down from the high valleys became less frequent. Stern decided to anchor for the night off a stretch of beach before the quick-falling tropical night made navigation dangerous.

In the brief twilight Tristam went ashore with a boat sent to retrieve palm leaves—a symbol of peace to the Varuans. While the men under the command of Osler went about their task, Tristam set out along the sand in search of something like solitude. He had never before realized how much he valued time alone. Living aboard ship was like returning to boarding school where privacy was almost unknown, but worse, for the ship was so small.

He felt the fine sand, flourlike and cooling, on the soles of his feet and between his toes. How very far he had come—halfway round the world—to this verdant green island floating in an endless sea, with its necklace of surf breaking on the reef. Part of him could hardly believe it.

He climbed slowly up a hand of rock, his limbs not yet back to strength, and sat at the top looking out at the quickly fading sunset, the broad turquoise lagoon, and the ship lying still at anchor.

Tristam ran his hand over the smooth stone—altered volcanic rock—and thought of the Varuans. No one among them did anything but the most basic crafting of stone, yet there was a great deal of stonework on the island, and Trevelyan suggested that there might be far more hidden beneath the luxuriant vegetation. It was believed that the Varuan culture was layered over another earlier society, the way streams laid down layers of silt, eventually to become rock. An earlier culture that understood some principles of engineering and knew how to shape and build with stone.

Darkness came swiftly at that latitude, flowing out from among the shadows as though the sun's setting was a signal, breaking the spell of light. A planet floated above the horizon, its disk almost apparent to the unaided eye. Lanterns appeared on the deck of the *Swallow,* the small flickering flames of men who feared the dark. Even Tristam, who loved the night, felt a bit uncomfortable alone with the dark, tropical jungle at his back.

He turned to look over his shoulder suddenly, as though he felt he were being watched, and was sure he saw eyes staring at him. Eyes that almost shone in a dark face and beneath a mass of tangled hair. And then this apparition was gone, with only the sound of branches swept aside and the quieter fall of a foot to assure Tristam that this had not been merely a figment of his imagination. It had been a man, dressed in strange, ragged clothing.

For a moment Tristam stared into the shadows, holding his breath, and then suddenly he leaped to his feet and made his way back to the beach and the small comfort of his shipmates.

FOUR

The country home of the Duke and Duchess of Blackwater had twenty-three sleeping chambers—a fact that kept popping into Alissa Somers' mind as she wandered through the maze of halls and rooms. In the winter season much of the old mansion was closed off, unheated, and largely ignored by both staff and family, and it was through one of these wings that Alissa explored. An explorer was how she felt, too, for the place was so vast, so labyrinthine that she truly believed she could be lost for days, and had brought no crumbs to leave a trail.

"A map would be appropriate here," she mumbled. The hall she walked seemed to be used for the display of family portraits thought to be of so little worth that they were not even given the protection of heat in winter months. One serious-looking youth appeared to be her own Jaimy, but when she stopped to look she discovered, in fact, that it was a painting of Erasmus Flattery, aged seven. This reminded her of her purpose and she walked on, the tap of her shoes on the wooden floor echoing in the cold hall.

She remembered how, as a child, her family home in Merton had seemed such a vast holding, full of secret places where children could play, far, far away from the adult world. The closet beneath the stairs. The hollow tree at the end of the garden. The tunnel into the ancient hedge. And best of all, the attic! How she had both loved and dreaded that attic! But the truth was her childhood home could be housed many times over in one wing of the Flattery family mansion.

She stopped to look at another portrait—her soon-to-be father-in-law. Not as handsome as his son, nor nearly as happy, judging by his countenance, but still a man of imposing bearing. She had begun to feel some affection for the old duke for he obviously had taken a great liking to this commoner who had lost her heart to his son—and the duke's response surprised her.

Well, I am not a social climber, and though I am sure there are many who could never be convinced of this, I do not think the duke to be one of them.

No, the Duke of Blackwater was not a poor judge of people, that was certain, and this astuteness concerned her a little. Unsure of what she had done to gain the duke's approval, she now feared that, through some equally unconscious action, she would just as easily alienate him. And here she was involved in this endeavor—trying to find out if the duke had hidden the writings of his famed uncle.

How Mr. Kent had drawn her into this she still did not know. The artist had appealed to some sense of justice that was strong within her, stronger than she had realized, perhaps. And then there was Kent's sincerity—one could not doubt that he was a man of honor—honor in the old style. Much like her own Jaimas and his cousin, who had intervened with her father on Jaimy's behalf and then set off on a voyage of discovery.

Of course, she had not taken on this task without spending some hours justifying her actions—if only to herself. The truth, she had decided, was that she was merely proving Mr. Kent's notions to be false. Thus she would perform a service to an old family friend, and do no harm to Jaimy's family in the process. Perfectly acceptable.

Perfectly acceptable until she had begun her detecting. She had befriended one of the servants—a girl close to her own age—there was a bond there almost immediately, no doubt because Alissa was not of the nobility herself. Over a number of conversations Alissa had learned that there was gossip among the servants about the estate of Erasmus Flattery. Much had been removed from the man's house under the direction of the duke and his secretary, or so it was claimed. Those involved had been sworn to keep silence on this matter—as though life below the stairs had suddenly changed its character and allowed secrets to be kept.

There was, Alissa knew, usually at least a kernel of truth in the whisperings of servants: enough that she had begun to wonder if Averil Kent's suspicions could actually have some basis. Enough that Alissa Somers could no longer be sure of the principle she served. If she was not clearing the reputation of Jaimy's family, at least in the eyes of Mr. Kent, then what in this round world was she doing?

She turned a corner into another hallway, dimly lit by bars of late afternoon light that fell through shutter slats, closed over tall windows at the hall's end. Somewhere here she should find the door she was looking for. The members of the Flattery family were born with such an all-consuming curiosity that they had, over several generations, accumulated a vast collection of books, monographs, periodicals, and pamphlets. The lovely library on the mansion's central courtyard could not begin to hold all the volumes that had accumulated over the years and Alissa had discovered that a second library had been created—not so elegant as the one she knew—to hold the overflow.

Alissa realized it was unlikely that, having taken the trouble to whisk away the writings of Erasmus Flattery, the duke would then simply store them in an unlocked library for all to read. But she knew no other way to begin than by eliminating the obvious.

Having assured herself that there was no copy of Dennis' *Moonlight at Winter's End* in the main library, Alissa then stated loudly at breakfast how very much she had always wanted to read this book. *"Might there be a copy somewhere in the house?"* The duke had immediately offered to have a servant search the closed library, but Alissa had insisted that this would deprive her of one of her chief pleasures in life—poking through shelves of books. The duke was far too much of a gentleman to deprive her one of life's greatest pleasures—as she had suspected. So here she was—feeling a bit clever, too.

She stopped before a pair of doors that were all of ten feet in height. If she had understood the directions correctly, this should be the library.

Pushing one heavy door open, Alissa found a scene she did not expect. Lamps blazed, lighting the white edges of shelves so that they framed staggered rows of book spines like the darkened pigments of ancient paintings. A walkway at the height of the second floor allowed access to the walls of books and, before her, a fire crackled in a carved hearth.

She paused for a moment, surprised by the light and warmth in a room she had expected to be empty and unused, but clearly the duke or the duchess had sent a servant ahead to make her visit pleasant. This made her smile, for the family were continually doing such things—to make her feel welcome she was sure.

Alissa pulled the door to, cutting off the cold breeze from the hallway beyond. At the sound of the door closing a man, hidden behind a wingback chair, leaned forward.

"Alissa?"

She let go of the door handle she had grabbed, so surprised that she was prepared to bolt. "Duke . . . ? You startled me."

"I do apologize, but you must rest assured that you could never come to harm within our walls, Alissa. You are too much of a treasure to us all."

The duke rose from his chair, a tall, well proportioned man, dark in coloring and handsome in his years. Gesturing to another chair, he said, "Come, sit by the fire. It is dreadfully cold, is it not?"

She pulled her shawl closer around her shoulders and nodded. Despite all his kindness Alissa remained somewhat intimidated by this man. He had been born to the highest rung of Farr society and had succeeded brilliantly—a man respected throughout the Kingdom.

Alissa was glad of the warmth as she felt herself perch, somewhat woodenly, on the offered chair. The duke took a moment to place another log on the fire, banking the coals expertly. And she could watch him, seeking the characteristics that he had contributed to his son. Certainly the duke's face was more strongly formed, and sharper featured, though that might be merely a result of age. In size and shape they were much alike, not that she was to notice such things, of course. The duke's hair was tightly curled and his beard he kept trimmed short, in the style of gentlemen. Despite this rather strong, masculine appearance, the duke moved with surprising grace, using his hands most expressively, and Alissa liked this contrast, this softening of his image.

Suddenly Alissa realized that this meeting was no accident, and the belated realization made her feel even more a country girl. Her lack of dowry suddenly loomed up, large, at least in her mind, for its embarrassment. How her father would lecture if he could read her thoughts! Wealth and titles were of no value in his scheme of things.

The duke returned to his chair, crossed his legs, and smiled in a manner she was certain was intended to reassure, though it did not have that effect.

"You have come down the 'hallway of unlikenesses'?" he asked, waving a long finger at the door, his mouth taking on the same near-smile that her own Jaimy affected when he thought he was being a wit.

She nodded, smiling to show she did not miss the humor.

"My family has a tradition of supporting failed painters." He shook his head a little. "And that is not said entirely in jest."

Jaimy took after his mother in coloring, but father and son had many mannerisms in common, and though their eyes were not the same in either color or shape, they both had a manner of crinkling them up, as though about to laugh, that Alissa found very endearing. Of course, the duke had many more and deeper lines than her Jaimy, though one day, no doubt, his face would be etched in a similar way. She would not mind.

"Of course," he seemed pressed to add, "there are

many paintings in the house that are very fine. There is no doubt of that. Occasionally my forebears did engage the services of someone with actual talent, though I think these instances were far too few and a result of a certain amount of luck." He shrugged. "We shall have to have you sit for someone of talent after the wedding. A future Duchess of Blackwater, and one so lovely, should certainly grace the walls of our home." He leaned forward slightly. "And we shall not relegate your likeness to a cold hallway, be assured of that." He turned his attention to the fire for a moment, propping his elbow on the chair's arm and placing a long finger alongside his eye, just as Jaimy did when lost in thought. "Certainly, if you have an artist that you would prefer ... I believe you have an interest in artists." He turned back to her, his face slightly more serious—the crinkles gone from around his eyes. "Did I not see you in the company of Averil Kent at the birthday celebration?"

She hesitated—a moment of guilt—but then hurried to answer. "Mr. Kent, yes. He is a friend of my father's. Why, I think I have known him all my life."

"No doubt. It is unfortunate he does no portraits." He nodded, as though agreeing with this statement. "He is a man of some interest, our Averil Kent ... though he does have some very odd notions." The duke looked off toward the windows where the last light of day was absorbed by gray mist and rain. This view seemed to hold his attention for a moment and then he spoke suddenly. "Kent once questioned me about my uncle, Erasmus Flattery.... do you know to whom I refer?"

Alissa nodded. No educated person could claim ignorance of the great Erasmus, but she felt she was admitting to more than just knowledge of his existence. Her perch on the edge of the chair felt suddenly precarious.

"Yes? Well, *'question'* is not truly what I mean. He virtually accused me of hiding Uncle Erasmus' papers after his death. I was the executor of the estate, you see." He shook his head. "I must say, if not for the man's great age and the esteem in which he is held by the entire nation. . . ." He left the sentence unfinished. "Of course, he is a friend of your family, and a good man, I realize, but ..." He raised his eyebrows and she could see a bit of tension in the muscles of his jaw. "As though I would steal from my own nephew, who was Erasmus' heir." He fell silent again, staring down at the pattern in the carpet.

Alissa wondered if the hairs on her neck could truly stand on end. Her mouth was completely dry, and she was quite sure the duke expected her to make some comment, though she was too frightened to speak.

Then the duke went on, to her relief. "Well, I suppose there were many who felt great disappointment that Erasmus destroyed all his work before the end. I confess, I was saddened by his decision myself. A lifetime of effort, and such a brilliant, even if erratic, mind. Terribly sad."

She could hear the rain on the window now, a soft sound that usually brought her comfort.

The duke looked up and smiled at her. "Individuals are viewed so differently by others." He waved a hand at the doors, and the hallway beyond, and his eyes crinkled at the corners. "Look at the portraits of anyone, even Erasmus himself. Each artist saw a different person. And it is often the case that one portrait is pilloried by friends and relations as being entirely false, while others, equally close to the subject, say the likeness is exact, even uncannily so." He laughed. "Different eyes see different things, apparently, and some people are less easily defined than others, I suspect. Erasmus Flattery was one of these. A man of infinite complexity and an equivalent number of moods. What painter could hope to understand all of that?"

Alissa smiled, she hoped agreeably: *what painter, indeed.* Deciding that she could not bear her perch a second longer, she rose to stand before the blaze. It would have been unforgivably impolite to turn her back on the duke, though she longed to do so. To hide her reaction. His eyes, though not unkind, seemed bent on looking into her innermost thoughts. Clearly she had not been as clever in her questioning of the maid as she had believed. *Idiot,* she thought. The Flattery family were obviously taking careful measure of their interloper. Undoubtedly the friendly maid had been sent Alissa's way. She felt a flash of anger—but then had she not been false to them? Was she not, in fact, here with a secret purpose? *Idiot,* she thought again.

Alissa looked off at the fading light, invisible rain spattering softly against the glass. "I–I am certain that many empiricists were hoping to learn much of the mysterious Erasmus Flattery from his writings, Duke. There were so many rumors about Mr. Flattery—his connection with Lord Eldrich, I am sure. . . ."

The duke nodded. "Exactly so. Rumors. Often begun by people who should have known better, as well. Poor Kent, I fear his disappointment was so great that it led him to speak rashly." He shrugged. "But that was some years ago now, and, of course, we are on the best of terms again. I don't mean to speak out against an old friend of your family, and not someone as good-hearted as our Mr. Kent." He reached to the small table beside him and lifted the cover of a book, tilting his head to read the cover page. Then he looked up as though remembering his point. "The duchess and I would very much like to engage an artist of reputation for your portrait, Alissa. You will be one of us soon—'Lady Alissa'—if you don't mind me saying so, for we do not mean to take you from the bosom of your own family. Not at all. Let the Somers and the Flatterys have great commerce between them. That is my hope, and the hope of the duchess as well." His eyes crinkled up as he smiled at her. "I dare say we could use the addition of a bit of substance. Too many generations of coddled aristocrats." He shook his head. "Bad for the blood."

Alissa nodded, tight-lipped. *Do you think me a brood mare, then?* she wondered.

"I shall leave you to your searching of the shelves, though it is my fear that you shall not find what you seek here." The duke rose from his chair and bent to kiss her hand.

A cool draft wafted in from the "hall of unlikenesses" as the duke left, making Alissa press closer to the fire. She turned so that she might more easily warm her hands and found herself staring at the portrait of a woman that hung over the mantel.

It may have been true that the Flatterys engaged some poor artists, but that was not the case here, though Alissa could see no signature. A woman of surpassing beauty seated on a divan, a cascade of dark curls framing a heart-shaped face. If this was a past Duchess of Blackwater, then Alissa would be embarrassed to have her own like-ness hanging in the same house.

But then the discussion of portraits had not been the true purpose of the conversation, she reminded herself. The purpose had been to warn her not to pursue Mr. Kent's suspicions. A gentle rebuff.

Alissa tore her eyes from the portrait and stared down into the flames. She felt her cheeks burning. *"Clumsy fool,"* she hissed. Jaimy's father would never trust her again. Not that he had placed any trust in her before, clearly. *Farrelle's blood,* she thought, *I allowed myself to be outwitted by a servant girl!*

Her eye was drawn again to the painting above the mantel. Whoever this woman was, or had been, she did not look the type to make a fool of herself in such a sit-uation. For the briefest second Alissa found herself think-ing that it would have been better if she and Jaimy had never met. Everything would have been so much simpler, and she would never have been involved in this scheme of Kent's. Her anger veered suddenly and fixed on the avuncular painter—but that could not last. She knew the decision had been her own.

Nothing to be done now but to carry on, to act in good faith with herself, and not get drawn into foolish schemes that Jaimy's family would not approve.

She turned her eye on the bookshelves. No doubt there was a scheme of order—she would have to learn the rules.

❦ ❦ ❦

An hour had passed and the only light in the room came from the oil lamps and the glow from the fire. Winter's darkness had descended on Deptford County like a black rain. Alissa had long since found the volume she sought but continued to search the shelves for the mere pleasure of it. Now here was something that would cause even her father to feel envy. This room, which apparently was largely ignored, was as full of jewels as the King's treasury—though jewels of literature, to be sure. The Flatterys were gifted in languages and the library reflected that—philosophy, novels, and poetry could be found in all the tongues of the Entide Sea, though, unlike her own home, the literature of empiricism was not so well represented.

Alissa had mounted one of the sets of steps that rolled along the shelves and was examining books, convinced now that life was far too short, for she could spend one lifetime reading in this library alone.

The sound of a door opening caused her to start, and she grabbed the steps lest she lose her balance.

"Alissa?"

It was Jaimy. She felt her face grow warm.

"Is that you, my darling Alfred?" she called, choosing a name at random.

"No. No, it is your poor fiancé. Alfred was detained elsewhere."

"Oh, well. You'll just have to do." She scrambled down the ladder, fearing that, in her haste, this was done in a less than ladylike fashion.

Jaimy stepped through the tall doors. He had been out to hunt with the neighbors that morning and was now, clearly, fresh from a bath. He had, no doubt, been sent to remind her of dinner, which would give them as much as half of the hour alone. One of the greatest pleasures of being engaged—they could spend some small amount of time together without the burden of a chaperon.

Jaimy took both her hands and kissed her, once gently on each cheek, and then on the lips. They embraced, far more closely than any chaperon would have thought proper, and she could feel the longing they carried within them, both by night and by day.

Not long now, she told herself, though she did not quite believe it. They had decided on a traditional spring wedding—some two months off yet. Mere weeks . . . but when had the week grown to such length?

Jaimy pulled back enough that he could see her face. His eyes crinkled at the corners but then he turned serious. "Is something wrong? You look as though you've seen a ghost."

Ah, yes, the other issue. In taking up with Mr. Kent's intentions she had not been honest to her betrothed—not that she had lied to Jaimy, of course, but still, honesty required that she speak of all things of import. Or so she believed.

She pushed her face into his chest for a moment. "Come and sit by the fire," she said, pulling back to meet his now concerned eyes. "I have a small confession. Nothing to cause you worry, so do not look so. Come." Alissa took him by the hand and led him to the two chairs that stood by the fire. As she had before, she perched on the edge of the nearer chair and Jaimy unknowingly took his father's place, though he did not look nearly so forbidding.

She gazed into the fire for a moment and then up at the imposing woman who stared down at her from above the mantel. "I had the oddest conversation with Mr. Averil Kent," she glanced over at Jaimy who nodded, apparently acknowledging that he knew Kent. "This was at the birthday celebration for the duchess." She bit her lip and then plunged on. "Do you know, Mr. Kent is of the opinion that the papers of your great-uncle Erasmus might have been . . . hidden away." Her gaze was pulled back into the flames. Suddenly she felt she had really betrayed Jaimy—saying nothing to him until now. "I should have told you," she said, her voice coming out as a whisper.

Jaimy continued to stare at her, his face unreadable she realized, and that struck her like a blow. Did she not truly know him?

She found herself staring down at the carpet—reds and

soft greens, an unfamiliar pattern. "I confess, I asked among the servants about this. There is gossip, as there always is, of course." Her voice evaporated for a few seconds, and when she looked up to speak again, she felt tears clinging to her lashes, about to run over. "The duke heard of my inquiries and spoke to me about them. Not harshly, but. . . ." She could say no more but only shrugged, stupidly, she thought.

Jaimy rose from his chair and crouched before her, taking her hands. He brushed a strand of hair back from her face and caressed her cheek.

"You have no need of tears, my dear Alissa, or embarrassment. The duke will have forgotten the incident by now. That is his way." Jaimy stopped, staring into her eyes and attempting a smile. "I have my own confession, far longer and more tangled than your own. Perhaps we can make sense of this together." He brought her hands to his lips and kissed each finger in turn. "It began in Merton last summer . . . my chance encounter with Tristam. He was there to help Dean Emin with Dandish's estate, as you no doubt remember. I sensed something odd when Tristam and I first met there, though I attributed it to grief at the time. I don't know if I told you that Dandish's house had been broken into, or perhaps you had heard through your father?"

Jaimy sat at her feet, staring into the fire, and as he told his story, she ran her hand gently through his hair. Jaimy tended to be serious so infrequently that she found this sudden change in his manner most unsettling, as though he had suddenly become ill. And the story was so very strange: a physic that kept the King alive; intrigue in the court; Professor Dandish, of all people, involved in a venture that was likely treason; the theft of the professor's journals; a correspondence with Valary the mage-scholar in which the name of Erasmus Flattery emerged. It went on and on, becoming more and more tangled and peculiar as it unfolded.

"I do wish you had not allowed Tristam to go off on this voyage," she said when Jaimy paused.

He squeezed her hand. "I fear that I was mistaken in

that as well. I pray he will come to no harm." He took a watch from his pocket and checked the time. "We must go along to dinner in a moment," Jaimy said; sadly, she thought. "But I must tell you about Kent before we go. The same day that he spoke to you, Mr. Kent rather rudely interrupted a conversation I had just begun with Sir Roderick Palle, who had taken me aside for a word. Not that Kent was rude in his manner. Obtuse is more the word I want. Interrupted our conversation as though he could not see we were intending to speak privately. Dragged Sir Roderick off to meet someone, too. Now Kent is very old, but he has the most genteel manners and a carefully cultivated sensitivity. Clearly he intended to keep Sir Roderick and me apart." He fell silent, and Alissa could feel the muscles in his neck had become hard.

"Now as to your own concern," Jaimy said. "I have listened to the servants' talk as well. I am quite sure that some things *were* removed from my great-uncle's home before Tristam came into possession. Perhaps the works that Kent seeks, but other things as well." He gestured up at the painting over the mantelpiece. "This canvas certainly hung in Highloft Manor in the days of Erasmus," he said quietly. "I know that for a fact. The Countess of Chilton. You know of her, of course?"

Alissa nodded, looking up at that too beautiful face. So that's who this woman was.

"There was some scandal. Perhaps scandal is the wrong word, but some . . . *involvement.* I can learn nothing for certain, but something occurred between my great-uncle Erasmus, Lady Chilton, Lord Skye, and, I have begun to suspect, Averil Kent." He paused again. "And there is more. This portrait has some significance to my father as well. He keeps a fire in this room, to protect the books, he says, and he comes here often. And this is a room my mother never ventures into."

"When I spoke to Kent . . ." Alissa began, but Jaimy hushed her with a finger to his lips and, as quickly, seated himself in the chair opposite. A soft knock on the door, and then it opened a crack, though no face appeared.

"I am sent to bid you to dinner, m'lord Jaimas. Lady Alissa." It was an underbutler, performing his duty with a little embarrassment, no doubt.

Alissa and Jaimy smiled at each other. She felt like a child caught breaking rules, though the use of the honorific—strictly premature—caused a second of confusion. As though she had been mistaken for someone else—someone far grander.

"We shall be along directly. Thank you."

The door closed.

Jaimy made no move to go but sat gazing at her; his face, usually so animated and full of life, appeared careworn and older than his years. "There is a part of me that would like to ignore all of this. I often tell myself that I have taken some small incidents and blown them all out of proportion, but my better half tells me that this is not true. And then there is Tristam, off risking much in this cause. Somehow I cannot abandon him. Farrelle knows whatever happens in Farrland will have no bearing on events halfway around the globe, but still. . . . If Tristam returns with several pieces of the puzzle, I shall feel I have let him down if I have done nothing. Do you see?"

Alissa saw completely. She crossed to Jaimy and kissed him tenderly. He could not imagine the relief she felt. Her deepest fear had been that her charming fiancé was not a man who would ever choose the difficult course, for comfort was too available to a man born into his world.

As she took his hands and drew him up, she felt a tear streak down her cheek like rain on glass, but she was not in the least sad.

FIVE

The road at least was reasonably well kept up even if it did wind and twist along the valley floor. Kent stared out at the stark, silvered-gray branches passing by, and beyond them a leaf-strewn bank rising steeply up toward sunlight and the blue he could almost sense somewhere above. On the narrow valley floor subtle shades of gray and brown and deep, living green must pass for color in a place where direct sunlight would not be seen all the long months of winter.

Glacial movement had formed this series of near parallel valleys between high ridges; or so Layel had conjectured, and that was all that Kent really knew. Geology was not the painter's great passion, nor, in truth, was painting—at least not in recent months.

Valary's letter had been so insistent, the tone so urgent.

Come immediately to Tremont Abbey. Waste not a moment! You must see with your own eyes what I have found.

Written as though whatever Valary had discovered was in imminent danger of disappearing; and perhaps it was, Kent did not know. The letter had hardly been effusive, but he and Valary were in this together, and though he was well aware that the old scholar was an eccentric of the highest order, Kent did not think the man would drag him halfway across the country without good reason—at least that was his hope.

He bent so that he might look up toward the ridge above. Yes, that might be the ruins through the trees, as though perched on a branch staring down, Kent thought, silhouetted against a chaotic sky. Another blast of wind shook the carriage on its springs, and Kent sat up to brace himself.

It couldn't be far now. He only hoped that there was a passable track up to the old abbey ruins. The prospect of climbing up out of this valley by his own efforts had no appeal. For the thousandth time he wished this matter had arisen when he was young.

To the road's left a narrow river swept along its twisted course, swift to carry away the winter rains, its surface scarred by ripples and eddy lines, and darkly pigmented with silt.

Deep in the valley, periods of utter calm were punctuated by fallwinds plunging down the valley walls, stirring the trees, and moaning horribly. Moss and dead leaves and broken branches would batter driver and team, rocking the carriage like a ship at sea.

It was the ragged end of another snowless February gale sweeping in off the open sea, some dozen miles to the east. Kent pulled his greatcoat closer about his neck. It was far worse for poor Hawkins, he realized, and did not indulge in self-pity. But this journey could not have been undertaken at a worse time of year—nor could it have been put off. Valary had discovered something. Something Kent desperately hoped would help them in this endeavor he despaired would ever come out right.

"Let it be worth the effort," he prayed, and as if in answer the horses slowed and then stopped. Kent threw open the window so that he might put his head out to see what went on. To the right, massive gate stones towered over the road, their gates long missing. Each stone stood at its own angle to the earth, leaving the impression that, over the ages, they had been pushed askew by the wind.

With some effort Hawkins began to work the four-horse team around the sharp bend and then up the sloping track. It was a difficult climb as the old carriageway was rutted and slick with moss and wet leaves. Kent braced

himself in his seat, wondering in the end, if he would not
have been better off on foot. But finally they came up
into the full daylight and the harsh wind of the sea, and
here, above the trees, the ancient abbey kept vigil, like
some mysterious standing stone. Its empty-eyed openings
stared off toward the gray sea, waiting for what, Kent
could not imagine.

The driver drew the carriage to a halt and Averil Kent,
pressing his tricorn down onto his head against the efforts
of the wind, stepped to the ground. He held on to the door
for a moment, though the wind tried to tear it from his
grasp, and stood with his cane in one hand, his coat blowing around him like the branches of a great cedar.

"What a foul wind, sir," Hawkins called as he climbed
stiffly down from his high-seat.

The painter nodded, moving his hand to his hat as a
gust struck. Closing the door, he stood away from the carriage and stared up at the remains of Tremont Abbey; the
ancient stone covered in lichen and vines and the hardy
flora that could bear up to the winter storms.

It was a pre-Farrellite abbey, Kent knew, though he
could remember little more than that. There were signs
that it had been torn down by the hands of men—though
the job had never been finished—and here and there the
stone was blackened as if the structure had once been
fired. It was an eerie, forbidding place, and not helped by
the day.

Kent turned and stared off over the downs toward the
distant sea, but his eye was drawn to the racing clouds
that chased the patches of sunlight across both land and
water. Great towering clouds, flayed to ribbons by the sea
wind, went scurrying inland as though in pursuit of the
parent storm that had left them behind.

"Shall I look about for your friend, sir?" the driver offered, though not terribly enthusiastically. The poor man
was undoubtedly frozen near to death.

"No. No, find shelter for yourself and the team." Kent
looked up to find the position of the sun. "It will be dark
in three hours. I don't know where we shall stay the

night, but let me only find Mr. Valary and perhaps I shall have an answer."

Kent set off immediately toward the ruin, thinking he would circle it once and see what there was to be seen.

"Hel-lo!" he called, but it seemed to him that the wind took his voice and stretched the words thin, drawing them up into the sky to chase off after the scurrying clouds. Even so he persisted, calling every ten steps or so. Stopping occasionally to listen. Where in the world could the man be?

The ruin appeared to be half-sunk into the ground, though Kent knew it was the ground that, over the centuries, had risen up. No doubt this ferocious wind deposited soil daily against the walls. It was a wonder the abbey could be seen at all.

The stonework was very fine, better than he expected, the openings all curving up to graceful peaks, and he could see that they had once been divided by fine stone traceries. In the structure's corners the walls ran off, curving down to the ground like ramps, though these features had been badly damaged. Kent climbed up a six-pace rise of soft ground and noticed fresh boot prints pressed into the dark earth. Valary must not be far off.

He bore on, around the far end of the abbey, where he found some protection from the wind, and then he heard, quite clearly, the unmistakable sound of metal scraping stone. The sound was not loud, but its sharpness echoed up among the shattered walls like a bell through fog.

Kent stepped into the protection of a doorway and stood listening. When there was a break in the work, the painter called out again and in a few seconds heard footsteps growing louder.

"Ah, Kent!" The head of Valary appeared through a hole in the floor some forty feet away. His hair was awry, like a skein of wool caught in the gale, his face smudged with dirt and red from wind or exertion, but all the same the old scholar looked well pleased with his lot. He continued his ascent—up a stairway apparently—and with each step Valary appeared more unkempt, more covered in grime. He wore a short coat of heavy oiled-cotton such as workmen favored, and, beneath this, hunter's heavy wool breeches. High leather boots completed this outfit—very sensibly, Kent thought.

The aging historian crossed to Kent, who had not moved from the doorway, and clasped the painter's hand tightly, as though unaware of how dirty his own hand was.

"Kent, you cannot begin to imagine how pleased I am to see you!" He broke into an awkward smile, so out of character for the serious scholar that Kent felt a smile appear despite his utter discomfort. "Or is it yet Sir Averil?"

The painter shook his head, sorry to be reminded of this.

"Well, either way, you cannot begin to imagine what I have found!" Valary stopped and peered at Kent closely, as though searching for the marks of some disease, but then his smile returned. "Oh, you needn't look so. I haven't taken leave of my senses, entire. Not in the least. No, my dear Kent, when you see what it is I have unearthed. . . ." Taking the painter's arm, he drew him into the abbey, into the excitement of his discovery. "Why, you will count your journey as easy coin for such a return, I can assure you."

Without further explanation he crossed the floor of the ancient building, now covered in grasses and stunted broom, and started back down the stairway. "Mind your step. The stone has been too long exposed to the elements and is much degraded. This one especially—it rocks badly. Place your foot squarely."

Kent braced himself against the wall as he descended, tapping each stone with his cane as though by sound alone he could test its potential for treachery.

The chamber below was small, though one wall had been partially broken down and opened into some larger area; too dark to tell how great. A vaulted ceiling was supported by pillars and solid responds that had once been much carved but were now broken and worn, though Kent, with his painter's eye for form, felt that he might be able to make out the design if only allowed enough time.

Valary fetched a storm lantern left sitting on the floor

and led the way through a low door into a dank passage, so small that Kent was forced to hunch over, soiling both hat and coat on wet stone. At a turn in the passage a rough square of stones had been removed, and Valary pressed through this opening. Almost immediately they were in a second stairway that wound down as though it burrowed deep into the hill.

The sound of scraping or digging came clearly up the well and grew louder as they went. Perhaps fifty feet down Kent followed Valary through a second opening broken into the wall, leaving the stair to continue its downward spiral. They picked through a rubble of dirt and rock, crouching to clear the ceiling, and then they slipped down from this into the chamber proper.

"You remember Laud?" Valary said, distractedly.

The scholar's driver, gardener, and sometime houseman tipped his hat to Kent, who had never actually heard the man speak.

"Of course." He nodded in return.

Valary stood and looked at him expectantly, the light of several lanterns turning his skin to darkened gold. Kent resisted the urge to wipe at the dirt he had acquired in his climb down, and instead turned slowly, gazing about the room. It was not large, less than fifty feet square. There was an open area obviously under excavation, and the gaunt Laud stood in its center; the walls were of smooth stone, not easily seen in the poor light. This ceiling, too, was vaulted, the supporting pillars six-sided and plain. Here and there Kent could find signs that the parts of the chamber had once been richly carved. Nothing extraordinary. Nothing worth rushing half the length of the Kingdom for.

Sensing Kent's disappointment, Valary spoke. "Do you not see it?"

Kent immediately felt a bit foolish, and a mild surge of annoyance as well.

"Look." Valary took him by the arm. "It is all around us." He dragged the painter into the excavation and across a stone floor half caked in dirt. "Look carefully at this wall." He grabbed one of the lanterns and held it aloft.

The wall the scholar indicated was a mass of broken and missing stones—astonishing really that it had not crumbled completely. Kent found himself looking up at the ceiling for signs of stress-cracking.

Valary took a step closer and held the lantern near to one of the sections where the blocks were missing entirely. "Here. The defacement was done in some hurry, I think."

Because the rows of blocks were staggered, Kent could see that some parts of a carved pattern remained on every second stone: a design that had run vertically up both sides of the area.

"It is floral," Kent said, pulling out his spectacles and having a closer look.

"It was indeed . . . once." He waved at the wall six feet away. "And there, another like it."

"Yes." Kent said, still not sure what it was Valary had found, though clearly the man was excited to the point of foolishness.

Between the two areas of missing blocks the wall had been shattered and broken so that it was impossible to tell what, if anything, had existed there. A trickle of water dribbled from the shattered stone and disappeared through one of the holes in the floor. At the foot of the wall the floor had been torn up and obviously Valary had been excavating here, for there was an opening going down some number of feet—difficult to measure in the dull light available.

The historian stood gazing at him, a look of expectation on his face.

"Well, what is it!" Kent burst out in frustration.

Valary took little notice. "Now, I will give you one more clue and then I suppose I shall have to tell you."

Kent shook his head. *Farrelle's flames,* he thought, *tell me and be done with it!*

But the old scholar was not about to let Kent off so easily. Valary had solved this puzzle himself, and he wanted to be sure Kent had that same experience. He crossed back over the dirt-covered paving stones and held his lantern over a spot on the floor where again the stones had been removed. He looked up at Kent who shook his head, though he felt himself drawn into the mystery again—his frustration replaced by a vague sense of what was perhaps familiarity.

A few paces to the right Valary showed him another such spot, and then another.

Kent suddenly stopped, drawing himself up in surprise. *"Blood and flames!"* he whispered.

He looked at Valary who beamed, no doubt enjoying the shock written on the painter's face.

"Is it an approximation of the Ruin on Farrow, but writ small. . . ?" He said it in a whisper, as though the discovery were so momentous that it should not even be spoken aloud.

Valary nodded; quick, jerky motions of his head. "Yes. Yes. That is it exactly."

"How in the world. . . ?"

"Endless searching and a stroke of sublime luck." The man almost pranced he was so delighted. "Oh, I have a tale to tell you, Kent. But first I must show you one last thing and then we will retire to better lodgings."

Suddenly showing signs of fatigue, Valary trudged back to the hole through which they had entered. As before, he held up his lantern and Kent could see that on this side of the thick wall there had been a proper doorway, with a richly carved lintel stone.

"Now, you are a naturalist, Mr. Kent, what do you make of this?"

The damaged carving of a bird in flight was positioned centrally over the opening, but despite its ruined state there could be no mistake. "A falcon," Kent said, and Valary nodded thoughtfully in response.

His elation had gone now and the exhaustion of long hours of effort drained off his animation. "Yes, and see this bit of the design left here?" He waved his hand vaguely. "It is mirrored to the right, but a different section has been left."

"A flower. A rose, perhaps."

50

"A vale rose, to be precise, or so I conjecture." Valary cast a glance at Kent and then back at the carvings above the door. "Let us go up," he said quietly.

❦ ❦ ❦

Just over the crown of the ridge Valary had established himself in partial comfort in a small cottage that had been built out of the path of the winter winds.

Kent sat at a table pulled up before the hearth where a kettle heated over a freshly banked fire. He was still cold and knew he would remain so for some time yet—age cooling the body's furnace. It was a brutal place, he thought, as the wind moaned over the hilltop.

Valary, somewhat washed and in cleaner clothes, stood at the table's head pouring boiling water into a teapot he had not bothered to warm. Unable to hold himself back any longer, Kent reached out and snatched up the man's smudged spectacles and, taking out his own linen handkerchief, began carefully to clean them. Valary did not notice.

"It was like so many things in my work, Kent. If you just keep digging. Follow every possibility, no matter how slim." He glanced up from his preparations. Even though he looked somewhat refreshed now, Kent was sure that Valary had lost weight—not that he was exactly thin, but he had obviously been pressing his inquiry very hard. Following every possibility, no doubt.

"I received a visit from an old colleague—Dolfield. Perhaps you know him?"

Only by name, Kent thought, but did not interrupt now that Valary had begun.

"The purpose of his visit, it came out, was to question me at length about some obscure events of the remote past. Not unusual, really. But Dolfield is the present expert on the abbey, and eventually the conversation came around to that, and what he had found up here in his recent explorations. Well, Kent, I tell you, I nearly fell out of my chair when he described that chamber. It was all I could do not to run out the door in the middle of the conversation I so wanted to see what he described with my own eyes." Valary replaced the steaming kettle on its hook, not interrupting his story, and Kent took this moment of distraction to return the spectacles to their place. Laud came in quietly with a pail of water from the well, fussed about in the corner, and went out again.

"Not quite able to believe what he had told me, I set out with Laud to see for myself, not wanting to trouble you until I had some more substantial evidence." The old scholar took a seat, propping his feet up on a low wooden stool by the fire.

"Do you know, I am quite sure that Dolfield does not realize what he has found." He looked over at Kent, his eyebrows arcing up almost comically. "It is one of the great discoveries of our time, in his field at least, and he has not yet seen it. Why, this was only one of a dozen things he spoke of, none of them even remotely as significant, but he just does not see—the tree for the forest, as it were." The old man shook his head, causing the woolly hair to bob. "Of course, there are still a thousand unanswered questions. I don't begin to understand what it all means." He looked over at Kent. "And that is where you come in, my dear Kent."

The painter tilted his head to one side, an odd motion he was unaware of. "In many things, Valary, I look to you for my answers. Mage-lore is your province—more than any man I can name, that is certain."

Valary looked up from his tea and raised a finger. "Any man, yes, I would agree. But there is one other who might add greatly to our knowledge."

Kent was taken unaware for a second until the words struck home.

Valary went on, apparently unaware of Kent's reaction. "I have long suspected that the Countess of Chilton might tell us much if she chose to. Not that there's much chance of that."

Kent sipped his own tea, not looking up. "The countess? This surprises me."

"Oh, yes. The countess may have a great store of knowledge, actually." He dropped his feet from the stool and turned so that he faced Kent, placing his elbows firmly on the table. "Did you not know that she had an ... *involvement* with Skye? And Skye, of course, was well known to Erasmus Flattery and perhaps to Eldrich as well. Now the countess corresponded with Eldrich, I know that for a fact, though of course one cannot hope for access to either set of letters. A terrible shame. There was some difficulty among this group. The countess, no doubt, or more to the point, the gentlemen around her. It needs looking into, I dare say. I do know that Erasmus Flattery kept a portrait of the countess in his home at Locfal. And not to stray too far from the point, also kept a residence on Farrow—near to the famous ruin. Do you see? It all fits so neatly together."

"Most intriguing." Kent shifted in his chair so that he almost faced the fire. "This man Dolfield ... what did he tell you?"

Valary was apparently easily drawn off the scent, for he responded to this immediately. "Dolfield, yes. Well, much that he said was not new to me. The abbey was built on the site of an earlier structure, for this has long been considered a holy place. The Oriston Monks, who disappeared before the birth of Farrelle, are believed to have constructed the abbey we see here—at least the part that is above ground. That is Dolfield's opinion, though what you and I have seen today could alter that considerably. The ridge was fortified at different times; pre-Farrelle and after as well.

"We know almost nothing of the monks—the followers of Farrelle were so damnably successful in eradicating our history!" He said this with the anger that only an historian could feel. "They traveled widely, though we do not know why, for their influence did not spread much beyond Kerhal, what is now Locfal, and perhaps half of Kerdowne. Barely a decent duchy, really. It isn't likely that they ever numbered more than a few hundred strong. Perhaps not even so many. Of their beliefs we know virtually nothing, though we do know from the journal of Aiden, the Farrellite Bishop, that it took some effort to 'cleanse' certain beliefs among segments of the population, though the monks had disappeared hundreds of years before Farrelle's birth. We also know that the Farrellites thought it important to occupy this site—making this a monastery of their own for some hundreds of years.

"Now, I cannot prove this, but it is very likely that they took the abbey from a mage—Helfing being the most likely candidate. There is no doubt that the Farrellites had to fight to gain control of the abbey, though if this was recorded in their history, it has been lost. Certainly the mages drove the Farrellites from this place late in the tenth century—one can easily dig up artifacts from the later battles and there are remains of those fortifications all around. Unmistakable." He looked off into the middle distance, his habit when drawing upon his prodigious memory. "But at least fifteen hundred years before that, the Oriston Monks dwelt here. Scholarly, prone to superstition, practitioners of the lesser arts, some say. And then gone." He snapped his fingers and turned his palm up as though he had performed slight of hand.

"Not much of a story, really . . . except for the *Lay of Brenoth*. Do you know it?"

"Just what every second-year man knows. It is only a fragment, I seem to remember, and the translation is rather . . . disputed."

"Yes, that's it. At least that is what we are told in the halls of Merton."

Kent could see that, despite his exhaustion, Valary's eyes had come back to life. He had a tale to tell, obviously, and was determined not to rush the telling. "You remember when last we met, I spoke of this young man, Egar Littel? Well, he applied some of his abundant intelligence to the *Lay of Brenoth* and the results were interesting. Not what we have thought for many years, that is certain. And not what the fine fellows at Merton and other such institutions wanted to hear either. All the same, Kent, I think it a work of interest to us. The *Lay* has long been thought a simple story of the heroic type, more valued for what it revealed of the ways of the

Oriston Monks than for its literary merit." Valary, considered a moment.

"An ancient sage of the Oriston Order is writing a scroll of unprecedented wisdom and clarity, but unfortunately his health is rapidly failing because of his great age. His followers are distressed beyond words, and send a young monk to seek an herb that will keep the ancient sage alive. A distant kingdom, said to lie beyond a range of impassable mountains, is the one place in the world where the herb grows, and one can find it only by passing through an immense, labyrinthine cavern. A cavern where strange things occur and nothing is as it seems. This kingdom, situated in a high valley, is always fair and green, untouched by the harsh mountain winters, for in this valley there is a power. The young monk, not the ideal choice for the job, it goes without saying, is sent off on his quest through all manner of difficulties until he finds the kingdom. Of course, this being the type of tale that it is, the real test is to leave this kingdom once it has been found, for the place is seductive, fair. No one is ever ill, or appears to age. And perhaps time does not run true there as well. The sage may be many years dead after only a few days there. You know the rest, I am sure."

"That story differs in significant details from the tale I remember," Kent managed, trying to dredge up the threads of the *Lay* from a time more decades off than he cared to consider. *Sent to look for an herb. . . .* He felt a strong urge to hurry to the countess with this. Did Valary know of Kent's involvement with the countess, then? He had not been careful enough. Kent felt a sudden surge of guilt at how often he had gone to visit her using this matter they pursued as an excuse.

"No, indeed. But is it not too perfect? Can you imagine? It has always been thought that the monk went in search of the 'plums of immortality,' but Littel's translation hinges on a few select words differently rendered. And through a cavern! That is different, as well. He believes. . . ."

"But, Valary," Kent hurried to interrupt, "who do you think built this chamber you have shown me?"

"Ah, now that is the question." The man rose from his seat and paced across the small room, hands clasped behind his back, head bowed. "Now, everything I have to say is only speculation—hunches, really—though what I am about to tell fills in an entire piece of a design I have been working on virtually my entire life." He stopped and turned to Kent. "I have developed a sense for these things, Averil. . . . I know this is hardly empirical, but even so. . . ." He moved to the fire and stood with his back to the heat. "In the years that I have pursued my vocation I have, on occasion, found references to a secret society. Now we are talking some good time in the past, mind you; the middle of the tenth century, I should think—five hundred years ago. *'That is hardly uncommon,'* you will say, but this society had an interesting purpose, or so I believe. Their intention was to learn the arts of the mages, and to that end, I fear, they had few scruples." Valary turned and sat on the stool on which he had so recently propped his feet. Clearly, not yet warmed from his hours beneath the cold floors of the abbey, he rubbed his hands together before the flames. "Of course, this was not the first nor likely the last group to have such an aim, I'm sure, but this one was formed by Teller, a man who likely served at least part of the lengthy apprenticeship with Lapin, a mage of note in the history of mages." Valary rose from the stool with effort, as though he had grown stiff as he sat. "It has always been that the few who undertook true apprenticeships with mages did not leave their master's service—another reason to believe that Erasmus Flattery did not apprentice with Eldrich. We are not sure if this was due to the effectiveness of the selection process—the mages simply did not choose anyone who would not suit the task—or whether some more arcane persuasion was used to assure loyalty. Either way, those who began apprenticeships did not stray from the course set by their teachers. Teller, however, is an exception, and I am not sure why. It seems most probable that Lapin died before Teller had completed his studies." Valary looked down at Kent as though he had just realized something as he spoke. "I think it most unlikely that the mages had no arrangement to deal with situations such as this. But somehow Teller slipped through the cracks, as it were. The mages had their own troubles at the time, of course, and the explanation may be no more mysterious than that. It is possible that Teller briefly fell into the hands of the Farrellites; an intriguing possibility. Think of it. How did the Farrellites battle the mages with such success? And I am talking about their true success, not their own false claims. They must have had methods of at least partially countering the powers of the mages. What other explanation can there be?

"In any event, there is no doubt that a society existed with the aim of learning the mages' arts and it is likely that this began with Teller, who must somehow have escaped the clutches of the church. Not too difficult, I would imagine, in light of what befell the Farrellites." Valary moved away from the fire, returning to his seat at the table where his fingers began to prepare his pipe slowly and apparently of their own accord. "Like almost everything in my field, little can be said with certainty about Teller's society. The Count of Joulle, the great Entonne historian, believed the society was destroyed by the mages prior to the Winter War, so sometime about 1415." Valary looked up and met Kent's eyes.

The painter blew out a long breath. "Destroyed? That says a great deal, Valary. The mages would hardly have bothered to do such a thing if this society had not ... offended them in some way. Farrelle's flames! They must have learned something."

The historian nodded. "Yes, and though the mages were not incapable of mistakes, it is unlikely that they made any in such matters." Valary rose again, lighting a taper from the fire, which he then used to puff his pipe to light. "Perhaps the only thing I know with any certainty is that Teller's society used as their token three vale roses."

"And the falcon?"

Valary stopped in mid-draw, clenching his pipe stem between his teeth. "I still don't know. A familiar, I suspect, though whose I cannot say. Many of the mages kept such creatures, though what significance they had, if any, is a matter of speculation only. Despite all the popular beliefs, we do not know the purpose of familiars, let me assure you."

It was Kent's turn to become agitated and he pushed himself up, using the table in place of a cane, and took up Valary's place, warming his back by the fire, his shadow wavering across the table. There was no need to say anything of the falcon which appeared to follow Tristam Flattery. "The missing stones in the abbey ... do you assume they were text of some sort?"

Valary nodded. "I think so, though, of course, only our knowledge of the Farrow Ruin would lead us to that assumption." The old man leaned back in his chair and rubbed a hand gently across his somewhat reduced belly as though he suffered some upset of the stomach. "If not text, then I don't even know where to begin speculating. Nothing we have found so far would give any indication, though I will say we have hardly begun to do the work that is needed. I intend to press on with it for some time yet. Poor Dolfield—I can't imagine what he will say when he returns to find someone has been busy in his own personal quarry. It will not be appreciated, and, of course, I would never have done such a thing if not for the gravity of the situation."

Kent found that his brain would not tackle all this new information in a useful fashion—it was like attempting to grasp a hot poker; try as one might, the hand would not close upon such heat. "But if this is some ... *cognate* of the Farrow Ruin, what does it mean? You still have not told me which tenant of the abbey would build such a thing?"

Valary put his smoking pipe on the table, thinking for a moment. "The island of Farrow was discovered four hundred years ago," he began, his voice slipping into the measured tones of a lecturer. "Teller may still have been alive, though I have no evidence of that. It would seem possible, though, that Teller or his followers did the work here. Several of the mages had a great interest in the Ruin on Farrow. It meant something to them, more than a mere curiosity, you may be sure of that—though for the life of me I do not know more." The old scholar tested his tea but found it cold and pushed it aside. "Could what we have found been built during the occupation of the abbey by the mages? Before the discovery of Farrow? With the little we now know I don't think we can rule this out. Is there a chance that it is even older yet? Created by the Oriston Monks? Or even someone who preceded them? By the same people who built the Ruin on Farrow, perhaps?

"This site. . . . it has long been important to the peoples who lived by the Entide Sea. Delve into the ground hereabout and there is no end to what can be brought to light. Men have been performing rituals in this place for longer than most imagine. And this hallowed ground was the object of bitter disputes since long before our own coming. One can find arrowheads of flint lodged in the earth here. *Flint!* And broken swords made of bronze. Helmets of strange design." He shook his head almost sadly.

"In truth, I do not know who built this artifact, Averil. I do not know. But if I was forced to guess, I would say that it is old. Older than our history, that is certain. Ancient. As old as the Ruin on Farrow. Perhaps even more ancient yet." He paused, pushing the tips of his fingers together and staring intently at Kent. "And Erasmus Flattery knew of it—years before Dolfield—of that at least I'm sure. Dolfield believes he was the first to find the chamber you saw, for it was carefully closed when he discovered it."

Kent leaned forward, his question unspoken, and in response Valary reached into the pocket of his waistcoat, removing some small object. He paused with this hidden in his hand, like a conjurer not willing to give away the secret before its time. "I found this two days ago, after I had sent word to you." He reached out his hand, still closed, and then slowly opened his fingers, revealing a small clasp knife, its bronze case scratched and worn but with a sheen like old gold. Turning it with a finger, Valary revealed two letters set into the opposite side in silver. The metal had worn thin, but the letters remained perfectly clear: *E* and *F*.

"I feel I place my foot into the boot marks of Erasmus at every turn," Kent said, his voice suddenly weary. "It is almost as though the man were still alive, and pursuing the same thread as we, but a few steps ahead."

Valary nodded. "A few steps, in a historian's view of the world . . . but Erasmus was here some forty years ago, I think. In the matter we pursue, Averil, that is too long. We are lagging far behind, I fear."

SIX

Gregory Bay lay in the ring of an ancient volcano which had been largely destroyed by a massive eruption some ages past. Arriving at yet another volcanic island was disturbing to Tristam, and reminding himself that this volcano had been dormant for thousands of years did little to alleviate his anxiety.

My course, he thought. *We can sail no other.*

In some age past, one wall of the crater had collapsed, allowing the waters of the lagoon to flow in on either side of a small, high-sided island that stood like a sentinel in the center of the pass. The volcano's rim had crumbled and natural erosion created a narrow, low-lying plain, backed by tusks of gray stone. The islanders called the bay *vaha nea:* the 'eel's mouth'—not terribly romantic, by Farr standards, but then the creatures that dwelt in the sea had a greater significance to the Varuans.

As the *Swallow* sailed into the bay in the early afternoon sunlight, Tristam stood at the crosstrees, enthralled by what lay before him. A lapis lazuli set in a ring of living, moving green, surrounded by jagged gray spires.

Beaches spread in a great circle, the honey-colored sands stretched taut against a backdrop of tall coconut palms, and above this stood Mount Wilam, the high peak of Varua, attached to the cloud by fine threads of drifting rain. Waterfalls of startling white twisted down the steep cliffs, looking like the fabric of clouds torn into ribbons.

Everywhere Tristam could see flowers: the exotic *frangipani* and the *tiara Varua* most obvious by their numbers, but innumerable other species displayed their colors as well. The warm trade stirred the scents of these in the great bowl of the volcano, creating a perfume of exquisite fragrance. A fragrance that Tristam imagined was worn by all the women of this beautiful island.

Osler stood beside Tristam, as silent as the naturalist, for there seemed to be no words for such an experience, no words for what they felt.

Halfway around the globe, Tristam thought.

The trade found its way into the bay as a soft breeze, where it rippled the water into fish scales and pushed the tall palms to and fro. A pair of double-hulled sailing canoes, with their strange twin-peaked sails, went skimming across the surface, like water spiders caught by a gust, their wake barely a scratch on the surface of the bay.

As the ship stood in from the outer lagoon, the islanders in the canoes suddenly put their helms over and came beating up against the trade, both men and women moving excitedly on the decks.

Immediately, people began to gather on the beach before the village at the end of the bay. With his glass Tristam could see the fales, the tall houses with their corner pillars of stone and roofs of sun-grayed thatch—the houses of the common people. Separated from the village by a stand of breadfruit trees, a marae stood in the shadows of towering trees, a stone platform, intricately carved with stylized animals. This was the stone work that so mystified the Farrlanders, for the present day Varuans did only the most crude masonry. *"Left by the servants of the gods,"* the islanders claimed, and that was all they felt needed to be said.

Above the lower village stood the City of the Gods, an almost flat stone plain three hundred yards across, the core of a secondary volcanic cone. Here stood the great house of the King as well as the larger marai used in important rituals. This City of the Gods had caused much speculation on the part of the Farrlanders. Who had built it?

When Tristam had questioned Stern about this place— not coming out and asking if it bore a resemblance to the

Lost City—the captain had guessed his concern immediately. Stern had laughed kindly. "Do not be concerned, Mr. Flattery. This so-called City of the Gods must have been home to the most rustic gods. No great towers or edifices. Nothing even remotely resembling the Farrow Ruin. Thatched houses typical of the rest of the island, though greater in size. A few remains of older structures, but these were not grand. No, the City of the Gods is largely a natural feature, though highly unusual, I must say. Only the stair leading to it is really of interest. Carved into a vein of basalt, I think, which stands proud from the softer rock around it. Lord Trevelyan believed it was made by a race that inhabited this island long ago. But who can say? Perhaps the Varuans have merely forgotten this craft."

Tristam had been much relieved by Stern's kind words, but even so he felt some anxiety coming here.

"There is no such thing as a coincidence in this world," Beacham had said that night on the pyramid. Tristam looked up, trying to catch a glimpse of this mysterious stairway, but it was hidden in the overwhelming green.

The Varuans believed the place was the work of gods and their servants who had dwelled there long ago. Gods who had left their home to a single servant who had remained to keep their houses, awaiting their return. Descendants of the servants of the gods, that was the claim of the Varuan Kings, and it was not so different than the claims of Kings in Tristam's own world.

The tropical day evolved beneath the floating sun, hot, languorous—sensual, Tristam thought. He fixed his glass on the shore again and saw the islanders pointing, children prancing across the sand, and others pushing outrigger canoes into the water.

Stern had ordered all the ship's colors flown, a gaudy, unnautical display, but designed for the eyes of the islanders. As the ship reached the center of the bay, two guns on either side were fired, and the great crash caromed off the crumbling walls of the ancient volcano, the echo taking an impossible length to die away. For a moment the islanders stopped, listening to this slow-dying report, but then they realized its purpose and laughed.

The Jack at the wheel put his helm down and the ship rounded slowly into the gentle trade, her sails backing, and as she lost way and began to slip aft, the anchor was let go into the glass-clear water where it could be seen to turn over and bury a fluke in the golden sand. The *Swallow* fell back onto her anchor cable, and hovered above her shadow like a kite.

Before the ship's boats could be lowered, the first canoe came alongside and the agile islanders climbed easily over the rail, as animated as excited children.

Osler slid down the backstay, but Tristam stayed where he was, immobilized by his disbelief. *Varua.* They had arrived. So much had been written about this island, and so idealized were men's descriptions, that it had become a place in a book—not real at all. Yet here it was, and more beautiful than any man's ability to express.

Swimmers began to reach the ship, which was now at the center of a raft of canoes, filled with smiling, chattering islanders. They delighted Tristam with their ease of manner, and the joy that shone in their beautiful round faces. Almost everyone that came aboard, even the swimmers, brought soft fruit or coconuts, flowers or shells. Soon the Jacks below had both faces and hands dripping with the sweet nectars of these gifts as they gorged themselves on the exotic fruits of the fabled land.

Tristam could see the duchess and Jacel hemmed in by both men and women, for the islanders had never seen a light-skinned woman before and always wondered why the Farrlanders sailed with only men aboard their ships. The duchess was trying to smile and retain some semblance of dignity; difficult, as the press around her was great, and so many hands reached out to touch and pinch her. Tristam could not help but smile.

A trill of laughter caused Tristam to turn, and there, perched on the yard behind him, sat two young women, dripping wet, though their luxuriant long hair (kept in a tight knot as they swam) was perfectly dry and drifted about their slim forms like fine grass moved by the wind.

Around their hips they wore pareus patterned in rich reds and blues and yellows, and about their necks and in their hair they had arranged flowers in flattering colors, their sense of style as refined as any woman of Entonne. But for these pareus they wore nothing, and their soft cinnamon skin, beaded still with jewels of water, glistened in the sunlight.

They eyed Tristam with good humor and spoke to each other in their melodious tongue, laughing and smiling at him as though he were a child too young to understand.

Self-consciously, he greeted them in their language and at this they laughed again, looking at each other in some amazement and then back to Tristam.

He went to move toward them but was stopped abruptly, and it was only then that Tristam realized he still kept a line tied around his middle.

ท ท ท

It was a strange assortment of gifts for the sovereign of such a tiny kingdom: a chest of overly-ornate silverware bearing the crest of the Farr Royal Family; a dozen parasols in shades of yellow, pink, and peach; a stock of canned foods (this in a place where food, both fresh and healthful, could be easily picked from the trees!); twenty bolts of cloth in colors not commonly seen on this island; feathers of the more exotic varieties (especially red ones); a looking glass; several books of engravings displaying the architecture of Avonel; two enormous rugs and many smaller ones; a box of combs, earrings, hair pins, rings, and other woman's jewelry; a leatherbound copy of the *Books of the Martyr* (a request of the Farrellite Church, but no one here could read it); various hand tools and sharpening implements, including hatchets, adzes, spokeshaves, saws, and caulking tools; and, atop everything else, an equestrian portrait of King Wilam before the fountains of the Tellaman Palace.

It was this last gift which drew Tristam's attention, not only because the scene depicted seemed so alien here, but because it showed the King at, perhaps, fifty years: half

the monarch's actual age. All Tristam had seen of the
King in the arboretum had been his hands, and the naturalist had been so afraid of discovery that he had hardly
noted how aged those hands had seemed.

Since their arrival, the Farrlanders had learned that
King Sala still ruled, and though he must be well past his
centenary, Tristam was not at all surprised—nor were
several others aboard, he was sure.

The great pile of booty had been ferried ashore and
carefully arranged on the beach, like goods in the market.
The Varuans stood about in awe, driven to silence by
such an abundance of riches. To Tristam's surprise this
scene caused him some distress—for these "gifts" were
not a hundred-thousandth part of the wealth of King
Wilam, and yet here they struck the population dumb
with wonder. It was beyond their imagining that even an
entire island should possess such abundance. And Tristam
knew that Stern kept more goods in reserve in case this
did not achieve the desired result.

There were other gifts as well, for the lesser chiefs and
the "Old Men," the *kenaturaga;* the Varuan shamans who
held great power on the islands.

"But where is the King?" the duchess asked. She had,
more or less, recovered from the affront of being misused
by the curious Varuans, and Stern had granted her an
honor guard of four large Jacks. The islanders were keeping a distance from the duchess now, but they were not
shy about staring openly. From the little Tristam knew of
their culture (from the little any Farrlander really knew),
they might now think the duchess was *"tapu,"* for Varuan
culture seemed to function within a complex system of
prerogatives and tapu. Tristam did not know if such
things applied to people.

The Farrlanders had been standing on the beach before
their offering for some time now, and it was not clear
where the Varuan sovereign was. "Hobbes said something
about a ritual," Tristam offered.

Something was not right; even the Varuans had begun
to look uncomfortable. They had recognized Stern and
Hobbes immediately and had greeted the two seamen

with obvious affection, but now they stood about, staring at the pile of gifts, speaking quietly among themselves and making the Farrlanders wonder if they had broken some tapu of which they were unaware.

Hobbes was endeavoring to discover the cause of this coolness, but he seemed to be having little luck, and Stern was capable of only a few rudimentary phrases of greeting and politeness. Llewellyn was by far the most fluent of them all, but Stern had told the doctor in no uncertain terms that he was not to speak unless asked. Stern, Tristam guessed, was concerned that Llewellyn's need for the *regis* seed not undermine his own purpose. Tristam could see that the doctor was almost twitching with his desire to use his command of the language.

"*Mr. Hobbes?*" A voice speaking perfect Farr came from somewhere in back of the crowd. "*Is it Mr. Hobbes?*"

The crowd of Varuans parted, and down the corridor they formed, strode a gangling Farrlander of middle years, incongruously dressed in a calf-length pareu and a ragged shirt. He was smiling such an enormous smile that Tristam thought his tanned face was in danger of actually tearing. He had seldom beheld such a look of delight.

"*Mr. Wallis!*" Hobbes said, jumping forward to grasp the man by hand and shoulder. "I thought I should never lay eyes upon you again in this lifetime!"

The man's grin widened as he took the master's large hand between both his own. "And I thought never to see another in this lifetime, as well, for all I could be sure of when the *Southern Star* sailed off was that I should die far from my own land." Perceiving the change in Hobbes' face, he hastened to add. "But I have not the slightest doubt in my mind that Captain Pankhurst did the right thing. There is no question but that I would have died on the return voyage, and who knows how many others with me? No, Mr. Hobbes, do not feel badly for a moment. It was the right decision in every way, and I would likely not be here otherwise." He smiled at the Farrlanders, as though absolving them of any sin.

"Excuse my manners, sir," Hobbes hesitated, glancing

at the duchess, and then gave a slight bow to his captain. "Captain Stern, commander of His Majesty's Survey Vessel, *Swallow.* I would give you Mr. Wallis, ship's artist on Captain Pankhurst's voyage."

"Madison Wallis, at your service, Captain." The man wrung Stern's hand as though he had just discovered a long lost cousin.

"Your servant, sir," Stern answered. "May I present you to the Duchess of Morland."

Wallis looked suddenly very awkward, glancing down at his clothing. "It is a great honor, Your Grace. Please, pardon my . . . poor showing."

The duchess took a step forward and took the man's hand, meeting his eyes with complete openness. "Make no apologies, Mr. Wallis, it is a miracle that you are here. You could not be a more welcome sight if you were dressed as a member of the royal court."

Wallis actually blushed at this, red competing with the deep color the sun had burnished his skin.

The duchess half-turned to Tristam. "And let me introduce my particular friend, Mr. Tristam Flattery, ship's naturalist."

"Your servant, Mr. Flattery. I cannot tell you all how quickly I have run to come to you." He laughed, and Tristam realized the man did look flushed. "Why, I have come half a league since first light, and on my own legs, too, for I was up in the high valley. Farrelle be praised, how good it is to feel my own language on my tongue and to hear it spoken true." He laughed again, apparently from sheer delight at finding people of his own land.

"I'm sure you have a tale to tell us, Mr. Wallis," Stern said, "but first, do you know why we have been received so coolly? We have not had so much as a message from the King. Is he not well?"

"Ah, you don't know?" and seeing the looks of the men before him he nodded. "The *mata maoeā* has begun." Seeing the incomprehension on the Farrlanders' faces, he went on. "A ritual of cleansing and purification. Began at sunrise yesterday. It is one of the great rituals of the Varuans, employed only in the times of greatest need.

The King and many of the Old Men shall be taken up with it for a fortnight, at least."

"A fortnight...." Stern did not hide his deep disappointment at this news.

Wallis nodded. "While the Old Men and the King are engaged in rituals, it is difficult to tell who is left in charge. Varuan society is not ordered in the same way as ours. The King here is jealous of his prerogatives, and, officially, no one is allowed to stand in for him." Wallis pointed out into the bay beyond the *Swallow*, anchored with her broadside aimed toward the village.

"Perhaps here will be the answer to your questions. Anua. Did you meet her on your previous visits? No? She is presently the King's most influential wife—not eldest, mind you, but her family have become very strong this past year."

A large, double-hulled sailing craft came gliding swiftly over the bay, sailors in their short pareus moving surely on the deck, and children peering from the bows.

The sailing canoe passed by the *Swallow*, and in contrast the islanders' craft looked like a water insect, light on the surface, quick of movement, with long spindly arms and steering oars like antennae. The double hulls came to a gentle halt a few feet from shore and the crew quickly slid a narrow plank out and into the shallows.

A woman of great dignity and indeterminate age, perhaps in her late thirties, led a small child down the plank, walking as though it were a grand staircase. This was the first woman Tristam had seen wearing the loose, sleeveless cloak of the Varuan nobility and the almost ankle-length pareu that showed her rank.

The Varuan equivalent of the peasants wore their pareus short, not touching the knee, and there seemed to be any number of intermediate steps.

Some of the islanders went forward to greet her, wearers of longer garments themselves, and there was much joy in this reunion. Tristam was sure, by their looks, that they spoke of the Farrlanders. After a few moments, the woman and child came toward Stern and Hobbes.

She spoke her own tongue, and then said, "I welcome

you," in softly accented Farr. She gestured to Wallis, and the castaway came to greet her, only slightly less awkward than he had been before the duchess. Like everyone else, he treated her with great deference, but also with affection. She spoke quietly to Wallis, smiling all the while, the child at her side staring wide-eyed at the strangers before him.

"Anua says that, no doubt, the King will be sorry he was not here to greet you. Most of the Old Men and the chiefs are either involved in the maoeā in the city of the gods or they are performing private rituals before their own. . . ." Wallis paused. "I think shrines would be our nearest word." The tall artist waved a hand at the mountain of gifts. "If these are for the King and the chiefs, then you must wait for the ritual to end before you can present them." Wallis looked a bit uncomfortable. "It would be unwise, Captain Stern, to give out any gifts before the King has returned." Tristam got the impression this was Wallis speaking, not translating for the Varuan noblewoman. "If you are in great need of stores, perhaps you might trade for them, but to open trade proper before the King has come would cause uncounted troubles. Things that could take months to work out."

Stern nodded quickly. "We will take your advice in this, Mr. Wallis, as no doubt we will in much else. I will have everything returned to the ship immediately. Please thank Anua for her kindness and say we did not know it was maoeā and hope we shall not upset the ritual in any way. If there are any special tapu in place for the duration, please tell us and we will obey them."

Wallis spoke to Anua, who did not seem perceptibly reassured by Stern's words. "Anua says that it is important that you not upset the balance of the community. No one should enter the City of the Gods—one must be properly purified to do so during maoeā—and your men must stay away from the marai, the stone platforms. They are used for the ritual and have been specially prepared." He glanced at the woman and then quickly back to the Farrlanders. "If I may say so, Captain, this ritual . . . imagine that it is like our own Days of Atonement. Even those not directly involved in the central rite make their own offerings, and the atmosphere of the island is generally subdued."

As Wallis stopped, the noblewoman spoke again briefly.

"Anua would like to introduce the Someday King—the Prince Royal, Ra'i Auahi. Her grandson."

The small child at her side was pushed gently forward, though he did not take his hand from her pareu nor did he remove his fingers from his mouth. Hobbes greeted him in his soft voice, and the child looked up at Anua in great surprise, making everyone laugh.

"Ra'i Auahi is shy, yet," Wallis said, smiling down at the boy.

Wallis then introduced the other Farrlanders, and it seemed that, like the other Varuans, Anua was most curious about the duchess and her maid. They spoke at some length through the efforts of Wallis, Anua asking many questions.

Tristam was introduced as well, and he made his best efforts to greet her properly in Varuan, which he saw pleased her.

Llewellyn took the opportunity offered by his introduction to speak the language of the islanders, feeling, no doubt, that this freed him of the strictures imposed by the captain. Wallis stood by ready to translate, but realized quickly that this would be unnecessary, and he began speaking with his old friend, Hobbes. Tristam listened carefully to everything that was said, trying to tease out words or phrases he knew, attempting to create meaning. At one point the smiles on the faces of the Varuans listening to Llewellyn disappeared, and the islanders looked at each other, obviously uncomfortable. He thought they shrank away from the physician.

But what on earth did he say, Tristam wondered?

❧ ❧ ❧

"I can't remember everything of my first days after the *Southern Star* sailed, for I was in a terrible fever." Wallis paused to think for a second, and the joy that seemed always apparent on his face passed.

They sat in the duchess' cabin, listening to the story of Wallis' time among the islanders. Stern had brought the artist new clothing, but he would take only the shirts, fearing that he might insult the Varuans by abandoning the pareu. Llewellyn had asked about his remarkable recovery, for Wallis had been left for dead when Captain Pankhurst ordered his ship to sea.

The castaway stretched his lanky frame out over a chair, as though he had lost the knack of using furniture. To Tristam, Wallis seemed a man reduced—as though his disease had left him thin and drawn. There was not an ounce of surplus flesh on his thin frame. Even the man's hair was lanky and sparse, bleached of its color by the sun, and his skin had been bronzed like dried leather.

"The Old Men tended to me, for the King himself had promised Captain Pankhurst that I should not be abandoned. They fed me and gave me the pounded roots and herbs and such that they use for physic here, and they chanted and sang over me. If I described some of the pagan rituals that were performed, well, you should think I had been in a terrible delirium ... though, in truth, at times I was."

The duchess glanced quickly at Tristam.

"I grew stronger," Wallis said quietly, simple words to describe the near-impossible. He looked at each of his listeners in turn, as though gauging their cynicism, and then went on. "At first I believed it was a miracle. Few survive the stillwater fever, though it is said some do. But now that I have lived among the islanders for a time I believe the Old Men cured me. They have herbs for mending, and ways that would seem strange to the medical men of our own land, but . . ." he looked at Llewellyn and shrugged apologetically, "they can accomplish much with them."

Stern glanced at Tristam as though to be sure the naturalist had marked this as he had, but nothing was lost on Tristam, not even the reaction of Hobbes, who stared down and became suddenly very still, as though afraid any movement would reveal what he was thinking.

"And so, I lived. But here I was among a strange people, speaking then only a few words of the language. At first I thanked Farrelle hourly for delivering me, I was so grateful to find myself alive. But then I began to falter, for I knew it could be some time before a Farr ship returned. Years perhaps. I began to imagine all kinds of things going on at home. War, plague, death of the King and change of government—anything that could delay a ship being sent to Oceana." He sipped from the mug of ale he had been given. "I had no family—no wife that is—but even so I was desperately lonesome for home. The Varuans would have none of that. They have a saying that does not translate perfectly. Perhaps; 'To wait for life is the pathway to death.'" He smiled. "They seem so childlike in their happiness and carefree ways that we cannot conceive of them being wise, but often they are.

"I was made one of the islanders. Taken in by a clan. Given the pareu; below the knee, too, if you please. A fale was raised for me, and a wife was found—or perhaps she found me." He laughed at this as though it were a private jest, and the look on his face changed, like the sun rising on a calm sea. "And, for good measure, we were given loan of a child, for the islanders could not believe we would be happy without children." He laughed at this, as well. "Some of their ways are terrible strange to our own way of going. I was granted a Varuan name: *Yawa Yanu.* 'Who knows distant islands.' For they cannot conceive that Farrland is not an island, you see, and there is no point in trying to convince them otherwise. I have a strange place among the Varuans, for I am thought wise in many things, and yet I do not have the most common knowledge; knowledge that children have about the fish that dwell in the lagoon, which fruits grow in various seasons. A bit like an old don who knows all the works of Boran and Halden and speaks Old Farr like a man of the past, but cannot perform the simplest day-to-day tasks." He smiled, not embarrassed by the admission. "I am a sage and a fool, and an artist as well, for I was left all my belongings. Most I gave away to those who helped me, but I kept my paint box. I have taught our language to some—the King's eldest son, Anua, and others. They are not the best students, for they do not have the habit of sitting and applying themselves to their studies as we do, but despite that, a few have learned rudimentary, but quite passable, Farr." He looked up at them, suddenly a bit embarrassed by what he was saying. "So, I have made a life here, and not unhappily, for some six years. I have painted much, and recorded all that I could of the language and the ways of the people and everything that I could learn of their own beliefs and history, though these are apt to be a little fanciful—in the way of tales, really."

He fell into silence looking down at the ale mug in his hand, realizing, perhaps, what the *Swallow*'s arrival meant. Tristam wondered what Stern would do. Could he leave Wallis here, against all orders? Tristam thought it unlikely, and felt some compassion for the man.

"But what of the islanders?" Stern asked softly. "Did they not contract your sickness?"

Wallis looked up, confusion crossing his features, as though he was not sure how he had come to be upon a Farr ship. "I was kept apart from the people. Captain Pankhurst had made that clear. As to those who tended me; they did not acquire the disease, nor did they spread it to others. You may rest at ease, Captain Stern, we did not visit a terrible plague upon them, as has been done in the past."

Stern nodded, a little relieved, Tristam thought. "Well, we must be thankful for that. You cannot imagine what a relief it was to find you, Mr. Wallis. And I'm sure you have learned much that will smooth our way here, so that there are no misunderstandings, as there have been in the past." Stern did not complete this thought. Everyone knew that once the guns of a Farr ship had been turned on this village.

Wallis nodded. He looked up at the doctor suddenly. "I must tell you, Doctor Llewellyn, although the Old Men of Varua are healers, it is not quite correct to give yourself their title. It means more than 'healer.' A great deal more."

Both Stern and the duchess turned accusatory glares upon the physician.

"I . . . I did not realize," Llewellyn said, shifting in his chair. "I had no idea."

ꙮ ꙮ ꙮ

The company for dinner had been carefully selected; the duchess, Tristam, Viscount Elsworth, Stern, and Wallis. To his consternation, Llewellyn was not invited. Stern had also taken the precaution of having Osler keep the quarterdeck clear. It would be as private a conversation as could be had aboard ship.

Wallis was a bit surprised not to find his friend and former shipmate, Hobbes, in attendance, but sensing the reaction of the captain when he mentioned this, Wallis fell to making stilted conversation. The man was no fool, Tristam realized. He knew something was afoot.

"Tell us about this ritual, Mr. Wallis," the duchess said, motioning to her brother to pour the castaway more wine.

Wallis did not lift his replenished glass, but stared into its ruby center as though it were a seeing crystal. "In matters of religion, Your Grace, it is always difficult for an outsider to discern exactly what the Varuans are doing. At times the religion seems little more than an expedient for maintaining the fortunes of certain groups. But at other times, I'm sure, it is meant to be quite sincere. An outsider, of course, cannot afford to flout the islanders' religion, no matter what we perceive to be its goals. But in this case I believe its intent is genuine." He interlaced his long fingers before him.

"There have been a number of strange incidents, here, that were taken as omens by the Varuans. Perhaps a month and a half ago, seven large whales somehow became stranded on the beach. There is not much tide at this latitude, so I can't explain how this occurred. The Varuans, as you likely know, view the whale as sacred. They are believed to carry the moon back into the east after it falls into the ocean in the west. This was cause for many sacrifices and the performances of rites, but the islanders, especially the Old Men, were obviously disturbed by this."

Stern looked a little askance at this information. "Mr. Flattery might owe his life to one of these sacred whales," he said suddenly, a hint of a smile appearing. "He bravely went swimming after a man who had fallen overboard, and we found them only because a curious whale circled around them, drawing the attention of Mr. Hobbes."

Wallis looked over at Tristam, oddly impressed by this information, and then went on. "Perhaps a fortnight after the whales were stranded, on a perfectly clear day, a series of great waves crossed over the lagoon. They were not catastrophic, but seven children who had been swimming, were lost. A terrible tragedy, for the people here love children above all else. And there was some damage, even here in Gregory Bay, especially to the canoes, and canoes are of astonishing importance to the islanders. The Varuans say there were seven waves, though, in truth, I think this might be a bit fanciful. Their superstitions will allow them to believe things without much critical thought. They also claimed seven canoes were destroyed, but it seemed to me there were several boats they did not really try to repair, thus reaching the magic number." He shook his head, clearly remembering the tragedy. "Again rites and sacrifices were performed, and ever since the King and the Old Men have been troubled. They began to practice augury, trying to see what might lay in the future, and several made journeys into the night world—a kind of trance where they're said to walk in the world of the spirits. Those who journeyed returned deeply disturbed, saying that the gods had turned their back on the people. Then, suddenly, a white bird—a raptor appeared on the island. And seven days later, the white-sailed *Swallow* hove into the bay. So you see, they do not really believe in coincidence, as we do." He glanced around the table, wondering how the others were reacting to this information, but no one seemed amused by the superstitions of the islanders.

"The Varuans have come to believe that the gods are displeased in some way—hence the maoeā, to appease the gods." He glanced up at Tristam, a bit unsettled, the naturalist could see. "This whale, Mr. Flattery, it actually circled about you?"

Tristam found himself shrugging, as though he had been asked for an explanation he did not have. "It appeared to, yes, though as you pointed out, one cannot rule out coincidence. But even if it was curious—well, certainly animals show curiosity often enough. I have often been followed by seals as I rowed a small boat on the coast, and anyone who has done so will have had the same experience. But I will say, it was a bit unnerving having a beast of such size so close, even though I was certain it meant us no harm."

For a moment silence smothered the conversation, each person appearing to take some interest in their food or their drink.

"Tell me, Mr. Wallis," the Duchess said, sounding like the polite hostess, "how have you managed, so far away from your own people, and immersed in such a strange culture?"

Wallis made an effort to shrug off his own seriousness—this was a social dinner after all. "I have managed very well, in fact, Duchess. The truth is that after a few years on Varua, some aspects of Farr culture have begun to look a bit strange to me." He laughed at this. "But your way of seeing things changes when you live here. Back in Farrland you spend most of your time dealing with the world of men. Pursuing your vocation, paying the rent, the taxes, going to the theater, to the butcher shop, and the baker, answering your post. It is an endless succession of duties, but most of them contrived by men. Here, on Varua, you seem to deal directly with the world itself—or, perhaps, directly with life. A more elemental life. You harvest food from the trees and the earth, fish in the lagoon, repair your roof after a storm, gather firewood, raise children, help your neighbor. It seems more genuine, somehow, and the world contrived by men seems very distant, and strange, and artificial. Oh, not that this life is all easy and good. I'm not a foolish romantic. I have lived here, after all, and can tell you it takes some work. And there are comforts you come to miss: books, a soft bed." He held up his wine glass as further evidence. "But, on balance, the things gained outweigh those lost. You cannot imagine how carefree and joyous the people are; and there cannot be a more beautiful place on this globe, of that I am sure." Wallis looked around as though challenging those present to name a place.

"I have no doubt what you say is true," Stern responded, clearly uninterested in the artist's philosophical insights. "Perhaps, with the knowledge you have gained in your time here, Mr. Wallis, you can answer a question. There is a botanical matter that concerns us," Stern said, broaching the subject at last. "There is an herb. . . . What is the islanders' name for it, Mr. Flattery?"

"Hei upo'o ari'i."

Wallis nodded his head like a man hearing long-expected bad news. *"King's crown or king's leaf."*

"Do you know it?" the duchess asked.

Wallis nodded his head again in the same sad manner. "Yes. Yes, I know of it. It is not a secret here." He reached forward, and took a drink of his wine, as though it would fortify him. "I will tell you, Captain Stern, there are no stronger tapu on the islands than those surrounding this herb. It is the property of the King and the King alone. To even touch it is to incur a penalty of death. Even members of the royal family have faced this penalty in times past. It is the most sacred object on this island. You would be wise not to even speak its name, here."

"But Captain Gregory was given some of the seed by King Sala to be carried to our own King. It was given freely."

Wallis' face twisted as though a sudden pain had announced itself. "King Wilam has it?"

"Yes," Stern said. "Has had it these many years."

"Farrelle preserve us," Wallis muttered, setting his

glass down too hard, and slopping wine onto his plate. "The Varuans believe, above all else, that king's leaf is cursed. It is the duty of the Varuan King, and the Old Men, to bear this curse for the people. Oh, king's leaf is said to give power, too—it is needed for much of the religious ritual—but it bears a curse which can never be entirely obviated, even by the strictest adherence to form and ritual. *'The curse of strength,'* it is called." The artist looked desperately around the table. "Don't you see? This was not a gift. It is a scourge, a blight. Far worse than anything we have ever done to the Varuans. It was revenge!"

🍃 🍃 🍃

Stern sipped at his brandy, clearly shaken by the conversation with Wallis, and since the castaway had left, he kept repeating the same phrases; "The man has gone a bit strange. His near-brush with death . . . and then living so far from his own people. Yes. A bit strange."

If the captain was shaken, the duchess was stunned, saying nothing. Perhaps it was Tristam's new found insight, but her face seemed easily read to him. The way she shook her head so minutely: *denial*. She would smooth her skirt, and press her beautiful full lips together, her eyebrows moving as she considered what the artist said in relation to everything else that she knew.

Tristam, however, was not even surprised. It had almost seemed to the naturalist that he had heard Wallis' warning before, but had temporarily forgotten. And look how many bore this curse now . . . ! In Varua it was just the King and Old Men. But in Farrland. . . . Even aboard the ship there were two—himself and Llewellyn. *Cursed*.

SEVEN

Five elaborately dressed palace guards escorted Averil Kent along a cold hallway devoid of functionaries. If he closed his eyes for a second, he could imagine that he was escorted only by sounds: heavy boots beating in time, the harsh strike of iron-shod heels followed by the squeak of leather soles. The hiss of fabric moving as arms swung through the air, and scabbards slapping thighs in perfect time. They were not comforting sounds.

An ancient suit of armor, wired together to give the appearance of a guard at his post, stood in the hall. The long coat of chain mail, the massive battle ax, and the blank emptiness of the eyes brought to mind a guard of the underworld, causing Kent to shiver as he passed.

The escort turned into a corridor lined with the busts of Farrland's sovereigns and before each bust the leader of the procession dipped his standard while the others clashed their sword hilts with metal gauntlets.

Obeisance to the dead, Kent thought, and felt like they were passing into the underworld indeed. He wondered at the lack of compassion he saw in the stone faces. Was it a trait of the Royal Family or was this supposed to be a regal attitude? There was not much to reassure him there either.

At the hall's end they stamped to a halt before a guarded set of doors.

"Who would pass into the palace?" a guard captain sang out in an expressionless voice which, nonetheless, echoed impressively in the near-empty hall.

"Mr. Averil Kent, escorted by the King's own guard."

"Is Mr. Averil Kent a peer or a freeman?"

"Mr. Averil Kent is this day, by the grace of His Majesty, Wilam VII, to become a Peer of the Realm."

"Then let Mr. Kent pass in."

A horn was sounded, loud in the hall, and the doors creaked slightly as they parted, a small day-to-day sound that seemed to stand against the solemnity of the occasion. Beyond the doors, the Honor Guard wheeled right and entered the Hall of Banners, tall and festooned with flags and standards, most old and torn, some stained by smoke and even the rust of ancient blood. These were the flags that had been carried into Farrland's most terrible battles, the pennants taken at great cost from enemy ships, and the colors won in the field or brought down from distant towers.

It was a somber hall, lit from dark leaded panes high up, the faded reds and blues and golds and greens hanging limp overhead, though in his mind Kent could see them all waving proudly in the breeze, colors untainted. For each tattered banner how many lives had been exchanged? And how many of those had been completely forgotten, never to be honored, mourned only by a few? No knighthoods for their great sacrifice. Each banner, Kent was sure, represented a thousand sad tales, despite the claims of courage and glory.

With some relief he passed out of the Hall of Banners and mounted a wide stone stairway that progressed from landing to landing, turning abruptly at each, until they had gone up three levels. It was brighter here, the hallway lined with a row of tall, mullioned windows. Every fifty feet a hearth kept the winter chill at bay and guards in purple snapped to attention, saluting smartly as the escort passed.

The trek through the palace was almost finished and Kent was glad of it. Had they waited another few years to honor him in this way, he would have had to suffer the ignominy of being carried to his own knighting. Not the first to be so treated, but it was an indignity he was relieved to have been spared.

Of course Kent was not convinced that this baronetcy had anything to do with his supposed accomplishments, though he would readily admit that others who had done less had been accorded far greater honors. But Palle had been the one insisting that Kent be raised up—and the painter was more than a little disturbed by Sir Roderick's support. Palle did favors for no one outside of his own circle.

Kent shook his head. Perhaps this honor was nothing more than it seemed. If Palle wanted to let Kent know that he was aware of his activities, why have him knighted? Absurd. But even so, he found the day disturbing.

With a precise stamping of feet the guard halted before a set of nondescript doors, which appeared to open of their own accord. Immediately the guard marched forward again, entering a small paneled chamber, not sixty feet long. Here, two simple thrones sat on a dais raised perhaps half a foot. Two fires burned in large hearths, and windows reached from floor to ceiling along one wall, letting in a thin light from the north. The carpets, Kent noticed, were very old though they showed hardly a sign of wear. It was a room that saw little use.

The honor guard escorted Kent to his place, seven paces before the thrones, and stepped back, arranging themselves behind him. This was one of many cues, and doors to either side of the dais opened and people filed in. Kent immediately recognized Sir Roderick Palle, two Gentlemen of the Bedchamber, an Official of Ceremony, a Chancellor, and several senior Ministers of the government. Each of these took up a position in relation to the thrones and stood, hands clasped before them, no one so much as nodding at the painter, as was proper. A page, standing just inside the door, announced in a clear youthful voice, "His Royal Highness, the Prince Kori. Her Royal Highness, the Princess Joelle. His Royal Highness, Prince Wilam."

All three members of the Royal Family entered, the young Prince Wilam giving the painter a quick wink, for they had met before and the young man dabbled with a brush himself.

The prince and princess took their places upon the thrones and everyone in the room bowed, Kent sweeping off his plumed hat, which a guard then took away.

The Official of Ceremony stepped forward. "Your Highness," he began, the singular encompassing all members of the Royal Family thus addressed, "Gentlemen. By the will of His Royal Majesty, King Wilam VII, Mr. Averil Josiah Kent, Esquire, in recognition of his great contribution to the arts and to empirical studies, is this day, the fifteenth day of March, 1560, to be raised up to the rank of *Baronet* of the peerage of Farrland."

A guard entered from either side of the dais, one bearing a low kneeler, the other a sword. Prince Kori took the sword and stood before his throne, looking once at the princess who smiled pleasantly, first at her husband and then at Kent.

The heir to the throne was not tall or of impressive bearing, as Kent had often noted before. He was, in fact, a nondescript man, having neither wise nor piercing eyes, nor indeed any other characteristic that people loved to associate with sovereigns. With the exception of one thing: it was very clear that Prince Kori knew his place well, and although not a pompous man, the prince expected all those around to defer accordingly. He was the heir to the throne of Farrland, at the moment the most powerful Kingdom in the known world, and he expected to be treated accordingly.

Kent, of course, knew much of the prince; knew his judgment was respected by those who governed the nations around the Entide Sea. Kent also knew that the man had almost no interest in art, but enjoyed music, often attending concerts in Avonel, and occasionally he was seen at the theater. Though the prince did not appear to be someone who could harbor great appetites, Kent knew that the prince had a mistress: a stunningly beautiful woman, who was said to be installed in a vast mansion at the city's edge. Kent often wondered if the princess knew of this arrangement.

The Official of Ceremony nodded to Kent who stepped forward, bowed to the prince, and placed one knee on the kneeler. The elaborately embroidered coat of arms cushioned his knee, and Kent found himself staring at the silver-buckled shoes of the future King of Farrland. He could, in fact, see his own reflection there, and, though distorted by the buckle's curve, the faces of most of those present as well. In this instant Kent felt as though he viewed the scene through a flawed glass, the men present standing over him, their bodies curving up unnaturally to macabre, nightmarish faces. And his own countenance seemed no less strange—overcome with fear as though this were a beheading.

The curved blade of the sword swept up and hovered above him for an instant, and then descended, crisply tapping one padded shoulder of his frock coat, and then the other.

"Arise, Sir Averil," came the prince's ordinary voice, and Kent looked up at the man's face which was creased by the slightest of smiles.

He gazed around at those present, all of whom seemed to wear a similar benign look. The Official of Ceremony made the tiniest motion with his delicate hands, and Kent understood that he still knelt and pulled himself up with less dignity than he intended.

It was, he realized, one of life's unreal moments. One of those occasions when you felt as though you were not actually present but perhaps caught in a dream. Even as the moment unfolded it seemed like an imperfect memory.

Someone led him forward and he kissed the hand of the princess, who made some brief comment that did not register, and then he made a leg before the young prince. Congratulations and the shaking of hands all around.

Then he was before Roderick Palle who held Kent's hand in his own soft grip. "So you see what all of your efforts have brought you to, Sir Averil?" the King's Man said, smiling, and those who heard laughed quietly.

"If you would, Sir Averil?" the Official of Ceremony said, taking charge of the situation. And Kent found him-

self walking behind his honor guard, through large doors
and into a brightly lit hall filled with people. They gathered in two lines down which marched the guard, Kent
reluctantly in tow. This was the simple ceremony he had
been led to expect? To either side, people nodded to him
and applauded politely, the tips of fingers slapping soft
palms. Kent really felt as though he were in a dream now.
The dream that you are the center of attention and everyone is staring at you expectantly, but you can't for the life
of you think why.

In the sea of faces there were many that he knew, each
passing like a wave: empiricists, fellow artists, scholars,
actresses, players, a conductor, philosophers, aristocrats,
and patrons. Kent's association was vast and well represented here. He continued to walk slowly down this ave-
nue of admiration, his head bobbing to either side like a
flower in the wind. Wondering if it was indeed a dream
and at the end of this corridor he would find two hooded
men waiting before a block, sharpening their axes.

He was halfway down the two rivers of faces when he
almost stopped in surprise, for there, politely applauding,
but unable to completely hide his look of distress, stood
Valary.

🐛 🐛 🐛

Kent laid his elaborate frock coat over the back of a
chair, and set his sword across the arms. A fire crackled
in the hearth and a single lamp wavered on the table. He
realized after a moment that he had simply stopped undressing, and stared off at nothing, like an old man whose
memory had begun to fail.

But it was not his memory he feared, it was his intelligence. *"Fool,"* he said, but could not raise his customary bile.

A knock at the door jarred him out of this, and the face
of his manservant appeared.

"A Mr. Valary to see you, Sir Averil. He is most insistent." The servant held out a calling card.

"I will speak with him, Smithers. Send him up."

Kent went to a sideboard and removed a decanter and two glasses. A moment later, Valary, his face flushed, hurried through the door.

"Will brandy be strong enough?" Kent asked, and the historian stopped in his tracks, unsure of the painter's mood.

"I felt there was little point in secrecy now. How in the world did they know of our association? I'm sure it wasn't me who let it out."

Kent waved a glass toward a chair. "Sit. Please. No, do not blame yourself, Valary. I don't know how Palle found us out, but do not for a moment blame yourself. It is far more likely the fault is mine." He poured two glasses of the amber liquor and took a second seat by the fire. "It is the damnedest thing," he said after a moment. "Before I saw you there, I was hoping, foolishly, that my knight-hood had nothing to do with our interests." He shook his head. "I'm sorry now that I dragged you into this, Valary."

The historian waved his hand. "No apologies. We're far from being children. I entered into this with my eyes open." Despite his words the historian looked decidedly frightened, his jaw muscles taut and his complexion near-ing gray.

Kent looked down at the fire, blinking like a man awakened from sleep. "*Benighted* is really the truth," he spat out suddenly. "Flames! How long has Palle been aware of us?"

Valary shook his head. "I . . . I hardly knew what to do. The Royal Invitation arrived only this three days past. I sent you a note upon its arrival, but. . . ."

"I'm sure it will be somewhere in the vast pile of let-ters of congratulations," Kent said. "There was nothing you could do. One can't refuse a Royal Invitation."

Valary sat stiffly in his chair, contemplating the worst, no doubt. Imagining the cells in Avonel's infamous tower, wondering if the horror stories of interrogations might be true. Kent had never expected the man to be brave—or at least he had hoped the scholar would never have to dis-cover if this trait lay dormant inside him.

"It must have been my contact with Varese," Valary said suddenly. "Obviously Palle would have taken an interest in the Entonne after that night at the Society. I wish now that I had never spoken with the man."

Kent nodded. Likely, Valary was right. And Kent was more glad than ever that he had never mentioned the countess to Valary. Perhaps Palle did not know that connection—not yet, anyway.

"What about our other friend?" Valary almost whispered. "The one who gave you the fragment from Lucklow?"

Kent shook his head. "I don't know. Perhaps that connection is still hidden. I hope. But I must have that fragment back. Best to be rid of it quickly."

"I have it with me," Valary said. Then sipped his brandy, maintaining his posture of injury. "Old men," Valary muttered.

"What?"

"Old men, Kent." The historian slumped down a little in his chair. "That's what we are. What hope do old men have in such a venture?"

"I don't know," Kent said, thinking how much he agreed. "But at least we're not in prison. Perhaps we can do something yet, though we will likely be under the eye of Palle's minions from this day forth. Still, I don't know how we can give up. I know no one as certain as you of the importance of our endeavor."

Valary reached over and hefted Kent's sword in its scabbard. "No, we can't give up. If you were not so famous, we likely wouldn't be free, but Palle can hardly throw the illustrious Averil Kent in prison. He has tried to frighten us off—two doddering old men, after all, how difficult could it be? He is trying to use me to threaten you. 'You, Kent, I may not touch, but your associates. . . .' But don't allow that to affect you. Without us, at the very least, there will be war with Entonne. And if Palle and his group manage to recover some of the arts that have so long been lost. . . . Well, prison might be a good place to be anyway."

Kent nodded. He knew Valary was making an effort to

raise his spirits, to assuage some of the guilt he felt at involving others. Alissa Somers had been there! Was that merely coincidental?

Valary waved Kent's blade, and made a halfhearted effort at a riposte, as though laboring to recall a lesson many years in the past. But it was lost, and the riposte nothing but an awkward thrust, and then the sword slipped from his hands and rang on the floor. He looked up embarrassedly at Kent, his face strained by fear and determination.

And there they are, Kent thought, *the key elements of courage. But what use would courage be if they had not the strength and skill to carry the day?*

❦   ❦   ❦

The lengthy celebration left Kent feeling a deep fatigue that sleep seemed to do little to erase—not that he had slept particularly well. He sat before the hearth in his small parlor, wearing a blanket like a shawl about his shoulders, his feet up, too tired to have even combed out his hair let alone donned a wig or neckcloth.

It was at moments like this, after some particularly taxing effort, that Kent felt his age. For some strange reason the arches of his feet ached so that he could hardly bear to put weight on them, and a sharp, hot throbbing pierced into his lower back, and sometimes stabbed down his leg like the blade of a rapier. As if that were not enough, his muscles were overly sensitive and weakened, leaving him feeling vulnerable and fragile.

But worst of all, on such days, he felt the fatigue settle in his once good mind, like a thick fog in which his thoughts lost their way, unable to connect one to another. And somewhere in there his memories wandered as well and, search as he might, they could not be located.

He sipped the coffee he cupped in both hands and closed his eyes, feeling the warmth from the fire, trying to will it into his bones as though it were a power that could flow, hot into his veins, like returning youth. But it did not seem to work—as though the cold in his limbs were infinite, absorbing all heat to no effect.

"Damn you, Wilam," Kent muttered. "Damn you to Farrelle's own pit of flames." His anger toward the King and what he had done could not be suppressed on days such as this; the King had brought so much into danger in his maniacal quest to remain young. *Damn you.*

When his mind was so fogged with fatigue, Kent always found it strange that random recollections from his youth would come to him, although the feelings once attached to these were now long forgotten. He did know that he had spent entire nights lost in passion, untiring, like some fine animal bred for that one thing alone. Flaming martyrs, he could name a few young women he had loved then. What were their names . . . ? But, sadly, he realized that even these memories did not stir him now.

I am far gone, he thought. *Far gone indeed.*

It was difficult to believe these things had taken place such a very long time ago. The events seemed distant, as though he had only read about them and not experienced them at all. He knew that at this point his death was far closer, far more tangible. That was something he could almost touch. One could feel one's mortal form progressing slowly to ruin, like that old abbey—the signs were undeniable. Things went wrong inside a man and did not come right again. That was the truth that hung over one's head like a blade. Injuries and illnesses were no longer easily repaired. And as with some part of a painting that he could never get right, the great danger was to see nothing but what was wrong. The trap of age.

He drank more coffee. That morning he had ordered it very strong, as though he could shock mind and body into alertness and activity. It only seemed to sour his mood though, touching neither the fog in his brain nor the enervation in his limbs.

Footsteps creaked on the old stair: Smithers. The man had been with him so long that Kent could tell Smithers' mood from how quickly he ascended the stair, the fall of his footsteps on the treads. And today his mood was sullen. His master was very recalcitrant—and on this day that should be so full of happiness, too. After all, had his master not been raised up? Had the King not granted him some five hundred new gold coins? Were not commissions flooding in? Poor Smithers, he could not fathom his master's mood, that was certain.

"Sir Averil?" came the man's ancient growl, like a wave on a pebbled shore. "There is a Miss Alissa Somers here to see you, sir."

"Have I forgotten an appointment?"

"No, sir. She has come unannounced. Most irregular."

Kent looked around the room, and then at himself in a glass. His long white hair spread out around his shoulders, across the blanket that he used as a shawl. *I must look like her old grandmother,* he thought.

"Oh, send her up," he said, unable to bear the thought of even rising.

"Here, sir?"

"Yes, here. And brew some more coffee. Try to put some teeth in it this time."

Kent shut his eyes and let his head fall back against the chair. I might as well be seen for what I am. An ineffectual, feeble old man.

A moment later two sets of footsteps could be heard on the stair, one so light that the ancient, creaking treads hardly noted their passing.

"Miss Alissa Somers, Sir Averil," Smithers growled, and disappeared.

Kent saw her hesitate at her first step into the room and the smile falter, followed by a narrowing of her beautiful eyes.

"Are you unwell, Sir Averil? I–I fear I have come at the worst possible time. . . ."

Kent tried to smile, though he feared he made a bad job of it. "No, I am perfectly intact. Only just worn out from all the excitement. A bit much for a man my age, I'm afraid. Do forgive me for not rising. . . ." He waved a hand vaguely. "My feet seem unwilling to bear me this day. Like bad tempered horses."

She came farther into the room so that the soft light filtering in the windows from the overcast sky reached her.

Youth seemed almost to radiate through her skin. He could not imagine a greater contrast: the ruin of an old man and this vibrant young woman.

She took the seat opposite him, setting a small hand-purse beside her. "Father suffers such pain in his feet and legs. I have often rubbed them for him with some oil but even just a rub can do wonders." She started to reach out tentatively. "If you think it might help ... ?"

Kent did not quite know how to respond and she took this as acquiescence. Her hands were warm, the skin soft as only a young woman's skin could be, and her touch gentle. He felt his lungs take a sharp, involuntary breath.

Praise the god of old fools, he told himself, *I thought never to feel a young woman's touch again in this life. It is almost as if she actually wanted to touch me—my withered ancient frame.*

Now don't be a perfect old fool, he cautioned himself. He wanted to close his eyes and just feel these soft hands gliding over his skin, bringing the nerves to a life they had not known in so very long, but at the same time he stared at her in wonder. *Why in this round world would you ever be so kind to a wrinkled old man?*

"Is this all right? It doesn't pain you?"

"No, no. I am sure my poor old feet have not been so well treated in some time." He did close his eyes, if for only a few seconds, but in that brief interval something was restored to him. He could recall now some of the feelings that had coursed through him so strongly long ago. A name came back to him: Lauron. Immediately he forced his eyes open and tried to smile, as though afraid his thoughts might be read on his face.

My word, Kent, you are becoming a deviant, he chided himself. *Sir Averil, indeed! She is hardly more than a child.*

"I'm sure that has helped a great deal," he said suddenly, disentangling his foot from her grasp.

"But I have only just finished the one."

"But the other is fine as it is. Thank you, my dear Alissa. I think you may have the power to heal in those perfect small hands."

"Well, your feet are colder than snow, and almost as white. If you can't bear to wear slippers, then you should prop them closer to the fire and wrap them lightly in a blanket." Saying this, she shifted his footstool so that it was nearer to the blaze.

"I think that Smithers shall bring us some fresh coffee momentarily," he said, at a loss for words.

"That would be very welcome, though I must tell you this is not a visit of a purely social nature. Though of course I do wish you joy of this great honor His Majesty has bestowed. A gentleman more worthy I cannot conceive of, Sir Averil."

Given his recent thoughts, Kent could not even bring himself to acknowledge that she had spoken.

Alissa looked down at her hands, turning them over slowly as though wondering if he had spoken the truth about their power. "Yesterday, at the celebration, I was approached by Her Highness, the Princess Joelle. Her Highness seems to have taken something of an interest in Jaimas and myself." She flushed the tiniest bit at this statement. "The Duchess, Jaimas' mother, and Her Highness are more than passing acquaintances, I collect. It is the second time the princess has spoken to me. The first was at the party where I had the honor of your company as well."

"The duchess' birth celebration?"

"Exactly." She fixed Kent with a look, and for that second he saw the determined child he remembered. "Her Highness asked if I would do the favor of delivering a letter to you, which I agreed to immediately. The princess also requested that I tell no one of this, and, naturally, I agreed to this as well. Her Highness has a certain way about her. . . . I think one would do much for such a woman and ask neither questions nor favors in return."

Kent nodded. He understood precisely what she meant, having known the Countess of Chilton for so many years. "You brought this letter with you?"

She nodded, removing a plain gray envelope from her hand-purse.

Kent took it, and turned it over once. It bore no mark, no address. Not even his initials.

"Please, don't mind me. It might be something needing a reply, which I would gladly carry."

Kent reached a bone letter opener from his side table and slit the envelope. Inside was a short note in a hand he did not recognize.

My Dear Sir Averil:

My warmest compliments. Your long efforts have only now truly begun to be recognized. And though no one deserves a rest so much, I do hope you do not intend to abandon your important work. Again, congratulations!

It was so good to see you at the palace, for you have not been to visit us nearly often enough, although we often hear about your doings: the manservant of your colleague the historian (I hope you will forgive me if I cannot remember his name) appears to have a friend in the palace.

I do hope to see you sometime before the season is over.

Respectfully,
J.

Valary's servant!? It was Valary's manservant who had betrayed them. Farrelle's flames, he must get a note to Valary immediately.

"Do you wish me to convey a reply?"

"I. . . . No. It is not necessary. Thank you, Alissa."

Kent stared at the paper a moment longer, not quite able to believe it. He wished that he could be alone to consider. Why in the world would the wife of Prince Kori send him such a note?

"Sir Averil?"

He looked up.

"Please excuse me, but there is one other matter I should discuss, if you don't mind?"

Of course. Erasmus' papers. "Please, say on."

"I am not quite sure where to begin. . . ." The way she avoided his eye made him fear the worst. He shifted in his chair, suddenly feeling warm for the first time in the day.

"To begin, I must say I broke my word to you, Mr. . . . Sir Averil. I would not have done so if I had not made promises to another before I made mine to you." She blinked, daring a brief glance at his face. "I can only say that I am sure that anything said to Jaimas, for that is to whom I spoke, will never be repeated." She smoothed her skirt carefully over her slim legs. "I made some queries among the servants of the Duke of Blackwater, in a manner I thought would not be noted, for little passes in a great house that the servants know nothing of. And this proved to be true, for there was a rumor that the duke and two servants had indeed removed some possessions from the house of Erasmus Flattery. But my inquiries went no farther than that." She shifted in her chair, and Kent could see a look of . . . what?—humiliation—pass across her face. "I suppose the Duke of Blackwater was . . . curious about this stranger who had stolen into their midst. My activities must have become known to him." She shook her head, a quick motion, and straightened in her seat. "Not that the duke reproached me directly. But he did make it known that he was aware of my interest in Erasmus." She paused, then looked at him directly. "Actually he told me that you had once all but accused him of hiding the work of his late uncle. And then he denied this allegation."

"I did nothing of the sort!" Kent blurted out before he could think, and then let himself sink back into the chair. He rearranged his shawl over his shoulders and stared for a moment into the flames. "I do apologize, my dear Alissa, for involving you in this matter which has, no doubt, caused you deep embarrassment. It was just that . . . my enthusiasm overcame my judgment. I am not sure now how I will make amends."

"Oh, Mr. Kent, you needn't concern yourself with that. It was my own foolishness that brought my efforts to the duke's attention. You can hardly be blamed for my clumsiness. No, no; don't concern yourself with it for a moment. You see, after my conversation with the duke, I spoke to Jaimy. And do you know he told me that he had long suspected that some things *had* been removed from Highloft Manner—the home of Erasmus—before Tristam took ownership. He indicated a portrait of a woman—the Countess of Chilton, I believe—that he was sure had hung in Erasmus' house."

Kent feared he did not hide his reaction well. He jerked his leg back as though he would rise, and hot pain shot both up to his knee and down his thigh from his back. For a moment he stayed rigid and then slowly forced his muscles to relax, easing back into his chair. He felt Alissa's hand on his shoulder, for she had risen.

"Are you all right, Mr. Kent? Shall I call your man?"

"No, I'm. . . . Stupid of me to move so quickly." *Farrelle curse this worn out body!* He opened his eyes and forced a smile. "A portrait, you say. Did you see it?"

Alissa looked carefully into his eyes, gauging his well-being, and then she returned to her seat, though she perched on the edge as though ready to rise at any moment: to call for assistance, no doubt.

I must look near to death to her, Kent thought.

"I did see it. The canvas hangs in a room in the Flattery country house." She described it perfectly. "Do you know it, Sir Averil?"

He nodded, meeting her gaze as coolly as he was able. "Yes, perhaps. But Lord Jaimas . . . he is not aware of anything else from the house of Erasmus?"

She shook her head.

"Well, it is very odd," he mused aloud. And what had the duke said? That Kent had once accused him of hiding Erasmus' papers! He had done no such thing! Oh, certainly he had once asked the duke if he thought Erasmus' papers had been stolen, but it was not an accusation—nor had it been taken as such, he was quite sure. *Throwing dust in this poor girl's eyes,* he thought. *I did not mean to pit her against such a formidable man.*

He looked over at Alissa. One thing was perfectly clear: being caught out by the duke had only strengthened her resolve. He could see the determination there: never would she be so foolish again. These Somers women had great character, that was certain. He wondered if young Lord Jaimas would be a match for her.

"We are not done yet," Alissa said quietly. "Though I am not certain what we shall do if we find Erasmus' papers. What terrible embarrassment that would cause the duke."

"But you must do nothing," Kent said quickly. "Nothing until you have spoken with me. As you say, we do not want to embarrass the father of your fiancé. Certainly we must approach this most circumspectly. I should not want the Flattery name to suffer. No. If any papers are found, first we must search through them to see if they're of importance."

She paused to consider his words. "Well, we shall simply have to deal with that in its time." She smiled at Kent. "I fear I have imposed upon you quite enough, Sir Averil. Do forgive me. I shall leave you to your much deserved rest." She rose from her chair. "No, no. Do not even consider rising. I shall find my way down." Saying this she clasped his hand, tenderly, he thought, and kissed him lightly on the cheek before letting herself out.

Kent closed his eyes and lay back in his chair, letting the touch of her lips fade away, like wind ripples on a pond.

After a moment he tried to bring his thoughts back to his real problem, but his mind was unable to take in all that was new, so he turned again to the letter Alissa had delivered. Princess Joelle. It was so improbable. Lady Galton had never for a moment even hinted such a thing, though they were cousins, but even so. . . . Well, Kent had not told Valary about the countess. It was just too improbable. The wife of the heir!

Well, there was really only one answer to the question. He must contact Lady Galton—most secretly if possible. And Valary! Farrelle's flames, had the man mentioned the countess before this damned servant?

If what the princess appeared to be saying was true, then Palle and his associates did not really know what it was Kent was up to. There was no time to waste in self-pity. No time to worry about age—all vanity anyway, or largely so. No, he must press on. There was still time.

Kent forced himself up and discovered that he had not lied entirely, his feet did not pain him as they had. And then he sat down again, almost collapsing on his footstool, but not from some failure of his body. One of his portraits. It had been in the possession of Erasmus . . . ? For how long, Kent wondered? Many years, perhaps. And now it hung in the home of the Duke of Blackwater. Farrelle's flames. She wove a spell that would last a hundred years.

EIGHT

*It is strange to think that I, of all people, became a smith
of the language, for my relations with human kind have
always been marked by a fundamental lack of commonal-
ity, as though I came from a distant land and spoke an
alien tongue. I have always looked at my countrymen and
thought that they slept as they walked: a sleep without
dreams.*

HALDEN, "To Sleep without Dreams"

Across the eastern horizon, sunrise seared the sky in a
narrow band, turning the clouds to molten copper, the sea
to lava. Tristam stood alone on the beach, having escaped
all and sundry, including his shadows, Julian and
Beacham. Immediately he began walking, putting as
much distance between himself and the party of
Farrlanders that had come ashore as he could. He was not
sure of the exact purpose of this escape, other than a desperate need to be alone.

He had brought his bag of naturalist's tools, but he no
longer suffered under the illusion that he had come to this
island to botanize: not since he had climbed up a flooded
stair and discovered a Lost City. Though why he was here
was still a mystery. He was no longer even sure the duchess knew—as he had long believed.

As he made his way along the beach, Tristam could see
the islanders going out to tend their gardens, to gather
fruit, and see to their livestock before the heat of the day
descended. They were graceful silhouettes moving beneath the trees. After walking only a short way, Tristam
decided that the Varuans were avoiding him. He turned
back and could see the other Farrlanders were the center
of joyful mobs of islanders—men, women and children.
Was he to be an outcast here as well? Had the innocent

islanders been infected by the superstitions of the Jacks? Flames! He would never escape those incidents.

Tristam took a path that wove its way up into the bush, hoping to meet no islanders, for he could not bear to be rebuffed again. He felt like a man accused, but never given a chance to defend himself. It disturbed him deeply.

He tried to turn his thoughts outward, and found himself alone in the jungle of Oceana, awash in its sounds and smells, like an island of Farr sensibility in this exotic world. Birds called in the trees, their songs unfamiliar, and the trade wind spoke its hissing language among the palms—which the Varuans believed signaled the presence of gods or the spirits of ancestors.

All around were the plants Tristam had studied with Dandish, and later found in the King's collection at the Tellaman Palace. While he had worked on Trevelyan's collection, Tristam often daydreamed of visiting this world, but he had never thought it would be anything more than that. Just a dream, not something that he would pursue. Tristam's life had never seemed the sort that could be planned—after being orphaned in childhood, plans seemed particularly suspect to him. Experience taught him that the future was uncertain and one could prepare for it only by learning indifference to disappointment and loss. It was, he sometimes thought, the defining characteristic of his personality.

The path slithered steeply up to the crest of the headland, and here, from a clifftop, he could look out over the aqua lagoon to the ring of breaking combers, and the shell-white crests of the trade wind seas.

He stood in the breeze, drinking in the rich aroma of the reef and lagoon, and the perfume of flowers. At that moment the world of Farrland seemed particularly distant and alien to him, as though he were no longer part of it, but a castaway on this pristine island, in the middle of an immense sea. A place where a man took his food from the trees and the lagoon, and never worried about the bill from his tailor. Even two days on Varua, and the contrived life that went with "civilization" as Farrlanders thought of it, seemed very removed from "reality." The words of Wallis seemed very wise at that moment.

Tristam laughed bitterly. It was all illusory, he was sure. Man, he suspected, had a particular genius for complicating things, for creating social hurdles that one must leap or be thought lacking. Wealth was clearly not evenly distributed on Varua—though to a Farrlander even a wealthy Varuan seemed to be living in poverty—and the poorer classes labored for the good of the chiefs and other nobility. Tristam knew it was not Farrland writ small, but he could also see that it was not the innocent paradise it had been painted either. In difficult times the Old Men were known to perform human sacrifice, and raids on neighboring islands saw the capture of slaves, who were the lowest caste on Varua. It was not quite paradise, though from his vantage it would be hard to believe otherwise.

For a while Tristam tried to botanize, identifying the plants and insects in the immediate vicinity, but he felt that he was only playing naturalist, the way one forced oneself to pursue the normal routine of life when tragedy struck. He was holding desperately to the familiar strands of his old life. *I am Tristam.*

He set out along the path again, following it down toward the beach. The conversation with Wallis the previous night kept coming back to him. The omens the artist spoke of did not seem so coincidental, for there was far too much coincidence in his life. Even a dedicated empiricist had to admit that after a while. The great waves Wallis spoke of almost coincided with the discovery of the Lost City—within a day either way, it seemed.

How can that be? the empiricist in him asked, but the voice was less strident, less sure.

A white flower caught his eye, but it wasn't Kingfoil. Tristam did not like the way his body responded to the mere thought of the seed—an immediate hunger as insistent as lust.

The craving had been much reduced, but it hadn't gone away entirely, and every so often it would return, as though it lay watching, waiting for a moment of weakness. He had begun to think that, as much as anything, it was his exposure to *regis* that had lost him control of his emotions. He still suffered from uncontrollable emotional tides: sudden anger, melancholia, great joy, and almost overpowering desire. There were times when he lay sweating in his cabin, his mind so full of the duchess' presence that he feared he was going mad. He imagined that he could see her in her cabin, undressing as she readied for the night.

It is the transformation, he thought, *but I will not give in to it.* With enormous effort he turned his mind elsewhere.

The forest thinned as he came down to the beach, and he walked through a stand of breadfruit trees.

As he came out on the beach, Tristam found a group of island maidens who had dropped their baskets of fruit and were staring up into the sky over his head. Tristam turned just in time to see a swift white form plunge into the trees.

"What?" he asked in his halting Varuan. "What was it?"

The girls began backing away from him immediately. One of the girls said something in Varuan. "Spirit bird," Tristam thought she said. And then they beat a quick retreat, clearly frightened.

Tristam found his field glass and began scanning the trees, almost afraid of what he would find. Among the foreign shapes and foliage, brightly colored kingfishers and lorikeets fled into shadows, as though something terrorized them. He kept sweeping his instrument back and forth slowly, and there, in the branch of a *mori* tree, half-hidden by leaves, he saw a patch of white feathers.

As silently as he could, Tristam moved forward, and then dropped to one knee, and raised his glass again. For a few seconds he thought the bird had fled, but then he found it, still partly obscured. Moving slowly, Tristam strung his bow, left his canvas bag on the sand, and taking his glass and two arrows, slipped forward.

The forest was so thick that he could not find an open

view of his quarry, though a relatively clear shot at the patch of white might be possible.

It cannot be a falcon, Tristam told himself. *There is not a white falcon in Oceana.* But if it was a falcon, he was going to put an end to the question of its origin. If it was merely flesh and blood, an arrow would bring it down, and at the very least, he would add it to his collection of skins.

As he raised his bow and notched an arrow, his hand shook, and he tried to calm his breathing and pounding heart. Taking a long, slow breath, and thinking, *pester me no more,* Tristam let the arrow fly into the jungle.

The sound of wings desperately beating the air came to him, and then silence. No cry. He was not sure his shaft had struck, and quickly he raised his glass to search. For only a second a white bird appeared above the trees, then plunged into the forest top.

An owl, Tristam was sure of it. A pale owl, hardly bigger than a songbird, with a heart-shaped face and golden eyes. An owl never seen before. An owl, he was sure, that would be unfamiliar even to the Varuans.

Tristam sank down on the sand, remembering the owl Beacham had seen as they ascended the water stair. What had it foretold? If this owl augured events even remotely as macabre, Tristam would almost rather die.

He looked out to the sea crashing on the reef. A fine mist filled the pure air, and this sight seemed like an escape, suddenly. If only the sea would take him, comfort him, as it had when he fell into its embrace at Bird Island. But he could not forget the outcome of that. The sea had refused, and returned him to his airy world—the world of living men.

An owl. Though he had been almost certain that the bird he glimpsed originally was larger, swifter, more powerful. A raptor.

Tristam took up his bag and trudged on, wanting only to escape. The moments of feeling a sense of release from this mad quest had been few. There was no escape.

The world around him was forgotten, and Tristam plunged back into a whirl of thought, like a man in the grip of melancholia. A relentless cycle, in which he went round and round, finding no escape, though becoming more and more desperate.

After a walk of indeterminate length, Tristam found himself at the mouth of a broad stream that spoke the peaceful language of brooks as it flowed joyfully into the lagoon. Here Tristam stopped to drink, trusting that the lack of fales in the vicinity would mean there was no one bathing or washing clothing upstream.

"There is a good place to make a bath, in the trees," said a voice behind him, and Tristam turned to find a young woman standing five paces away, twisting together the stems of bright flowers with barely a glance at her swiftly moving fingers.

"You speak Farr," Tristam said, surprised, though perhaps equally surprised that she did not run from him as did the others.

The girl shrugged her bare shoulders. "Wallis teached me.... Taught me?"

"Taught, yes."

Tristam was not sure of the girl's age, barely twenty he thought, perhaps younger, for girls became women early on Varua, having children when they would have still been considered children themselves, had they been born in Farrland. She had the friendly, pure white smile that all the Varuans seemed blessed with, and a face slightly less round, framed by thick, dark hair pulled into a knot at the back of her head. The young women seemed to compete over the length and beauty of their hair. Her pareu fell below the knee, though she wore no tunic, leaving her torso covered only by her hair and a necklace of flowers.

One of the qualities of the islanders that enchanted Tristam was their lack of self-consciousness, and this young woman stood before him, stripped to the waist, and regarded him with utter candor.

"Are you the son of a great chief?" she asked suddenly.

"I . . . No, not at all. My father is dead," he said, thinking immediately that this was a foolish answer.

The woman nodded, as though it were a sensible answer after all. "Wallis says that you . . . the *dausoko* who are clean and do no work, are the sons of great chiefs."

"Ah. Well, we don't have chiefs in the same way, but what Wallis says has some truth. My family are . . ." Tristam searched for a word, "influential." He saw that she did not understand. "They have some wealth." Still, he was not making himself understood. "My uncle is a great chief," he conceded.

She nodded at this. "My aunt is Anua. Do you know Anua?"

"Yes. Yes, we were introduced." Tristam searched for a phrase that could not be misconstrued. "She is very wise."

At this the woman nodded, clearly both understanding and agreeing. "Very wise. Yes."

"My name is Tristam."

She nodded.

"Can you tell me your name?"

"Faairi."

Tristam smiled. "It is similar to a word in our language."

"Yes. Wallis told me. A small person with magical powers, like a spirit. It makes me very sad that I am not a small person with magical powers." She continued to regard him, her expression hardly changing, as though he were some mildly interesting phenomena, or perhaps a beast she had never seen, and though she had been told it was harmless, was taking no chances.

She shifted her concentration to her work, suddenly, as she finished twisting the flowers together in a garland. This she held out before her for careful, if quick, examination, and then, with the first sign of anything resembling shyness, she proffered it to Tristam.

The naturalist was completely charmed. It was, of course, a modest gift, something which the islanders made in minutes, but it was the gesture that mattered, its spontaneity and lack of guile.

Tristam bent and let her slip the necklace over his head. Immediately he felt that he should give her something in return. Metal was much prized by the natives and iron spikes had become so common as the price of a woman's favors that Farr captains had made the removal of iron from the ship a crime almost as serious as mutiny. Otherwise the ships would fall to pieces in the lagoon from loss of structural integrity due to lack of fastenings. Somehow, despite what he knew of this practice among the islanders, Tristam thought it would be an insult to give this generous young woman a piece of iron. It would be construed as a suggestion, and though Tristam thought she was very beautiful, still he could not shake his Farr standards of conduct.

He opened his canvas bag and rummaged among the contents, looking for something he could part with that would not affect his ability to carry out his studies (another idea that he could not give up, despite circumstances), and finally realized that he had several small hand lenses. More than he could ever use, or lose, for that matter.

He produced a palm-sized leather case and held it out to her, not sure what the reaction would be. A great smile appeared on her face, and she met his eye with a quick look of such intensity that he felt a surge of desire. But then she hesitated, and he could almost see her suspicions forming by the changes on her face.

Thinking that she did not know what it was, Tristam opened the case, revealing the circle of glass inside. He raised up one of the blossoms from his necklace and looked through the glass at it, moving the lens until he found the point of focus. He turned the lens toward the woman and motioned for her to look. Tristam had the definite impression that curiosity overcame some reluctance. He moved the lens slowly up and down, hoping the flower would come into focus for her, and when it did she exclaimed; some Varuan word he did not know.

Tristam picked up a scrap of dried palm frond from the sand and focused the sun on it. Faairi stood close to him, watching intently, and the scent of the flowers and the oil Varuan women used for perfume caused Tristam to take long deep breaths, drinking in this aroma. Her bare arm touched him as she stood and Tristam caught himself before he moved away, as he would be expected to do in Farrland.

A small circle of the leaf began to blacken and a tiny feather of smoke appeared, presaging diminutive flames which sputtered in the breeze.

Faairi turned to him in great delight. "It is *makawa*," she said, and made no move to claim the offered gift.

"I don't understand?" Tristam said.

"Old Man's work," she tried.

"Ah," Tristam said, with a sinking feeling that she meant necromancy. "But it is just a piece of glass. Nothing magical or forbidden. I have several."

He still held it in his hand, not quite offering it to her again, afraid that there might be some tapu involved, but hoping she would take it, as it hung in the air between them. He thought she seemed overly impressed with this display of Farr technology—or white skin's magic.

"The day is very hot," she said, glancing toward the sun. "Will you come and bathe?"

How easily such a suggestion was made, Tristam thought. He tried to imagine Jenny saying such a thing. But then he remembered the evening he had spent at the duchess' and realized that there were places, even in overly-proper Farr society, where the rules and expectations were flouted. A foreign visitor would likely never see such things, and would come away with a completely different picture of life in Farrland.

Tristam followed Faairi up a narrow path that bordered the stream, her supple waist and the tight wrapping of her pareu around her buttocks drawing his eye. The contrast between this young woman and the duchess struck him as they walked. Her dress seemed almost a symbol of the difference between the two women—a simple piece of cloth made from the inner bark of the paper-mulberry, *Broussonetia papyrifera,* wrapped simply about the waist and held in place without fastenings. It seemed as though the layers of artifice that Farr culture required were peeled away with each layer of clothing. Tristam thought of the whalebone corsets that Farr women once used to squeeze their figure into the fashionable shape, and here was Faairi, who wore little more than a string of flowers. And she had spoken to him, not needing a "proper" introduction. Tristam realized he was shaking his head in disbelief.

Her strong back and square shoulders moved with such ease as she went, and Tristam found himself wondering what it would be like to kiss that perfect golden skin.

They found the pool, created by a dam of rocks—not a work of nature at all, Tristam was sure. Faairi laid her necklace carefully on the ground, and stripped off her pareu, laying it over the branch of a bush. Reaching back to free her hair raised her breasts in the most enticing manner, though she did not seem aware of this. She waded into the pool, casting a look over her shoulder at Tristam, as the water distorted her perfect legs.

He began pulling off his clothes, realizing that he had stood entranced, watching her. Tristam's clothing seemed absurdly complex and impractical, suddenly, and his life even more so. How he wished that he could peel away the layers of complexity, sloughing them off like old skins.

Before entering the water, he set the magnifying glass on the ground near Faairi's necklace of flowers, leaving her to take it or leave it, whichever she chose.

He plunged into the water, trying to hide his rising desire. The pond was just deep enough to swim and he struck out for a dozen strokes and then stopped, his feet finding the soft bottom.

"You swim," Faairi said, clearly pleased. "How is it that your sailors cannot?"

"Many people in my country believe swimming will make them ill," Tristam said, a bit embarrassed at the foolishness of his countrymen. "Of course, the water in our land is much colder than here."

Faairi smiled and shook her head, trying not to laugh, he thought. "Farrlanders believed many strange beliefs," she said. "There are only two women on your ship, and so many men. It must be very . . . lonely."

"Well, in the past there were no women at all," Tristam countered.

She nodded, her look unreadable, as though she consid-

ered this carefully. "These women ... the old one is
Stern's woman, and the other is whose?"

"The old one," Tristam tried not to laugh at this term,
"the Duchess of Morland, is not Stern's woman. She is
like a great chief herself—like Anua—a woman of wisdom who is much respected in Farrland, and who is also
a great friend of our King. The young woman, Jacel, is
her servant. Do you know 'servant'? Someone who does
your work; brings your meals, cleans your clothing, heats
the water for your bath."

She nodded, although heating water for baths seemed
unlikely work here.

The slow current drifted Tristam down toward Faairi,
and she held her place, watching him with that same look
of odd detachment.

"When you walk in the dream world, have you come
often to Varua?" she asked suddenly.

The words did not convey meaning to the Farr mind,
but Tristam was afraid that he understood her only too
well, though he was curiously reluctant to admit it. He
nodded, saying nothing.

"Once I saw a woman in the lagoon."

"Who was she?"

Tristam shrugged. "I don't know."

"Did you ..." she searched for a word, "have the love
with her?"

Tristam laughed. "I confess, I did."

"Ah," she said, as though it were approval. "What did
she look like?"

Tristam laughed aloud this time. "She had long black
hair, brown eyes, skin the color of yours."

Faairi shook her head. "Wallis said that our people are
much alike to your eye." She regarded Tristam. "Your
people are not so much the same, I think. Taller, shorter,
hair like sand, eyes that are green or the color of the sea."
She cupped water in her hands and lifted them, letting the
water run out in a glittering stream. "In the world of
dreams I have walked in your land," she said, "though
only one time."

"And what did you see?" Tristam asked quickly.

"A village of stone, and beasts like giant pigs that drew people in *wagons*, I think. Smoke rose out of the roofs, which were smooth and black. It was like the paintings that Wallis showed to me, but everything moved and I could hear the sounds and smell the smells." She wrinkled up her nose. "In your village the earth found its way through stone only in small places. The ground was very hard. As I walked, the sun set and I came upon a house that had fallen. Such a large house that it looked like a mountain of broken stone, and among the stone a small boy was hiding, though I think he was a *tamaroa mo'e*."

"What does that mean? A boy? Some kind of boy?"

She shrugged. "One that cannot be reached. A boy who lives in the world beyond."

Tristam nodded. Wallis had shown her some illustrations of Farrland, apparently, but he guessed there was no ghost boy in them, nor would there likely be the ruin of his father's theater. Who was this woman and why had she, of all the Varuans, come to befriend him? "Do you have such dreams often?" he asked, instead of his real questions.

She shook her head. "My sister is a dream walker. She is lost in the dream world, now. They could not call her back to her body, and she is lost forever. But this cannot happen to me. Look." She stood taller in the water, pointing to a small blue tattoo between her breasts. It was all Tristam could manage to glance at anything beside the glistening dark nipples that seemed to bob on the surface. The tattoo was a small diamond shape, intersected with many lines.

"It is my star," she said, "so that I might always find the way home." She settled back into the water, to Tristam's disappointment.

"That would do it," he said, hoping as soon as the words were out that she would not take offense, but irony did not translate easily.

"I would like to regard your hand," she said, which made Tristam smile.

He raised his hand, dripping from the water.

"No. Another hand."

He hesitated. Had she seen his scar as he undressed? Reluctantly he raised "another hand."

She took hold of it softly, turning it over so that the scar was exposed. For a moment it was as though she had forgotten him, she stared so intently at his wrist—like a doctor examining a wound. Then she laid the palm of one hand gently over the scar, and though she raised her head, her eyes remained closed.

Tristam was not sure what she intended, but for some reason her touch seemed cool upon the wound, and the desire for *regis* seemed to diminish. He closed his own eyes, and breathed out slowly, unsure of what was happening—not certain it was anything but imagination.

Then he opened his eyes and found Faairi gazing at him, her look full of curiosity. Her grip had shifted so that she held only his fingers, and her manner was less grave. "You walked near to the burning gate and returned," she said. "So very few have done this thing. Were you not afraid?"

"I am not sure what happened," Tristam heard his voice whisper. *What am I saying? She is not making sense!*

She nodded. "Memories do not always return with us from the dream world."

Tristam said nothing, only shutting his eyes. What was she talking about? Did she really understand what had happened to him? He felt a hand touch his cheek.

"You must be careful to not let yourself slip away. If you turn your back on the world of the sun . . . I saw it happen to my sister. You must keep hold of this world, Tristam. Do not let it go." She squeezed his hand tightly as she said this, and then raised it to her breast, slipping close to him. He felt her legs wrap around his waist, and her arms encircle his neck. Desire took hold of him. It was like sinking into a *regis* dream. A feeling that he lost himself, or something else took control. He felt his own personality submerging, as though it were driven down into the depths. A cry sounded loud in his ear, and though he thought it was Faairi, it became the cry of a bird of prey.

* * *

Tristam woke to find himself lying on a bed of flowers and leaves on the edge of the pond. For a moment he felt a terrible vertigo and then this passed. He turned his head and saw Faairi stretched out on her back upon a rock, her soft belly arching, the muscles pulled taut, her small breasts flattened. She turned her head to him and smiled, though there was some concern there.

"Are you returned?" she asked.

"I think so, yes."

She rolled over and came near to him, laying a hand on his chest. "You must learn not to let the other master you," she said.

"What? What happened?"

"Shh," she said softly, and then moved to sit astride him. "You must not take your eyes from mine. We will go very slowly." She reached down and helped him into her, and he felt the warmth and softness embrace him. "So slowly. You are Tristam," she said, beginning the slowest rhythm. "Tristam. And we are here on Varua, in the world of the sun—the waking world. *Ohh.*" She closed her eyes for a second in pleasure, and then snapped them open. "Stay with me."

He reached up and touched her face, and she kissed his fingers. Again her eyes closed, and she moaned, but opened them again quickly. She moved his hand to her breast and he rolled the nipple in his fingers. Something stirred in him and Tristam recognized it as that force, the desire that had overwhelmed him. With some effort he struggled to keep control, feeling his hips rise to meet Faairi as she moved.

I am Tristam, he said to himself. *Tristam.* I am not a mage. No matter what they want, I will not become that. He kept his eyes fixed on the beautiful face above him, and then saw the tiny star tattooed between her breasts. She was his star at that moment. His point of contact with the world of the waking. He brushed his fingers over this mark, and she took his hand and kissed the scar on his wrist.

"Tristam," she whispered, and then words in her own language that he did not understand, but which sounded soft and fair.

NINE

Ceremonies for graduating scholars had taken place annually in Merton since the founding of the university some five centuries earlier, and, as things did in Farrland, the rituals had become quickly entrenched.

A member of the Royal House of Farrland did not necessarily graduate from the university even once in a generation, but even so, there were rituals to deal with this eventuality, too. Although there were no invitations sent, certain segments of Farr society were expected to turn out for the royal graduation—those of the right strata of society or of the correct association simply knew—while anyone appearing who should not would be marked for life for their presumption.

The graduation of Prince Wilam, the son of the Prince Royal, appeared to follow the expected course, flowing as predictably as the River Wedgewater, which had not overflowed its banks in living memory.

The official reception after the ceremony was held at the home of the University Chancellor, a man who had been born at a level in society that would have required his attendance on this day even if he had not been presiding over much of the ceremony.

Sir Averil Kent had twice put himself in the path of Roderick Palle, only to have the King's Man turn aside to greet another—not snubbing the painter openly, but Kent knew the man avoided him. Kent was not even sure why he was going out of his way to greet the King's Man, just some strange urge. A desire to let Palle know he was not intimidated—to leave the King's Man wondering why he seemed at ease. He wanted a little revenge on the man for the misery that his knighthood had caused. But Palle was not about to give him the opportunity, it seemed, and the painter decided it was time to stop being so childish, and continued on his rounds through the crowded rooms.

He had already stood in line to pay his respects to the Prince and Princess on the graduation of their son, and Kent was sure that, as the Princess took his hand, he had felt an almost imperceptible increase in pressure—a message. There had been no other sign, that was certain. The Princess was no more cordial with him than with anyone else who came before her, and Prince Kori was as amiable, and at the same time as distant, as always.

This small incident with the Princess, a minute caress of his hand, had left him feeling somewhat elated, even protected here, as though no evil could befall him—an illusion he knew, but even so, he felt it strongly, and this was a vast improvement over the gnawing anxiety he had known these past months.

Passing into a large ballroom Kent stopped for a moment to survey the crowd. It was an odd mixture of Merton dons, uncomfortable in their formal clothing, aristocrats, and scholars attended by their friends. The scholars wore robes of deep crimson trimmed in gold, and carried old fashioned tricorns tucked under their arms. They were flushed with elation, and in some cases drink, their clear pink complexions glowing, reminding Kent vividly of his own graduation, so many years ago.

Too many members of Kent's own year had passed on, too soon, he thought. He didn't like to count. A point would come when there would be more dead than remained alive, which Kent felt had some terrible significance—those remaining would be thought "survivors." But, Farrelle bless them, these young men and women he saw here had no fears of growing old and dying—an event that no doubt seemed impossibly far away.

Thoughts of mortality soured Kent's mood a little, for it always brought up the questions about *regis*—the great temptation that Valary had once spoken aloud; to use it themselves if they were ever to have such a chance. Valary was certain the physic would drive anyone who did not know the arts of the mages to madness, as it apparently had Trevelyan. Poor man. No, Kent knew he would have to grow old as gracefully as he could—there was no alternative for him.

"Sir Averil, is it?" a familiar voice said. "You haven't forgotten your old friends though, I hope."

Kent turned to find Professor Somers, Alissa's father, making his way through the press, smiling as he came. "Professor. Please, no need for the title. We both know, only too well, how these things are usually acquired, though mine was truly a surprise, I will say in my own defense."

"Which goes without saying. Titles *have* been awarded to deserving individuals occasionally, and I don't mind using the honorific; for you, of all people, have my respect." Somers took Kent's hand warmly. "My Alissa has said you have very kindly come to her rescue at various social functions, and I must thank you for that." His face changed then, a hint of worry appearing.

"Oh, hardly, hardly. She is perfectly able to carry these things off without help from me. But I congratulate you on Miss Alissa's coming marriage. I know your feelings about the aristocracy, Somers, but I will tell you, I think this young man is a fine gentleman and will do everything within his power to make your daughter happy. It is a good match, and she will rise to the social demands with ease, I'm sure. The Flattery family are people of substance, as you must have realized, and not caught up in the more superficial parts of the aristocratic life. The Duke of Blackwater is a man I esteem greatly, and his wife, though not well these past years, is a kindly, intelligent woman. You are not seeing her at her best, but let us hope you will."

Somers nodded, clearly glad to hear these words from an old friend. "I'm sure you're right, Kent. It was a bit of a shock, I will admit." He shook his head, and then a bemused smile appeared. "You have not the blessing of children, Sir Averil, but no matter that one thinks one knows them better than they know themselves, they will surprise you—force you to admit that they have lives of their own." He glanced quickly about the room, as most people did occasionally, looking for friends they had not seen in some time, or others they felt some social obligation to greet. "I must tell you, Kent, there are some I miss at times like this—Dandish most of all."

The painter nodded. "Yes, he was not a social man, but those of us who knew him realized his value."

Somers swept his gaze around the room again. "I pass his house occasionally and it always affects me. Whoever bought the old place, though, is tearing it to pieces; digging up all the gardens, ripping out the interior. Madness! It was a perfectly lovely home as it stood."

"Tearing up the garden?" Kent said, too quickly. "Who bought the place?"

Somers shrugged. "Dean Emin could tell you, I'm sure. Ah, there's my future son-in-law now." The professor nodded toward the far end of the room. "I have grown fond of him, I will admit, though I can't help but wish Alissa had fallen for the young lord's cousin. A solid young man and an empiricist of some promise. Do you know him? Tristam Flattery?"

Kent nodded, keeping his face carefully neutral. "I do indeed. Perhaps when he returns, he will capture the affections of another of your lovely daughters." Kent followed Somers' gaze, and there was Lord Jaimas talking to a group of young men about his own age.

"I would not be against it, though he does live rather far off, in Locfal. Do you mind, Kent? I should speak to Lord Jaimas for a moment. Come by if you can. The house is full of people, as you might imagine, but everyone would dearly love to see you."

Somers set out into the sea of faces, bumped and buffeted like a boat on the waves.

Tearing up the garden? Kent wondered how soon he could politely escape. Dandish's house seemed to be an object of continuing interest. But to whom?

Kent was about to turn and leave when he noticed a

woman exiting by another door; the sight stopped him, like a bird striking glass. All he had seen was a cascade of shining black curls, but this had brought back a memory so powerful that for a moment he thought he had wakened from a dream of being old to the sight of the woman he cherished retreating from the room—retreating from his life.

"Flames," he whispered. Too many memories lurked in the depths, surfacing unexpectedly, some like old leaves, rising dark and shapeless from the bottom, others like blossoms, appearing, bejeweled in beads of water. His memories of the countess were of both types, some dark and despairing, others so full of light it hurt to recall them, though he often did, and bore the pain. He could not help it, the currents that brought memories to the surface were inconstant and mysterious.

❦ ❦ ❦

As the Ambassador of His Imperial Entonne Majesty, Count Massenet had carried both gifts and expressions of his King's great respect to the Farr Royal Family, and he was now doing the two things he did best in the world, charming women and seeking information he was not supposed to be privy to. Lady Galton did not appear in Farrland very often, preferring her adopted home, the island of Farrow, and the count did not want to waste an opportunity to speak with her. There were two reasons for this: the lady admired him extremely (unfortunate that she was not still young and beautiful), and she was the cousin of the Princess Joelle.

"I have not had more than a moment to speak with the Princess. Her Highness is well, I hope?"

Lady Galton's eyes lost focus briefly, as though she were a little bored with questions about her royal cousin. "I believe Her Highness is well." Suddenly she looked sharply at the count. "Though I thought you should know better than I."

Massenet did not blink or hesitate. "I am at the palace often, it is true, but seldom do I see anyone of any interest or real charm. Ministers and officials and so on. I wonder sometimes whatever led me to take this position."

Lady Galton laughed softly. "Because intrigue is your nature, Count Massenet," she said, her smile remaining, her still-beautiful eyes laughing, "as it is a bird's nature to fly. When you were pushed from the nest, I believe you landed in the royal court. But am I being unfair? Perhaps you were not pushed, but jumped?"

Massenet bowed his head in surrender. How he loved intelligent women!

But Lady Galton was not done. "And intrigue offers such possibilities, for it comes in so many varieties; political, courtly, social, intrigues of commerce, intrigues of the bedchamber. Variations without end."

Yes, Massenet agreed silently, *like women.* "Though I hate to dispel any myths concerning my origin, I fear that ambassadors are not born, Lady Galton, but merely appointed. I understand that Farrow was graced this autumn by the Duchess of Morland. There is no end of speculation as to why the lady set out on this remarkable voyage."

"I thought everyone knew ..." Lady Galton said ingenuously. "She seeks youth ... in the form of a young empiricist. What was the young man's name?"

Massenet attempted something he found difficult—he tried to look foolish, as though he could not think who or what she meant, exactly.

"Well, that's my guess at least. It is a flaw some cannot overcome. They pursue youth." She waved a hand at a gathering of young women who kept glancing coyly toward the count. "They may not think that is their purpose but ..." She shrugged. "But such pursuits end in tragedy, Count Massenet. We will all grow old, as I have, or die young. No artifice can change that." She reached out and touched his arm. "I am called away. It has been a great pleasure." She curtsied like a girl, no small effort for her, he was sure, and swept away in the wake of a Royal Page.

Youth. He glanced at the group of young women, but they had gone, and in their place was a single woman, who stared at him openly, her look amused as though she had heard the entire interchange and understood its undercurrents completely. And she was an astonishing beauty! She bent her long neck toward him as though in acknowledgment, a dark cascade of hair moving like something in nature, and then she went off in the same direction as Lady Galton. Massenet, to his surprise, merely stood and watched her go, watched everyone step aside as she passed, as though she were the Queen herself.

"You look as though you've seen a ghost."

Massenet turned to find the Marqeuss of Sennet staring in the same direction as he.

"But who was that woman?" Massenet asked, his voice coming out as though the wind had been knocked from his lungs.

"Well, if I am not mistaken, that is Angeline Christophe. Though I am surprised to see her here. Perhaps she knows someone who is graduating."

"Really." Angeline Christoph was the woman rumored to be Prince Kori's mistress. "Well, I should very much like to meet this young woman. Will you be so kind as to introduce me?"

Sennet smiled, perhaps enjoying the count's candor. "I have never had the pleasure myself. She is something of a recluse, I understand. I don't know a soul who claims to be her friend. So you shall have to be bold, Count Massenet. I dare say you are able."

❦   ❦   ❦

Jaimy walked in the garden, listening intently to his companion, becoming more and more alarmed at what he heard.

"It was almost an impossible task to translate. They would allow me only a copy of the original text and this had been broken up into fragments and given to me in an order that would make it difficult to recognize as one piece. These men, Wells and Llewellyn, attached themselves to me as I worked and I began to realize, by their endless questions, that they must be attempting a translation of some sections of the thing themselves. But their attempts to hide the nature of the text were rather futile. Anyone would eventually realize what it was." Egar Littel looked around the garden as though suddenly afraid. "I insisted that I must come to Merton to search the library—told them I couldn't continue otherwise. I am still amazed that I managed to give them the slip." He stopped, clearly frightened. "You're sure we're safe here? There are any number of people coming and going." He looked back to the lights of the house. Dark shapes could be seen moving in the windows.

"Try not to worry, Egar. If any of your tormentors arrive, Alissa will alert us. But what will you do now?"

The young man began to pace again, staying to the shadows of the trees and hedges. "I don't know. I must get away. Out of the country if I can." Jaimy could tell the man was staring at him suddenly, trying to read his face in the darkness. "I shouldn't have come to the professor's house like this, but I really didn't know where else to go. The Somers' were always so kind to me in my time here."

"Don't apologize, you've done absolutely the right thing, though I think we should not bother the professor about this just now. I will tell you more once we have you out of Merton. We need to decide on a course of action, though." There were any number of places he could hide the young man. Even Tristam's home in Locfal. But out of the country might make the most sense. Entonne, probably. Egar's skill with languages was such that he could probably pass for a native. But there was more to it than that. Flames, he wished Tristam were back! Here was another piece of the puzzle, falling into his lap unexpectedly. But what did it mean exactly?

"This text, Egar, what did you make of it? Ancient, you say. But who wrote it, do you think?"

The young man put his hand to his forehead. "I can't give you a name, if that's what you mean. Its purpose isn't even perfectly clear. It's stranger than you can imagine, and, of course, I saw it all out of order with some crucial sections excised. It is both prose and verse, dissertation and syllabus, and it is not all in the same language, even. The subject is necromancy—I don't know what else to call it—though I don't know who could ever make sense of it. There are continual references to things—herbs and I don't know what else, like *belloc root,* and *kilsbreath,* and *kingsblood.* They do not translate into modern Farr, and what they are, we don't know. But the subject is definitely the arts of the mages, and written, I would say, by someone intimate with its practices."

"A mage."

"I would assume so."

They paused at the end of the garden for a moment and the young scholar lit a pipe with a coal from the smoldering incinerator. Jaimy could see the hands tremble in the hot glow of the pipe. He realized the young man could not bear up much longer.

"And the worst thing is," Littel said suddenly, clenching the pipe between his teeth, "these men—Wells and Hawksmoore and Noyes—they take this all so seriously. It is not just scholarly interest. They really believe they can rekindle the arts of the mages. In this day and age, if you can believe it!"

"Well, if they kept you half a prisoner, they must have some reason to think this. They aren't foolish men, Egar."

The scholar said nothing, but gave Jaimy a quick glance that almost spoke anger.

"Listen, Egar, there is someone else I wish to involve in this. Someone who knows more about these men and these matters than I can claim."

The young man nodded, his pipe bobbing like a ship's lantern in a seaway. "Who?"

"I hesitate to say until we have you safely away."

Littel stopped, removing the pipe from his mouth slowly. "I would like to know who you are involving. It is my safety in the balance."

"I understand." Jaimy looked up to find a star had appeared through a hole in the cloud. "Do you know Averil Kent?" he said quietly.

"The painter?"

Jaimy nodded.

"Only by reputation. He will help us? I thought he had just been knighted at Palle's insistence. Didn't I tell you that Palle was part of this?"

"You did, but I can assure you that Kent is no friend of the King's Man, despite appearances. I can explain further, but it will take time."

Littel walked a few more paces. "It seems very odd to me. You're sure of the man?"

"Quite sure," Jaimy said, though in truth it was only a hunch. "Kent's in Merton now, or was earlier today. I'm sure I can track him down, but we need to hide you away. I'm staying with Flinders. Do you know him? No? Good. I'll tell him you're an old friend and there isn't an inn with a free room in the town. He won't mind in the least. Flames, I wish Tristam were here. He would give anything to see this text. Unfortunate that you couldn't have spirited it away with you."

"But I did." The scholar looked quite surprised. "Don't you know? I can recall entire books without error. It is my memory—I seem to be unable to forget anything, no matter how trivial. It would take me a few hours, a day at most, but I can copy out this text, and my translation of it. Would that interest you?"

"Interest me!? Farrelle's blood, Egar, you can't begin to imagine what an unlooked for miracle you are."

❧   ❧   ❧

Kent elected to walk the short distance from his inn to the house that had once belonged to Professor Sanfield Dandish. The streetlamps here were far apart and the night sky was half blinded by drifting cloud, so the streets were dark, and still damp from an afternoon rain. The small storm lantern Kent carried would have lit his way had he not chosen to keep it shuttered so that only the faintest glow escaped along with a feather of smoke.

It was a night of celebration in Merton, even the scholars who were not graduating used the occasion to justify their revels, but in this corner of the city things were relatively quiet. Kent found himself taking more and more care as he went. He did not put his cane down with the customary tap, and set his boots lightly, though the leather squeaked all the same. For some reason he thought that he was being watched or, more to the point, followed. Twice he turned quickly only to find a darkened street. His imagination tried to make something out of the shadows, but even with his imperfect eyesight he was almost certain he was alone. He heard nothing, and his hearing was not failing as quickly as his sight.

No light showed at the windows of Dandish's old residence, but Kent decided to circle the block and enter through the alley. The gate set into the hedge was not locked, and Kent stepped through it quickly to pause in the shadows, listening. Even in the poor light he could see the garden was in ruins, as though an excavation was underway. There were piles of dirt and rubble everywhere. Only the majestic trees had been spared, and they stood over this carnage, stretching their bare limbs up to the sky in silent lament. Kent could not help but think that this would break poor Dandish's heart.

After five minutes he was sure he was alone, and began to pick his way across the garden, using his walking stick to probe for open pits and to locate obstructions. Once he was forced to open his lantern, a brief appearance of light, like the moon emerging from behind a cloud, but then he closed it again, not wanting to draw anyone's attention. He was still not absolutely sure who was responsible for this travesty. He had sent a note off to Dean Emin but didn't expect a reply until morning.

The back doors to the house had been broken during the excavations and nailed hastily shut. Using his walking stick Kent had one ajar in a moment. He squeezed through the crack and opened his lantern to find that the house had been treated like the garden. Laths and plaster had been ripped from the walls and the flooring torn up, exposing the joists and beams. Inside, the house had been reduced to a skeleton. He could look between bare ceiling joists into the upstairs rooms.

Kent felt a need to sit. "What in Farrelle's name?" he said aloud. Someone had been desperately looking for . . .

what? He stepped out gingerly onto some planks that had been laid across the joists, and could see down into the cellar bellow.

The entire house had been treated the same; only the main stairway was left intact. Kent went from room to room, remembering each as it had been when Dandish still lived—and on his last visit after the man had passed on. The professor's involvement with the court and *regis* was still causing ripples on the pond. Was this the work of Palle, trying to be sure that Dandish left no information, no trace of his efforts? Or was there someone else who Kent was not even aware of (one of his great fears)?

The painter made his way down the stairway, which seemed to stand almost unsupported, as though it were the spine of this skeletal house.

"Mr. Kent?"

Kent was so startled that he nearly missed the next step. A young man stood on the bottom tread, and for a moment Kent thought he was looking at Tristam Flattery.

"Lord Jaimas! What a start you gave me."

"I apologize, sir, I was surprised myself."

"What on earth are you doing here?" Kent came down to the young man's level and reached out to take his shoulder, as though reassuring himself that he was substantial.

"I went to Dean Emin to ask if he knew where you were lodging and he mentioned that he had a note from you inquiring about Dandish's house. When I could not find you at your inn, I thought I would come here, as it was so close by. Isn't it a crime? Look what they've done to poor Dandish's home!"

"But who did it, do you know?"

Jaimy shook his head. "I haven't the faintest notion." He looked around the entryway, then back at Kent, catching the man's eye. "Sir Averil, I have talked to Alissa about your request of her, as I think you know, and I believe that we have a common cause; you, and Alissa and I, and my cousin Tristam, as well as a few others. I do not want to say more, here."

Kent almost smiled. "Let us go out by the back," the

painter said, holding up his lantern so that they could both see the way. They came out into the dark battlefield that had once been Dandish's precious garden, and as they stepped onto the brick terrace, a child bolted out from behind a pile of rubble and shot through the gate, though the gate was quite clearly firmly closed.

❦ ❦ ❦

Kent sat before the fire in the drawing room of a friend of Lord Jaimas'—he had not caught the man's name— but, anyway, he was conveniently out. For a moment the painter closed his eyes, listening to the voices. His stomach had taken to burning as though he had swallowed mild acid, and the pain flared up now—a sign of his distress. Things were much worse than he had imagined. How he wished Valary were here!

"It is nothing like you imagine, Miss Alissa," Egar Littel was saying. "The text, even if perfectly translated, which we are not yet capable of, is so ... arcane, so dense and convoluted." He paused, searching for words that would convey his meaning. "You would almost think it had not been written by a man at all but by some being from a nether world with an entirely different mind. It is in no place clear and logical or linear. It is as though the sentences were taken and randomly mixed."

"But did you not say they had given it to you in fragments, out of sequence so that you would not understand what it was you read? Could Wells and his group have merely mixed the sentences?"

"No," he said emphatically, and then stopped at the corner of the room to which he had paced. Kent watched the young man, could almost feel him thinking, with his thumb hitched in his waistcoat, his other hand to his forehead. He was surprisingly presentable for a scholar, the painter thought, attempting to make the most of his looks. To think that he had been telling Valary only weeks before that they must make an effort to find this young man, and here he was. Not out of the country at all, as they had been led to believe. Kent almost smiled. *You are too clever, Palle, but luck has favored me this time. Your genius escaped and came directly to me!*

"When I say it has no logic, that does not mean it has no pattern." Littel looked a bit ill at ease as he said this, as though stating this contradiction was like admitting he sometimes had the urge to do terrible things. "I cannot explain this, but there is some deeper pattern. I sense it more than see it, but I'm sure it's there. And I'm certain that Wells did not jumble the order of the sentences. You would have to see it yourself, but they follow, in their own strange way, from one to the next."

"I am dying to see it," Alissa said. "We will have to lock you in a room somewhere until you have reproduced it."

Littel drew himself up to his full height. "I have already been locked away in a room somewhere. I came to you to avoid that in the future."

"Oh, certainly, Egar," Alissa hurried to add. "It was just a figure of speech."

"Alissa is right, though," Kent said. "We must get you away, and you absolutely must reproduce that text. It is imperative that we know what Palle and his group possess. And Valary must see it." *And the countess,* Kent thought, bringing back a vision of the woman he had glimpsed earlier in the day. Had she really looked so much like the countess? Absurd, of course. If he had seen her face, the illusion would have been dispelled.

"I can give you some sense of what it is—at least my opinion. I believe it's a description of a ritual." Littel looked around at the others. "An incantation, a chant of warding, a procedure to create some kind of physic or elixir, and instructions for making an offering, perhaps even a sacrifice. That is what I think they possess."

Flaming martyrs! Kent thought. "What do Wells and the others think?" Kent realized suddenly that he was very tired. It would soon be light.

"They do not say, but I have come to believe they think it is a ritual that opens a portal or a gate."

"What gate?" Jaimy asked.

Littel shrugged. "I don't know."

"But what is behind the gate?" Alissa asked. "What is it they seek?"

Littel rubbed his eyes for a second, almost seeming to cover his face in horror. "I don't know that either, though whatever it is, they seek it desperately." He lowered his hands, and Kent thought his face suddenly looked quite pale. "Desperately enough that I fear what they might do if they find me. And I regret extremely my part in their scheme."

"I think we should get you away tonight," Kent said, his mind made up. "They must be seeking you even now. When I was young, there was a walking trail from Merton to Bothwell. Is it there, still?"

"Most certainly," Alissa said, almost jumping up. "I have walked it myself. Five brisk hours in the daylight."

"I can't stay in Bothwell," the scholar protested. "There aren't two hundred people there, all of whom know each other's business."

"No, you mustn't even enter the town, but I will meet you on the high road with my carriage and take you on. I have a place in mind. . . ."

A great thumping at the door stopped all conversation. Everyone looked to Kent, their alarm apparent. Littel stepped behind the back of a chair as though it would protect him.

"Your sight is better than mine, Lord Jaimas," Kent said quietly, forcing confidence into his tone. "Will you go to a window and see who it might be?"

The thumping came again, and everyone sat in silence but for Jaimy who sprinted up the stairs. In a moment he was down again, looking perplexed. "It's a man, alone apparently. It seems to be Prince Wilam."

Jaimy went and spoke through the door, then immediately threw it open, bowing quickly to the King's grandson.

"No time for that, Lord Jaimas," the prince said. "Palle and some others are on their way." The prince dropped a bag to the floor and then pulled off a heavy cloak. Beneath the cloak he still wore his graduation robes. "You're Littel, I collect?" he said matter-of-factly.

The scholar was so stunned he could not answer, but managed to nod.

"Put this on," the prince pulled crimson robes from his bag. "And you as well, Lord Jaimas." He bowed to Alissa. "I do apologize, Miss Alissa, but I have no costume for you." And then he turned to Kent. "I will leave you to see Miss Alissa home, Sir Averil. But we must meet later, though I'm not sure where to suggest."

Kent stood looking on, weighing this twist in events, gratified at how little it surprised him. It all fell neatly into place—made sense somehow. There was no choice but to trust the prince, if for no other reason than he was more his mother's son than his father's.

"At the Bayswater Bridge, before the track joins the high road to Avonel. I have a place to hide Mr. Littel."

"It will take us a few hours." The prince turned toward the others, dressed now as graduating scholars, and still young enough to be believable.

"Your Highness?"

The prince turned back to Kent.

"How close is Massenet on our heels?"

"Quite close."

"Then we should be on our way. Please, lead on."

TEN

Kent had made his way through the streets crowded with revelers, delivering a somewhat worried Alissa Somers home, and then had gone back out into the fray, struggling on to his inn. He was surprised as he entered the lobby to find Dean Emin and Professor Somers waiting rather impatiently.

"Ah, Kent." Somers was out of his seat much more quickly than the aging dean. "I have lost a wager due to your timely arrival. But never mind. You can spare us a moment, I hope?"

Kent stopped in his tracks. He had no moments to spare. The thought of letting Littel fall back into the hands of Palle and his company was propelling him along at new found speed. Farrelle's blood, this young man knew what Palle and Wells were working on!

"A moment . . . ?" He looked at the worried faces of these two good men. "Can you come up?"

They ascended to the painter's rooms in cold silence.

"Won't you sit," Kent said as a servant came in to light the lamps.

Dean Emin took a chair, but Somers stood, clearly agitated. "I prefer to stand, thank you," he said, a bit coolly, the painter thought.

As soon as the servant was gone, Somers raised a finger. "It is time we knew what is going on, Kent," he said emphatically. "Palle has been to my house asking after you and one of my former students, who showed up at my door earlier this evening looking like a man who'd just escaped the gallows. Lord Jaimas and my daughter took this young man off before I had a chance to find out what was going on, and now all three of them have disappeared. An hour ago Prince Wilam himself came by asking for Lord Jaimas. And your note to the dean would indicate that you have a continuing interest in Dandish and his doings. Perhaps you even know why his home has been destroyed." He paused looking suddenly weary. "I am worried nigh on to death about Alissa, Kent."

"She is at your home, Professor, perfectly safe. I delivered her there myself not half the hour ago." Kent poured three brandies and passed two to his guests, though he was sure it was he who was in need. "Mr. Littel is safe as well, I hope. Which is to say he was not, when last seen, in the company of Palle."

Emin and Somers glanced at each other. "It seems that the King's Man has had a hand in much of this, Sir Averil," the dean said quietly, his manner subdued, as though he would make up for his companion. "Though Dandish's home was purchased through a barrister, it was this man, Hawksmoore, who had the house stripped to the bones. He was not so clever as he thought. I saw him there myself."

Kent paced across the floor. Too many knew too much already. "I wish I had an explanation . . ." Kent began, but could go no further. He desperately needed a moment to think. And even more desperately, he needed to get away!

"Was this flower that Dandish grew so very important?" Emin asked innocently.

Kent stopped abruptly, looking at his companions with surprise.

"So important that Palle would have his house torn to pieces . . . searching for what?" Somers said. "And was it the King's Man who took Dandish's journals?" Somers paced away suddenly, too upset to continue, it seemed.

"We would not be so worried, Sir Averil," Emin said, almost apologetically, "but the Flatterys are involved—relations of old Erasmus—one of whom is to marry Somers' daughter." Emin looked over at his colleague with some concern, and then went on. "Tristam Flattery was here last summer after Dandish died, and even then was involved in some affair that unsettled him greatly. Something to do with the palace arboretum, I realized, though he would not speak of it. And this young man, Littel, Somers tells me, has some tale of being held a near-prisoner while he translated an ancient text, which, if he is of sound mind, is quite an astonishing claim." Emin shook his head, saddened. "And Palle has been about Merton this evening, in a flap, asking after you and Littel. What in the name of sanity is going on here, Sir Averil?"

Kent slumped down into a chair as he looked at his two inquisitors. Good men, he had no doubt, but they would be better off knowing no more—better to know less than they already did, in fact.

"I should not tarry here with Palle looking for me, gentlemen. If you let me escape this night, I swear I will return when I can and tell you the whole long tale."

Somers stopped his pacing. "But what of my daughter, and Lord Jaimas? Are they involved in this madness in some way?"

Yes, Kent thought, *what of them?* "I will try to dissuade them from further involvement, Professor, though they are adults now and may not listen to me."

Somers stabbed his finger in the air. "Lord Jaimas may have reached the legal age of majority but that is not true of Alissa. I will not have her in danger, Kent! I will not."

Kent nodded, feeling a pang of guilt. Her involvement was his doing. "I understand, Professor. She is, I am sure, in no danger. Miss Alissa is one day to become a Duchess of Blackwater. Palle may be willing to bully a young scholar like Egar Littel, who is not well connected, but the daughter-in-law of the Duke of Blackwater he would bow to if she picked his pocket. You need not worry. Of that one thing, at least, I am sure."

The heavy thump of boots came from the hall, and then a solid knock at the door. All three men fell silent, not even daring to move. Kent took a long breath. "A moment!" he called. And then, quietly, to his guests. "I don't think there is any point in hiding."

As he crossed to the door, Kent realized that he had spoken with some degree of confidence, something that he did not feel. Was it only a few hours earlier that the Princess Joelle had squeezed his hand, imbuing him with a sudden feeling of invulnerability? What a delusion that had been! Flames, it might have been a warning!

His hopes that it would be some innocent caller were dashed the second he opened the door. Despite the fact that they were not in uniform, Kent was sure he confronted three Palace Guards in the hallway.

"Sir Averil Kent," one said, "you are to accompany us."

Kent looked at the men, all large and young enough to be strong, yet old enough to not be cowed. "And what reason would I have to do that? Are you officers of the peace? Have I been charged with some crime?"

Only a second of hesitation. "Sir Averil, I am to bring you by whatever means necessary," he glanced at his companions, who seemed eager to carry out such a threat, "and we will do that, if forced to."

Kent nodded, not surprised. It was the damndest luck that Somers and Emin had delayed him—but it had to happen in time. Foolish of him to have thought he could escape. "May I gather my things?"

"We'll see to those," the officer said.

"And my guests?"

"They are free to go."

❧ ❧ ❧

Prisoner in my own carriage, Kent thought.

They were on the road back to Avonel, pressing the team cruelly. Poor Hawkins; he could not bear to see animals mistreated so, and here he was forced to do it himself. One guard rode before them and two behind. Kent could just make them out in their dark capes.

It had not happened quite the way Kent had imagined—and he had imagined his arrest over and over. He had expected to be taken quietly, without witnesses.

They let Emin and Somers go! But had they really, he

wondered, shuddering at the thought that evil might have befallen his friends.

Palle was either desperate or supremely confident. There would be a hue and cry at Kent's "disappearance," that was certain. *Unless they intend to charge me with treason,* he thought suddenly. What in this round world had led him to have dealings with Massenet?

"Fool," he whispered.

Leaning forward he peered out the window at the passing scene, trying to gauge their progress. A stand of beech trees glided by, barren of leaves, their silvered bark just visible from the coach lamps' glow. The bridge should lie just beyond. How he hoped that Lord Jaimas and Littel would not be recognized . . . if they had managed to get this far. Could they still be with Prince Wilam? Unlikely. But if so, Kent was sure that Palle would not dare to interfere with the prince—unless he had specific orders from Prince Kori.

Rain had begun to fall, yet Kent opened the carriage window, hoping to show himself to Lord Jaimas and Egar Littel. They wouldn't be foolish enough to shout to him? Kent decided he had to take the risk.

He clutched a glove in his hand into which he had stuffed a note he had written with difficulty in the moving carriage. The glove was almost black, but even so Kent feared that the riders behind might notice what he did. He looked back again and felt a little reassured. The road was wet, the riders were keeping their distance so that they were not covered in mud thrown up by the passing carriage. It was unlikely they would see the glove.

For a moment he considered jumping but decided something as large as a man would likely be seen, and he would undoubtedly be injured as well.

Ahead, at the roadside, Kent could make out a lantern, and then the shape of a large coach. The rider leading them slowed and Kent feared he would stop, but he spurred his horse again, and hurried on.

Kent could see only a driver down on the roadside, no one else, and then the carriage was alongside. But what if this isn't whom I think? He pushed down his doubts and threw the glove as best he could, hoping it would hit the driver or land near enough that he would be aware of it. And then they were crossing the bridge, the clatter of hooves on granite echoing like fireworks.

❦ ❦ ❦

Despite utter exhaustion Kent could not sleep, and stayed awake watching the darkened miles slip by. A cruel drizzle fell for much of the trip, and the night was cold. The painter shivered under a heavy fur rug, aware that poor Hawkins hunched out in the cold and wet, driving his team on in a manner that must pain him terribly. Their ghostly outriders kept their stations. *My carriage to the netherworld,* Kent thought.

Perhaps three hours before sunrise they came to Avonel, and Kent forced himself to sit up and monitor their progress, wondering where he would be taken. Palle's home? Or some more neutral place. To his surprise the rider led them straight to the Tellaman Palace and stopped unexpectedly by a side gate.

Flames, he is bold, Kent thought. *What control he must feel he has to bring me here, to the center of all intrigue in the kingdom.*

Kent got stiffly down from his coach, casting a brief glimpse up into the tortured face of Hawkins. One of the riders came and supported Kent, taking his arm strongly and causing him to hurry more quickly than he was really able. How he did not fall in the dark was a wonder. Through a door, not lit with lanterns, and then into a hallway. A single dull candle far off. Through locked doors, and into the arboretum.

As exhausted as Kent was, he could not help but look around him. The famous arboretum. The place where the King grew his cursed *regis*. But the light was so poor, and his eyes so tired.

And then the sound of water running, and Kent was allowed to sit on a rough wooden bench, his guide standing silently at his back.

After a moment of slumping, eyes closed, overcome by

fatigue and the pain of being thrown about and frozen for so many hours, Kent forced himself to look around. The scene was unreal, enchanting, as though he really had been transported to another world, but not a terrible place at all. He sat near to a waterfall and a small pool. Beneath his boots he could feel sand, and near at hand there was vegetation—exotic and aromatic. A shuttered lantern hung a dozen paces off, casting more shadows than light.

A sudden shuffling sound, accompanied by breath roughly drawn and muttered curses, came to the painter.

It can't be, Kent thought, and realized that he was suddenly sitting up straight.

Three men appeared, two guiding another who seemed to be blind. They took him to a chair set not far off. And then they stepped back, standing at attention. The seated man cursed and muttered again, struggling for breath.

"Kent?" came a terrible voice, ruined and guttural, almost unable to pronounce human sounds.

"Your Majesty." Kent bowed his head, unable to rise. The lantern was adjusted so that some light fell on Kent. Immediately he was reminded of his interviews with the countess. He could not see the man in the shadow.

"Flames, man, you are old. How long has it been?"

"Twenty-some years, sir."

Perhaps the head nodded. "Twenty years . . ." the voice said, as though testing these sounds for meaning. "I am lost, Kent, overwhelmed," the King said suddenly, as though remembering the purpose for this meeting. "Lost. Disappearing. And now that Elorin is gone . . . So many are gone."

Quiet. Kent could almost hear the man searching for the thread of his thought.

"If you are weak, it makes you mad eventually. Like Trevelyan. In the darkness I see . . ." Nothing. No sound. Just a man breathing. "The seed has grown scarce. Fallen to the frost, like all things. Too weak to resist. And I will follow." Kent could tell by the sound of these last words that the King looked directly at him. "Do you fear death?"

Kent was taken aback but hurried to recover. "Doesn't everyone?"

"Yes, but not all men will sacrifice everything because of it. These two behind me . . . they fear death; I'm sure of it, but they would die to keep me alive. Do you see? And I would let them do it, even if it was the death I deserved. That is the lesson." A wheezing that might have been a laugh . . . or a sob. "There is something that you must do, Kent. A last royal request. . . ."

"Anything Your Majesty could ask, I will do."

The waterfall continued to whisper, the endless pouring forth of water from the bones of the earth. One of the guards shifted his feet in the sand. Kent was sure he heard fingers snap.

"Though I cannot sit for you, you will paint my last portrait, Kent. Concentrate your mind, for you shall have only this one sight of me."

The lantern was carried forward. Kent prepared himself, ready to observe, fumbling with his spectacles. Without warning the light was cast upon the seated man. And Kent stopped, hearing his own gasp, barely muffled, then looked away. It was all he could bear.

🍃 🍃 🍃

"He was cadaverous, Valary!" Kent stood by his fire, swaying from fatigue. "Unimaginably ancient, and hideously so." He raised his hands to rub his eyes, but instead merely covered them in horror. "We have been wrong all along. Martyr's blood, but I expected him to be young! At least younger than his actual age. Every rumor we have ever had from the palace. . . ." He lowered his hands and stared at his companion, thinking that he was so tired and so overwhelmed that tears might come.

Valary looked down at the paper on which he had been writing, forcing Kent to recall every word that had been said. "You're sure the King said; 'And now the seed has grown scarce. Fallen to the frost, like everything. Too weak to resist. And I will follow.'?"

Kent nodded. "More or less; yes."

Valary puffed out his cheek and drummed the end of his pen against it. "What in this round earth did he mean?" the historian muttered.

It was morning, a gray light streaming into the room through swiftly moving clouds. Outside the door, footsteps squeaked on the stairs, and then came Barnes' familiar knock.

"Yes?"

"I have posted your letter to Merton, Sir Averil," the servant said, puffing to catch his breath. "Mr. Hawkins is in a hot bath, as you ordered, sir. Food and coffee will come directly."

"Excellent, Barnes. See that Hawkins doesn't nod off and drown, he must be beyond exhaustion. Put him to bed and have the doctor around this afternoon. It will be a wonder if he doesn't take sick from this. Double pneumonia, at the least."

Barnes nodded and retreated from the room. Kent raised a hand and rubbed his forehead gently. "That should stop Somers and Emin from raising the alarm, I hope. Now what were we saying?"

"I was puzzling over the King's words," Valary said, still staring at what he had written. "But perhaps he is no longer lucid. What did you think?"

"Well, it was a strange audience. . . ." Kent thought for a moment, remembering the meeting. "I did not get the impression that His Majesty was mad so much as unable to . . . focus his mind. Do you know what I mean? Like a man overly tired, as I am now, though more so. But, no, I can't say he was not in his right mind." He looked over at his companion. "The point is, Valary, King Wilam does not appear young. It has, all along, been one of our central assumptions. And if that is wrong, then in what else are we mistaken?"

Valary looked up at Kent as though he had finally registered what it was the man was saying. "Did I not quote Holderlin's letter to you? 'To live to the age that some have, one must follow the art with an unwavering, iron discipline, else one would pay a terrible price.'"

"What are you saying? That what I saw was a man who had paid that price?"

"So it would appear. The King is not, to the best of our knowledge, in possession of talent."

"But I have spoken with reliable people. They swore that, to all appearances, the King had not aged beyond sixty or at most sixty-five."

"And at the time they saw His Majesty I would conjecture that they spoke true, Kent. But that was some time ago—at least five years. Who knows what stages this habituation goes through? If one does not follow the larger art, perhaps the seed ceases to be effective after some time. There is certainly evidence that King Wilam has dramatically increased his use of the physic over the past two years. As it ceases to have the desired effect, perhaps the only answer is to take more. But how much can a body tolerate? Do you see? I think what you saw was undoubtedly true, but it does not negate what was observed by others. Not at all."

Kent went to a chair. He was so exhausted he could barely stand, but he could not sleep either.

"Let me read this back to you once more, Averil. Listen carefully, it could be very important." The historian read the conversation once again, slowly and clearly, like a school boy at his lessons, and in the middle of it, Kent fell deeply asleep.

🍃 🍃 🍃

The three young men piled out of the carriage, and watched the coach disappear across the bridge. "But that was Kent, I'm almost certain," Jaimy said. "Why did he not stop?"

Prince Wilam stood beside him staring down the now dark road. "Because he was accompanied by guards. I'm quite sure of it. Though they wore no uniforms, they were Palace Guards. Palle's people, I'm sorry to say."

The driver came up then, having calmed his team which had been stirred by the other animals racing past.

"This glove was dropped from the carriage, Your Highness. Or more rightly, thrown, I think."

Littel almost snatched it from the man's hand. "Ah! Look at this!" he said. "There is a note stuffed into one finger." They took it forward to the carriage lamp and huddled over it.

"What species of hen scratched this?" Jaimy asked, for the note was barely readable.

Littel took a small magnifying lens from an inner pocket. After a moment he shook his head. "Well, it is signed with a 'K,' but it makes no sense to me. *'If you need refuge: the home of the lady who dwells with your looks.'* What in Farrelle's name?"

"That is helpful," the prince said, "we need a riddle right now. I suggest we move on before Palle or my own father comes along."

"I agree," Littel said, obviously still frightened. "Let us be on our way."

"Could it say 'books'?" Jaimy asked suddenly. " '. . . who dwells with your books'?"

"Yes, I suppose, and would mean just as much," Littel said, putting a foot on the step of the carriage.

"How in this round world would Kent know that?" Jaimy asked, addressing the night, it seemed.

"Never underestimate Averil Kent's knowledge," Prince Wilam said. "Do you have some idea what this means?"

"I know exactly what it means," Jaimy said incredulously, "though I should never have thought of it in twenty lifetimes. But I don't know how we shall travel there."

"It doesn't matter, get in," Littel urged. "We'll play thirteen questions as we go. Come on."

❦ ❦ ❦

Kent could rouse himself only to semi-consciousness, just enough to recognize the two men responsible for waking him—Valary and Barnes.

". . . from Professor Somers, sir," Barnes was saying, "he's here in Avonel."

Kent realized he lay on the sofa in his sitting room, though he could not remember how he got there.

"I'm fully dressed?"

"Yes, sir," Barnes said solicitously.

"The duke requires a reply, and quickly, I think," Valary said.

"What duke?" Kent sat up, suddenly afraid that things of import had been occurring while he slept. It was daylight.

"The Duke of Blackwater, sir," Barnes said, obviously repeating himself. "The butcher boy just came with the meat and he also brought a note from the duke and Professor Somers."

"Ah, a note. Let me see it."

Barnes hesitated.

"It's in your hand, Averil," Valary said softly.

Kent realized that he did indeed hold a piece of paper. His servant handed him his spectacles and Kent read, trying to force his mind to awareness.

To the Manservant of Sir Averil Kent:
  Sir:
  I have come to Avonel with Professor Somers searching for your employer. Do you know Sir Averil's whereabouts? Please send an answer back with the boy who bears this note.

  Edward Flattery,
  Duke of Blackwater

Kent looked up at his companions. "Apparently my letter did not reach Merton before they acted." He removed his spectacles, and gently pressed fingers to his eyelids. "A pen and paper, Barnes, please." He looked up at Valary. "They must believe Palle has set a watch on my home, and I'm sure they're not wrong." He tried to push some of the fog from his mind. "Have we had any word from Lord Jaimas?"

"None," Valary said. The historian was still dressed as

he had been when Kent had roused him so early that morning. Was this the same day?

Taking paper from Barnes, Kent asked, "What is the day?"

"Sunday, Sir Averil. Sunday the sixth."

The date meant something, Kent was sure. "Are they not opening the iron bridge today?"

"They are, sir. The festivities must already have begun."

Kent wrote quickly.

I am perfectly hale, and flattered by your concern. Wise to stay away from my home, though. I will attend the iron bridge festivities, which will allow me to speak with everyone.

ಶ ಶ ಶ

From where Kent's carriage stopped, the dark framing of the bridge looked like a section of web made by some monstrous spider of prehistory, cast across the gorge to snare the unwary. The painter could not tell if he was filled with admiration for its simple, functional beauty, or if he was disturbed by the image it brought to mind. The bridge, however, was not the work of some prehistoric monster, but of man. One man in particular, for it had been conceived and designed by the redoubtable Mr. Wells. The same man who had been working with Littel to translate the mysterious text. Apparently he did not lack intelligence—of a certain kind, at least.

Kent was still so tired he felt as though he remained half in the world of dreams, and so stiff that just getting down from his carriage seemed like the descent from a precipice.

Valary had accompanied him (and poor Hawkins had insisted on driving), and now the two gentlemen stood on a rise by the river, staring out over the gathered crowds, toward this "great monument to man's ingenuity," as it was being called. The day was blustery, but more spring-like than winter, and the sky was a riot of cloud, thrown hard up against the winter blue.

"Sir Averil," called the Marquess of Sennet as he came along the cliff top. The man smiled giddily, and waved a field glass toward the bridge. "Is it not a wonder of the unnatural world?"

Kent introduced Valary, and the three men turned their attention back to the bridge.

"But why not a bridge of stone?" Valary asked in a small voice.

"I am told that this was done merely to prove the principles—hardly an essay in the craft. Much larger spans are possible, larger than have ever been managed with stone. This, Mr. Valary, is the bridge of the future—to the future, in a way. They say Wells is planning a great building on the same principles." The marquis searched the crowd with his field glass. "I think everyone but the King has come out," he said after a moment, and then added, in a tone far more serious than was common for him, "may Farrelle restore him."

"What's that?" Kent asked quickly, as alert as ever to the subtleties of conversation and tone.

"Surely you have heard the rumors, Sir Averil?"

Kent raised an eyebrow toward Valary. "Even I do not hear rumors before you, Lord Sennet."

The marquesss laughed with some delight at having surprised Kent. "It is said that the King has taken leave of his senses. I expect a regency to be declared by the senior ministers and the palace at any moment. Perhaps by week's end."

Kent leaned a little more heavily on his walking stick. The exhaustion of his night's drive came over him like a shroud. "And who will be named to the regency council?"

Sennet lifted his glass to his eye again. "That is the parlor game of the moment—guessing who will be named. Certainly Prince Kori." He stopped his searching. "Yes. There is the heir assumptive, now. You get no credit for guessing that correctly, of course. Then I would say this nondescript man I have in my glass now."

"Certainly not Palle?" Kent said. "He is the King's Man and should perform the same role to the council."

"Yes, it will be a break with tradition, but I will risk my money there." He moved his glass on. "And the third? Well, that is the hardest to predict. Every group is trying to have someone from their own faction appointed—even the reformers. I think I will not commit myself on this yet." He lowered his glass but continued to stare toward the bridge. "You are coming to the festivities at the Winter Garden, I assume?"

Kent nodded distractedly. The crowd before the bridge suddenly began to move, like a great army of ants, and the vanguard of this army set out onto the bridge, dark silhouettes, tiny at this distance. The first carriage rolled out onto the deck, and the sounds of the crowd moving swept down the river gorge like a torrent.

"I shall get back to my carriage," the marquess said, "for I don't want to miss my chance to cross over. Will you join me?"

Kent stared out at the great web and felt a chill run through him. Without even consulting Valary, he answered. "We will go back as we came."

❦ ❦ ❦

Alissa Somers was fortunate to pick the correct entrance, and her patience paid well, for she was certainly the first person to find Kent. He almost hobbled in the door in company with a badly dressed man whose hair seemed to have been cruelly punished by the wind—a scholar, she was certain, and she was overly familiar with the type.

But poor Kent! The man looked like he might expire right on the spot. His face was bleached of all color, and she could see his neck tremble just to hold up his head. He looked infinitely worse than when they had last met, and she had been most concerned about him then.

"Sir Averil." She curtsied quickly, and then took his arm.

"Miss Alissa," Kent said, his voice barely audible in the din of the hall. "May I introduce Mr. Valary."

"A pleasure, Mr. Valary. Now, you, Sir Averil Kent,

will come with me." His hand was so cold it did not seem to have life in it, which alarmed her terribly. "I know a quiet place where you may sit by a fire, and I shall see you are brought tea and hot food."

Kent seemed about to protest, but then acquiesced, having lost the strength to resist.

She led the two gentlemen into a hallway just as they had a glimpse of the main hall, and the crowd swarming about the model of the iron bridge.

Not too far along this hall the Duke of Blackwater had reserved a room for the use of his family, and Alissa found the door and eased the ailing painter in.

With Valary's help, she lowered Kent to a chair, and sent servants scurrying for food and drink.

"Oh, Mr. Kent," she said, no longer able to hide her distress. "I have no idea what you have been up to, but you will not stand another day of it, I am absolutely sure of it." Alissa realized that she was almost in tears seeing this dear man in such a state.

"This young woman is right, Kent, you need rest." Valary looked concerned as well.

Alissa pulled a chair up to the painter's. Leaning close, she spoke quietly, her voice full of concern. "And no one has heard from Jaimas since we parted last night. Do you know where he is? Is he safe?"

Kent lifted his hands in a gesture that seemed a little helpless. "I am not sure. He is almost certainly safe, for you know whose company he was in. We shall hear from him soon, I think."

Alissa was only slightly comforted by this. She did not like what was going on around Kent. She looked at the man again. He was so very frail. How in the world had he become caught in the center of Farr politics?

The door banged open, causing Alissa to jump.

"Father!"

Professor Somers closed the door quickly. "Alissa. Kent, how in the world did you get free? I was sure you were freezing in some prison cell." He stood shaking his head in both disbelief and admiration. "I don't know how you did it."

"I shall have to explain another time, Professor, it is a long tale."

Somers seemed to realize for the first time how frail Kent actually was. "Did they harm you, Kent? Do you need a physician?"

"No, I need rest, that is all. I travelled all night to Avonel, and nearly froze into the bargain. I shall be myself in a day or two."

Somers perched on the edge of a chair, looking solicitously at the painter. "It is unfortunate you are not well. There is a mad struggle over who will be appointed to the regency council. You've heard about the King?"

"It is not just a rumor, then?"

"Apparently not." Somers shook his head sadly. "The duke is at work as we speak. There must be someone on the council to balance the prince and Palle."

"Who is most likely, do you think?"

"Lord Harrington is the prince's choice, but there is a strong resistance to this. The duke supports Galton."

"Stedman Galton?" Kent asked. "But he is one of Palle's inner circle!"

Somers sat back in his chair, surprised. "Galton? But the duke is most adamant that he is the man for the job."

Kent made to rise from his chair, but found he could not, and felt a cold sweat seep from his pores. "Where is the duke? I must speak with him."

"Somewhere in the building. I might find him, I suppose." Somers did not seem inclined to do so, and looked at Kent oddly, as though the painter had ceased to make sense.

"Please, Somers do that. Warn him about Galton, and tell the duke the claims about the King are entirely false. His Majesty is perfectly coherent."

"What are you saying, Kent?" The professor seemed sure that Kent was not making sense, now.

"I was in His Majesty's presence this very morning. Spoke with him, in fact. Tell the duke that this is nothing more than a palace coup. Tell him, Somers."

ELEVEN

The feast was small, for the ritual of *maoeā* would allow only the most modest expressions of welcome, and to perform even these required appropriate rituals and sacrificies to be sure the gods would not be offended. Only the Farrlanders who had been to Varua on earlier voyages realized how subdued and modest this affair was. The others were so taken with their new surroundings, the beauty of the music, the vivacity of the women, and the exotic fare laid before them, that they thought they had made a landfall on paradise indeed.

Tristam sat on a plaited mat before the "table," long mats laid end to end and decorated with flowers and vines. The sun had set only moments before, beyond the high peak of Mount Wilam, and the moment of twilight was passing quickly. The trade continued to blow, warm from the lagoon, and the evening was perfumed with a thousand scents both exotic and familiar. The pungent odors of smoke, sand baked beneath the tropical sun, the perfume of flowers, and the smells of the salt lagoon. The Varuan women all wore flowers in their hair and about their necks, as well as scenting themselves with sweet oils that they kept in shells and applied occasionally. The breeze would blow, sweeping the air clear, like water cleansing the palate, and then would come some new treat for the senses. The smells of the freshly cooked food, fish and meats baked in the ovens in the ground, actually caused Tristam to salivate.

Fires offered only dull light, but the stars were quickly

appearing. The moon, perhaps two days past the quarter, hung high overhead, its oddly unbalanced shape offering some cool light. Tristam had been told that this was the night of a ritual dance, and the visitors were extended the honor of witnessing this rite.

Each Farrlander seemed to have been adopted by a Varuan family who looked after them, making sure they were never without food, or sweet coconut milk to drink. Tristam's own hosts were a man and wife whose two daughters sat on either side of him and plied him with morsels, some of which he was expected to eat from their fingers, something he found very odd at first and then a bit erotic.

These young women flirted with him quite openly, and not only did their parents not mind, they seemed to encourage it. Often Tristam felt a bare breast press softly against his arm or his back, and hands brushed him suggestively. He thought he must be recovering his health, for despite his tryst with Faairi that morning, he felt a growing charge of desire.

He kept searching the faces in the crowd, hoping to find Faairi, though he was a little apprehensive about her reaction to his present situation. Although visitors to Varua always wrote that the islanders appeared to never suffer from jealousy, Tristam could not quite believe it.

Occasionally he caught the duchess gazing at him from across the mounds of food, and she appeared to be amused. *"Do not miss your opportunities among the young maidens out of some misplaced sense of obligation to me,"* she had said as they came to the feast, leaving Tristam wondering, as usual. But how would she respond if she knew of his afternoon's encounter?

The duchess is trying to rid herself of me, he thought suddenly. But then he wondered if that were true. It seemed more a statement of the nature of their involvement—he was not to expect matters to run in the normal course. This was not courtship leading to marriage, as one would expect in Farr society. But where was it leading? The true nature of their involvement was still a mystery to Tristam. If there were rules, then they were known only to the duchess.

Tristam realized that his morning of love with a complete stranger, rather than damping his desire, had increased it. He found himself wondering what the duchess would look like dressed as an island maiden. The thought excited him. The duchess displaying her charms with the utter candor of the island women—something Tristam was sure she could do easily, if not for the impact on her reputation. He suspected that the duchess, given the opportunity, would be as free with her favors as any island girl. It was part of the reason that he desired her so— because she would occasionally reveal this secret side of herself to him.

Tristam smiled at the women beside him in turn. What would Jaimy think if he could see Tristam now, seated between two beautiful young women who were bedecked in flowers and scented with oils, barely half-dressed, their hair caught by the breeze and teasing about him? It was a dream that many a student had nurtured, Tristam was sure.

Tall torches were lit as the sky faded and the smell of burning pitch was added to the evening's complex perfume. Shadows moved and flickered in the light, disturbing Tristam, who found the effect too much like his recurring dreams of wandering through darkened ruins. Despite the warm evening, he shivered, and wondered if the shadows were real or if they were merely a product of his own state.

He suffered waking dreams still—the dream world that Faairi had spoken of—though less frequently, but they were not unlike this, a feeling that his senses were overwhelmed and could no longer separate the myriad sights and sounds and smells.

He turned to one of the women at his side, hoping for reassurance, hoping there would be no signs of distortion. She smiled at him in the partial light, and this lifted his heart a little. Leaning forward she spoke close to his ear, her breath tickling his neck. She whispered in her musical language and Tristam only understood one word:

nehenehe, which meant handsome, he thought, and hoped she meant him. The look she gave him afterward assured him that she did, and then a shadow crossed her face, though it was not real.

I am Tristam, the naturalist thought, unreality laying its cold hand on him.

Food was being cleared away and the crowd rearranged itself in a large circle. Shadows began to take on substance for Tristam, as though they were ribbons of smoke, spreading throughout the scene, painted across the people in irregular bands, like random applications of charcoal. But they moved. Tristam closed his eyes and felt himself floating, as though he had taken the *regis* physic.

He felt one of the young women put her hand on his back, almost tenderly, and she sighed, her breath catching. Even though the waking dream pulled at him, Tristam felt himself respond.

A sudden gust of wind hissed through the trees, like the night's whisper of desire, and drums began a slow rhythmic pounding in imitation of the surf.

Tristam tried to find the other Farrlanders in the crowd of faces, but the shadows moved like a stain floating on the surface of his eye, allowing him only glimpses. He could feel the excitement of the crowd more than he could see what occurred.

Into the circle came a dancer, a lithe young woman, not twenty he was sure, a small, white flower behind her ear.

"Pōti'i mo'e," the woman near to him whispered, pressing herself closer.

What? Had she said 'lost girl,' or 'ghost girl?'

Tristam felt himself pulled further into dream, the ground beneath him less solid. The blossom behind the dancer's ear could have been *regis,* but in his present state he could not be certain. *Regis!*

The drums began to beat a more demanding rhythm. Tristam was no longer sure if it was the wind sighing in the trees or if he heard his own breathing.

One of the women ran her hand up to caress his neck just as the dancer began to twirl, her fine combed skirt of grasses fanning out, her neck arched back so that the long shadow of her hair seemed to spin outward, joining the darkness. Her hands and arms moved with such supple grace that they were almost tendrils. Shadow seemed to wrap itself about her like a web, but Tristam could not tear his eyes away.

She is being consumed by shadow, he thought suddenly. *I am falling into a regis dream. I have been given the seed.* But this knowledge did not move him. He stayed, fixed to his place, watching the dancer in the midst of the growing hallucination.

A male dancer in a long-beaked bird mask leaped into the circle, as though he had alighted from the sky. Across his shoulders and arms stretched a cloak of feathers creating the effect of wings. Wings that cast shadows upon the ground and the wall of faces.

Through some artifice the beak moved and produced a sharp clacking sound as it snapped shut. The two dancers continued their movements, separated by a dozen paces. Tristam felt a finger gently trace the curve of his ear. The trade wind combed through the palm fronds like a quickly indrawn breath.

Shadows flickered, painting the dancers and the open circle of ground with undulating bands. Suddenly the drumming stopped and the bird-man spread his wings, turning slowly. He had discovered the other dancer, who froze in mid-step.

And then the drums began again, the dancers moving swiftly about the circle, the bird-man in pursuit, clacking his bill. What Tristam saw being enacted was sexual pursuit, like animals courting. Aggressive display and posturing from the male, coy tempting from the woman.

But what did it mean? What myth or legend was being played out here? A ghost girl and a bird-man. Tristam's head whirled. The two women beside him pressed closer now, excited by the dance, by the pulsing beat of the drums and the sighing wind in the trees.

Tristam felt out of control, he reached to balance himself and touched soft skin. Someone whispered in his ear. Foreign words. And then a soft kiss.

The dancers had come closer now, not touching but

their pelvises were only inches apart, their hips moving in a frenzy, driven, like copulation. He could see the sweat on their skin, on the woman's quick moving waist.

The drumming was fierce, reaching toward a crescendo. Tristam could see other couples touching, pressing near. And then, as the performance came to its climax, the bird-man stopped suddenly, turning about toward his audience, toward Tristam, and ever so slowly opened the great bill, and inside there was a second mask, half consumed by shadow—the face of a man, tattooed like the skin of a snake. The woman took the white flower from behind her ear and dropped it into the long beak, which clacked closed with finality.

Tristam was up then, pushing through the startled islanders. Staggering into the darkness, tripping as he went into the shadows. The two women were beside him, supporting him, guiding him, as though somehow they understood his panic.

"Blood and flames," Tristam muttered. "What the hell was that?"

"Only a dance of transformation, Mr. Flattery." It was a man's voice. "Nothing more. Are you ill? Shall I call your Doctor Llewellyn?"

"No!" Tristam turned toward the voice. Wallis. It was Wallis, he was sure, though the man's form contorted in the dark like the stuff of nightmare. "No. I need only be alone for a few moments. Some water, and a place to lie down."

Wallis spoke a few words to the women, who did not answer, but Tristam felt himself guided suddenly to the left. "I know a place," Wallis said. "Leave it to me. Not forty paces."

Tristam realized they were in a glade of trees, walking along a twisting path. He was all but blind and let himself be led by the women, who seemed to have no trouble seeing in the dark.

Wallis spoke again, words Tristam did not catch, and suddenly he was being supported by the artist alone, the women gone. "Not far now," Wallis encouraged. "You can manage."

Flames appeared—a low-burning fire—and around it men hunched down into the moving shadows. Tristam tried to stop, but the gentle strength of the artist carried him forward. "Not to fear, Mr. Flattery. I have not brought you to harm. Please. . . . Sit quietly."

Tristam felt a hand on his shoulder, pressing downward. He sank to the sand, looking around him, trying to make out who these men were, but his vision was too clouded now. The nightmare was overwhelming him. The flames from the fire, thick with smoke, seemed to dance about him.

"These are *kenaturaga*. Old Men," Wallis said. "Do you know what I mean? Yes? They mean you no harm, but wish to ask you some questions."

Wallis had seated himself a few feet away from Tristam, as though disavowing any connection between them. The Old Men did not speak, but stared. Seven still figures, like carvings, Tristam thought, except that the shadows they sat in writhed. He could see little of their features, and he was not sure if the dark patterns on their faces were shadows or tattooing, but they seemed to swirl and undulate, as though resisting the firelight.

Finally one Old Man pointed with a carved stick and spoke.

"Show them your hand," Wallis said, just as Tristam realized he had understood some of the words.

"Why?" *Faairi.* She had betrayed him!

"Mr. Flattery, they mean you no harm, but they will not brook insubordination. These men are powerful, here. You must answer to them. It will prove the easier course, believe me."

But still Tristam held his hand close to his body, the sleeve pulled down, as he always kept it.

"Mr. Flattery. . . ." Wallis said, the warning in his tone compelling.

Tristam leaned toward the flame, reaching out his clenched fist.

The Old Man swung his stick aside as though to be sure it did not touch Tristam, and then moved forward to stare. He nodded to another who took hold of Tristam's elbow, jerking it forward until the naturalist could feel the hot breath of the flames. His shirt was yanked up, revealing the scar. Tristam tried to pull back, but the man was immensely strong.

"They're burning me!" Tristam appealed to Wallis.

"Hold still, Mr. Flattery. They will soon be done."

Tristam smelled the hair on his hand begin to singe.

"Martyr's blood, Wallis!"

"Be still. They are not patient."

The others moved forward, their gazes fixed on Tristam's hand. Suddenly one barked a single syllable and they all began to mutter.

Tristam looked down and then closed his eyes, trying desperately to pull his hand back. *The tattoo had reappeared!* It seemed to writhe across his wrist in the inconstant firelight and it *burned,* like a hot lash.

"Sweet Farrelle preserve us," Wallis intoned.

Suddenly Tristam's hand was released and he pulled it away from the flame, cradling it with his other arm. Holding it, throbbing with pain, near to his heart.

The Old Man who had held his arm leaned over the fire, extended his hands palm down, and passed them through the flames once, twice, and then a third time. He did not move quickly nor did his face display anything but concentration. He then went back to his place, and sat, not even glancing at his hands.

The Old Man with the stick addressed Wallis, speaking too quickly for Tristam, who was still absorbed in his pain—the pain of seeing the tattoo return.

"How did you come by this tattoo on your wrist, Mr. Flattery?"

How had they known about the tattoo at all? Faairi had seen only a scar. But then Wallis must have heard the story from the Jacks. Perhaps she had not betrayed him after all, he thought with some relief.

Tristam felt trapped, not knowing what it was these men wanted of him—if it would be prudent to lie, and if so, what lie to tell. Tristam felt the *regis* dream was sapping his energies, eroding his judgment. Certainly Wallis had heard much of the story already.

"When I said they were not patient, Mr. Flattery, I was quite serious," Wallis cautioned.

"I don't know where to begin ..." Tristam said, his memories confused by *regis,* he was sure. "We were pursued ... into the Archipelago by corsairs, as you must have heard." And he proceeded to tell the tale, his audience listening raptly to Wallis translate this story of the strange doings of men in a world far beyond the reef. When he finished, the Old Men spoke again among themselves.

There was a silence then; only the whisper of the trade in the trees, the far off roar of the surf, and the crackling of the fire. The singing had stopped at some point—Tristam only now noticed.

In this silence the Old Man who appeared to be in command, spoke in an ancient voice. Wallis listened attentively, his entire manner suggesting the demeanor of a retainer, making Tristam wonder where the man's loyalties lay.

"*Toata Po* asks why you have come to Varua," Wallis said.

"Certainly, Mr. Wallis, you have already told them our purpose."

"They want to know *your* purpose, Mr. Flattery, not the purpose of the voyage."

What to tell them? That, in truth, I am not sure? My course was chosen for me? I am drawn along, toward some end I cannot see?

"Mr. Flattery?"

"I serve the King, Mr. Wallis, and I mean no one harm. You may tell them that."

The artist seemed to consider this a moment, and then, with a show of reluctance, he translated for the Old Men, who spoke quietly among themselves again, for some minutes. Finally one addressed Wallis.

"Mr. Flattery? I assume as ship's naturalist you have been given the duty of searching for King's leaf. But you must not even consider attempting this. If you were to find this bush growing naturally—unlikely in the extreme—even to touch it would put everyone on your ship in peril. Do you understand what I'm saying?"

"But will the Varuan King not give some of this seed to us?" Tristam asked.

Wallis may have shrugged in the darkness. "The King is involved in the *maoeā*. Who knows what he will do when he returns? But I can assure you, you would be better to take none of it back. Farrland would be better without the fruit of this flower."

Wallis was interrupted then and he listened respectfully for a moment. "They want to know about Doctor Llewellyn. He claimed the title of 'Old Man' when he arrived here, and the Varuans can see the marks of the seed on him. What is his place? Is he your teacher?"

"My teacher?" The question seemed absurd. "You must tell them that Llewellyn is only a physician. An employee of the duchess. Nothing more."

"Mr. Flattery . . . it is obvious that he is something more. These men before you are wiser than you seem to realize."

Tristam tried to make his mind work. What to say? "Llewellyn is a minion of Sir Roderick Palle, but I don't know his purpose. There appears to be a struggle in the court. I understand little more that that."

Wallis was silent a moment and then he began his slow translation.

"What did you tell them?" Tristam asked suddenly.

"Only that Llewellyn supports a courtier of the King who has his own desire for power. On Varua the families of the King's wives vie for power through the succession. They are familiar with such things."

Tristam searched around the faces, thinking that perhaps the shadows were retreating a little—becoming merely absence of light. The feeling of nightmare was loosing its grip—a little.

Tristam thought he could feel the distant pounding of the surf transmitted through the earth. If he strained to listen, he could hear it, a din like a crowd where no single voice could be distinguished—no sound of individual waves, just the constant rumble. A force so consistent, so elemental that to Tristam it seemed geological—the rumble of the slow, incontestable movement of a landmass.

The youngest man present began carrying half-coconut shells around the circle, stopping before each Old Man, who would clap his hands loudly three times. The man who bore the cup would then speak a few words, and present the shell with both hands, the gesture oddly formal. One came to Tristam—a musky, pungent odor rising out of the dark bowl. He looked at it suspiciously.

"It is *kava*," Wallis whispered. "Made from a root. We drink it as one, all of it in a single draught. It is the custom."

A few words were spoken by one of the Old Men—half prayer, half-toast, Tristam thought—and he copied the others, lifting the shell in both hands and draining it completely. He almost gagged. A bitter taste of roots, spicy, warm, bits of sinuous pulp catching in his teeth.

One of the Old Men spoke quietly and the others nodded.

"I will guide you back, Mr. Flattery," Wallis said.

"That is all? Will you not explain why I have been brought?" He held out his right hand, shaking it in the firelight, causing looks of distress among the Old Men. "Will no one tell me what this means?"

Muttering all around now, men moving back from the fire, deeper into shadow.

Wallis pulled Tristam to his feet. "This is not the place." He almost pushed Tristam, placing himself between the naturalist and the others. "You will get no answers like this."

The artist was stronger than he looked, and Tristam found himself guided out into the dark beyond the fire where again he was without sight. He stumbled and Wallis bore him up. The ground tilted, first this way and then that. The fine sand of the beach came under foot, and Wallis stopped, balancing Tristam like a pole on end, testing to see if he could stand on his own.

The soft night wind swept across the lagoon and the stars hung in the sky, so clear that Tristam could feel the great depth of the heavens swaying above him. For a moment he felt a sense of vertigo, as though he could topple over into the stars, and then his rump hit the soft sand.

"You'll feel all right in a moment," Wallis said, gently. "It passes quickly." The man stood for some time, a moment—an hour—Tristam could not be sure. "Will you wait here, Mr. Flattery? Don't go wandering off without me."

Tristam made a noise that had been meant as words. His lips were numb, as was his tongue; thickened flesh in a dry mouth.

Wallis headed off down the beach and Tristam toppled backward so that he was lying, staring up at the moonless sky. Patterns of stars, moving, fading, then returning. A sound approaching. A large part of the sky turned to black and then Tristam realized a person stood over him. *Wallis,* he forced himself to remember the man's name. *Whatname Wallis.*

Cool hands touched his neck and forehead, and soft hair drifted over his chest.

Not Whatname, Tristam registered. Then a voice, speaking Farr.

"Is he all right?"

Wallis.

"Yes. I believe yes," A woman's voice, softly accented. He knew that voice. "He drank the kava for the first time?"

"Yes, but it is the *ari'i* he was given," and then he added something more in Varuan.

An indrawn breath. "He is not ready for this, I think."

Tristam felt a soft hand caress his face. *Faairi.*

"Best to keep him ashore until you are sure he has recovered. Will that cause trouble?"

"No. He is largely independent of ship's discipline. I'll see to him. I have a canoe."

The woman stood, said something in Varuan, and to Tristam's disappointment, was gone. He listened to her steps retreat across the beach, like the rhythm of his heart. From somewhere he heard singing.

"Mr. Flattery?" It was Wallis, his tone concerned, tinged with guilt, perhaps.

"I'm not quite ready to move." The stars were spinning and Tristam closed his eyes. "Tell me about the dance. The dance of transformation." He desperately needed to hear someone speaking.

He heard Wallis settle himself on the sand. "Well, that is easy enough." The words arched out toward Tristam like a lifeline. "It is an old legend of the islanders. In the ancient times they believe spirits took the form of animals. The dancer you saw tonight—the man—portrayed a bird now seldom seen, they say; a great sea eagle. It came to Varua long ago, where it saw a beautiful young maiden with the white flower behind her ear. Because the moon was not yet full, the spirit did not realize that the maiden was actually a ghost, wandering in the darkness. She is called the 'dream girl' sometimes, though it is not meant as we mean it.

"The spirit thought this maiden surpassingly fair and pursued her in the manner of his own people, the people of the sea and air, but he could never touch her. Determined to win her, the spirit transformed himself into a human man, only to realize then that the woman was a ghost and had no substance in this world. He could not reach her, nor could he transform himself back into an eagle. So he became the first Varuan man, named *Tetarakihiva*. The islanders say the ghost of the girl is still seen on occasion, and none can wear a white flower unless chosen to dance the part."

"But the face, the inner mask. It was tattooed like the skin of a snake."

"Was it? Well, it was very dark. Part of the drama is that you cannot quite see the man within. Can you rise?"

"Not yet. The white blossom. Was it *regis*?"

Wallis hesitated. "It was," he said softly.

Tristam looked up again at the stars, but they still would not remain still. "Tell me another legend—it will help me." Tristam needed the voice to anchor him.

"There are many. Surprisingly many. For a people without writing, they love tales. My favorite is the explanation for the moon rising and setting. Of course they know the world is a globe and floats in the heavens, and the moon circles round it. They even have the solar year, believe it or not—something we've had for only two centuries—so in some way the story is independent of that knowledge. I don't really understand.

"The Varuans say that the moon falls into the ocean at night where it is swallowed by a great whale, one of two whales who were once lovers. There are constellations named for them—one seen in the extreme east just after sunset, another in the west. One of the whales swallows the moon and swims under the waves across the ocean to the eastern horizon where it then blows the moon back into the sky with a great breath. When the moon is waning, the whales, who are very hungry from their labors, eat a piece each night. But when it is all gone and there is blackness—the new moon—they become so frightened that they make it again; regurgitating a bit more each night until it is whole. I think the moon is a great lump of ambergris." Wallis gave a small laugh of pleasure.

"While one swims east bearing the moon, the other sleeps, overcome with exhaustion from their labor. But when one arrives with the moon, the other must immediately set out to the west to be ready to catch the moon as it falls—they do it turn about. Because this great journey is so difficult they can never pause to speak as they pass but must rush past each other, only gliding close so their flukes touch. If you stand on the outer beach, just at moonrise, sometimes you will hear them touch—a soft sigh hard to distinguish from the sounds of the wind and waves, though the Varuans have no difficulty."

"What happens to the sun?"

"What? Oh, who swallows the sun and carries it into the east? I don't know, Mr. Flattery, but surely the sun is very hot. There will be another explanation for that. I will ask." Wallis chuckled. "Are you well enough to rise?"

"In a moment." Tristam opened his eyes and was relieved to see the stars hanging above him, clear and still. He wondered which cluster would be the whale.

"There was one other question that the Old Men asked, Mr. Flattery," Wallis said slowly, as though not quite sure he should say this. "I had difficulty explaining to them that the Viscount Elsworth was no relation to you. At first I simply thought they believed the duchess to be your wife and the viscount your in-law—brother-in-law, as it were. But it came out that they believed the viscount to be your brother, and I had trouble convincing them that this was not so. In truth, I'm not sure they believed me. You speak some Varuan; do you know the word *va'ere?* No? I think it is made up of parts of the words 'spirit' and 'dark.' Dark spirit." Wallis was silent a moment. "Let me tell you one last fable of the Varuans. Once there was a very powerful chief who had a beautiful daughter who was not happy among her people. No one knew why, for she had not been ill or unlucky in love. She was young and might still have babies, so no one understood her dissatisfaction. One day she disappeared and was nowhere to be found. Her father could not be consoled, but one night while he sat weeping on a rock by the lagoon, a dolphin came to the surface but a few feet away. 'Do not weep, father, for I am happy at last,' the dolphin said, and the man knew that his daughter had been transformed by some spirit, and now dwelt among the people of the sea. 'But daughter, I miss you, and I will never sleep for fear of what has befallen you. You live now in the world of the shark and barracuda.' The daughter blew a little fountain of water into the air. 'But, father, a shark is always a shark and barracuda always a barracuda. You know what they are and what they will do. But on land sharks and barracuda go about disguised as men. They are difficult to recognize and unpredictable in their cruelty.' " Wallis shifted on the sand. "Do you take my meaning, Mr. Flattery? The Varuans have ways of knowing these things. This Viscount Elsworth, he is a *va'ere*—something vicious dwells inside him."

Yes . . . and what dwells inside me, Tristam wondered. The viscount was another man transformed. The bird-man of the dance came back to mind, leaping high over the sitting audience to land in the circle. It made Tristam think of the bird-viper in the Lost City. The stars wavered, but Tristam forced himself to remain calm, breathing evenly. A dance of transformation. What had Wallis said? "You cannot quite see the man within."

ꙮ   ꙮ   ꙮ

A pounding in his ears brought Tristam out of sleep into a state of immediate reactive anger.

"Mr. Flattery?" came a demanding voice. "Captain wants you. In the duchess' cabin, double time, sir. He's in no mood to be kept waiting. Mr. Flattery?"

"Yes. Yes. I'll come along directly."

It was broadly light—late morning. He sat up, assessing his state. Something near to normal, he thought, and he was awake—fully awake.

Tumbling out of his hammock, Tristam stood for a moment, dazed. Yes, fresh clothing. He had fallen asleep in his clothes the night before. But how had he even come aboard? Wallis! Suddenly he remembered his meeting with the Old Men.

They had given him regis. And his tattoo had reappeared.

Tristam held up his hand and found the tattoo had almost faded to invisibility again, though not quite, and the hair on the back of his hand was singed short. It had not been a dream.

Fearing that he looked badly disheveled, and feeling some apprehension that he might have caused the voyage trouble, Tristam took himself out to meet the captain.

"Mr. Flattery," Stern said as Jacel let the naturalist in. "Be warned that we are at stations this morning."

"Stations. . . !" Tristam said. He looked over at the duchess who seemed uncommonly subdued.

"Yes. We lost two men last night." He nodded to Wallis who sat by the table, clearly distraught.

The artist glanced up at Tristam, his eyes rimmed in red. "Two men were caught in the City of the Gods last night. They had entered the house of the most powerful Old Man, Toata Po, which they were searching. For

King's leaf, it is claimed. They were executed on the spot."

"Flames!" Tristam said. "Who?"

"Garvey and midshipman Chilsey," Stern answered softly.

"Chilsey! But how could he even know?" Tristam blurted out, and then realized the answer. *Hobbes!* Garvey was the master's mate. Blood and bloody flames! Hobbes! Tristam could not help but look over at the duchess. She must realize as well. But the duchess would not meet his eye, looking down at a handkerchief she had twisted tightly around one hand.

"Sorry fools," Stern spat out. He looked up at Tristam. "You have not spoken of *regis* to anyone? To Beacham, perhaps?"

"Not a word, sir."

Stern shook his head and began to pace, his coat thrown back where he pressed a fist to his hip. "What do you think the Varuans will do, Mr. Wallis?" he said after a moment.

Tristam looked over at the painter who seemed to hang over the table like a man exhausted by life. Stern obviously did not consider for a moment that the castaway's loyalties could be with the islanders—the people who had saved his life—not with those who had left him to die.

"I cannot say, Captain Stern. I suspect that nothing will be done until the King has completed the *maoeā*. I have tried to argue that these men were not acting on your orders, but if you demand reparation for their deaths. . . . That will indicate otherwise. You must make a public admission that their act was a crime."

Stern stopped abruptly, looking down at Wallis. "Are you suggesting that I allow these savages to murder two of my crew and simply let it pass?"

Wallis looked completely taken aback. "They broke two of the central tapu—laws—of this society, Captain. You must realize. . . ."

"And you must realize that I will not allow my men to be murdered without trial on the word of someone I have never even heard of! I cannot allow it. No, they should have been brought to me, and I would have dealt with them. Navy men meet navy discipline."

"But, Captain, if this were Entonne, you would not expect any of your crew who had committed serious crimes to be turned over to you. They would be subject to the justice of Entonne."

"Yes, Justice! A trial at which they could be properly represented. Not summary execution for a crime they may or may not have committed. For martyr's sake, they might have been lost. They might have had an assignation and gone to the wrong fale. There might well have been an explanation, but we will never know."

"They had seed in their possession, Captain, taken from the Toata Po's fale. I had warned you about this seed, Captain Stern, and Anua asked that no one enter the upper city."

Stern did not answer. Tristam could see that the captain was in a rage. He also realized that the crew would expect him to respond.

"There is more to consider here, Captain Stern," the duchess said suddenly. "We have our obligations to King Wilam. Directly to King Wilam. His Majesty expects us to succeed."

Tristam remembered the duchess' reaction after he had saved Pim: *'You risked everything for the life of a cabin boy!'* It was not likely that she would worry much about the loss of the two seamen. Not where her own purpose was involved.

Garvey and Chilsey . . . had Hobbes put them up to this? Martyr's blood, Chilsey was hardly more than a boy. And his father was a captain in the navy, too. Someone Stern would know.

The thought of the captain turning the *Swallow*'s broadside, even as small as it was, on the village caused deep revulsion in Tristam. The Varuans had acted according to their own laws, their own interests. Tristam had seen the same thing the previous night when he had been taken before the high court of the Old Men.

"Is there no appeal to the Varuans under their own customs?" Tristam asked.

"They view their laws differently than we do ours, Mr Flattery. There are no mitigating circumstances, no trials in our sense. Whoever caught your men last night executed them on the spot—they did not go looking for higher authority. The laws are the laws. Not all laws affect all the people, that is true, but everyone is subject to the rules that govern their caste. Even the Royal Family. Even the Old Men live by specific laws."

"And exactly which of their laws govern us, Mr. Wallis?" Stern demanded.

"It is difficult to describe, Captain Stern, for it is still not perfectly clear. In laws of what you would call 'property,' you are largely exempt. The Jacks go about picking fruit without ever asking who might have rights to a tree. But in tapu of religion you are subject to the same laws as everyone but the Royal Clan, the chiefs, and the Old Men. They will not exempt you there, I fear. It is possible that you might be able to negotiate reparations for some other transgressions, just as we pay fines back home. But in religious matters, and certainly anything to do with King's leaf. . . . Well, I don't think Varuan customs would allow any exemption. You must realize they feel bound by their laws." Wallis slumped in his chair, lost in thought. "I don't know what to do, Captain Stern. The Varuans are strange to our way of seeing things. They will have great regret over the deaths last night, and at the same time feel they were completely justified. Do you see?"

Stern paced the small cabin, like a man imprisoned. "The Jacks will expect me to exact some retribution for what they will see as murder; the laws of the Varuans seem foolish to them. We have that to think of. We cannot afford to alienate the crew, not this far from home."

"And I'm sure your only chance of acquiring King's leaf is through the goodwill of the Varuan King." Wallis stood up, ducking his head beneath the beams. "You will have to find a way to mollify your crew, Captain Stern, or you will sail home empty-handed."

Stern was taken aback and stood glaring at the castaway with both surprise and anger. "Let me assure you, Mr. Wallis, that I have no intention of sailing home empty-handed. You might tell that to your Varuan friends."

TWELVE

Midday found Jaimy and Egar Littel riding cross-country with a cool wind at their backs. They had purchased riding horses and tack as well as more useful clothing, but were still underprepared for this journey. Jaimy thought it a blessing that it was not raining. Littel, it turned out, was a passable horseman and a good companion except for his overwhelming fear of being apprehended by Palle. *"I spent much effort in appearing so obtuse as to be no threat to anyone,"* he had said, *"but now they must realize I understood more than they thought. They will want me back."*

Jaimy was becoming slightly less worried about being apprehended as each mile passed. The real concern now was finding the place Kent had indicated, for Jaimy had only the vaguest idea of where the Countess of Chilton lived.

Egar glanced back over his shoulder as he had been doing periodically the whole morning.

"No army in pursuit, I hope?" Jaimas said, hoping to bring a smile to the worried scholar's face.

"I am not being foolish about this," Egar said, perhaps thinking Jaimy made fun of him. "I'm quite sure Roderick Palle sees my flight as betrayal, and men of his type do not accept disloyalty easily. They have absurdly misplaced importance on this text. They will make great effort to have me back. I tell you this for your safety as well as mine."

Jaimy nodded. "I did not mean to make light of what

has happened to you, Egar. I agree that we should take no chances, but speed you to safety, which is what we are doing. No, I understand your concerns."

It was partially a lie. Jaimy was now almost certain they had slipped away unnoticed, but it seldom paid to mock a man's fears.

This journey with Littel reminded Jaimy of his many rides with Tristam, which set him to wondering where his cousin was now. Was he on some exotic isle surrounded by beautiful maidens, indulging his passion for things natural in a new way?

They came to the crest of a hill where Jaimy pulled his horse to a halt. He surveyed the surrounding countryside—beautiful even in late winter when the trees were bare and the colors muted. "That will be Coombs to the east. You can see the smoke rising in the draw." He pointed. "We will want to give that a wide berth. There is an inn on the Postom Road, where we can likely stay quietly."

"Lord Jaimas," Littel said, his voice almost a whisper.

Jaimy turned to find his companion staring back the way they had come. There, passing across an open pasture between two small woods, a clutch of riders could be seen, looking at a distance like a many-legged beast scuttling across the landscape. And before this beast went smaller creatures, bounding and baying: *hounds.*

"Hunters, do you think?" Littel said.

"Yes," Jaimy said, standing up in his stirrups, "but they do not hunt the fox. We are their quarry, I fear. Come on, we must get off this hillside."

They rode quickly down, finding a path winding among ancient elms. They stopped before a low stone wall at the bottom, and Jaimy could see that Littel was desperate, casting his gaze from side to side, like a fox at bay.

"Which way?" Littel said. "Which?"

"Let me think."

"Think! There is not time!"

"Yes, there is time now. Later we may not have the luxury." Jaimy looked up the slope and tried to estimate how far ahead of their pursuers they might be. When they had left the town they had set out on a west-going road, and then doubled back overland, so that anyone asking after them would be thrown off. But it had not worked. Someone had likely seen them leave the road.

Jaimy tried to pull a map together in his mind. The River Whipple would not be far to the north, and could only be crossed at its bridges or fords. There were three towns of any size nearby, all best avoided now.

"Our horses will soon tire," Jaimy said, thinking aloud.

"They will not have a chance to tire if we stay here."

"We must stay on our course north as though we are making for the Wye Bridge and Caulfield Town. Once it is dark we'll turn east and south, for Avonel. That's not what they'll expect."

"But what of their hounds? Dogs aren't likely to care for their master's expectations."

"No. We will have to throw them off somehow. But right now, we need to stay ahead of them. They're a larger party and will go more slowly if the land is not open, though our horses are hardly racers. I wish we were riding my best jumpers, we would quickly leave them far behind."

They cantered beside the wall until they found a gate, then set their horses to a good pace to cross the open meadow. Once they were in the shelter of pine trees, Jaimy dismounted and slunk back to see how close their pursuers were.

"Just starting down the rise," he said as he returned and mounted, spurring his horse on. They pushed their horses as much as they dared considering that they would not have fresh mounts for some hours—if at all. Jaimy hoped that their pursuers had found their mounts at the same inn as he and Littel, for they had taken the best horses there by far.

"Once they see we have begun to press our pace, they will realize we have seen them and guess their purpose," Jaimy called back over his shoulder. "We must try to keep this distance between them and ourselves." How he wished they had bows. He had never thought of shooting at a man, but it might come to that. Even a warning shot might have some effect. Were these men armed? If they were guards, they would likely have blades. More than he and Littel could claim.

At the far side of the wood they came out into the open and were faced with a fen, stretching on to a distant line of willows, lit by a shaft of sunlight so that the yellow of their drooping branches stood out against a dark cloud.

"Dare we cross?" Littel said.

Jaimy could see what he thought was fenberry growing, and in places, cattails. He wished that Tristam were here. Just by looking at the flora, the naturalist could usually tell how wet such a bog would be.

"I don't know, Egar. We'd better skirt the edge, I think. It looks shorter to go east-about."

They hurried in earnest now, spurring their horses on. Jaimy was certain that the dogs belonged to a local man, someone who would know the land well—know whether he could cross such a bog. Jaimy looked up to find the sun, judging the hours of daylight left. Two hours. They could not turn east yet, that was certain. He didn't want the hunters to know they were heading toward Avonel.

They would have to keep going north. Jaimy wished he were in country that he knew. Anywhere near his family's country home he would give their pursuers the slip with ease. But what did these men plan? Would they take Egar prisoner, with the son of the Duke of Blackwater as witness? Certainly they would not dare to harm either of them. No, likely they would take Littel on some false charge, that would be their likeliest route.

The fen curved north now, and they pressed their horses to keep moving, feeling exposed here in the open, their eyes fixed on the line of trees ahead. An eerie call, like a badly sounded horn, was carried on the wind, and Jaimy knew that sound well. The baying of hounds. Their pursuers were closing in.

Without being told, Littel spurred his horse to a gallop, jumping a fallen tree as he went, landing badly but keeping his seat. They were almost past the bog now, the trees rearing up before them like a row of massive hairy beasts.

As they slowed to push through the hanging branches, Jaimy turned and saw the hunters follow their hounds straight into the fen without pausing. They could have crossed, but had lost that time.

For the first time Jaimy felt truly frightened, wondering what these men intended.

Beyond the willows lay a narrow track running east-west, and they pulled up their mounts here, looking around as though searching for a place to hide. Beyond the road lay a small lake, perhaps a quarter of a mile across. Jaimy wheeled his horse east and called for his companion to follow. If they did have better horses, perhaps they could put them to advantage on the road.

The dull drumming of hooves on mud; and distant, the shouts of men and baying of hounds. The wind whipped at the drooping willow wands which swayed out into the track like grasping tendrils, making the riders work their horses lest they shy.

So this is how the fox feels, Jaimy thought as he struggled to keep his horse moving and beneath him. He made a silent vow that he would never ride to the hounds again.

A mud farmyard appeared, and a cottage and ramshackle buildings. They barely slowed, scattering fowl before them. Then suddenly out onto a proper road. Jaimy did not hesitate to consider, but turned his horse north. He looked back at Littel, and realized that neither horse would go much farther at this pace.

"Off the road," Littel called. "We must get off the road."

Yes, but where? The underwood here was dense, and no paths could be seen opening into its inner halls. Jaimy didn't know what they should do. Ride on as long as their horses could stand. That was all they could do.

They galloped round a bend and came upon three men, two mounted and one standing by his horse. Before Jaimy could react, one man lifted a bow. He turned his horse then, and plunged blindly into the wood, staying low to the horse's neck, clinging to the mane, letting his mare find her way. Certain that at any moment a branch would crack his skull.

There were sounds of someone behind him and Jaimy hoped it was Littel and not one of their pursuers.

Someone had made to fire an arrow at him! And at that distance might have killed him easily. Killed him!

The bush thinned just perceptibly and Jaimy dared to raise his head, he could feel his horse laboring to breathe, her chest heaving beneath his knees. A quick glance behind and he saw that he had Egar in tow, his face set and grim.

The trees thinned again, and the underwood all but disappeared so that they were galloping over a soft cushion of decaying leaves. A low stone wall, almost buried in a thicket of vines, rose up before them and without thinking Jaimy made his horse jump, and heard a loud grunt as Littel landed behind him. Jaimy turned again and found his companion still in the saddle and flailing with his foot to retrieve a lost stirrup. They were in another wagon track, and turned again to follow, not knowing where they would go or what they would do. Only keep to the saddle and run their horses until they dropped. That was all they could do now.

Out of the bush ahead a fox suddenly appeared, some small rodent in its jaws. For the briefest second it paused on the road, staring at the riders bearing down on it, one dainty foot raised, and then it bolted into the bush to the left. Jaimy almost let out a whoop.

Hoping Egar would have the presence of mind to follow, he turned down the track of the fox, forcing his horse to keep her pace. Branches whipped him, tearing at his skin and clothing. His cheek was raked terribly, and he rode with one arm up before his face, barely able to stay in the saddle. Then the fox appeared again, and Jaimy swerved off, leaving it to go its own way.

At the bottom of a steep embankment he found a shallow stream and turned to follow it, his horse slipping and stumbling on the smooth stones. After half of an hour of this he stopped and his horse stood panting, fighting her bit to drink, which he dare not let her do.

Egar Littel came up beside him, gasping almost as hard

as his mount. He had suffered worse than Jaimy and one eye was almost closed by a cruel welt.

Not far off, hounds bayed.

"We should not stop," Littel managed.

"No, listen.... They are going north, chasing our fox. With luck he will drop his prey and that will cause even more confusion. They are spoiled for chasing us now. The riders will take hours to pick up our trail again, and by then it will be dark."

Jaimy slipped out of his saddle and into water to his knees. Tired of struggling with his horse he scooped up some water in his cupped hands and let her take a little. "Come, we will walk them so that they don't cool too quickly. I think we must stay to the river a bit longer, though it can't be good for our poor mounts. We will go up the bank just at dark. I think we would be best to go east, and then north. I'm afraid to go toward Avonel now in case we meet reinforcements for the dogs." He waved off toward the baying hounds.

Littel almost fell from his saddle, splashing down into the stream bed. He looked hardly able to continue, despite his fear.

"Best we move, Egar," Jaimy said softly. "You saw them aim an arrow at me. I am not convinced they wouldn't have shot either."

"At you?!" Littel said, incredulous, and then turned his shoulder toward Jaimy. He pulled at his coat, displaying a ragged hole in the sleeve. "Did that arrow come this close to you?"

Jaimy stood, a bit stunned, as the realization made its way through the layers of fear and confusion. *They had tried to kill them! Tried to kill them rather than let them escape.*

THIRTEEN

Sir Roderick Palle was not at peace with the world. He stood on a balcony in the Winter Garden, looking out over the crowd gathered to celebrate the opening of Wells' bridge of iron, and something about the sight of the milling masses unsettled him. The people below seemed so ... rudderless. So lacking in real purpose. They had been told that Wells' bridge was a marvel of the modern age and, dutifully, they had come out to celebrate this auspicious event. The King's Man suspected that not more than half a dozen people in this whole great building understood what it meant.

The hall, Sir Roderick believed, was filled with the benighted. Fashionable aristocrats who saw this as merely another social function, no different from the theater or opera. Perhaps there were even some softhearted transcendentalists and nature lovers staring up at the model of the iron bridge and shaking their heads in dismay, and for no reason other than this concept was new. Palle was sure that even many of the empiricists present did not fully comprehend what had happened right before their eyes.

We have broken away from stone, the King's Man thought, *weaned ourselves of the material of the ancients. Hundreds of years ago we delved down into the earth and wrested something new from her aged bones. We smelted and refined until we found the essence of the earth's strength. And now, through an act of creative genius, we have built a structure of this material. A structure that balances the forces and stresses in such a way that it supports itself. And it is only a beginning. We have broken away from stone.*

But Palle could see that these vacantly smiling faces, these mouths that spoke nothing but gossip, did not realize they stood at a crossroads of history. What would they say if they knew Wells was certain ships could be built of iron? Ships of iron that would not only float but repel cannon shot!

This lack of understanding made the King's Man uncomfortable. These people could misconstrue anything. Pledge unwavering support to the worst tyrant, vilify the most honorable minister. Even a man such as himself could fall victim to these people. All it took was some rabble rouser to stand up and convince them his lies were true. Never mind that Roderick Palle had given them over a decade of security and good government. They would march in the streets, chanting his name as though he were a demon in need of exorcism. He had seen it happen to others.

Oh, today the crowds had come to celebrate the iron bridge, but they might just as easily have come to tear it down as a symbol of their oppression . . . or some such thing. One could never be absolutely sure. And anyone who was, soon came to a bitter end.

He suddenly realized that he was beginning to think like Rawdon, and this caused him to shake his head. He was sure that the Royal Physician was actually superstitious and believed that if he never became overconfident, as long as he always believed that the worst could happen, then it would not. The King's Man smiled. Perhaps the doctor was right in this belief and was averting disaster with this regimen. In which case, it was good that the doctor laid awake at night looking out for their interests through his program of constant anxiety. Palle never lost sleep over his choices. Or very seldom anyway.

It was true that he had not slept soundly the previous night. But then who would have? Littel gone, and Averil

Kent disappearing from Merton—hardly a coincidence, he was sure. Kent had something to do with Littel's disappearance, unquestionably, but he was not sure what he could do about it. Valary's man-servant swore that there was no one staying in Kent's home but the two elderly gentlemen. So if Kent did not have Littel, where was he?

Kent was fortunate that Palle was a civilized man. In times past many of those designated as King's Man had not been so discreet, nor did they care much for the reactions of the people—which had brought many of them to their demise. Roderick knew; he had made careful study of these matters. As things stood he was not quite ready to weather the storm that would result from apprehending Sir Averil Kent. Oh, he wasn't really worried about what the people milling about below him might think. They would likely accept whatever explanation they were given, especially if it somehow fit their expectations. But there was a group who would not believe Palle's explanation, and that group concerned him. He couldn't afford to offend them. Not at this point anyway. And there *was* the unreliability of the crowd to consider. . . .

It was the problem with Farrland; the country was governed by compromise. Compromise between this group and that. Between the industrialists and the merchants, the landed gentry and the Farrellites. And now even the reformers were beginning to play a part! A development he looked upon as benignly as a surgeon looked upon gangrene.

He gazed out at the people gathered on the floor of the Winter Garden's great hall and thought that, except for small, temporary setbacks, things proceeded as they should. This very day would see the formation of the council of regents—in fact if not in name. Official announcements would come soon enough. Best to tidy up the loose ends first. He didn't want Egar Littel galloping about the countryside telling what he knew—not that it was likely that many would believe him. Still, there were some. . . .

Noyes appeared at his side, quietly, his tall somewhat comic form standing a head above the King's Man. There could be few men in all of Farrland whom high fashion suited less. It was unfortunate that a man with such an intellect should persist in looking so foolish.

"I think it is all but done, Sir Roderick," the empiricist said, smiling broadly.

"The duke has agreed?" Palle asked, betraying a bit of surprise, he realized.

Noyes nodded solemnly, although this solemnity did not erase his smile entirely. "Not only has he agreed, but Galton was one of the names the great duke put forward himself!"

"Do not laugh, Noyes," Palle said quickly. "Let no one see you laugh." Palle turned to look out over the hall, feeling a great easing of tension in his body, like a carriage spring relieved of its load. "I can't believe it came so easily," Palle whispered, almost speaking to himself.

"Nor can I, Sir Roderick. Nor can I." Noyes shifted on his feet, and spread his large hands out on the railing. "There is only one condition. The Duke wishes an audience with His Majesty."

The King's Man nodded. "I'm sure Doctor Rawdon can arrange a meeting that will convince the duke our claims are true. At His Majesty's convenience, of course."

"I will inform the duke. Will you bear the news to Galton or shall I?"

Palle looked around and saw the governor seated near to his wife, speaking with a group of young nobles. "I shall inform him of his most recent honor."

For the briefest second Roderick felt suspicion take hold of him. The duke had put Galton forward? But then he smiled. All those years on Farrow had made Galton seem the most innocent of men. Clearly he had no greater ambition than to help the people of Farrow, which he had done in great measure—especially his efforts toward rescinding the Daye Laws which apparently had a devastating effect on the economies of certain of Palle's friends.

Palle turned away from Galton. The good news could wait until the governor was alone, it would give the

King's Man a few moments to savor it. Such moments were like fine wines, not to be rushed.

Noyes continued to stand at his side, saying nothing, perhaps enjoying the moment as Roderick did.

"Sir Roderick." It was one of his secretaries.

The King's Man turned.

"A messenger has come from Mr. Hawksmoor, sir."

"Yes."

"He will deliver his message to no one but you, Sir Roderick."

Roderick nodded. "Well, bring him along, then."

"Sir, he has been riding hard for several hours." The young man looked around, a bit apprehensively. "Perhaps you would prefer to meet him more privately?"

Roderick nodded, waving the man to go ahead, and taking Noyes in tow. Now what in Farrelle's name went on here? He did not have long to ponder this for Hawksmoor's messenger was waiting in a nearby alcove. Roderick's first thought was to commend his assistant for recommending that he meet this man in private. The messenger was covered in mud and grime, his clothing torn, and he looked entirely out of sorts, like a man who had, by good luck and hard riding, escaped highwaymen. He bowed quickly to Roderick and passed him a letter closed with Hawksmoor's seal.

Sir:

After a difficult chase, we caught up with Mr. Littel. I regret to say that Mr. Littel and his companion fought quite fiercely and, in the heat of the moment, both were killed. As Littel was last seen in the company of the son of the Duke of Blackwater, I fear the very worst may have occurred. I am hurrying now to the scene of this tragedy, and will relay more information as soon as is humanly possible.

I remain your servant,
E.D.H.

Palle found he could not move, but stared at the note as though certain these words were somehow misarranged. It simply couldn't be true.

"Sir Roderick?" Noyes said quietly. "What is it?" The empiricist reached out toward the letter, and when Roderick did not respond, he took the sheet of paper from the man's limp fingers.

"We are undone," Noyes whispered. He lifted a hand toward his face but then let it fall.

Seeing the reaction of his companion, Roderick suppressed his own emotions. "Were you involved in this madness?" Palle asked the messenger.

The man nodded, apparently too frightened to speak.

"Did anyone know these men you captured?"

The man shook his head. "Two young gentlemen, sir." The man's voice was so hoarse he could barely be heard. "We had been pursuing them for the entire day. Hunting them with hounds, sir. Caught them just at dark. I was sent off to Mr. Hawksmoor immediately, and then he had me come here."

Palle turned away, taking the letter from Noyes as he did so, concealing it quickly in his coat, as though just being seen in its possession could bring calamity.

"Noyes," Palle said, turning to his confederate, speaking so no one else could hear. "You must take charge of this. At the gallop. If it is the young gentleman that Hawksmoor suggests, then you must take every step to be sure that no one—no one—will ever know." Palle reached out and took the man's forearm. "Do you understand? If the duke were ever to learn of this, it would not matter that too little evidence could be found to convict us in court. The entire nobility would be raised against us." Palle looked around quickly to be sure no one could hear. "Whatever steps necessary. Our survival depends on it."

Noyes nodded a bit tentatively.

"Mr. Hawksmoor will be there to carry out whatever measure you deem necessary, don't worry. Your own hands will stay clean." Palle turned and looked out toward the great hall. "If this proves to be true, then it would be best if we were to hunt down the boy's murderers ourselves. Hawksmoor will understand."

Roderick thought it best if he returned to the celebrations. He had good news for Galton. The other matter he would keep to himself, for now. Even his closest associates might lose their nerve if they heard about the duke's son.

Roderick wondered if the duke would expect him to pay his respects, but decided there would be nothing odd in his not doing so. Galton was acquainted with the nobleman, anyway, and would be better suited to expressing appreciation.

For a few seconds Palle felt pity for the duke. The poor man had lost his only son. That would be hard. Roderick wondered if it would ever be possible to trace the murder back to him. They needed to find out how Littel had escaped Merton. That was the key. He had been there, in the company of this young lord—this cousin of Tristam Flattery!—and then he had disappeared, and no one knew how.

Kent had been seen walking through the city, and then he, too, had slipped away. Palle had only this rumor of Kent seen, apparently alone, in his carriage heading for the Avonel Road. But this was just a rumor.

Roderick made an effort to calm himself. Panic stopped one from making intelligent decisions—he knew this well. He had made a reputation for coolness under fire, and was damned if he would falter now. He smiled at some passersby, not entirely confident that his face was not still betraying his recent shock.

Rawdon appeared out of the whirl of faces. Here would be a test. The physician knew him as well as anyone and would notice immediately if something was not right.

"Sir Roderick." Rawdon bobbed his handsome head.

Occasionally Palle felt jealous of Rawdon's appearance, having been born so plain himself. "Doctor. I thought you had been detained with your patient. Everything is well, I hope?"

"Well enough, I think." The doctor looked around, then bent his head closer to the King's Man. "Though I have a fear that something might have happened at the palace last night."

"Things happen at the palace all the time, Doctor. Speak more plainly."

Rawdon cast a look around. "The King went down to his waterfall very late in the night."

Roderick nodded. "Unusual, I agree, but not terribly so."

"I spoke with a chambermaid this morning who was in the garden last night, and said she saw someone being taken from the arboretum. Someone quite elderly, she thought."

Roderick was truly alarmed now. "The King is there still, is he not?"

"I attended His Majesty this morning. But, do you see, he might have met with someone. That is my suspicion."

"Well, it is slim evidence, Doctor, but I understand your concerns." *Kent?!* Could it have been Kent? "I'll look into it when we return. We'll speak to this chambermaid together. If she was about at such a late hour, then there must have been a young buck as well. Or an old one. And who assisted the King? He could not have gone so far on his own—not these days. We will soon get to the bottom of it."

The doctor looked so kind, and had suffered so many troubles of his own that Roderick found he wanted to confide the news about the duke's son. But he stopped himself, knowing what such news might do to the doctor's fragile mental state. He had suffered badly from melancholia this last year—ever since his wife had fallen ill.

"It is likely nothing, as you say," Rawdon conceded. "I worry overly, as you have often noted, Roderick."

At the extreme end of the great hall a drunk stepped up onto a chair and began to harangue the crowd, much to the amusement of many. Officials began to push through the gathering toward this man, but he did not seem to notice, or perhaps care, and carried on in a deep powerful voice. The noise in the hall began to drop as more and more became aware of the disturbance, and as the crowd fell quiet Roderick began to make out some of the man's theme.

". . . houses of iron, and iron ships with terrible weapons." The man slurred his words and stretched his vowels comically, but his tone was so full of dread even Roderick could feel it. "And iron nannies will care for your children, suckle them on molten metal until they grow souls like engines ticking inside them. Where will this bridge take us? Can you see that distant shore, darkened by a cloud of sickly smoke? Can you see yourself in chains of iron? Can you see your children?"

It was then that the officials reached the orator and hauled him down bodily, carrying him away, shouting and struggling. There was a moment like an indrawn breath, and then the chaos of several thousand people talking at once.

Rawdon looked over at Palle and shrugged, but the King's Man could see the doctor's face had gone white. He thought Rawdon might collapse where he stood.

"I think you should sit down, Benjamin," Palle said, taking him by the elbow and steering him toward a seat.

The doctor sat down, and laid his head back for a moment, closing his eyes. Roderick was afraid he'd lost consciousness, but then he roused himself and managed a weak smile.

"Forgive me, Roderick, I don't know what came over me."

"Far too many sleepless nights caring for your patient. It is unfortunate that we lost Llewellyn. I would prefer to see you with some reliable assistant."

"No," the doctor said with surprising firmness. "There are too many involved as it is." He took three deep breaths. "I am recovered. Don't be concerned." He made an effort to force off his normal manner of distraction. "Tell me how things proceed. We have worked out this problem with Mr. Littel?"

Roderick hesitated. "I'm not sure," he said evenly.

"Well, offer him more. A title. An estate. You have been too tightfisted with him, you will excuse me for saying, Roderick, but that's what I think. I realize he isn't one of us, but it hardly matters. We need him yet, or at least that is what Wells says. Our Mr. Wells may be the great polymath, but Littel is certainly unparalleled in his field. A genius, really."

"Perhaps you're right, Benjamin. I shall do what I can when next I see him."

Benjamin nodded, happy to have set the King's Man straight in this matter.

ॐ ॐ ॐ

The Entonne Embassador had rushed through his official responsibilities as quickly as decorum would allow and now his attention could be devoted entirely to his latest interest. He had been, almost desperately, trying to meet Angeline Christophe, the mistress of Prince Kori—or so everyone said. Massenet was no stranger to blinding passions, but this one, he was quite aware, was even more misguided than usual.

She is the mistress of the prince, who is about to become the real head of the Farr government. He had repeated this to himself countless times in the past thirty-six hours, but it did not seem to have any effect on his behavior.

I just want to speak with the woman, he told himself, *to see if she is as beautiful as I first thought—which I'm sure she can't be.* The young woman he had seen was something of a goddess, he had thought.

But that look she had given him. . . . Just the memory of it had the most stunning effect—as though, when he drew a breath, it went right through his entire body, even right out to the ends of his limbs. Like breathing a draught of distilled life. It was remarkable.

Massenet, of course, was no young fool. He even thought that he had become somewhat jaded these past years. Not only had he become adept at predicting the behavior of others, but he could predict his own behavior just as well. He no longer surprised himself. It was one of the saddest things about aging.

The count was well aware that he took a particular

pleasure from cuckolding husbands. He had admitted this, at least to himself, long ago. And the more accomplished and successful the man, the more Massenet enjoyed stealing his wife's affections (of course such men tended to have the most beautiful wives, as well).

It was not a particularly personal thing. Some of the husbands Massenet cuckolded were quite decent men; acquaintances whose society he enjoyed. He also made every effort to be sure they did not discover the truth. He did not, after all, wish them ill. He could enjoy his little triumphs quite privately.

And now he knew part of what was driving him was the desire to cuckold this fatuous little prince. She could not possibly desire the man! It was only his position. His power. Massenet had a great deal of information that made him quite sure of this.

She had looked at Massenet with such . . . interest. He knew that look. He had seen it, perhaps more often than any man in Farrland. He knew it.

"The pleasures of the day to you, Count Massenet," a voice said in perfect Entonne.

"Bertillon! Pleasures indeed." Massenet smiled warmly, though he kept glancing off, searching the crowd for those dark tresses. "I am surprised that a miracle of metal would interest you, Charl."

"It seems everyone assumes I have no interests but music and the arts, which is not true. I believe I might find clients in this mass of intelligent and cultured people."

Massenet smiled. "Money, then?"

"In a word. And you, my Count? Searching for the woman who will measure up to your ideal? What would this ideal maiden be like, if I may ask?" Bertillon, too, kept searching the crowd.

"I hate to disappoint you, Charl, but it is not anything so romantic. I am too old and jaded. Have you heard who will be named to the council?"

"Galton?"

Massenet laughed. "Foolish of me to think I could surprise you, Mr. Bertillon. Perhaps you know something about last night's events in Merton? Palle was searching the town. Kent was one of the people he sought, but he was not the only one. I confess I was unprepared. Hawksmoor is seeking someone still, I think."

"I will see what I can learn." Bertillon was about to leave but hesitated. "I have just learned the oddest thing. Not useful, I'm sure, but interesting. I just watched Princess Joelle very intentionally steer her son away from a young woman—the intended bride of Lord Jaimas Flattery—and the look on the young prince's face! He tried to hide it, but . . ." Charl shrugged.

"You think there is some involvement there?" Massenet asked, his interest suddenly piqued.

"No, in fact, I don't. I think there is youthful infatuation. Something to be marked. One might note the qualities of this young woman. They can't be so unique that we could not find another with similar charms. It is at least a possibility."

The count pondered this for a moment. "Perhaps the son will take after the father," he said after a moment. "Do you know this Angeline Christope?"

Bertillon shook his head. "She is hardly ever seen, apparently. I don't even know who her friends are, apart from the obvious, that is." Bertillon turned to his companion, his manner suddenly grave. "You will be careful there, Count Massenet. Whatever could be gained would be lost ten times over if your interest were discovered."

Massenet realized he had drawn himself up, and fixed Bertillon with his most imperious glare, but he managed to catch himself and soften his tone. "I'm sure you're right, Charl. I am merely making the most delicate investigation, that is all. Nothing to fear." Massenet looked around the hall. "I have not seen our favorite artist here. Would you speak with him? I would dearly love to know what went on in Merton."

Bertillon bowed and went off on his rounds, leaving the ambassador feeling somewhat chastened. The musician was right; he should forget about this woman. It was unfortunate that this was the one area in which Massenet's phenomenal will often could not be brought to bear.

❦ ❦ ❦

Alissa sat near to her father in the Avonel residence of the Duke and Duchess of Blackwater. Despite the reassurances of Averil Kent, she was worried to near madness about her missing fiancé. And she could see that the duke was as concerned as she, which was even more worrying. This was not a man who revealed his concerns.

"If Kent gets himself in too much trouble, I'm not certain that I will be able to extricate him. What do you think he is up to, Professor?"

Somers shrugged. Alissa noted that her father was always a little uncomfortable in the duke's presence, which she had originally thought indicated that the professor was intimidated by the great man. She had come to realize, however, that her father was actually uncomfortable with his reaction to the duke. He liked the nobleman. Respected him, in fact. It was a difficult thing for a dedicated reformer like her father to discover that this wealthy aristocrat had concerns for others. Had thought deeply about the nation and its people, and had grave concerns about the unfolding future. Of course, her father was a mild reformer. He shuddered at the blood shed in the streets when the mobs marched. The deaths distressed him terribly.

"I don't quite know. Kent has managed to avoid telling me anything on two occasions now, and I am not sure I will ever learn more than that. I'm not even sure that Emin is telling me everything. I must say though, that Kent was distressed to hear what had been done to Dandish's home. I think he is afraid that Hawksmoor found something there. Some information about the inquiries that the professor pursued in private. Emin spoke with Dandish's old cleaning lady who told him that she and your nephew had opened a locked room in Dandish's home. Apparently, according to the woman, Dandish had been very secretive about this chamber. But all that was found inside were empty planting boxes. Nothing more." Somers' eyes looked off through a wall as though he imagined the room in Dandish's home, and perhaps might conjure up its past contents. "It is all very odd," he muttered.

Alissa looked away from her father to find the duke's penetrating gaze on her. She looked away immediately, and felt a slight flush on her cheeks. No doubt the duke was wondering about her involvement with Kent, and she cursed herself again for being caught like a fool.

She leaned forward and poured herself more tea, hoping to hide her reaction. A fear that the duke might know she acted as Princess Joelle's liaison with Kent was taking hold of her. *Don't be absurd,* she chided herself. *Even the duke cannot read thoughts.*

"Kent is adamant that he did not engineer the disappearance of Jaimas and this other young gentleman?" The duke addressed this question to no one in particular.

Alissa said nothing, hoping her father would answer. She did not want to lie, and now that she had not heard from Jaimy, she wanted to tell the duke the truth, hoping he might help. Afraid that if she kept her secret she might be endangering Jaimy. But Kent had been adamant. *No one must know of the prince's involvement.* And she understood the importance of that. She had worked up her nerve to approach the prince at the Winter Palace, but he had been surrounded by courtiers and other hangers on, and she could see no way for them to speak privately. The prince had noticed her, though. Their eyes had met, and she had felt the look a bit disturbing; she could not tell why. As though he were trying to tell her something. It had made her quite afraid.

"Apparently so," Somers said. "Alissa, you spoke with him."

"Sir Averil assured me he did not know their whereabouts."

"Palle would not dare to harm my son. . . . But I still wonder about this young man. Littel you called him?"

"Egar Littel. He used to come around the house to my Friday evenings. Something of a savant in linguistics, though I suspect his real reason for coming was Alissa's older sister."

The duke nodded, glancing again at Alissa.

"I promised the duchess that I would read to her this evening," she said, rising abruptly. "If you will excuse me, Father. Duke."

She could not help but feel the two men stared after her as she made her escape. It made her feel so stiff and awkward that she almost tried to draw her back in closer, as though protecting the area from a blow.

Once out into the hallway she sighed audibly. She went first to the chamber she was now becoming accustomed to sleeping in while visiting Avonel, and here she found a shawl and the book of poems she had taken from the library. Before leaving she stood looking around the room, which was vast by her standards. The maids had turned down the bed and lit the lamps for her, and there were fresh flowers from the greenhouse. Yellow winter roses in arrangements with a delicate fern. For the briefest second she longed for her small room in her family home, and the comfort of her sisters' warm laughter. Despite the fire, this room seemed awfully cold.

Squaring her shoulders Alissa set off for the chamber of the duchess.

A maid sat in a small antechamber. She let Alissa in immediately, smiling at her warmly. The staff were always so welcoming and kind—even the ones who weren't spying on her. The duchess lay beneath a heavy comforter of goose down, though the room was not cold. Her eyes were closed, but her face did not seem peaceful. Alissa looked at her, feeling sad and helpless. This woman had been so kind to her, and she seemed to be having her life drained away. It immediately made her fear that Jaimy would one day suffer the same fate—and it did not help that the woman's face on the pillow bore such a similarity to her son's. The duchess' hair was the color of Jaimy's, or had been before gray had begun to appear—silver locks among the gold. And she had the eyes almost exactly. Alissa so wanted to make her well.

"Duchess?" Alissa whispered, and those fine eyes flashed open. They were so rimmed in red that Alissa thought the duchess had been crying.

"Lady Alissa," the woman said, and her voice, though subdued, did not betray signs of recent tears. Her face brightened somewhat, and a smile appeared.

"I am not Lady Alissa yet, Duchess," Alissa said, and took the offered hand in her own. The duchess' fingers were so cold—like barren branches.

"Will you not indulge an old woman in her dreams? I have so wanted a daughter I could fuss over, and whose marriage I could ruin with constant meddling." She gave a small laugh. "You must not hesitate to remind me that you are mature enough to make your own decisions, and that I have grown old and meddlesome."

"The Duchess is neither old nor meddlesome. In truth I will accept all the guidance you would care to offer." It was true that the duchess was not old—not fifty years—but her constitution was so delicate, and she had been a near invalid for so long.

The duchess squeezed her hand, meeting her eye and holding it as she often did, her gaze not searching but filled with affection. It was no wonder the woman was adored by so many.

"There is no word from Jaimas?"

Alissa shook her head, not meeting the duchess' eye. She thought for a second that a tear might escape, but it did not. The duchess squeezed her hand again.

"No doubt he will turn up in the morning, and I shall upbraid him terribly for worrying you so. Such selfishness is not characteristic of him, I want you to know." The duchess looked off toward the fire for a moment. "You brought some poetry?" she said, her voice sounding utterly fatigued, suddenly.

"I must warn you, it is modern. . . ."

"It does not rhyme? I am scandalized." She settled back into her pillows and closed her eyes. "Read to me, Lady Alissa," she whispered.

Reluctantly Alissa released the cold hand of the duchess, just as it had begun to take on some of her own warmth. She opened the book, turned slightly so that the light fell on the page, and began.

"*I lie down at the gnarled foot of an oak
And watch the ants explore the vast desert
Of my cast off cloak.
What treasures might they mine from pockets
To return, triumphant, to city and queen?
        High summer passes in Wicklow County.*

*I spent my morning
Watching the salmon spend their too short lives
Against the rocks and falls of Wicklow River.
Battered and rotting, they skulk in shallow pools
Gathering strength in sullen silence.
I watched them brood, and hover,
An insolent flick of a still powerful tail.*

*Sailors return from the open sea
To die upon the grass,
And have their ashes spread
On the slow currents of rural streams.
One must wonder why, when they say
Men buried at sea are reborn
As dolphins.*

*I am caught in a back eddy,
Floating in the shallows of this field
Spinning slowly, beneath the summer sun,
Pockets emptied.
Who carried off the treasures of my life?
        Once bright memories, fading.*

*Rest a moment, rest.
Soon we must begin,
The struggle again.
A last leap
Into the empty sky.*

Alissa closed the book gently, her gaze coming to rest on the duchess' face.

"Lord Skye?" the duchess asked softly.

"Yes."

"He makes it sound so easy," the duchess murmured, not opening her eyes. A tiny smile appeared on her still beautiful lips, and then her breathing became regular and the lips suddenly relaxed, drawing open a fraction. Alissa thought that all the skin on the duchess' face went slack, like a pavilion when the ropes were loosed, and this seemed a picture of death to her. She stared at the duchess for a moment, distressed, almost frightened, and then, carefully, she tucked the woman's cold hand beneath the covers, and pressed the comforter gently around her white throat, so that no currents of cold air might touch her.

FOURTEEN

Tristam stood at the rail watching the tropic birds perform their mating flight over the clear lagoon. It was an astonishing display, these cloud-white birds, dark eyed and red billed, their two elongated tail feathers streaming like blood-red banners. They fanned the air with elegantly curved wings, cocked their tail to one side, and flew backward through the air.

Tristam had been watching carefully, and was quite sure past observers had not exaggerated; the birds actually propelled themselves backward. Tristam was not sure how impressive this was to a prospective mate, but it certainly astonished him.

Across the lagoon the village was still empty, though at this time of day it did not seem so strange, for during the heat of the afternoon the Varuans usually rested or slept, and the village could be very quiet. The people had fled to some hiding place in the interior, expecting the Farrlanders to turn their guns on their homes, as had been done once before. The abandoned village seemed both very picturesque and a bit forlorn, bringing up unexpected emotions in Tristam. It reminded him again of Kent and what the painter had said that afternoon they had met. *Isollae.* Loneliness in the face of beauty.

A Varuan rail emerged gingerly from behind an empty fale. These flightless birds did not commonly come near to dwellings of men, but here it was, tentatively exploring among the abandoned fales. It made Tristam realize, again, how quickly man's works went back to nature.

There was a call from the masthead lookout, and Tristam moved a little along the rail to get a better view. From the breadfruit trees behind the village, appeared two groups of islanders wearing crowns of green leaves and bracelets of white flowers. They walked close together, their steps measured and slow, and among them bore two burdens covered in red tapa cloth. Red, the color of prestige and wealth.

In the central common the two groups laid down their burdens—two bodies, Tristam was certain. The Jacks had gathered at the rail, and Tristam could hear them muttering ugly threats. The duchess suddenly appeared at his side.

"Farrelle rest them," she said softly. "Is it Garvey and Chilsey?"

"So I hope," Tristam answered, not thinking how odd this might sound. He was afraid that this might be two Varuans, sacrificed to mollify the Farrlanders. The Varuans did not sacrifice humans often, unlike the inhabitants of some other islands, but in desperate times even they would resort to this terrible practice.

The Varuans stood in rows on either side of the draped bodies, looking down at them silently. Then they clapped three times in perfect unison, and one man spoke, his voice loud, almost chanting. The man's speech was brief and the speaker too distant for Tristam to discern any words, and then they began to sing softly. Tristam was not sure, but it sounded almost like the song that Teiho Ruau had sung as the *Swallow* departed from Farrland, and this chilled him a little.

Wallis came up on Tristam's other side.

"What is this song, Mr. Wallis?" Tristam asked.

"It is sung at the outset of a voyage, Mr. Flattery, such as the islanders have made through all their history. Great voyages, as you know. It is a song of sadness, and of hope. They sing it as part of their funeral rite, as well, not so incongruous to them, for death is thought to be the beginning of a voyage to the sacred island—the 'Faraway Paradise,' they call it." Wallis listened for a moment, and then began to recite, slowly, as though he were translating what he heard.

> *"The mother wind carries us*
> *Into the distant west*
> *The great whale appears*
> *With the sun's last rays.*
> *And stars light to mark our way*
> *Like islands cast upon the sea.*
>
> *Gently sings the mother wind*
> *Across the lapping seas.*
> *Gently sings the mother wind*
> *Of islands far away.*
>
> *The whale appears to call its mate*
> *Lonely beneath the waves.*
> *And we follow passing moons*
> *Their sails bright in the sky.*
> *Slowly we're drawn, by moon and sun,*
> *Into the distant west.*
>
> *Gently sings the mother wind*
> *In our swelling sails.*
> *Gently sings the mother wind*
> *Of islands green and fair.*
>
> *May you find clear lagoons,*
> *Protected from the storms*
> *And may the maidens think you fair*
> *And sing you welcome songs,*
> *Across the seas you take our hearts,*
> *To keep until we meet again.*
>
> *Gently sings the mother wind,*
> *Gently."*

The painter fell silent. In the distant village the islanders finished their song and from baskets began to scatter something over the bodies. Again they stood looking on for a moment, then clapped their hands loudly, and turned and went back as they had come, in two lines, as though they still shared a burden among them.

"First murder them, and then honor them," the duchess said so that only Tristam might hear. "Though they would rather have life than honor, I think. How very sad."

❦ ❦ ❦

Only the few animals that had been left behind wandered the village, a sow and her young rooting about in a taro patch, fowl waiting for their feed of coconut shards. The bright fabric of pareus left out to dry flapped lazily in the trade, large strange blossoms. The party from the *Swallow* went through the empty lanes and open areas between the houses with a sense of foreboding. Tristam couldn't help but think of the Lost City, abandoned as well, and these thoughts did not comfort him.

It was late afternoon, and the shadows of the palm trunks elongated impossibly across the sand, like crooked fingers pointing toward their fallen shipmates. Stern had sent a party ashore to retrieve the bodies and to make contact with the islanders if possible: Wallis, because he was half an islander himself; Hobbes, whom the islanders treated with affection and respect; Beacham, to add numbers and because he was level-headed; Tristam, because Stern thought the naturalist uncommonly lucky; and the viscount, because the duchess had insisted. Tristam's shadow, after all.

Hobbes walked a few paces ahead, keeping intentionally to himself. Since they had landed on the beach the ship's master had not spoken a word, though he was supposed to be in command of this party.

Stern hoped they might somehow reestablish relations with the Varuans, but the islanders were not to be seen. They were up in the hills, Wallis said, in secret caves used to hide women and children from invaders. Tristam wondered if they realized there were limits to the range of the ship's guns—they would have been safe just beyond the village.

Tristam wondered again what part Hobbes had played in the deaths of Garvey and Chilsey. Had the master schemed with the two and sent them to look for Kingfoil? Or had he merely been careless—talking too freely about the conversation he'd overheard—and the two sailors had taken it upon themselves to search for *regis*? Tristam could not decide, but one thing was certain—Hobbes bore a great burden of guilt over the deaths.

Tristam had never seen the ship's master so distracted. Didn't Stern realize Hobbes was presently unfit for command? But no doubt the captain thought Hobbes was affected by the death of Garvey, the master's mate, and a fine seaman. It would be expected. It would also be expected that an old sea dog like Hobbes would rise above his grief.

The entire party slowed as they came nearer the bodies, as though they were already part of a funeral procession. A sweet smell of blossoms came to Tristam and then the putrid smell of the dead, left out in the tropical day. Hobbes clapped a square of cotton over his mouth, and stopped six feet away. Tristam could almost see a panic in the master's eyes, as though he would not be able to face it—to face what he had done.

The others passed Hobbes by, and came and stood by the bodies, as the Varuans had earlier. Under patterned tapa cloth Tristam could see the forms of the men, like the geology of a land beneath a covering of vegetation. Tristam reached down and gently pulled the cloth away from one of the faces, and found Jon Chilsey, blood matted in his hair where his skull had been broken. Beacham sobbed, and turned away to hide his face.

Garvey had been treated the same. Delicate white shells had been laid over their eyes—the paper nautilus, Tristam noted automatically, *Argonauta argo*—and upon each cheek the Varuan symbol of the sun had been tattooed. Between the lips of the dead men the delicate petals of pale blossoms appeared, as though they had taken root in the sailor's souls.

The scene was so reminiscent of the ritual in the Lost City that Tristam was shaken. He knew the others must be thinking the same thing. And then the naturalist in him noticed the blossoms, and he almost snatched one up. They were *regis* flowers. Tristam removed the shells and the blossoms from the men's mouths, putting them into one of his pockets, as though the honor the Varuans offered these two men were an offense.

"Farrelle protect their souls," Wallis said. "These are Varuan funeral rites. The stone adze in the hand is for the making of boats and fales. These plants set by their feet are young breadfruit and coconuts to plant when they reach their destination, to sustain them in the life to come, as are the sacrificed fowl and pigs."

Hobbes had walked away some ten paces, turning his back on the scene. Tristam saw him press thumb and forefinger delicately to the bridge of his nose, and then realized that the man wept, absolutely silently, as though a lifetime aboard His Majesty's ships had taught him that skill as well.

The viscount had turned away from the bodies, and stood staring at Hobbes, as though the master were a specimen pinned to a board. Tristam looked away, unsettled by the viscount's apparent fascination with the master's grief.

Wallis continued, almost reciting, it seemed. "When people are laid out in this manner, beneath a coverlet of blossoms, they are being honored, not treated as enemies. There is regret over these deaths."

"Then why did they murder them?" Beacham asked angrily. He knelt near to the body of his fellow midshipman, so filled with anguish that he moved his limbs without focused control, puppetlike.

Wallis shrugged. He was near to tears himself, Tristam thought. "They broke the tapu, Mr. Beacham. A serious tapu. The islanders who did this would have felt that they had no choice in the matter."

"No amount of debate or anger will bring them back," Tristam said suddenly. "We must bear them down to the shore, so they can be taken for burial."

Beacham glared at Tristam, his anger suddenly fixed on the naturalist, but rather than speak, he jumped up and walked away twenty paces, where he began to pace back and forth like an agitated guard. Hobbes did nothing to marshal his party.

Tristam was left with Wallis, who crouched on the ground five paces from the dead men. He tucked the elbows of his spindly arms between his knees and twined his hands together. He looked down at the ground before him and then up at the dead, repeating this action again and again.

"I don't think you will find what you want here, Mr. Flattery," the castaway said suddenly, keeping his voice low, and not looking up at Tristam.

"What I want? I have lost any sense of what I want, Mr. Wallis. I wish only to perform my duty and return to my home."

"But that's what I mean, sir. I don't think the islanders will give you the seed. Even if it really is meant for your King, the Old Men would never give it to you."

"And why is that, Mr. Wallis?"

The castaway looked up, a bit of surprise registering. "Is it not obvious, Mr. Flattery? A series of omens the islanders find quite unsettling, and then you arrive with this strange tale of a Lost City. A whale saves you from being lost in the vast ocean." He nodded at Tristam's hand. "And this. . . . The islanders fear you, Mr. Flattery, they can't imagine what it is you want here. They have enough troubles without someone such as yourself appearing."

"Bloody foolishness!" Tristam spat out.

Wallis rocked back on his heels, dragging his finger tips along the ground. "But how else would you explain what happened in the Archipelago? And the other things are equally strange. Did the sea not give you back your life? Float you to a ledge?"

Tristam gave the painter a withering stare. "I don't understand why these things have happened to me, but let me assure you, Wallis, that they are not of my choosing. And I want no part of this Kingfoil. I would rather not even touch it." Tristam kicked at a stone suddenly. "Let's carry these men down to the beach. I can't bear to see the flies on them any longer." Tristam called to the others.

It was not a pleasant task, bearing the bodies of men with whom they had sailed. And it was made worse by the fact that the men had been dead some hours in the tropical heat. Beacham retched as they went, but did not falter. Hobbes looked as though despair had overwhelmed him entirely, but he did not falter either, though he let Tristam take command of the party, saying nothing.

When the bodies had been laid on the tide line and a boat had put out from the ship, Hobbes turned away and disappeared back into the empty village, saying nothing. The viscount stood watching the man go with unnatural interest. When he realized Tristam was watching, the viscount turned away, bending suddenly to pick up a shell from the beach, as though natural history had suddenly taken his interest.

"He is taking this very hard," Wallis said, quietly.

No one responded.

Wallis turned to Tristam. "I think I should go up to the caves alone, Mr. Flattery, and speak to the villagers. With the King and most of the Old Men involved in the *mata maoeā*, things are confused. There is really no one in command. It makes everything more difficult. I will go up and see what I can do, and at least I will know the mood of the people when I return. But someone must speak with the captain. What the islanders have done—carrying these men here, and treating them with honor—it is as far as their customs will allow them to go. Stern must realize that they would rather die than violate their own tapu. If he demands more, there will be terrible and senseless fighting, Mr. Flattery. Any hope Stern has of success will be lost."

Tristam looked about for the master who should really be the one speaking with Wallis, and giving him permission to go. "I will tell Mr. Hobbes where you've gone," he said after a moment. "And I'll speak to Stern, if I can, Mr. Wallis, but I'm sure these words would have more weight coming from you." Tristam looked up into the trees. "You don't think you're in any danger?" The sight of the two dead sailors had shaken Tristam. The friendly islanders suddenly seemed capable of the worst treachery.

"No, I'm sure I'm not. Nor do I think you are in danger. But don't stray far, and if you meet islanders, don't chase after them. Hold up a palm branch and wait."

Tristam hated to see Wallis leave. The man's understanding of the language and customs of the Varuans was so much greater than his own, and he felt at least a little protected when he was with him. "Good luck to you, Mr. Wallis."

Beacham came and stood beside Tristam watching the lanky figure of Wallis disappear into the village. "I don't like the feel of this place, Mr. Flattery. All empty and forbidding." He did not need to say, "too much like that other city."

"No, I don't like it either. Let's go up as far as the edge of the village and sit out in the open. If nothing else, Wallis will see us when he returns." Tristam looked along the beach. "Where is Lord Elsworth?"

Beacham turned around, a bit apprehensive. "I don't know, sir."

Tristam thought that Beacham looked as alarmed as he felt.

ᵛ ᵛ ᵛ

At dusk Stern sent a boat ashore, but Tristam felt they should wait for their shipmates, and sent this message back to the captain. They built a fire on the beach so that they would be visible to the watch, and made a dinner of what fruit they could find near at hand.

Darkness, Faairi's "other world," descended and Tristam wondered where she was now. Hiding with the rest of the people he was sure. Tristam longed for her as much as he did for the duchess—no, that was not true. His obsession with the duchess invariably left him confused, his encounter with Faairi had been calming. She seemed to understand what was happening to him—had even tried to help him. Tristam closed his eyes and thought of her lovely face, moving above him, how she had called to him and kept him present. The star between her breasts was like a talisman. He wished she were here now, as the darkness gathered around him.

The wind in the palms whispered in the speech of the night. The Varuans believed that Old Men could understand this speech, and would relay messages from the spirit world. A small gust sounded the beginning of some sad tale.

Tristam was reminded of the dream he had in Avonel—how familiar the wind in the palms had sounded. He found himself looking around, afraid the spirits that inhabited this world would appear on the edge of the firelight.

If Beacham would only speak, but he did not—absorbed in his own thoughts, apparently, and Tristam could think of nothing to say himself. The two sat listening for footsteps. Hoping for the return of Mr. Wallis and their shipmates.

Tristam was worried about Wallis, the man's loyalties were so divided. And then there was the viscount. Where in Farrelle's name had he gone, and to what purpose? The man was such a ghoul. Tristam even wondered if it had been the sight of the dead bodies that had set him off—a thought that caused some revulsion.

He remembered the blossoms in his pocket; both male he thought, but wished he could take them out to examine them more carefully. But why? he asked himself. More and more he was convinced that he would be best to have nothing to do with *regis*. He should have thrown the blossoms away.

Looking out toward the ship he thought he saw a slim figure pacing in the great cabin, crossing and recrossing the small distance before the windows. The duchess. It was difficult to image that a woman with such poise could fret—it just did not seem in character, but he could almost feel her anxiety and worry from the way she moved. It was like finding an actress backstage—imperious before an audience but frightened and vulnerable behind the curtain. He felt his heart go out to her.

He closed his eyes for a moment and felt the flooding

of his emotion, like a tide running through his being. How did one swim when the tide was inside?

"What?" he heard himself say. Beacham had been addressing him.

"Perhaps there will be time to teach me to swim," the midshipman said.

"Perhaps." Tristam looked out at the ship, though stare as he might the duchess could not now be seen. Had he fallen into a brief sleep?

The night sounds of Varua, unfamiliar and exotic, surrounded them: the constant voice of the trade, though softened after sunset, and the sounds of insects, as discordant as a tuning orchestra.

Something moved on the edge of the firelight, but when Tristam turned, he could make out nothing. *I must shake off this mood,* he thought. Fear of slipping back into the dream state induced by *regis* haunted him. He tried to call up Faairi's star, but it no longer seemed so clear.

"Tell me, Mr. Beacham, how did you come by the name Averil?" Tristam asked suddenly.

Beacham looked up, a bit surprised, perhaps even a little apprehensive. "You've found out my secret. I hope you won't let on, sir. I've suffered all my life for that bloody name. Life aboard would become very unpleasant if the others should find out. It is an old man's name."

Tristam took a long breath, and let it out under perfect control. "There are just the two of us here, Beacham. No one to hear. Averil Kent and his interests are known to me." He tried to say this last with confidence, for he was really not sure. In fact, for a moment he wondered if he sounded a little unbalanced—if he *was* a little unbalanced.

Beacham stared out over the bay for a moment, then turned to speak, faltered and went back to looking at the darkened water and the stars. "My father is an artist in the Admiralty, a cartographer, but a painter as well. Over the years he has been much encouraged by Mr. Kent, though he actually paints very little. Gifted with skill but not inspiration. Mr. Kent has always been something of an uncle to me. Thus the name. But I know nothing of Mr. Kent's ... 'interests' as you call them—except for nature and art."

"That night when we were hunted by the corsairs. You knew what was going on with the viscount and Kreel. But you said nothing to the captain."

At the mention of the viscount, Beacham looked over his shoulder, obviously uncomfortable. " 'Keep out of the business of your betters,' my father always told me, Mr. Flattery. I think it good advice."

Tristam looked out over the bay, to the small ship swinging to her anchor, the web that was her rigging just visible in starlight. "All right, Jack," he said with resignation. "Tell me only this. Do you have information about my situation? You were with me in the Lost City. You've seen what has happened around me—and to you, now." He held his hand out into the firelight, but the tattoo remained drawn back into the vein. "You were there when this happened. I'm struggling in the dark, Jack. I don't know what's happening to me." Tristam closed his eyes. "I don't know what's happening to me," he whispered.

A log shifted on the fire sending up a spray of sparks like an offering to the stars. Beacham moved, almost squirming, took a breath as though to speak, and then said nothing. The silence stretched on. "I can tell you this," Beacham said after a long struggle. "There are rumors among the Jacks about this ... herb. It is said to cure any illness, extend one's years, command a vast fortune for only a few seeds. The miraculous survival of Mr. Wallis has turned many who scoffed into believers."

"Farrelle's blood!" Tristam said. "How in the world ... ?" but he hardly needed to finish.

Beacham shrugged. "Ships are small," he said, keeping his eyes fixed on the bay.

A land crab scuttled along the edge of the firelight, causing Tristam to start. The naturalist pulled his knees up and wrapped his arms around them, burying his face in the circle of his arms. Stern apparently did not know this. Blood and flames, the poor captain was out of his depth. Tristam looked out at the ship, half expecting a mutiny to break out as he watched.

But there was some truth in what the Jacks believed—that was the irony. The worth of the seed was almost incalculable. There were any number of Farr adventurers who would lay this island to waste to get their hands on something of such value—if they only knew.

What have we unleashed on these poor islanders? Tristam thought. It was no wonder the Varuans believed the seed was a curse.

"We have to tell Stern," Tristam said. "He will have a mutiny on his hands, and no warning."

The midshipman became utterly still for a moment. "You could tell him, Mr. Flattery . . . and leave me out of it."

Yes, the code of the sailors. Beacham could not tell—caught as he was between being a seaman and an officer. "All right, though it is likely he will guess where I've learned it. Blood and flames, what a situation. Already we've lost two men. That is enough. We should sail from this place. Set out tomorrow and forget this fool's quest."

Beacham nodded. "Yes. None of us knew what we were sailing into, and it has turned out to be strange territory." Beacham put his hands near to the fire as though he had grown cold.

"That night at the temple, Mr. Flattery, when we were poisoned, did you dream?" He said this with such unguarded concern that Tristam feared the worst.

"Yes. I dreamed. I dreamed until I finally regained the world, and even now dreams still haunt me. And you as well?"

Beacham nodded. "Yes," he almost whispered. "I dreamed that I was standing before the entrance to a cave, and inside a fire was burning. I could see the dance of the flames. Feel the heat, like hot breath. Although I was more afraid than I have ever been, I walked forward. I could not stop myself, Mr. Flattery. As I drew closer, I heard the hiss of the flames, as though the fire were alive. Against my will I went inside. But when I had passed in, it was to the outdoors. And I saw a city in flames, the people blackened, screaming silently, and toppling like burning trees." Beacham kept his eyes fixed on the horizon, his voice had become flat. "I thought it was the Lost City before me, but it wasn't—it was Avonel. And then I saw someone, someone who was afire. He walked toward me through the flames, and in his arms he carried a burden. A burned and burning man. A man who wore a crown that shone white in the red of the flames. Suddenly I could move, and I ran, into a tunnel. An endless tunnel. I was thirsty and weak, and lost and frightened. But finally I saw another—in the distance. It seemed to be a child, and I followed him into a small opening in a wall of solid stone, and when I emerged, I was swinging in a hammock, muttering something, looking up at the face of Llewellyn."

Tristam said nothing. He could not offer the common reassurance; *It was only a dream,* for he did not believe that. These were more than dreams.

He moved and felt the delicate shells and blossoms that rested in the pocket of his shirt—miracles of nature. Frightening miracles.

An urge to get up and walk along the beach whispered to Tristam, but he looked out into the darkness and realized he was afraid of what might wait in the night world of the islanders.

🍂 🍂 🍂

Hobbes crawled forward the last few feet to the cliff edge, and felt the salt wind on his face. Below he could see the pale, luminescent crests of breaking waves undulating along the base of the cliff some hundred feet below. His breath came with difficulty, and this was not due just to the hour's hard march.

"Blood and flames," he said, *"you deserve such an end."* His fingers curled over the edge of the damp rock and he stared down to the sea boiling among the rocks. A man might jump clear of that and into the deep water, where death would find him swiftly, painlessly. It was here that the Varuans sent captives of war to death—any

escaping the rocks were said to be swept away by strong currents, where they fell easy victim to sharks.

"Let the sea take me," he said, barely able to catch his breath. "Flames, Chilsey was only a boy!" The ship's master felt the sting of tears, and not just from the wind on his face. "Not fit to command, nor fit to be master. And Garvey, a man with family." He wanted to scream, but instead fought to catch his breath. "What a ruin of a life . . . and it should never have been so. A curse on every desk captain in the Navy Board!"

He stared down, almost hypnotized by the flow and ebb of the pale crests in the starlight. *What an end,* he thought. *But all I deserve now.*

"Do you seek death, old man?" came a near-whisper, barely audible above the sounds of surf.

Hobbes turned his head, startled, sitting back quickly from the cliff. He recognized that voice: Elsworth.

"I know him," the voice continued. "Know how hard he can be to find. But I know a way."

Hobbes searched in the darkness, and now he could see the viscount, hunching down in shadow. He felt his skin crawl. It was the viscount, wasn't it?

"I can help you, Hobbes," the voice went on, oddly full of emotion and strangely like a priest. "Make it easy." He paused, drew a sharp breath. "Wrestle with me, Hobbes. One of us will fall. If it is me, you will know it's not your time." He heard the man shift, move closer. "You seek death, don't you?" he said, almost too quickly. "Atonement for those two who've gone before you—innocent as you believe they were. Let me help you. Or you might be spared, Hobbes, and he might take me. . . . But one of us can end our suffering. End it this night."

The viscount moved again—almost seemed to slither closer. Hobbes could hear him breathing, like a man overcome by passion. The breeze suddenly seemed chill, drying the sweat of his forced march. He moved back from the cliff involuntarily—the instinct for self-preservation strong.

"Don't show him fear, Hobbes! Not that. Do you feel

him? Here, with us." Again the viscount slid closer, his form indefinite, like a shadow octopus.

"Come no nearer!" Hobbes said, suddenly, surprising himself.

"You have thought too long. Thought weakens the resolve, Hobbes," the viscount went on, as though he had not heard. "It will force you to live in growing misery, until he comes for you—which he will do in time. But you aren't afraid of death, Hobbes. I've seen you face him. Stand strong before him in the midst of battle. You were unwavering. Come—one of us can make an end." And then more quietly, "Perhaps me. Or perhaps I will escape ... again. Come, let us see who he will choose this night, for my sins are as great as yours."

The viscount was close enough now that Hobbes could make him out, like a darker shadow, moving slowly through shadow. The master no longer tried to escape, but waited, terrified, relieved, fascinated—like some poor beast at bay before a predator.

Death. Was that not what he sought? And here it was, in the form of this mad viscount. Now it would not matter if his nerve failed. Elsworth would see to that.

"Push me off," he heard himself say, the words coming out in a whisper.

"No! Hobbes, wrestle with me. Let me feel his hand. His breath upon my face. Let me see if I am still his servant."

Hobbes felt a hand grasp his forearm in a bone-hard grip. He twitched, but then held himself in check.

"It will soon be over, Hobbes. See if he will absolve you of your sins, and take me. See if he will do that, Hobbes."

The hand on his arm loosened a little, held him almost tenderly, and then the man was upon him, immensely powerful, smelling of sweat and fear. Hobbes fought back, struggling under the man's weight. Rolling toward the edge.

Yes, he thought, *let us see who he will take.*

A hand so strong it could have been a machine wrenched an arm behind his back, twisting it painfully, an arm took him around the chest, crushing the air from his lungs. The viscount tried to shuffle him toward the cliff, to lift his feet off the ground, but Hobbes reached back and took hold of the man's hair, and kicked at him with desperate force, twisting free. They fell, landing hard on stone.

"Feel his breath," the viscount whispered. *"We are before him."* And the man grappled with him again.

A life at sea had toughened Hobbes far more than his appearance revealed. He met the man, head on, holding his ground. The viscount tried to knee him in the groin, but Hobbes twisted away, losing his balance so that they fell again.

And then the man's mouth close to his ear as they struggled. *"Pray he will reward us both,"* he said. *"Take us both from our misery."* He tried to pin Hobbes' arms to his sides, and the seaman dug his heels into the ground and pushed, only managing to move them along the stone. Where was the cliff edge?

Hobbes brought his knee up hard and then broke the circle of the man's arms. He tried to turn away, and the viscount grasped at his waist and then drove forward, tumbling Hobbes onto his side.

Age betrayed him then. Hobbes struggled for breath, and felt his strength beginning to fail. The sound of the surf came to him.

The viscount butted his head down, smashing his forehead into Hobbes' ear. He lunged ahead now, dragging Hobbes under him, and the master felt his hands scrabble desperately, seeking a hold on the stone, until his fingers curled around a hard edge.

Again the viscount tried to drive him forward, but the master's grip held.

"I am his servant," the viscount hissed. *"Let yourself go to him, Hobbes."*

The viscount tried to tear his hand free and Hobbes let go suddenly, driving his elbow back quickly into the man's forehead. Twisting around, he grabbed at the man's throat, and the viscount let out a scream of anguish such as Hobbes had never heard. And then he was writhing, twisting, pulling free, in the grip of madness. The viscount's strength seemed to grow while Hobbes' waned. Suddenly the viscount had the master by the throat, lifting his head and driving it back against the stone with such force that Hobbes was left limp, barely holding onto consciousness. And again.

It is over, the seaman thought, and felt himself sob.

Again the viscount raised his head, and then his hands slipped off and he toppled forward, burying Hobbes beneath his enormous weight. They both lay still, Hobbes fighting to breathe, to maintain consciousness, to live.

The weight came off slowly as the limp form of the viscount was dragged to one side. Hobbes lay gasping sweet salt air. He could see blurred lights—stars overhead. Someone else was there, standing over them in the darkness.

"You shall not go so easily," a ravaged voice said.

Death. Only death could have such a voice.

"Live with your misery, as I've lived with mine. And damn you for it!"

Gone. The thing was gone. He could hear it shuffle noisily into the bush like some drunken beast.

For a moment more Hobbes lay drinking in long draughts of air and then, almost desperately, he began to crawl back into the dark jungle.

FIFTEEN

After forty-two years of marriage Lady Galton believed she could almost read her husband's thoughts—or at least read his mood and, with what she knew of events, predict what was on his mind. She watched him fuss about at his desk, pretending to be absorbed by work and avoiding her eye. But he was uncommonly agitated, and it was not very well disguised as concern over work. His breathing was quick and shallow, louder than usual, and he could not keep his hands still. There were other little betrayals of his true mood, around his eyes, and his jaw clenched stiffly shut, not noticeable to most in that round, fleshy face. He had learned something today that was upsetting him terribly.

Of course he had been named to the Regency Council, though not officially, and that had to be taken into account. But even beyond that, something was very wrong. So wrong that he could not discuss it, even with her.

Lady Galton turned the page of her book, no more reading than Sir Stedman was working. She would wait a bit and then ask. The time was not yet right. And there was always the chance that Stedman would broach the subject himself—which would be a relief, for it would mean that whatever had occurred was not so very terrible, but only blown out of proportion. Though she was afraid this was a vain hope.

Galton continued to fuss, periodically releasing a loud sigh, as though he struggled with some problem that frustrated his every effort. Once she saw, over the edge of her book, that he darted a glance her way, gauging the success of his charade. There was, perhaps, a little guilt in that look.

"It is cool here, isn't it?" she said after a moment.

"Shall I bank the fire for you, my dear?" the governor said quickly.

"No, no. It is fine here by the fire, Stedman. I was thinking more of you, over in that dark corner."

He smiled, affection showing on his round face. "You are so kind to an old man. Whatever did I do to deserve such a wife?"

She gave a tiny smile, and turned the page she had not read. "You were young, and charming, and quite handsome, I thought. But it was really the young Stedman's open heart that won me—open and trusting and a bit naive. As though he wanted so badly to believe in the good of his fellow men, that he would bare his breast to their blades. I could not refuse that."

Stedman Galton slumped just perceptibly in his chair.

"Do you think you might tell me, sometime, Stedman, what it is that is causing you such distress?" She still kept her attention on her book, but she could feel his eyes on her.

Galton sat for a moment and then he rose and very slowly came and settled on the end of the divan, not too close, and that presaged something bad. Lady Galton put her book aside and braced herself.

He took a moment to start, but she waited, almost holding her breath. "I found out today that this young scholar, Egar Littel, was being . . ." he paused, searched for a word, "coerced into translating the text."

That was bad enough, but there was worse, she realized. Something much worse. She nodded, encouraging him to speak.

"He contrived to escape just recently. Slipped away from the library at Merton College." Galton turned away, staring at the fire, his face stiff. He closed his eyes. "In their attempt to apprehend him, some of Palle's minions . . ." A long exhalation. "Farrelle preserve us, they *killed* the poor boy." These last words were barely sounded.

She drew in her breath quickly, her hand going involuntarily to her mouth as though she were trying to suppress her own response. And Stedman was not finished. There was something yet to come, something that was going to hurt her terribly—she could read all the signs.

"Littel had a companion," the governor gave way to his distress now, and his voice trembled, as he fought for breath. "Farrelle protect him, it appears to have been Lord Jaimas Flattery, the son . . ." But he did not finish, a muffled sob escaped Lady Galton.

Galton reached out to comfort his wife, but she brushed his hands away, standing quickly with her back to him. But she did not move further, only stood, sobbing quietly.

"Heartless scoundrels!" she managed after a moment. "Beasts!"

"You have been right all along, my heart," Galton said softly. "Sir Roderick has lost all sense of honor—of what is right. And I have gone down that road with him—too far. . . ." There was anguish in his voice as he said this.

"You are not like him, Stedman!" she said emphatically. "Nothing like him."

He shifted along the divan, closer to her, and she did not move away. He reached out, but checked himself, afraid to lay his hand on her lest she shake it off, which he could not bear a second time.

Neither of them spoke for many minutes and Galton found this excruciating, fearing that he had stepped beyond the distinct moral lines drawn by his wife. She was very rigid in this, and the thought that he had disappointed her pained him terribly. His great fear was that what he had done was irreparable.

"I have straddled the border long enough," he said firmly. "I must declare myself in this."

Lady Galton turned to him then, staring down at the man sitting in abject misery before her. If he had tried to justify what had happened. . . . But no, Stedman was too good for that. Too noble. He would always shoulder the burden of his mistakes. "You must not declare yourself to Palle, Stedman." She sat down facing him, and took his offered linen to dab at her still flowing tears. But they did not touch. "He must be stopped—stopped utterly—and I can see no other way. I am frightened by the risks, but you must conspire against him, without revealing your true allegiance. It is the only way to remove the taint of this murder." And then, "Do the duke and duchess know?"

He shook his head. "Everything is being done to hide the truth." Neither of them spoke for a moment, realizing what this could mean.

"I will speak with the princess, and then, perhaps, I will go to the duchess. We must be careful. If the duke accuses Palle of this murder, well, the time is not right for such a thing." She stopped to think and felt a hand take hers tentatively, tenderly, and she squeezed this, massaging the fingers gently.

"I was blinded by my passion for the Ruin, for the knowledge," Galton said.

"Yes," she whispered. "I know."

"I should never have ignored your counsel." He took her other hand.

"No, you shouldn't have."

"I will not be so foolish in the future."

"You are not foolish. You are many things, Stedman Galton, but never foolish. We will find our way through this. We owe it to those young men. Farrelle rest them. The poor duchess almost died to bring that child into this world, and now he is gone. She will never survive it, Stedman. Palle might as well have put a blade in her heart. I shall not forgive him this," she said, surprising her husband with the bitterness in her voice. It was as though Palle had just murdered the child they could never have.

SIXTEEN

The prince had always wanted a room in a tower, ever since he was a child, and his corner room, high up in the palace, had been made to feel as much like a tower as was possible. He sat in the alcove of a window, wiping condensation from the glass, gazing down into the darkness. A black fog had slipped, dripping, into the garden, and remained—like a part of the night that had begun to solidify. The prince could make out the shapes of trees, and rectangles of open lawn. Perhaps that line was the edge of a pond—or was it a hedgerow?

The shapes were so indistinct, almost varying shades of darkness, that it occurred to him that anyone unfamiliar with this view might imagine an entirely different scene. But after living in the palace all nineteen years of his life, he could not look at it with an outsider's eyes.

"Grays," he whispered. The world was composed of grays, with almost no white and even less black. As a king, he would one day be dependent on his ability to differentiate between the myriad, nearly identical shades of gray. The prince stared down into the garden with renewed focus.

If he leaned back from the grass a little, his reflection appeared, smeared with the beads and rivulets of condensation that streaked the glass. It was like looking at himself through tears, and he suddenly had a strong premonition—one day someone would look at him this way.

I will break a heart, he thought, though he could not

imagine how. As much as he was aware, it was not some-one else's heart that was in danger. He stared at his re-flection, which seemed to float on the surface of a pool of darkness. What did Alissa see when she looked at him?

"Had I only met her first," he said aloud, and then al-most winced.

But he had not. He leaned forward again, his shadow obliterating his reflection. Perhaps she thought him young, though, in truth, he was two years her senior.

He didn't need to close his eyes to call up an image of Alissa—standing beside the Duchess of Blackwater at her birthday celebration. He hardly had eyes for anyone else, still . . . what a contrast that had been! Alissa seemed al-most to be aglow with life and youth, while the duchess' fires had burned low; there was barely a flicker when she smiled.

And then they had spoken at the opening of the iron bridge. Prince Wilam felt a bit of embarrassment, even here in the privacy of his own rooms, at how quickly his mother had whisked him away. Anger flared in him for a second. He hoped Alissa had not suffered embarrassment over this. The fault was his. He was the one acting like a lovesick puppy. Alissa had never been less than lady-like.

She must think me an idiot.

What is it I want from her, he asked himself again. He was quite certain that she had not entered into her en-gagement with Lord Jaimas for any but the most genuine reasons. So what *did* he want?

He placed his forehead against the cool glass, and shut his eyes, Alissa appearing in his mind as he best remem-bered her. He had passed a note from his mother to be de-livered to Averil Kent. For the briefest moment this young woman's forthright gaze had met his own. And he still felt that no one had ever looked at him like that. She had looked at *him.* Not at a prince of Farrland. Not at a future king. But at him. He could not imagine giving that up. Giving that up for a life of polite smiles and measur-ing gazes. Measuring gazes.

And what *did* he want? Only to tell this young woman

what he felt. To tell her how much that had meant to him. He hoped that she might give him some indication, even the smallest sign, that she shared some of that feeling. Even if they both knew that her heart belonged elsewhere. That was what he desired—just a simple moment of clarity in this existence. A moment where every other consideration was stripped away, and two people revealed their hearts. A moment of truth to sustain him through all the years of lies that were to come.

He leaned back and stared at his reflection again, distressed to realize that his own gaze measured as coolly as any courtier's. Certainly that is what Alissa had seen. He couldn't change that, but it was his hope that he could explain and she would understand.

The gentle double tap on his door was so familiar that he knew immediately who called. He stared only a second more, and then swung off the window seat and crossed to the door.

"Princess," he said, bowing to his mother.

"Prince," she said, curtsying in return. "I thought you would be awake yet." She tilted her head toward the room. "May I?"

Prince Wilam stepped aside, and his mother came in. Normally she entered a room as though she owned it—no one had as much right to it as she—but tonight she clearly entered his room. Her manner was subdued. She took a seat by the fire, like a guest.

"You think I was rude to Miss Somers," the princess said, not allowing an awkward silence to take form between them nor resorting to meaningless pleasantries. She was always so forthright with him, at least since he had become an adult. It never failed to flatter him.

"I am to blame," he said quietly. "We should not embarrass Miss Somers for my foolishness."

She did not answer, neither agreeing nor disagreeing. For a moment she stared at her son, then took a long breath, turning to look toward the dark window. "She is charming." She shook her head. "No. That belittles her. She is more than charming. Alissa Somers is intelligent, poised, entirely genuine, charming, and quite lovely to

214

behold. Everything a Farr princess should be." She turned back to her son. "Everything we would want in a future queen."

A small silence began to coalesce between them, but beyond it Wilam saw the compassion in her face. "There will be others, Wilam. I know that must seem impossible, now, but it is true. Alissa Somers could never sit on a Farr throne, nor do I think she'd want to. I am not saying that, if circumstances were different, she could not have feelings for you. But the reality of ruling Farrland requires that we choose our alliances with great care. I would never want you to marry against your will. I would not see you condemned to that life. But there are many eligible young women. It is not as though there were only three to choose among." She tried a smile. "The life of a queen requires a certain preparation, Wilam, preparation that begins almost at birth. You would not want your bride to live unhappily, surely?"

The prince shook his head. "No. I wouldn't," he said quietly, knowing it was the truth.

"Have I ever told you that you are noble in more than birth?" she asked, a slight quiver of pride in her voice. She smiled at him for a moment, and then her manner became more serious. "I wanted to speak of this before I told you what I had learned." She paused, drawing a breath. A look of great sadness spread across her face, the tiny lines of beginning middle age appearing around her eyes and at the corners of her mouth. "Although you did everything you could, Palle's minions caught Lord Jaimas and Mr. Littel." She looked up, meeting her son's eyes, tears forming. "They killed them both, Wilam. Murdered them rather than let them escape with what they knew."

Wilam felt a rush of hope—far less than noble in its origin. And then the realization, and the sadness. A thought of Lord Jaimas laughing—a young man he both liked and felt enormous jealousy toward. He imagined Alissa, suffering her loss, and felt his heart go out to her.

"You realize what this means, of course, and so will Alissa. The palace had her fiancé murdered. We did not sanction it, you or I. Even my pathetic husband would not have approved, I'm sure, but it does not matter. Your father's weakness allowed this to happen. *Your* father. And you appeared to rescue them, Wil, then sent them off to their destruction. Imagine how it looks." She reached out and grasped his hand, holding it tenderly, sharing the pain. "I want you to promise me—you will maintain your distance from Miss Somers. No matter what you feel, no matter what your instincts, you must stay away. There is no comfort to be had from a murderer's son. Promise me," she said squeezing his hand and forcing him to look at her. "Promise," she said but it came out as a whisper, her voice failing. Tears streaking down her face, like rain on glass.

He nodded.

She cleared her throat. "Whatever happened, Wil?" she asked, her voice small and full of despair. "He was not always like this. Not always. . . ." Words failed her altogether.

Wilam shook his head. The son did not understand the father, nor would he forgive. Not this.

🦑 🦑 🦑

A ribbon of starlight twisted slowly as it fell through the forest. Prince Wilam held a taper before him, and made his way slowly through the vegetation toward the pool. Overhead he could see the clouds had fled, and faint stars splashed their light on the wet glass overhead and the waterfall below.

He came to the edge of the forest just as Teiho Ruau began another song. The pure tenor seemed to belong to this place as much as the call of a bird or a breeze sighing among the trees. Prince Wilam stopped and listened, closing his eyes so that he might concentrate more fully on the music. But as soon as his eyes closed, the image of Jaimy Flattery appeared, lying in a field, staring up at the sky—and then Alissa, her sorrow hidden by a veil.

Close to the waterfall Wilam could see his grandfather seated on a bench in the near-darkness. The old King slumped like a sleeping drunk. Wilam knew his grandfather found the songs of Oceana comforting, but he often wondered if the King really heard them, if he actually listened. There was certainly no sign that this was so, lost as he was in the dreams brought on by the physic.

The scene suddenly seemed pathetic to him. Sad beyond measure. What a price this man had paid for his extra years. Had it been worth it? Certainly not now that no amount of physic kept the aging at bay.

For a moment Wilam struggled with his conflicting desires—he both wanted to stay, and wanted to turn away. But as the song ended he went forward.

"Grandfather?" he said, surprised at how youthful his voice sounded.

Silence. Wilam was sure he had not been heard. The dream state was like that. The King would be neither asleep nor awake, but absorbed in his dreams, eyes wide open, staring.

"Wil?" the King answered, something like tenderness in his ruined voice.

The prince smiled with relief. "I need to speak with you, Grandfather."

A longer silence this time. "I am not well, child. Wilam? Is that you?"

The prince reached out and laid a hand on his grandfather's arm. "It is me. I. . . . I need to speak with someone, Grandfather. It is important." He sat near to his grandfather on the bench.

"Ah. . . . Important." A dry hand found the prince's in the darkness—a touch like parchment, ancient and fragile. "I will try. Please, leave us," he said to his attendants and the singer.

Wilam leaned close. "They have killed Lord Jaimas Flattery," he said close to the old man's ear.

"Who has?"

"Hawksmoor's men."

"Palle?"

"Yes." Wilam could barely see his grandfather in the dark, but he could hear him fighting for every breath. Knew the look of confusion that appeared when he struggled to come back to this world—even for a few minutes.

The prince closed his eyes. It hurt him to find his grandfather like this, enslaved to the seed, aging daily now.

"Wil?"

"I'm here, Grandfather."

"What? What did we just say?"

"Palle killed Lord Jaimas and Egar Littel."

"Yes." He paused. "But why have you come?"

Wilam swayed where he sat.

"There is something else. . . ." The prince wondered if they were making sense to each other at all. The King's concentration would not hold for a long explanation, as necessary as one might be. "I am in love with the woman who was to be Lord Jaimas' bride," he blurted out, realizing that this misrepresented his situation entirely.

The King nodded, as though he considered solemnly. "You can't have a man murdered and then marry his fiancée. Wouldn't look right."

"Grandfather . . . I didn't have anyone murdered."

The dry hand squeezed his. "I know, Wil. I know, but it was done by the palace, and you are to be King one day. Do you see? If she knew—if anyone . . . does the duke know it was Palle?"

Wilam hesitated. "I'm not sure."

"Let us pray he learns the truth," the King whispered. He seemed to look at his grandson for the first time. "Don't say a word, Wilam," he pleaded, and then began to wheeze. "I must have my physic. They will take it from me."

The prince put his hand on his grandfather's shoulder. "No one will take your physic, Grandfather. I promise you."

The King nodded, making an effort to calm himself. "Where is Ruau?" he said peevishly. "Where is my physic?"

Wilam rose, waving to one of the attendants he could see silhouetted in the starlight. "Ruau is coming, Grandfather. Calm yourself."

The dry hand took hold of his wrist suddenly, the grip surprisingly powerful. "When you are on the throne, Wil, see him gone. See his reign ended. But don't endanger my physic. There's a good boy."

The prince listened to him wheeze in the darkness, fighting for air, for one more breath. "Goodnight, Grandfather."

The hand released him, the King already slipping back into his waking dreams, drawn away from the world of men.

As the prince walked back into the forest he found Teiho Ruau, standing still and silent among the trees.

"Ruau," Wilam said nodding to the Varuan.

"My Prince," the islander said, his voice filled with music even when he spoke. They stopped, perhaps feeling it would be polite to speak, but neither knowing what to say. "He will have to pass through soon," the Varuan said suddenly.

"I don't understand."

"Mr. Ruau!" came the voice of an attendant.

"Soon," Ruau said, and set off toward the king, beginning to sing as he went.

❦ ❦ ❦

Prince Kori looked with despair on the first few lines of the letter he had begun hours before. His hand was atrocious, he knew, but this was not a letter he could have his secretary copy. He began to read again, trying to put himself in the position of the woman he addressed, attempting to measure the impact of each word.

My Dear Angeline:
  It has been such a long time now since we met and there have been so few letters. I wonder, often, about your well-being, and where you are. Recently, I was told that you had returned to Farrland, but I have missed seeing you. Are things so bad between us that you do not even send the prince a note?

He crumpled the page, crushing it between his fingers. How despicable that the future King of Farrland was reduced to writing letters like a jilted schoolboy. And he had so little skill with words—words of love, at least.

It seemed ironic that he was able to maneuver his own people onto the regency council—against powerful men who had spent their lives in politics! And yet here he was, reduced to the same circumstances as any man in Farrland—on bent knee before a woman who spurned him. Spurned him!

And she had seemed so . . . intrigued by him upon that first meeting. Three years past, now. The memory was so fresh. The midsummer costume ball. He had found her alone on the balcony, holding a mask in her hand, the white of her shoulders like snow against the blackness of her gown and the night. He could not remember feeling so nervous. And she had turned and smiled at him. Those beautiful lips parted, and she had smiled the way a kind woman will when she sees you are uncomfortable. He had felt like a schoolboy, even then.

Later he had taken her to the arboretum, and they had talked for hours, sitting on a hard stone bench, walking along the narrow paths. And then she had allowed him to kiss her. Those perfect soft lips, the curve of her neck. He had felt like a man granted the greatest privilege in the kingdom. When he had placed a hand on her breast she had demurred, in the most charming way. And they had sat longer still, speaking quietly, and then, strangely, he had fallen asleep, waking later to find her by the waterfall, chatting with the King, as though they were old friends.

To the prince's surprise his father had said nothing of this night—not even a censorious look—which was very odd when one considered the great favor the King showed Princess Joelle. But then the King's own married life had not been beyond reproach.

Angeline had exhibited no surprise at the relative youthfulness of the King, and had laughed when he tried to swear her to secrecy. Kissing his cheek, she had agreed, her manner mockingly solemn, as though she were humoring a child. And then she had disappeared. Disappeared utterly. They had exchanged letters. He had even spoken of her to his friends—intimating that he had a mistress of surpassing beauty and charm—but they had not met again. She had gone abroad. Then returned to care for an ailing aunt in the country. And then the letters had stopped altogether.

The prince could not understand how she could be so indifferent to his position; as though he were just another man. He often wondered what he had done to chase her off. She had seemed so enamored of him at the time (and he had told his friends as much!). Every word that he could recall of their conversation had been analyzed over and over. In the end he decided that he had bored her. The prince knew that he was not a fascinating conversationalist, nor was he terribly attractive. At least his wife did not find him so. The princess had clearly been bored with him for years.

Prince Kori pressed the heels of his hands to his eyes and leaned back in his chair. Why he struggled with this world of women he did not know. It was not for him. He did not speak the language, and remained a foreigner, always, with all the attendant feelings of being in another culture. The awkwardness, the embarrassment, the feeling that you were never seen for what you were.

The prince took his watch from his pocket, remembering that he must meet with Sir Roderick. Casting his failed letter into the fire, Prince Kori went to the bookshelf and removed a volume, a vast tome of great reputation which he had never read. He opened it to a random page and tried unsuccessfully to read, but could not see beyond the image of that beautiful face looking at him with apparent adoration.

"I see Your Highness is enjoying Halden," Sir Roderick said when he arrived. "He always leaves me feeling so . . . inarticulate. It's his ability to look inside and express things I was convinced there were no words for, until I read Halden."

"I feel much the same," the prince said, closing the book and looking up at the King's Man. "You have the proclamation?"

Roderick waved a large, rolled document. "According to the letter of the law." They spread it open on the desk and went over every word together—comfortable words of law.

The prince nodded, reading through the text one last time. He dipped a pen in ink, and signed, aware of how poor his hand appeared. "Read it in the house tomorrow." He clapped Roderick on the shoulder. "We reign both in fact and in law. I had anticipated more of a struggle, but it was hardly even sport."

The King's Man blew on the wet ink, then rolled the proclamation, closing it with a purple ribbon. "Win often and handily enough, and your opponents learn the futility of opposition." The King's Man pursed his lips in what passed for a smile with him. "I have been to see Wells and Galton. They will soon have as complete a translation as is possible. We might have to act more quickly than we anticipated."

The prince placed the pen back in its stand. Any talk of this text brought up thoughts of the duke's son. The most unfortunate accident. What had the boy been doing, in the company of that traitor? It was very sad, but then the security of the nation sometimes required sacrifice. It had always been so, though the prince had great hopes for a period of security—a Farr peace that would encompass all the nations of the Entide Sea. "I thought we were still months away."

Roderick leaned back against the desk, an uncharacteristic act for an ex-military man. No doubt he was exhausted from his constant efforts. "Littel was in the company of the Duke of Blackwater's son. If what he knew was passed on to the duke. . . ." Roderick paused as though considering whether to continue. "I have learned something from Wells; something he did not immediately realize was important. Littel was more than a savant of language, the man had a genius of memory such as I have only read of. He forgot almost nothing. Although we are certain that he took no copy of the text on his flight, it is very likely that, given a few hours, he could have produced one. If that is true, it is possible that our enemies no longer have just vague suspicions about our activity.

"There were some that placed young Flattery in the company of Averil Kent the night that he and Littel fled Merton. All three of them disappeared for a time—Kent and Littel and Flattery. And then there is this servant who saw an old man being led from the palace—secretly. We still do not know who that was, though for my money it was Kent again." Palle put his hands on the desk as though to steady himself. "There are the Entonne to consider, as well. We still don't know what they plan, or even what they know. I think we must be prepared to act."

The prince realized he felt a certain sense of alarm. Like one might feel at the moment of declaring war. It was one thing to discuss the possibility, but to actually give the order. . . . The moment had always seemed so remote. Perhaps he had never believed it would arrive. "Well, better sooner than later," the prince said quickly. It was his role as regent and heir to the throne to be decisive, and he believed it was his skill as well.

The prince looked over at a painting on his wall. A hart staring out from the trees over an open field toward a village, half-shrouded in smoke—the world of man from the point of view of the animal. How bewildered that poor beast looked. "I have been wondering about Kent. Have you learned anything more?"

"He is harder to keep under one's eye than one would think, considering his age. But I have not lost sight of him altogether. I am almost certain that he is involved with Massenet, and I think we should not let that progress too far."

The prince raised a hand. "A few months abroad— Farrow, perhaps, or Doorn. But only if we absolutely must. He is old and if he were to die while in exile. . . . I have enough troubles without that." The prince shook his head. Kent was admired by every member of his family: the King, the princess, his son. Harm a hair of that man's head and he would hear howls from all over the kingdom, and from within the palace loudest of all. Never mind that Kent was almost certainly committing treason!

Palle considered this a moment. "I shall do everything in my power to see that he does not come to harm, but we both know what is at stake. I was far more willing to indulge *Sir Averil*," he spoke these words with some disdain, "before I realized that he had fallen under the influence of that Entonne. . . ." Words failed him.

"Perhaps a brief tour abroad would be best," the prince said, not liking Palle's qualifications. "Something restful. Could the crown not gift him an estate on Farrow? And send him there to see it? He could stare at the Ruin then, and consider the folly of his ways."

Palle raised his eyebrows. He was silent a moment longer. "But we would be thought cruel in the extreme sending such an old man to sea before the storm season had passed. I have heard experienced captains complain of that passage in winter." He seemed to notice the mood of the prince for the first time. "But spring is not so distant. I could set things in motion, and hope Kent does nothing foolish between now and then."

Left alone, the prince paced almost silently around the room, stopping to look down into the fog-enshrouded grounds. He paused for a moment and examined the painting of the hart, wondering what the animal saw. What did the activity of men look like from a distance? He realized that he could not imagine.

Returning to his chair, he hefted the book he had taken up earlier, though he was not sure why; he no longer had Roderick to impress. Perhaps it was merely because he felt he would not sleep easily that night.

This collection of Halden's essays was the most quoted book in Farr history, the prince was sure, yet he had never been able to sustain an interest in the author's vague dissection of a human life. It said almost nothing about the true arena of man's endeavors—statesmanship. The prince flipped through thick chunks of pages, pausing to read a few lines wherever his eye fell, hoping to find some way into this great tome—for in truth he felt a bit embarrassed that he claimed to have read it. And then a line caught his eye and he began to read:

SEA WITHOUT A SHORE

I sometimes rise late in the night beset by anxieties, thinking that my heart is about to stop beating; that robbers lurk outside, seeking entry; or a terrible storm is about to send lightning down upon me. I am convinced my talent has withered, and I have grown old and foolish; that women laugh cruelly when they speak of me; and all my careful investments have collapsed, leaving me a pauper. I imagine that a terrible war has begun that will sweep away all we know, and silent lines of soldiers pass by in the night. I worry that lack of rest will bring my health to ruin.

And then, when I can bear it no more, the terrible, infinite depths of the night sky turn stone gray, and the sun rises again, lifting up above the horizon like a bright promise, and I realize the condition from which I suffer is but the human condition. Our solid lives are balanced on the edge of calamity, so much so that we do everything possible never to think of it, for contemplation drives one to despair. Despair that there is nothing we can do except promote the illusion that all is well, though we live with the secret knowledge that this is not so.

We wake in the grip of terror, the night telling us that we are utterly alone, our safe lives nothing but dreams. And our greatest fear of all—that we will be released from this world of anxiety and terror. The sun will not rise on the morrow.

The prince let the book slip into his lap and gazed at the darkened window, imagining that silent companies marched by toward a distant city, shrouded in smoke, aflame at its center.

SEVENTEEN

The guards sent Wallis on, and the painter continued through the darkness, up a narrow stair cut into stone. The tropical forest moved around him, the shadows stirring in the constant trade. Unlike the Varuans, Wallis was not uncomfortable in the darkness. He did not hear his ancestors whispering from the edge of the forest, or feel the presence of spirits—the coolness on the skin that announced their presence.

Of course, his years on Varua had done much to strip away his condescension toward the islanders' beliefs—he had certainly witnessed things that he could not explain, even if he was not always ready to accept the Varuan explanation. But fires wandering through the forest at night, burning nothing; the green sea light enveloping holy men; people cured of the most dire illnesses; these could not be ignored. Even so, the night did not frighten him.

Wallis slipped sideways through the narrow gap leading to the ledge before the caves—the "stone haven" as he translated the Varuan name.

"Anua," he said to the first person he recognized, and she pointed. As he walked, the castaway searched for his wife, looking for her friends and family, for that is where she would be. But he could not see her, nor could he hear her gentle laughter.

There were several fires burning low, the smells of cooking. He could sense the numbers of people around him, the entire village and more, huddled here in fear of the Farrlanders' vengeance. But despite the numbers in such a small place, Wallis knew that there would be no flaring tempers over space or supplies of food. The Varuans would not only remain at peace, but they would turn it into an outing, a picnic. Released from their normal routines, they would sing and have love, dance and laugh, talk, weave, cook and eat.

Despite the crowding here, there was no terrible odor such as one would expect if the same number of his own people were equally confined. He thought of His Majesty's ships and their stench. Here a clear stream ran down from the mountain and a pool had been built where everyone managed to bathe at least once a day if not twice.

Anua, he found, had set up court in a comparatively quiet corner, beneath the branches of a small breadfruit tree. A group of young people were singing not far off, their sweet tones carrying softly through the encampment—*like the perfume of flowers,* Wallis thought.

The King's senior wife waved him forward. She sat with her sleeping grandson in her arms, rocking to the slow rhythm of the music.

"Wallis," she said in her own language. "I have been hoping that you would come."

"I could not get away sooner, Anua, I apologize."

"What are the *dausoko* doing?" she asked; a polite term meaning "sailor." "Are they going to set their great guns to fire on us again?" He could hear the concern in her voice even if he could not see it on her face.

"No. I don't think so. Though Stern has not decided on a course." Wallis shifted where he sat. "He is like a King who mustn't lose the respect of his chiefs and his people. His followers think we have committed murder, for their tapu are different than our own. The sailors, perhaps even some of the officers, think Stern should respond by pounding the village to ruin. But Stern, despite his anger, is a civilized man. He does not want innocent people to suffer. But he cannot afford to lose the regard of his men. Do you see?"

Anua nodded. "Yes. It is a hard choice. If it was a fleet of our canoes lying off a distant island, I'm not sure we would be more understanding. Leaders must not lose face." She fell silent, stroking her grandson's hair as she rocked. "But we cannot give up the men who killed the two thieves. They acted according to our laws—they acted correctly. If only the King were here." She shifted the boy's limp weight, but he did not stir. "What about this one, Flattery? What do you think now?"

Wallis thought for a moment, considering the quiet naturalist. He seemed to bear such a burden, this young Flattery. "I'm sure that he is in some way part of what was predicted. And I am even more certain that the date of his discovery of the Lost City and the day of the seven great waves were the same. The Old Men were not wrong about some things, that is certain."

"But what is his purpose, Wallis? Can you guess?"

Wallis picked up a small stick and began to draw in the dirt. "I don't yet know. Nor does he, I think. Certainly Tristam means no one harm—I'm sure of that. Though that is no guarantee, I realize. I am beginning to believe that he does not understand his own purpose—or perhaps is unaware of it." Wallis realized that he was sketching his own fale. He would be able to go to his wife and children soon—when Anua finished questioning him. The thought of his family caused Wallis a moment of distress. He had not realized how much he had come to take their presence for granted.

"This story that he told the Old Men. . . . I do not understand."

Wallis nodded. "The world beyond the lagoon has its own laws, Anua. In my land the stars in the sky are not the same stars we see here. What happened at this Lost City—it is not easily explained in our own terms. My view is that the power is the same, but the way men find it varies from place to place, as does their use of it and even their beliefs concerning this power. Here a tree is a being. A spirit, that exists in this world in the form of a tree. In Farrland people believe that trees have no spirit. They are cut down without ritual or concern, and used for any purpose without thought for the spirit's dignity. An ancient tree, many times older than our oldest village, might be made into fence rails. No one would think it the slightest bit odd. The world is strange."

"How could anyone not realize that a tree has a spirit?" Anua said with some disbelief.

Wallis shrugged. "They find our beliefs equally hard to comprehend."

"But certainly the trees that have been made into their great ships—the builders knew their names and blessed their spirits?"

Wallis shook his head.

"How is it that they sail so far? Have the Farrlanders' gods no care for their charges?"

"Different people, different gods, Anua."

She kissed the head of her grandson, and nuzzled his hair with her cheek. "Has the King misunderstood the signs?"

Wallis stopped his drawing, considering what to say. "I don't know. The Old Men did not see Tristam Flattery on their journeys. Only one warned us of the snake."

"Perhaps Flattery was able to hide himself from us?"

"Tristam has no such control. Not yet, anyway."

"I think it could still happen, Wallis. The spirit within might do it."

"Perhaps."

They were silent again, and Wallis listened to the music. He had often heard his wife sing this same air when she was happy and content—though, oddly, it was a sad song.

"Faairi tells me that Flattery cannot control the power within. It can overcome him."

Wallis stopped his drawing. "How does she know that?"

"She saw, Wallis. Faairi was there, with him, when he was overpowered."

"He'd taken the King's leaf?"

He saw Anua shake her head in the dark, as she kept rocking her child.

"I am worried," Wallis said suddenly.

"Yes. We are all frightened. But it is worse. This bird that came with the ship. . . ."

"The falcon."

"Yes. Flattery transformed it. Faairi saw, as did several others. He put his power into an arrow and shot it into the falcon. It burst into flames, they say, and out of the smoke came the spirit transformed into a ghost owl."

Without realizing, Wallis brushed his stick across his drawing. "But what does it mean?"

Anua brushed strands of hair back from her grandson's face, and looked out into the darkness. "The snake will come. As Vita'a said. And there will be nothing to stop it. Will not this *dausoko* who calls himself an Old Man teach the young one?"

"I don't know. I think he is not what he claims."

The singing continued, unaffected by Anua's pronouncements. Wallis sat very still and listened. A small gust of wind began a recitation in the trees, and this stopped even the singers. It died away after a moment, and a single voice picked up the tune again—one woman—but no one joined her for some time.

When finally the others began to sing again, Anua turned back to the castaway. "You must be anxious to see Hau and your children, Wallis. I have kept you too long."

"It is all right. I will go to them in a moment." He made no move to rise. "Have you thought more about ... ?" He did not finish.

Anua looked into his face. "You must obey your chief, Wallis. If Captain Stern agrees, you may stay with us, but you must live by his word."

Wallis looked down at his half-erased drawing. It was the order of the King of Farrland that no man be left on the islands when the ship sailed.

🦂 🦂 🦂

Tristam lay staring up at the stars, thinking of the tattoo Faairi had shown him. The star by which she found her way back from the world of dreams. Part of him thought of this as the most primitive superstition, but to another part it made perfect sense. He wasn't sure he did not need such a talisman himself.

Tristam closed his eyes and saw the column at the ruin on Farrow and its particular view of the heavens. Did it represent a view from a specific place or a time? If it was a place, what did it signify? He had not made a careful examination of the sky while they were in the archipelago, but was it possible that he might have seen the view recorded on the Farrow Ruin?

He opened his eyes at a sound, but it was merely Beacham, muttering quietly in his sleep, troubled, perhaps, by the dreams that had started that night in the Lost City. Sitting up, Tristam cast his gaze in a circle. The fire had died to coals, and still there was no sign of their shipmates. He worried most about Hobbes. Not only was the master out in the dark alone, with the mood of the Varuans unclear, but the viscount was out there as well. Tristam was sure that nothing would happen to Julian. The truly macabre seemed immune to misfortune—as though their twisted spirits were misfortune enough.

A sound behind caused Tristam to turn, staring into the darkness. There was someone there.

"Tristam," came a whisper.

He rose to a crouch and froze. "Faairi?"

"I don't wish to be seen by your fellows," she said. "Can you come with me?"

Tristam hesitated, looking at the sleeping Beacham, and then out to the ship. And then he moved quietly into the darkness. He almost believed he could smell her perfume, the scent of her hair.

They found each other in the shadow of the trees, and clung together fiercely.

"I snucked away," she said, as pleased with herself as a truant. "No one is to be here but the watchers."

Tristam laughed, feeling great relief to be in her company.

She took his hand. "Come with me. I have something to show you."

He resisted the tug of her hands, looking back to the beach. "I am concerned about Beacham."

"He will be safe. The watchers will let nothing befall him."

"The watchers?"

"The men who watch the ship. They will keep him safe."

"But Faairi, what will happen now? Two of our crew have been killed. Your people hide in the forest."

Tristam could not see her, but he could sense her seriousness in the dark. She became very still. "It has not to do with us, Tristam. Your fellows defiled the fale of an Old Man and came into the Sacred City against the King's wishes. It was their fate. Your captain should see that."

Tristam stood, realizing that she did not know what her people planned, or would not say. Somehow he trusted her to tell him if he were in danger—though he did not know why. The insight the seed had given him, perhaps.

She led him surely through the trees in the utter darkness, onto a narrow path where Tristam stumbled occasionally. After a reasonably long climb he heard water running, and stars appeared overhead through a tear in the trees. They went on another fifty yards, or perhaps a hundred, Tristam could not be sure. She stopped several times and kissed him tenderly, promises of what was to come.

Finally they emerged into a clearing where Tristam could see something almost white, twisting like a ribbon in the darkness. This narrow fall of water seemed almost illuminated by the starlight, and for a second Tristam wondered if there could be some luminescent life that dwelt there.

"Do you see?" she said, clinging to him. Tristam could sense her excitement. The vapor cooled the air, and Tristam felt a refreshing mist reach out to him.

"It seems to glow in the darkness," *Ghostly,* Tristam thought, and shivered.

"It is the starlight," she said, her voice full of awe and pride, "it falls into a pool high up on the mountain and, on certain nights, spills over into the stream. It trips and falls and runs again, until it pours into this pool—the pool of fallen stars. From here it goes into the sea where you can see it glowing sometimes as the fish pass, or along the line of surf."

Luminescent phytoplankton, Tristam thought. But this. . . . He could not explain this. The falls did seem to be illuminated somehow. Faint moving threads of silver, as though the entire falls were crystal, and refracted some source of the whitest light.

"Sometimes the moonlight is caught in this same falls, spilling into the pool. I have seen it glow white, like the moon soon after it has risen, huge over the eastern sea."

She released him, suddenly, and left him standing, staring at the ribbon of falling water. He could almost believe it *was* starlight. A moment later she returned, a coconut in her hand. With Tristam's knife she opened it deftly, sharing the sweet milk with him. She scooped the soft flesh out, and they ate that as well, licking each other's fingers and laughing. Faairi had him strip off his clothes, and leaving her pareu on a branch, she led Tristam into the shallow pool.

Chanting something in Varuan, she began to fill the empty nut with water from the falls.

"Star water," she said.

"Good for many things, I'm sure," Tristam said, bending to kiss her neck. He felt the "other" stir within and he almost stepped back, struggling with a surge of fear.

Perhaps sensing what happened, she embraced him, repeating his name softly, over and over, like an incantation. She placed the coconut carefully on a rock and gently pushed Tristam back into the falling water. It rained down upon him, cool in the tropical night, like the weight of the sky. As though the falls were a column, upholding the dark dome of the star-scattered night.

The water seemed to glitter as it fell, twisting coils of silver disappearing into a luminous froth at his feet. Tristam realized that he was sobbing, though he did not know why—adding the salt of tears to the stream flowing out toward the moving sea.

He felt that the water flowed into him, and had done so for an endless time, like water wearing away the soft stone of the earth. Something was carried away, leaving him with a strange sadness, a hollowness that echoed with memories, though they were memories of dreams. His uncle sitting at a desk covered in snow. A woman rising from the water, lifting a white blossom in her perfect hands. Following a small boy through twisting, darkened streets. He opened his eyes and the world seemed to have shifted. Did he see the silhouettes of massive structures not far off? And was that a small boy scurrying along the water's edge? A clear tenor came to him, singing a sad air, and a young man clung to the hands of an old man.

"Tristam?" It was Faairi, but he could not see her.

"What has happened," he heard himself say. "Where am I."

"The world of the night," she answered. "The world of dreams."

"Why have you brought me here?" The water continued to fall—the ancient song of water running over stone.

"To help you find your way. What do you see?"

Tristam searched the darkness. Around him there was whispering, the scuttling of creatures. A snake's tail disappeared into a fissure of darkness. An owl's barren call. A woman walked at the edge of the pool, unaware of being watched. She swished her long skirts and her hair moved with the breeze. The duchess, he realized, but then a second woman appeared, younger, he thought, though they were far off. They stood facing each other, neither speaking nor moving. And then they reached out their hands as though to touch, but the hands passed through each other, causing them to search more frantically. Ghosts.

A bell rang, echoing down the stone streets of a great city and a single carriage, drawn by a gray horse, passed slowly through an empty square. Tristam could see no driver, and the passenger was hidden by a veil.

"Tristam?"

"Avonel. I see Avonel. A funeral."

He saw men climbing a long stair, bearing a living man laid out like a corpse. Stars appeared, as though he stood on the top of high hill. Stars like he had never seen, arrayed about him, almost close enough to touch. Below, a procession of carriages moved slowly along a valley floor, a twisting road following a twisting river. A ruin stood atop a long ridge that curved like the back of a giant beast.

"I am afraid," he said, but then a star rose above the hills, and he felt his spirits lift also. It floated high, increasing in brightness as it went.

He lifted on a breeze, following this star. Over water, which lay still and heavy, like mercury dyed the deep purple of dusk.

And then the island appeared below, and a white light like a star reflecting on a pond. Tristam was under water, trying to rise, but could not move. Nor could he breathe or call out.

Then the darkness gave way to indistinct points of light which coalesced into stars. Someone's face hovered over him.

"Tristam?" It was Faairi, her voice full of concern.

He was lying on his back, staring up, his heart pounding and his breath coming in gasps.

"You are safe," she said, laying her hand on his cheek. "My star brought you back." She pressed his hand to her tattoo, holding his fingers there. She was warm and real. Then she bent and he felt her soft breasts press against him, and her arms gathered him and pulled him close to her. Her star had led him back, but from where?

EIGHTEEN

Whatever plans they made, though all makeshift, came to nothing. That was Jaimy's realization that morning. As though events conspired to limit their choices. To avoid the men who they were sure were seeking them, they had been forced to abandon any ideas they had of going to Avonel and instead had ridden around the countryside like men bewildered. Somehow they had avoided capture.

Although there were men about in numbers, at a certain point they seemed to stop searching. The hounds were called off. But, still, they kept seeing groups, or even single horsemen moving about. For the life of them they could not guess what transpired.

In the end they had been driven so far off their course they decided to return to the original plan and follow Kent's advice. They were so afraid of capture, however, that they stayed off the roads, going cross-country. On the second evening they stopped at the most isolated farmhouse they could find, and only because their horses could not go on. They purchased hay and grain and the farm wife made them a perfectly awful meal of rabbit and last summer's root crop.

They slept until two hours before dawn, and then continued slowly, riders and mounts still, exhausted. Finally they came to the county where the Countess of Chilton was said to live. Jaimy was afraid to go asking about after the countess for fear that they might still be pursued, but finally they broke down and asked a boy they found cutting peat on the edge of a bog. Everyone, it seemed, knew about the countess, though no one had seen her for decades. She lived on quite a sizable estate not five miles off.

In the end they walked on blistered feet the last few miles, leading dispirited horses, hungry and exhausted. The weather had not been perfectly cooperative, either, for they had been the victims of a fine drizzle most of that morning, which, finally, had mercifully stopped.

Littel was quiet and sullen, much affected by their suffering, which, in the larger scale of things, Jaimy thought was not really so great. He tried to imagine what a war would be like. Even Tristam, on his voyage, was no doubt suffering worse privations than this. He kept reminding himself that it was not really so bad. But such suggestions, he soon learned, were not appreciated by his companion.

They came across the fields of what they believed to be the countess' estate and, finally, by a small lake and wood, they discovered the manor house. They could see the stone walls and slate roofs above the naked branches of the surrounding trees.

Jaimy was suddenly beset by a fear that he had misread Kent's riddle. What if they had come all this way and he was wrong? What a fool he would feel. And Littel would never forgive him, that was certain—even though the scholar would certainly have been captured without Jaimy's help.

If the countess turned them away, Jaimy was not sure how they would proceed. It might be foolish to send Littel back to Avonel now. Better, perhaps, to spirit him out of the country, though with what he apparently knew, it might not be wise to send him to Entonne—hadn't Kent asked the prince about Count Massenet?

Tristam's home in Locfal was beginning to seem a good possibility. If they could buy fresh horses, it was only four to five days' ride. Jaimy would have to find a way to send a message to Avonel, or perhaps he should return and let Egar go on alone. It would almost be safer. Their pursuers were after two young gentlemen, not one. And if Jaimy turned up in Avonel, that would likely confuse things. They might try to murder him out on some lonely heath, but surely no one would be so foolish as to try it in Avonel. Littel, however, was another matter.

Each time they came out into the open, Littel would start glancing behind them. Jaimy could almost see the man fighting this urge, but then he would give in, snapping his head around as though afraid that a dozen mounted men with hounds had somehow snuck up behind them. It would normally have made Jaimy smile but he was too exhausted, and, now that they had almost certainly escaped, he bore a smoldering anger over what they had been put through. *How dare they?* he would find himself thinking. *How dare they? Hunt us like common criminals!*

"There is someone walking along the shore," Littel said, one of the few times he'd broken his silence all day.

Jaimy could make out a figure, dressed in black, moving slowly along the shore. "Let us speak with them."

The woman, for Jaimy was almost certain it had been a woman, disappeared behind some small pines, and they adjusted their course to intercept her. Though the clouds were beginning to break, Jaimy could not yet tell where the sun might be. There could be two hours of light left, not much more.

They came up to the stand of pines and picked their way over a bed of damp moss. So silent did this make their passage that when they emerged from the trees the woman was taken completely by surprise. She stopped on the gravel path which bordered the waters, and glared at them without the slightest sign of fear.

Before Jaimy could speak, she seemed to recover. "Well, I would take you for highwaymen if you rode better horses. So I must take you for fools, ruining those poor beasts, and then showing your faces here, where you certainly are not welcome."

Jaimy was almost unable to respond, guilty as he was over what they had been forced to do to their poor mounts. But there was more. He was certainly in the presence of the loveliest woman he had ever seen. Those eyes! The lashes were so lustrous and dark, and the eyebrows so perfectly arched. Her anger had heightened her complexion a little and Jaimy found this almost irresistible.

"Excuse our terrible manners," Jaimy said, gently. "We didn't mean to alarm you. We're looking for the estate of the Countess of Chilton."

"And who might you be, sir?"

"Lord Jaimas Flattery." He hesitated, not wanting to use Littel's name, though not sure why. "We have been sent by a friend of the countess'."

"This friend, has she a name? For I know all of the countess' friends."

Jaimy was not sure how to proceed. He had this terrible feeling that to make an error here would send them back out into the fields, where hounds and men might find them yet. "Sir Averil Kent is his name."

"Kent . . ." she said, and he could see that this truly surprised her. "Why has he sent you here?"

"You will excuse me, Miss, but I am to speak of this only with the countess."

"Well, come along. I don't know if the countess will be able to receive you, but let us see."

ꙮ ꙮ ꙮ

It was well past dark, and Jaimy and Littel had not yet seen the countess. They had been given rooms in the vast old mansion, allowed to bathe, and then provided with clothing of the finest quality, though thirty years out of date and ill fitting, having once belonged to someone larger in both stature and girth. Jaimy thought they both looked a bit buffoonish.

"You don't think we've been betrayed, and are merely sitting here, comfortably, waiting for Palle's men to arrive?"

The thought had occurred to Jaimy as well. "I don't. Our choice is to wait out in the cold, prepared to leap into the saddle of our exhausted horses." Jaimy blew on a spoonful of soup. They sat in a cavernous dinning hall before a tall hearth in which blazed a fire of good sized logs. It dated from a period when ancient castle architecture had been the rage. The room seemed extremely out of place in this elegant old manor house, but Jaimy found he liked it.

"I think I shall copy his room when Alissa and I find a house. It has a certain charm, don't you think? Perhaps it is just the ride that we have survived. Doesn't it seem fitting that we would end up here? If we only had a few horns of ale to quaff."

Littel looked up from his food, raising an eyebrow. "I don't know how you can jest. This has been the worst three days of my life. I've sometimes wondered if I wouldn't have been better off as Palle's prisoner. Yes, I know what you will say; men have gone to war throughout history and experienced things infinitely worse, but that was bad enough for me. I have saddle sores that will leave me scarred for life, I'm sure."

Jaimy laughed, though not mockingly. He felt somewhat relieved to be here, though he was not sure why. "I can't believe we did not ask her name," he said suddenly.

Littel shook his head, as though his companion had gone a bit mad. "You can't really be thinking of that!" he said reproachfully. "Especially in your betrothed state."

"Curiosity only," Jaimy said. "One has to wonder how a woman of such astonishing beauty could go unknown in Farrland. She must have lived the most sheltered life."

"She was something of a vision, I will grant you that." Littel said a bit wistfully. And then turned back to his meal with a distracted air.

"If we are certain this will be a haven for you, Egar, I think you should set straight to work on reproducing this text."

He looked back at Jaimy, and then registered what had been said, and he nodded quickly.

A servant came in to clear the table, and he bobbed his head to Jaimy. "When you are done, sir, Lady Chilton will see you."

Jaimy immediately rose. "We are quite done, aren't we Egar? Do lead on."

They were taken up to a small withdrawing room, lit

only by a single lamp and the flames in the hearth. The servant was quite adamant about which chairs they should take, and before he left lit the burner beneath a warmer that stood beside a decanter of brandy and two snifters.

They sat silently for a moment, heating their glasses alternately.

"This seems very odd," Littel whispered. "What do you make of it?"

Jaimy looked around the room, at the chair just visible in the shadow cast by the screen. "The countess is a recluse—has not been seen in decades. I assume she is making certain that does not change."

Littel leaned a little nearer to his companion. "She is even more eccentric than your friend Kent."

"You think Kent eccentric . . . ?" but he did not finish, for the sound of a door opening hushed them both. The lightest step crossed the floor behind the screen and then a woman dressed in a black gown took the shadowed chair.

"I am not quite sure if I should bid you welcome, Lord Jaimas, Mr. Littel," came a flat voice, almost devoid of expression. "I do not care to have my solitude interrupted." She paused and Jaimy waited, not certain if he should speak. He found that he was uncharacteristically nervous.

"What reason did Kent have for sending you to me, and what message did you bring?"

Jaimy took a breath, and then another before he started. "We have only this note, thrown to us by Sir Averil as his carriage passed, escorted by three men we could not identify in the darkness." Jaimy took the scrap of paper from a pocket, but was not sure what to do. He did not feel he could approach this woman who made such effort to hide her face. Her hands almost reached out, he could see them covered in white lace.

"Would you read it?" she said.

"Yes, certainly," Jaimy held the note closer to the firelight, and realized, suddenly, how absurd it would sound. *"If you require refuge: the home of the lady who dwells with your books."*

"That is it? On the strength of that you came to me?" There was just a little color in the voice now, and it was the crimson of anger. "Have you your books here, and I am unaware?"

"I believe Kent is referring to a portrait of Lady Chilton that hangs in our library. In fact, I am quite sure of it."

She was silent for a moment. Jaimy saw her hands, which had gestured in anger a second ago, fall to her lap. "The portrait that Erasmus kept," she said quietly.

Jaimy nodded.

She drew in a long breath. "You should begin your tale from the beginning, Lord Jaimas. Leave nothing out. I must hear every detail, even those you think too small to warrant mention. Perhaps, especially those."

Jaimy took a moment to marshal his thoughts, realizing that Egar was unaware of much of this. "It began last summer, Lady Chilton. I was in Merton ... I confess I had lost my heart, and my suit was proving unsuccessful in the extreme. In the midst of this, my cousin Tristam Flattery appeared, completely unlooked for." The story was longer than he realized and much of it he had to dredge up from unclear memories. He had only seen the letter from Valary to Dandish that one time, for instance. He could not see the reaction of the countess, who sat perfectly still and asked no questions until Jaimy related how he had come by Kent's note, when the painter was escorted past by horsemen the prince was sure were palace guards. Here she raised a hand to her heart, as though it suddenly raced.

"Kent has been taken by Palle?" she said, not even her flat tones disguising her fear and concern.

"So we conjecture, Lady Chilton, but we have no evidence other than what I have just related."

"Please," she said, calming herself, the hand returning to her lap where it clasped the other tightly. "Continue."

The countess remained in that pose for the rest of the story, though, at each new revelation Littel became more agitated.

Jaimy thought he saw her long hair move, as though

she shook her head, when he related the attempt on their lives, but he was not completely sure of that. Finally he came to the story's end. "And so we came to your estate, Lady Chilton, and so exhausted and beset with fears were we that we didn't ask the name of the kind woman who took us in."

The countess said nothing, but sat with one hand twisting a lock of ebony hair around her fingers, over and over. "This boy gave you directions to my home—tomorrow we must find him and see how many others might know of your arrival here." That said, she fell to thinking again. Jaimy had a terrible feeling that she would say nothing more, but rise and leave them, wondering.

"And the text," she said at last, "Lord Jaimas says you can duplicate it, Mr. Littel?"

"I can, Lady Chilton," he answered, with more deference in his voice than Jaimy would have expected from a reform sympathizer.

"Will you do that immediately? This night? It might be more important than we know." She thought a moment more. "I will find out what has happened to Averil Kent," she said softly. "Pray that he has come to no harm, for it has been a formidable task, and he is no longer young."

"Lady Chilton?" Jaimy said, a bit surprised at the meekness in his voice. "We do not understand what we have been caught up in. Do Palle and his group believe they can learn the arts of the mages? Is it possible?" Jaimy was sure that the shadow stared at him. Almost, he could see eyes in that darkness.

"It is the question we are all asking. I am anxious to see this text Mr. Littel has been translating. Though you have not yet finished, I collect?" she said to the scholar.

"No, not yet. It is a difficult task, and has become more so at each stage. I don't know if I shall ever render it exactly or completely." He shrugged.

"I hope you will not object to continuing, Mr. Littel. I realize you've been through a terrible experience and would like some peace."

"I. . . . If it will assist you, Lady Chilton, I will gladly do it, but I fear I must ask leave to sleep a little. I can barely keep my eyes open, I apologize for saying."

Jaimy thought she nodded assent. "Certainly. Sleep, but not too long," she said, warmth lighting her voice like a wick giving birth to flame.

❦ ❦ ❦

Egar Littel had not exaggerated his exhaustion and went immediately to his chamber and bed. Jaimy, though hardly less affected by their flight, could not sleep and finally rose and dressed. He paced across the cold room, for despite the fire in the hearth the night wind seemed to penetrate the walls.

He did not light the lamp but measured the length of his floor, back and forth, by the light of his fire. Occasionally he crouched before the hearth and warmed his hands as though by a fire in the woods. He was concerned about his family and Alissa, who had not heard from him in three days, and it would take more than a day for a letter to reach them—if a letter was advisable. He would have to ask the countess.

What a strange audience that had been, almost a bit comic, though somehow the voice that came from the shadows did not inspire laughter. What terrible vanity, though. To hide oneself away for decades because one had lost the beauty of one's youth. It seemed so very odd, for Jaimy would expect such a person to be . . . well, strange. Some of that vanity would seep into the conversation, but the countess had seemed positively genuine, even modest. Not at all what he would have expected.

His thoughts returned to the woman they had encountered by the lake. The countess had not fallen for his ploy and supplied the woman's name. *You are engaged to be married to the most delightful young woman you have ever met,* he reminded himself. That did not mean he stopped feeling attraction for other women, however. He was, after all, not yet twenty-four. He couldn't stop himself from feeling admiration for someone's beauty, but it must not go beyond that.

He moved to the window ledge, pulling the curtain aside and feeling the cold through the glass. There were other lights still on, but only a few among the myriad blind openings. Bare branches twined around his window, clutching to the cold stone. Tristam would have named the vine, but Jaimy could not, and marveled again at how little he had managed to learn in his years at Merton.

Someone moved at a window, one floor higher and at such an angle that he could make out no more than a shadow—which seemed to be the way things went in this place. For a moment he waited, wondering what this person would do. Wondering if it was the countess or the young beauty, staring out into the night. A small bird sat on that window ledge, or so it seemed. It was so still it might have been only an ornament chiseled in stone. After a moment he felt as though he were imposing on someone's privacy and decided it was time to wake Egar. The work must begin.

❦ ❦ ❦

A servant had been detailed to see to their needs, coffee being chief among them. They worked at the same table where they had eaten their dinner, side by side, their backs to the fire. Egar had turned a page on its side and ruled it neatly into thirds. The first column he began to fill with rows of odd characters, as unlike the script used by the people around the Entide Sea as Jaimy could imagine. The second column was direct transliteration of the characters into the common script, but the language was unknown. The third column was reserved for the translation.

Jaimy's task was to make a fair copy of the second and third column, for his hand was much finer than Egar's. The work did not progress quickly, but it seldom halted, Littel's memory being every bit as phenomenal as he had claimed. As the night wore on, the scholar did begin to falter, and at one point he laid his head down on his arm on the table and fell asleep for thirty minutes, like every student had done at some time or other.

There were still two hours of darkness left when they finished. Egar sprawled in a chair near to the fire and sipped a brandy, his eyes red and puffy, his jaw a little slack.

Jaimy tried to make his exhausted mind grapple with what he read. The text was long, almost twenty pages, and oddly cadenced and phrased. Most of it was in one of two languages, but there were bits of other unknown tongues as well. In places Littel had used Entonne to translate words or phrases, and in a few others he had used the language of Doorn. Sections, some quite large, were left untranslated, although a few of these bore notes suggesting what they *might* refer to.

"But what in Farrelle's name does this mean?" Jaimy exclaimed. "Who could make sense of this? It does not seem to have been written for men at all, but some other race whose perception of the world is not as ours."

"Exactly. That is how it seems. Did I not warn you?"

Jaimy nodded, his eye running down the page. "But listen to this:

> *"Lifesblood blossoms, bear up, blood white*
> *Spring snow. Gathered then, palely gathered.*
> *Rose thorns stab, heather heals*
> *Gather with the new moon's light.*
>
> *Snow bears moonlight.*
> *Starlight, in the winter rain,*
> *And clearly run to Terhelm Spring*
> *Where the singer awaits*
> *The secret song."*

Jaimy almost threw the page onto the table. "What is that supposed to mean?"

"But you've chosen one of the simplest passages. Merely a set of directions for gathering herbs or some such things. When it should be done, and where. It also tells that starlight and sunlight can be collected from a spring, for they are contained in snow and rain. And this is what Palle, and Wells, and even Kent and the countess seem to take so seriously. For this, someone attempted our murder!"

Jaimy picked up another page. "And you've used so much Entonne," he said.

"Yes, it is very odd. Some of it translates better into Farr, and, in other instances, the Entonne words are a much closer fit. Or so I imagine. It is almost translated more by intuition and inspiration than by pure scholarship. It might take years to do it properly, but Wells and his companions wanted something immediately. In many places I have translated the sense of it more than anything else. But it is shoddy scholarship, I am well aware."

"And listen to this," Jaimy said. "It wounds like a children's rhyme:

> *"Owl's song on whispered shores*
> *Where the silvered sea dies*
> *Along the wake of a running moon,*
> *Moontide and magic rise."*

"Yes, and there are four verses like that. All in what seems to be a different dialect. And that is not the only place I have encountered them. In the *Lay of Brenoth* one of those lines appears again, almost word for word: *'Beyond the wake of a running moon.'* Far too close to be accidental. And I think it was preserved elsewhere, in one of the songs of the Carey minstrels. And from there it found its way into a poem by an obscure Doornish poet. Who knows who will use it next."

Jaimy stared at his companion. "Flames, Egar, you are the Tristam Flattery of language!"

"What?"

"My cousin Tristam is like you, except his province is birds, and trees, and insects. He has a head stuffed with the most amazing facts. I am in awe of him, sometimes, as I am of you."

Littel shrugged and tried to smile at what he hoped was a compliment.

"But I can't make any sense of this," Jaimy said turning back to the text. "This is what everyone is struggling to possess and it is gibberish, as far as I can tell."

"To you, perhaps." The woman they had met by the lake was standing by the door. Jaimy had not heard her enter and had no idea how long she might have been listening. She smiled at the two of them, though there was no joy in this gesture, and she crossed to the table. Jaimy had not marked how gracefully she moved before, as though she were a virtuoso of that one act, had studied it for years.

"It is complete?" she asked looking down at the sheets spread over the table, but she did not move to touch them.

"As complete as I can make it at this time," Littel said, his voice changing in the presence of this woman. "I would need access to quite a library to go much farther."

She nodded, not taking her eyes from the pages. "This is the fair copy, without the characters?"

Egar nodded. "I will add the characters, though I am not sure I can do it tonight. I am all in, I fear."

She turned a genuine smile on them both then, with the result that they suddenly felt their energies return. "You have done more than can be asked: both of you." She pulled out a chair and sat. "I will fill in the third column. And I will be as meticulous as you would be yourself, Mr. Littel. You may review my work when you have rested. I do not think you will have cause to criticize."

As though they were the most fragile of ancient documents, she reached out and slid the pages toward her. And then she looked up at the two men staring at her. "Sleep, gentleman. You have completed your task, and difficult it was, too. Sleep, and when you have risen tomorrow, at your leisure, and broken your fast, I will have someone show you our library. Now, sleep well, and long. You are safe here."

The two gentlemen went reluctantly to the door, and as Littel passed through, Jaimy turned, almost leaning out from behind the door.

"I could sit with you a while. Perhaps there is something yet that I might do."

The woman looked up from the table, forcing a smile

as she took up a pen. "Rest, Lord Jaimas. You must rest. We don't want you returning to your fiancée, and then hearing that we mistreated you. Sleep the sleep of the innocent and I shall see you on the morrow."

Jaimy nodded, and backed out the door closing it softly behind him. When he reached the foot of the stair, he realized he still did not know her name.

Back in his chamber, Jaimy resumed his pacing. For a few moments he lay down on the bed, staring up at the ceiling. What had she said? "Sleep the sleep of the innocent and I will see you on the morrow,"? A phrase he had not heard in many years. His grandmother had used it. It was a sign of the life this woman led, shut up here with an old woman who hid herself from everyone's sight. What a life! He felt a wave of pity for her.

I am engaged to be married, he thought, *I should not be affected so.* But when he closed his eyes, he saw that extraordinary face looking at him. There was no sense of vagueness to this image—it was as sharp as if the woman stood before him. The nameless woman, with her high forehead and prominent cheek bones. Almost the same face that looked down from the mantle in his father's library. Almost. She wore her hair up, and that changed her look, but even so, the similarity was striking. He had been truly exhausted not to have seen that immediately. The countess' daughter, he thought, though she must have been born late.

He wondered if Alissa ever met men who had this same effect on her. Somehow he thought she would not let herself have these feelings, and his guilt increased. He rose after a while, stiff with cold, and went to the window, looking for signs of the morning light. Darkness still prevailed.

He began to undress, but instead of going to bed when he finished, he put on his own clothes that had been returned, clean and mended.

"I will look like a fool," Jaimy said aloud, but the idea of being thought foolish by a woman was a bit alien to him. It had happened so seldom.

The hallways were lit only by candles, spaced at some

distance, but Jaimy made his way down the stairs,
through the silent mansion. No light appeared below the
door to the dining hall, and he almost did not go in. But
then he turned the handle and stepped into the room. It
was dark but for a dull glow from the coals in the hearth.
He crossed to the table, placing his hand on the back of
the chair where she had sat. He reached out and brushed
the table, but his eyes were not wrong: the text was gone.

"It is safe with me," came a near whisper from behind,
making Jaimy start.

"Lady Chilton?" Jaimy said, turning to the sound. The
countess sat in a high-backed chair by the hearth,
wrapped in a dark shawl or a blanket. In the slight glow
from the fire he could see long curls, and it brought to
mind sculptures he had seen. It brought to mind the portrait in their library that his father made pilgrimages to
view.

"Yes."

She seemed to be huddled in the chair, drawing into
herself, like someone left to die of the cold.

"Shall I rekindle the fire for you, Lady Chilton?"

"No. I am not bothered by the cold."

"You have read Egar's translation?" Jaimy asked, surprised at how softly these words came out.

"Every word," she said, her voice even more flat, if
that were possible.

"What . . . what does it mean?"

She shifted in her chair, he could just make out her
head turning toward the fire. "It means many things. It
means that the mages failed in their last great endeavor.
That is its central meaning. It also means that a way once
denied at great cost, might now be opened again."

"Egar said it was a ritual—perhaps to open a gate."

She waved a sheaf of paper which he had not realized
she held. "Oh, this will not do that. No, this is far simpler, though it is complicated enough. This . . ." she
shook the papers slightly, "is merely the end of a string.
What you will find when the string is drawn in, that is my
fear."

"And what will we find?" Jaimy asked.

She shrugged, Jaimy was certain.

"Tell me about your cousin Tristam. Were you with him when he was approached by the ghost boy?"

"No," Jaimy said, disappointed that she had avoided his question. "No, I was not. And he does not like to speak of it." Jaimy stared into the barely glowing coals, which looked to him like cooling molten lava. "Kent thought he saw the ghost boy, though."

"You did not tell me *that*. When?"

"As we left Dandish's ruined house the night we made our escape. As we stepped out onto the terrace, a child bolted across the garden and out the gate. Kent was quite shaken, and certain that it was not a natural child."

"Poor thing," Jaimy thought she whispered. "Did this boy open the gate to pass through?"

Jaimy hesitated. "He did not appear to."

"But still, you do not believe?"

Jaimy said nothing.

"I must find out what has befallen Averil," she said, as though to herself. He thought her voice quavered just slightly as she said this. "If you would like to send a message to your family, I will have it delivered, but I fear you must stay here for a few days, at least, until we know more of what goes on beyond our gates. Write something quickly and I will have a servant collect it from your chamber, though say nothing of being here with me." She looked at him now, he could tell by the sound. "And then you must find rest, Lord Jaimas. We must all harbor our strength. I cannot predict what will be asked of us before this is over."

He did not move immediately, and a hand emerged from the shadow into the dull light, a graceful hand, and it waved him away as one might a child. He almost smiled, and for some reason thought the countess did, too.

The clatter in the courtyard below brought Jaimy to his window. He had written quick notes to both his mother and Alissa, with instructions that both could be delivered to either, and a servant had rushed off with them.

In the courtyard below he saw that a good-sized carriage had been pulled up before the door, and servants were bustling about with baggage. Four horsemen stood by their mounts, wearing capes against the weather, reminding Jaimy immediately of the riders who had accompanied Kent—poor Kent. Jaimy hoped that no harm had come to the man, but considering how casually his own murder had been attempted he held little hope for the painter.

The door to the entrance hall opened and someone emerged. Under the roof of the carriage entrance he could see only the hem of a dark coat, and a woman striding quickly the few paces to the carriage, which barely jiggled when she boarded. There was a moment's fuss while everyone found their places and then the carriage set out, preceded by two of the horsemen. He watched the carriage lamps disappear in the slight mist that hung beyond the courtyard, the sounds of horses coming up to him even through the cold glass.

NINETEEN

Lady Galton did not look well that afternoon. Alissa had heard that the woman lived on Farrow because the island had the climate required for her health, and wondered if the poor woman had been away from her adopted home for too long. Her color was high and she seemed somewhat short of breath as they ascended the stairs to the duchess' private sitting room.

"The duchess is well, though? Her nerves not too frayed?" Lady Galton asked, as they paused on the landing.

"The duchess seems very well today, but perhaps Lady Galton knows how nervous excitement does affect her. They live very quietly here, and I fear the coming wedding has been more than enough excitement."

Lady Galton put her hand to her forehead as though she had a sudden pain.

"Are you well, Lady Galton?" Alissa asked, concerned. The older woman nodded, still not revealing her face, and when she did look up, her eyes were rimmed in red.

"You are such a sweet child," she said with greater feeling than their brief association would seem to support. They had met only once before.

They continued up the stairs, slowly, for Lady Galton seemed almost to be carrying a burden, something that weighed heavily upon her. Alissa thought the poor woman seemed overcome with sadness, and she wondered what had befallen her. Despite what Kent claimed about this woman's husband, Lady Galton seemed very kind and warm.

"It is not much farther," she said quietly, and Lady Galton nodded in response, keeping her eyes cast down.

They paused again at the head of the stairs, so that the older woman might catch her breath, and she tried to smile at Alissa, though it was a very weak smile. Finally she nodded, and they set off along the hallway. Never had the passageway seemed so long. With each step Lady Galton appeared to become more reluctant, and when they finally came to the door, she paused, straightening her posture, and taking control of her breathing. Alissa got the impression that she was gathering her resolve.

They found the duchess sitting in a chair by the fire, reading by the fine sunlight that blessed them that day. Her pale face lit with a smile when Lady Galton appeared, and a decade of cares were erased in that instant. She rose to meet her old friend, and to Alissa's surprise the two women fell into each other's arms like schoolgirls, both of them shedding tears.

Alissa stood by, a bit embarrassed, a bit charmed by the scene, and she found her own eyes damp. Jaimas always teased her for crying so easily, though she knew he loved her for it.

Reluctantly the women released each other and sat, dabbing at their eyes and laughing a little at their show of emotion.

The duchess reached out and took Alissa's hand. "You have met Lady Alissa before? You see, Margel, I finally have a daughter, and I shall embarrass her by saying I could not be more pleased if I had brought her into the world myself. Bless her poor mother, gone now these many years."

This reference to Alissa's mother, for some odd reason, seemed to steal the joy of the reunion from Lady Galton's face, and a tear welled up in each eye, causing her to blink.

"I cannot bear this task I have been set!" she said suddenly, looking at the two women with such compassion. "I am the bearer of the worst news, for both of you." She leaned forward in her chair, reaching out and taking both women by the hands. She moved her mouth to form a word but no sound came, and Alissa suddenly felt a chill of fear.

"I have received news, I cannot begin to explain how, but your son, Anthia," and she cast a look of pity toward Alissa. "Your dear son, and his friend as well, were found . . . found dead in County Coombs." Her voice disappeared again, and then she managed. *"I am so sorry."*

The duchess put her hand to her heart, all color draining from her face. "But this can't be. When? When was this to have occurred?"

"Two days past."

The duchess let out a long sigh, and a tear slipped down her cheek. "But we have had word from Jaimas this very morning. She reached over and lifted a sheet of letter paper from her reading table. "Here it is, dated yesterday. And Alissa received a letter as well. There can be no doubt." Her face fell a little. "Unless there is a mistake in the date, or something has occurred since then."

Lady Galton hardly knew what to say. "No. No, it was two days past, I am quite sure. You are certain this is from Lord Jaimas?"

The duchess nodded, vigorously. "Absolutely. He has a very distinctive hand and manner of expression. No, there is no doubt." The duchess looked over to Alissa for confirmation, and she nodded quickly. Her own letter, she was a bit embarrassed to think, was tucked inside her bodice near to her heart. She dearly hoped she would not be asked to produce it!

Lady Galton sat back in her chair, though she did not release their hands. She looked as if she would be the one needing comforting. "But how can this be?" she said to herself.

The duchess was obviously shaken by the news, and Alissa was certain that she would take to bed again for several days.

"I'm quite sure our letters were written yesterday," Alissa said firmly, "just as the dates indicate. Jaimy said explicitly in mine . . ." she felt her face color a little, "that he has missed me terribly these three days. That would be correct. I last saw them in Merton on Saturday, the fifth. Yesterday was the eighth, and that is the date on the letter. And you think something befell them on the sixth, Lady Galton?"

"Yes, the day the iron bridge was dedicated." Lady Galton appeared confused and upset that she may have borne this terrible news falsely, carrying doubts to these poor women.

"Then I think your information is not quite correct, Lady Galton" Alissa said, taking the duchess' hand, which remained limp.

"Alissa," the duchess said, a bit pitifully, "are you certain?"

"Absolutely. Jaimy would never mistake the date by two days. And he said that they had found refuge after some difficulty, and that he expected to return in a few days, perhaps at the week's end." Alissa turned on Lady Galton. "Perhaps, Lady Galton, you would explain what has led you to bring us this news."

The old woman looked as though she would expire on the spot from embarrassment and guilt. "I hardly know where to begin," she said.

ॐ ॐ ॐ

Jaimy walked along the path that traced the lake's border. On the opposite shore, a hawk sat high in the bare branches of a tall tree and turned its head slowly, as though it stood vigil. Spring, that day, was a rumor whispered on the breeze. The sun, too, hinted at the coming season, and snowbells appeared, pixielike, in the grass and moss.

Jaimy kept scanning the edge of the lake, but the tall figure he hoped for could not be found. He went another forty feet, and stopped to survey the scene again, feeling a bit like the hawk across the waters.

The servants had told him the countess had gone away for a few days. *And the other woman?* She was indisposed at the moment; they would tell her he had inquired.

He had learned only one thing; the woman's name was Angeline, and the servants said she was the daughter of the countess' cousin. All that day Jaimy had spent in contemplation. He was surprised to find that he was glad to have an excuse to spend another day or two here, and this made him wonder if he was in fact the rogue that Professor Somers had initially taken him for.

Did he not love Alissa? Or did he not love her enough? How he wished Tristam were here so that he might speak of this with someone. Littel was cooped up in the mansion's impressive library, wallowing in books. Jaimy had always heard that the countess was known for her beauty and her wit, but had not realized that her interests were so broad. He thought of the woman who had questioned them that night—she did not seem the type to collect books merely to impress others. There appeared to be no others to impress.

He took a seat on a bench and stared out over the water, which held the sky and the trees of the other shore. He worried about Tristam, and every new thing he learned made this worse. What he most wanted was to gather everyone together; Kent and the countess, and this man Valary, and Littel—and find out what they all knew. It was like a children's treasure hunt, with clues buried all over the countryside. And he was getting frustrated from pursuing them. And now someone had attempted his murder. So casually attempted it!

A figure appeared across the small lake, causing him to sit up, but immediately he recognized the walk—Littel had torn himself away from the books. Jaimy smiled. One sight of the countess' library and the trials of the past days had been forgotten. To find such a library the scholar would have braved their cross-country chase without hesitation. Braved it daily! Now that Littel was recovering from his fright, Jaimy found he quite liked him—and not just because he reminded Jaimy of his cousin, whom he missed terribly.

It occurred to him suddenly that perhaps Angeline was more interested in Littel, for she seemed to be something of a scholar as well.

"You are acting the fool," he chastened himself. He wondered if Alissa was worried about him. If he were causing her distress. And yet he had no desire at the moment to rush to her, and this made him wonder exactly what kind of man Jaimas Flattery was.

TWENTY

Kent was still far from recovered, despite the fact that he had nearly slept the clock round, but he felt such a need to speak to others. As his actions were the subject of much scrutiny, the only way to do this was in public. Preferably some place where he could speak with as many people as possible, so he could bury the important conversations amongst fifty others that were of no import whatsoever.

The opera was almost perfect, for many of the people he really wanted to see would be there, and afterward anyone who was anyone would collect at a select few homes in the city—and Kent, of course, had standing invitations to all of these.

He surveyed the crowd from his box in the balcony, noting those he wished to see, and those who he might speak with to confuse anyone watching. There were certain people to be avoided—anyone who would try to monopolize him, certainly—but he knew how to steer through such situations. He also knew where most of the important people habitually gathered at intermission—everyone had their favored place.

He saw that Alissa Somers was present in the box of the Duke and Duchess of Blackwater, but she was accompanied only by Lady Galton. On the same level he saw Count Massenet in the company of two beautiful young women whom he did not recognize; one blonde and one dark.

The place glittered with jewelry (an Entonne passion

adopted by the women of Farrland), and was as colorful as any summer garden. Kent delighted in the sight, considering how it could be represented on canvas, the rows of colors making random patterns, broken by the balustrades and gilt columns and balconies. But what could never be represented was the excitement. Even an old man could feel it. Everyone in their finery. Beautiful necks and shoulders, bared by the recent fad for low necklines. The pleasure he could see in the shining eyes. The feeling was so strong, it made the courting of spring birds seem subdued.

He turned his attention back to the stage where a young Entonne singer was exercising her magnificent soprano. And even here he could not escape it, for she wore the most revealing gown of all, he was sure. So low cut that he could have never raised his opera glass to look, despite his eyesight, lest others should see him. Instead he consulted his list of players, and found her name: Tenil Leconte.

At moments like this he thought it a cruel trick that his youth had fled. He could feel this tangible sexuality, but it was past for him—oh, not the feeling certainly, but his time. He was nothing but a ruin of an old man, not even a prize for an elderly lady.

For a moment he shut his eyes, unable to bear the beauty spread before him any longer. The singer's voice seemed to pierce him, cut through the facade he had built to protect himself, and the notes of her sad song seemed to be a requiem for his lost youth. It brought to mind his response when Alissa Somers had rubbed his aching feet—physical, beyond his control. It was like falling victim to a spell that one could hardly bear, it was so compelling and yet so painful. Like the obsessive, unrequited love he had experienced when he was young.

"Kent?" It was a whisper—a man's voice.

The painter turned to find Bertillon standing in the shadows at the back of the box.

"May I join you?"

Kent waved him forward, feeling a bit of embarrassment, as though afraid Bertillon would know what he had been thinking—or feeling, in fact.

Bertillon took a seat, and Kent leaned a bit toward him. "This girl is magnificent! Have you heard her before?"

"Heard her?" Bertillon smiled. "Indeed."

Kent turned away from this handsome young man, realizing that the woman was his lover, or had been at some time. He felt a moment of outrage, focused on Bertillon, but it was merely life he felt this anger toward. Outrage that this disease called age should befall him.

"Our friend would like to meet with you. It's very important."

Kent nodded. "As you must have realized, Palle is watching me. A meeting now would not be wise."

Bertillon nodded, and then began to applaud as the air ended. He leaned close to Kent's ear. "Five minutes of your time. No more. At the Earl of Milford's tonight." He stood, continuing to applaud, and much of the audience followed.

During intermission, Kent made his way out into the upper lobby, packed with tight knots of people, alive with the buzz of conversation—like putting one's ear to a hive and giving it a tap. The painter did not feel quite so tired, society was ever rejuvenating, and people greeted him with smiles rather than with looks of concern. He must not look as though he was about to expire, as he had since his return from Merton.

Picking his way carefully among the people, Kent finally found Sennet, who detached himself from his group at a nod from the painter.

"Sir Averil. I must say you are looking more hale tonight. I confess I was concerned."

Kent smiled and shrugged. "I cannot go without sleep as I did when I was young." Pleasantries were brief between the two. They had known each more decades than they cared to count, and were well aware of each other's interests.

"Would you have guessed the governor would be appointed to the council?" Kent asked, and Sennet, surprisingly, shook his head.

"Not at the time we last spoke. I was taken unawares." He laughed as though this gave him pleasure, as though the antics of court and government were not to be taken too seriously. "If all goes as planned, they shall announce the council tomorrow, though who will be surprised other than illiterate shepherds in northern Locfal, I can't say." He drew himself up in mock outrage, though it seemed he was ready to burst out laughing. "Many are predicting a long regency. Do you know some young wit had the effrontery to offer odds that the King would outlive *me!* And while I was present, too!"

Kent could not help himself; he laughed.

"Do not laugh, Kent," the marquis said seriously, "I got better odds than you," and then when he saw the look on the painter's face, he could contain his laughter no longer. "I tell you, Kent," he managed after a moment, "this younger generation, they will turn anything to profit."

They laughed a moment longer, and then Kent stopped, surveying the room. "The Duke has seen the King, then?"

"This very night," Sennet said.

Kent squinted. "Is that Lady Galton, by the stairs?"

Sennet raised himself up on his toes. "I believe it is, accompanying the young woman the prince is so taken with."

Kent must have revealed his surprise. "Alissa Somers?"

"You know her?"

"I should say so. Have known her many years. Her father has a chair at Merton. But she is engaged, you know, to Blackwater's son."

Sennet's smile was huge. "Lord Jaimas? Of course. Well, her fiancé should watch himself. Not, of course, that I doubt the intentions of Miss Somers. The daughter of a don, you say?" This seemed to please him immeasurably. "That would set Prince Kori and the princess into a spin!"

Kent felt a little horrified. He should never have told Sennet that this was Alissa. The man really was a terrible gossip. But he was so well connected, and far more shrewd than most realized.

Kent took his leave of the marquis, crossing the room at an opportune moment, wanting to speak with Lady Galton, but not wanting to share her with others.

"Sir Stedman has not accompanied you?" Kent asked after he had kissed Lady Galton's hand.

"No, he was called away by other matters," Lady Galton smiled with affection. "No doubt you've heard," she said, not meeting Kent's eye.

"Yes," he said quietly.

Lady Galton raised her head, her look a bit defiant, perhaps. "But Stedman seems to be over this strange condition that has plagued him these past few years—he has hardly been himself. But he is recovered, now."

"I am so glad to hear it," Kent said, perhaps not hiding his surprise as well as he should. "I can't tell you how I have worried about the governor." So the duke was right! Galton was no longer supporting Palle—and obviously Palle must not know.

Lady Galton reached out her hand and offered Kent a folded card—an invitation. "I don't think you will have a more interesting time anywhere else this evening," she said, just as the bell rang to call everyone back.

Kent returned to his box and, before the performance began, took out his spectacles and read his invitation. Inside there was an unfamiliar address, and the invitation also named Valary. The writing, however, was well known to him. It was the hand of the Countess of Chilton, though she had not signed her name. *The countess, in Avonel!* To the best of his knowledge she had not been in the capital for decades. He tried to imagine what had drawn her from her fortress, and found the thought ruined his ability to concentrate on the remaining performance.

❦   ❦   ❦

Kent peered out the back of his carriage. There was no breeze that evening and the smoke from a thousand chimneys settled into the streets and alleys and commons. It seemed to grow thicker around the streetlamps, where it gathered like silt in a river's eddy. He could not be absolutely sure they were not followed.

"I'll have Hawkins let us out a few blocks away from our destination, Valary, and we will walk the last bit. Easier to see if we are unaccompanied."

"You are being rather mysterious, Kent," Valary said. He had been deep into his pursuit when Kent arrived, trying to convince himself that some long past event was merely a coincidence. "You have me a bit nervous. We're not going to meet the King, are we?"

Kent shook his head, still staring back into the smoke. "The city is awful when it is like this, is it not?"

Valary realized his question had not registered. They went along in silence another block.

"Do you remember, Valary, the last time I visited, you said there was someone who might know more about the mages than you?"

Valary looked confused for a second. "The Countess of Chilton?" he said suddenly. "That isn't who we're going to meet?"

"Well, it is."

Valary touched the painter's shoulder. "How in the world did you arrange that?"

"It is a long story, Valary. I will try to explain later."

Kent had Hawkins stop, and the two men stepped out onto the wet cobbles. The driver went on, with instructions to return to this spot in one hour. They were not so far from Kent's own home that he did not know the area, and he took them into a darkened side street.

"Are you sure this is wise, Kent?" Valary almost whispered. "I should stay out in the light."

"I think it's a small risk only. We mustn't be followed. Better to be set upon by cutpurses than let anyone know our business tonight."

They stumbled up a flight of stairs where they surprised a group of young boys drinking sour smelling wine. The second the gentlemen appeared, they took to heel. At the stairhead they found themselves back on a lit circle, where a single carriage made its slow way around the central park, almost disappearing between streetlamps, its progress marked only by the sound of iron-shod hooves on stone. Kent and Valary stayed in the shadows, watching the coach pass, and then draw up before a house where a gentleman and two children got down, talking in hushed tones.

When the street was empty, the two men set out briskly along the walk until they found the address they sought. It was a three-story townhouse, with a broad stair to its entrance and an ornate iron fence protecting it from the street. They tugged on the bell pull and waited.

Kent found he was a little nervous. He also realized he did not want to share his privilege of visiting the countess with another. Did not want to spoil whatever intimacy there was in these meetings. He was also terribly anxious, simply from wondering what would bring the countess to Avonel.

The door opened, and to Kent's relief, a servant he recognized stood in the entryway.

The room was different from the one Kent was used to—this was a small library—and there was a single lamp, though well shaded and burning low, not casting even a shadow beyond the table on which it was all but hidden. The fire flickered, almost ready for a log. Not far from the hearth, a screen patterned with irises stood, and two chairs sat on either side of a table which held a pair of glasses, as well as brandy and a warmer.

"Will they not bring us another lamp?" Valary asked.

"No," Kent said. "I should have warned you, Valary. Lady Chilton does not allow herself to be seen. Please, indulge me in this, and do not rise from your chair. Your trouble will be amply rewarded, I can assure you."

The historian did not respond, but sat staring at the fire, his face set in concentration, as it was when he was seeking some bit of information from the vast storehouse that was his memory. Kent noticed that he rather furtively pushed his shirt cuffs into his jacket, and then tried to tame his unruly hair. Kent was so used to the man wearing frayed clothing and looking like a distracted don that the painter had become convinced the man never gave his appearance a second thought.

He is old enough to remember, Kent thought. When she withdrew from society, the countess was still the most beautiful woman anyone had ever seen. That was the image she had fixed in everyone's mind—he glanced at the screen—and she was not going to ruin it now.

Kent heated his brandy, turning it slowly over the blue flame until the aroma of it filled the room. It was comforting, familiar, a part of the ritual.

A door opened and he heard the light footfall, the swish of a gown, and she was sitting opposite them, dark in the shadows.

"Averil. Mr. Valary," came the flat voice. "I am so glad to meet you at last."

Valary bowed his head, unable to speak.

"And Averil, I received your gift. I hardly know what to say. . . . Wherever did you come by such a stone? It must be. . . . Well, it is overly generous, I think."

Kent waved off her protest. "Not at all, it was left to me by an admirer. What in the world was I to do with such a thing? No, I'm a bit ashamed to admit it cost me nothing. I hope you will accept it."

He could not see her reaction in the darkened room, but she seemed to hold him in her gaze a moment, and then she nodded, as though she had not the words to express her gratitude. Kent took a long breath of relief. It was out of his hands now, and he had profited by it not at all.

"Lord Jaimas managed to bring Mr. Littel through, Averil," the countess said, "though it was a near thing. I was more than a little surprised that you would send them to me, but when I saw the text Littel had been working on for Palle. . . . You certainly did the right thing, and as far as I can tell, no one realizes where they are."

"You have seen the text?" Valary blurted out.

Kent was sure she smiled. "I have, Mr. Valary. And if you agree, soon you shall see it as well. Though I warn you not to agree too quickly. Palle tried to kill Lord Jaimas and Littel so that no one else might possess it."

Kent was more than a little taken aback by this. Thank

Farrelle they survived! He had assured Somers and Alissa that no one would dare harm the son of the Duke of Blackwater. He felt as though he had seated himself at a gaming table, and, too late, discovered the stakes were beyond his means. He gave voice to the fear that had been plaguing him. "Lady Chilton is certain they were not followed?"

Tentative. "Yess.... As sure as I can be."

"I will see this text, Lady Chilton," Valary said suddenly. "I will take the risk gladly."

"I thought you might, though I'm not quite convinced you understand what is involved, Mr. Valary." Kent saw the tips of her fingers come together. Her hands seemed so small. He did not think of her as frail. It was the illusion that he carried, as did many others, that she was still young. An ideal, after all, never changed.

"If you go to the table behind you, I have laid the text out there. The translation, as you will see, is not complete, and may never be. But it might be enough, or is very nearly so. I am interested in your response, Mr. Valary. Please," she said, gesturing with a lace-covered hand.

Valary seemed curiously reticent, now that he had been invited, but Kent put this down to mere anticipation. The man had spent so much of his life waiting for a moment like this, and now that it had come it would take on that unreal quality that Kent had felt when he was knighted. One felt no need to rush; time seemed to slow down in fact. For a second he wondered if they would be disappointed.

The two of them bent over the papers spread on the desk. "This is a copy only," Valary said, speaking to himself.

"That is true, Mr. Valary, but this young man Littel is possessed of the most remarkable memory. Nearly infallible, as far as I can tell."

Valary reached out and so very gently pressed down a corner of one page, his eyes darting back and forth as though he tried to take it all in at once.

Kent, too, stared at the text: a column of unfamiliar

characters, what he took to be a transcription into the common script, and then a translation, though incomplete.

Valary let out a long sigh, as though he had been holding his breath. He glanced at Kent, excitement lighting up his face. "This is exactly what I tried to explain to you that night, Kent. Littel is a genius. Look at this! Assuming he's correct, this would have taken anyone else decades. I can't imagine how he did it." He turned to the countess. "Did Palle and Wells find a key, or some samples of an intermediate language?"

"No, this is the work of Mr. Littel, assisted by Wells ... and Stedman Galton, I regret to say."

Galton, Kent thought. His wife claimed he was no longer with the King's Man, and she had carried the note from the countess. Pray she was right.

"Look at this," Valary said, pointing. "It is almost an incantation. And this is a description of a ritual, I would say. And here a verse fragment. Farrelle's flames, is it whole or is it several fragments thrown together?"

"That is what I hoped you would tell me, Mr. Valary. My own feeling is that it is whole. The mind of a mage was not the mind of a normal man, I can tell you that, nor did their ritual and cant follow anything like logic."

Valary picked up a page and held it closer to the light. Kent could see him shaking his head. "Forty years I have searched for something like this. Look, here, a warding chant. I knew such things existed, but never did I think to hold one in my hand."

Kent looked at the sheet Valary was holding. It was hardly more than gibberish to him. "But what would happen if this were ... performed by a person with talent? What would result?"

"There is more to it than that, Averil," the countess said softly. She had risen from her chair and stood warming herself by the fire, though she kept her back turned to them.

From where Kent stood, she could be the same woman he had known so long ago. The thick dark hair, though shorter now, and dyed he was sure. The slim form, not what had been thought ideal before the countess had swept Farr society before her.

"There are many elements required, and even this text is not complete enough, I suspect." She returned to her chair, and Kent tore his gaze away, looking back at the text. Valary had pulled out a chair and sat poring over the first page.

"Here, a reference to the serpent and the hunter," he said, as though Kent would understand the significance.

"Yes," the countess said. "The falcon Averil saw."

"Tristam's falcon?" Kent said.

"Yes," she said sadly. "His hunter. His champion in the struggle to come."

"It *was* a familiar, then?" He could just make out her shrug in the darkened room.

"Familiar? We don't know exactly, but probably all of the mages had one. Sometimes it was a wild cat or a wolf. Some believed the emerging mage created the hunter unknowingly. Others said it was a natural creature, transformed as the mage was transformed. But it is all speculation."

The countess was revealing more than she had in the past, which surprised Kent. He thought she had opened the door to some memories kept hidden, and now that it was open they floated out like old ghosts.

"Eldrich had a wolf. Massive, beautiful, supremely wild. It followed him—almost haunted him—appearing at the oddest times. It even came into his home, prowling the hallways at night, as though it searched for something—like a mother seeking her cubs."

Kent could hardly believe his ears. In all the years he had known her, she had barely said two words about Eldrich. He sometimes believed it was only gossip that connected her to the mage.

"What think you, Mr. Valary?" she said quietly.

Valary adjusted his spectacles, and sat back in his chair, tearing his gaze from the text with some difficulty. For a moment he sat staring blankly. "I suppose we shall never see the original," he said wistfully, "but even so, my first impression is that the document is authentic. Of course there have been many hoaxes, but I doubt this is one, if for no other reason than it is so very . . . odd." He removed his spectacles and rubbed his eyes with the back of his wrist. "I am surprised to find more than one language here—two main ones, it seems. Once one has Littel's work in hand, one can begin to see the way of it. How words might have evolved into our own ancient tongues.

"There were, to the best of my knowledge, nine books of lore, although I believe they were really compilations, each devoted to some study or art. One to herb lore, for instance. Some of these were books of history, and were constantly added to, I believe. Others were books of ritual, or incantation, or what have you—the arts. But these were the nine disciplines of the mages. And all of their knowledge fit into one of these. Each book had a name, and I have discovered four of them, or so I think, though little good it does us, for they tell us nothing. *Owl Songs,* I believe, was one, and the book of herb lore, I am almost certain, was called *Gildroth.* I have puzzled over that word for years: I should like to hear Mr. Littel's thoughts on it. *Gild* would seem to be an early form of 'gilt,' ancient Farr for gold. But then *ildroth* itself might be a root word. There is a village called Eldrith not far from Tremont Abbey, oddly enough, and I think there was once a wood of the same name there, though centuries ago, for there are references to it in old songs. Tremont, is clearly from tree mount, as I'm sure the hill was once called. And Eldrith may resemble Eldrich only by coincidence, one cannot be sure. *'Golden wood?'* The north road passed through both wood and the town of Eldrith, and perhaps the road took the same name in that area. It was commonly so. 'Golden way?' 'Golden wood?' 'Golden Road?' Do you see all the possibilities? One can spend the night tracing these words toward their sources: like grasping the very top branch of a giant tree, the roots lie somewhere deep in the earth.

"Eldrith has an interesting possibility—'elder,' which has 'eld' as its root. *Ellaern* was the name of a small, white-flowered tree. We call it 'elder' now or even 'elderberry,' though I am not convinced it is the same tree at all. The name 'Elorin' is from the same source."

"The Duchess of Morland's given name," Kent said, and Valary nodded.

"Do not assume these names are mere coincidence," the countess said softly. Kent glanced over, but she was invisible in the shadow now that he had come into the lamplight.

Valary nodded agreement. "Be that as it may, I believe the book of herb lore was called *Gildroth,* probably meaning 'the golden wood' or even 'the golden tree.' There is a reference in here to this book, and it is almost like an instruction: 'Get this part from the book of *Gildroth,*' though it is not quite so plainly said. Very few would even know the word, so I can't think it is a forgery.

"And then there is a verse fragment that begins," he leaned over and picked up one page, " *'Owl's song on whispered shores.'* One book, as I said, was called *Owl Songs.* There may be more such references, I would need to spend much time searching." He studied the page a few seconds longer, then picked up another. "And this section near the beginning, Lady Chilton. It is a warding, or so I think. Done almost as a preamble to the longer ritual." His brows pushed tight together, and he thrust out his lower lip. "I need much more time. . . ."

"Time is the one thing that we do not have, Mr. Valary. Let me tell you what I think, and then you may have until morning to examine the text." The countess shifted in her chair, turning almost sideways, one lace-covered hand cupping her knee. "Erasmus Flattery believed there had been a struggle among the final generation of mages. Those who followed Lucklow, and believed their time was past—though Erasmus did not know why—and those who worked against this decision, though to all appearances agreeing. I do not know what the mages found or did or perhaps foresaw that led to their decision, but whatever it was must have seemed truly terrifying. I knew Eldrich—oh, not as well as some think, but I knew him. One of the few things I learned from this brief association was that mages were not known for self-sacrifice.

They were willful, self-centered, arrogant, selfish, and less concerned with the affairs of men than many think. Much of what is thought to have been done for the benefit of humankind was really secondary to the benefits gained by the mages—or perhaps even one mage.

"This text that we have, it was somehow hidden away, left to be found, when all the mages were gone. And that was no easy thing, for every effort was made to guard against this. They left Eldrich behind, who was trusted. But this text, Averil, Mr. Valary, I fear it is like an island, just over the horizon. One performs the ritual and the next island in the string will appear, and then the next. At the end could lie anything. Even that which caused the mages to bring an end to their own kind."

❦ ❦ ❦

The Duke of Blackwater visited his wife in her chamber every night, though their times of intimacy had become few due to the duchess' health, but the duke still yearned for her company and required her counsel. This evening he arrived late from his appointment and found her sleeping, the lamp turned low, and her pale, thin face ghostlike. For a moment he stood staring down at her, almost overcome by melancholy. Her face had become so thin that he could see the structure beneath, and though this was thought beautiful by many, to him it was a sign that she wasted away. He remembered how different she had been when they first met, gangly children then. Full of life and vital in the extreme. How unfair it was that she had fallen victim to this wasting condition that sapped her vital energies and caused her such pain at times.

Aging is like slow robbery, he thought. *All of the skills we spend so many years acquiring and perfecting are stolen from us one by one.*

The duchess stirred then, and he gently lowered himself to sit on the bed's edge. Her eyes opened, and for the briefest second he saw confusion and pain, and then a smile appeared—real for the most part, but also partly feigned, he knew: it was the mask she hid behind.

"Edward," she said, reaching out and finding his hand. He brushed his fingers across her cheek then bent and kissed her. In the warm lamplight her color appeared almost healthy, and he felt a stirring.

"And how is my love today?" he asked.

Gently, she put her hand on his heart. "My love is never the problem," she said, and smiled again. "In truth I have had an unusual day." She stopped then, examining his face as though she did not need to inquire about his own well-being, but only look for a moment. "Your meeting with the King has left you troubled, Edward."

He looked down at her hand, resting so lightly in his. "Yes," he said quietly. "Yes. I remember His Majesty, thirty years ago, when he was thought miraculously well preserved. . . . He had an impressive mind, which one cannot always say of kings. What I saw tonight . . . His majesty's once fine mind has been overwhelmed by a terrible dementia." He looked up and met his wife's eye. "It was like looking into our futures—your future, my future. Dementia and helplessness. He was once the most powerful man in the known world. . . ." He fell silent. "It doesn't matter. We suffer the same end as our gardener."

"Yes," the duchess whispered, taking his hand in both of hers, "but before that comes we are fortunate to live lives our gardener can only dream of. It is all the compensation that we have, but it is more than enough, I think. We should never complain."

He brushed hair back from her forehead. "You have made a religion of never complaining. I am not nearly so skilled in this area."

"I have never known you to complain . . . unless it is about this one thing. We will grow old and pass through. I like it no more than you." She reached back and plumped her pillow so that it lifted her head. "His Majesty is no longer competent: Palle is not lying?"

The duke shook his head. "The King is mad, there is no doubt. He did not even recognize me, though of course we have not met in many years. He called me Kent, of all things, and kept raging about his portrait. 'Where was his portrait? How did I expect him to go on without it?' " He looked over at the book lying on the night table. "The audience was very short, but I am satisfied, at least, that it is not a palace coup, though the result is much the same."

They were silent for a moment; almost awkward.

"Will you stay with me this night?" the duchess asked. "I wish to keep you near."

She sensed that he might be the one needing comforting, he realized. "Yes, give me but a moment."

When he returned the duchess seemed to be asleep, and he almost retreated, but then she opened her eyes, and stretched like a child, beckoning him. He slipped into the bed beside her and was shocked at how cold she was, here beneath this weight of down quilts. She wriggled close and nestled her head on his shoulder, so that her mouth was close to his ear.

"We must send someone north to County Coombs," she whispered so quietly he almost did not hear. "Two innocent young men have disappeared there—murdered, I fear. It is possible that Palle thought they were Jaimas and a young man named Littel, though our son and his friend are safe."

She felt him stiffen, and soothed him. "Shh. Jaimas is safe. Do not be concerned."

"How do you know this? Palle would never do anything so mad."

"Madness awaits us all, some sooner than others. Palle's madness is caused by a belief that he is smarter than all others. This friend of Jaimas' escaped from Palle with something the King's Man valued extremely."

"How did Jaimas get involved in this?"

"I am not certain, though I suspect Alissa may have some part in it."

"Alissa!"

"Shh. Yes. But I will deal with it. I forbid you to put servants to watch her again." She shook her head. "I absolutely forbid it!"

He did not argue. There was no point when she used that tone. He tried now to hide his growing rage. If what she said was true, Palle did not realize what an enemy he had made. *He tried to kill Jaimas!* No, he would not become angry until he knew more. He would send someone to Coombs in the morning.

"How did you learn this?"

"Galton has come over, as I told you he would."

He lay still for a few seconds, considering this news. His duchess was seldom wrong when it came to people. "You astonish me, my love" he whispered, but her breathing had become regular, and she slept.

❦ ❦ ❦

Kent listened to the lonely sound of his team making its way through the dark city. It was now very late, and a fog crept in off the bay, compounding the effects of the smoke. Kent was now sure that he simply could not be followed, the pall was so dense that one could not see beyond the horses, who plodded on, gingerly, into the obscurity. Sounds seemed to come from all directions at once, and Kent was certain the only way he could be followed would be by someone holding on to the back of his carriage, and he had checked for that.

He had left Valary alone in the countess' library, looking over the ancient text, and gone off to keep his appointment with Massenet, though it was now so late he was sure the count would be gone. Even so, he thought it best to go. His conversation with the countess made him realize how desperately they needed to know the extent of the Entonne knowledge. He had been lulled by the fragment that Massenet had shown him, but there really was no reason to believe the Entonne did not want to recover the arts of the mages. Especially if they thought Palle and his followers were close to doing so. And there was Bertillon. . . . The countess and Valary had been more than a little shocked when he told them of the musician's trick with the flaming rose. It now seemed possible that Massenet had someone with talent, and—more than that—he had some knowledge of the mages' arts. These damn smooth Entonne! Bertillon had been so convincing when he denied possessing any real talent.

They needed to find out the extent of the Entonne

knowledge. And they desperately needed to discover the origin of Palle's text. Could there be more? He prayed there was not.

Lights were still burning at the home of the Earl of Milford's, and carriages lined the curb, the drivers huddled round a charcoal brazier, shoulders hunched against the cold and damp, talking quietly.

He almost sent Hawkins over to ask if the ambassador was still inside, but decided against it. Drivers gossiped, and no one had more carriages and drivers than Palle. Better simply to go in.

The earl had come into his title and fortune early, and was now only in his late twenties. His home was the haunt of the more willful sons and daughters of some of Avonel's leading families. But Kent knew the earl was also a devotee of the theater and the opera, as well as a patron of the arts, so he could not fault the man entirely. The painter also remembered that he had spent many an evening at just such houses when he was younger, and did not seem to have suffered greatly for it.

Despite the hour, the house was nowhere near empty, laughter and conversation coming from every room. The aura of sensuality that he had sensed at the opera was even more tangible here. He sometimes wondered if humankind had another sense for these things.

He had not gone far into the mansion before realizing that, at this hour, he was by far the oldest person present, by quite some number of years, too. He hoped he could find Massenet and escape quickly, for he felt rather removed from these beautiful young women, and the dandies scattered among them. It was not the kind of gathering where one expected to find Averil Kent—and this concerned him.

The sound of a pianum drew him, and as he expected, he found Bertillon, surrounded by admirers, most of them women. Kent leaned against the door frame, and felt a wash of envy. He was so tired he could hardly think of anything but rest, and here was this young musician who, no doubt, had not even begun the exertions of his evening.

"Sir Averil Kent?"

He turned to find a young woman, her hands clasped together, her manner prim and timid, though her dress contradicted her manner most strongly.

"Yes?"

"I can't begin to tell you how much your paintings mean to me," she said, coloring a little. Her accent was Entonne. "I have dreams of walking in your garden—vivid dreams. I hope you will paint your garden again."

Kent smiled, and bowed his head. "You are very kind. I think you are right—I have not given my garden the attention it deserves. One or two paintings only, though I have perhaps a dozen studies. Wherever did you see my garden paintings?"

"Count Massenet owns one, and the other is here, in a room upstairs."

"Ah," Kent said, "I didn't realize the count possessed one of my paintings."

"He has three, I believe. Three in Avonel. His collection at home is said to be vast, so he could easily have more. But three paintings by Sir Averil Kent is treasure enough for one man." She paused, a bit awkward yet. Kent would soon have put her at ease—he was used to admirers, after all—but he hardly had the time. It was late, and he needed to find Massenet, if the man was still here.

"Did you enjoy our performance this evening? You were at the opera?" she said.

"I was, indeed, and I enjoyed it enormously. You are a singer? I confess I do not recognize you."

She gave a small laugh. "I was the heartbroken lover, but without the makeup I am very plain."

"That is not true at all," Kent said. "You are far more beautiful when playing only yourself."

She curtsied. "Be careful, sir, I admire you extremely, and even the slightest hint of compliment may raise my hopes."

Kent laughed. He realized Bertillon was watching, and

the musician smiled, and inclined his head toward the singer, his meaning plain.

"May I accompany you, Sir Averil? I shall introduce you to anyone you might want to meet."

Kent held out his arm. "I cannot be properly introduced by someone who keeps her name from me."

"Oh. I am Tenil Leconte; and please call me Tenil."

"Well, Tenil, if I were blessed with grandchildren, I would want them all to be just like you. Even the boys."

They made their way through the mansion, Tenil making only occasional introductions. This was the younger set, but Kent had watched many of them grow up. He was always shocked at how adult these children had become in so short a span of time. They seemed to remain children for years, and then, in a matter of weeks, transformed into adults—young adults, certainly, but unquestionably no longer children.

The young woman who held his arm seemed to be quite pleased to be in his company, as though she was escorted by a new beau of whom she was particularly enamored. He had realized years before that there were young women in society who truly loved art, and held great admiration for those who produced it. Kent had known this kind of admiration before, but he no longer allowed himself to believe that such a young woman actually felt something for him. If he had not been a famous painter, she would have thought him just another feeble old man. It was his art she was enthralled with, though she might not distinguish the "singer from the song," as the saying went.

It was common, though. Many artists, or singers for that matter, were not particularly admirable human beings, in Kent's view, but they still had their followers. It was a bit perverse, he had always thought.

Tenil smiled up at him. She was not tall, or fine featured, but her roundish face was still very beautiful with the most striking dark eyes, and a mouth and smile that he thought perfect. Her revealing gown tugged at his eye, like a line in a painting, leading one irresistibly into the composition.

They made their way up the stairs, Kent following, assuming that Bertillon's nod meant she would take him to Massenet. She stopped and opened a door a crack, peeking in, and then opened it quickly, drawing Kent in behind her. It was a small, dimly lit sitting room, which had obviously been recently used, for there were wine glasses and bottles on a table by a divan that had been pulled up before the fire.

Laughter could be heard, and Kent was sure it came from behind a second door.

Tenil smiled. "I will interrupt him, as he so wants to speak with you." She squeezed his arm and left him standing in the middle of the room. The laughter stopped abruptly as Tenil rapped on the door.

"Yes," came a man's voice.

"It is Tenil. The count's guest has arrived."

Rustling followed by a footfall. A moment, and then the door opened, and the count appeared; behind him Kent could see a bed, and unbound hair, both blonde and dark, and ivory bare arms, and there a leg.

The count had obviously thrown on his breeches and shirt, and stopped now to pull his hose quickly over white feet. He waved toward the door and Tenil went into the room he had just left, clearly to be sure no one tried to leave, or listen.

"My dear friend," he said quietly. "Just let me bolt the door."

Massenet came back from the door and took a seat on the divan, pulling his shirt into order as he did so. Kent looked at the man sitting near to him, his usually perfectly groomed hair mussed, a light in his eyes—that unmistakable light. There was also a poor attempt to hide the smugness. Kent wondered why he had come.

"There was a terrible fuss in Merton, just a few days ago," the count began, speaking low, leaning close to the painter. "What in Farrelle's name was going on?"

Kent said nothing for a moment, staring into the man's dark eyes. "How much more of the Lucklow correspondence have you uncovered?" he countered.

The count did not answer immediately. He rose and

picked up a wine bottle, tilting it to measure its contents, and then he poured some of the liquid into a glass, chosen at random. He looked up at Kent. "I have no clean glasses, I apologize. Shall I call for wine?"

Kent shook his head. "I have not come for wine."

Massenet returned to the divan, lost in thought. "You have lost confidence in my intentions, Sir Averil," he said at last, almost as though this hurt him.

"Perhaps I need to be reassured," Kent said. "Answers to my questions might restore my faith."

Massenet nodded. "The letters Varese spoke of at the Society, which I believe your Mr. Valary has seen. Other than the revelation that Varese unleashed that evening, they contain very little but for a bit of insight into his sexual interests. We discovered a few entries in a diary kept by the marchioness, and the fragment you saw. Nothing more. The letters, by the way, are authentic, just as Valary no doubt has told you. Boran really might have been inspired by a mage, though his reputation is safe. I will destroy the letters soon enough."

"But Bertillon. . . . He performed a rite at the house of the Duchess of Morland. Where did he learn that? And how much talent does he possess?"

The count sipped his wine. "We have a fragment, about nine pages from one of the so-called books of lore. I suspect it is from the same source as the text I assume Palle possesses. You have heard of Teller? It is our belief that he managed to hide a few fragments of what he learned. Concealed them here and there, so that the mages could not trace them all. Or perhaps they were hidden by one of the mages. We don't really know." He looked up at Kent. "Our fear, Kent, is that there might be one fragment that is a key—leads to the others. Or perhaps each has that potential, if it can be unraveled. You cannot imagine how . . . arcane the text is. We have hardly begun to understand."

Kent was sure this was not true. "Bertillon performed a rite, Count Massenet."

The count nodded. "Yes. It is not really a rite of the mages, so much as an artifact of the lesser arts, as they are called. Healing, and augury, things of that nature. It was known to those who opposed the mages. One does not need to be a mage or even possess much talent to perform it. We have another who can do it just as well. You might be able to master it yourself, Sir Averil." Massenet tasted his wine once more, grimaced, and dashed it in the fire. "Does that satisfy you? I am not seeking to bring the arts back, but if Palle manages to do so . . . well, we must be prepared to defend ourselves. But answer my question now—what did happen at Merton?"

"I will merely be confirming your knowledge, Count Massenet. Littel did escape. He is safe at the moment."

"You have him?"

"He is safe. I can say no more, for his own safety, which I'm sure you can understand."

"But did he have the text? Have you seen it?"

Kent hesitated and feared this would tell the count more than a lie. "He did not carry it with him, so we have only what he can remember, and his own thoughts on its purpose."

"But is it a key? Flames, Kent, should we be sitting here talking so calmly?"

"Even if it is a key, Palle still lacks someone with talent."

"Are you sure? Have you a source in Palle's group? That is how you got this Littel away?"

Kent shook his head. "Littel managed his own escape. How I wish I had someone close to the King's Man."

"But the King's Man is about to become King—or at least a third part of a King. When will the regency be announced?"

"As soon as tomorrow. Not later than a few days from now." Massenet certainly knew this; he was using an old trick. Ask questions to which he knew the answers, and if he heard lies, then his source could not be trusted.

"They might find someone," the count said, almost to himself.

"Talent, I am assured, is very rare. The one man we know to possess it is on the other side of the world."

"Doing what?" Massenet said quickly. "It is a constant

fear of mine. Why did they send this Tristam Flattery so far away?"

"I am not sure," Kent admitted. "Not because he is a promising empiricist, that is certain. They have something in mind."

"And that is why we must be allies, Kent. Palle is not pursuing this out of curiosity. We both know this knowledge should never see the light of day. We must take this matter into our own hands, and end it as it should have been ended, long ago."

Kent felt a bitter smile tug at his mouth. "And when we have this mage lore in our hands, how will we destroy it? Will you merely trust that I will put what we have to the flame? You will keep nothing back in case we are not acting honorably?"

The count cast a look back at the sleeping chamber door. "You have struck to the heart of the matter, Sir Averil. That is why I chose you. Someone who would understand what must be done. Someone I hope I can form a bond of trust with. If we cannot do this, Kent. . . ." He did not need to finish. "You should go," he said.

Kent nodded.

Massenet rose and stopped as he began to turn back to his bedchamber. "Tenil is your great admirer, Sir Averil. I'm sure you could entice her to accompany you home tonight, but I will tell you, if it is not already obvious, that she is an agent of the Entonne government. Take her into your house with that in mind. You see, I will try to be as forthcoming as I am able." With that he bowed, and went back to the door.

Kent sat staring at the empty wine bottles, the smeared goblets, a hair ribbon and a lace garter. He thought of it as a still life. *The Seduction* he would call it.

Tenil reappeared, the awkwardness she had shown upon their meeting having returned. "I see the Count has been a terrible host, Sir Averil. Is there anything at all that I might bring you? Wine? Something to eat?"

Kent tried to smile but found he was too exhausted. *Sleep*, he thought. *I must have sleep.* But it was not possible. He must return to see how Valary was progressing.

If only I were younger, he thought, looking up at the beautiful woman before him.

"You seem very tired," she said suddenly.

"Yes," he said, "I suppose I am."

She crossed over to him. "Stay a while more, Sir Averil. I will make you comfortable here. You can close your eyes, and let your worries fall away."

Kent could hardly answer; there was nothing he wanted more than to close his eyes and sleep, even for half of the hour.

"Put your feet up and lie back," Tenil said.

He struggled within. It would be folly to stay here. He looked up at the lovely face of the singer, filled with apparent concern for him. "But you must wake me in an hour," he said quietly.

"I promise." She removed his boots and fetched a light coverlet, and then banked the coals in the fire herself and put more wood to burn. She removed his wig with the expertise of someone who worked in the theater, and then lifted his head, but instead of a cushion, she slipped under herself, lowering Kent's head gently to her lap.

"In one hour I will wake you. There is a clock on the mantelpiece." She began to stroke his face tenderly, running her fingers through his thinning hair. "Sleep. . . . Sleep," she breathed, and then very softly she began to sing. And to his surprise, Kent began to drift off into a languid dream, her song echoing among the trees of an exquisite garden.

He awoke to the moans of a woman in the grip of pleasure. The lamp had burned out, and the room was lit only by the fire, burning low. He could feel Tenil's breathing, responding to the sounds from the next chamber, where Massenet lay with his two lovers.

The fingers of her right hand had taken hold of his shirt and they curled, almost quivering, as she listened to the other woman's orgasm.

She realized then that Kent was waking and released her grip, pressing his shirt flat against his chest. Coyly, she leaned over to look down into his eyes. "Your hour is yet ten minutes off, Sir Averil," she whispered, trying to control her breathing now.

Kent found that he, too, was excited by the sounds. How many years had passed since he had held a woman in his arms while she shuddered in pleasure and cried out like that?

"The sounds of love," Tenil said, a small laugh escaping. "We are like animals there. We hear them, even in our sleep, and our hearts respond." She laughed again and brushed a lock of hair back from his forehead, then kissed his brow. "The count has intimated that you might, in the near future, come to live in Entonne, which would be an honor for my country, not to mention what it would mean to your admirers."

Kent sat up abruptly, almost pushing her away, as though he were overcome by claustrophobia. "No," he said, shocking her with his response. "I will not."

❧   ❧   ❧

The night was still windless, and the fog and smoke so thick that Kent wondered if they would even be able to tell when the sun rose, which could not be more than three hours off. Hawkins took a convoluted course through the city, stopping here and there to see if anyone would appear out of the murk behind them. Finally he dropped Kent near the countess' home and in twenty feet dissolved into the murk.

The city seemed deserted at this hour, abandoned and dreamlike. Perspective and depth were erased by the fog and darkness, and the street lamps illuminated nothing but the fog itself, like small moons behind thin clouds. Kent waited a few moments in shadow, until he was certain he was alone, and then set out for the countess'. His hour's sleep, and the sweet kiss that Tenil had given him as he left, had rejuvenated Kent more than he would have expected. There was almost a bit of spring in his step. But this was tempered by what she had let slip. There could be only one reason for Massenet believing Kent would take up residence in Entonne. He trusted the man even less, now.

He found Valary still studying the text, an untouched cup of coffee, now cold, balanced on the table's edge. A second lamp had been provided and both were turned bright, illuminating the room, including the countess' empty chair.

Valary looked up as Kent came in, confusion written on his face. "Kent?" he said, as though they had not seen each other in thirty years.

"What have you found, Valary?" Kent asked, pulling a chair up beside the scholar.

"What an astonishing document, Kent!" he said, his voice filled with awe. "I count myself blessed to have lived to see it. And this man Littel. . . . I don't know how he did it! I really don't know."

"Yes, but what is it? What is its purpose?"

Valary's enthusiasm waned a little. "Well, that is not so easily answered. I am not entirely sure I agree with the countess, you see. I'm not even convinced it is of a piece, though it is difficult to tell. There are four stanzas of verse, and each is like an epigraph to a section, but if you put the verses together in the order in which they are found they don't really flow smoothly, or at least that is my impression. They seem to go much better like this.

> "Owl's song on whispered shores
> Where the silvered sea dies
> Along the wake of a running moon,
> Moontide and magic rise.
>
> Beyond the sea without a shore
> The choral stars in silvered verse,
> The white bird rides the sailor's wind
> O'er spoken sea, and silent curse.
>
> The ancient tongue of sea worn words
> Sighs along the brittle shore
> And broken stones speak naught to man
> Of ancient sites, forbidden lore.

The journey out through darkened lands
A way beneath the vaulted hill
The tidal years sound elder bells,
Though falcons cry and thrushes trill."

"Does that not sound right?" Valary said looking up to Kent and raising his eyebrows so they arched over his spectacles.

"It does seem to flow more easily, but Valary, you know far more of these matters than I."

The countess' odd voice seemed to echo out of a shadow, though she did not appear from behind the screen. "I think you are right, Mr. Valary, and it might help our understanding substantially."

"It would mean the warding remains where it is, at the beginning, but the section that describes the collection of herbs is now second rather than last; although this same section appears to tell how to collect moonlight and starlight. I don't really know what this reordering signifies precisely, but do you see, Kent? At least we will be reading it in its proper order." Valary picked up a page and shook his head. "But this. . . . It is in a different style, with unusual phrasing. Much of it remains untranslated. I would dearly love to speak to this young man Littel about it." Valary looked up at Kent, and then over at the screen. "But if it leads to other similar documents. . . . I can't say. It could be the work of years to understand such a thing, not hours."

Kent saw the countess' gloved hand take gentle hold of the top of the screen. "Would you consent to stay here for a few days, Mr. Valary? I have sent for Mr. Littel, and you could work with him here, uninterrupted."

Kent felt a flash of jealousy.

"Yes." Valary began bobbing his head quickly. "Yes, indeed."

"But I must warn you. Do not become too enamored of this task. This text must be destroyed, sooner rather than later. I am reticent enough to have anyone see it, but we must know more of its purpose. And there is one copy that I can't yet see a way to destroy, even though it must be done."

TWENTY-ONE

Galton sat staring at Sir Benjamin Rawdon, who looked more distressed than he could remember, and that was saying quite a bit. Rawdon might be the most celebrated physician in Farrland, but he was a man beset by melancholia, a man easily overwhelmed by life's hardships. "A poor swimmer," Lady Galton would call him, an odd term in a land where few swam at all. But Rawdon was a man who could barely keep his head above the tides and currents of human affairs.

Galton had known the doctor for many years now, had consulted him, in fact, and knew there was more to Benjamin Rawdon. In the company of Lady Rawdon, or several other women Galton knew of, the doctor was transformed. A poor swimmer returned to solid ground. From nowhere, a delightful wit appeared, self-deprecating, yes, but informed by great insight. In the company of women, the Royal Physician's conversation was filled with intelligent observation, even wisdom. He smiled often and laughed in all the right places. He was not this distracted, awkward man Galton saw before him. The governor could not begin to imagine why, but Rawdon could never be comfortable in the company of men.

"I am distressed beyond measure, Stedman. I can't begin to tell you." Rawdon shook his regal head. "These men. . . . What on this round earth were they thinking?"

Galton shook his head as well. "Thinking? Clearly, they took no time for that. The son of the Duke of Black-

287

water. They might as well have murdered the heir to the Entonne throne. If the duke ever learns who did this. . . ." He did not need to finish. That very day his wife had gone to see the poor duchess. Galton was not sure it had been wise, but had kept his own counsel. He'd been wrong often enough these past months. In the morning Lady Galton would return, and he would learn how the duchess was faring. Her only son, and she would never bear another.

Rawdon looked up, and managed a wan smile. "Sir Roderick assures me that nothing like this will ever happen again. But this man Hawksmoor. . . . I tell you, Stedman, I have never liked him. People talk of Elsworth as though he were some sort of monster, but Hawksmoor. . . . I'm convinced he would throttle me if he thought it would please Roderick." His mouth twisted in disgust.

Galton looked up at Rawdon, wondering if this was genuine disillusionment. "I know what you mean. I feel much the same. Our good Roderick is a little blind in this, but Hawksmoor's utter devotion to him must seem such a useful quality at times."

Neither man spoke for a moment. A slow measured dripping of rain could be heard leaking from the gutter pipe.

"How go things with Wells?" Rawdon asked, obviously changing to a less disturbing subject.

Galton shrugged. "Not as quickly as we hoped, I fear. We need Mr. Littel more than Wells ever admitted."

"I am not surprised to hear it." Rawdon shifted in his chair.

"Do you ever have reservations, Benjamin?" Galton asked suddenly, almost certain that this was a safe question under the circumstances. "Does your conviction waver?"

Rawdon raised his dark eyebrows. "Yes. And more strongly now, after what has happened. I don't care who their fathers were, these were worthy young gentlemen with bright futures ahead of them. It simply cannot be allowed to happen again."

"I agree. I will not condone it twice. Noyes is not pleased either. He had to deal with the situation, and now lives in terror that the duke will learn of it. He will not put himself in that position again, and has said as much to Roderick."

"I have expressed my concerns as well. Roderick is not a monster, Stedman. It was a terrible mistake—one cannot justify it—but it will not happen again. I have Roderick's solemn word on that."

Galton stared at his companion. Not a very strong ally, he thought. Probably not strong enough.

TWENTY-TWO

Kent awoke in a darkened room. He felt uncommonly warm and pushed the coverlets away, trying to remember where he was.

"Averil? Are you awake?" It was the expressionless voice of the countess, quite close by.

He realized that she held one of his hands, and Kent turned his head, looking into the utter darkness of the room.

"How do you feel, Averil?"

"What happened?" he asked.

"You collapsed. Fell hard to the floor. You must tell me how you feel. Is there pain?"

"Pain? No." He stretched his limbs, searching for anything untoward. He realized that the duchess' hand was quite warm in his. "I seem to be whole."

She squeezed his hand and then released it. He heard her move away and realized there was a high-back chair set near to him. "I want you to sit up now."

Kent lay for a second, feeling there was something strange or out of place in this situation, though he could not say what. He felt completely odd, as though something were missing. He pushed himself up, and drew a quick breath.

"Averil?"

Kent turned his focus inward. "I seem to be ... I feel perfectly hale ... I feel vital." He looked up at the shadow before him. "What has happened?"

"It will not last long—a week, perhaps two—and then

you will pay a price for it, Averil, I'm sorry. But we cannot fail in this. I realize that, more than ever, now." She fell silent, then found his hand again in the dark. *"I'm sorry,"* she whispered, and Kent felt that she was apologizing for something more. For all the mistakes of their long lives.

He could not answer. They clung to each other in the dark, her warm, still-soft hands in his. He could not remember the last time they had touched. So long ago that the time would be measured in decades.

"Have you given me the seed, then?" Kent said, dreading the answer.

"No! No, I should never do that. I. . . ." She did not finish.

"Eldrich," Kent said, the word coming out unbidden, like the name of an illness. *She had learned this from Eldrich! It was necromancy. Magic!*

They sat, holding each other's hands tightly. He thought he felt a slight trembling, as though her shoulders shook, as though she wept in the darkness, and the overwhelming sadness flowed down her arms into her hands and his.

🐚 🐚 🐚

Kent's carriage wound slowly through the mist filled streets of early morning. How different this fog looked in the silver morning! How different the world looked.

It is the enchantment, he thought, though it hardly dimmed his spirits. Kent had left the countess' home, all his questions unasked. He still did not dare to presume too much, there had been so many years without word from her. He could not bear that again, even if the years remaining to him were few.

And the truth was that he probably did not need his questions answered: he likely understood only too well. And this understanding left him with a feeling of such profound emptiness—as though her secrecy were a betrayal.

Eldrich had passed at least some of his knowledge on

to the countess. There could be no other explanation. Despite the task that Eldrich had been sworn to complete, he had given up some of what he knew. In Kent's mind there could be only one explanation, and he was sure it was not merely jealousy.

The duchess had been the most beautiful woman Kent had ever seen. Eldrich may have been very old, but Kent knew that age didn't prevent a man from feeling desire—and apparently even ancient mages had ways of increasing their strength. If it had been within Kent's power would he allow that beauty to fade? It had been like art, it was so perfect. In his own life he had watched so many things fade and decay. He knew, absolutely, that he would give his life for the countess. What might Eldrich have given?

Did she take the seed? Did she still appear youthful to the eye? Could that impossible beauty still live? Kent could hardly bear the thought of it. As though some part of his youth still existed, though out of reach.

Of course, at the moment, he too felt youthful—or at least middle-aged. He could not remember feeling so strong, and so at peace—that feeling in the body that one experienced after good strenuous exercise. And his desire had come back as well, rising at the thought of the countess. It was his one great regret, that they had never been lovers. Part of him wanted to go back and storm the walls of her resistance.

Could she really still appear as he remembered? Was that possible? Or, like the King, was she aged and decayed beyond her years? Had the seed betrayed her, too?

The carriage stopped before his house and Kent jumped down to the ground, and then looked around, wondering if he had been seen. Better to lean on his cane a little, though he wanted to vault up the stairs two at a time.

Smithers met him at the door. Despite the hour he had obviously been awake.

"There is a young woman here for you, sir. I could hardly turn her away. She has been waiting some time."

Alissa, Kent thought, and then cautioned himself—best

not to let her rub his feet today! "Did she tell you her name?"

"Miss Leconte, Sir Averil."

Kent stopped as he went to hand Smithers his walking stick. "She came alone?"

"Yes, sir. She's in the library, sir. I've just served her tea and biscuits."

"Thank you, Smithers."

Kent paused at the door to the library, wondering how he looked after his near sleepless night, but then decided he did not care, and opened the door. Tenil rose as he came in, and stood with her hands clasped together as she had before. For a few awkward seconds, neither of them spoke.

"You understand my involvement with Count Massenet?"

"You are his agent?" Kent said.

She nodded. "The count believes that, because I am young, you will be easily influenced by me."

"He is not always subtle," Kent said, feeling her beauty so strongly that it almost touched him. "What do you expect of me?"

"To be honest, I expect you to send me away. And I will remind the count that not everyone suffers from his own weakness."

Kent stood gazing at her, the short curls that fell about her exquisite neck. Something like defiance in her manner. He felt the habits of decades struggling with the energy of his returned youth. "But would you not like to see a painting of my garden before you go?"

She brightened, then hesitated before answering. "You are being too kind."

Kent laughed. He could not help it. The situation seemed so absurd. "Miss Leconte, I could never be too kind to you, try as I might, it would be less than you deserve. Come with me. This house is awash in my paintings and sketches. The attic is so filled with things I am trying to forget that I cannot bear to go up there."

Kent took the young woman on a tour of his paintings and if her interest was feigned Kent thought she was a better actress, even, than singer—and she was a beautiful singer.

In the seldom-used studio, they went through the canvases stacked against the walls and she made the most appreciative sound.

"But this is a child," Tenil said, surprised. "I did not think you were interested in the human figure?" Tenil was still dressed in the clothes she had worn at the Earl's, and as she bent over the canvases the beautiful curve of her breast was revealed to the very edge of her nipple.

"Oh, but I am. She was the daughter of an old friend. It is a study only. But she was playing in my garden and I could not resist. Do you like it?"

"Like it? It is beautiful? Look at her face. She is an angel."

On impulse he said, "If you will sit for me, Miss Leconte, I will gift it to you."

Tenil straightened up, her look very serious. "But it would be an honor to model for you. I could not take this. It is a treasure."

"But I insist," Kent said taking her hand. "You must have it."

Her seriousness did not waver. "Then I will sit for you, in return." She rose up on her toes and kissed him on both cheeks, as the Entonne did. Kent felt such a surge of desire, it was all he could do not to reach out and take her in his arms, even knowing she was an agent of Massenet. And then Kent remembered the countess and his suspicions there.

"I must change and wash," he said. "Would you mind? Shall I have Smithers prepare you something? Are you hungry?"

"No. May I not stay here?" She waved a hand at the paintings yet unseen. "I shall be very, very careful."

Kent nodded.

He ran up the stairs, only realizing it at the top. It had been some years since he had done that. He called for water and washed quickly, setting aside his wig, ignoring strange looks from Smithers.

What on earth was he doing? He should send this girl

off immediately. She might be truly an admirer of Averil Kent, but that would not likely affect her loyalty to Massenet. Women simply did not betray the count.

There was so much for Kent to do. He needed to speak with the Duke of Blackwater. He must find out what Palle was about now. Did the King's Man still believe that Littel was dead? How long would that last?

Kent emerged from his bathing room still rubbing his face with a towel, and there stood Tenil, wearing only her undershift.

"Where shall I stand? Or would you prefer I lie down?"

This was not quite what the countess had in mind when she imbued him with such vitality, he was sure. Unable to stop himself, Kent crossed to her. Without a word he took her in his arms. He did not care if she found his body beautiful, or that she was an agent of the Entonne government. Nor did it matter that this was a false spring, brought about by enchantment. He did not care if her admiration was genuine or if she despised his art. He did not even care if his heart gave out. Nothing mattered.

Kent was not sure how this enchantment the countess had laid upon him worked. He felt strong and vital and young, but he was not sure what the effects of strain might be on his bone and muscle, so he stopped himself from doing some things that came to mind. Even so, he had not had such pleasure in many years.

Her skin was soft and yet it had that tautness that only the young possessed. And she responded to him as Kent had thought a woman never would again. He thought her cries of passion were the most beautiful music he had ever heard—more beautiful than her singing by far. Her caresses seemed to bring his flesh to life—as though she were possessed of magic herself.

Kent's own climax seemed to surge through him like some strange force, like the crashing of waves on the shore. And when it was over he lay gasping, awash in such pleasure. What in the world had the countess done to him?

"You put young men to shame," Tenil whispered,

squirming beneath him. "To think that earlier this night I thought you would fall where you stood."

It was like a slap reminding Kent of what his true task was. "Yes. Look what you've done for me. I feel like you have brought back my youth."

She raised up her head, looking at the clock, and then let it fall back. "I shall have to sit for you some other time, I'm sorry to say. The opera company calls." She giggled. "Though I would rather lie for you, if I have my choice."

When Tenil had gone—slipping out the back, for whatever good that might do—Kent stood at the window looking down into the street. He had slept only part of an hour that night, had love with a woman a third his age, and he felt well. Oh, he was tired, but not devastatingly so. And best of all, his mind felt clear, alert. What was Massenet's reason for sending this woman to him? What else did the count want from him? And why was he so sure that Kent would one day move to Entonne? Kent shook his head. His mind might feel clear, but he could not see the count's design—not yet.

A knock sounded at the door, and at a call Smithers appeared. Kent could not tell if it was disapproval or astonishment on the man's face. "You are awake, sir."

"Yes," Kent said. "I must break my fast, Smithers, bathe, and then sleep for two hours—not a minute more."

Kent turned back to the view as the servant left. A neighbor woman was walking her small dog along the walk, and she bent with each step, leaning heavily on her cane. Kent felt great pity for her, aged and frail as she was—and then he remembered that only a few hours earlier he had looked much the same. He realized that age had always felt like an illness to him—he always expected to recover and feel as he had—as he should. And now it had actually happened. *A week, perhaps, two,* the countess had said. Already that seemed like a sentence— life in the prison of his failing body.

Kent closed his eyes. What would he not do to have his

youth returned? It was easier to say no before he had felt as he did now. He had forgotten what youth was like.

The countess must be near in years to this woman he watched make her slow way along the street. Had she betrayed him and taken the seed? Taken it perhaps for years? But where in the world would she have found it? Where did the mages find it?

Kent felt suddenly a little small for having love with Tenil, for despite the obvious reasons, he was sure his feelings of betrayal had pushed him into it. Young. Did the countess feel like he did now? Had she been so for all these years? And if so, how did she deal with the desires of youth? It was a painful thought, and unworthy, but Kent could not help himself. Of all the women he had known, only the countess brought up such feelings.

TWENTY-THREE

At sunrise Tristam emerged from the shadow of the trees onto the shore of the calm bay. Beacham paced back and forth along the water's edge, occasionally glancing out to the *Swallow*, which stood dark and angular against the blossoming sunrise. Tristam came slowly down the quiet beach, feeling tired and empty and oddly sad after his night journey.

"Ah, Mr. Flattery. Quite a fright you've given me," the midshipman said, obviously relieved and resentful at the same time.

"I'm sorry, Jack, I should have woken you." He realized he did not know what lie to tell, not knowing how long he had been missed. "Have you been awake long?"

"Long enough," Beacham said curtly, and then his gaze fixed on something down the beach. "Is it Mr. Hobbes?"

A lone individual was making his way along the water's edge, limping awkwardly, his shirt flapping lazily in the breeze. Tristam could see that the man staggered.

Without another word the two set out, almost trotting they were so concerned, and as they came closer, their concern grew. Hobbes appeared to have been savagely beaten, his face bruised and stained with blood. He cupped one elbow as though the arm and shoulder was injured, and walked with such a terrible limp that he looked as though he might not manage another step. His clothing was torn and soiled, and smeared in places with crimson.

"Who did this to you?" Beacham asked as they reached the ship's master.

"No one, Mr. Beacham," Hobbes said, his voice sounding dry and broken, like a man overcome by grief. "I went searching for our Varuan friends, hoping to meet some that I knew, and got myself foolishly lost in the dark. I fell—thrice, I fear—once down a steep ravine. Just an old fool, lost in the dark. Nothing more."

Tristam might have believed this had he not developed this strange insight that plagued him. "Did you encounter the viscount on your travels?" he asked quietly.

Hobbes looked at him sharply, but then turned his eyes away. "No, no. Is he not with you?"

"He went off into the dark just after yourself," Beacham said, offering the master his shoulder for support.

"Well, no doubt he will turn up, unless he is foolish enough to go up into the city."

A boat put out from the *Swallow* just then, oars flashing out in unison, and pulling the craft forward toward the trio hobbling along the beach.

"We'll have you aboard in a moment," Beacham said.

"Yes," Hobbes replied, his tone a little distracted, "let's get that over with."

The scene that met them as they scrambled over the bulwarks was not what Tristam had been expecting. Every soul aboard ship stood on the deck. The silence that met their arrival was disturbing. Tristam thought immediately that this reception was meant for them, but then he realized that all the officers and guests stood upon the quarterdeck, and the Jacks had gathered below in the waist—split into two groups that kept a distance from each other. Into the ten-foot gap between the Jacks and the quarter deck the men recently returned from their night on the island stopped, looking about in bewilderment. Beacham gave Tristam a gentle nudge toward the quarterdeck, and it was then that Tristam realized what was in the wind.

As he came to the top of the stairs, Osler unobtrusively put a blade in his hand. Stern looked at the ship's master for the briefest second, and then turned back to the gathered men on the deck. The silence persisted.

A hand touched Tristam's shoulder, and he turned to find himself looking into the eyes of the duchess, who was more alarmed than he ever expected to see her. Her lips formed words, but she dared not utter a sound: *"Where is Julian?"*

Tristam shook his head and shrugged, hoping that his look was sympathetic. *Take a look at Hobbes,* Tristam thought, *that should answer your question.* Had the master managed to do the monster in? Highly unlikely, Tristam thought. Monsters were never so easily vanquished.

"Go on, Mr. Kreel," Stern said, nodding to the large forecastleman who stood half a pace before his mates.

Kreel turned his straw hat carefully in his hands, uncharacteristically subdued. "If we were to find a treasure or take an enemy ship, sir, there'd be prize money for all. That is all we're saying. If this flower is half as valuable as is said ... well, it should not be kept from us who've taken risks equal to the officers and guests. We're poor sailors, Captain Stern. We only want what's fair." He looked up and met Tristam's eye, perhaps by accident. "That's all."

Stern did not answer but raised his eyebrows as though acknowledging what had been said. "There's nothing more?" he said, his voice so quiet that even Tristam found it menacing.

"Well, there is Garvey and Chilsey, sir. Their murderers have not met justice. Not by a long stretch. These heathens had best not get to believing they can kill His Majesty's seamen, sir, or none of us will be safe. They sacrificed men before we Farrlanders came, and made a feast of them, too. And now they are murdering our shipmates, and keeping this flower for their own, as well. We may not be a sloop of war, Captain, but I reckon we can still show them the error of their ways, and should do it, too, before they forget what they're being punished for."

"Is there anything else, *Captain Kreel,* or does that complete your list of demands?"

Kreel looked up sharply. "I've just been picked to speak by the drawing of lots, Captain Stern. I am no more the leader than. . . ." Words escaped him. "I'm just speaking up so we might avoid trouble, sir."

Stern nodded. "I will take everything you have said under consideration," Stern said, addressing the entire gathering. "I will tell you true, though, that there is no special prize being offered for anyone on this voyage. I doubt I shall even make my post for such a voyage, and if things continue as they are . . ." he did not need to explain what that meant, "I may retire from the sea altogether." He raised a hand. "Be about your duties, and I shall give your requests my full consideration. But let me say this. Don't think for a moment that a ship of mutineers can find a place to hide where the women are comely and a man's livelihood can be picked from the trees. The Admiralty knows that if such a thing were allowed to happen once. . . . Well, let me just say that the world is not so large as you might imagine."

Stern stood his ground, staring down his crew, and slowly, in twos and threes, they went back to their duties, nothing being said, but many a look exchanged.

Stern turned immediately to Osler. "Keep a presence on the deck. No change in the duty or shore-leave rosters. No idle hands, Mr. Osler." He half-turned toward the ship's master. "I will begin with Mr. Hobbes," he said curtly, and then disappeared below, the old seaman in his wake, trying to hide his limp.

Tristam stood for a moment, still holding the sword that Osler had given him, suddenly feeling the endless leagues of ocean that separated them from Farrland. A terrible row broke out below, obviously muffled, but not nearly enough. Stern was taking the ship's master to task for dereliction of duty. Poor Stern. This was not the moment when he could afford to have his officers falter.

"Where has he gone?" the duchess whispered to Tristam.

"Julian?" He shrugged. "He and Hobbes disappeared just at dusk."

"He left you alone?!" she said, and Tristam could not tell if she was angered or terribly disturbed by this.

"I was with Beacham."

She turned away as though to hide her reaction. "I must find him," she said suddenly.

"I am not sure that Stern will let you ashore given the circumstances."

"I do not depend upon Stern to approve my decisions," she said angrily. "Look how he has mismanaged things thus far."

Tristam shrugged. "Though it was likely Hobbes overhearing your conversation that set this all in motion."

She looked up reproachfully, as though hurt that Tristam did not support her as she obviously believed he should. Her surprise was so great that she didn't respond for a moment. "Young Varuan maidens will not get you through what is to come, Tristam," she said suddenly. "Do not for a second doubt that." And she spun away quickly and went down the hatch without looking at him again.

Osler came up then, and took the sword from his hand. He raised his eyebrows at Tristam, obviously having witnessed, if not overheard, the exchange with the duchess.

"The favorite of the King," Osler said quietly.

"It must have slipped my mind," Tristam answered, the sarcasm not very well masked.

"The captain will want to speak with you soon, I imagine. What in the world happened to Hobbes? Did the Varuans attack him?"

Tristam shook his head. "I don't know. He claims he got lost in the dark and fell several times, once down a ravine."

"Hobbes, lost?" Osler said, clearly not believing for a second. "The man has a binnacle in his head. Have you never heard of his feat when his ship foundered? Sailed the ship's boat across the Gray Ocean and made his landfall at the very mouth of Wickham Harbor in the fog! Don't tell me he was lost."

"I am only repeating the master's own words," Tristam

said, and then noticed the captain's steward motioning to him. "My audience, I think."

Stern was in the great cabin with Llewellyn and the duchess. The captain had taken up a place before the open transom windows, and stood with his coat thrown back and his fist on his hip, as he did when his temper was in ascendance.

"Our voyage is in great peril," he said, keeping his voice low so that he would not be heard on deck, but hiding none of his anger. "Two men dead, and every man in the crew demanding 'prize money' for this seed we seek. This secret seed. I, for one, let no word of this matter escape," he said, the accusation clear. He paced quickly across the small open space, then stopped and looked at each of the others in turn. "Landsmen believe discipline on His Majesty's ships is insured by dire punishments, but this has never been the truth. No, it is fairness and concern for the men's well-being—mixed with a just use of the lash, to be sure—that keeps a ship safe from the crew's worst impulses." He pointed a long finger forward. "Those men before the mast, they have not a hope for anything in this world but poverty and the succor of drink. Not one in a thousand will make the rank of master. And here they see a chance for some small sum— though a fortune to their eyes. They might buy their way out of the service and have a bit of land and a cottage, for there is commonly no prize money to be had on a voyage of discovery. And they feel it more on this voyage where the dangers they have met are not of the natural kind. Lost Cities, and strange peoples, necromancy, and death at the hands of "friendly" natives. They feel the injustice of this. They feel they're owed something for standing brave before such madness, for any Jack would face a thousand battles before they'd choose to face anything deemed unnatural. And now what am I to do?" He glared at the others, obviously believing they were the cause of his problems, mere landsmen who did not have the least understanding of the ways of the navy.

"I cannot, by order, admit the existence of this seed. And even if I did, I can't, on my own authority, give them prize money for its procurement. Yet, have they not stood their ground in the face of the one thing that they fear most? Is there not some justice in their demands?" He turned and stared out over the lagoon, lost in his dilemma.

"I could offer to reward the crew at the voyage's end," the duchess said quietly. "Ten gold crowns for each man, or even twenty, from my own purse. I'm sure the King would approve."

Stern turned and eyed the duchess for a second, then shook his head. "I did not mean to suggest such a course. It is against regulations. If we begin offering bribes to every crew that threatens mutiny.... Well, the Admiralty would never allow it. I will keep discipline in my crew, though it shall not be an easy task now."

The duchess almost took a step toward the officer. "But, Captain Stern, you said yourself that the Jacks deserve something for what they've done, and I think you were right. It has been a disturbing voyage for them in many ways, with all their superstitions.... A few crowns at the end of it all would seem like a small return. And it would come from me personally, not from the Admiralty. A token of my appreciation, not something that others would expect from their captain. We dare not endanger the voyage . . . for the King's sake."

Stern had gone terribly quiet, his anger apparently past. "No. Leave the crew to me. I will deal with them without resorting to bribery. I did not for a moment mean to suggest it." He looked down at his hand, suddenly, turning it over and flexing the fingers as though doubting their sureness or strength.

The duchess looked as if she would speak but chose to say nothing.

"Doctor Llewellyn," Stern said, "will you see to Mr. Hobbes, and then relate the conclusions from your examination back to me?"

The doctor nodded, obviously glad to be released. Stern thought briefly, then drew himself up to his full height. "I shall send a party ashore to find Lord Elsworth.

Duchess. Mr. Flattery." He went quietly out, all of his bluster gone.

Tristam waited for the duchess to speak, but when she did not: "You did not press your offer of gold with much conviction, Elorin," Tristam said.

She moved to the seat by the transom window and drew her knees up so that she turned sideways and stared out over the lagoon, her beautiful chin propped on one hand. "Give me credit for knowing something of the ways of men, Tristam. Just the crew's knowledge of the existence of *regis* spells the death of Stern's career. And I'm sure you're right—it was not Stern who let this knowledge slip. But to stoop to having a woman bribe his crew to avoid a mutiny. . . . Well, the captain has some pride left. This might be the last voyage of his ill-fated career, but he will not have it said that he required a woman to bribe his crew so that he could make port. Poor Stern could not bear that. I'm not sure what we will do, for the men certainly do feel they have a right to some part of this treasure we seek—though of course they have no idea what is really taking place."

"And what is taking place?" Tristam said. "Why *are* we really here?"

She turned away from her view, examining Tristam with that disinterested look that she had perfected. "Will you go ashore with me, Tristam, and search for Julian? Did he do this to Hobbes? Is that what you think?"

Tristam shrugged, not much willing to cooperate when his question was so obviously ignored.

"What led to the two of them going off? Did they go together or did Julian follow?"

Tristam hesitated, but the duchess' real distress touched him. "Hobbes looked as though he were entirely overwhelmed at the deaths of Garvey and the young midshipman, which makes his involvement in what befell them almost certain. Once we had borne the bodies down to the shore, he disappeared into the forest. I didn't see Julian go, but I think he followed."

The duchess nodded, closing her eyes for a moment. "Do you think Hobbes could have intended to take his own life? Was his despair that great?"

"It is possible, I suppose."

She nodded. "It probably began innocently enough. He would have gone to watch Hobbes make his end."

"That is your idea of innocence!?" Tristam blurted out, his offense at the very idea obvious.

The duchess turned on him. "For Julian, yes. But it might have gone wrong, somehow. We absolutely must find him." She put her fingers to the ridges above her eyes, and tears appeared, though she made no sound.

"I will go with you," Tristam said quickly.

"Thank you," she managed and then turned her head away, propping her chin on her hand, and staring out across the azure lagoon as though she watched the white terns awash in the wind.

Stern did not protest as Tristam expected him to, but then perhaps the captain was beginning to have his own suspicions about the viscount and would rather the duchess dealt with her brother. The duchess and Tristam went ashore with a party of reliable men, all armed. Beacham and Tobias Shuk and three stout Jacks who earlier had stood apart from their mates during the confrontation with the captain.

They did not go thirty paces into the village before they saw the viscount, sitting on the trunk of a felled tree, staring down at the ground like a man in a state of catatonia. He did not hear the others approach, and when they were fifty paces off, the duchess raised her hand.

"Lord Elsworth is sometimes subject to fits of melancholia," she said, as though revealing this secret to her closest friends. "Perhaps it would be better if we did not all approach him. Tristam? Would you accompany me?"

The naturalist followed the duchess, who made every effort to move silently. When they were a few paces away, she stopped Tristam with a hand on his arm, and went forward alone.

"Julian?" she said pleasantly, keeping her voice quiet and calm. "Julian. It is Elorin." The viscount did not move or show any sign that he had heard.

Tristam found that he had become quite tense, and

gripped his walking staff with both hands, as though he would be forced to go to the duchess' aid at any second. How unpredictable was this man?

The duchess crouched down three paces before her brother, and smiled at him. "Julian?" she said softly. "It's all right. It's me. I've come to take you home."

Tristam realized that he felt a certain revulsion at this sight. How could she do it? The man was a ghoul.

Lord Elsworth raised his head a fraction, but Tristam could not see if his eyes were opened or closed.

"Nothing is amiss, my dear. Come along and we will find you a bath and a meal. No harm was done, Julian. Come along, now."

The viscount took a sharp breath, and shuddered as though he had been touched by a ghost of a breeze. "I'm no longer his servant, Elorin," he said as though he referred to a tragedy beyond imagining.

"Julian! You promised never to speak of this again," she said sharply.

"But he would not take me," he went on in the same voice. "Neither of us, worthy of him."

"Let this go, Julian," she said, an edge of desperation in her words.

He raised his hands, which had been clasped between his thighs, hidden by the sleeves of his shirt. One hand was red with blood, and the other held a dagger.

"My word! Julian? What have you done?" The duchess moved forward instinctively, but the viscount's head snapped up and she froze in place.

"Put it down, Julian, I beg you. Put it down, please."

"I am cast out," he said, a note of desperation entering his voice, and then he began to sob, sob with the abandon of a child whose heart had been broken.

The duchess moved forward then. Prying the dagger from his fingers, she cast it away and tried to pull his hands from his face. "Help me, Tristam, please."

The naturalist went to her assistance with no enthusiasm. He could hardly bear to witness this scene, let alone become involved.

The duchess had pulled the viscount's bloody hand free,

and tried to open it, searching for a wound. Wiping at it with Tristam's handkerchief, she revealed a hideous gash. The viscount had tried to incise the radial artery. And around the wrist circled the bloody form of a snake, carved raggedly into the skin with the point of a knife.

The duchess led her brother through the trees to one of the bathing pools the islanders used, and here Tristam helped her undress and bathe him, while the others discreetly disappeared. The viscount was like a man who had slipped half into catatonia, hardly aware of what was done. He clasped his hands together obsessively, as though he held something of immense importance there.

With her own hands, the duchess rinsed her brother's soiled and bloody clothing and spread it over the bushes to dry. The viscount sat in the shade, his hands still clenched, the only sign that he recovered was a loosening of the knotted muscles. Tristam gathered some fruit and opened a drinking nut, but the viscount could not be induced to take any sustenance.

"Let him be for a while," the duchess said. "He will come around on his own." She looked toward the trees. "Do you think the others can see us?"

"I'm sure they have no desire to witness what is done here," Tristam said, immediately worried that his honesty would not be appreciated, but the duchess just nodded distractedly.

She began to open her blouse, and in a moment had slipped out of all her clothing and went to the edge of the pool, tying her hair into a knot as she went. Tristam could not take his eyes from her. He thought immediately that she had lost weight from worry, for she seemed tall and willowy. For the life of him he could not imagine why such a woman was worried about the effects of age. She was so perfectly beautiful.

She waded slowly into the water, brushing her fingers across the surface and then settled down with the water just lapping about her shoulders. She turned back to Tristam, a tiny bit of her worry washed away by the immersion in water. "I am not entirely sure why Palle sent you, Tristam," she said suddenly, as though she had just registered his question now. "He clearly did not want you to find the seed for the King, but what his own purpose was, I cannot guess. Llewellyn must know but, of course, will never say. Although everyone thinks that I convinced His Majesty to allow me to come on this voyage, it was the King that sent me."

She moved her hands just beneath the surface, as if treading water, though Tristam knew her feet touched the earth. "As you heard me say, 'we follow Tristam's course now.' You are their lodestone, Tristam. Palle has sent you to begin some process. For a time I thought that the things that happened to you in the Lost City were the events they hoped for. Your part might be done. But Llewellyn, in a fit of anger, said something that made me think this was not so." She took two steps toward him, looking around as though her words might be overheard. Tristam could see her body through the clear water. It distorted slightly in the light slanting into the pool, as though part of her existed in another world—a world that had its own physical laws.

Tristam waited for her to tell him what Llewellyn had said. He leaned forward in expectation.

The duchess examined her brother who sat unmoving on the bank. Then she turned back to Tristam. "If I can take the seed back to the King, I will, but I can't help but feel that this is not the reason we are here. History, Tristam, is like the web of a spider. Those who are ensnared never see it until too late. The web is ever-expanding, ever more complex, growing as history grows. Without our realizing, some strand, some event from the past, reaches out and wraps about us. Struggle against it as we might, we cannot escape. Why we are chosen is a mystery, but there is nothing we can do but try desperately to see the pattern in which we have been caught.

"This is what I think has happened, Tristam. Some strand of events from the past has wafted out on the breeze of time, and has us in its grip. Our own lives and intentions have become unimportant. History has chosen us, and there is no hiding, no shirking. We must somehow attach this strand to the future, though where in the web we choose to do this may have the most unexpected repercussions." She came up to the edge of the pool and reached out with her dripping hands to take hold of Tristam.

"But what is at the center?" Tristam asked. "What is the spider?"

She shook her head. "We are only human, Tristam. How can we know that?" She took his hand and kissed it. "The mages did not regard time as we do. They lived long, and began enterprises to be executed over generations. They are gone, but who knows what enterprise they might have left behind, unfinished, waiting for others to complete."

"That is what you think? We are fulfilling some plan initiated by a mage?" Tristam did not like even the sound of this. Already he felt that he walked a preordained line, that free will had been denied him.

The duchess shrugged. "I think there is more to all of this than anyone realizes. Consider what happened in the Lost City. Did it not seem that those people had been waiting for you? Think of it: the Ruin of Farrow perched atop a temple in an unknown part of the world. And we found our way there. Found our way to that one island in a chain of a hundred thousand such islands. Sir Roderick Palle is the most ordinary of men with the most ordinary aspirations. He had not the slightest idea that such a thing could occur, let me assure you. Llewellyn was staggered by what happened. Absolutely staggered. I saw it."

"But the mage who set this all in motion . . . what did he intend?" Tristam said, his voice subdued and small.

The duchess rose up out of the water and embraced him, encircling him with her soft arms, dripping water on his face, pressing her wet body close to him. "I don't know, Tristam. That is why we must stay close together. Support each other, at all costs. We are caught in a mystery and need all of our wits and strength."

Tristam closed his eyes and felt this woman close to him, her wet skin cooling his like a refreshing breeze, even as he warmed from desire. "But why . . . ?" he whispered. "Why in this round world did Julian cut his wrist in imitation of mine?"

"He wants to be like you. Free of his demons. Free."

No, Tristam realized, filled with sudden insight. *He believes he has lost his master and seeks to draw mine.*

Tristam had escaped the glade of the bathing pool, leaving the duchess with her brother. As he came out into the village, Tristam found Tobias Shuk standing over the almost-completed hull of a canoe. The carpenter bent over, examining the craftsmanship, but he would not lay his hands on the wood.

"You have found your priest-builders, I see," Tristam said.

Tobias looked up. "Their work, at least. Abandoned when they fled our revenge."

Tristam looked down at the great hollowed tree, carved without proper tools. "Are you well pleased with your noble islanders?" Tristam asked.

Tobias squatted down on his haunches, as Tristam had seen the islanders' do. "I would be better pleased if they had left our shipmates alive. But, yes, they are much as I hoped. Not perfect, of course, and they have the same misguided idea of inherited worth: aristocracy. But do you see how genuine are their concerns and lives? Not taken up with the polish and scroll work. Their time is spent on the important things—food and shelter and spirit and children, singing and dance and. . . ."

"And love," Tristam said.

"And love, yes." Tobias turned back to the canoe, rising to sight along one gunwale. "Though I shall not fault their morality until I have some proof that it brings them harm. So far, it makes me question our own practices." He moved to the bow to examine the head carved there, an elaborate, long-necked sea creature. "This flower that everyone speaks of . . . is it the herb that friend Llewellyn needs to affect his cure?"

Tristam was not sure what to answer. The carpenter turned his large, sincere eyes on Tristam. "There is an herb the Varuans value above all else, Mr. Shuk. Only the

King and his high priests may possess it. Any other who so much as touches it is put to death. Garvey and Chilsey did not know this. Do not seek it for Llewellyn. I am not sure the doctor is being entirely honest with us when he speaks of his condition. Do not risk your life for Llewellyn, Mr. Shuk, he may be less of a friend than you suppose. Do you take my meaning, sir?"

Tobias nodded. He opened his mouth as though he would speak, but a call cut him short.

"Mr. Flattery!"

They turned to find Wallis crossing what was almost a common in the center of the village.

"I hope you bring us good news, Mr. Wallis," Tristam said, realizing that the look on the man's face did not indicate that his mission had met with great success.

"Well, there are no signs that the islanders want anything but peace, that is certain, but they can conceive of no way in which that peace can be achieved but for your captain to admit that his men were in the wrong." Wallis looked a bit distressed. "The King might find a way around this, but he remains entirely taken up with his ceremonies."

"But how long can they stay up in the forest, Wallis? Certainly they must come down eventually."

"They are patient in ways that we are not, Mr. Flattery, and what would seem hardship to Farrlanders is hardly inconvenience to them."

"Can no one see that both sides are wrong?" Tobias said, his voice filled with sadness. "Garvey and Chilsey should never have broken the tapu, and the Varuans should not have killed them so needlessly. But now what do we do? The crew are calling for revenge for their mates, and the Varuans are unable to admit that their laws are arbitrary, and should not have been so callously applied to guests who did not understand the consequences of their actions."

Wallis sat down in the shade of a palm. "What you say has some truth to it, Mr. Shuk," he conceded. Clearly he understood both sides too well to be able to see a solution. "Anua asks that you make yourself available this evening, Mr. Flattery. I am to make this request of Captain Stern if necessary."

"What does Anua want of me?" Tristam asked, his suspicions rising.

"She would not say, but I am certain she means you no harm. After all it would be easy to send a party down to fetch you off the beach right now, if she wanted to take you against your will. Do not be afraid. Anua is a woman greatly honored by her people. You will be under her protection. She also asks that the viscount accompany you."

"The *va'ere?*"

Wallis looked up at him, clearly uncomfortable. "Yes."

TWENTY-FOUR

Bertillon did not like mornings. The light pained his eyes, his mood was never anything but sour. People seemed bent on tormenting him, asking him foolish questions, bringing him things he did not want. It was only after two terrible hours that he began to feel more himself. Women with whom he had spent the night said he was transformed in the morning—the kind of man they would never have consented to spend the night with, had they but known. Fortunately the world seemed to take its proper form by the time the sun was a little above the bell towers, or Bertillon would likely have slept alone for the rest of his years.

The morning was not that far advanced, unfortunately, and the musician wasn't happy to have been summoned at such an hour. Of course, Massenet didn't need to sleep, or so it often seemed to Bertillon—and the count was almost twice his age!

"Bloody fog," Bertillon said as he looked out the window of his carriage. In truth, it was beginning to clear, but he ignored that. Better to vent his anger on the fog than the count.

The musician wondered what had led to the hasty summons. Although he made no attempt to hide his connection to the ambassador, Bertillon was careful to disguise the nature of that connection. It was, after all, one of the ambassador's duties to promote Entonne culture in Farrland, and it was well known that Count Massenet was a lover of music—especially beautiful young singers. So it was not at all unusual for Bertillon and Massenet to meet often. But to call Bertillon to his home early in the morning—that was not necessarily wise. The musician did not like it. He was not a member of the embassy staff—which meant he had no diplomatic protection. A charge of spying would likely mean his death, unless his Imperial Entonne Majesty could be convinced to pay a substantial sum into the coffers of the Farr government. Something Bertillon dearly hoped the aging monarch would do.

The carriage pulled up sharply before Massenet's residence—no apartment in the embassy for this ambassador, who liked to keep many of his activities from the prying eyes of even his own people.

Bertillon found the count sitting at a table, all the news and magazines of Avonel spread out before him, coffee steaming in a bowl.

"Ah, Charl! You can't imagine what I have learned this morning." No apology for dragging the musician out so early, or for compromising his safety. The usual Massenet. Whatever he had learned seemed to delight him more than a little.

"Well, if I can't imagine, you will have to tell me."

The count poured his guest coffee. "You saw Kent last night at the opera?"

"And gave him your message, yes." Bertillon settled back in his chair, sipping his coffee, hoping the world would soon undergo its daily transformation and become a reasonable place once again.

"And how did he seem to you?"

"Exhausted beyond measure. I am concerned about him, in fact."

"And what would you say if I told you that not long before sunrise, after being out the entire night, this same Averil Kent had passionate love with a woman a third his age. Not just passionate, but prolonged."

Bertillon stopped with the cup at his lip. "Kent? But ... the most accomplished actor in the world could not have been so convincing. The man had no hint of color in his face. He trembled to raise his opera glass."

"Exactly so. When I saw him, I thought our alliance would be brief, for he must surely expire within weeks. I can't believe such a thing could be feigned."

"Nor can I. He even appeared to be making an effort to *hide* his infirmity rather than convince others of it." Bertillon set his cup back on the table. He realized he must look a bit stunned. "Is he taking the seed, or is his infirmity an act? And if it is an act, why?"

Massenet rose from his chair, crossing the room slowly. The sun penetrated the fog then, casting its pure light through the large windows. The count appeared to examine his shadow, as though to be sure it really was his own. "I can only think that he has been careful to hide his vigor from us. That, or he came so near to collapse that he began to take the seed. Though I don't know when, or how long it takes to have an effect."

"It is a difficult thing to give up, once begun," Bertillon said. "Youth is a difficult enough habit to break."

Massenet looked up as though he thought he were being criticized, but he saw Bertillon lost in thought. "It does make me wonder about the intentions of our ally," Massenet said quietly.

Bertillon nodded. "But what a temptation. . . . Could you resist it?"

Massenet looked down at the musician, squinting in the sunlight. "I must," he said, "for I was not born with talent. But Kent has been giving in to temptation lately. He might begin by telling himself it is only so that he might complete his task, but it will not end there, I think. Don't forget that he took a large diamond as the price for his loyalty. Temptation. He is cooperating with a foreign government."

Bertillon looked up at Massenet, wondering if his utter shock was apparent. "I am quite sure Averil Kent is an honorable gentleman. He truly believes that Palle's intentions are a threat to everyone. Otherwise you would never have caught him in your snare, which I'm sure you know."

Massenet raised a finger. "But he did not return the stone."

Bertillon paused, and then said quietly, "Well, it is of enormous value. Such a thing might prove useful one day. After all, Kent may be forced to fly if things do not go as we hope." Bertillon looked down at the papers spread across the table. It was utterly like Massenet to perform a seduction and then think less of the person who had fallen to his overture. Not that he ever let anyone know. Bertillon was certain that Massenet was never less than polite to any woman who had shared his bed—he might act as though it had never happened, but he was charming about it.

And now Kent was being viewed in the same way. The painter had been taken in by Massenet's cunning, and how could the count maintain his regard for someone like that? It occurred to Bertillon at that moment that Massenet might view him the same way. How would he ever know? As long as he went on being useful, the count would treat Bertillon like a colleague of great value. As he would Kent.

"If you were Averil Kent, where would you hide Mr. Littel?"

Bertillon looked down at his cup. "I told you that Noyes was dispatched to County Coombs with some haste. From all I can learn, there has been some commotion there. Are you sure Mr. Littel really did escape? Kent is not lying in this?"

Massenet paced to the window, folding his hands at his back. "I can think of no reason for him to lie."

"Unless we have not taken his measure at all. What if he desires this knowledge for himself? After all, you think he might be taking the seed."

Massenet nodded. He did not answer Bertillon for a long moment, and then spoke almost to himself, his voice sad. "Why did he take my diamond?"

❦　❦　❦

Littel had been anxious most of the journey. Only when they entered Avonel's city limits did he begin to relax. Jaimy decided not to tell the scholar that this was the part of their journey that caused him the greatest concern. He pulled the curtain back an inch and looked out. Lamplighters were setting their globes aglow, and dusk came over the city like a gray bird settling onto her clutch of glowing eggs.

"Not far now," Littel said.

"So I assume," Jaimy answered, though they had not been told their destination. They were joining the countess in Avonel—nothing more.

Now that they neared his home Jaimy had begun to feel some guilt about his attraction to Angeline. He had done nothing wrong, of course, but there was a nagging thought that undermined this justification somewhat. Had the opportunity arisen, he wasn't utterly convinced that he would have kept his vow to Alissa. Even now he hoped that he might see Angeline again.

There had been less conversation during the journey than Jaimy had expected. Littel had been fretting silently, and Jaimy had been thinking about women. Now the scholar stretched and his face lit with a smile.

"Do you think Palle and Wells will try to perform these rituals?"

"Rituals? Was there more than one?"

"I'm assuming the text Wells worked on was a ritual. He would not speak of it, but the questions he posed, the odd word or line he asked my opinion of—they led me to believe it was a ritual."

"I can't imagine what they're planning," Jaimy said.

"The countess, she seemed to take these matters as seriously as Wells and his group."

"You don't take it seriously?"

Littel seemed to consider for a moment. "I didn't really worry too much about that, to begin with. It was the most fascinating linguistic challenge I had ever encountered. I had never even dreamed of finding such a thing! And here it was, unknown to other scholars. I am not one to worry overly about recognition, but I have suffered more than my share of abuse from the conservative element of my profession. But this text! It would make my name. No one would be able to criticize my theories after this." He paused, perhaps going over events in his mind. "I thought I should talk them out of their intention of keeping it secret. They were intelligent men after all. But then, even before I talked to you, or met the countess, I had begun to have doubts. It was the text itself. . . ." A look of frustration crossed his face. "I can't really explain, but the longer I worked on it the more powerful it seemed. As though it started out a work of fiction and then began to take on substance. I began to see the world described, hear the characters' voices." He shrugged. "I was very slow to realize that they would not let me walk away, knowing what I know. They treated me well enough, chiding me, offering me money. Hinting at even greater rewards. But it was not until they tried to murder us on the road—murder us in cold blood—that I realized they were not merely eccentrics, deluding themselves about the mages. These were powerful men willing to do whatever was necessary to keep this knowledge secret. Even going so far as to murder the son of one of the kingdom's most powerful men. I woke up then. They did not do that without reason." Littel turned and looked at Jaimy. "I have to thank you, Lord Jaimas, for getting me through this ordeal. I didn't thank you properly before, but I realize, now, what you did. I was no friend in trouble, but a complete stranger. Though I hope that has changed now." He smiled.

Jaimy tried to smile as well. "Changed utterly, Egar. We are more than friends. We are fellow fugitives. Did you not play at being highwaymen when you were a child? Well, our lot is far worse than that, and I can't see how it is going to change."

❦ ❦ ❦

"Believe us dead?" Jaimy sat in his chair looking toward the countess, who not only stayed in shadow but appeared to wear a veil. "How in the world did they come to believe that?"

The flat tones of the countess revealed little emotion. "They murdered some innocent young men, I fear. I am not sure who they were. It is a terrible thing, but it means they have given up searching for you—at least for now. No doubt these poor young men will be missed, and then. . . ."

Jaimy looked over at Littel who sat with his eyes pressed shut.

"Do not lose sight of the truth, either of you. These deaths were none of your doing. Palle and his followers bear full responsibility. Do not forget that."

"And Mr. Kent?" Jaimy asked.

"He is well. You might see him soon. But I stress, you must stay hidden. I am not even sure you should return to your home, Lord Jaimas, despite your desire to see your family and fiancée."

Jaimy considered her words, but did not protest. Was Angeline here, in this house?

"There is someone else whose acquaintance you shall want to make." She rose gracefully from her chair. "Come," she said, gesturing for the others to go ahead.

They went through a door into the next room, almost as dimly lit as the first, though there were two shaded lamps set on a table, and someone hunched over there, working. At the sound of the door he looked up, his spectacles crooked on his nose, a skein of loose hair projecting out from the side of his face. Jaimy thought he had seldom seen anyone who looked so comic, but then the man's eyes suddenly focused, and his look was so serious, so intelligent, that Jaimy's smile disappeared.

"Mr. Valary," the countess said, lingering in the shadowed doorway. "May I introduce Lord Jaimas Flattery, and Mr. Egar Littel. I think you are aware of each other?"

The man named Valary almost bounced from his chair. "I have looked forward to this moment more than you can imagine." He actually shook hands with Egar first, clearly not much impressed by the son of a duke. "I have admired your work for years, sir. And this. . . ." He turned and gestured grandly toward the papers spread over the table. "It is a work of genius, I can tell you, and I know something of these matters."

"Mr. Valary is our resident authority on mage lore," the countess said. She had taken a seat away from the light.

Valary bowed toward the countess. "I am but one of two," he said with great courtesy.

"I had hoped the two of you might make some sense of all this. We need only Kent and we shall have all the pieces we have gathered in one place."

The countess gave Littel and Valary leave to examine the text together, which only their good manners prevented them from doing. The two huddled over the table, and Jaimy took a chair opposite them, pushing it back so that he did not exclude the countess who sat across the room, listening to the conversation.

Valary explained his reordering of the text, surprising Littel. The younger man pored over the pages, considering.

"I take your point, Mr. Valary. It does make more sense, if 'sense' is a word we can use in describing this." He brushed a hand over the pages.

"Did the others, Wells and company, have this exact translation?" the countess asked. "You made no progress of which they are unaware?"

"No. I'm afraid I hid nothing from them. Wells and this man Llewellyn were often at my side, and by the time I had decided to escape them, I had completed almost everything you see here."

"How capable is Wells, do you think?" Jaimy asked.

Littel stood for a moment considering. "Capable enough. At the risk of sounding vain, he learned much from me. But he is not intuitive. 'Plodding' is the word I would choose to describe him, but he will eventually get the job done. Of course, we do not know the length of the text he held back. It could be quite short. It would make sense that Wells kept the simplest sections to tackle alone." Littel considered a second. "My contribution to their endeavor was in the translation of the sections that were meant to be spoken—by far the most difficult parts for they were in a much older language. Wells and Llewellyn were not of one mind on the usefulness of this. Oh, certainly they wanted to know what was being said, but Dr. Llewellyn believed it was not strictly necessary to the performance of the ritual, for it was meant to be performed in that language, if you see what I mean. And he seemed quite certain that he knew the purpose of the ritual, though he never elaborated around me. But the sections in what they called the 'mage language'; I gave them those, I'm afraid."

Valary stood, looking around at the others. "If I may explain a bit more. . . . The text appears to be broken into a ritualistic chant—what is said by the person performing it—and description of physical aspects—the parts of the ritual that must be performed—and these are in vastly different languages, or so it appears." He looked over at the young scholar who nodded distractedly. "One language is not so different from our ancient tongues—once one sees some of it translated, it begins to make sense. Fortunately Mr. Littel is possessed of extraordinary recall, but normal men, like Wells and myself, must spend hours sifting through old books and manuscripts searching for words that might be descendants of the words in this text. Some have no descendants, we so must fill in around them and hope that, eventually, their meaning will become clear—difficult when a word is found only once or twice in the entire text. In a way it would be easier if we had more. If we had the piece Wells is working on, or some other text, it would pose more problems, but provide solutions to others."

Littel was nodding his head in a agreement. "Though I wish it were true that I had no need of references. Unfortunately I'm almost as dependent upon them as the next scholar. There are any number of words here that I have not yet deciphered." He looked down at the text, a bit unsettled perhaps. "It is the greatest mystery," he said quietly. "The greatest mystery."

ೀ ೀ ೀ

Kent had slept two hours that morning and arisen with a smile on his face, and no sense of exhaustion or nagging pain, as was usual. Two more hours were given over to a sketch of the King, while the memory was fresh, and then the artist had taken himself off to his club, hoping to find some of his compatriots and perhaps learn something about what went on in Avonel.

He took his usual table by the window and watched gentleman stream in. Talk, it seemed, centered on the just-declared Regency Council, and the state of the King's health—a subject of constant speculation.

The artist ate alone, trying to graciously deflect invitations from several tables. There were only certain individuals with whom he wished to speak. A grand coach arrived at the doors below, reminding Kent of his meeting here with Massenet. And this brought up thoughts of Tenil, which caused a strange sense of physical pleasure and euphoria to tide through his body. It was an effort to hide his vitality and sense of well being.

Although he half-expected Massenet to emerge, to Kent's surprise Sir Roderick Palle stepped down from the carriage, and only a moment later a servant approached his table.

"Sir Roderick is asking if he might join you, Sir Averil."

Kent tried to show no surprise. "Of course. It would be my pleasure."

Kent rose and made a leg to the new regent, and Palle waved him to his seat. There was a brief silence in the room as the gathered gentlemen witnessed the arrival of their new ruler—one of three, at least—and then the hum of conversation began again. Recent change of rank aside, Palle was not a new face here.

"You look well, Sir Averil," the King's Man offered. "You are one of the few people I know who appear to be getting younger. Massenet is another. But then I am told his youth is a gift from enchanting young singers."

Any hope that Kent had harbored of this being a chance meeting was dispelled.

A servant asked Roderick's pleasure, and the King's Man turned back to the painter. "I think it is time for us to speak candidly, Kent. If I may borrow an image from the natural world, for some time we have both been sitting like spiders at the center of our respective webs, our fingers on the strands, alert to every vibration. And we are not alone in this endeavor—our friend, the charming Count Massenet has been similarly engaged." Wine arrived and the King's Man took a moment to taste it and have glasses poured for them both. "The King's health," Palle said, raising his glass, and Kent joined him, dearly needing something to moisten his suddenly dry mouth.

Palle smoothed the tablecloth before him, not raising his eyes. "Within the palace walls, Mr. Kent, you have several admirers, which makes charging you with treason more than a little difficult. But not, I will tell you, entirely impossible." He looked up, meeting Kent's eyes, and it was all Kent could do not to look away. "It isn't a course of action I wish to take, of course. You are a national treasure, Sir Averil, and I am well aware of it. You are also acting from a misguided sense of honor. I despair to think that you trust my intentions less than those of Massenet." He looked down again, shaking his head sadly.

Kent glanced out the window, looking for the palace guards that would take him away. He felt his palms begin to sweat. *Treason.* They could behead a man for treason.

"Let me make one last effort, Sir Averil, and I do hope you will give what I say your most serious consideration. My loyalty is to Farrland, and to the royal court. My endeavors have no purpose but to protect those interests. Although I hardly expect to be believed when I say this; I am willing to give my life for my principles.

"I am not a terribly appealing man, I realize. Women have never found me fair. My conversation is not spiced with wit, and I was not born with a surfeit of personal charm. I am well aware that I cannot appreciate art as it should be appreciated. But I serve, Mr. Kent. I serve the interests of my nation. And in this it matters little what people think of me. Men like Massenet are able to turn others to their purpose by the sheer force of their personality. But Massenet is not to be trusted. I'm sure you are aware of the truth behind Lord Kastler's suicide? Our charming Entonne does not lay awake nights, suffering for his part in this tragedy, I can assure you."

Palle turned and stared out the window for a moment. He was like a man performing a task that he found terribly distressing. A bearer of the worst news. Then he turned back to Kent, looking suddenly tired. "I look at you, Sir Averil, a man suddenly restored to strength. No. Make no explanation. I have seen this before. I also know where it leads if one does not posses certain qualities and knowledge ... and what happens when the physic is withheld. It is terrible, Kent. I should not like to see anyone suffer such a fate—especially one I esteem." The King's Man lifted his spoon unconsciously, staring at his reflection in its bowl, as though trying to see what it was that he lacked that he should be so mistrusted. "I shall make you an offer, Mr. Kent, in good faith. You may speak to Rawdon about it, or Wells, or any other who might reassure you of my sincerity." He looked up at Kent with his blank, unreadable stare. "I will offer you a place on our council, not the regency council, but the true cabinet. You shall have your say in all matters, and do not think that we are so united that you will never be heard. We are not of one mind, I will tell you. Whatever we learn in these matters that so concern you will be put to your judgment. I will even offer you the position of liaison with Massenet, so that he will be assured that we do not seek the domination of Entonne, which I tell you we do not. And finally, Kent, I will offer you your continued vitality, if that is within our power. You may live as you do now for some considerable span of years. Your art will be renewed. You might have all the young mistresses you desire, for you are much admired. Think of it, Sir Averil, double your span of years, perhaps. Like being granted a second life." He sat, staring at the artist, gauging the effect of his words.

"But how do you know I will cooperate? I might say 'yes' only for my own purposes, and to avoid this undeserved charge of treason."

Palle nodded. "I will need assurances, Sir Averil,

though your word will be chief among them. It can be done."

"You will excuse me for bringing it up, Sir Roderick, but if I do not control the physic, I control nothing. Once habituated, a man must have his physic at all costs." *Why am I discussing this?* Kent asked himself. *Because I must. If I refuse, I will be in the tower by nightfall.*

Palle looked down at the spoon, as though the face he saw reflected there was unfamiliar. "When there is no trust, these things are always difficult. Obviously we must give you the plants and let you cultivate them yourself."

"But I have no talent. Will I not suffer as the King suffers?"

The hesitation this time was long. Finally Palle spoke. "I cannot guarantee it, but we think there might be a way past this," he said softly, as though admitting his blackest deed.

Kent's next words came out as a whisper. "But can you make the plant bear?"

Palle nodded his head with that same air of sadness.

"Then why . . . ? Why did you send Tristam Flattery to Oceana?"

Palle looked up. "I can tell you nothing more, Sir Averil, until I have been assured of your cooperation."

Kent nodded. "Of course," he said softly. He shut his eyes for a moment. Palle was offering him a second life! He could feel the way he did now for how long? Fifty years? Sixty? And offering him a place in his cabal, a say in their decisions. It was beyond imagining.

"You hesitate, Mr. Kent. . . ."

"I am being asked to betray those to whom I have given my trust."

"And thereby saving them much misery, Sir Averil. I will give you my word that none will come to harm. At the worst a comfortable life in the country. Excuse me for pointing this out, but it is your association with our Entonne friend that has endangered them."

Was Palle bluffing? Did he have enough evidence? Did he even need it? Kent decided it was time to let the

King's Man know that he had taken precautions against this very eventuality.

"You should know, Sir Roderick, that the Entonne government has a root that extends right to the heart of the palace. I can cause enough scandal to bring down your regency, and have not done so only to protect some who are dear to me."

Palle nodded, not meeting Kent's gaze. "Becalmed beyond cannon range. Is that the situation?" He looked up, his gaze still mild, frighteningly so, Kent thought. "So you refuse my offer?"

Kent did not answer immediately, and then he glanced out over the men sitting in the room. Did they wonder what this conversation was about? He suspected they could not imagine. Who would control the knowledge of the mages; that is what they bargained here. And Kent was being offered a part in that decision.

"Do you mind if I speak with Wells and Rawdon, and perhaps Galton?"

Palle made a tiny motion of his head, as though granting permission. "But quickly, Sir Averil. I find my faith in others is eroding as I grow older. Delay will make me suspicious, and I despair of losing my faith in mankind altogether."

"May I not be the cause of that," Kent said.

Palle raised his glass for a second time. "Long life," he said, and Kent raised his glass as well. He could not help himself.

❦ ❦ ❦

It was late afternoon. The fog had retreated out to sea and gathered on the horizon where it swirled slowly like cream poured into a glass of coffee. Tongues of gray lapped at the sky and the almost calm sea. A few ships hovered on the edge of the fog, their sails barely drawing, their wake invisible at a distance.

Kent had intended to throw off the men who followed him and make his way to the home of the countess, but instead instructed his driver to go out to the headland that overlooked the sea at the harbor mouth. He sat in his carriage as it jogged along, gripping his cane as though it were his only hold on sanity.

The thought of his night with Tenil seemed so present, as though her body had left an imprint on his. He could smell her perfume. Imagining her voice caused him to catch his breath. He was being offered this. He could have his life back! His true life. The life he had been deprived of by this disease called age.

All the way out to the park Kent remained in terrible turmoil. What a temptation he was being offered. Had the countess kept her youth? Was it possible that they could still find a way to be together? It seemed as though fate were offering him a second chance. Would he not be a fool to refuse?

The carriage rolled to a halt and Kent stumbled down onto the grass, instructing his driver to wait. He walked out into the damp sea air. The sun had fallen to the horizon where it plunged into the moving mist, lighting it from within.

Was Palle speaking true to him? Were his intentions so honorable? His *intentions,* perhaps, but what of his actions? The King's Man had murdered two young gentlemen thinking they were Littel and Flattery. Murdered them rather than endanger his schemes.

Kent tried to square this with the man who had sat across from him in his club—a model of moderation and dedication to duty. *Overzealous underlings,* Kent told himself. Roderick would never have allowed these murders.

Kent came to the cliff top, and stopped, looking out over the still sea. The glowing fog bank stretched across the horizon, and the undersides of clouds turned to near-crimson. The sky to turquoise. It was a scene that seemed tranquil, yet was also powerful and strange. Kent was transfixed, memorizing every detail—the habit of a lifetime.

"How many more sunsets?" he said aloud. He had come to expect there would be few. Very soon a day would come when the sun would rise, though Averil Kent would not see it, nor any thereafter. "It is close," he whispered. "And I have it within my power to change that. To escape the grip of death, for a while, at least."

But he would betray the countess. A woman to whom he had been loyal his entire life, even when she had spurned him.

A gull cried, as though it had found itself soaring over a barren world.

But what had she been doing all these years? She had contacted Kent again after decades of silence and sent him on this quest to stop the recovery of the arts of the mages—and yet she practiced them herself! She let him age while she herself, he had begun to believe, remained young. She was letting him die, and preserving herself. Was her purpose even what she claimed?

A few days earlier Kent was sure he would give his life for the countess and her purpose. But now. . . .

"*She* betrayed *me*," he said, looking up at the white bird floating overhead, "and chose another. And now betrays me again, letting me age and die, while she keeps the bloom of youth alive."

He sat down on a lichen-stained rock and watched the sunset burn to glory, and then fade to darkness. Stars appeared, giving faint light.

"It was not a betrayal," he whispered after a time. "She chose another. I had no promise from her, other than the one I hoped for, the one I imagined." He placed his elbows on his knees and felt his shoulders sag.

After an hour Kent rose and returned to his carriage, wondering to what lengths he would go to cheat death. One thing was certain; no matter what he did, he could not lie to himself about the decision—that *would* be a betrayal.

❦　❦　❦

Jaimy sat quietly listening to the two men discuss the problems, trying to follow their speculation. The Flattery family were known for their gift with languages, so Jaimy did better than many might have, but he had not studied the ancient tongues, and they were most relevant here. His smattering of Old and Middle Farr was of little help. Whenever possible, he searched through books for the two scholars, seeking references they vaguely remembered, or perhaps merely hoped for. Littel had brought a trunk of books from the countess' library, but they were wishing for more before an hour was out.

Egar wrote out all that he could remember of the lines and words Wells had brought him from the secret text, and he and Valary pored over these.

"Did Wells bring them to you in this order, do you think?"

Littel nodded. "Yes, but I would not attach too much significance to that. You know how these things go: you work away at what you can, not necessarily from beginning to end."

Silence, as the two stared at the page. Jaimy rose to pour himself more coffee. A servant had stayed awake to provide for their needs. Taking up a sweet tart, Jaimy paced into the next room through the open door. Valary had come in here and slept for an hour earlier. The man looked so disheveled, clearly sleeping only when he could not go on, and paying no attention to the time of day or night. Jaimy was about to turn back to the other room, deciding he did not need to sleep yet, when he realized someone was sitting before the fire in one of the high-backed chairs.

"Lady Chilton?"

Angeline leaned out, her look serious. She put a finger to her lips. "I confess, I am listening, but did not want to disturb you in your work."

Jaimy took the other chair. "My work? I am hardly of any help at all," he confessed, and then laughed. "I pour the coffee."

She said nothing, looking down into the fire.

"How is it that I have not met you before?" Jaimy asked suddenly. "Do you never travel in Avonel society?"

She cocked her head to one side, exposing the lovely curve of her neck, causing her hair to move in the most delightful way. Jaimy wondered if everything this woman did appeared seductive.

"I have had enough of Avonel society, I fear. I prefer a quieter life."

"A scholar's life," Jaimy said. "Isn't it true that you understand what Littel and Valary are doing—far more than I can comprehend?"

She looked up at him, a bit surprised, but did not answer.

"Why do you hide your skill?"

"They are each more expert than I."

"But you have knowledge that they don't possess— isn't that so? From the countess. . . ."

She turned back to the fire. Jaimy could hardly take his eyes from her. She stood out in that somber room like a blossom in a shaft of sunlight. A single large emerald hung at her throat on a silver chain, complementing the green of her dress. He wished she would turn her eyes back to him—as dark as a night filled with soft rain.

"You mustn't do this," she said, looking at him, her eyes pleading. "It is futile even to begin. A young bride awaits you, and I will soon be gone." She rose suddenly, causing Jaimy to sit back in his chair, staring up at her. "It might be best if you returned to your family," she said and almost fled from the room.

Jaimy sat in confusion. "What in the world?" he said to himself. He wanted to go after her, though he was not sure where she had gone. Something stopped him. *She feels something for me,* he thought. *Flames!* Yet even that realization would not let him go in pursuit.

Sometime, late in the night, the countess reappeared. The gentlemen were suddenly aware that she sat in the corner.

"Have you learned anything new?"

"Only that 'buoh' is the root of 'book' and perhaps the name of the fifth book of lore," Valary said, clearly in his element.

Littel looked up from the text. "No, we have learned more than that. Mr. Valary has done much to make the purpose clear, and this has helped with my translation. This warding at the beginning, I now believe, has two purposes. *'The spoken flame burns before me, and at my back the cold fire seals the path.'* Mr. Valary has suggested that this somehow protects whoever performs the ritual as he advances forward—perhaps the advance is not actually physical. The word I have translated as 'path' is problematic. The original document was damaged in places, difficult to read. The word is, at best, a guess. It could also have been 'pattern' or even 'gathering,' for the ancient words were alike enough."

Valary was nodding as Littel talked. "And we are now almost certain that the text Mr. Wells was keeping to himself was part of this one. The more I study this, the more likely it seems that there was another section which fit on the end, for our text does not seem complete somehow—stops in mid-stride, as it were." Valary picked up a sheet of paper and gazed at it for a few seconds. "These are the lines and words Wells questioned Mr. Littel about, and we have little idea what they might mean. One phrase, though, does not bode well: *'the hidden world in all its terror.'*" He looked up at the countess. "I think we need to find this text Mr. Wells is so carefully hiding."

The countess nodded. "Yes. Do you think, Mr. Littel, that with the work you have done, Mr. Wells will manage to put the entire text together? Will he see the pattern you and Valary have discovered?"

The young man nodded grimly. "I would like to say that without me there is no hope of that, but I fear it is not so. They could have a translation sooner than we hope. It seems likely, now that I have thought about it, that Wells would keep the shortest and simplest section for himself. And we mustn't forget that Stedman Galton has come from Farrow. Wells spoke highly of the governor's skill."

The countess seemed to consider this. " 'The way beneath the vaulted hill.' Is that not the line?" And then almost to herself. "How in the world did Erasmus know?"

TWENTY-FIVE

Tristam went ashore two hours before sunset, accompanied, against his will, by a somewhat recovered viscount. At Stern's insistence, they had dressed formally, and even though the sun was waning quickly, the clothes were unbearably hot.

A party of Varuans met them—six men dressed in their pareus with garlands of leaves about their heads. Special marks had been painted on their foreheads, and these looked disconcertingly like ghostly owls. They greeted Tristam with formality, ignored the viscount as though he were a lowly slave, and taking up positions around the naturalist, led off into the jungle.

They were soon on a track that twisted and crossed others so confusingly, that Tristam was certain he would never be able to find it again. The path led inevitably up, through a gap in the granite spires, crossed a falling stream, and then cut a diagonal line across the mountain's lower slopes. The Farrlanders removed their coats, waistcoats, and neck cloths, but even so they were soon dripping with sweat, and panting from exertion.

The Varuans stopped and waited silently while the two foreigners caught their breath, and then pushed on at exactly the same pace. Tristam had not expected the hiding place of the Varuans to be so far away. After an hour they came upon a tiny village, the inhabitants watching silently as the party passed through, and making Tristam feel like a condemned man on his last journey.

The track became less clear, but the Varuans never faltered or even stopped to consider which way it might go. Tristam, who believed himself skilled in the forest, could never hope to duplicate this feat.

A sudden downpour caught them, and the Varuans cut down massive leaves and gave one to each Farrlander as an umbrella, and the entire party continued, walking beneath their absurd parasols.

The sun was setting somewhere beyond the island's opposite shore when they came out into what, in Farrland, would have been called a hanging valley—a shallow valley slung between two shoulders of the mountain, and opening over a steep cliff. The valley looked out across the bay and lagoon, over the seemingly endless expanse of ocean, east to the distant horizon. A dark squall moved across the purple waters, like some hunting creature, Tristam thought.

He turned away from the view. A more beautiful setting was difficult to imagine. A stream wound through the glen, gathering momentum before it threw itself off the cliff. The trade wind picked up the spray from this cataract and spread it across the lip of the valley, so that leaves glistened and dripped as though in constant rain. The air was cooled by this continual drizzle, and Tristam stood breathing in the moist air, feeling the oddly cooled breeze slowly loosen his shirt from his sweating torso.

Tristam thought it was a beautiful fertile vale—a botanist's dream—but if the Varuans hid here, there were no signs. Only a single, somewhat dilapidated fale, half buried in the trees.

With a bow, the Varuans motioned Tristam forward, and then quickly faded back into the darkening forest.

The viscount gestured toward the fale, but waited to follow Tristam's lead. The dressing that encircled the viscount's wrist drew Tristam's eye, and he found himself hoping they were not alone in this place.

There is nothing to fear, he chided himself. At least so he had been told. Tristam started forward, not resolutely, but with a certain sense of inevitability. As though this place had long been awaiting him.

The quick twilight of the tropics came over the scene

at that moment, like the shadow of a great wing, and as they came closer to the fale, a sudden light came to life within. It flickered desperately, like a butterfly set aflame, and then settled to a steady light, casting a shadow which moved slowly across the inner wall.

"*Hel-lo,*" Tristam said quietly, and when this received no response he approached the nearly-open side of the house. It took a moment for his eyes to adjust, and then he realized that a ship's lantern hung from the ceiling, and before a rough plank table, a ragged man hunched, working at something in the shadow.

"Hello," Tristam tried again, and the man stopped, raising his head so that the light shone off his beard and hair, unkempt and streaked with gray.

"You're not Mr. Hobbes," the man croaked, his voice broken and distant, and deepened, Tristam immediately thought, by sorrow and regret. Tristam had heard that terrible voice before, in the palace arboretum. And this, too, was a Farr voice; here in the back country of this impossibly distant island.

"No. No, I'm not. I'm Tristam Flattery. And who might you be?" Tristam asked, the words sounding absurdly normal in this situation that was anything but normal.

This stopped the man for a second. "Some relation of Erasmus?" he said, then, nodding his head, went back to what he had been doing. "How did you find me?" the man asked, and Tristam realized that he struggled for each breath.

"The Varuans brought me up here ... with the Viscount Elsworth. And who might you be, sir?"

The man paused to concentrate his efforts on grinding. "The Varuans ... call me *Matea.*"

Tristam thought he should know this word. "But you are Farr?"

"Was, long ago. I'm barely more than a ghost now." He waved a hand at a bench opposite him. "It is a long climb. Rest your legs. The descent is more difficult yet." Tristam stepped over the bench and sat down. The man continued his efforts, using a bone pestle, perhaps a rodent's femur, to crush some substance in a shell.

"Wallis has never mentioned you, sir," Tristam said. The man was either extremely eccentric or a little mad, Tristam could not decide which. Even across the wide table he could smell the man; sweat and smoke and mud and worse. His clothing was in ruin, and he was wrinkled and creased by what appeared to be several ages of men. This was unquestionably the man Tristam had seen the first night they had landed on Varua. A Farrlander . . . here, without the admiralty's knowledge.

"Wallis? Pankhurst's artist? The one they left here to die?" This produced what might have been a laugh—like a rasp being worked against a bone in the throat.

"You don't know him?"

"Nor does he me." He finished crushing whatever he had in the shell, and looked up at Tristam, his eyes squinting, head cocked to one side. The man was such a ruin Tristam could hardly bear to look at him.

"Erasmus," the castaway whispered, and shook his head in disbelief. He pushed himself up from the table and made his way to a door-sized opening in the back of the structure. Here Tristam could see him bend over to retrieve a kettle from a firepit built up with rocks. He shuffled back across the small room and found three rough pottery vessels which he brought with him to the table. He set himself down with obvious relief.

"If I may ask," Tristam began, thinking how absurd this politeness sounded here, "how have you come to be here?"

The man appeared to have fallen into a brief sleep, and jerked his head up when Tristam spoke.

"How? I was carried here by folly. Nothing more, nothing less. The folly of man." He turned away, and put his head in his hands for a moment. Quiet. Only the sounds of the small fire and the voices of insects and frogs. Water plunging over the cliff. Far off, the surf battered the reef without respite.

"There should be three for a tribunal," the man said softly, breaking the eerie quiet, "but then perhaps I shall be the third. I outrank both of you, that's certain." He looked up at Tristam, and then over at the viscount, who still stood, leaning against a post in the opening, the near-full moon rising behind him.

"Your shadow," the ragged man said, with some distaste. "Tried to murder Hobbes. . . ." He shook his head, and wiped his sleeve across his mouth. Sitting upright, he combed his fingers into his beard, as though aware suddenly of his appearance.

"You were on one of Gregory's voyages," Tristam said suddenly. "That is why you know Hobbes. That's how you got here."

The man looked at Tristam, then carefully picked up the shell he had been using as a mortar. With a tremulous hand he began shaking the powder, equally, into each vessel. It was a laborious process, and the man concentrated on it as though to misapportion would be a sin.

He poured the water from the kettle into the cups with the same exaggerated care, his shape distorting behind a cloud of steam. He leaned as far as he could to the right, managing to get his fingertips on a dagger, and with this he stirred each cup.

"You will join me?" he said, obviously an afterthought.

"What is it?" Tristam asked, his body reacting on its own to the smell.

"What you've come so far seeking, Tristam Flattery," the man said, pushing a cup across the table for Tristam, and then moving the other in the viscount's direction. Tristam closed his eyes, willing his body to be still. The odor alone wakened something within him and he thought of Faairi's star. Tried to focus on it. His right hand twitched as though some other will struggled to move it, and Tristam removed this hand from the table. With effort he opened his eyes.

"It is Kingfoil," Tristam said, regretting even inhaling the vapor.

"Kingfoil? Yes, that's it. King's leaf." The man raised his cup and sipped as though it were fine brandy. In the glow of the lantern he could see the man's eyelids flutter and then close.

"All right," he whispered, his breathing already eased, "I'm ready to begin."

"Your name; Matea," Tristam said, the cup still sitting before him like a taunt. "It means what?"

"Death," the man said, drinking again.

Tristam closed his own eyes. Why had he been brought here?

"But I have not always been named thus. I was once known as 'Tommy boy,' to a mother who is long dead. And then 'Master Tomas.' 'Midshipman,' for a time. 'Lieutenant.' Then Captain Tomas Gregory, of the Royal Navy."

"You aren't Gregory!" Tristam said, the denial coming out in a burst of resentment.

The man half-opened his eyes, and his face changed, the mouth tightening a little. "No. I'm merely a half-mad castaway the Varuans do not speak of because they fear me. Because they call me 'the matea,' and leave offerings at the head of my valley. The valley of death."

Tristam almost rose from the table, unable to bear the man's presence. This was not Gregory! "Why did they bring me here?" Tristam asked, fearing the answer, and more than a little disturbed by the man's claim.

"Because they would like to be rid of me, but are too superstitious to do the deed themselves. It is a test. Let me see this mark on your hand."

"How do you know about my hand?" Tristam asked.

"Even death has his followers," the man said, sitting forward and opening his eyes. He sipped his drink again, gazing strangely at Tristam, as though he almost recognized him. Then his eyes darted to the left, and Tristam realized that the viscount had come up beside him.

Before he knew what he did, Tristam snatched up the cup that had been left for the viscount, just as Julian reached for it. Tristam glared up at the man, who stepped back quickly.

The old castaway was nodding his head as though now he understood. With effort Tristam set the cup back on the table, beside the other.

Tristam tried to control the surge of rage that had taken hold of him, and when he turned to find Julian, the man was no longer in his place; standing guard.

"Show me what was done to you," the castaway said again, his tone more insistent, edged with a little hysteria, Tristam thought.

Unsettled by his response, the naturalist hesitated, then drew his sleeve back and extended his arm, afraid to look himself.

The old man leaned forward, forcing his eyes open. He turned Tristam's hand over, the touch of his fingers like wood. "It disappears if you have not had the seed?" he said, and Tristam nodded.

Taking up a cup of the tea he splashed some of the physic over Tristam's wrist, the liquid still painfully hot. Tristam tried to jerk his hand back, but the old man proved to be stronger than he looked. He held Tristam's hand, apparently with little effort, staring at it as though his own future was to be revealed.

With each flicker of the lantern's light the snake became more distinct, its raptor head appearing as though it were rising up through murky water. And then it surfaced, welt-red, coiling out of the vein, and appearing to move in the inconstant light. Tristam closed his eyes, and the man released his hand.

"And what did they look like, these men who did this to you?"

"I didn't see them," Tristam said, drawing the hand back close to him. He opened his eyes and saw the surprise on the man's face.

"Didn't see them?"

"No."

The man sat back, reaching for his cup impulsively, appearing shaken. In that second Tristam could see the illness in him: habituation to the seed. The man was as much a ruin as this house that sagged around him, and almost as empty within.

Tristam turned so that he looked out over the vale toward the sea. A cluster of stars hung on the horizon, forming a pattern that Tristam felt he should know—like so much that occurred on this voyage.

"The ruin of my ship lies beyond the reef," the man said quietly, "in deep water. All hands . . . wandering with the dolphins now. They mutinied, you see. Tried to take the ship so that they could have the seed. Wanted to live forever: the dream of even humble men. A group forced their way into the armory and magazine. I was on the quarterdeck with my officers—those who had not joined the mutineers. I was killing my own crew. Putting them to the sword." He had closed his eyes again, and spoke in a near whisper, his voice oddly devoid of emotion, as though he could not tell the story any other way. "We'll never know what happened. Perhaps they broke a lantern. The explosion blew me clear and I landed in the dark water among a rain of debris. And there, bobbing on the sea, lay the ship's yawl boat, which had been towing astern, ready to sound the pass." Silence. He combed the fingers of both hands into his hair, pulling it hard back from his face. In the orange glow of the lamp the man's features contorted, as though he watched the entire scene again.

"I came ashore like a ghost," he hissed. "Farrelle bring them peace. The Varuans had never seen anything like it—a ship blown to hell in a blaze of flames. They have stories of fiery mountains exploding; caused by the gods, of course. They cannot imagine that such a violent end could have had any other source. Thus the Varuans fear me. And call me 'death'—although I alone lived. And so I sit here in my valley and watch the ships come and go, while something feeds on my soul. I don't know what: the cursed seed, or my own remorse. How can I know? Seventy-five men. . . . All dead. My command. *Mine*." He looked at Tristam, the flame from the lamp flickering in his eye. "The most distinguished naval career of my time. And now I cannot even make an end of it." He looked down at the cup he cradled in one hand, a thin serpent of steam rising from its depths. "Denied even that. Robbed of one's will. Robbed of one's life."

"Tell me, truly," Tristam said. "Who were you?"

"Were?" The man shook his head. "No, you have it right. I was someone. Someone else. I am death, now. A walking corpse, with only memories circulating in my veins. Memories and this elixir I must have. I came back to Varua to have this seed for my own use. That is the truth. Trevelyan and the King had kept it for themselves, and I, who had gifted it to them, was left to death. A seaman without influence. Never mind that I had braved all the unknown terrors of the world. Never mind that I brought my crews back entire. 'Legend' they said of me. 'Hero' I was named then. But the word got out among the Jacks, many of whom had sailed with me before.

"The King was denying life to me, and I, in turn, was denying it to my pitiable crew. My own betrayal was to be secret, for it began with a mutiny in my heart, but the Jacks were not so cunning. They knew they could never bring the seed back to Farrland and hope to keep it. No, they would have to wrest it from the Varuans, and then find some island of their own to live out their long lives. What reason had they to return to Farrland and the lives of poor men?"

He sipped his physic, stopping to look into the steaming cup as he swallowed, as though realizing what he had just done. Then his eye fell on the cup that Tristam had refused. Again he looked up at the naturalist, something like wonder in that gaze. "Can you truly refuse it?" He reached out and raised Tristam's cup, tilting it precariously over the ground. "Say yea or nay."

"Spill it," Tristam said, forcing the words out. "I will have none of it."

The old man began to tilt the cup further, but when a drop escaped the lip and ran down onto his hand he relented, returning the cup gently to the table. As he did so, a sweat broke on the man's brow, as though simply raising a cup was exertion. For a moment he struggled to regain his breath.

"All around me on the dark sea, the body of my ship lay," he said, drawn back to the vision that clearly haunted him, his terrible voice echoing up from the emptiness within, "some of it aflame. Men floated nearby, staring down into the fathomless depths. Men who had dreamed of living forever. I stood in the rocking yawl boat, helpless, not a living soul to save. Left alive myself by some vengeful god who wished me an eternity of torment. And I knew why. Knew as though I had been told in words.

"Everywhere my ship had sailed I sowed the seeds of ruin. All of the peoples I had discovered were destined to be overwhelmed, their ways lost, their gods put aside. Replaced by the gods of the peoples of the Entide Sea: reason and commerce, progress, empiricism. Possessions and wealth. For this, the gods of the islands and the sea punished me.

"I think the gods fled, then, to some distant corner of the world. And now the Varuans sense the change. The King and his sorcerers have retreated up into the ancient city, hoping to call their gods back. Hoping to keep their people alive."

He stopped and looked at Tristam. "And they want me dead. They sense that the gods' disfavor has something to do with my presence here—little do they realize. But they cannot kill the bearers of the curse, those they have allowed to take the seed. It is tapu. But you.... What you do affects only yourself and the people of your own land. It is nothing to them."

"But I will not commit murder," Tristam said. *Especially one as pitiable as yourself,* he thought.

The old man, whom Tristam feared might actually be Gregory, drained his cup, staring down into its emptiness. Then he rose, standing more erect. "Let me show you," he said, and motioning for Tristam to follow, they stepped out into the moonlit valley.

The viscount was nowhere to be seen, which Tristam did not like. But he followed the old man, treading along a well-worn path that led into a copse of breadfruit trees. Here the man stopped before half a dozen neat rows of *regis* plants. Tristam could see their pale blossoms in the moonlight.

"My greatest victory," the man said, the irony clear.

"You take the *regis* physic," Tristam said, "but you are not young. How is that possible?"

The man stood staring at his plants with such a mixture of emotion that Tristam wondered how he remained even as sane as he did.

"If you have not the ways of the Old Men, the makings of a mage, I have come to believe, then the seed betrays you. Sooner or later. You require more and more, yet you age. Eventually, there is no amount of seed that will keep time at bay. And I have so little left. *Look at them.* As innocent seeming as children. Yet even this viscount was a child once. As sweet as any, I'm sure." He reached out and gently turned one of the flowers up, as though it were the face of a child. "This is what you came for?"

Tristam did not answer. Here it was. *Regis.* And not in the possession of the islanders. With only a few plants and some seed he could return to Farrland a hero. Wealth, a title, and the gratitude of the duchess.

A bat flitted over the garden, once, twice, its flight erratic. An owl hooted, causing Tristam to look up. Was this the owl he had seen? His owl?

The naturalist let the silence go on, afraid to speak. He wanted no more answers from this man. Nor did he want to consider any of his requests.

"Yours," the old man whispered hoarsely, "if you want it."

"I cannot do what you ask," Tristam said.

"But can you not help me?" the man said, suddenly turning on Tristam, pleading. "You are a relation of Erasmus. You understand these things. Will you not take pity on a sorry shell of a man? Help me regain what I have lost. The Old Men could do it, but they have changed toward me, and will do nothing to assist me, now. But you, Tristam Flattery, are my countryman, and I was once counted great among the citizens of Farrland. I do not wish to die ancient, and infirm, and without all honor. Was it such a terrible thing I did? Many a commander has lost a ship, yet retained his honor. Many who had accomplished less than I. Do I deserve such an end? Do I, sir?"

Tristam did not answer, but shook his arm free of the man's grip. "I am not your judge, Captain Gregory, or whoever you are. And, contrary to what you think, I understand almost nothing of these matters. I could not help you if I wanted to, and that's the truth of it."

The man turned back to his plants, his shoulders sagging. Again he reached out and caressed a blossom. "Even if what you say is true, Tristam Flattery, you could help me still. Would you not put a beast from its suffering? I am such a beast."

"*No.* You are speaking to the wrong man. Talk to my shadow. Did you know he cut a bird-serpent into his arm with the point of a knife, and slit his wrist as well?"

The man nodded. "*Despair.* He can never be you, so he attempted self-murder. You ... you can live to thrice the age of men, have the love of his adored sister, and are free of his particular demons."

Clearly this man knew more than he claimed. "But what are these demons?" Tristam asked. "What drives him to be as he is?"

"I heard him speak with Hobbes. He believes he is the servant of death."

Tristam turned away, unable to bear it any more. *No more!*

If I accept the seed, the quest will be over and this madness will be done with, he told himself. But he could not—he believed now that it was a curse. Look at what it had done to this man. Could he truly have been Gregory?

Tristam walked back toward the fale, led by the flaming butterfly in the ship's lantern. A few steps into the shadow of the trees, he came upon the viscount, standing silent and still. Tristam almost stopped and spoke, but instead went on. They had a pact, these two: *Death* and his manservant.

Reaching the edge of the trees he stopped, morbid curiosity gaining the better of him. He saw the shadow of the larger man standing before the aged seaman, and then the viscount dropped to his knees. Tristam turned and fled toward the single light.

Tristam did not know how much time had passed. He sat, staring out toward the stars that lifted slowly above the sea, his mind in such confusion it was its own kind of emptiness. Finally a noise startled him, and the viscount stood in the door, bearing the limp form of Gregory in his arms.

Tristam rose from his seat, pulling back a step, staring at this horrifying sight: the viscount holding the man as tenderly as though he were his own dead father. In the faint light Tristam could see what appeared to be tears on the viscount's face.

"Lay him here, on the table," Tristam said, and the viscount did as he said, arranging the man's hands on his breast, brushing the strands of hair back from his face.

Tristam reached the lantern down. "Set it afire," he forced himself to say. He went out, crossing the vale to the stand of trees. Hanging the lantern from a branch, he stared at the plants a moment, the blossoms like tiny bells in the moonlight. "I have come for you," he whispered, and went quickly to work, removing each plant, taking care that no seeds fell to the ground. He imagined he could feel the plants exerting their primitive will toward him, trying to stop him. Tristam's longing for the physic grew, and his hands trembled, but he would not relent. Behind him the dry thatch of the fale caught, going up with a high, crackling hiss. The light of the blaze caused the shadows of the trees to battle around him, like enormous many-armed warriors.

The fale was an inferno when Tristam returned, and the viscount stood there, too close, as though paying honor to a dead hero. Daring the scorching heat, Tristam cast the *regis* plants on the flames, where they twisted and sizzled in the blaze.

The viscount pounced forward, trying to rescue the Kingfoil, but he pulled away, the heat too much for him. *"What have you done?"* he said, grabbing Tristam roughly by the front of his shirt.

The two men froze that way, their faces inches apart. *"Take your hands off me,"* Tristam said with controlled rage, feeling something stir within him, something frightening. And to his surprise, the viscount let him go, stepping back quickly. Tristam shrugged his shirt back into place. "It is a curse," he said, moving away from both the viscount and the heat of the fire. "I will have no part of it. Nor will I take it back to Farrland, King or no. I will risk prison before that."

The viscount stood glaring at him, and Tristam took another step back, suddenly afraid of this madman, unsure of the source of his apparent immunity. Gregory had suggested that the viscount was jealous of him. Jealousy caused madness to take hold of *sane* men.

But then the viscount nodded. "You understand these things, Tristam," Julian said, his tone almost subservient. He looked over his shoulder at the burning structure. "He was a father to me," the viscount said, his tone eminently reasonable, "demanding sometimes, but just and fair. . . ."

Tristam scooped the lantern up off the ground and fled, searching desperately for the path to the lagoon, wanting to hear no more. No more.

🥀 🥀 🥀

The darkness among the trees was so dense it resisted the moonlight, and Tristam was soon lost, finding himself on steep slopes, where he could barely make his way. For a long time he followed the flaming butterfly, but finally the lantern flickered out, empty, and Tristam sat down in the dark and tried to catch his breath. Was the viscount searching for him? Yes. Tristam was quite certain he was.

He lay back on the soft earth, listening, attuning his ear to the sounds of the forest—the running of a stream somewhere nearby, the sound of the wind among the leaves. Insects sang their high, strange songs, and occasionally came the sound of an owl, like a question. *Where? Where are you?*

For a long time Tristam listened, and then he heard the sound of the Tithy running outside his home in Locfal. His uncle walked there, by the brook, lost in thought. Tristam threw open the window of his room and cupped his hands to his mouth. *"What is it you want of me?"* he shouted. His uncle looked up, as though vaguely aware of a sound, and then went back to his musing. A falcon cried from the aviary.

* * *

Tristam awoke to first light, the sunrise smeared across the eastern sky like a swelling wound. For a moment he could not think where he was or how he had come there, and then he remembered.... The night in the valley. A man who made impossible claims.

"Blood and flames." He sat up quickly, and found that a dagger lay in his lap. Tristam cursed, snatching up the weapon, which was still stained with dried blood. He looked around, suddenly frightened, still half in the world of dreams. This was the dagger that belonged to the man who had claimed to be Gregory, and only Julian could have carried it down. Tristam shuddered at the thought of the viscount near him while he slept. He looked at the knife again, and found the letter 'G' engraved on the handle.

For a moment he shut his eyes, seeing the pathetic creature who huddled over his physic, having lost all sense of himself—all honor, all pride. The shell of Tomas Gregory, the greatest explorer in Farr history. This is what the seed wrought in men. Unless they had the talents of a mage—and then Tristam suspected the effects were even worse.

"I can deny myself anything," Tristam told himself, though his obsession with the duchess made this half a lie.

He staggered to his feet, and immediately set off along the hillside, feeling relief in movement. The events of the previous night seemed like a nightmare to him—the kind of nightmare you couldn't shake in the morning, and which left you feeling strange and tainted, somehow.

The terrain forced him up, and repeatedly he kept encountering slopes too steep to descend. Three hours found him looking over a bluff into a deep valley, not sure where he was or how he would get down.

He thought he heard his name echo across the valley, and he went out to the edge of the cliff, hoping to catch sight of his rescuers.

Again the call repeated up the valley, to be lost among the trees. Tristam answered, reminded immediately of his dream. *What is it you want of me?*

It was half of the hour before Tristam realized that it was Faairi searching for him, and longer than that before she managed to find him. She smiled with relief when she finally saw him, but there was some underlying anxiety that this smile could not erase.

"Tristam," she said, hurrying up through the trees. "You must hurry. There has been fighting on the ship."

TWENTY-SIX

Tumney paced the width of the arboretum, stopped, and stared out over the neat rows of plants. He removed his hat and turned it slowly in his hands, as though searching with his thumb for irregularities in the headband. He realized he was not comfortable here alone at night. These plants had always seemed strange to him. "Foreign" was what he thought of them. Peculiar. But tonight this did not seem an adequate explanation. "Aware" was much more what he thought, though he would never admit it to anyone. Brooding. Intent on a purpose he did not understand, he who knew plants well.

The waxy leaves of *regis* glistened dully in the lamplight, and the silence in the room almost felt like patience. They seemed a bit like murderous innocents to him; raised apart from others, never learning right from wrong. They had a purpose of their own, and like everything in nature but man, did not care how they achieved it. Perhaps it would be more true to say that some men cared.

Tumney shivered suddenly, and turned away, crossing to the small planting boxes, but he stopped a few feet short, keeping his distance. These were the seeds planted by that young naturalist months before. Tumney had tended them, as the duchess had asked, but nothing had happened. And now virtually every box had the beginnings of a Kingfoil seedling, erupting out of the earth like small green hands, reaching for light and air.

"Unnatural," he muttered. There was no explanation for it. None.

He heard a door open and turned expectantly. A moment later Princess Joelle arrived accompanied by the young prince and Teiho Ruau. The gardener bowed as best he could, gratified by the kind smile from the princess. She always called him 'Mr. Tumney,' and even, on occasion, 'sir,' which he liked more than a little, the princess being born to such a high station and all.

"Mr. Tumney," she said, nodding her head to him. "I do apologize for leaving you waiting. We came as soon as we were able."

He shook his head, not sure how to respond. Certainly the princess should not be apologizing to him. Not wanting to keep the princess so late at night, he led them immediately to the planting boxes. For a moment no one spoke and Ruau reached out and touched one of the emerging seedlings. He glanced up, sharing a look with the princess, and then took his hand away.

"These were all planted by Tristam Flattery?" the prince asked quietly.

"Yes. Just before high summer. Almost eight months past." The gardener took a step away. "There is something else." He gestured with his hat.

They followed him down the rows of Kingfoil, the princess waving off his expressed concern for her shoes. He crouched by a plant and took the end of a branch, lifting the flower that grew there. "It is a girl," he said. "The first female flower in months and months. There will be seed from this." He pointed to some other buds on the same plant, and others nearby as well. "All females," he said, a bit in awe. "And I take no credit. I can't begin to explain it," he said.

Again the Varuan and the princess shared a look.

"Tristam Flattery," the prince said, staring down at the flower. His mother looked at him sharply, and he said nothing more.

"You're certain, Mr. Tumney, that no one knows of this?"

Tumney nodded. "Sure as sure, ma'am."

She considered this for only a second before speaking. "Destroy the seedlings," the princess said firmly. "Cut every female bud and flower off and put everything into the fire. No one must know what has happened."

"But ... we have hoped for so long!" The gardener didn't go on. The look on the princess' face told him that he had spoken out of place. "Excuse me, Your Highness. Old Tumney speaks before he thinks. Excuse me."

She reached out and put a hand on his shoulder, an easy gesture, for the princess was considerably taller than the old gardener. "I know it seems mad, Mr. Tumney, but you must do this for me. It is for everyone's good. Don't ask me more."

The gardener nodded. "I'll do it this night."

The princess mouthed the words, "Thank you," though no sound came. She took Ruau and her son in tow, and left Tumney alone in the arboretum.

For a few moments the old gardener stared at his charges, wondering how they would react to the coming assault, but he shook his head. "Don't be an old fool," he chided himself, and went to get his tools, though not without a feeling that he was being observed.

ᵛ ᵛ ᵛ

The prince looked over his sketch. He thought it might have been good fortune that had him born a prince, for he clearly didn't have the talent to be an artist. Though, to be fair, Averil Kent had said his own early sketches showed little promise. Of course, the artist might have been merely trying to encourage. One could not rely on others to be truthful about their abilities.

He wondered if the eyebrows should not really be so arched. He closed his eyes and tried to summon up a clear mental image of Alissa Somers, and though he was able to do this easily, when he tried to concentrate on specific features, the whole picture seemed to lose focus.

He thought her high forehead and eyebrows must represent perfection of form, the skin unmarred by even a hint of a line, as though she had never worried in her life. But then she had not been born into a royal family. When people spoke to her, it was likely that they felt no need to speak anything but the truth.

He opened his eyes and looked with some despair upon his creation. Perhaps she was not really so perfect, but he had made her so in his mind. People did this; he had seen it. As though the world of humans was created from their desires as much as their perception—an issue the empiricists tried to deal with in their natural philosophy.

Although he realized this was a trivial truth, still, trying to comprehend the reality of a situation was his constant activity. He could not necessarily trust the word of ministers, who all had their own purposes; nor what his mother might think, for her own perception was colored by her desire to see people in certain ways. One did not trust the periodicals, certainly, and pamphleteers were never disinterested. Everyone seemed to see the world and events a little differently, depending on their own personal mixture of desire and pragmatism. In history there were any number of rulers whose perception of events was so far removed from reality that it led to calamity. Prince Wilam did not want to be one of those—at any cost. Even if it meant giving up the world as he desired it to be.

He looked again at his drawing. Well, she might not be quite the paragon he wanted to believe, but Alissa was certainly more beautiful than his sketch indicated. That, at least, he knew for truth.

His mother's signature knock sounded on the door and he turned his drawing facedown before answering. It was late, but it seemed that both he and the princess were managing with limited sleep these days.

"Princess," he said, following the ritual they had long ago evolved—"Princess" was not a proper form of address.

"Prince." She entered his room with more assurance than last she had visited. The princess scanned her surroundings quickly, no doubt taking notice of his sketch, turned over on the desk. "Wilam, I have been torturing my brain trying to understand the significance of the *regis* flowering at this precise point in time, but I can arrive at no explanation. I am quite sure there is no empirical explanation. I think we need to consult with Averil Kent. Will you go to him in the morning?"

The prince nodded. "Yes. Of course."

The princess nodded, giving half a smile—worry obviously preyed upon her. "I have tried to find some explanation that does not rely on logic, but once the borders of rationality have been removed I cannot imagine what should take their place. How does one begin to measure? What standards should one apply?"

The prince understood what she meant. Once reason was no longer your guide, you were like a man stranded in a featureless landscape. There were no landmarks to use. One direction was as likely to yield results as any other. Even so, the prince found he had a hunch, though it was not more than that. Certainly he could not justify it. "I understand what you're saying. I don't know why, but I feel sure, somehow, that this sudden flowering has something to do with Tristam Flattery. It is not rational, I realize. Flattery has not set foot in the palace in months, but, still, I think it."

"Perhaps you are right. Intuition is not to be discounted; no matter that it is not empirical. Talk to Mr. Kent. He knows more than most realize."

The prince nodded. The two stood awkwardly for a moment, not knowing what to say.

"I have kept my word regarding Miss Somers," the prince began, trying to make his voice calm and adult. "But I find that I am concerned. It might give me some peace to know that she is well. Is that possible?"

The princess stopped in the middle of the room, gazing at her son with a serious look that he could not read. "I've received a note from Lady Galton, and will dine with her tomorrow. Afterward, we can speak." She reached out and put a hand on his shoulder, then kissed his cheek and left without another word.

The prince went back to his desk and flipped the drawing over. It was not only a poor likeness of Alissa Somers, but it was a poor representation of his own idealized image. And to think a real portraitist captured not only a person's likeness but something of their inner being as well. His sketch showed a woman stiff and wooden, perhaps a little apprehensive. This was not the Alissa he knew. Not even remotely like her.

🍂 🍂 🍂

Despite the return of his vitality, Kent was miserable. He could barely meet the eyes of his friends, and slumped in his chair with his hands jammed into the pockets of his frock coat. His meeting with Palle had left him feeling morally tainted. The man was a devil incarnate!

"If there was any way at all for us to see it," Valary said. "Though I am sure that Wells and Palle have taken every precaution to keep this away from prying eyes."

Kent could feel the countess look at him, even if he could not see her clearly. Her lifeless tones came out of the darkness. "What do you say, Averil? Is it possible?"

Kent found that this question robbed him of his desire for humor. "Possible. . . . Perhaps. There would be some risk involved. As things stand now, Galton will alert us if Palle and his group decide to attempt this ritual. I'm not quite sure what we will do, but at least we will know. But if Galton is found copying this text . . . Wells is distrustful in the extreme, and his experience with Mr. Littel will have only made that worse. I would dearly like to see this text myself, but to endanger Galton. . . . I'm not sure it is wise.

Silence. Kent thought he could hear a clock ticking.

"I think Averil is right in this. We have a man in Palle's inner circle, now, and that may prove to be the more valuable thing—at least for the time being. If Palle suddenly decides that he must act. . . ." The countess looked around at the men present. "Well, then I am not sure what we shall do."

Kent rose out of his chair. "We have stronger allies than most realize. We need only prepare them. Which we must do rather quickly, for we cannot know when Palle and Wells will act. I will need the assistance of Lord

Jaimas, if he will not mind being made a mere messenger."

❦ ❦ ❦

When Smithers appeared at the door to his study, Kent hoped it would be to inform him that a young woman from the opera had come calling. It was relatively early in the morning, really too early for visitors, but then these were not normal times.

"There is a young gentleman to see you, Sir Averil."

"And what name might he go by?"

"He would not say, sir, but gave me this envelope, insisting that you would see him." A second of hesitation.

Kent took the envelope from the silver tray and slit it open. "Show him up immediately ... and, Smithers? The proper form of address to use is 'Your Highness.' "

The servant hurried from the room.

Kent removed his spectacles and rose from his chair, stretching his arms to loosen his shoulders. He had been working on his sketch of the King, though when he would ever have the leisure to paint a portrait he did not know. A moment later a somberly dressed young prince was shown into the room.

"Your Highness," Kent said, making a leg. "It is a great honor."

The young man grinned a little self-consciously, as though he suspected Kent of making sport of him. "The princess has sent me to ask you a question, Sir Averil."

Kent gestured to a chair, and the two sat, Kent leaning forward, his hands on his knees, ready to offer whatever service he might to the princess.

"But before I speak further, we must reach an understanding ..." The prince gazed at him, turning his head slightly to one side. "Although the princess has the highest opinion of you, Sir Averil, as do I, we have had no formal declaration of your intent or loyalty."

Kent nodded, thinking immediately of his conversation with Palle. Everyone else trusted him so completely. Did they not know that there were things that could tempt even Averil Kent?

"It is my intention to see that knowledge thought lost for many years is not recovered. I am opposed to Roderick Palle and his colleagues."

"One of whom is my father," the prince said.

Kent hesitated barely half a beat. "One of whom is the prince. Yes," he said quietly, realizing that these words still seemed true to him, despite what he had been offered.

"And what are you prepared to do to stop these men from regaining the lost knowledge?"

"Whatever I must," Kent said without pause. And this seemed true as well.

The young man nodded. "Then we are of one mind, Sir Averil," he said, staring down at the floor for a moment, losing his focus. "Last summer," he began suddenly, as though remembering his purpose, "while staying in Avonel, Tristam Flattery planted *regis* seeds in the arboretum. On the instructions of the Duchess of Morland, the gardener watered these seeds but otherwise left them alone all these months. A few days ago they began to sprout."

Kent sat back in his chair.

"That is not all. The *regis* plants in the arboretum have begun to bloom: female blossoms."

"You're certain?"

The prince nodded, carefully gauging Kent's reaction.

"My word," Kent muttered.

"What does it mean, Sir Averil?"

Kent rose from his chair and paced across the front of the hearth.

"Simply started growing, you say? The gardener did nothing different?"

"According to him, nothing."

Kent dearly wanted to go and see this for himself, though he knew there would be no point. "What do Wells and company make of this?"

"They don't know. The princess had the seedlings destroyed. And all the female blossoms and buds were pinched off."

Kent stopped, staring down at the prince. "You're sure Palle doesn't know? Few things pass in the kingdom without his knowledge, and we're talking about the palace. Ostensibly his home."

"I'm certain he does not know. Even the King has not been told."

Kent reached back and put an elbow on the mantlepiece. "You may not be able to keep it secret for long. *Regis* seems to have a mind of its own, or nearly so."

"You have no idea what this might mean, then?"

"Mean? I dare say it means that the things we have struggled to keep from waking have begun to stir. It could be due to events here in Farrland, or it might even have some connection to Tristam Flattery, wherever he might be."

The prince nodded, as though this corroborated his own thinking. "Is there any way we might discover more certainly?"

Kent considered a moment. "There are several people who might cast light upon this. Two I will consult, but the third is Stedman Galton. You might tell the princess that I think she acted wisely," Kent added. "I think it is best to keep the plants from flowering. Anything that might give us an advantage over these others. Even the smallest thing."

Smithers knocked on the door, apologizing profusely. "A young lady to see you, sir. Shall I have her wait or send her on?"

Kent felt his heart rise, and then sink. She was an agent of the Entonne government, and the future King of Farrland sat in his study speaking openly about the most sensitive matters. Smithers must have understood his master's hesitation.

"It is Miss Alissa Somers, sir."

"Ah. Bring her up, Smithers. Send her along immediately."

Kent noticed that the prince's color changed, his face becoming a little bright.

"Perhaps I should . . ." the young man started to rise, but the sentence trailed off and he did not move. An awkward silence ensued, reminding Kent of what Sennet had told him.

Have they arranged an "accidental" meeting at my home?

A moment later Alissa Somers burst through the door and answered Kent's question; her face changed utterly when she saw the prince, and she faltered. Stopping self-consciously just inside the door.

"Your Highness," Kent said, "I believe you have met Miss Alissa Somers, the future Duchess of Blackwater."

Alissa curtsied quickly and the prince bowed more deeply than he strictly should have. The poor young man looked so out of sorts. Torn between wanting to leave and needing to stay.

"It is the greatest good fortune that I find you both here," Alissa began, then she looked at them in turn as she spoke. "Do you know the whereabouts of Jaimas? Is he truly well?"

The prince turned away at this, stricken with pain and remorse, Kent could see.

"Lord Jaimas is perfectly well."

She paused for a moment. "You are absolutely certain?"

"I have seen him with my own eyes, Miss Alissa. He might well be home to you this very day."

She put a hand to her face, and Kent saw her eyes brim with tears. The prince had turned and was staring at him in disbelief.

Kent felt himself floundering, wondering how he might save the situation. "Fortunately, Your Highness managed to spirit Lord Jaimas and Mr. Littel away, or who knows what might have happened. As it was, Palle's minions committed the foul murder of two young gentlemen by mistake, and believe that Lord Jaimas and Littel are dead."

Alissa turned her lovely eyes, still glistening with tears, on the prince. "How terrible for these young men," she said. "I–I owe you a great debt, Your Highness."

This simple declaration melted Kent's heart entirely, and he could only imagine the effect on the prince. The poor young man looked as though he would never find words to answer.

"Certainly my part was very small," he managed.

The prince and Alissa stood on either edge of the rug, as though it were a chasm between them, looking at each other, their eyes filled with questions.

"I am glad you have come, Miss Alissa," Kent said. "If you don't mind, I would have you carry a note to the duke."

Kent's words seemed to break the spell, and the two began a show of acting normally. Kent offered them tea, wondering if he was furthering a romance, feeling a bit sorry for Lord Jaimas—a bit guilty.

🥀 🥀 🥀

The prince's carriage stopped and rolled back a foot. Alissa glanced out at the facade of the Flatterys' Avonel residence—it seemed so grand, and it was not a palace. She looked back to her companion. She dearly hoped they would not be seen.

"Your Highness has been very kind," she said, looking down at her hands which were clasped tightly on her knee. There had been only stilted conversation after the prince offered to return her from Averil Kent's. She had seldom felt so uncomfortable. A footman opened the door and lowered the step.

She forced a smile at her anxious looking companion, and then turned to go.

"Lady Alissa?" he said quickly, a hint of urgency in his voice. "I wanted to apologize for what happened at the iron bridge celebration."

She put on her most naive look and then caught herself. For some reason she could not make herself pretend that she didn't understand what he meant—the princess steering him away.

"No need to apologize," she said, warmth coming through.

"It won't happen again. I . . . It won't happen, I promise."

She nodded.

"My mother," he paused. "She is too perceptive sometimes." He meant to say more but could not choose among the endless possibilities, and he ended up shrugging foolishly.

"It's all right," she said softly, looking down so that her thick lashes hid her eyes. "My heart . . . it belongs to Jaimas, but if it did not. . . ." She met his eye. *"Thank you,"* she managed, and then reached out to squeeze his hand before leaving.

The prince raised her hand to his lips and kissed her fingers. "Thank you," he said.

She nodded, and stepped down to the ground, turning once to wave, conscious of his gaze as she mounted the steps.

He thinks he loves me, she thought. *Farrelle save us, he is a prince of Farrland!*

Inside the door she gave her cloak to a servant and then, looking up, she was greeted by the sight of Jaimas coming down the stairs. She did not wait but rushed up to meet him.

The story took some time in the telling, and Alissa clung to his hand through much of it. Although she had been certain that Lady Galton's news was wrong, she had not slept that night for worry. And now here he was, returned to her, returned from the dead, almost.

"I can't imagine how you escaped," she said. "It was clever of you to set the dogs off after the fox."

Jaimas nodded his head, his look distracted. "You know, when that fox appeared, I had the strongest impression that it was not an accident."

"You're saying that it came to rescue you?" She poked him in the ribs with a finger, as she liked to do when they teased.

"Not quite, but I don't believe it was an accident either."

She laughed, she was just so overwhelmed with happiness to have him back. "You will become superstitious next."

"But I already am. I believe I found you when I was following a hooded crow that seemed to be carrying a silver ring, and hopping furtively from branch to branch."

She laughed. "Well, my life has been less eventful, I will say."

"Oh? And whose great carriage brought you home early this morning, my dear?"

"I was delivering a message to Mr. Kent," she said, trying not to sound too serious. "Prince Wilam happened to be there and kindly saved me from hiring a hack to get home."

"Accidental meetings with royalty? Hardly uneventful."

"I suppose," she said, more seriously. "I think the prince is lonely, you know. Perhaps lonely is not the right word." She turned a lock of Jaimy's hair around a finger. "He does not have what we have: people around us who care for us enough to be critical when needed. People whose reactions we trust."

"Yes," Jaimy said. "I need someone to be critical of me occasionally. Left to my own devices, I would make a perfect fool of myself." He thought of Angeline and closed his eyes, embarrassment and guilt causing that strange tightness, as though something inside him cringed.

"I hardly think that. Jaimas? I believe the prince is sweet on me." She paused for a beat. "Now don't laugh."

"I am not laughing. It's very likely true. We don't need to change our marriage plans, do we?"

She laughed and kissed his cheek, then turned his head and kissed him sweetly on the lips. "No. I think we can go ahead. At least I haven't had a better offer yet." Then more seriously, "I feel a little sorry for him, as absurd as it is to pity an heir to the throne."

Jaimas pulled her closer and she put her head against his shoulder.

"Isn't it odd, Jaimas, that your great-uncle had the portrait of the Countess of Chilton, and then Kent sends you to her home? I wish you had seen her. Imagine hiding away from the world for so many years!"

Jaimy shrugged. He dearly wanted to examine that portrait. Did the countess' niece really look so much like her? Almost too uncanny to believe.

❧ ❧ ❧

The carriage moved quietly through the streets of Avonel, and the prince stared out the window at the people going about their daily business. A world so far removed from his that the glass he looked through might have been a magic mirror, showing scenes of another land.

The words of Alissa Somers echoed in his mind. *"My heart ... it belongs to Jaimas, but if it did not. ..."* And then she had thanked him. For what? Was it a compliment that he had paid her? Not by the standards of gentlemen—expressing one's feelings for another man's fiancée! But she had thanked him, and he was certain it was not just for escorting her home.

He wondered if that had been the moment he dreamed of? The moment when two people ignored all propriety, and spoke from their hearts. Yes, perhaps it was. And if the world did not seem overly changed by it, that did not matter. It was precious to him all the same.

"But if it did not," he whispered, and laid his head against the seat, curling up like a child, pressing his eyes closed as though he could shut out the coldness of world and somehow inhabit those five words.

TWENTY-SEVEN

The words on the page had begun to blur and Stedman Galton closed his eyes, feeling a mild burning sensation behind the lids. He had not slept enough these past nights, and his lung condition was not liking the dampness of the late Farr winter. The only good news had been the assurance of his wife that Lord Jaimas Flattery and Egar Littel were still alive—though who the two unfortunates in County Coombs had been was still a mystery.

It did not matter to Galton that it was not Lord Jaimas and Egar Littel who had been murdered. Palle had let his people commit this crime, and their intended victims had broken no laws. And then there were these poor young gentlemen who couldn't have had the slightest idea of why they were attacked. No, Galton had no second thoughts—when he woke up to the truth of what was happening around him he had awakened completely. There was no rest for him now.

"Shall we give it a rest, Sir Stedman?" Wells asked solicitously.

Galton's eyes snapped open as though he had been startled as he dozed. "No. I can go on bit longer yet. We are so close." He forced his eyes to focus on the text before him.

Wells leaned over the table as well, sighing a little as he moved. After a brief silence he said, "I still think that 'gwydd' will prove to be the root of 'wood.' The 'g' became silent, as we know, in words like 'gnarled' and 'gnat.' Consider the root of 'gnat': 'gnætt.' It is almost a perfect

363

model. So 'gwyddhyll' is 'woodhill' or 'wooded hill.' 'Tree mount.' We know that Kent and this man Valary visited the abbey."

Galton nodded blankly, even the simplest things taking a moment to coalesce in his exhausted mind. They were debating a passage that described the ritual, written in a different tongue than the chant of the ritual itself. "That might be true, Wells, but Sir Roderick sent a man up there to search the place and he reported nothing out of the ordinary. It may not be the site we're searching for."

"Yes, but would this man have known what to look for? It might take more knowledge than he possessed."

Galton had been doing everything in his power to slow Wells' progress, but feared that his purpose would be perceived if he was not careful. There were times when he needed to agree, even make a small contribution so that he did not fall under suspicion, for Wells had become very suspicious, guarding the text as though it might walk off of its own accord.

"I take your point, but there must be five hundred 'wooded hills' or 'forest hills' or variants. Yes, Kent visited this one, but it might have been only coincidence. Knowing we look for a variant of 'forest hill' is about as exact as knowing we look for a town with a name ending in the suffix 'field' or 'bridge' or 'ford.' They are countless." He paused for a moment. He had been trying to put Wells off this inquiry all evening. "Do you think it important?"

Wells considered for a moment. "It depends entirely on how we interpret the writings on your Ruin, Stedman. If we must go to Farrow, as you think, perhaps it will not matter. The journey to Farrow this time of year, though, is many more days than to any place in the kingdom—assuming the 'gwyddhyll' is in Farrland. If Valary and Kent are involved with the Entonne, as Roderick insists, then it is possible that Massenet could make use of the abbey site while we were at sea on our way to Farrow. It is a risk."

They both heard the steps in the hallway, and paused, wondering who it might be. The door opened without a knock and Sir Roderick stopped in the opening. *"Littel is almost certainly still alive,"* he said, and Galton half rose from his chair. It had happened sooner than he'd hoped.

"But how can that be?" Wells said. "Hawksmoor's men. . . ." He stopped, not liking to use the word "murdered" or "killed."

Roderick shook his head angrily. "I don't know who they were, but they were not Flattery and Littel." He looked up and caught Galton's eye. "Farrelle rest them," he added quickly.

"But where is he, then?" Galton asked, fearing the answer.

"Kent has him, I'm certain. Or will know where he is. I have Hawksmoor out now. We will apprehend Sir Averil and his driver, and whoever else is unlucky enough to be with him. That Entonne-loving historian, I hope. That will be a start." He began to pace across the room. "I can't arrest Massenet, but we can apprehend his agents. We will see." He looked up at his colleagues, something like alarm on his face. "What the duke will do when his son returns with his tale of being hunted by Hawksmoor's people, I don't know. If we are very fortunate, the duke will be satisfied with just Hawksmoor." Palle appeared to see the two men before him for the first time. "Have you both given up sleeping?"

Neither man answered.

"But there can be no rest for any of us now," Palle went on. "We might need to act immediately. Is it possible? Are we ready?"

Wells looked down at the pages spread across the table. "To be honest, Sir Roderick, we don't know. It isn't really a matter of translation at this point so much as interpretation. This is what I have been saying to Stedman. We must perform the ritual correctly: the language—the part that is spoken—is recited in the original tongue. That is not the problem. It is the other elements of the ritual that are not clear, and that is simply because the text is so . . . vague. It speaks in allegory and strange images. We are only guessing at what much of it means."

Palle collapsed in a chair, thinking. "If we perform the ritual incorrectly, what will result?"

Wells looked over at Galton, raising his eyebrows, and then back to Palle. "We are not sure. Perhaps nothing will occur. It's possible that the warding will protect those involved, even from their own mistakes—or it might have another purpose altogether."

"I would venture that there is substantial risk," Galton said quietly. "We are a bit like children playing with a water-driven loom—it is so powerful and our understanding of its mechanisms and purpose so imperfect. There is every chance that it will catch hold of us and drag us in, with tragic results, I fear."

Palle gripped the arms of the chair with his soft hands. "Even so, I don't think we dare delay, Stedman. If the second earth tremor on Farrow meant what we thought, then Tristam Flattery was well along the path we foresaw. Assuming that Llewellyn can do his part, how long could they be?"

Galton shook his head. "Augury is an inexact art, and we are only novices in its practice. I am concerned that we'll rush into action before we're truly prepared to do so. Even if Kent passes Littel's knowledge on to Massenet, are the Entonne better prepared than we? Would they dare perform this ritual so soon? Have they someone with adequate talent?"

"Have we someone with adequate talent?" Palle asked. "That is my fear, though I understand your concern. We might bring ourselves and our purpose to ruin, leaving Massenet the field. But what else can we do? If the Entonne gain this knowledge before we do. . . ."

Wells went to a sideboard and filled three glasses with wine from a decanter. Passing each man a glass, he said, "There are precautionary steps we could take. There is the Ruin on Farrow. Can we not place it under guard so that others cannot employ it?"

Galton shook his head. "Not without drawing great attention to ourselves. Farrow is so small—no matter how quietly this was done, people would soon know."

Wells was staring at a map hanging on the wall. "There

must be several sites around the Entide Sea where the mages performed their rituals. After all, they were practicing their art long before Farrow was discovered." Wells looked back to his companions. "There is this other possibility we have been puzzling over," he added. "The 'gwyddhyll.' My wooded hill."

"You've not given up on the old abbey, then?" Palle asked.

Wells shook his head. "No."

Sir Roderick rose from his chair, gesturing with his glass. "Valary's servant claimed that Kent and his master were extremely excited by what they had discovered up there, but he was not absolutely clear about what it might have been. The man is thick, even for one in his position. I had Hawksmoor send someone up to look, but he reported nothing extraordinary."

"But as I have said to Galton, would they have known what to look for? It might take someone with the knowledge of Kent or Valary to understand what they were seeing." Wells pressed his fingers to his eyes as though he could not bear to have them open a second longer. He did not like to admit that this man Valary might be as knowledgeable as himself. He gave his head a shake, and turned his reddening gaze on each of his companions. "We should send someone to the abbey immediately," he said. "We need to know if something significant lies hidden there."

Palle stopped to consider this, staring into the bowl of his glass as though events were revealed to him in the blood-red light. "No," he said, his voice surprisingly soft. "There is no one we might send who has the knowledge necessary for a proper inquiry. We must travel there ourselves. It is impossible for me to believe that Kent and Valary journeyed so far in winter for no reason. This servant of Valary's is no genius, but his eyesight is perfectly fine. He described a cellar where many carvings had been destroyed. 'A room like a temple apse,' were his words. Nothing left now but scars where its various elements once stood. A number of holes set in the floor, a wall with stones removed or chiseled clean of their design.

Signs that a stream of water had once poured forth from an opening in the rocks and disappeared through the floor." He looked up, his face a bit drawn. "It is likely what we seek, don't you think, Sir Stedman?"

Galton tried to respond accordingly, though he wanted to weep with frustration. "It seems possible. I just don't want to see us wasting time. We know the Ruin on Farrow will suit our purpose."

Palle nodded agreement. "I am more concerned that the site in the abbey is no longer fit for use, if it is in ruins."

Wells shook his head vigorously. "I am sure that it will not prove a problem. It is the place, I think, not the decoration. The stage is the thing here, not the set. Do you think that Kent has told Massenet about this?"

"I fear it is likely. But I think we shall soon be able to ask Kent that very question. Don't be too concerned, Mr. Wells, at least for the moment. As of an hour ago Hawksmoor's people had our good ambassador under his watchful eye. But we must not rely on that continuing," he said. "We must proceed while others talk. Risk is hardly to be considered now. There are too many working against us." He looked pointedly at Galton and Wells. "We will know when Tristam Flattery has completed his task, will we not?"

Wells nodded, lost in thought himself. Then he stirred. "You are right, Roderick. We might wait years to gather all the information we feel we need. There comes a time when we must act or lose our advantage."

❦ ❦ ❦

The door was not locked, but the two young guards stationed outside seemed more than capable of stopping an aging painter from escaping, even in his revitalized state. Kent paced back and forth, swinging his arms, and occasionally muttering in anger.

"I should be frightened," he said aloud. But he was not. Anger was what he felt. He stopped before the window and looked out over the grounds toward the lights of the palace. Occasionally a large carriage would sweep along the lighted carriageway to the main entrance, passing through the trees like the shadow of a hunting owl. There was a function at the palace tonight, but what was it? A ball he thought, though for the life of him he could not remember what had occasioned it.

Kent turned the cold bronze handle of the window and found that it was not locked. He swung it open and stared down. One floor—perhaps twice the height of a tall man. If the ground was soft. . . . But no, it was unlikely that his old bones would stand it. He must not let his temporary return to youth make him take foolish risks.

There was still a chance that Palle merely wanted to speak with him. Most likely he would demand Kent's response to his offer a bit earlier than he had arranged.

But then the guards who had apprehended him had taken Hawkins as well. Pushing the poor driver in with his master and putting their own man to drive. And then, when they arrived here, they had led Hawkins off in a different direction. It did not bode well. *Poor Hawkins,* Kent thought. He hoped he had not put the man in danger.

He crossed to a sideboard and poured himself two fingers of brandy. This was obviously the apartment of a senior officer in the palace guard. There were three badly painted miniatures on the mantlepiece depicting a stern looking woman, and two unremarkable children.

Kent began a thorough search of the room, wondering what he might find that could aid him. A cherrywood box on a small table was a sword case, but it contained no weapon. He pulled open cupboards and drawers and found nothing of import. The occupant of these rooms was apparently named Ceril Hampton, Colonel Ceril Hampton, though that knowledge did him no good. There were Hamptons to burn in Farrland.

Kent stood in the center of the room and glared around him. There were not even bed sheets to tie together to make his escape, as there would be in any good story.

The door opened at that moment, and Kent must have had such a look on his face that even the King's Man hesitated in the doorway. But the hesitation was brief. Palle was accompanied by Noyes, wearing one of his typically outlandish outfits, and two guards.

"Mr. Kent," Roderick nodded.

Kent said nothing but continued to glare. Noyes would not meet his eye.

"Why am I here?"

Palle gave a tight smile, as quick as a blink. "Let us not waste time, Sir Averil," the King's Man said, his voice showing no signs of anger. The guards took up positions to either side of the door. "Will you not sit?"

"I prefer to stand."

"Very well. I am looking for a young scholar named Egar Littel. Only a few days past you helped him escape from Merton. He is wanted for a terrible crime, Mr. Kent. It would give me confidence in your intentions if you would tell us where this man is hiding."

"Littel? I meet so many people, and the name is not uncommon."

A look of pained distaste registered on the face of the King's Man. "Mr. Kent. No one knows where you are." He waved toward the door. "These men are entirely loyal to me. They would torture Princess Joelle if I commanded it. Will you tell me what I want to know, or will I resort to more extreme methods? And do not forget that I have your good driver as well. Perhaps he will be more willing to reveal where Mr. Littel is hiding."

"He does not know," Kent said quickly.

"Ah. . . . Then you do. Please, Kent, consider the heartache you will bring to others." Palle took a chair and folded his hands in his lap. "You should have taken my offer, Kent, rather than trying to continue in your path. It was an offer made in good faith."

Kent stared down at Palle for a few seconds, but the man's face remained impassive, registering nothing—like a page before it is written upon. "I could not ally myself with murderers," Kent said, turning toward Noyes, who looked away immediately.

Palle nodded, as though everything were clear now. "Recently a young Entonne opera singer was seen calling at your home, Sir Averil. This young woman is an agent of Count Massenet. I must say, she is being much more cooperative than you. Earlier, she told me that her sole reason for visiting you was to retrieve a certain letter that Count Massenet desired; which she did. What was the significance of this letter?"

Kent wondered if his alarm showed. He took a seat as casually as he could manage. "I cannot imagine."

Palle laughed softly. "What was it Massenet gave you that made you think you had acquired some form of *diplomatic protection?* Was this the 'root' that you said reached right to the heart of the palace? That would cause enough scandal to bring down the government?" Palle tilted his head as though encouraging an answer. "Massenet is entirely treacherous, Mr. Kent. Loyal only to his King and to his appetites. You see, you should have taken my generous offer." Palle traced a circle on the arm of his chair. "I will make you my final offer. Answer my questions, and I will let you retire honorably to your home in the country. In time you may even be allowed to return to Avonel. Refuse to cooperate with me, Mr. Kent, and I will deprive you of your physic. Consider the fate of poor Trevelyan." He looked up. "Where is this man Littel? Have you passed his knowledge on to Massenet?"

Kent looked over at Noyes, but the man still would not meet his eye, which told Kent only that he felt enormous guilt. Kent shifted in his chair, trying to look as little like a cornered beast as was possible. "Littel is in Locfal, at the home of Tristam Flattery."

Palle looked over at Noyes, then back to Kent. "I wonder if what we learn from your driver will corroborate this. And Massenet?"

"He knows nothing of Mr. Littel, I assure you."

Palle raised his eyebrows as though to say, *"really."* "Then what is the count planning?"

"I'm sure you know as well as I, Sir Roderick. It is you he despises and would thwart at any opportunity. He wishes to stop your *great endeavor,* obviously. But you say you have one of his agents: what does she tell you?"

"A great deal. It is remarkable how informative fear of

beheading will make a person. Treason, Mr. Kent; we tolerate it no more than the Entonne."

Kent knew he should say nothing, but he could not help himself. "And what will you do with her once she has told you everything she knows?"

Palle met Kent's eye, but his look was not so unreadable now. There was amusement there. "That depends on how truthful you are with me, Mr. Kent. I place her life in your hands."

TWENTY-EIGHT

The Duke of Blackwater followed his servant to a small withdrawing room on the main floor.

"What is the hour?" he asked, more than a little irked by being wakened.

"Half twelve, sir."

"My word," the duke muttered.

The man awaiting him was a complete stranger, a servant, the duke realized immediately. Perhaps sixty, balding, utterly fastidious in his modest dress. The man seemed almost overcome with worry. As the duke entered, the man rose and made a leg.

"Sir, you are using the calling card of my friend, Sir Averil Kent. Can you explain this?"

"I am Sir Averil's manservant, Your Grace. I apologize profusely for waking Your Grace at this hour, but I am following Sir Averil's express instructions."

The duke nodded and waved the man back into his chair, taking a seat himself.

"My instructions from Sir Averil were precise. Whenever he leaves the house, he gives me an exact hour by which he will return or send a message. If at any time he fails to do so, I am to take a certain letter and bring it to Your Grace immediately."

"To me?" the duke said, caught by surprise.

"Yes, Your Grace."

"I see. Well, perhaps I should see this letter."

Smithers reached into his coat, a look of great distress on his face. "I retrieved the letter, as instructed, sir, but I could see immediately that the envelope contained nothing." He passed an envelope to the duke, who looked at it, still completely taken aback by what was happening—it was indeed empty. The envelope bore the name of Count Massenet, and the hand seemed vaguely familiar.

"How long is your master overdue?"

"I expected him some hours ago, sir. He has never failed to send a message in the past."

"What ... what did Sir Averil expect of me?"

"I don't know," Smithers said, looking both embarrassed and deeply distressed. "He said that Your Grace would know."

The duke nodded, staring at the writing again. "Sir Averil disappeared not long ago, when he was visiting Merton, and then reappeared unharmed. Perhaps that will be the case again."

"I hope Your Grace is correct, but I think circumstances might be different. As I slipped out the back of our home, a group of men arrived. I stood in the shadows, not too far off, and watched them, trying to determine if they were friends of Sir Averil—perhaps bearing a message. When they finally managed to raise the housemaid, they thrust her aside and forced their way into the house. From the sounds, and what could be seen at the windows, these men appeared to be searching the house quite thoroughly. I slipped away then and came immediately here."

"And you did not know these men?"

"I did not, but if I had to guess, I would say they served the King's Man."

"Where had Sir Averil gone, do you know?"

"He seldom says, sir."

The duke nodded. "I think you should stay here for the rest of the night, Smithers. I will do what I can to locate your master."

The duke sat thinking after the manservant had been led away. For a moment he considered waking the duchess, but decided to let her rest.

When the servant returned, the duke considered a moment longer. "Wake Lord Jaimas and Miss Alissa," he instructed, and the servant backed from the room, exhibiting no surprise at this request.

A quarter of the hour went silently by before the two arrived, looking more anxious than sleepy.

"Is it Mother?" Jaimas asked immediately, making an effort to sound calm.

"No. No, the duchess is perfectly well. It is Kent." He related what had happened.

Alissa and Jaimy looked at each other, not liking what they heard, he could see.

"Where had Mr. Kent gone off to?" Alissa asked.

"The servant did not know. Kent wisely tells him little, I think."

Alissa bit her lip, lost in concentration. "When I visited him this morning, he said nothing that would indicate his plans." She looked at the duke. "Did the letter I brought offer any clues?"

The duke considered a moment. "He wrote to inform me that the plants the King keeps hidden in his arboretum had begun to flower. Do you know what I refer to?" Jaimy and Alissa nodded. "He indicated that Palle's group did not yet know of this, but once they did, he believed, it would set them on a course that would endanger all of Farrland. Kent is not known to be melodramatic. I'm sure what he says is true."

"Do you think the palace has taken him?" Jaimy asked.

For some reason the casualness with which this was said made the duke very sad. The statement spoke too much truth about Farrland at the present. "It is quite likely. I will find out. Better sooner than later." He picked up the empty envelope, glancing at it again. "This hand . . . it is familiar. . . . He proffered the envelope to Jaimas, and he and Alissa bent over it.

"The princess," Alissa blurted out.

The duke looked at her, more questions in that gaze than anything. "You're certain?"

"Yes. The duchess could confirm it, but I'm quite sure."

The duke shook his head. It was not what he was expecting to hear. Kent had possessed a letter from the princess to Massenet. But the letter had been stolen, apparently, the envelope left in hopes that Kent would not notice the theft immediately. And this letter was to come to him if anything happened to Kent. It suggested innumerable possibilities.

"I should get a message to the Countess of Chilton immediately," Jaimy said, thinking aloud.

The duke nodded. "Yes. There is a ball at the palace," he said suddenly, "I will go see what I might learn."

Alissa rose from her chair. "I'll look like a country cousin, but I could be ready almost immediately."

The duke considered this a moment. "Yes. As quickly as you can. And Jaimas, you will accompany me, also. Let us see what effect that has on the King's Man."

ਹੈ   ਹੈ   ਹੈ

Prince Wilam was trying to escape two very pleasant sisters, daughters of a marquess, who unfortunately bored him into somnolence. He kept trying to catch the eye of a young naval officer whose express duty that evening was to intervene as subtly as possible when such things occurred. Unfortunately the man was suffering a similar fate himself—the daughter of an admiral had his undivided attention—leaving the prince alternately furious and trying not to laugh at the absurdity of the situation.

The more he tried not to laugh, the more fragile his control became. The more fragile his control, the more animation the sisters forced into their conversation, looking distinctly uncomfortable at the prince's reddening face.

"Eh-xcuse me," the prince said, turning a laugh into something resembling a sneeze. It was at that moment that the Duke of Blackwater entered the room, accompanied by Alissa Somers and Lord Jaimas. All feelings of levity fled. Ignoring his companions, the prince began to search the room for Palle and spotted the King's Man just as one of his assistants brought the duke to Sir Roderick's attention.

Palle's face did not change when he turned his gaze on

the duke and his, undeniably, living son, but it froze for just a moment, as though he had been stunned into immobility—like a man who has seen something horrific in the midst of battle. And then he turned away, speaking close to his assistant's ear as he swept out of the room. Noyes followed in his wake, looking back over his shoulder once, clearly frightened.

"He is wearing a sword," one of the sisters whispered, and the prince followed their gaze, realizing that they referred to the Duke of Blackwater. Since Beaumont had written his scathing attack on the barbarians who strode about bristling with weapons—and had not been challenged to a duel for it—the wearing of swords had fallen out of fashion, and the duel had almost disappeared. But here was a most civilized man wearing a rapier at his hip, and it did not appear to be a dress sword.

"Flames," the prince heard himself say.

Alissa and Jaimas made their way immediately toward Princess Joelle, and as the prince's eye followed them, he realized that his father, Prince Kori, had disappeared at the same time as the King's Man.

"I must congratulate Lord Jaimas on his coming marriage," the prince lied, and with a smile frozen in place, escaped his sleep fairies.

The prince could not make his way through the crowd quickly enough to reach his mother before Alissa and Jaimas, but he was only seconds behind them.

"Kent is gone," his mother whispered as soon as he was close enough.

Alissa did not meet his eye, but Jaimas' bow and the look on his face spoke of no animosity.

"If he is on the palace grounds, we know where they would keep him," the prince said. He looked quickly around the room and realized that several prominent lords had gathered around the Duke of Blackwater. "We should waste no time. Let me collect our loyal few," he said, and hurried off.

🦅 🦅 🦅

The guards were taken aback when they opened the door. Princess Joelle stood there, dressed for the ball and wearing a lord's fortune in precious stones. Beside her a young lord and the Duke of Blackwater stood silently, their stance determined: both carried swords.

"You will release Sir Averil Kent to me immediately," the princess said, her tone suggesting that compliance was not optional.

"Sir Averil?" the senior guard said, almost stuttering in his surprise.

The princess stepped aside so that the guard could see she was not without armed Palace Guards of her own. "Take these two men into custody. They have broken their oath and the laws of the Kingdom."

The sound of a sword being drawn hissed in the darkness. The lords of Blackwater pushed the door open and the guards on duty fell back, drawing their weapons. They may have been well trained in their duties, but their instructors had never imagined that they would be confronted by a member of the Royal Family. The two parties squared off, and, just when it seemed they would acquiesce, Palle's men chose which side they would back.

The struggle was brief, and the guards who came running to the clash of swords were so surprised by the situation that the building quickly fell to the princess and her supporters.

As soon as the fighting stopped, Princess Joelle entered the house, but was stopped by what she saw, color draining from her face. One guard lay unmoving on the floor, a small pool of blood forming slowly beneath him, and two others clutched wounds, anger written on their faces.

"It has begun," she said softly, and a single tear clung to her lashes, quivering there like a jewel taking form from the substance of human sadness and remorse.

They found Kent standing before an open window, staring down into the darkened garden. He spun quickly upon hearing the door, and for a second seemed disoriented, staring oddly at the rapiers, drawn and stained. His manner changed, becoming stiff and formal, his face grim with knowledge.

"Your Highness," he said, bowing formally, his voice laden with concern. "I prayed it would never come to this."

The princess seemed affected by Kent's reaction, and she stood for a moment as though overwhelmed by doubts. "We must hurry, Sir Averil," she said. "Nothing is settled. We may all be under armed guard before the night is over."

🐛   🐛   🐛

The ball continued, music drifting through the doors and into the myriad hallways of the palace like faint ghosts. No one was quite sure what would result from their actions, not even the princess. The unspoken rules that governed Farr politics were being broken by all sides. Palle and his supporters had attempted to murder the son of one of the kingdom's most powerful lords, and then they had abducted one of Farrland's most famed citizens—and all for their own purpose. And now the duke and a princess royal had risen against them, which would divide the government, at the very least. But everyone realized that they could not afford to lose their nerve now.

The princess gathered her supporters at the guard house and marched on the palace, armed almost entirely with the element of surprise. In consultation with the duke, they had agreed that immediate action was their only option. If Galton would side with them, and they could produce the King during a lucid period, they could then claim that Palle and Prince Kori had usurped power in the kingdom, keeping the King under the influence of a powerful physic. The regency could be dissolved and, at the very least, Palle brought down.

It was a dangerous gamble. Everyone understood that it could mean their own imprisonment, or even civil war. Their best chance lay in taking Palle and Prince Kori immediately, before they realized what was planned.

The Duke of Blackwater and guards loyal to the princess led the way into the palace through a little-used door. They swept into the larger hallways, surprising servants and guards as they went, taking them all in tow so that they could not sound the alarm.

They came into one of the main thoroughfares and saw, in the distance, a lone woman, dressed for the ball. She paused, shocked to see a band of armed men proceeding down the hallway, but just as she turned to flee, she hesitated. Wavered so that she almost lost balance.

"Lady Galton!" the duke called, and the woman's shoulders could be seen to sag with relief. She came hurrying down the hall as quickly as her elaborate gown would allow.

She was out of breath when she arrived. "They ... have fled," she managed, and the princess and Alissa pushed through to take her arms, offering her support. Assisting her to sit in a chair.

She looked up at them, terribly distressed. "All of them ..." she said. "The prince, Palle, Wells. . . . Gone. And they have Stedman with them."

"But where?" the duke asked, bending to one knee. "Where would they go?"

Lady Galton raised a hand, nodding, clearly indicating that she knew, but must catch her breath before speaking. She turned away from the group then, removing something from the bodice of her gown. She handed several folded sheets of thick paper to the princess, who opened them quickly.

"But what is this?" She showed the pages to the duke who waved Kent forward.

The painter took one look and turned to Lady Galton. "The missing section of the text?"

She nodded, still unable to speak.

"But where has my husband gone?" the princess asked.

"Tremont Abbey," Lady Galton whispered, barely managing to find enough breath.

Palle and his group had indeed fled. The princess and her followers secured the palace while most of the people in attendance at the ball had no idea that anything untoward occurred. Others, slightly more in the know, realized that something was happening and speculated endlessly in whispers. A third group knew that there was a struggle in the kingdom that had just broken out in actual hostilities, and they had slipped out of the palace quickly, and were desperately trying to gather information on what transpired.

No doubt, some of these were committed to one side or another, but many were waiting to see which way the struggle would go before declaring themselves. It was not important to them who won, as long as they were, in the end, aligned with the winners.

There was a very small fourth group who actually were players in the drama, and most of those had gathered in a state dining room on the ground floor. It was not a large gathering, Princess Joelle and her son, the Duke of Blackwater and Lord Jaimas, Kent and his rescued driver, Lady Galton, Alissa Somers, the Marquess of Sennet, several officers of the Palace Guard, the Sea Lord and his wife, and one Entonne opera singer, who looked decidedly frightened and out of place.

Sennet was sitting on the edge of his chair, shaking his head, not in disbelief so much as awe. "And I thought I knew what transpired in the Kingdom." He kept glancing up at Kent with something like admiration, a bemused smile spreading over his face.

A map lay on the table and the duke and Jaimy were leaning over it, occasionally tracing some significant line with a finger. Alissa sat with Lady Galton, who was recovering and trying not to be seen watching the beautiful young Entonne girl who sat by herself, looking entirely dejected. Kent had spoken to her earlier, not unkindly, but their conversation had been in Entonne—something about a letter—and Alissa had not caught it all. The woman had shown great difficulty meeting the painter's eye, and had been near to tears, Alissa thought. Very odd, but then everything about the situation was extraordinary. She was not sure that anyone really believed what had happened. In less than an hour their entire world had changed, and they were the agents of this change.

Alissa wondered if she would not have been better off staying in Merton and marrying some young scholar, as her father had wanted. She had enough knowledge of what went on to realize that if this rebellion failed she would likely be charged with treason. It was frightening knowledge to have.

In its absence, the powers of the Regency Council would normally devolve to Lord Harrington, the Chancellor of the Exchequer. Alissa remembered Kent pointing out Lord Harrington at the duchess' birthday celebration. He was a very small, dapper man, known for his brilliance. If he had a weakness as a politician, it was his alleged single-minded drive to increase his personal fortune—not that this was uncommon among ministers, Alissa was given to understand.

At the moment no one knew Lord Harrington's whereabouts. *"Probably plundering the treasury,"* someone had suggested, but it had sounded too much like gallows humor, and the laughter had been bitten off short. Alissa sensed that there was nothing that worried the people present so much at this moment, unless it was the sudden disappearance of Palle and his entire cabal.

Jaimy stood with his father speaking in low tones, both terribly serious, but there was something else in their manner.

She felt at that moment that these men were strangers to her. Men who discussed the fate of the kingdom as though it were not absurd to be doing so. As though it were not unnatural. She was overcome by a feeling that she did not belong in this room. Perhaps did not want to belong here. This was not the insular world of Merton where politics was another subject for discussion, like literature, or philosophy. In this room politics had ceased to be theory.

Jaimy's belief that he could avoid the responsibilities of his position was proven naive here, and this, she found, caused her great distress.

Alissa was also aware that the prince occasionally looked her way, as much as he tried not to. Oh, he did not stare, nor was he obvious about it, but he could not stop himself from glancing at her. Alissa sensed this more than saw it, for she would not meet his gaze. If this rebellion actually survived the night, the prince would be put forward to succeed the King, rather than Prince Kori. No one had said this, but it was obvious. Prince Kori would have to fall with Palle and the others—abdicate in favor of his son. This young man who was infatuated with her would be next in line for the throne.

The door opened and a woman was allowed to enter. Everyone turned toward her, but no one spoke or made any gesture of welcome.

"Lady Rawdon," Lady Galton whispered near Alissa's ear.

The woman who had stopped inside the door was not beautiful, but she had such bearing and poise that she drew the eye all the same. Alissa did not know Lady Rawdon, but had heard she had been very ill only the previous year. For some reason Alissa was interested to see the woman who had captured the heart of the royal physician, for Benjamin Rawdon was one of the most admired men in the kingdom; by the ladies at least. He was certainly one of the most handsome men Alissa had ever seen, though aloof and distracted in his manner.

The duke greeted her, acting as the princess' representative—a sort of Queen's Man.

Lady Rawdon did not speak, but stood looking about her, as though suddenly and uncharacteristically unsure of herself.

"I wish to speak with the princess. I beg your indulgence, Duke, but it is concerning a matter of some sensitivity."

The duke glanced at the princess, who nodded, and he waved Lady Rawdon forward. As she passed, Alissa saw that she had the most intelligent look. As though her mental acuity was so strong that it almost shone in her eyes, the way self-doubt did in others.

Lady Rawdon and the princess went to the far end of

the long room, and spoke quietly before the hearth. The
princess stood aloof from this woman—unquestionably a
sovereign being petitioned by one of her subjects, and not
necessarily one she felt any warmth or compassion toward.

Thinking that it was impolite to stare at this private interchange, Alissa looked away, but noticed that the duke
stared openly, his manner intent. Alissa was certain that
he could not be concerned for the princess' safety, and
wondered what it was that caused him to act so.

Suddenly he turned and crossed to Lady Galton. Bending down close to her he whispered, "Did Rawdon cure
his wife with this seed?"

Lady Galton's head snapped up at his question, and she
met the duke's eye. "You would be wise not to pursue
this," she said quietly, a slight quaver in her voice, her
head shaking as she spoke.

"It is true, then?" the duke said, ignoring her admoni-
tion.

Lady Galton did not answer, but her eyes searched the
duke's as though she were deciding what he might do
with this information.

The princess left Lady Rawdon standing by the hearth
and returned, walking directly toward the duke and Lady
Galton, gesturing for her son to follow. Alissa stayed
where she was, and realized she had not been so close to
the prince all evening, even though he purposely stood on
the opposite side of the circle.

"Do not rise, cousin," the princess said to Lady Galton,
who held so tightly to Alissa's hand that she could not
rise either, though no one seemed to notice. "Lady
Rawdon claims that her husband is disillusioned with Sir
Roderick and the prince. He is nearby, she will not say
where, unwilling to leave the King, who is his charge.
Rawdon is prepared to give his support to us, and Lady
Rawdon has told me Roderick's destination to prove her
good faith."

The duke cast his gaze toward the woman standing
near the fireplace, but she had her back to them and stood
hugging herself, her head to one side, staring down as

though lost in sad memories. The duke turned back to the princess. "Lady Galton has already told us their destination. Why did Palle fly when he did, leaving only Rawdon behind? That is the information we require. If she will tell us that, I will look more kindly on their defection, for it is remarkably convenient that she has come to us now. If we carry the day, they will be safe, and if we do not, they will claim that they had no choice but to make concessions to preserve the King." The duke stopped to think for a moment. "I also fear that Rawdon will control the King's mental state with this physic, as Your Highness has suggested that he does. If we cannot prove His Majesty to be competent—our resistance will be treason."

The princess stood with an arm folded across her breast, the hand supporting the opposite elbow so that she could stroke her chin with the free hand. "Only Rawdon truly understands this physic. It has all been kept such a secret. I do not know what will happen to the King if we do not have Rawdon to attend him. I tend to think that Lady Rawdon is sincere. I have never known her to be otherwise. And if that is true, we could certainly use Rawdon's voice to support our claims."

"I have never thought anything but the best of Lady Rawdon," the duke conceded, "and before his support of Palle, I always thought highly of her husband. Will Rawdon sign documents that explain how the King has been kept in a state of near madness and dependence? Will he name Palle and Prince Kori as the instigators?"

"Yes," the princess said. "He will denounce the regents and swear that the King is competent still. My husband asked the doctor to stay to watch over the King. Say what you will against the prince, he has not allowed the King to suffer any accident, which would have been the easiest way to power. Apparently regicide is beyond even him."

The duke looked over at Lady Rawdon again. "I say we should accept their pledge of loyalty, but keep them under careful scrutiny. If we are to claim that Palle and the prince seized power from a competent King, then His

Majesty must appear competent. That is the one certainty."

Both pain and exasperation were revealed in the princess' next words. "Then we cannot allow the King to continue this overindulgence in the seed. Palle and the prince fostered this dependence and now Rawdon must bring it under control, without endangering the King's life."

Alissa wondered immediately how much the duke's own interest in the seed had colored his judgment. It was obvious that his questioning of Lady Galton was not innocent.

The princess put her hands together. "Then we agree," she said. "But we mustn't forget that we are restoring power to the King. It is our only chance of survival. If Lord Harrington is confronted with a King restored in both mind and position, then he will be taking the greatest risk to not pledge his support. We must move quickly to legitimize our position and gain recognition from the senior ministers."

With that the princess crossed back to Lady Rawdon and took her hands, kissing her on both cheeks in the Entonne manner. They spoke for a moment, and then Lady Rawdon hurried out, leaving the princess to return to her supporters.

"Lady Rawdon says that Palle and his followers fled Avonel the moment they learned that Count Massenet and this Entonne doctor, Varese, had slipped away and gone north. Palle and the prince were convinced Massenet was making for Tremont Abbey, and they went in immediate pursuit. It was only coincidental that the duke arrived at the same moment."

Kent bobbed his head. "Yes. Yes. That makes sense. My own colleague, Mr. Valary, believes the abbey was once used by the mages for certain rituals, before it was destroyed by the Farrellites. . . . And maybe even after. I have seen it myself. In a hidden chamber in a deep cellar there was once a close copy of the Ruin of Farrow." Kent held up the pages that Lady Galton had given him. "Mr.

Littel and Mr. Valary must see this. They are the authorities."

"And the Countess of Chilton, Lord Jaimas tells me," the duke added.

Kent nodded, obviously still unwilling to name the countess.

"We need their counsel, then," the princess said quickly. "Can you have them brought here?"

Kent nodded. "Though I cannot speak for the countess. She has remained aloof these thirty years. I don't think she will emerge, now, no matter what goes on in the kingdom."

"I will write the countess myself," the princess said. "We must draw upon all the wisdom we can in these matters. We have not a moment to waste. The struggle for the kingdom may be waged far away."

The dining room had been chosen because of its proximity to both the apartments of the King and to the arboretum where His Majesty spent much of his time. The princess and her followers could not risk having the King fall into the hands of their rivals, and so put this area under control of those Palace Guards who were most trusted.

Kent and Sennet had commandeered a separate table, and immediately set about gathering information on the state of the capital. A constant stream of supporters came and went, reporting everything they learned. Alissa was astonished by the number of informants the two gentlemen could call into service on such short notice. Every so often one or both of them would report something to the duke and the princess, and occasionally the duke, would go to them with questions.

Alissa had the distinct impression that the individuals gathered in this room were like people walking in the dark, listening so intently that their own heartbeats were almost too loud, overwhelming the faint sounds they sought so desperately. She felt they attempted to sense vibrations, movements in the air, and even tried to look into the pitch-black night. The tension in the room was captured in this forced silence.

Somewhere in the city of Avonel, officers loyal to the Regency Council might be gathering an army. Lord Harrington could be plotting to take the palace, even now. The princess had secured the grounds, but at this point it was impossible to be sure of the loyalty of every guard. It would take only a single man opening a gate, and everyone in this room could find themselves in prison.

"You must turn your mind elsewhere," Lady Galton said, regaining her breath finally. "There is no profit in dwelling on what might happen, Lady Alissa. We have taken a leap into the darkness, unsure of where we will land. But there is no way to turn back in midair. We must land where we will land, and try to keep our feet. There is nothing else for it. That is all we can do." She squeezed Alissa's hand and smiled kindly at her, which touched the younger woman. At a moment that would be written in Farr history, this woman had taken time to comfort her. It showed a kindness and compassion that Alissa thought she would never equal.

An hour later Sir Benjamin Rawdon arrived in the company of his wife. The physician appeared troubled and more than a little apprehensive. He made a leg to the princess, and, very self-consciously, swore an oath of loyalty to the King, renouncing his allegiance to the Regency Council. After this formality, Prince Wilam and the duke accompanied the princess and Sir Benjamin to visit the King.

It was near to morning by this time and people were leaving the ball; most still completely unaware of what had gone on, which Alissa found astonishing. But then, only a year earlier she would not even have received an invitation, let alone known what transpired behind the closed doors of the palace. She was a little saddened to realize how far even the educated of Farrland were from the true workings of government.

Jaimy was sent as envoy to the Countess of Chilton, and Alissa accompanied Lady Galton, who had been summoned to the famous arboretum. Alissa thought she would never look pityingly at an elderly person again. The older generation in the persons of Lady Galton, Kent, and Sennet, seemed to be proving their mettle tonight.

A guard led them down a path that wound its way through dense jungle. Despite the season outside, beneath the glass it was almost hot, and quite humid. Alissa wondered if any of these plants were kingfoil; but none seemed to fit the description Tristam had given Jaimy. The sound of water falling and then a sweet tenor floated through the branches, sounds as ethereal as the flight of a butterfly.

They found Rawdon seated on a stone bench, listening to Teiho Ruau, who stood by a small pond, singing as though his heart would break. The music touched Alissa immediately, though she could not understand a word. Her eyes adjusted to the poor light, and she realized that Prince Wilam sat beside someone slumped on a cushioned bench, almost hidden by the darkness. Close at hand the princess was seated in her own chair, and beside her the duke.

Rawdon gestured to them, and gave up his bench. For a few moments Alissa sat, transported by the singing. She had heard Ruau perform only once, and that had been Farr and Entonne music, but this was a sweet foreign tongue, a song of heartache, she was sure; of loss or parting. The staccato of falling water, and the sweet perfume of exotic flowers combined to make the situation seem entirely unreal. It was almost impossible to believe she was in Farrland in late winter.

The song ended, much to Alissa's regret, though it left an ache in her breast that would not be easily erased.

The Royal Physician escorted Lady Galton forward to take the prince's place. Prince Wilam bowed to his grandfather and turned toward Alissa. She realized that he was going to come and sit beside her—he simply could not help himself.

Neither of them spoke, though he motioned for her not to rise and curtsy, so they exchanged nods only. Above the sound of the tumbling water Alissa could hear the mumble of conversation between Lady Galton, the King, and the princess. His Majesty's voice was a deep, disconcerting rumble; a sound no human throat should have been capable of producing.

Rawdon caught Alissa's eye and whispered to her. "We will see Lady Galton safely returned."

Prince Wilam rose immediately. "It would be an honor to escort you back, Lady Alissa." He offered his hand, and she accepted it to rise but purposely did not take his arm as they left.

"I had not heard Teiho Ruau sing in his own tongue. Very beautiful," Alissa said as they passed into the jungle.

"Yes. I have found that not understanding the words is a small impediment—the sentiment is conveyed perfectly. Dr. Rawdon's associate, a man named Llewellyn, spent some time translating the lyrics, and though I found these of great interest, my appreciation of the songs was not greatly increased. It occurred to me that one could translate the words of our best Farr songs into an unknown tongue and they would affect the heart just as strongly. Music is a conduit for emotion." He cocked his head at her. "Do you play?"

"Not well, though I enjoy it a great deal. And you?"

"Poorly. I have often though that I was born with the temperament of an artist, but none of the talents." She could see his smile in the poor light.

"Perhaps you have not found your talent, yet, Your Highness."

"I would like to think that is true, but I suspect it's not. I will have to learn to be a passable King, I'm afraid."

An awkward silence fell, as false as the conversation that had preceded it. Alissa could not bear empty conversation, and wondered how she would survive as a duchess of Farrland.

The prince began to speak, but Alissa raised her hand. "Say nothing, please. Let us have silence that is true: like music without words."

The prince nodded his head, and they walked on in silence. Alissa knew what emotion this silence conveyed, and felt deep regret that she could not respond.

ṽ   ṽ   ṽ

Lady Galton found that the arboretum had a surprisingly kind effect on her breathing. Heat and dampness hardly seemed a physic for improved breathing, but then perhaps it was really the soothing sounds of the falling water, the charm and serenity of the environment.

"I will die without it," the King said to the princess. "Look. Look what want of it has done to me already. I am living my death. Who can even bear to set eyes on me? NO! I must have more, not less. More!"

"But if the Ministers of the Government cannot be convinced that His Majesty is competent, then Prince Kori and Palle will return, and the seed will fall under their control again. They will let you slip back into your world of dreams, while stealing the kingdom."

"But I am old, old. What need have I to govern? Let me have my physic. Have I not earned my rest? A century I have labored. A *century*."

The princess was near to tears, Lady Galton thought. This terrible, willful old man would condemn them all to prison or worse if he would not cooperate. The princess had underestimated his desire for the seed. It was greater than his desire to do well by his kingdom. He had sacrificed everything to it, why not his daughter-in-law and grandson? Had he asked them to stage this rebellion?

"Your Majesty must remember that Palle would withhold the seed when he wanted to bend you to his will. Withhold it and make Your Majesty suffer. I ask only that you reduce your intake until we have proven your competence. Once there is a new King's Man and the succession is arranged to Your Majesty's satisfaction—the throne going to Wil—then you may do as you like."

"*I will do as I like now!*" he raged in his terrible voice.

"But they have set out to retrieve the knowledge of the mages," Lady Galton said suddenly. "What will we do if they accomplish that?"

The King shook his head, rubbing his brow gently. "Yes. I remember. Yes. That young Flattery came, and then they sent him on their errand. Has the time come? Has Elorin fulfilled her promise?"

"What promise?" the princess asked.

"Where have they gone?" he asked, suddenly calm, almost interested, "Palle and the others?"

"Tremont Abbey."

"I see. Yes. Then we must go as well. Bring my physic, and Ruau, and this treacherous doctor, too. He keeps my physic from me. Ready my carriage, bring a company of loyal guards. We must leave at first light, but don't forget my physic. And my portrait. Has Kent finished my portrait? There is no hope without him. There is nothing more certain than that."

"But, Your Majesty," Princess Joelle said soothingly, "we must convince the Ministers that you are lucid, and that the Regency Council is unnecessary."

The old man shifted on his bench so that he looked at his daughter-in-law in the darkness. "My dear Joelle," he said, a sudden clarity of thought apparent in those terrible tones, "if we do not arrive at the abbey before Sir Roderick; who controls the kingdom according to the law will be of no importance whatsoever. All will be lost. Ready my carriage. If we ruin a hundred horses, we must be at the abbey before Palle, or everything I have planned will be lost. Ready yourself in all haste. I leave in three hours."

❧ ❧ ❧

Alissa sat by the window watching the sun rise through the mist which hung in the garden like a thin wash of paint smeared across the air. An arrangement of purple iris and pale yellow roses stood before the window in a simple vase, catching the morning light. One particular rose had opened far beyond maturity, as though attempting to reveal its heart, and appeared almost languid, the largest outer petal falling away like the train of a lady's gown. She admired the way the light and shadow fell among the petals. How the fluted edges caught the sun and rippled through the shadows like movement on the surface of water. Astonishing that the flower had achieved this moment of intense beauty only an instant before its petals would fall. The slightest breeze would carry them away—a door opening too quickly, a child running near.

"Everything is so fragile," she whispered.

Jaimy found her there some time later. The morning sun had risen, like a ship's flare, and hung burning beyond the park, casting a golden light over Alissa, illuminating the straying strands of her auburn hair. She sat on a divan, her arms around her drawn-up knee, her skirt trailing like a fan to the floor. She cradled her head on her arms, and Jaimy thought he had never seen such dejection.

As he took a seat beside her, she raised her head: obviously she had not been sleeping, as he thought.

"You look very dejected, my love," he said softly.

"Dejected? No, I am merely adjusting to what I now perceive as the real world."

Jaimy reached out and put a hand gently on her back. "Yes. It has all changed in so few hours. Suddenly we are risking everything over this matter, though it is not entirely clear what it all means."

She looked at him closely for a moment, and then took his hand and wrapped his arm around her, turning away and pressing her back against him. "That is not the reality I speak of," she said. "If we survive this, I will become a real duchess—not just one in name. We will be embroiled in the intrigues of the court, the social life of the aristocracy, the constant concern for power and place. We think we can avoid it and live quietly, but we cannot. Without your father, tonight, what would have happened? And it is the duke's place you take, with all its attendant responsibilities. Our lives will not be our own."

Jaimy put his cheek against her back and heard the slow measured beat of her heart, or was it his own? He could not be sure. "Although my heart would be broken, utterly, Alissa. . . ." For a second his nerve failed, but then he shut his eyes and continued in a whisper. "I would release you from your vow if you will not be happy in our life together." It was said. The heartbeat did not alter but continued to measure the endless silence.

"I will consider your offer," Alissa said in a small voice. "Jaimas?"

"Yes."

"I love only you."

The sun continued to wash them in the colors of a late winter morning, and they sat unmoving, not wanting to give up the other's presence. A petal fell from the rose, turning once slowly in the air, before landing without a sound.

❦ ❦ ❦

Tier and Tarré draw near and far
While starlit gates await the hand
The moon shall sail o'er hidden realms
To seek the heart of mage and man.

Valary pushed ineffectually at his unruly hair, and stared down at the pages Lady Galton had delivered. "Tier and Tarré are the names of stars, I believe, but possibly names of places as well. There are other references to them, you see. Lapin mentioned Tier in the presence of Dunn, who recorded everything he could remember the mage saying, though he did not understand the reference. A star, a place—those were his guesses."

Littel sat massaging his temples, his excitement only somewhat blunted by his obvious exhaustion. "The translation is competent. I see a few things that I would dispute, but largely it is good." He placed his finger on one page. "This line is certainly open to argument, but then. . . . It is hard to be sure."

"But what do you think it means?" It was the princess speaking. The room had been cleared of everyone but the princess, Prince Wilam, the Duke of Blackwater, Kent, Lady Galton, and Sennet, and the countess, who sat in a corner of the purposely darkened room (her face hidden by a veil) where she was the object of deep fascination for everyone there.

Valary straightened up, rubbed his eyes for just a second, and then looked around the group. "My best guess is that it is a ritual for opening a portal—'the way beneath the vaulted hills.' I've now come to believe that Tier is the site beneath the ruin of Tremont Abbey. I have several reasons for this. . . ." He lifted a finger like a lecturer and then saw the look on Kent's face. "But I can explain another time. This text seems to imply that two such sites must be employed simultaneously." He pointed to the pages on the table. "It states several times that one must heed the words of Tarré. We might ask Lady Chilton, but I think this would mean the rite is performed turn about. The person performing the rite at one site taking his turn and then the other."

"But where is the other site?" Kent asked. "Farrow?"

"It seems most likely."

"I think you will find that the site is on Varua, Mr. Valary," the countess said, her flat tones catching everyone's attention so that they turned toward this apparition in the corner, intensely fascinated. The countess raised a gloved hand. "That is what the signs mean, I think. The *regis* blossoming. The appearance of the ghost boy to Sir Averil and Lord Jaimas. This earth tremor on Farrow. Tristam Flattery has begun the transformation from human to mage. This ritual will be the culmination of that process, or so I surmise."

"But what of all this talk of gates? To where do they lead?"

"Perhaps the question might be to what do they lead, Mr. Littel. Knowledge, I fear. The knowledge we thought lost."

"My uncle, Erasmus Flattery, believed that the mages were involved in a great undertaking," said the duke, causing Kent to turn suddenly. "An undertaking that absorbed almost all their efforts for some time. Decades, he thought. My uncle didn't know the precise nature of this endeavor, but Eldrich apparently referred to it as 'the grand exploration.' It was Erasmus' obsession, though I am not sure how much he actually learned in the end."

"Well," Sennet said, speaking for the first time since

this group had gathered, "it seems clear that we cannot let Palle or Massenet have whatever knowledge there is to be found. We must have it first."

There was a moment of silence and then Kent said kindly, "No one must have it, Sennet, absolutely no one. Not even someone as kindly and honorable as yourself. That was what the mages learned in the end, though we have only suspicions of why. But rest assured, we do not race Palle and Massenet to gain the knowledge ourselves. We go to destroy it forever."

Sennet looked as though he would protest but finally nodded. If he was embarrassed at his mistake, he did not show it.

"Kent is absolutely right." Valary opened a small box that lay among the chaos of his papers. With great care he removed a yellowed scrap of paper from a stiff envelope. "I am absolutely certain that this is authentic. These are the words of Lucklow:

I have been a witness to this horror and can tell you that our colleague exaggerated nothing. Children armed with fearsome weapons roam the streets as brigands, killing man or woman for little gain—often enough for none at all. Sky choked with a yellowish pall, noxious and unwholesome to the lung, it blots out the blue by day and the stars by night. The poor starve on the paving stones, and citizens shut themselves up in homes that have casements barred and doors of iron. In our darkest times we have not known such calamity, and this is the common day in this benighted land! At all costs we must end this fool's endeavor! We are tainted enough as it is."

Valary looked up at those gathered around the table. There was a profound silence, broken only by Lady Galton's breathing.

"We believe that this 'fool's endeavor' Lucklow refers to is the same matter spoken of by the duke," Kent said quietly. "We may never know what it was the mages encountered, but by all accounts Lucklow was a man of considerable brilliance. If it frightened him, then it terrifies me. We would not easily make a decision to bring Farrland to an end, yet that is, in effect, what the mages chose to do. By refusing to train the generation to follow, they brought an end to their world. Imagine us choosing to bear no children, and letting the human race come to an end. That is what they did. And, as Valary has said, we may never know why. But this knowledge is enough for me."

"Where in the world did you come by that?" Littel asked, incredulous.

Kent looked directly at the princess as he answered. "It came from Count Massenet, though we are sure it is no forgery."

This brought a second silence, not quite as deep as the first. Everyone in the room wondered how in the world Kent had managed to come by this document, yet no one wanted to hear the answer. The name Massenet was used in the palace to conjure visions of betrayal and treason.

Jaimas broke the silence. "Sir Averil? Does Roderick have someone who can perform this ritual? I thought that was the role they had hoped Tristam would fulfil."

Kent shook his head. "I don't understand it either." He glanced at the princess, and then Lady Galton. "I thought that they were seeking someone with talent as well. Perhaps they seek only to stop the Entonne."

"Baron Trevelyan," Lady Galton said. "He was their last resort if they could find no other."

"Trevelyan?" Kent said, shaking his head sadly. "No. The poor baron is quite mad."

"Not at all times, and Stedman thought that Palle could control this condition, at least for short periods of time. Rawdon would know."

"And the Entonne have Bertillon—and Varese filling in for Mr. Valary and Mr. Littel—though what they hope to accomplish, I cannot say." Kent looked down at the pages spread over the table. "Have they discovered some text we know nothing of, or did they manage to steal the work of Wells and Galton? I will ask this young Entonne singer, though it is unlikely that she will agree to answer." Kent closed his eyes for a second, as though fatigue had caught up with him as well.

"Perhaps they mean to damage the site at the abbey in some way. Make it unusable for others?" the duke suggested, and then turned to ask a question of the countess. "But where has Lady Chilton gone?"

Her chair was empty. The guard at the door reported that the woman in the veil had left several moments earlier, though no one in the room had noticed.

Kent immediately went in search of the countess and soon learned that she had left the palace, and, to his utter astonishment, taken Tenil with her. The painter sat down on a bench in an alcove, looking out over the gardens. The countess had gone without so much as a word, and taken with her Massenet's agent. He had never mentioned his dealings with Massenet to the countess, but she would soon know. Tenil would not be able to keep anything from Lady Chilton, he was sure of that. The countess would even learn that Kent and Tenil had spent the night together. She would realize that it was the first thing Kent had done with his restored vitality.

"I *felt betrayed,*" he whispered. But how would the countess feel when she found out? Likely she would feel nothing. Kent did not wish anyone pain, but could she not experience just a little?

ಶ್ ಶ್ ಶ್

The King proved determined to make the journey, and though no one thought it wise, especially the Royal Physician, even he had to concede that it was less dangerous for all involved to take the King with them—providing His Majesty survived.

In the end the princess pronounced. "If we are restoring power to the King, then we must abide by His Majesty's will in such matters."

And so the King's carriage took its place in the cavalcade. The princess and Lady Galton and Alissa traveled together. Kent, Valary, and Littel took another carriage. The King traveled with his doctor and Ruau, while various servants and functionaries followed, and Palace Guards went both before and behind. The duke, Jaimy and—after a heated battle with the princess—Prince Wilam, set out on horseback with a company of Palace Guards, in hope of overtaking the other parties and delaying them in the name of King.

The Marquess of Sennet was appointed King's Man and left behind to deal with Lord Harrington and to spearhead the restoration of power to the King, something, the duke confided to his son, that should not be relegated such a minor part in the bigger scheme. Even with signed letters from the King, the Duke of Blackwater, and the princess, Sennet would be trying to garner support for the King while unable to explain the sovereign's absence.

If Massenet and Palle had left agents in the city, which certainly they had, they could not miss the parade of carriages leaving Avonel escorted by armed Palace Guards. Whether these agents could catch their masters to warn them was the question.

Kent worried that they would never make it to the abbey in time. This convoy would not travel quickly, despite the King apparently swearing they must not rest until they had overtaken their rivals.

"What do you think the King knows about these matters?" Kent asked his companions, not because they were likely to know more than he did, but because he could not bear to be alone with his questions any longer.

Littel shrugged. "You have spoken with His Majesty, Kent, you should know if anyone does."

"Yes, I should. But, unfortunately, I don't. I shall have to corner Rawdon. Despite his apparent defection, the good doctor is not being generous with his knowledge unless it is specifically asked for. I don't care for his attitude." Kent looked out at the passing scene. "I have often wondered if His Majesty sent the Duchess of Morland on this voyage of discovery, or if it was her own initiative. Certainly she would never have gone if she had not believed it was of the utmost importance. But was the King involved in the decision?"

Valary touched his arm, drawing his attention back

from the passing scene. "According to Lady Galton, His Majesty has waking dreams. Portents of what is to come. The King has been taking this seed for some years now. Even if his talent is very small, I think this could well be true. Lady Galton assures me that Wells and company believe they have foreknowledge. Events were foreseen, and this led them to send Tristam Flattery to Oceana. And the King may have sent the duchess as a result of his own intuition. Palle certainly has people aboard the *Swallow* who plan to exploit the situation, just as the duchess must be hoping to do."

"Valary, what in the world are we heading into?" Kent said with feeling. "Even if we are able to stop Massenet and Palle, will it matter? The real threat may be this young Flattery. Did the countess not say he had begun the transformation from human to mage? Were those not her words? And that is exactly what we have struggled against. That fragment of Lucklow's letter . . . I have seldom read anything so ominous. And the countess, despite her tendency to secrecy, is convinced that a rediscovery of the arts will bring about a cataclysm. And she knows more than we."

Valary nodded. "Yes. And where has the countess gone, that is what I'm wondering? What was said that set her off so quickly?"

Kent wondered the same thing. And why had she taken Tenil? It seemed very odd. Had Tenil actually been watching Massenet for the countess all along? And watching Kent for both of them? He just did not know.

"You're our authority on Tremont Abbey, Valary; what do you think the mages used it for? Was it required for their arts in some way?"

Valary considered a moment, running through the countless details of the history in his mind. "It is difficult to answer, Kent. There were times when the Abbey was not controlled by the mages—some quite long stretches—so it's impossible that it could have served for something so central as the rites of initiation, or some such thing. The discovery of the Ruin on Farrow was only four hundred or so years ago, and the mages certainly did not build that. It now appears that they were as fascinated by it as anyone. I'm beginning to believe that the purpose of the two ruins was realized after their discovery. Perhaps long after. It had something to do with their great endeavor, and then the fragment written by Lucklow. But what that great endeavor was, is still a mystery."

"Not to Lady Chilton," Littel said firmly, surprising the other two.

"Did she say something to you that I did not hear?" Valary asked.

"Not really, no. It is what she did not say, coupled with the strength of her conviction. I am certain she knows. Knows even more than Wells and company. More than this man Massenet. That is why she ran off. I'm sure she is on this road before us, journeying north with all speed. Faster than we will manage, that is certain. Only the duke and the others have a chance of catching her. No, we will arrive after it has all been decided, I'm afraid. And then, perhaps, we will find what this has all been about. I pray we have not done some terrible evil with our efforts, Valary. I could not live with that."

TWENTY-NINE

Even with Faairi leading, it was not an easy hike down to the village on Gregory Bay. Tristam scrambled along after his Varuan maiden as best he could, but her legs were more accustomed to roaming the island than his, and he barely kept up. An ominous rumble, like thunder, tumbled up the slopes from the bay, and they both stopped in alarm.

"Was that your ship's guns?" she asked.

"I'm not sure," Tristam said, almost certain that it was. There was no thundercloud in the sky that he could see. They carried on, Tristam pushing himself now, and neither sparing breath to speak.

As they approached the abandoned village, Faairi took them off the path, and they crept quietly through a grove of trees. And here, hiding in dense bush, they found some of the *Swallow*'s crew. The viscount was there, standing near to his sister, and Stern was crouched down behind the foliage, staring intently out through the branches toward the bay.

"Tristam!" Some part of the duchess' apprehension disappeared as she noticed the naturalist. "I have been worried unto madness. You are well? You look exhausted." She eyed Tristam's companion dubiously.

"Perfectly well. What in the world has happened?"

"We've had a mutiny," the duchess said, placing a hand on his shoulder as though assuring herself he was real. "At first light. Somehow Llewellyn got word of it, and we were lucky to escape into the boats. We got ashore, but then they drove us away from the boats with cannon fire. We wait, now, to see what they will do."

Tristam looked around, making note of who had come ashore: Tobias Shuk; Jacel, of course; Beacham; Osler; Llewellyn, but not the ship's surgeon; a dozen Jacks; Pim; the captain's steward; a few others. Not quite half the crew, Tristam could see, and they were poorly armed. Only a few swords and short pikes among them. Some of the Jacks had made spears by sharpening poles, and this gave Tristam no confidence at all. Stern had been caught completely unawares, despite his confrontation with the Jacks.

Wallis caught Tristam's eye and nodded, looking more anxious and despairing than anyone present.

"Who was it led them?" Tristam asked. "Kreel?"

"Hobbes!" the duchess said, her own shock and sadness apparent.

Tristam sat down on the stump of a felled tree. "Hobbes?"

"Yes. We still cannot believe it. The master will have this seed for himself. That is what Stern thinks. They will take it by force from the Varuans, if need be, and with such women as they can tempt along, will set off to find an island of their own in unknown seas."

Faairi brought Tristam an opened drinking nut, receiving another strange look from the duchess, though the islander did not seem to much care. Tristam searched the group again, and found Julian standing near to Stern, now, the most dangerous position, without a doubt—as near to death as he could be. Everyone focused their attention on Stern and what was happening in the bay.

"Elorin," Tristam said, keeping his voice low. "Julian tried to murder Hobbes."

Her manner became suddenly guarded and stiff. "Did you see this?"

"No, but I spoke with another who did. I don't doubt his word. And it might explain things. After the deaths of Garvey and Chilsey, Hobbes intended self-murder, but could not go through with it. Julian attacked him. Now Hobbes must believe his life is in constant danger, and that we harbor a murderer." Tristam moved his head toward the viscount, almost without meaning to. "What little loyalty Hobbes might still have for Stern and the service has been destroyed utterly. He has chosen to live. And if he cannot go home to Farrland with honor, then by Farrelle, he will have this seed we seek and live long among the islands."

The duchess looked distant, as though she were barely able to contain her anger—but it seemed to Tristam that he was the focus of this rage, not Julian.

"They're coming ashore," Stern said, raising his voice enough to carry to his supporters. "Move back. Mr. Wallis, can you lead us to a safe place? We are outnumbered, and poorly armed."

"Yes. Certainly, yes. Come along quickly."

Stern began shepherding his charges back into the forest, glancing back over his shoulder. "They will take the ship's boats now," he said to Osler.

"There's nothing for it, sir. They will drive us back with cannon fire if we attempt the beach again."

Out on the lagoon Tristam caught a glimpse of a manned raft made of barrels. It bobbed precariously as the Jacks paddled toward shore. At the mention of danger, Tristam found that his exhaustion passed. He could easily have outpaced the others but followed up the rear of the party with Stern.

"Osler tells me you are a swordsman, Mr. Flattery?" Stern asked, his manner calm.

"Of sorts," Tristam said quickly.

"Doctor?" Stern called out. "Would you give Mr. Flattery your blade?"

Reluctantly, Llewellyn paused to let Tristam catch up. The man was obviously terrified. He pressed his sword into Tristam's hand and the naturalist realized that it was his own blade, from his cabin. And Llewellyn carried Tristam's canvas bag, as well.

"I managed to rescue a few thing from your cabin, Tristam," the doctor said matter-of-factly. "Shall I keep this safe for you for the time being?"

Tristam was too surprised to feel anger. What was the

man up to? Certainly Llewellyn did nothing for anyone but himself. "Yes," Tristam managed, "do that, Doctor." And Llewellyn hurried up to the front of the group again, showing no signs of shortness of breath.

Stern looked back, exhibiting some reluctance to retreat. "Let us stop here, and watch what they do," he said suddenly. "Mr. Wallis. Take everyone on. I wish to see what they intend."

Tristam found himself in the company of the captain, Osler, Beacham, and an ominously silent viscount. They slipped back down the path toward the bay, keeping well to cover, catching occasional glimpses of the turquoise water.

"You haven't your glass, Mr. Flattery?" Stern said.

"Llewellyn might have it, sir."

"Mr. Beacham," Stern said, "run along to the doctor and fetch back Mr. Flattery's glass, if he has it."

Without a word, Beacham was off.

"They are in no hurry," Osler said. "Look at them."

"There is no officer present," Stern said, "so they take their time. Such laxity may prove to our advantage. We will see how they keep their watches."

Tristam moved to a position where he could see through the foliage, and, just as they stepped ashore, he spotted the mutineers. The word had such infamy attached to it that he half-expected to see some band of terrible cutthroats. But there, on the beach, were the men he had sailed with these past months, appearing no more treacherous or fierce than usual. Not one of them looked the part, he thought. Some were so young that they had only recently begun to shave. And others had families waiting back home. Yet every one of them faced hanging if they were captured, now. They had made an irretrievable step. There was no choice for them but to pursue their course with total commitment.

Beacham delivered Tristam's glass to the captain, and then bent double trying to catch his breath.

"There is Mr. Hobbes," Stern said, "standing on the quarterdeck. It is a hard way to come by a command," he said with feeling. "They are getting ready to push the boats out, now. Tell me, Mr. Osler; what would you do if you were in Hobbes position?"

"Tie a pig of iron around my neck and step off the rail, sir," Osler answered, but there was no humor in his tone. "They want this herb. That is their goal. And the sooner they get their hands on it, the sooner they can make their escape. If I were the master, I would come ashore late tonight. The Varuans are superstitious about the darkness and do not like to be about. The crew could slip up to the Sacred City and find what they're after, or perhaps take some hostages they can use for trade. But if the King and the Old Men leave the city . . . well, there will be no finding the Varuans in the bush, Captain. I'm sure of that. The crew will have to come ashore this night."

Stern passed the glass to his lieutenant. "You're right in every way, Mr. Osler. If we can get Wallis to convince the Varuans to put aside their superstitions, we have a chance of taking the *Swallow* back. Otherwise we will be here until the Admiralty sends a ship to search for us."

❦   ❦   ❦

Tristam sat in one of the abandoned fales, staring out at the *Swallow* with his Fromme glass. It was late afternoon, and there seemed to be every indication that Stern and Osler had predicted Hobbes' plans correctly. The crew were preparing arms on the deck—swords and bows and short pikes. But most frightening, they had lowered one of the small cannon into a boat, as though they meant to use it as a field piece.

Immediately Tristam had sent Beacham off to inform Stern, and while he sat waiting for the officer, the mutineers began climbing down into the boats.

Stern and Osler both came at a run, careful not to be seen by the men on the ship.

"Well, Hobbes will not waste a moment," Stern observed. "I sent Wallis up to warn the Varuans, but I do not know what they will choose to do. They might help us, but they have such a fear of our guns that it is just as likely that they will let us work this out ourselves." He borrowed Tristam's glass and focused on the mutineers as they pushed away from the ship.

"We might try to retake the ship while they are gone," Osler suggested.

"No, they've rigged boarding nets and left enough men aboard to man the guns. Even under cover of darkness I fear we would suffer great loss of life, and with little chance of success." Stern passed the glass to Osler. Tristam thought the redness of the captain's face was suppressed anger, but his manner was calm.

Stern seemed to be struggling with a decision, though Tristam was not sure what this might be.

"Though it seems the Varuans have abandoned us," the captain said finally, "we cannot abandon them to these men—we don't know what atrocities they might commit. If we are cunning, we might slow their advance to the upper city, and perhaps there is still a chance they might listen to reason. There must be a few among them who are having second thoughts about what they have done."

"Too late for second thoughts," Osler said. "You might offer them amnesty, Captain, but the Admiralty will not be so kind. They must realize that, if they surrender to you now, they will hang."

Stern nodded, not quite listening, Tristam thought. "Yes, but the duchess has offered to guarantee the King's pardon to any man who gives up this madness. And there could be a reward as well. Hobbes, of course, I cannot save, but he has long put the welfare of his shipmates above his own. I have hopes that he will do so again." Stern moved back out of sight, and stood to full height. "Come away. It will take them two trips to bring their party ashore. We must meet them at the stairs to the Sacred City, and make it known that they will pay dearly for every step."

They retreated back into the trees and found the rest of their party. It was in Stern's mind to separate those who could not fight, and send them up into the forest, but it was decided that the duchess must be present to make the King's pardon sound credible, and Llewellyn, to Tristam's surprise, would not be sent away. That left only

Jacel, and a few of the men who had sustained slight injuries as they escaped the ship, and none of these wanted to be separated from their fellows.

Tristam had not yet seen the stair to the city. When they found it, he felt his heart sink a little, for it was stone, though not carved into the rock, but carefully built by master masons. Thankfully no water flowed down the steps.

Stern had his crew take up anything heavy that could be found—stones, lumps of wood, even fallen coconuts—and this debris he piled on the first landing where it could be thrown down upon any who advanced.

Tristam had one of the few bows in the group, though hardly enough arrows, and these were meant for taking small specimens and doing as little harm to the skin as possible. Not really the best weapon for repelling mutineers.

Tristam understood Stern's feeling of responsibility toward the islanders—this was, after all, his own crew advancing with both weapons of steel and a cannon—but there seemed little chance that the mutineers could be stopped by a party so poorly armed. Nor was anyone sure how the Varuans would react when they found the Farrlanders battling at the gate to their most sacred shrine.

The landing on which they made their stand was all of twenty feet square, and crowded once Stern's people had assembled there. The captain sent those less fit for battle up the next flight of stairs, gathering his strongest men around him.

Like everyone else, Tristam realized that they stood little chance. Their only hope lay in Wallis convincing the Varuans to come to their aid, but with the King cut off from what occurred, it seemed highly unlikely that the Varuans would come to a decision quickly enough to make any difference. And everyone knew that one shot from the mutineers' cannon would send an army of Varuans scrambling for cover. The islanders were said to be fierce warriors, but having once seen the devastation wrought by cannon, they would not stand against it again.

"There!" Beacham said suddenly, pointing. "To the left, in the trees."

A line of men could just be made out, advancing slowly but purposefully. Two Jacks appeared ahead of the others, scouting, and when they saw Stern's party on the stair, one set off at a run.

"The flag," Stern said, and Beacham passed him a staff bearing the remains of a white shirt. "Duchess. And Mr. Flattery. If you will.

Taking the duchess' arm, Tristam fell in behind Stern. He had to keep his eyes on his footing and did not see the mutineers draw up, a hundred feet from the base of the stair.

Tristam felt the duchess holding tight to his arm, her usual confidence apparently having abandoned her. This group of men she found unnerving—she who knew so much about the ways of men. Their eyes met once, and Tristam realized that he had never seen her look so frightened, not even when they had been pursued by corsairs.

She does not believe this will work, he realized. And this increased his own fear tenfold. If the duchess was frightened, then there was reason to fear.

Stern stopped without warning, a dozen steps remaining to the ground. He stood there, with one foot a step higher, half-turned a little to the side. Tristam thought he cut a fine but tragic figure there, with the tatters of a shirt in his hand, his uniform torn and dirty, and the light of late afternoon slanting down through the trees at his back. It would make a memorable painting. *"The final stand of Captain Josiah Stern."*

Hobbes stepped through the crowd of Jacks, his face grim, but his manner resolute.

"Mr. Hobbes," Stern said, nodding and the master nodded in return, though he said nothing, but stood sullenly waiting, a sword gripped in one powerful hand.

"Mr. Hobbes . . ." Stern began, "all of you. I implore you to reconsider this course you follow." He paused, looking over the group, his manner one of concern for their welfare. "The Varuans will never give up this herb. They have been warned by Wallis, and the King and the

Old Men have fled into the forest. There is no point in going further." Again he paused, letting his lie sink in. "I know you believe you've gone too far to turn back now, but that is not so. The Duchess of Morland will guarantee the King's pardon to any man who will give up this madness now. The King's pardon. . . ." He paused again, but only for a second. "You will be able to go home again. You will have a country. But those who refuse will be pursued for the rest of their days. No land will be safe, for the navy will not rest until you are brought to justice. And you know what that justice will be." He paused again, looking the men over, gauging the effect of his words. "In all honesty, I cannot guarantee this pardon to you, Mr. Hobbes, but consider your shipmates. Consider the life you lead them to. It will be as brief as it is desperate. I know you don't wish to bring them to ruin, Mr. Hobbes. Let them make their own choice. Let them become citizens of Farrland again. Rescind the sentence of death that shall be decreed for each and every man."

The mutineers stood shoulder to shoulder, glaring darkly at the captain.

It is not working, Tristam thought, and he could not understand why. Had not the captain's claims been perfectly true and logical? Could it be that an appeal to their reason would not be listened to? It was madness.

Hobbes looked down for a few seconds at the sword in his hand. "You offer us pardon?" he said suddenly, his soft voice quivering with long-suppressed anger. "It should be you, Stern, and your precious Admiralty, who stand trial." He pointed his sword at the captain. "But you will feel the justice of the Admiralty soon enough, for they will come for you, Stern." Hobbes lowered his sword. "*You* bring a murderer among us," he said softly, waving his sword up the stairs. "A man who murdered Dakin, and tried to kill both me and Kreel. And you dine with him evenings while your crew lives in fear of this monster." He paced to one side, agitated, enraged, filled with despair at the truth he spoke. "You carry this spawn of a mage, who will bring our souls to what kind of ruin we cannot imagine; and you speak to us of justice?" He stopped and looked up at Stern, such loathing in his eyes that the captain actually wavered. "We have all risked much to carry this herb back to the worthies of Farrland, who sit in their palaces and fine mansions, awaiting this gift, this elixir that will extend their days of pleasure, and keep them from the ravages of disease. And what will we gain? The men who risk their short, hard lives, and the ruin of their souls? The wages of poor men, and no hope for any life better. There is your justice, Stern! And it will be meted out to you, in your turn. Your career is ended, Captain. I know your masters well. I have felt their justice. You will pay a price for failing them. You will give all, Stern." He turned and looked at the men who stood behind, listening and nodding their agreement.

And then he looked back at Stern, his anger tempering to pity. "No, we will not take the *justice* you offer. We will make our own laws and trust that they will be fairer than those of your masters. And if the navy finds us one day, what of it? To live in our own way, among these beautiful islands, for even five short years, would provide us with more joy then we would find in three lifetimes in Farrland. That is the truth. And if they never find us . . . ? We both know the ocean is vast. Men have disappeared in it before." Hobbes stood, taking the blade of his sword in his free hand, standing with his legs apart, facing the captain squarely.

"Let me make an offer to you, Captain. It will not profit you to return to Farrland. Disgrace awaits you. No reward, no pension from the crown. You will find this much-vaunted justice you speak of; meted out by men who have never been to sea, and done at the bidding of others who have never known discomfort. Join with us," he said, raising his voice, to be certain that all of Stern's crew would hear. "Join with us and take the risk of living for a century in paradise. That is your real choice. Risk creating your own future, or return to the *life* prescribed for you by those who profit from your efforts and sacrifice. I extend this offer to everyone, but especially to those who have nothing to gain by returning to Farrland."

A long silence. Tristam could sense the men above

them on the stairs reconsidering their choice. And now that he had heard the master speak, Tristam was not sure what he would choose for himself, if he were one of them.

"And if we do not join you, Mr. Hobbes?" Stern asked.

Hobbes stepped forward. "Do not stand between us and what we have come for, Captain Stern. We wish no one harm, and will leave everyone present untouched, unless we are forced to do otherwise. I will even say freely, that any man who so wishes may cross over and join you." He turned to the men behind him. "Any man who will accept this King's pardon, do so now. But do not stand against us, or I cannot guarantee your safety."

For a second there was no reaction, then men began shaking their heads and muttering their refusal. No one moved to cross the sea of sand.

"That is your answer, Stern. Now I will have mine."

The captain hesitated, as though desperately hoping for a way through this, but finally he shook his head. "We cannot do as you ask, Mr. Hobbes. I cannot stand by and let you bring harm to the islanders. I am sworn to protect them from the follies of my crew. We will stand against you, Hobbes, and may Farrelle forgive you for the souls you take."

It was said, and everyone present felt the impact of these words, as though the sentence had been passed down—death for some; though no one could predict who. The captain looked over his shoulder at the duchess, almost an appeal.

"There is something you don't know about this herb," Tristam heard himself say, his voice, though quiet, carrying in the terrible silence. "It will keep you young only if you have the knowledge and talent of a mage." He paused, trying to discern the impact of his words. The sun dipped behind the mountains then, plunging the scene into shadow, and it seemed as though a pall had fallen over the mood of the mutineers. "If you don't possess that knowledge, the physic will drive you into a terrible madness, and rob you of your will. Our own King is enslaved to this herb, and though he has lived long, he bears the burden of those years like a great weight. I swear, it will not profit you to take this seed from the Varuans. You can neither use it nor, in your situation, can you sell it. Your desire to possess it has already brought you to mutiny and sentence of death. And if you don't turn aside now, it will only become worse. This seed is a curse. If you will not accept the King's pardon, then at least save yourselves from this one fate. Sail away. Sail away this moment. Hide yourselves in some corner of the globe. But I will tell you, as surely as my uncle served a mage, if you continue this pursuit of the seed, it will bring about your ruin." Suddenly he raised a dagger up for all to see. "This blade belonged to Gregory. It bears his initial and crest. The islanders have always known his fate, but superstition kept them silent." Stern looked at him, eyes wide, as though he thought Tristam had taken leave of his senses. "His ship lies in deep water beyond the pass, where mutineers brought about its wreck. Mutineers who wanted this seed for themselves, not realizing it was cursed. That is the fate that awaits you." Tristam tossed the dagger into the sands before them, where it landed point first. No one moved to examine it.

These words had impact on the sailors. In the diminishing light, Tristam could see some making warding signs. Others were muttering, and they had begun to shrink back.

"And that is why you have traveled so far to have this herb, Mr. Flattery?" Hobbes said, his tone mocking. "Gregory's dagger?" He laughed. "The King bears the burden of this seed so heavily that he has sent you to bring him more? And the Duchess of Morland has taken ship with a bunch of ragtag sailors because she feels this seed is of no value; that it is a curse?" He laughed, and Tristam could see the men at his back, nodding, the doubt he had sowed being stripped away like newly planted seed torn up by a storm. "Make your decision, all of you. Either join us, or step aside. Duchess, please. Do not stand with these men. If they do not surrender the stair to us now, the cost will be great."

Tristam saw the duchess shake her head minutely, and

then turn her gaze down. Stern lifted his tattered flag, and pointed up the stair, sending Tristam and the duchess up before him. At his back Tristam heard Hobbes order the gun brought forward, the master's voice heavy with emotion.

Night was not far off, Tristam knew, and darkness would fall swiftly. Hobbes would want to climb to the stairhead while there was still light.

Tristam thought of Gregory. *Greed and folly,* he thought. The fire of the crew's resentment had been kindling long. Ignited by the injustice of being born the sons of the poor, fed by the knowledge of what they were deprived. Hobbes's words had contained much truth—that was the power of them. Justice was an illusion—a luxury of the educated classes.

They came up onto the landing, puffing from the exertion. Beacham and the viscount stood at the edge, peering down.

"Lie down," Stern said. "Lie facedown and cover your heads." The captain crawled to the edge of the landing so that he could see what transpired below. Tristam dropped down, and lay there, smelling the indescribable smells of stone and sand. Impossible that stone could have an odor.

He felt the duchess take his hand, and he looked over at her frightened face. *Madness,* he thought she mouthed, but could not be sure.

The sound of the cannon firing caused everyone to flinch and press themselves into the rock. An instant later stone exploded above them with an ear-splitting crack, and dust and pieces of shattered rock rained down on them.

"Up!" Stern yelled. And those who were not undone by fear grabbed up some of the rocks and lumps of wood and cast them down the stair toward the advancing mutineers.

Tristam jumped forward and loosed an arrow toward the men who cowered below, and then a second, and a third. He could see the mutineers had halted, and some were even falling back, and then Osler shouted for everyone to get down again.

The gun sounded before many were prostrate, and this time the ball struck lower down, whistling close over their heads, and impacting the stone with such force that it shook the landing. Tristam heard people moaning and crying out, and only half the number rose to meet the men advancing below.

The mutineers had gained more stairs than Tristam expected, and then crouched down, exposing only their backs to the rain of stone and debris. Tristam realized that, even with the stone broken by cannon fire, their supply of debris to throw down was almost at an end. Suddenly, Stern called for everyone to climb up, and they turned and fled up the stairs.

Ahead of Tristam, people stumbled and fell in the failing light, and others tripped over them, yet somehow they scrambled upward. When the cannon fired, fear propelled everyone up a few extra steps, and the stone exploded behind them, fragments knocking people to the stairs. Several struggled to rise and were left on the landing, no one stopping to tend to them or to help them go on. They were running for their lives before cannon fire, and Tristam thought their fear was no different from that of the poor Varuans who had encountered it for the first time.

They came to another landing and though Stern tried to muster them here to make another stand, many simply ran on.

"The trees will offer . . . some protection," Osler said, gasping for breath.

Only half a dozen had rallied on the landing, and Tristam looked down the stairs. Their pursuers were swarming up the steps now, but there were no shouts of triumph at this rout of their former shipmates. They came on grimly, determined to have it over with quickly.

The trees arching over the stairs hid much of what went on from those manning the cannon below, and they held their fire, lest they gun down their own shipmates.

Tristam sent two quick arrows into the ascending mutineers and those around him cast down their few stones and bits of the shattered stair, but the men below hardly slowed.

"What happens when we come to the city above?" Tristam heard Beacham ask, no doubt thinking of the fate of Chilsey and Garvey. No one had an answer.

The brief tropical twilight fell then, which meant darkness was only moments behind, and Tristam was not sure if this would be to their advantage or not. He leaned over the side of the stair to see if it was possible to escape. A man might climb down off the stairs, but it would be onto a steep slope, and even a ledge might not lead them to any kind of safety—though it might well be their only option.

"We'll keep going up until we meet the guards at the stairhead," Stern said. "Perhaps they will let us through, or stand with us. I don't believe they will allow mutineers into their most sacred site without resistance."

The cannon sounded just then, and everyone with presence of mind dropped to the stone. There was a crash in the trees to their left, and Tristam actually saw sparks where the iron ball struck stone. The island night had fallen.

There was a sound similar to arrows in the air, and the shouting and cursing of men. After a few seconds of confusion, Tristam rose and tried to make out what went on down the now darkened stair. In the gathering gloom he found the mutineers retreating desperately under a hail of stones which seemed to be coming out of the trees.

"Blood and flames!" Osler said. "The islanders have come to our rescue. They're using slings."

Even in the fading night Tristam could see men falling senseless to the stairs, some rolling limply down behind their fellows. The cannon had fallen silent, and Tristam wondered if it had been fired so erratically because the crew manning if had been attacked as well. The mutineers kept falling back, their numbers thinning rapidly. And there among them went Hobbes. He came to the rear and clambered down behind the others, as though he could shield them from the lethal missiles with his great frame. Tristam could see the master flinch and stumble as stones struck him, but he did not give way to panic and kept his place. Tristam saw the master's head driven forward suddenly, and then he toppled, arms outstretched like a wounded bird. He toppled into the darkness and the mass of falling bodies before him.

Stern stood looking down for the moment, rigid, like a man helpless to stop what he watched, though every muscle strained with his desire to act.

"We must gather up those who are left," Stern said, his voice thick and subdued, and then he turned away, motioning the others to go before him.

"But will they show them no mercy?" Osler cried out suddenly, still unable to see his former shipmates as enemies. He looked at Stern as though appealing for him to intervene.

"None, I fear," Stern answered, marshaling them up the stairs. So they turned away from the screams and curses of the Farrlanders and began to climb, unsure of what lay ahead for them.

"You must understand, Lieutenant," Stern said quietly, all signs of anger gone, "the so-called city above and this ritual are deeply sacred to the Varuans. They would die rather than see them desecrated. It seems they would even face darkness and cannon fire."

"And what of us?" Beacham said, glancing back over his shoulder.

"They have not turned on us thus far, so I hope that bodes well." Stern paused for a moment. "But I would be a liar to say that the islanders' actions are so easy to predict."

They found the other victims of the mutiny huddling on the landing before the final flight of stairs. They apparently already knew what had happened below and were now waiting to discover their own fate.

Stern stood before the remains of his crew, his clothes tattered, and his face bruised and bleeding. Tristam thought the captain looked like a man with little hope, yet he would not shirk his duty. Like Hobbes, Tristam was sure Stern would put himself between his crew and the missiles of the enemy. "I think our mutiny is over, though what will be done with us I am not sure. They have not attacked us yet, when they could easily have done so, and I hope this means they will leave us unharmed. Perhaps we will be returned to our ship this very night. I cannot say. If the Varuans come to us armed, remain calm. Show no anger at what they have done, but do not show them fear either. I will try to get us out of this. Dr. Llewellyn? We may have need of your linguistic skill. And where has that Varuan girl gone? Mr. Flattery?"

"I don't know, sir."

Apparently no one knew. She had disappeared not long after the first cannon shot.

"Where is Mr. Wallis?" Llewellyn said, coming forward with obvious reluctance.

"I wish I knew," Stern said, turning back to look down the stairs.

Night had fallen completely, and a net of stars appeared through the trees. The trade began its nightly abatement, and the surf, beating down upon the reef, could almost be felt, like the heartbeat of this exotic island. No sounds of fighting came up from below, and most of the crew crowded to the back of the landing, where they remained uncommonly silent. Everyone strained to hear, wondering what went on in the dark. No one even dared whisper lest they miss some warning sound.

A silvery glow spread across the eastern horizon, and then the full moon floated up, released into the sky by a giant whale.

"Captain," Beacham hissed. "I think I hear someone coming."

Stern went forward, with a terrified Llewellyn at his back. Tristam came up beside the captain, thinking that his own limited knowledge of the language might be needed if Llewellyn lost his nerve.

"Captain Stern?" came a man's voice out of the dark. "It is Madison Wallis."

"Mr. Wallis? What has happened? Are my men . . . ?"

The sound of footsteps on stone came softly up the stair and then the gangly form of Wallis appeared in the moonlight. He moved slowly, as though bearing the weight of what he had just witnessed. Instead of coming up onto the landing, he stopped several steps down, as though afraid the Farrlanders would not welcome his presence.

"I think they are all dead, but one, Captain Stern. I cannot be sure because of the darkness. One Jack had been rendered unconscious, and I think I managed to intervene when he was discovered alive. At least he was alive when I began to climb up." Wallis sat down heavily on a step and put his head in his hands.

Tristam heard muttering behind him, partly from relief that they had been delivered, partly from horror. Their former shipmates, all dead but one.

"What will they do with us, Mr. Wallis?" Stern asked. "Do they understand that we came up the stair only to keep the mutineers from entering the City of the Gods? Our intentions were to protect the Varuans."

"That is what I assumed, Captain, and is the case I have made, but I'm not certain what they believe, and the Varuans will not tell me what they intend. They have sent me only to instruct you to keep your people where they are. Do not, under any circumstances, try to go up into the city. Only stay where you are, and I will try to find out what they will do."

"We will not move, Mr. Wallis. Please, do everything you can on our behalf. I have no intention of allowing my people to desecrate their sacred sites. We want only to go about our business and then be gone. We wish the Varuans no harm."

"I will convey your message, Captain. But it is your business that is at issue. You may be forced to renounce your quest for this herb. That is what I think, at least."

The duchess came forward when she heard this, suddenly more concerned with what was being said than with their situation. Tristam did not think she would give up so easily.

THIRTY

Baron Trevelyan had not really slept, only dozed lightly between lurches of the carriage. But all the same he had dreamed. Dreamed he had been ascending a stairway, dressed in a white robe, a cold glittering stream flowing about his ankles. An owl had called in the darkness, its sound almost human. Then the carriage had swayed and cracked his head against the window frame.

His eyes focused on Roderick Palle who sat staring at him with that same measuring gaze that he habitually turned on the poor, unsuspecting world. The carriage hit a pothole and the two men bounced several inches out of their seats. The pounding of hooves over the earth's drum was loud.

"Are you feeling more yourself, Lord Trevelyan?"

"Has my lunacy passed, do you mean? For the moment, it seems. But this state of grace will disappear the moment you deprive me of the seed again."

"We have no intention of depriving you of the seed ever again. Once you have performed your task for us, Lord Trevelyan, you shall have physic enough for the rest of your years, if that is what you choose."

Trevelyan was certain that his suspicion was not well masked. "I saw what happened to His Majesty. I require just enough to keep the madness at bay—no more. Over-indulgence is a vice easily learned, and its effects are devastating."

"But what of your youth, Lord Trevelyan? Do you not want your vitality restored?"

The baron attempted to hide his disgust for Roderick. The King's Man was such a master at discovering men's weaknesses. But the baron would not be tempted again. Palle and his group had betrayed him once, and he was not sure they had any intention of honoring their bargain this time. "Tell me about this rite you wish performed."

Palle smiled at him, or tried to—the King's Man was famous for this grimace that he thought was a smile. "It is a simple enough thing. Mr. Wells will instruct you." He nodded to Wells, who lay unconscious in the corner. The man was either exhausted beyond measure, or could sleep through a cataclysm.

"I think it will be small service for your return to sanity. And then you may take up your work again, and every man in the Society will sing his praises for the great Trevelyan's return."

"You make it sound so easy, Roderick. And what will you gain from such a *simple* task?"

Roderick shrugged.

"Do you actually know what you possess? A text, I assume. Do you even understand its purpose? Let me see it."

"Soon enough, my dear baron, soon enough."

Trevelyan knew he would get no more from Roderick. The King's Man had spent his lifetime harboring secrets, rising through the court by trading what he knew to advantage. He was a merchant of secrecy, Trevelyan thought, keeping every bit of knowledge, no matter how inconsequential it seemed, increasing its value by its scarcity. Palle could have been rich beyond imagining if he had chosen the world of commerce, but the coin he valued was not gold.

"Why do we race on so, Roderick? Who is it we are hoping to best?"

Palle looked at the baron for a moment, never embarrassed to stare at a man's face for any length of time, though it was considered most impolite in Farr society. "Massenet," he said, finally, deciding it was not information that he could trade, and so gave it away, probably interested in Trevelyan's reaction to the news.

"Ah. I might have known." The baron pushed himself back up into his seat and gazed out the window. The day was clear and somewhat cool, with a harsh wind from the north. The carriage was as uncomfortable as a ship beating into a gale, and the wind whistled as though it blew through the rigging, moving the barren branches so that they clattered against each other horribly.

"He does not know we follow," Palle said. "It is to our advantage. With a little luck the count is not racing north as we do, but is taking his own good time. We might hope that he finds an inn where the serving girls are fair. That could slow him substantially."

Obviously the King's Man thought of this information as a peace offering. It was *information*—the most valuable commodity Palle could conceive of. Trevelyan should be honored; but the baron knew that if there was something he truly needed to know, Palle would certainly hold it back, for use later. The baron was not deceived. He had run afoul of the King's Man before, and paid a terrible price for it. He would not make that mistake again.

The carriage came to a halt, and the shouts of men up and down the line replaced the thrumming of horses' hooves. Palace Guards rode past, and then one stopped and dismounted by the carriage. Palle allowed the door to be opened.

"It is the ford, Sir Roderick. It has swollen." He looked a little abashed explaining this, as though, somehow, he were responsible for this setback.

Palle cast a look of annoyance at Wells who sat up, rubbing his eyes. "Let us see what this is about."

No one protested, so the baron followed the others out of the carriage, stretching his great frame, stiff and bruised from their mad dash. The carriage of Galton and Noyes had stopped behind a farmer's wagon filled with grain. Guards on horseback were milling about ineffectually in an attempt to look as though they were doing something useful. One officer, more imaginative than the others, was coaxing his horse out into the current.

The river was certainly high, flooding back into the

trees, running swiftly, catching the sunlight on its endlessly changing surface. A gathering of small gulls circled over the ford, calling and diving in the sunlight. Occasionally one would light upon the surface and bob along the small waves like a toy, making a mockery of the men standing timidly on the banks.

Trevelyan breathed in the fresh air, unable to express the relief he felt at finding himself released from the prison of his madness. With all of his heart he did not want to be serving these men, but the thought of returning to his cell of darkness terrified him utterly. *Better anything than that.* To think that he had possessed one of the most celebrated minds of his generation. He was sure that he could never perform at that level again, but just to be able to think clearly! To look around him and see the world for what it was! It was enough. He did not care if he would die in his own time. Just let him be sane for a few years. Let him have the dignity of that, and he would do whatever Roderick required.

The rider was struggling out in midstream, but managing. His mount was being swept somewhat downstream, apparently its natural buoyancy was having an effect and the beast was beginning to float, losing its footing. But then it passed the deepest point and found the earth again. A few more yards and the horse began to surge forward, gathering its powerful haunches, and driving toward the bank. The other guards cheered.

Roderick, Trevelyan realized, was paying no attention. Instead, he was walking around the farmer's wagon, examining it as though it were some innovative carriage he had discovered.

"The rider has crossed, Sir Roderick." said one of the guards.

"Proving only that a horse and rider can manage," Palle said without bothering to look at the man. "Mr. Hawksmoor!"

The minion of the King's Man stood nearby, ever attentive to his master's needs. "Sir?"

"This will serve nicely. Send it across."

The farmer who stood by suddenly realized what was

in the wind. "But, Your Grace, it is the end of last season's grain, sir. For market. . . ."

Guards moved in on the man, and he fell silent with fear.

Palle raised his hand and the guards stopped as they were about to grab hold of the frightened farmer. "Pay this man for his rig and grain, Mr. Hawksmoor, and then get a driver aboard. We have no time to waste."

The farmer scrambled up into his wagon to rescue a few of his effects, while Hawksmoor counted out some coins. The baron was sure the farmer had been well compensated, but the man stopped and stroked the noses each of the big draft horses, and spoke softly to them.

One of the guards removed his sword and hat, climbed up onto the loaded wagon, and started the horses forward.

"We might use this team to draw each wagon over, sir," Hawksmoor said, looking at the massive work horses.

Roderick nodded distractedly, his eyes fixed on the wagon as it rolled into the water. Two mounted guards, carrying coiled ropes at the ready, followed, prepared to cast a line to the driver if things did not go well. Like almost all Farrlanders, these men did not swim, and though the ford was not overly deep, the current was strong and could sweep a man off his feet.

"It is odd that the sky is clear, and the earth dry," Wells observed to Noyes. "There has been no rain here for several days, I would venture."

Roderick waved a hand vaguely upstream. "It is from the Camden Hills."

The wagon had rolled forward until its hubs disappeared, a moment more and the water reached to the wagon body. Without pause the draft horses kept pulling their burden forward. The water would not affect them so much, Trevelyan thought, for they each stood eighteen hands, he was certain.

The team reached the river's midpoint, where the current ran most swiftly, and still they plodded forward as though they were some great beasts of the river or the intertidal zone. Another two yards and they began to rise up the opposite slope, and the men watching all began to relax, suddenly aware of how intently they had been observing.

It was just then that the wheel broke, or perhaps the axle, and the rear of the wagon swung sharply downstream, sinking as it did so. The horses' rear quarters were swept to the side and they stumbled over each other and fell, struggling, the wagon dragging them in harness, spluttering and crying out, trying to keep their heads above the surface.

The driver tried for a moment to control the situation, but then realized what had happened, and managed to take hold of the rope thrown his way and jump clear of the flailing horses.

The rickety wagon began to break up, and as it did so, one horse shook itself free, suddenly surging toward the same shore it had left. Seconds later it pulled up onto the bank, where it stopped and whinnied to its trace mate, gone now into the deeper water beyond the ford. Pulled under by the remains of the wagon and the harness wrapped about its limbs.

The horse came trotting along the bank, hanging its head, back to its former master, where it stood trembling and agitated. Trevelyan thought it looked at the men with reproach, perhaps anger, and the poor farmer could barely speak, his voice thick with emotion, as he tried to calm the beast.

"That answers our questions, I think," Palle said. "We must detour to the Tainsill Bridge, though we will lose much time." He turned to go back to his carriage when Hawksmoor stopped him.

"What about this horse, sir? We paid gold for it."

"Oh, let the poor man have it!" Galton said, raising his voice. "I will repay you the gold myself." And he went over to the farmer, who stood wretchedly by his horse, and gave him some coins. Trevelyan could not hear what the governor said, but his tone was kind. There was one among them, at least, who had not lost his compassion entirely. It was good to know.

❦ ❦ ❦

The night was chill. A tear of molten silver had frozen on the icy sky, and as this near-full moon lifted above the surrounding hills it cast a faint light into the vale. People did not come to this place at night. The local shepherds would not even leave their herds to graze past sunset. There were terrible stories of those who had, by accident or bravado, defied this simple rule. Ghosts of the men lost in battle haunted the night, and mages on gray horses galloped silently across the hilltops. Green light was seen emanating from the ruin of the ancient keep, and beyond this the middens themselves lay, like the backs of green whales. It was said that no tree ever took root there, nor would burrowing animals make their homes in that terrible field.

Count Massenet was not frightened by the tales of shepherds, but he had learned too much of arcane matters these past years to discount everything. It was, he admitted, if only to himself, a disturbing place.

"Can we not draw the water from here?" Bertillon whispered. "It is the same water."

"No, it must come from the falls," Massenet said, purposely speaking in a normal tone. "Do not offer me an argument based on logic, Charl, it has nothing to do with logic. Or reason, for that matter. The text says it must come from the falls, and so it must come from the falls."

"The count is absolutely right, Mr. Bertillon," Varese added. "We must not deviate in the slightest from the instructions."

Bertillon shook his head. "I still can't see how this water could differ from the water a hundred paces downstream ... but I bow to your superior knowledge." He tried not to make this last sound sarcastic, but didn't quite succeed. The count did not take offense. It was an unsettling place, and perhaps even more so for the musician. Bertillon's talent would lay him open to things others would not feel. The truth was, Massenet did not like this place either.

"Indulge us, Charl," Massenet chided him. "It won't take long."

They didn't carry a lamp, as Varese was sure that the light of stars and moon must be kept pure, so they picked their way through the darkness beneath the trees, stumbling occasionally. Bertillon wished that he had brought a blade from the carriage, but he had been afraid the others would laugh at this impulse. He would have felt better, however, to know he carried steel at his side.

Their path followed a small stream that ran through the forest like a black artery, carrying the vital fluids of the earth among the trees. Twisted roots emerged through the surface to trip the men who trespassed here, as though the interlopers could be kept at bay and the source of the forest's elixir protected.

A breeze like a chill breath would sigh through the wood occasionally, rattling the dried leaves that still clung to the branches.

"Do the leaves not fall here?" Bertillon asked.

"These are oaks, Mr. Bertillon," Varese answered. "They keep their dead leaves till spring. It is most common."

The musician had never noticed. *Oaks.*

Occasionally a bird would call—a soft, falling tone that would die without echo, as though absorbed by the darkness. Bertillon thought it a call of profound sadness.

The spattering of falling water began to distinguish itself from the other night sounds, and a small breeze stirred among the trees, the dried leaves scraping together in a most unsettling manner. Bertillon was surprised by a strange rattle, followed by a distinctive croak. A raven. Birds, at least, did not fear this place.

The trio plunged on, tripping as they stepped into shadow, then making good time as they crossed starlit glades. The path suddenly stepped upward among a jumble of large rocks where the stream dropped from one small pool to another. They were panting when the path leveled again, and the night seemed suddenly warm.

Again Massenet led them into the shadow of the twisted ancient oaks; trees that had stood in this place during the battle of the Midden Vale itself. Trees that had watched silently while Dunsenay rode out alone against the host of Farrelle. Witnessed the green sea-light form about the mage, and then the coming of the storm, summoned in strange tongues. Massenet had always thought the tale fanciful, but was no longer quite so sure. And this power that Dunsenay wielded was not lost! If only the count had more talent himself!

The air grew damp as they made their way further into the stand of oaks and young pines, where the scent of pine needles was fresh and fair, in contrast to the age of the forest. Beneath the trees the men progressed slowly, Massenet waving his hands before him, feeling carefully for each step. Bertillon held tight to his coattail and no doubt Varese had hold of the musician—like the three blind men of fables.

A dim light tempted them forward, and the sound of water rushing increased in volume. Perhaps a dozen paces would take them to the pool. Massenet felt some apprehension, as though they were engaged in an endeavor that was somehow deeply wrong. *Like thieves in the night,* he thought suddenly.

The pale light of stars and moon glittered on water, and Massenet caught a glimpse of the stream, erupting from an opening in a limestone cliff. It glittered like a column of liquid crystal.

They emerged from the shadow of the trees on the edge of a pool, and there, before the falls, knee-deep in water, stood a woman, ghostly pale. She half-raised her hands, and chanted as though standing before an altar. Dark curls fell down her naked back like a twisted vine.

Varese stumbled at the sight. *"A ghost!"* he hissed.

The woman whirled about, clutching her arms to her breasts. Massenet was transfixed. Certainly this woman was too perfectly formed to be anything but a vision. He heard Varese gasp and step back, fearful, but unwilling to bolt alone into the shadows.

The woman regarded them, saying nothing, but not frightened, now that she saw them. Shadows played across her face and her body, but even so Massenet could see the heart-shaped face was lovely, her lips full and sensuous. A large stone hung from a chain around her neck, and this seemed to be as full of starlight as the falling waters.

"Count Massenet," she said, surprising the count, who had half-expected her to vanish, or step back into the waterfall and disappear. "I think you do not understand what is taking place here," she continued, her voice lovely and melodious, but commanding all the same.

Massenet took a step forward. "I know you . . ." he said, certain he had seen this woman before. "You are Angeline Christophe," he said, a little triumphantly, but she did not seem to hear. The woman continued to stare at him, apparently unaware of the chill in the air and the water.

Massenet realized then that she held a small glass bottle that glittered as though many faceted. "What do you do here?"

She said nothing, though she did not look frightened into silence.

"Prince Kori has sent you," the count said. He moved forward again, about to step into the water.

She raised her hand quickly. "Do not sully the waters. They are pure, untouched by men." Angeline pushed the hair back from her face with one hand, lifting a breast enticingly, and then she cast her eyes down as though suddenly shy.

Massenet thought she was maddeningly beautiful. To a man who thrived on the new the situation seemed charged with eroticism. A wraith of a woman, hiding none of her charms, here in this forbidden wood, alone. She was like a creature from a fable; a water nymph. He could barely take his eyes from her. But certainly this meant the prince and Palle were preparing to complete their plans. And this woman was somehow part of them.

She looked up, though only barely raising her head. "You have given in to the temptation, I see," she said quietly, and then nothing more.

"I could find no other way to stop the King's Man . . ." the count said, speaking before he realized that he had begun to justify his actions to this young woman who stood before him so immodestly.

She raised her head just a fraction of an inch, meeting his eyes, almost taking his breath away. "The temptation is great. Imagine; power, knowledge, youth. . . . I hardly blame you, though I had hoped you would be wiser."

"You presume to know a great deal," the count said, still not sure what to do.

She shrugged at this, apparently unconcerned that she might insult the ambassador of Entonne. Nor did she seem particularly afraid to be revealing herself as his adversary, as though meeting three men in a dark wood was not cause for alarm. *"Youth,"* she almost whispered, "it holds such promise." Then she turned and took three graceful steps up onto the opposite bank. She turned and looked over her shoulder. "In the next village there is an inn. Perhaps we might continue this discussion there?"

Massenet knew that he should not let this woman escape, with her star-water and obvious knowledge of the arcane, but he was so used to women desiring him. He could not believe that her suggestion was anything but what it seemed. She would succumb to him—as other women had. Women with marriages and places in society. Women who had much to lose, but simply could not help themselves. He felt both his desire and his pride swell. Angeline Christophe was not indifferent to his charms after all.

He could see her now, half hidden by shadow, moonlight falling upon her through the branches. She took up a black shift and let it slide slowly down over her curls, so that darkness seemed to envelop her. The white of her face appeared and she shook her hair free.

"Count Massenet," she said, nodding her head. "Gentlemen." And she turned and walked into the shadows and shattered moonlight. For a second Massenet thought he saw a child at her side, but he blinked and she was gone, disappearing into the shadow-wood.

"Prince Kori's mistress . . ." Bertillon said.

"That woman is no mistress of that fatuous little prince," Massenet said derisively.

"You—you shouldn't have let her escape," Varese said, finding his voice. "She was collecting water from the falls, as do we."

"But we will meet her in the next town, Doctor," Massenet said.

"She will never be there," Bertillon said firmly.

Massenet turned to the musician, whose skin appeared even paler in the moonlight—as though he were a ghost himself. "Of course she will be there, Charl. Of course she will."

    ❦   ❦   ❦

Massenet sat in a large chair, sipping wine. His companions had been invited as well, to his disappointment, but he was sure that he would be alone with Angeline soon enough. If anything, it allowed him to savor the moment a little more. Both Bertillon and Varese were nearly speechless in the face of this woman's beauty, and this made Massenet smile. They were like boys. Massenet turned his gaze on Angeline, who stood at a side table pouring a glass of wine herself. There were no servants present. Massenet savored the sight for a moment, imagining what he would do to her once they were alone, imagining her response. Massenet had made the closest study of what gave women pleasure—it was one of his areas of vanity.

The shape of her bare shoulders attracted him, promising some strength. Her hair was pulled back from her face with silver combs, falling in thick dark curls. Massenet knew enough of such things to realize that she had done very little to prepare herself for this evening. Her black dress was simple, and her use of makeup so sparse that she might not have bothered. Yet she was as striking as any woman he had seen.

She passed a glass to Varese who took it quickly, obviously uncomfortable. Raising her glass, Angeline met each gentleman's gaze for the briefest second. "To chance encounters," she said.

Massenet smiled broadly and drank. It was at that moment that he realized the stone Angeline still wore around her neck was the very diamond he had given to Kent. His smile disappeared. *Kent?*

For a moment his confidence wavered. What was her involvement with the old man? Obviously she had both talent and knowledge—but what did she intend to use them in pursuit of? He realized that his evening of much-anticipated pleasure might be extremely unwise. He was not about to allow anyone to endanger his purpose. Did she realize that?

"So," Angeline began, taking a seat opposite Massenet, "we are all on the same quest, it seems. No, I suppose that is not really true. You have decided that you will seek ... what? Dominion, Count Massenet? Is that it? You will command whatever power your discovered text leads you to?"

"I seek only to retain the balance of power in the nations surrounding the Entide Sea, Lady Angeline," Massenet made an effort to sound casual. He refused to look as foolish as his companions simply because she was beautiful! "What is it that you and my friend, Mr. Kent, hope to gain?"

She did not look surprised, and he was happy to see she was not so easily thrown off. Massenet could not bear to win too easily.

"It is Kent's desire to find his lost muse, Count, if you must know. He would sacrifice much to this end." She held up her glass. "To the muse."

Massenet lifted his glass and stared into its dark center. A moment later he realized that Angeline stood before him and had just removed the glass from his fingers. She leaned over and placed a hand on his forehead, mumbling words he could not catch. He reached out for her and then realized that his hands had not obeyed the command. He felt cool lips brush his forehead, and then Angeline rose and moved away. He tried to turn his head to follow but found he could not, and his eyes were closing, as though gravity had suddenly chosen to increase its force at that moment.

From some distance Massenet heard more mumbling in

a strange tongue. *I have been drugged,* he realized. He struggled to open his eyes, and force his head to turn. Despite blurred vision he could see that Angeline now sat speaking with Varese. They appeared to be examining something. Papers. Distorted vowels and sharp consonants reached him, as though the words had been broken as they passed through the air, and his mind could not put them right again. Sometimes the voice was soft and melodious, and at other times it was deeper, and the deeper voice went on at length.

He is telling her everything, the count thought, but he could not move nor even speak. His eyes closed, and the voices continued, like chanting. There were moments when he could almost make sense of what was said—almost. He forced his eyes open and found the blurred form of Angeline standing before him looking down upon him as though he could not see her in return—as though he were not really present.

He tried to force his lids to stay open. Angeline turned away, and in two steps she had gone out of his narrowing field of vision, and he could see only the shadows of someone moving. Then she reappeared to take her place on the divan, facing Bertillon. Massenet could see her smile—and still she ignored him. She was speaking earnestly with Bertillon, her hands moving. Occasionally she would touch his arm, and even in his drugged state the count could see the musician was affected. More and more frequently Bertillon would nod, reluctantly at first, but less so after a while.

Massenet's eyes closed and he fought to keep his focus, his mind slipping off into dream. He wakened to find a naked Angeline standing before him, but then his eyes opened and revealed a second truth. She still sat on the divan with Bertillon, but they were not speaking. The musician stared down at the cushions, in the grip of indecision. He looked up once at the count, his gaze cool, unreadable, and then he turned to Angeline and nodded. She leaned forward and kissed him on the corner of his mouth.

Massenet realized the grunt he heard was his own

curse, and this caused the woman to raise her head and look his way. For a second she leaned toward him, but seemed to decide he was no threat and turned back to Bertillon. Massenet's world went dark again and anger fled like a winged creature. He fell.

"Count?" Massenet tried to stir, wondering who called him. *"Count Massenet?"* He forced one eye open, and found Varese bent over him, his manner filled with concern. "They've gone," he said, as though Massenet would know who he meant. "Gone. And taken the text with them."

The count sat up. "Who?"

"That young woman and Bertillon. And our text has disappeared with them," he said again.

Massenet put his face in his hands. Yes, he remembered. She had drugged him and then. . . . Had he dreamed everything else?

"Do you know what happened? Did she learn everything?" The look on Varese's face answered the question before it was out. Massenet stood, too quickly and sank back into his chair. *She made a fool of me,* he thought. *Made a fool of me!* "She drugged the wine."

"I think she did more than that." Varese shook his head, obviously unsettled. "I fear we have met someone who knows more about these matters than we can claim ourselves. It was a mistake to let her escape the pool, though perhaps we could not have stopped her." He shook his head again, as though he had just predicted the end of the world.

"You can ride, I assume," Massenet said, and it was not a question. Varese nodded. "Good. We'll catch them before they reach the abbey."

THIRTY-ONE

Jaimy wondered if their escort of out-of-uniform Palace Guards deceived anyone. Perhaps here, a day's ride from Avonel, people wouldn't recognize the soldiers so readily: Palace Guards, after all, tended to stay near to the palace. The lieutenant approached their table, stifling his automatic desire to salute and bow to the prince.

"Massenet took rooms here last night, Your. . . ." The guard cleared his throat. "He was entertained by two ladies who had arrived earlier—a woman who kept her face hidden behind a veil, and a young companion. Massenet left this morning, on horseback rather than in his carriage, but was not accompanied by the younger of the two Entonne gentlemen who traveled with him. No one was quite sure when this young man left the inn, though some are of the opinion that he went off with the two ladies."

"The Countess of Chilton and her niece," Jaimy said quietly.

"But who was the younger man?" the prince asked, keeping his voice low. The inn's common room was not empty and the locals exhibited some interest in the gentlemen traveling with their armed escort.

"Did Kent not mention Bertillon, the musician?" the duke asked, and Jaimy nodded agreement.

"So, they are ahead of us by several hours yet," the prince said. "And where are Palle and my father, I wonder?"

No one answered.

"Best that we continue," the duke said, wiping his

mouth with a threadbare piece of linen. "Do we have fresh horses?"

The lieutenant nodded.

"Gentlemen . . ." the duke said, as though insisting they enter a door before him. Jaimy knew his father well, though, and this lightness of tone was meant only to raise spirits. The duke was more concerned than Jaimy had ever seen him.

They mounted horses, and as they waited for the guards to finish adjusting saddles, Jaimy caught his father's gaze. "Uncle Erasmus had something to do with this, didn't he? Were there writings, after all?"

The duke's temper, usually kept in close check, flared, but then subsided just as quickly. "If there is an opportunity, Jaimas, I will try to explain," he said softly, then looked off at the facade of the inn. "And apologize to Lady Alissa for terrorizing her unjustifiably." He nodded to his son, motioned to the lieutenant, made sure the prince was with him, and spurred his horse onto the road.

Jaimy followed, purposely riding alone. He wondered how much his father knew about this business. The portrait of that too-beautiful woman in the library was something of an obsession of the duke's, Jaimy was aware, and now perhaps he would learn why. He tried to remember if his father had spoken to the countess at all when she came to the palace. But other than the introductions, he could think of no instance—and his father's reaction to the woman had revealed nothing. Unless not speaking to her at all could be considered revelatory.

But they were not too far behind the countess now— only a few hours—and Massenet was somewhere in between. It was difficult to imagine that the countess was allied with the Entonne, but why else would Bertillon have accompanied her? If the countess was interfering in the affairs of the Entonne ambassador, Jaimy thought she was in some danger.

He carried a sword on his saddle—not a weapon designed for the duel, but a sword meant to take punishment without failing. He touched it quickly as he rode, but this did not bring the comfort he hoped.

❦ ❦ ❦

Alissa worried constantly about Jaimy, though after what he had told her of his flight from Palle's men, she knew he was more capable than she had realized. And he was with the duke, of course, as well as a detachment of Palace Guards.

He would release me from my vow, she thought suddenly, and that thought came like sudden rush of fear, followed immediately by a feeling in her chest—a hollowness she could not adequately describe. She wondered about Jaimy's loyalty to her. He had seemed a bit distant since returning from his time with the countess. But he had been through a great deal. She should be a little more understanding. *But can I be a Duchess of Blackwater,* she asked herself? It was a question difficult to answer. She realized the few months of her engagement had changed her more than a little.

Just look at her situation at that very moment. She rode in a carriage with Princess Joelle and her cousin, Lady Galton. Even if Alissa had never aspired to such company, still she had to admit it was flattering. Perhaps more than flattering, she felt as though her relationship with the world had changed. After all those years of listening to endless discussion of politics, here she was, involved at the highest level. It was more than a little flattering, and seductive as well.

But was it truly the life she desired? Alissa remembered that she had rather quickly gone through the childhood phase of playing princess. Other things had interested her more.

Alissa gazed out at the passing road, realizing that Jaimy had ridden this way only a few hours earlier. How could she let him go? As mad as it sounded, she would be happier if he had been born to more humble circumstances. . . . But he had not, and she had not been born to this world in which she now found herself. *I am an outsider here,* she told herself, *and likely will always feel the same.*

Where was Jaimy now, she wondered? *Pray that he is safe,* she thought, though it was only a reflex: she could not pray.

Perhaps it was the young prince she should be worried about, though by the look of great distraction on the face of the princess, it seemed she had that area well under control. Unless she fretted about her husband? How in the world was the princess making peace with that situation? Or had that been done years before?

Alissa had no doubt that her party, those who accompanied the King, were bringing up the rear in this race to Tremont Abbey. It seemed rather futile. She could sit a horse—not with any grace, but she never fell or lost control of her mount. If only she had been allowed to go on with Jaimy and the duke. Occasionally she thought it something of a curse to have been born a woman.

The driver called out to his team, and the carriage swayed and rocked as it came to a halt. She pushed the window open quickly, wondering what had stopped them here, apparently near no human habitation.

She heard men talking, but no one came to the carriage to explain their situation.

"Let us see what goes on," the princess said suddenly. "Cousin?" she said to Lady Galton, the single word standing in for the entire question.

"Go along," Lady Galton said. "I'll sit quietly here. Go along."

A footman jumped down and lowered the step for the ladies who quickly descended onto a dry, dirt road. Forty paces along, the track disappeared beneath a flowing river.

Kent came walking up from his own carriage, swinging his cane like a man about town, two ragtag boys running at his heels. "Brookford," he said smiling. "Apparently a wagon was swept away here just yesterday."

"Grand folk set it out into the flood," one of the boys piped up, looking at the two women with awe. "The King's own Man, they say. And you can see the wagon washed up on the bar, with Burnett's old Ned lying there, drownt."

"Goodness!" the princess said, looking down at these children as though they were pixies, so strange were the sons of farm laborers to her. "Someone died?"

"I believe he means a horse, Your Highness," Kent said kindly, causing the boys to step back a bit. They knew enough to realize that Kent's form of address indicated this woman was of very high birth.

"Can we not cross, then?" the princess asked.

"We're just trying to determine exactly that," Kent said, then bent down to speak with the boys. "Has anyone crossed since the wagon foundered?"

"Wha?" the boy said, fingers in his mouth.

"He means since the horse drowned yesterday," Alissa offered, thinking it her place, as resident commoner, to translate. "Has anyone crossed the river since then?"

"Just Burnett's Bill, and Foster's cattle, Yer Ladyship."

The princess smiled. "But any horses or carriages?"

"Burnett's Bill, Your Majesty," the boy managed.

"Let's go have a look for ourselves," Kent said. "Now tell me, lad, what happened with the King's own Man, yesterday? Jog your memory and I shall give you a coin for your troubles. I'll give you each a coin."

They walked to the edge of the river, the boys chattering away about the "grand folk" who had come to the ford the previous day, unaware that the woman who walked nearby was a princess, and inside the curtained carriage the King of Farrland slipped in and out of his waking dreams. As they passed the carriage of the King, Alissa thought she heard soft singing.

Alissa noted that a line of debris, leaves and twigs and seeds, no doubt deposited by the river, lay now far above the level of the waters. "It has gone down about two feet, I should think," she said, pointing to the evidence, and impressing the princess with her powers of observation. Her Highness might function at the highest level in the world of the palace, but apparently her experience of the real world was limited.

A guard was leading his horse out into the middle of the river. Downstream, Alissa saw the remains of a wagon stranded on a gravel bar. As the boys had said, a horse lay there, beneath a covering of crows, which moved like a feathered cape in the breeze. Each bird bobbing and moving like an automaton, an unfeeling machine, sun glinting off metallic feathers. For a second the birds interrupted their gluttony to look up, assessing the visitors with their dark glinting eyes.

Alissa turned away. All she could think of was the two young men who were murdered when mistaken for her own Jaimas and Egar. It could have been Jaimas, lying in some unknown field, left for the roving bands of cutthroat crows. It could be, yet.

"I think it is perfectly safe to cross today," Kent said, watching the guard walk easily to the other shore. "Palle will have been forced around to the bridge at Tainsill. They are not so far ahead of us now. If we can just keep moving. How fares the King?" he asked Rawdon who had joined them.

"His Majesty is growing tired. He is not fit for such a journey." Rawdon looked a bit pale himself. Perhaps he was regretting his defection, considering that Palle was not so far ahead of them.

"We must find a place for the King to await our return . . ." the princess began.

"The King will not be left behind," the physician said firmly. "His Majesty has stressed this to me over and over. It is not just his wish to go on, he commands it. No matter what, His Majesty will go on."

Alissa saw Kent and the princess exchange a look, though she could not quite tell what it meant. Alarm, perhaps. Concern. But it may simply have been a question: *What is driving the King on like this?* Although Alissa believed that all parties were keeping their own secrets, apparently Kent and the princess didn't understand the motivation of the King.

"As pleasant as I am finding not being dashed against the hardest parts of my carriage," Kent said, "I think we must carry on."

Kent found Valary and Littel engaged in heated discussion by the roadside, and herded them back into the carriage. They had been studying Wells' text, and working on it as they could in the moving carriage.

"But if it is not the Midden Vale, then how do you explain it?" Valary was asking, his tone almost accusatory. Obviously being shut up in a carriage for hours on end was having its effect.

Littel shrugged, apparently tired of arguing.

"Kent," Valary said, turning to the painter. "You remember the sections of the text that dealt with the gathering of starlight and moonlight?"

"Captured in snow and water, I seem to remember."

"Well, not quite, but close enough. The text speaks of a spring where snowmelt and rain water meet. We have been puzzling over the location of that spring forever. But it occurred to us that the ancient word evolved into 'mogdynge' in Old Farr, and that is midden. The Midden Vale, don't you see."

Kent glanced over at Littel who shrugged. The young scholar may have been a genius with language, but Valary had been studying these matters longer than Littel had been alive. Kent had begun to think the old scholar's intuition in these matters was a bit uncanny.

"The road branches not too far off. If Palle has taken the fork to the Midden Vale, or even sent others in that direction, it would indicate something. But what are you suggesting we do, Valary?"

The man looked a bit surprised, as though it were merely academic debate—he expected no one to act on his discoveries. "I–I don't really know. I am merely trying to puzzle it out."

Kent nodded. The water would be necessary to perform the ritual. If he did not have it, he could not be tempted— not that they would ever be there in time. No, he had been offered his chance to keep his youth, and thrown it away. His thoughts turned immediately to the countess and the question that plagued him. *What had she been willing to do to stave off age, if indeed she was still young?*

❦ ❦ ❦

The dried oak leaves scraped together like the carapaces of a cloud of insects. It was not the usual sound of a breeze passing through the forest. Galton, oddly enough, had the best vision in the dark and led the way, probing the trail with his cane like a blind man. As usual, the governor was breathing with difficulty, but their pace through the darkness was such that even Galton was not taxed overmuch.

Wells and Palle supported the baron, who made his slow way down the narrow path. A stream rushed along to their right, though the hollow sounds of water lapping and splashing over rocks did not seem to fit with the mood of the place. This water came from the spring in the Midden Vale, which would make it unwholesome by Galton's reckoning.

The prince and Noyes had remained with the guard at the carriages, as Palle was unwilling to allow the prince to participate in this endeavor. Despite great expressions of confidence, Galton knew that no one was really sure what would happen tonight. Up until now it had been all theory—no one had yet tried to apply what they'd learned. He was distinctly uneasy, himself.

The governor was not sure how he could thwart Palle now. He was beginning to realize that unless Lady Galton managed to send Kent and the others to his rescue, the governor would be forced to tip his hand at some point. And that could prove extremely dangerous. If he could only think of some way around this, but he was so fatigued from his endless efforts on the text that his poor mind did not even offer him possibilities to consider.

"Do you think it is far?" Trevelyan asked, his voice taking on the pitiful tone that had characterized his madness.

"Not too far," Palle said, making his voice kindly. "Do you have your part, Lord Trevelyan?"

The baron grunted.

"I hope this is really necessary," Galton managed.

"Utterly necessary, my dear fellow," Wells said. "Have no doubt of it."

They trudged on, saying nothing. The leaves scraped their dried bodies together again, and Galton gave an involuntary shudder. Bits of cloud drifted across the sky at intervals, increasing the shadow under the trees. A storm was in the air, Galton was certain. Tiny flashes of light, like sparks from a distant fire, punctured the darkness on the southern horizon. Lightning, the governor was sure, and though he could hear no thunder he could sense something deep and powerful approaching—like a hound seemed to hear thunder long before its master. The air had that feeling of odd dryness and gathering galvanic power that accompanied a lightning storm.

Like an agitated bull, Galton thought. The charge would come soon.

The path crossed a glade, faintly lit by starlight, and then was absorbed into the shadow of the wood again. A moment more of fumbling through total blackness and the path began to rise. Galton was forced to stop and catch his breath, giving poor Trevelyan a rest at the same time.

"Not far, I'm sure," Palle said.

"And we still have the holyoak to find," Galton said, and then regretted it. It would be better if they had forgotten.

"Don't worry, Stedman," Wells said. "It grows in several places along our road."

They felt their way up the last steps, crouching and feeling the path with their hands. The sound of falling water was loud.

A pool appeared through the trees, like the forest's dark eye, staring up, glittering with the tears of reflected stars. Galton glanced up and realized that cloud had covered the moon and stars, but that did not matter in this place. Their light had been captured, and spewed from a fissure in the cliff, down a pillar of water into the pool below.

Galton stood transfixed. It was like a column of glittering ice, turning slowly in the darkness.

Wells stopped beside Palle, staring at this scene, almost

imperceptible in the darkness. He searched the sky for a moment. "Do you see? The starlight appears in the water even when the sky is blanketed with cloud! Natural philosophy will never explain this!"

"We must not tarry," Palle said quickly, unsettled by what he saw. "Lord Trevelyan."

"I am to climb naked into this pool of ice melt?" Trevelyan said, a little outrage creeping into his whimpering.

"Remember our bargain, Lord Trevelyan. The sooner you are done, the sooner we will be away from here and back to a warm carriage. There is an inn not too far off. We will stop there for a few hours. Help him, Wells, we haven't the entire night to wait."

Wells and Galton began assisting the baron with his clothes, coaching him in his part as they did so. The cloud opened a little, like a wound, revealing a scattering of stars, and bleeding a cool, brittle light into the pond. The oaks that leaned protectively over the water took on definition now, their leaves like remnants of dried skin on ancient bones.

"All right," Trevelyan said after a moment, "I'm ready. Flames, it is cold! Where is the jar?"

Wells passed him a glass jar, the stopper removed. Bending to touch the water with a finger, Trevelyan began to recite the lines he had memorized. He touched the finger to his lips, and spoke again, his voice gaining a bit of strength.

Galton thought the old man looked more than pathetic as he waded tentatively out into the pond, his massive bulk like an overgrown grub in the moonlight. He had barely gone three paces when a fox appeared at the water's edge. It stood with one delicate paw raised, as though surprised in mid step. Palle took a sharp breath, and Galton thought he was about to shout, but Wells touched his hand.

"It is all right. That will be Trevelyan's familiar. A good sign."

"But I thought nothing was to sully the waters?" Palle whispered.

"The fox is an extension of Trevelyan, in a way," Wells said, the excitement clear in his voice. "It will cause no harm."

The fox seemed to keep its eyes fixed on the strangers as it bent to the pool. A small tongue flicked out once or twice, and then the fox raised its head again. Trevelyan was not the object of its attention, but it eyed the others as though they were not to be trusted.

Trevelyan lumbered ungracefully across the pool, nearly falling with each uncertain step, dragging his feet beneath the water, slipping on submerged stones. He kept looking up at the falls as though it posed a threat. Galton saw the baron shiver, though he was not sure if it was from the cold or from fear. The fox seemed to become less sure as Trevelyan progressed, leaning more toward the shadowed wood, as though it might seek safety at any second.

Trevelyan finally came to the foot of the falls, where he stood, unmoving, his shoulders fallen like one who had lost confidence entirely. Galton thought the baron would not continue, but then Trevelyan raised his fat-laden arms, his stance changing, and he called out in the strange tongue of the mages.

"Tandre mal!"

Galton heard Wells catch his breath. But nothing changed. The pale light of the almost full moon and the stars still fell into the glade, the falling water glittered as it had. The fox, though, bolted into darkness, and Galton wondered what that could mean.

A breeze caused the leaves to rasp together, like a shaman's rattle, and Galton felt his hair take on a charge, the strands clinging together unnaturally. Trevelyan's voice fell to a chant now as he continued with the ritual.

Reaching down into the pool, the baron brought up water to anoint his own shoulders and brow. It appeared to Galton that Trevelyan began to coalesce in the poor light, and he believed that direct moonlight had found its way through the trees to illuminate the scene. But when he looked up, he recoiled before he was able to control himself.

"Sea fire," Wells whispered.

The light appeared to cling to the tips of branches like some luminescent green lichen. Slowly it grew, slipping down the branches, springing from one tree to the next.

Trevelyan droned on, apparently so caught up in the rite that he saw nothing else. The sea fire continued its descent, the three men watching with fear and fascination.

Trevelyan stepped forward and filled his jar from the falls, still reciting the words of the rite.

A deep rumble of thunder boomed somewhere beyond the vale, and Galton felt an echo in his own chest. The three men watching this scene had all moved closer together, their shoulders touching. The sea light spread down to the forest floor, and suddenly touched the baron where he stood completing his ritual.

"Impossible," Wells whispered.

The baron continued, as though unaware that he had been enveloped in pale green light. Another rumble, closer this time, and a gust of wind rattled through the trees like hail.

Trevelyan finished then, and lightning stabbed the forest not far off, thunder booming through the wood like cannon exploding. The sea fire intensified, flaring up, jumping from treetop to treetop, then blinked out, leaving darkness but for the glitter from the pool. Clouds had covered the stars, plunging the wood into renewed darkness.

The baron seemed stronger and less hesitant as he waded back across the pool. Galton threw a blanket around the man, who seemed dazed, not quite aware of what went on around him. Wells could not pry the jar from his grasp and was forced to stopper it while still in Trevelyan's hand.

"The fire is gone," Wells said. "It touched you, Lord Trevelyan. Did you feel it?"

"What?"

"The sea fire. Did you not see it?"

"Yes, I saw," the baron said, covering his face with his free hand. "The dreams. . . . The dreams of my madness. Not dreams at all," he whispered, horrified. He began to shake, and Galton thought he would collapse. Lightning flared again, so close that they all flinched. Palle managed to take the jar from the baron and stepped away from the others.

"Come, Trevelyan," Wells said. "Dress quickly. We must get away from this place. The sea fire. The storm. It is too much like the battle of the Midden Vale. The spirit of Dunsenay is said to ride the hilltops at such times." He began helping the frightened baron into his clothes.

Again lightning struck, so close that they were nearly blinded by its flash. Their courage gave way then, terror taking hold. The baron had begun to weep, falling to his knees. Wells and Galton pulled the man to his feet, throwing his coat over the blanket, and leading the poor baron away, barefoot.

He whimpered as they made their way through the dark, flinching occasionally as though warding off a blow. But even worse; Galton realized that not all the words mumbled were from familiar languages, nor were they all from the ritual the baron had memorized.

Galton began to feel his own fear taking hold of him, overcoming his reason. The darkness seemed frightening, and each time the lightning flashed he expected to see some terrible spectacle—an army of ghostly warriors surrounding them silently. Or something even worse.

Trevelyan fell repeatedly, and cried and whimpered in his fear, making no sense now at all. The wind whipped the branches in frantic circles so that they creaked and moaned, the dried leaves almost hissing as they moved.

The path had begun to seem endless, and at times they lost it completely. When a flash of lightning revealed them on it again, Galton thought it nothing short of a miracle. A light flickered in the trees ahead, like a flame brought to life by a lightning strike. It appeared to waver and then disappear as though floating through the trees.

"Is it a lantern?" Galton wondered aloud, hoping it was nothing unnatural.

A moment later, in a lull in the storm, they heard Noyes shout, and they all answered in unison. Prince Kori and Noyes appeared, looking distinctly disturbed in the light of their storm lantern. The fury of the storm was such that no one tried to speak when they met, but Noyes turned and led the way back through the trees. A branch split with a crack and fell across the path twenty feet ahead, and the air was full of the dried leaves of oaks, torn free by the storm, battering against the men like a plague of insects.

Finally, they came out of the trees, and the night was revealed in all of its horror and glory. Lightning flashed continuously, far off on the horizon, and close by. A fire seemed to be flickering on the hillside, and the men could not look into the wind, which hurled bits of the valley floor against them.

"Fire writing!" Trevelyan shouted, pointing at the lightning filled sky, and then he stopped as though transfixed, his eyes wide.

The drivers and guards struggled with the horses, though they seemed hardly less frightened themselves. Rain fell, propelled by the wind so that it struck man and beast like gravel. Galton and Wells managed to push a struggling Trevelyan into the rocking carriage, and then crawl up behind him. Palle went to his own coach, and the drivers sent their charges forward, and as soon as they were given leave to move the horses bolted in terror.

The darkness inside the carriage was held at bay by the continual lightning, and over the sound of the rain and his own breathing Galton could hear Trevelyan muttering—some of it in the strange tongue of the ritual.

The governor of Farrow was deeply distressed by what had happened. Surely they could not go on. . . . It was completely clear that they did not understand in the slightest what they were involved in or what forces might be involved. Had Trevelyan somehow unleashed this storm and the sea light?

"Lord Trevelyan," Wells said, shouting over the cacophony of nature, the mad drumming of horse's hooves. "You must take hold of yourself, sir. We are not finished, yet."

"Oh, we are finished, Roderick," Trevelyan said, his voice strange. "We are quite finished. *L'achevé.*"

❧ ❧ ❧

Massenet pulled his horse up at the top of the hill, and sat waiting for the others. He could see the road ahead in sections: usually where it climbed a hill between hedges and rows of trees. The hills would then hide the track for a stretch, and it would appear again, brown against the emerald fields and gray woods, a light strip of green up the road's center like the stripe on a snake's back. For the most part the road was empty, though the low light of late afternoon created dense areas of shadow which hid much.

They were not far behind Angeline Christophe and Bertillon now, but they were narrowing the gap at a maddingly slow pace, despite pushing their horses cruelly. Varese, of course, was not the best horseman, but he was doing all he could, and not complaining. He said little each time they stopped, though he did not hide his growing pain.

The count looked up at the sun, and realized that he would have to give up his hope of catching Lady Angeline and Bertillon before nightfall. All of the things he had considered doing and saying when finally he faced the woman would have to wait. He wondered if they would stop for the night, and the thought that she might spend the night with Bertillon caused his anger to surge. He tried to calm himself. This was a time when he needed to think clearly, though he still felt his anger burning slowly beneath the surface. He did not know exactly what this woman intended, but clearly he could not let her arrive at the abbey before him. He could not understand why he was not gaining more ground in this race, and it unsettled him. Riders were faster than carriages, after all.

Varese and the others came up then, and Massenet nodded to the doctor.

"Why do you think she took Bertillon?" he asked Varese suddenly.

"To stop us," Varese said quickly, obviously having considered the same question.

"Yes, but why take him with her? Could she not have poisoned us all, or just Bertillon, for that matter?"

"Perhaps she is not so made, Count Massenet. Not everyone is capable of murder."

"No. Surely. But is there some other explanation? Does she need Bertillon? Are we missing something obvious?"

Varese shrugged.

Far off, on the most distant curve of road, a carriage appeared, accompanied by horsemen. Even at a distance they could be seen to be making good time.

Massenet said nothing, but spurred his horse forward, determined to resolve this situation. He was not used to being made to look a fool.

❦ ❦ ❦

Bertillon realized that the dark objects he stared at were women in veils. He shut his eyes tightly and wondered how, exactly, one forced one's eyes to focus when they refused to cooperate. Opening them again revealed the scene a little more clearly.

"Can you hear me, Mr. Bertillon?" said one of the women. Her tone was musical and pleasant, and somewhat familiar. He found it stirred him in an odd way.

"Yes." His voice came out as a whisper. "What has happened? Where is Massenet?"

"Be at peace, Mr. Bertillon. Your mind will clear in a few moments. Do not be alarmed."

He tried to nod his head but was unsuccessful.

A carriage. He was in a moving carriage. The blinds were drawn almost completely, and light found its way into the coach only when the curtains swayed. Parts of the interior were illuminated by quick moving javelins of light that appeared and disappeared abruptly. It was as though reality had been shattered into fragments, and all the normal relations of time and substance no longer existed. His confused mind struggled to pull these fragments into a coherent pattern. Two women, dressed in dark clothing, wearing black veils and gloves.

They are like visions of death, he thought suddenly, and felt fear flash through him. Angels of death, and the final journey to the underworld. He felt sudden nausea.

"You do not look well, Mr. Bertillon. We could stop, though only for a moment."

He nodded. "Please."

The light outside the carriage was blinding, the late afternoon sun casting long shadows. Two men appeared and supported Bertillon while he urinated. For a moment he thought he would be ill, but when he appeared to recover, the men helped him back to the carriage.

"A moment more," he said drinking in the pure spring air.

"We have not a moment to squander, Mr. Bertillon," the woman said again, and the two men helped him up into the carriage against his will, though he had not the strength to resist.

"Do you feel better?"

He nodded, laying his head back against the swaying seat. "Am I ill?"

"No, Mr. Bertillon, you took the physic. More than you have in the past. You don't remember?"

"Massenet. . . ? We left him at the inn?"

"Yes, he is not far behind us, now."

That seemed to be correct, though Bertillon was not sure why he thought that. "We're going to the abbey?"

"Yes, it is not far off. I think we should be there by morning."

"The count. . . . It seems unlikely that he will let us escape. He is a skilled rider."

This statement caused brief laughter, though he could not imagine why. "So I have heard. He will not overtake us, do not worry. Do you remember our agreement, Mr. Bertillon?"

"I–I don't." *Agreement?* What had been done to him? He could remember nothing.

"Wait a few moments, and it will all be clear. Breathe

deeply. Be at peace. Sleep if you are so inclined. You are quite safe. I will wake you when it is time."

Time? the musician thought. Time? What had he agreed to? When he shut his eyes, the strangest visions appeared before them. A persistent scene of him having love with a strikingly beautiful woman, which was powerfully erotic even in his present state. The vision seemed to draw him in a manner he could not describe, as though it had significance he could not quite grasp—it seemed more a ritual than a night of pleasure.

ಌ ಌ ಌ

They had stopped again, and Kent could not bear it. If only he had gone with the duke and his son. But, despite his feelings of vitality, that might have been tempting fate. Better not to have taken the chance of slowing the duke's progress. Horses were being replaced and people were seeing to their necessities. Kent had wolfed down some food earlier, not wanting to be responsible for slowing their progress.

"Sir Averil?"

Kent turned to find Princess Joelle approaching him. In the golden sun of late afternoon she looked years younger, as though human concerns could not stand up to such light. "Your Highness," he said.

She nodded in a way that seemed to speak familiarity, though was no less regal for all that. Beside Kent she stopped, shaded her eyes with one hand, and looked off down the road. "What do you think Massenet intends?" she asked quietly.

Kent shook his head. "I was hoping Your Highness would know that."

She looked down at the ground, and then up again at the road, as though following it from her feet into the distance, ascertaining that there was no trick to this route. "Men are commonly more predictable."

"I am not sure how to broach this subject, Your Highness." Kent paused, looking for a sign that she knew what he referred to, but she kept her gaze fixed on the distance.

"Massenet gave me a letter. A letter that I thought indicated he had the trust of someone . . . someone in the palace."

She nodded, but Kent was not sure what that gesture might acknowledge. "And where is this letter now?"

"It was taken from my home, by an agent of the count's, or so I assume."

"He has a way of winning people's confidence, but his true intentions are never revealed. If he arrives at the abbey first, is there some way that he can render the site unusable?"

"Valary does not think so."

She raised her hand to shade her eyes again, hiding her reaction to what Kent had said. "Then one would be inclined to believe that the count has every hope of recovering this knowledge for his own use, or the use of his government."

"I'm afraid I must agree."

"We must pray that the duke arrives first. May Farrelle speed them."

Kent nodded. She did not mention her concern for her only son, and that touched the painter strongly.

The princess nodded to Kent and went off to see to her party, leaving Kent wondering what she had meant exactly. *"He has a way of winning people's confidence, but his true intentions are never revealed."* It would appear to be a lesson learned at first hand.

Kent could see Alissa sitting alone on a bench beneath a tree, lost in thought, probably thankful to have a moment alone. Kent decided not to interrupt. Being shut up in a carriage for so long was affecting everyone.

Valary waved to him then and came striding across the open yard before the small inn. "Kent, I've been thinking. I am more and more convinced that I'm right about the Midden Vale, do you see? I don't think I'm merely being pigheaded."

"Well, it seems that Palle and his followers went that way. I take that as a fairly strong indication that you are right."

Valary nodded, suddenly distracted, as though he had

forgotten why he had come to speak with the painter. He stood struggling for a moment and then picked up the thread of his thought. "I think we may have made a mistake, Averil. We should have gone to the vale ourselves. If there is no way to stop the others from recovering the lost knowledge, it might be better that we possess it ourselves. Do you see? Better us than Palle or Massenet."

Kent did not respond for a second. "It hardly matters, Valary. We shall be there long after everyone else. We must pin our hopes on the duke, or perhaps the countess. I have begun to wonder why we make this journey at all. Perhaps the King truly is mad. What in the world does he hope to accomplish?"

Valary looked thoughtful for a moment. "It is not inconceivable, Kent, that the others will fail. You must realize that we are not at all sure we can perform this ritual in a manner that will yield results. We can't, of course, be sure what Massenet might know, but from what Littel has told me, I would give Wells and company no better than even odds. We might not be there first, but we might be the ones to succeed. If only we had gone through the Midden Vale. We would need water from the spring and certain herbs that grow there. And there is something else. . . . The more I look at the text that Wells had, the more I am convinced that it is not complete. Could they be holding back a section of the text? Something neither Galton nor Mr. Littel knew anything of?"

"Why would they do that Valary?" Kent asked, a little alarmed at the suggestion.

"I don't know, but I have the worst feeling about this. I have developed quite a sense for these things, Kent, and if I am right about there being a missing section, I don't like to think what its purpose might be."

Kent found Valary's reaction deeply disturbing. The only one who might be able to tell if the text was complete was the countess, and she had run off without explanation—not for the first time.

People were beginning to board their respective carriages, and Kent motioned Valary back to their own horse-drawn cell, as he was beginning to think of it. He went to climb up behind the scholar, but his leg gave way as he put his weight on the step. If not for the quickness of the guard holding the door, he would have fallen. Mounting more carefully, he sat heavily on the seat and broke into a sudden sweat.

Was the countess' enchantment weakening so quickly? Was the disease of age about to invade his body again? He shut his eyes for a moment, but could not bear the darkness.

THIRTY-TWO

Bertillon was still feeling at a remove from the world of common perception, as though his awareness had sunk deeper into his skull and peered out at the world through narrow tunnels. Despite all the assurances he had received from Massenet, the musician now regretted his decision extremely. If not for Angeline, he was not certain that he could have dealt with the effects of the physic—especially in the quantities this endeavor was to require. Either Massenet had not known, or he had not been completely honest with Bertillon, and the musician would not have been surprised to find it was the latter. He had been drawn in by a promise that he would be able to extend his years—his productive years—but now he was not so confident of his decision.

He paced purposefully across the grass and scrub before the abbey, stepping carefully among the sheep droppings. He stopped and searched the horizon, assessing the weather the sea would send that afternoon. It was best to keep moving, and try to focus his mind on something, otherwise he would drift into the unsettling, waking dreams that the seed generated.

"There is no road back," he whispered, as though addressing the distant gulls that rode the breeze. Perhaps one of these would be his familiar. Angeline had said to be on the watch for such a thing, but so far any animals he had seen seemed perfectly natural.

Massenet would arrive soon. He could not get over how little concern Angeline displayed over this—her mind seemed to be on other matters. Bertillon was not sure whether this was a display of confidence or a measure of her nerve. Did she actually have the cards or was she merely bluffing? Bertillon did not know her well enough to guess. There was no doubt in his mind that there was far more to Angeline Christophe than his few hours of observation would reveal.

The count would be in a rage when he arrived—a controlled rage, perhaps even silent, but it would be a rage nonetheless. She had stolen Bertillon away, and perhaps even worse, had done it by suggesting she was available to the count. Massenet's great vanity in this one area would make him now very dangerous. It was not a good idea to make a fool of Count Massenet.

If at all possible, the count would have his revenge for this affront. Bertillon could not return his support to Massenet now, even if he wanted to.

Angeline claimed that Bertillon was under no enchantment and that he had made his decision freely. In fact, she claimed that the ritual could not be performed successfully by someone who was doing so under duress—but he wondered if this were true. He was not sure what it felt like to be bespelled, so he was not sure if he were making his own decisions or not. But then, there was more than one type of spell that such a woman could cast, he was sure of that.

A gust of wind made his coat flap, and he felt for a moment like a scarecrow, standing guard over the ruined abbey, keeping at bay all the humans who flocked there, drawn by its strange promise.

"Already you are thinking of them as human," he said aloud. It was an odd feeling. *I will not be a true mage,* he reminded himself, and that was some comfort.

He turned away from the view to find Angeline staring at him, her gaze measuring him disinterestedly. She had shed her veil and gathered her hair in a ribbon of black velvet. She was dressed simply, and Bertillon saw grime from her forays into the abbey had left a stain on her shawl. The wind colored her face, making the blue of her eyes even more striking, and Bertillon found he could not easily pull his gaze away.

"They are nearby," she said, and Bertillon did not need to ask who she meant. "You don't need to speak with him, Charl, if you would rather not."

"No. I will stand with you, if you will let me."

She smiled as though the seriousness of his tone or perhaps his choice of words amused her. "We'll make our stand together, then," she said, though it was not mockery. "Come." She inclined her head toward the spot where the road emerged through the trees.

They walked silently to the top of the track, and waited expectantly. Bertillon did not bother to ask how she knew "they" were arriving now. He had learned that Angeline knew many things that could not be readily explained.

It did not take long. As Bertillon expected, Massenet was ahead of the others—incautious when it came to his own safety, as usual. He was leading a horse that looked like it might not manage the last few yards. Even Massenet looked filthy and fatigued—a sight Bertillon had never seen before. By contrast, Angeline appeared as though she had merely stepped from the front door of her home.

"Count Massenet," she said, her tone perfectly warm, "we have been awaiting you."

The Entonne Ambassador stopped, his legs spread as though to keep his balance, and regarded the pair before him with obvious disdain. Bertillon did not like finding himself facing that glare.

"Are you happy in your new country, Charl?" the count asked softly.

Bertillon did not know what to answer, but found he could not continue to endure that terrible stare, and looked away, feeling a quick flush of shame.

"There is more at stake than you realize, Count Massenet," Angeline said, her voice still calm. "More at stake than our vanity." She smiled charmingly as she said this.

But Massenet did not rise to the challenge. Bertillon knew the count loved a strong woman—one with wit and confidence—but Massenet's look of anger and disdain did not change.

"I have not come this far to banter with traitors and girls. I have every intention of completing my task," he turned to Bertillon, "and you will help me, Charl."

Bertillon hesitated only a second, then shook his head. "I cannot," he said quietly.

Angeline spoke just as Massenet opened his mouth, his temper flaring. "Allow me to explain, Count Massenet," she said, her voice infinitely reasonable, and still showing no signs of concern about Massenet's threats. "And Mr. Varese; you must hear this as well."

The Entonne doctor had struggled up the path, looking far worse for his journey than the count. He sat down heavily on the ground, staring up at Bertillon and this woman before him, his mouth open and his lungs drawing in great heaving draughts of air.

"I have seen the text that you posses, and the text of Roderick Palle's group, and they are not the same." Angeline crossed her arms, a stance of complete defiance, Bertillon thought. "These texts cannot be employed independently. You were not meant to have this power you dream of, Count Massenet. Even if Charl agreed to cooperate, you would succeed in accomplishing nothing but Charl's own horrible ruin. I believe I can convince Doctor Varese that what I claim is true, if you will allow me to do so."

Massenet looked over at Varese who considered a moment and then shrugged, as though passing the decision back to the count. "We have some hours before the ritual can be performed," Massenet said, "but I warn you, Lady Angeline, if I suspect you are attempting to subdue us again, by any means, my response will be immediate and extreme."

To this threat she merely smiled sweetly, and then motioned the count toward the abbey, as though inviting them into her manor house.

In one corner of the ruined building shepherds had thatched over a frame of poles before an ancient hearth, providing rough shelter. A bench, low table of old planks, and a few rough stools were scattered about, and a kettle hung from a rusted hook over the fire. The servants and horsemen who had accompanied Angeline left immediately, the riders taking up stations not far off, like well-trained guards, Bertillon thought. The other lady, the one who did not speak, was not to be seen.

Massenet took a stool at the table, across from Angeline, and Varese sat just at his shoulder, like an advisor. It was impressive to see how quickly everyone learned his place in Massenet's scheme of things. Bertillon thought it must make his own apparent betrayal all the harder to accept. Men who were used to subordinating others to their wills were invariably surprised by rebellion—as though this imaginary prison that they created was, in fact, real.

"You are not innocent of the mage's arts," Massenet said, going immediately on the offensive. "Where did you learn them?"

Angeline smiled as though the count had said something witty, and that was too much for Massenet. He half-rose, pulling back his hand to strike her, but something dove at the count's face, causing him to pull back.

Massenet put a hand to his cheek and came away with a jewel of blood on his finger. Bertillon glanced up at the stone wall and caught sight of a small bird, almost invisible in the shadows.

"Please sit down, Count Massenet," Angeline said. "You are far from your lair in Avonel and have come here with little strength and nothing to bargain with. It is an unusual position for you, I realize, and therefore, I will forgive you this one indiscretion. If you attempt violence against me or anyone in my party again, one of my guards will put an arrow in your heart. Do you understand? You are present at my sufferance only. I have absolutely no need of you."

Massenet lowered himself back to his stool but said nothing, his face revealing even less. Bertillon wondered if Angeline had any idea what she had just done. She had better have every bit of power that her manner claimed, or Bertillon did not want to contemplate what awaited her.

She rose from her chair, turning her back unconcernedly on the count, and poured water from the kettle into a battered teapot. "I don't suppose I can interest you in tea?"

"I've had your wine," Massenet said, eliciting only a shrug from her.

As she returned to her seat, Angeline began to speak. "It will come as something of a surprise to you, I think, but this text that you have come to possess—you were intended to find it. Oh, not you, necessarily. Let me try again. The discovery of the text suited another purpose, but it was not meant to serve yours. Nor could it, I must tell you."

Varese leaned forward to speak, but Massenet silenced him with a gesture.

Was I like that, Bertillon found himself wondering, *so utterly subservient?*

"And whose purpose is this all in service of, may I ask?"

Angeline shrugged. "I will tell you honestly that I am not absolutely sure myself."

Massenet leaned back from the table. "But you.... You did not acquire your skills by some accident of nature. Where did you learn them? You asked me here to listen to an explanation, but I begin to think you are merely wasting time. Whose purpose does the Lady Angeline serve? And who are you? Why is it that no one can name your parents or family?"

She looked up and met his gaze without blinking. "Some of these things will become clear to you in time," she said quietly. "Who do I serve? That fragment you gave to Averil Kent, Count Massenet: I serve those who understood what that vision meant."

Bertillon watched Massenet closely. He could not help himself. It was fascinating. Like watching a predator realize that it was being hunted. He had shifted almost imperceptibly back from the table, as though suddenly wary of the woman who sat across from him.

"I see. And what will you do?"

"We will seal the power away, forever if we can. And I think we can."

"What do you want from me?"

"Your cooperation, Count Massenet. Others will arrive soon. There is nothing we can do until everything is in place. But I appeal to your reason. Better no one have the lost knowledge than it fall into the hands of Palle or some other. I think you will agree. I want nothing for myself but to complete a task begun long ago. If you threaten my purpose, you increase the chances that this power will come into someone's possession. Quite likely someone you would rather see without it."

"Why do you not merely render me obedient? You could do that, could you not? Is it because you need Bertillon's willing participation? Are you afraid that you will lose it if you act against me?" He turned suddenly to Bertillon, his manner determined as only Massenet could be determined. "Charl, do you see? We are being manipulated by a master; an enchantress. She is a loyal Farrlander. Do not doubt it. We await others, she admits, and we know who those others will be: Palle and his prince. We are being duped, Charl. Made fools of. Palle will arrive, and she will surrender the arts to him. It will mean the ruin of Entonne. She claims that this is not so, but are you willing to take such a risk?"

Bertillon struggled for a moment. He had not realized how difficult it would be to break free of this man. How much he wanted to please him. "I think Angeline tells the truth, Count Massenet. There is much more to what goes on than we ever suspected. Let Angeline and Doctor Varese speak and I think you will see."

"She has influenced you, Charl. We were all drugged. . . ."

He did not finish, for the sound of horses and men's voices caused them all to stop. The count cast an accusatory glance at Bertillon. "She has delayed long enough," he said.

A moment later the Duke of Blackwater appeared around the end of a stone wall, and Bertillon heard the woman beside him sigh with apparent relief, causing Massenet to shift his gaze back to her.

The duke stopped, observing the scene, and his son and Prince Wilam appeared at his side.

"Lady Angeline," Jaimy said, bowing quickly, "it is a pleasure to see you again so soon."

The duke nodded to Massenet, and then turned to Angeline, his gaze searching. "We arrived before Palle and the others." It was half a statement of the obvious, and half a question, for nothing could be sure in this matter.

"They are behind you, though not so far."

"And the countess?"

"She is preparing for the ritual."

Bertillon thought this duke looked more like Massenet than not, and though his bearing was less haughty, his mannerisms were not so different. *Two powerful men,* the musician thought, *and neither is entirely sure why they are here, nor what is about to occur. Drawn, almost instinctively, to a struggle over power.* The duke kept his gaze fixed on Angeline, ignoring Massenet, although Bertillon knew this did not necessarily indicate the duke's interests or concerns.

"I have been ordered to secure the abbey until the King arrives, and I will use my guards to insure this."

"You will receive no opposition from the countess, Duke. We await the King, as well. It is the King's Man and Prince Kori who are the threat. I understand they travel with a guard."

Bertillon had made a study of the count's most subtle mannerisms, and he could tell now, simply by the stiffness of his body and the position of his hands, that the count was near to exploding with frustration. Bertillon almost smiled. Not only was Massenet not in control of the situation, but he did not even fully understand what was going on. It must be driving him mad.

"And Count Massenet? What is the ambassador's intention?" the duke asked.

"The Count can do nothing without my cooperation, Duke," Bertillon offered, "and I have agreed to assist

Lady Angeline." And the countess, he thought. Whoever she was.

The duke glanced at Massenet, as though assessing his reaction, and then turned back to Angeline. "I will post guards in the abbey, then."

Everyone stayed in their place for a moment, all the unasked questions struggling to take form, and then the duke turned away and began giving orders to the palace guards. Angeline rose to show him the entrance to the lower levels, and Bertillon found himself alone with the count.

The second the others were out of hearing Massenet turned to him. "I can do nothing without you, Charl?" he said, cocking his head to one side. "I had not realized your opinion of me was so low." He rose and walked out from under the shelter with what Bertillon knew was a tightly controlled fury.

It was probably nothing more than a boast, an attempt to make Bertillon worry, but he would warn the duke and Angeline. Better to underestimate anyone but Massenet—many would attest to that.

❦ ❦ ❦

Kent emerged from the woods, his spirits raised a little by the signs of spring, the buds on trees and bushes, the buzz of insects, the scent of newly emerged flowers, and the excited songs of birds. *The power of the earth reawakening,* he thought.

They had stopped at a roadside spring to water the horses, and the carriages were drawn up haphazardly, the teams led away. Guards and drivers were busy with their charges and the passengers lounged about or, as Kent had done, answered the call of nature.

A guard officer approached Kent.

"His Majesty requests you attend him, Sir Averil." The man inclined his head away from everyone, not looking in that direction himself. One did not look at the King.

Under the spreading branches of a cherry tree that was just coming into blossom, sat the King on a stone bench.

His back was to everyone, and he wore a heavy coat thrown over his shoulders, but there was no doubt of who it was. The sovereign of Farrland was bent over, as though the weight of the coat was more than he could bear.

Kent approached, making as much noise as he could, as there seemed to be no one at hand to announce him.

"Your Majesty?"

There was no reaction for a few seconds, and then the King lifted his head, turning it slightly from side to side.

"Your Majesty?" Kent said, louder this time.

The King raised a hand and motioned the painter to come around before him. "Is it Mr. Kent?" His voice did not seem quite so unearthly, though Kent wondered if it was the setting.

"Yes, sir." Kent made a leg before the King, who squinted at him in the bright sunlight.

"Imagine coming to a point in one's existence," the King said, "where one shunned the light of the sun."

Kent nodded, not sure what to say.

"Well, I am a little more myself, though I suffer terribly for want of my physic. You know about my physic?"

"I do, sir."

The King looked sour. "It seems everyone knows. Secrets are not what they once were, Kent, I'll tell you that. In my day I knew men who could keep secrets! But they are all gone now. I'm the only one left. Once I'm gone there will be no one who can keep a secret, and everyone will know everything." The King looked up at Kent, and a terrible smile appeared on the ruined face. "Don't look so, man; I jest. You have the painting?"

"I have only a sketch, Your Majesty. I could show it to you."

The King raised his hand quickly and shut his eyes, turning his head away. "No. No, I don't need to see it. It will do, I'm sure."

Kent stood in silence—one waited to be addressed by the King—but the silence stretched on so that Kent wondered if His Majesty had slipped off into one of his waking dreams.

"Kent?"

"Your Majesty?"

"Do you fear death?"

He had asked this same question of Kent before. "I do, sir."

The King nodded, his head shaking just perceptibly, as though he were palsied. "Is there anything you would not do to evade it?" he said quietly, as though he would be ashamed to have anyone hear.

"One can never know until faced with the choice," Kent said, thinking of Palle's offer.

The King nodded his head again, keeping his eyes shut, agonizing over his choice, Kent thought. *"Yes,"* he whispered. "Do you think our 'age of reason' is an improvement, Kent?"

The painter considered for a moment, wondering what this conversation was really about. "I think it promises more than it will deliver, but, in balance, I think it will lead to a better world, a fairer world."

"Fairer? I wonder if the mages would agree," the King said. "But then you mean more equitable and just, don't you? Not 'beautiful.' I sometimes think, Kent, that I will be looked upon as the last of the Farr Kings before the 'age of reason.' The last unreasonable King. Do you think history will deal kindly with me?"

"I am sure that historians will deal with you very kindly, Your Majesty."

"Perhaps," the King said softly. He opened his eyes suddenly, and nodded up at the tree. "Is this a hawk?"

Kent followed his King's gaze. "A kestrel, sir."

"It appears to be watching me," he said, and Kent could not tell if this were another jest. The King closed his eyes and turned his face up, something like a look of peace on his horrible features. "The caress of the sun, Kent. The sounds and perfumes of spring. These are the things I could not bear to lose—yet my craving for the seed, in the end, saw me shut up in the darkness. My world reduced to a mere imitation. Think of all the years I have lost—though I believed I had gained those years.

Well, we are only hours away now. Not too long. Thank you, Kent. Keep my portrait at hand. Thank you."

Kent bowed, though the King's eyes were closed, and then backed away. This audience, he felt, was only slightly less disconcerting than the last. Just the man's appearance was horrifying! But the terrible voice had lost some of its hollowness and strange distance—a result of Rawdon controlling the physic, no doubt. Kent was now quite sure that the enchantment of the countess was wearing off, but any temptation he felt to accept Palle's offer of the physic was erased by his meeting with the King. What could be worse than ending up like that? Even if it was years off.

Had the countess enough talent or training to avoid the King's fate? The question never went unasked for long, and now that they drew near to their destination, Kent's curiosity seemed to be increasing—as his vitality ebbed. *Soon,* he thought. *Tomorrow before sunset. We will see what has transpired in our absence. If the duke was swift enough. And I will see the countess again, and have an answer to my question.*

"Sir Averil?"

Kent turned to find Alissa Somers standing behind him, her lovely brow creased with worry. "Lady Alissa, you look positively distressed. Will you tell me what an old man might do to help?"

This brought some response, not a smile, but a softening of her appearance, as though muscles had relaxed. "Sir Averil, I must confess that my life has become more complex than I ever anticipated. It has become impossible to make any decisions at all. I am no longer sure even who I am. People constantly refer to me as 'Lady Alissa,' yet even if I am to marry, I shall never feel that anyone could be addressing me in this manner." She looked up at Kent and bit her lip.

Kent noted the words she used—'even if I am to marry'—and thought this did not bode well for poor Lord Jaimas. And Alissa looked almost overwhelmed with distress, which touched him in some way he could not explain. "Although we are taught that certain kinds of promises are inviolate," he said, "I think it is too much to expect that someone sacrifice their happiness for the sake of a promise." He thought of the countess' decision, all those years ago. "If you really cannot go on, Alissa, be honest with your young man, but treat him as kindly as you can. You will be glad of it in the future, and so will he. I myself. . . ." He found he must close his eyes for a moment.

"Mr. Kent?"

He opened his eyes and smiled as best he could, blinking back a tear. "This may sound rather foolish and overly romantic, but do you love this young man?"

"Without question," she said solemnly.

"Well, then you know something for certain. One must predicate one's decisions on something. Of course, there are many who have made their decisions on just such a foundation and will tell you that they brought their lives to ruin. But I can tell you without a doubt—if you decide that other factors are more important than what you feel for Lord Jaimas, at the very least you will always wonder if you have made the right decision. When you grow old, such questions will plague you, like repeating nightmares. Be sure you know what is important to you, before you decide."

Alissa nodded and looked away from Kent's gaze. "I'm sure you're right. I am to tell you the princess would like to speak with you."

Kent found the princess in her carriage, the door open to the spring air. She was making a lunch of bread and cheese, apparently not too concerned that she wasn't surrounded by a bevy of servants.

"Ah, Mr. Kent," she said as he appeared in the open doorway. "You have spoken to His Majesty?"

"Yes, just now. Remarkable to find him outside, out where others might see him."

The princess nodded. "It is more than remarkable. Doctor Rawdon tells me that His Majesty is hardly less morbid, however, and still speaks constantly of death.

Can you tell me if anything was said of which I should be aware."

"The King was concerned that I brought the sketch I had made. Otherwise I think the conversation was of little consequence."

"I wish I understood what the King hopes to accomplish, Mr. Kent. I dearly wish I did.

"I am told that, if all goes well, we may arrive at the abbey tomorrow afternoon. Do you think the duke has managed to stop Palle?"

"I hope so, Your Highness. If Roderick and the others have managed to win through and perform their ritual. . . . Well, the world seems little changed to me."

"The world has a history of such deceptions. Many a ruler has sat, unaware, in his palace while outside the world changed irrevocably. King Ambray had been deposed for three days before anyone bothered to inform him. He was playing the pianum for his grandchildren at the time. But who is it that plays on, foolishly, here? Is it my husband? Or is it me?"

Kent wondered the same thing himself. "The Duke of Blackwater is a resourceful man. He traveled with loyal guards. I think that the day seems innocent because that is the truth of it. What has happened at the abbey I cannot say, but I suspect if anything arcane had occurred, the King would have sensed it. His Majesty gave no indication to me of having done so."

"I hope you're right." The princess looked at Kent suddenly, squinting a little in the light, and then she shut her eyes briefly. He realized she was near to tears, from constant anxiety, no doubt. "That fragment from Lucklow," she said looking away; "what did it mean? What was this a vision of?"

Kent touched a hand to his cheek. "I have wondered long over this same question. Valary believes that the mages had a limited skill at augury—some were likely more able than others. Perhaps it is the future—or a possible future. Though it is worded in such a way as to make one believe it is another land that Lucklow spoke of. As though he had traveled there himself, and seen it with his own eyes. Whatever the case, clearly he feared that this same tragedy could come to pass here."

The princess considered a moment. "It is too altruistic," she said firmly. "The mages were not known for their concern for others." She shook her head, with resignation, Kent thought. "There is more hidden here than we guess, Averil. Does the countess not tell you her thoughts?"

"The countess tells no one her thoughts, Your Highness," Kent said, again surprised by the bitterness that crept into his voice when he spoke of the countess.

The princess did not respond to this, as though he had not spoken, but in truth he had revealed something too personal. One should not presume such familiarity with the princess.

"When can we get underway?" she asked suddenly. "These constant delays will be our ruin."

"I will see to it," Kent said, bowing stiffly, and making quick his escape. *No one understands,* he thought. *Has there ever been such an occurrence in known history? The powerful of two nations racing toward a ruined abbey for a purpose that no one can articulate. It is like a madness.*

THIRTY-THREE

Jaimy had never been to a military staff meeting, but even so he was quite sure this one deviated from the pattern. The senior ranking officer was a lieutenant of the guards with a mustache like the bottom two inches of a broom. The man had every sign of being a fop, but Jaimy knew that there was a tradition among the guards: they were the best riders and most skilled swordsmen in the kingdom. Their training was said to be so demanding as to be just short of brutal, and the guards were renowned for courage and toughness. It was no wonder that over the years they had been instrumental in deciding several struggles over the throne.

Colonel Townes sat on his stool, leaning over the low table as though a map had been laid there. His uniform jacket was open at the collar—the only concession he made to their exhausting ride, for though he had ridden as far as everyone else, the miles did not leave the same mark on him. His shoulders did not sag, his gestures were precise and strong, and his wit did not seem to have been dulled by lack of rest.

Like many military men Jaimy had met, Colonel Townes seemed to believe that hesitation of any kind was a sign of weakness. Only an inferior man had to stop and "think," a good officer simply "knew." Despite this, the man did not seem a fool. Perhaps his experience and training had better prepared him to meet such situations.

But then Jaimy was quite certain there was nothing in the officer's manual that would cover what was about to occur here. The members of the legally constituted Regency Council were about to meet a force representing a King whose supporters claimed he was fit to rule, as well as reign. And all parties had gathered in this out-of-the-way corner of the kingdom to perform an arcane ritual of indeterminate purpose. Under the circumstances he was performing his duties with elan.

"If we do not take Prince Kori's party, Your Grace," the colonel said to the Duke of Blackwater, "then what will stop them from simply retreating and gathering reinforcements? We have the element of surprise, and it seems imprudent to squander it."

"I don't think they will surrender the abbey to us so easily, Colonel Townes," Lady Angeline interjected. Her manner was patient, as though she were practiced at dealing with men whose grasp of events was inferior to her own, and this had the effect of heightening the color of the officer's face.

"But if they do, they can gather any kind of ragtag army and easily overrun our position here," he said, his voice remaining calm and reasonable. He was too much of a gentleman, and too impressed with this woman's beauty, to disregard what she said, though, clearly, he thought her understanding of military matters was imperfect.

"Not before we have completed our task," Angeline answered quickly, as though even her patience could wear thin.

"But we will lose the kingdom to Sir Roderick if we do not take this opportunity to arrest him. Is what you do here more important than the kingdom?"

"Yes," she said without hesitation.

That brought a moment of silence. The colonel cast a glance at the two officers who accompanied him. They knew what awaited them if this rebellion against the Regents failed. He then turned his eye on the duke, perhaps hoping a man would better understand their position.

The duke did not appear to be worried by the officer's concerns. "My instructions from Princess Joelle were to secure the abbey until the arrival of the King. 'Secure the abbey at all costs.' That, Colonel, is the will of the King. It is your duty to consider all possibilities, Colonel Townes, but trust that securing the abbey is of ultimate importance. I would lay down my own life to stop these others from wresting control of this site."

"Then I can do no less, sir," the colonel said quickly. "I would still suggest that we can best secure the abbey by arresting the King's Man and his followers."

"Something that cannot be done without some risk," the duke said, "especially as we do not know the precise size of their party. We are few, Colonel. I think it would be better to continue to barricade the abbey as best we can, and hold it. I will try to reason with Prince Kori; after all, he has a kingdom to lose, and little of real worth to gain. If reason does not work, we will do everything within our power to hold the abbey for the King, who, I believe, travels with enough troops to deal with Palle."

The colonel looked down and tapped a finger on the table, as though pointing out something crucial on a map displaying the arrangement of armies. "Accepting your argument that holding the abbey for thirty-six hours is our primary function, Your Grace, then I would agree. I fear what will happen to the kingdom of Farrland, but I will put my guards to work again, as tired as they are, and we'll finish doing what we can to fortify the abbey. And that is very little, I fear. We should be prepared to retreat down into the cellars to defend the critical chamber."

The colonel bowed, and retreated with his officers, leaving the prince, Jaimy, his father and Lady Angeline to wonder if they had made the right decisions.

The three sat, saying nothing, the last light of the evening soft and warm on their careworn faces. To all appearances it was a situation where, all having been said, people sought comfort in each other's company, but Jaimy knew this was not so. He wanted desperately to speak privately with Angeline, and was certain she must sense this.

He remembered the night at the countess' house. *"You mustn't do this,"* she had said. *"It is futile even to begin."* Now this admission of her feelings seemed to lay between them like the map Townes had imagined—it was etched with the beginning of a path that they could choose to pursue or abandon. Jaimy wished his father would leave them alone, even for a moment. When he thought he could bear the silence no longer and had decided he must speak, Angeline rose, bid a hurried good night, and slipped away, though not before Jaimy saw the blush of red that colored her cheeks.

He watched her go, his eye following until she disappeared around the end of a wall. And then Jaimy realized that his father was staring at him. "I'll help the guards barricade the abbey," he said quickly.

"No need, Jaimas. There is little that can be done, and all of that is near complete. I expect we shall see Palle before the night is over, and there is something that we need to discuss before then." The duke moved closer to his son, his manner changing. He met Jaimy's eye, his look suggesting that he was surprised to find himself speaking with a man and not a boy. "If fighting breaks out, one of us must try to bring down Prince Kori; it may cost us dearly, but it has to be done. Do you understand?"

Jaimy nodded, hardly believing what he heard, but realizing the utter, cold logic of it.

"It is unlikely that the prince will expose himself to danger, but one never knows. I will attempt to do what must be done, but should I fail. . . ." The duke looked down at the table, lost in thought and concern. "Anything can happen in battle, Jaimas. One can never predict. If the fighting goes against us, you must escape with the prince. No one is more important." He looked up at his son. "Do you understand? No one."

Jaimy felt that distancing from reality that one experienced upon receiving bad news. "That is not true for me, but I understand, and will do as you say."

The duke gripped his son's shoulder, but it turned almost to a caress, the hand suddenly resting lightly. "Sennet will bring forces to Prince Wilam's banner, if it comes to that. Even if Kori is brought down, war might still come. If Palle can seize the King, he will have a chance, don't doubt it. We must hope for the best, but plan for the worst." The duke tried to smile.

"I want to protect you from this," he said suddenly, "but you are a duke's son. . . ." He gave Jaimy's arm a last squeeze and then withdrew his hand. "I will tell you my secret hope, in case things do not go as we wish." He lowered his voice to something just above a whisper. "I believe Rawdon cured his wife from a terrible illness using this seed. My uncle, Erasmus, had a similar theory about the Countess of Chilton. This physic—it might restore your mother to health. She has been so ill for so long. . . ." He fell silent as though he had lost his train of thought. "A cure for your mother. . . . Imagine," he almost whispered.

"If circumstances require," Jaimy said, not liking even the sounds of this phrase, "I will pursue this matter."

A soft smile appeared on the duke's face. "I rest easier knowing that. And seeing the man you have grown to be. You make us proud, Jaimas. You make us proud."

🍂 🍂 🍂

To the east the moon, one day shy of full, floated free of the ocean, casting a path of porcelain shards toward the Farr shore. In the west, the very last light of a warm day fled over the horizon. The wind fell silent, then would speak in syllabic gusts, muttering like an old man in his sleep.

Jaimy paced back and forth across the ridge top beyond the abbey and its surrounding trees. The vista was spectacular, and occasionally he would tear his focus away from his concerns and gaze out at the distant coastline, the shimmering ocean, and the strands of cloud illuminated at their edges by the newly risen moon.

How quickly and surely it floats heavenward, Jaimy thought, *like the pendulum of a celestial clock.* The only thing of which we can be sure—time passes—everything else is vanity.

The smell of smoke reached him, and then the odors of cooking. There were no more sounds of guards at work.

Earlier they had felled trees and hauled them into place with teams. Rocks had been skidded on makeshift stoneboats, and all the gaps in the small building had been roughly closed. All was in readiness—as ready as could be made under the circumstances. Everyone still expected to retreat to the lower chambers, and there they thought they might hold out for some time, for the openings and hallways were narrow.

The area around the abbey had begun to take on the appearance of a military bivouac, though a small and somewhat odd encampment. There were no tents or pavilions or machines of war, but there were men gathered about fires, guards posted, horses tethered, weapons being tended. Here, in this somewhat forsaken district of Farrland, assembled the oddest collection of scholars, nobles, reclusive legends, foreigners, and renegades. It would become a story told over and over down through the years; and Jaimy was here, part of it.

"If I do not hang," he whispered.

Palle and Prince Kori could not be too far off now. If they didn't stop for darkness, they would likely arrive this night.

Jaimy was not sure what his father could say that would sway Prince Kori or Sir Roderick Palle. These were not men used to being thwarted in their desires. And after Jaimy's brush with Palle's followers, he realized there was little the man would not do to achieve his ends.

He stared out over the sea, and thought of Tristam, sent to gather more of this plant that was so valued. The countess had said that Tristam had begun the transformation from man to mage. What did that mean for poor Tristam?

My brother, he thought.

Tristam was to have gone off on an adventure and Jaimy was to have remained quietly at home to marry. But it had all gone wrong somehow.

Jaimy wondered if he was still about to marry. He had offered to free Alissa from her vow, and she had agreed to consider his offer. He closed his eyes. Had he done this because he had met another? Was this truly what he wanted? The idea that Alissa would spurn him and find another caused his eyes to suddenly burn. How could he possibly want that?

His thoughts returned to Angeline Christophe. Their paths kept crossing, yet never ran together for any distance. What was this man Bertillon to her? The duke was certain that Bertillon was, or had been, an agent of Count Massenet. How had she convinced him to change his allegiance? Anger and jealousy boiled up in him as his imagination took hold.

I am still betrothed to another! It was almost a cry of anguish. This was how the Countess of Chilton had affected men in her day. Men whose names she did not even know would abandon their wives for love of her. And now the niece had brought out this madness in him.

I am hardly worthy of Alissa, he told himself angrily. If she knew. . . . This thought brought despair. He could not bear the idea of bringing Alissa pain. *Perhaps, after we are married, we should go abroad for a time, to allow this madness to work its way out of my blood—if we are married at all.*

"Lord Jaimas?"

Jaimy spun around to find Bertillon standing a few feet away, ghostlike in the moonlight.

"Mr. Bertillon."

They stood for a moment like that, eyeing each other, somewhat less than politely.

"Warn the duke that Massenet is not to be trusted," the musician said quickly, as though once he had decided to speak he wanted it over with as soon as possible. "He would never passively accept being bested. It is not in his nature."

Jaimy considered these words for a moment, keeping his eyes fixed on the man. "Massenet thought he would gain this power through you. . . . But how was he planning to insure your allegiance?"

Bertillon looked at Jaimy oddly, as though searching for mockery in the question. "Count Massenet does not admit the possibility of independent will. The world is full of people who do not yet realize that they long to subject themselves to the will of Massenet. His vanity is unimaginable. But that is no longer my concern. I believe that Lady Angeline is right—this knowledge is best left hidden, destroyed if at all possible. You must warn the duke."

"Why don't you speak to my father yourself?"

Bertillon hesitated for a moment, and then jerked his head toward the trees. "I saw a child prowling through the trees a few moments ago and followed him. He came and stood at the edge of the wood, as though watching something. When the moon rose, I realized it was you he watched, Lord Jaimas. As I slipped closer, he became aware of me and looked my way. Light did not seem to reflect from him as it should, and then I saw that he cast no shadow. He slipped back into the darkness, more cunning than any wild animal—became part of it, really. But he had been watching you, is probably doing so at this moment. I thought you should know, in case you were unaware." The Entonne bowed as though he had just finished a recital, and acknowledged the chorus of applause. He walked back into the wood like a man who had no fear of ghosts.

Jaimy stood a moment, staring at the dark line of trees, the deep blue of the shadows, but once Bertillon had been absorbed into that liquid darkness, he could see nothing. No eyes staring out.

But we are so far from Merton, he thought. *It couldn't be the same specter following me.*

There was a shout, and he heard a horse coming up the track from the valley below. Forcing the thoughts of ghosts from his mind, he found the footpath through the woods and plunged into the pool of shadow, somewhat apprehensive of what might lurk there. A moment later he emerged gratefully from the wood and found the camp alive.

"My father is here," Prince Wilam said as Jaimy appeared, and the young royal seemed truly dismayed. Jaimy thought everyone else was equally alarmed, but even so, there was no chaos. The duke and the colonel had been preparing for this eventuality. Jaimy scrambled up a rough ladder to take his place on the wall, throwing aside his coat so that his sword was easily reached. The guards wore helmets and swords, and some took up pikes. Horses were quickly saddled and mounted, and the group of riders faded quietly into the trees. The colonel wanted to maintain some element of surprise, Jaimy guessed, but perhaps these men had some specific purpose.

He wondered how much strength Palle's followers would have when they arrived. They had been racing across the Kingdom themselves. Apparently Palle had set out with a small party, preferring speed over numbers, but the precise size of the party was unknown.

Jaimy knew this was a decisive moment, and not just because it would tell who controlled the abbey, but because it could mark the beginning of civil war. It was not a moment of normal life, but an instant in history, and he wondered how he would acquit himself, and whether his name would one day appear in history books.

If the Regency Council retreated, claiming the King had been abducted by parties wishing to usurp the legal right of the Council, many would support them. It was, as the colonel had pointed out, a terrible gamble. The duke was counting on a stand-off, betting that Palle would be unwilling to surrender the abbey, and would, therefore, take up a position nearby. Before Palle could find reinforcements, the King would arrive, and whatever needed to be done would be quickly concluded. It was the ragged end of a plan, cobbled together, as everyone realized, but fortunately Palle would have had no way to prepare a counter plan—completely unaware as he was of what went on at the abbey.

Jaimy found the prince at his side, holding a sword slightly away from him as though he feared it, or what he might do with it. No doubt the prince had fenced at the university, as everyone did, but this was not the practice floor. The two young men locked gazes briefly: some strange unspoken acknowledgment, and then the prince nodded.

He is in love with Alissa, Jaimy realized, the thought stabbing into his consciousness like a blade. But there was far more to it. Prince Wilam did not wish him ill. No, they were here, cast together by their common cause, their fear of the coming confrontation, and apparently by the love of the same woman. The possibility of losing Alissa became real for the first time and almost overwhelmed his fear of the coming confrontation.

The sounds of horses came up the track from below, refocusing Jaimy's mind on the present events. Fear. Jaimy felt some, there was no doubt. Men had tried to kill him before. It was no longer beyond imagining, as it might still be for the prince. But Jaimy had also learned an invaluable lesson during that cross-country chase: he knew that survival would depend on keeping his wits about him.

Jaimy also knew that the prince was about to face a situation he could hardly imagine. Prince Wilam's father was about to become his rival.

My father and I stand side by side, Jaimy thought. *The prince's father will ride up this trail, and realize the betrayal.* Jaimy offered up a silent prayer thanking whatever gods there might be that he was not forced to this same experience. Halden had written that all young men must vanquish their fathers, but he had not meant it so literally. Would Prince Kori send troops against his own son, Jaimy wondered? If the moment came, could the son raise the sword to the father?

"Will you fight, if that is what comes about?" Jaimy asked suddenly, keeping his voice low.

The prince nodded, his look sad. "Anyone but my father. But I hope it will not come to that."

"I know these men," Jaimy said. "They tried to murder me once. They are more determined and less concerned about lives than we might imagine. If you find yourself crossing swords with a man you recognize, do not count on him respecting your royal person. Take whatever advantage is offered, and strike with all force. But for now put your sword in its sheath until we see what occurs."

The prince looked down at his sword with some misgivings, and then returned it to its sheath.

The first horseman, a Palace Guard, appeared at the top

of the road, riding bent over, sore and tired. Seeing armed guards of his own company before him he pulled up, dazed. The third man to appear took one look at the situation, wheeled his exhausted mount, and tore off down the trail. Jaimy heard the horse stumble and fall, but all the same, Roderick and the prince would know the situation in moments. There was a madding quarter hour during which the sounds of horses and occasionally men could be heard, though no one appeared.

Jaimy had been given a bow, a weapon he had been forced to master by his cousin Tristam. He stood atop the trunk of a tree that had been braced up against the wall at such a height as to allow a man to look over. The abbey roof had fallen in decades before, leaving the structure much like a walled keep, though with the gable ends still in place, their glassless rose windows, complete with stone traceries, still intact.

"Imagine that we defend such a place with our lives," Jaimy whispered to the prince, wanting to hear someone speak.

The young royal looked over at him, perhaps a little relieved to hear a voice. "Yes, but we are not the first to do so. Over the centuries countless lives have been squandered to control this site. Whatever is here does not go away—the attraction always returns."

Jaimy looked down the line of men at the wall, their faces illuminated by moonlight. They stared out at the shadows, searching for attackers, desperately wondering what Palle's men were preparing. Even Jaimy found himself hunkering down, exposing less of himself, imagining an arrow coming out of the darkness to pierce his face.

At that moment a rider on a gray horse appeared, an officer of the Palace Guard. He did not even bother with a flag of truce, but came out into the open, holding his head high and his back straight. Even his horse held itself proudly, as though mimicking its master's mood.

The officer stopped his horse in the open area, and for a moment stared at the abbey, using the opportunity to assess the situation.

"I am Ceril Hampton, Colonel of the Palace Guards,"

he called out, his voice confident and filled with authority. "I accompany Prince Kori, and members of the Council of Regents. You were once my fellows, my brothers in both arms and purpose, but if you do not lay down your weapons and surrender this site to us, you will become nothing more than criminals—failed mutineers—who bring dishonor to your uniform and your oath."

"You have said enough!" the duke called out suddenly. "The Regency Council has been dissolved, and the King rules again in Farrland. Sir Roderick Palle is the King's Man no more, and it is you in danger of being named 'mutineer.' I am Edward Flattery, Duke of Blackwater, and I stand beside Prince Wilam of Farrland, sent by the King to represent His Majesty's will in this matter. A loyal army will reach this place within hours. You have no choice but to surrender. No Palace Guards will be held responsible for their actions until this moment, for you have opposed the King's will unwittingly. But now you have been warned. The powers of the King have been restored. Continue to support the members of the dissolved council, and you will be rebels. The palace guards are sworn to guard the King—not those who would usurp His Majesty's throne. You have sworn fealty to the King. Act according to that oath, or declare yourself this moment."

Jaimas could sense the officer wavering. His silence was caused by doubt. The Duke of Blackwater was known as a man of honor. Not a man who haunted the halls of the palace, seeking power for himself.

"And who has appointed you abbot, Duke?"

Jaimy knew that voice. It was Palle. And then he appeared, mostly obscured by the rider and his mount, for he was protecting himself from bow shot. Obviously the King's Man hadn't guessed there were mounted guards in the wood.

"Have you really the prince with you?" he said a bit mockingly. "Come down, Your Highness, your father awaits you."

"I will not come down," Prince Wilam called out, barely hesitating. "I follow the orders of the King, whom you formerly served. You are no longer a Regent of

Farrland, Roderick, nor are you King's Man. Surrender yourself now, before you are branded a rebel and lose more than your position."

Palle said nothing. Jaimy was almost certain he heard men speaking in the dark.

"But I know the voice of my prince," Palle said, as though this were friendly banter. "Know it well. That is not Prince Wilam. What lie will you threaten the King's Man with next, Blackwater? Will you tell me the King rides at the head of this phantom army? *Give this up!*" he shouted, his voice suddenly harsh. "I have come with a force of my own. You are no match for us. Many lives could be lost. Perhaps you have your own son with you? Do you really wish to endanger his life so pointlessly?"

"He survived your first attempt at his murder, Roderick. Do not think we Flatterys are so easily murdered."

The King's Man may have been about to answer when suddenly a woman appeared in the moonlight, walking calmly to the center of the open area. She stopped before a fire that had burned down to coals. Jaimy could see her silhouetted against the dull red, an almost invisible plume of smoke rising before her.

"Do not look so, Roderick," the countess said, for Jaimy recognized her voice immediately. "Let us end this charade. Come out from behind your brave knight, *Sir Roderick,* and speak with me. I shall not hurt you."

"Who are you, lady?" Palle said, his voice suddenly quiet.

The countess reached up to her veil and pulled it free, folding it back over the rim of her hat. Her back was to the abbey, but even so, Jaimy felt himself lean forward as though he might catch a glimpse of this legendary face.

Palle emerged gingerly from behind the rider. *"Lady Chilton?"*

Jaimy saw her head nod once. "You are no fool, Roderick, you must guess why I am here."

Roderick neither spoke nor moved. Clearly, even the King's Man could be shocked into silence.

"You cannot have what you've come to claim," she

went on, as though instructing a child who would be terribly disappointed. "Even if I were to step aside, you could not have it. But no one else will possess it either. I will seal it off, Roderick. Seal it off from anyone's reach." The fire at her feet roused itself, coming back to life with a sound like an exhalation. A narrow tongue of flame wove up, licking the air as though tasting the night. "You have Trevelyan with you. Bring him to me, and I will save his mind. Take pity on the poor man, he has served you as best he could."

Palle reached out and put his hand on the horse's flank, as though he would steady himself, but instead the hand reappeared holding a sword, and the King's Man backed quickly in behind the rider.

"You are the one Eldrich left. Not Erasmus," Palle said, his voice rising. "Stay back from me! I saw you gesture and the fire come to life. I know what you can do with fire." He was retreating quickly now, and the rider was backing up his mount, protecting his master from this unarmed woman before them. At that moment armed men rushed out of the shadows, coming to Palle's aid.

"Protect the countess!" the duke shouted, and Jaimy let an arrow fly into the midst of Palle's men, unsure of the result.

Horses erupted out of the wood, but before they could engage the opposing guards, the fire before the countess blazed up once and a thick black smoke spread across the meadow like an advancing wave. Before it men fled, though the smoke was so thick Jaimy could see nothing more.

A hand gripped Jaimy's shoulder, and he found his father beside him.

"Massenet has disappeared down into the abbey. I can't leave the wall. Go after him, but be careful."

Jaimy jumped down to the ground and quickly gathered the three others his father detailed to him, one of whom was the prince, and sprinted for the stair down into the cellars. Behind them they could hear horses galloping, and the shouts of men.

They took a single lantern, turning the flame low so

that it did not make them such a target, and made their way down the stairs into a narrow passageway. Jaimy had been down here once, only as far as the door to the crucial chamber, but the route was not difficult to remember.

He wondered what the Entonne count was up to. Without Bertillon, Jaimy thought the Entonne were effectively neutralized. But then Bertillon had warned him. Trust an old tactician like Massenet to wait quietly until such a moment to move.

At a turning in the hall Jaimy stopped, not sure if he heard a sound beyond, or if he was listening to his imagination.

"Did you hear that?"

The prince nodded. A guard brought up the rear, hovering over the prince, obviously not happy to find a member of the family he was sworn to protect in such a position.

Jaimy realized the lantern cast their shadows on the wall, so that anyone ahead could see their every movement. He made his shadow move as though he were leaping out into the hallway, and an arrow shattered against the stone, bits of wood striking Jaimy.

"Stay back," the guard cautioned unnecessarily. "If they block the opening to the chamber, I think it could be held for some time. Even to get near enough to force our way in we will need to fashion shields, or lose many men to arrows. We can do nothing," he cautioned. "We are only three."

Jaimas considered for a moment. As much as he would like to report that he had retaken the chamber from Massenet, he believed the guard was right. Massenet was no fool. "Then go up to my father and tell him what has happened. I do not know if Massenet can make use of the chamber on his own, but if not, the count will want to negotiate. Tell the duke that."

Jaimy and the prince crouched down keeping their swords ready. They both strained to hear the smallest sound on the stairs below. Though the silence was tangible, the silence between them was greater.

Almost as though the presence of Alissa could be felt, as though she had come and sat between them.

"Do you think, Lord Jaimas," the prince whispered suddenly, "that you will be happy in your future life?"

To Jaimas, to whom happiness never seemed to be in doubt, the question sounded very odd. "I have always assumed so. And Your Highness?"

"I . . . I do not make that assumption." The prince kept his gaze fixed on the stairs below. "I have often thought that if I find a bride, she will merely share my unhappiness—a terrible fate, I think."

Jaimas nodded. Alissa. The prince wanted her to be happy. In his awkward way, that is what he was saying.

"I would not want my bride to be unhappy either," Jaimas said quietly. "I would rather she change her mind than be unhappy."

The prince nodded once. "My feelings as well."

And the silence returned. Not quite so filled with things unspoken.

THIRTY-FOUR

The moon lifted up above the distant sea, but overhead a tattered cloud rained a constant drizzle down upon the party in the valley. Palle stood beneath a tarp that had been suspended between the prince's carriage and three saplings freshly cut for the purpose. Just beyond the shelter, a fire sputtered pathetically, sizzling as the rain fell into the flames, and smoking terribly. In this situation the Regents of Farrland met to discuss the future of their nation. Not quite what they were used to.

Stedman Galton was cold to the bone, damp, and only slightly relieved that the duke had arrived first. He looked around at the others, wondering what they would do. Palle especially worried him. The man was resourceful in the extreme, and especially so when threatened.

"How long has the countess been involved in this matter?" Prince Kori asked, his tone clearly accusatory. "I thought you had agents, Roderick. I thought you knew what transpired in my Kingdom."

Palle did not seem overly intimidated by the prince's manner, however. He stood, unmoving, his hands jammed into pockets, his features almost hidden in the collar of his greatcoat, though they were hardly less expressive for this. He was obviously lost in thought, hardly paying attention to what was said.

"Is it a bluff, do you think?" he asked suddenly. "This army the duke claimed?"

This thought seemed to unnerve the prince enough that he dropped his accusations, and fell to thinking himself.

"It would make sense," he said after a moment. "Obviously my traitorous wife has joined the duke in this—that is why the prince is here, doing his mother's foolish bidding. But it would be reasonable to assume that, as the duke outraced us here, the princess raised an army to send to his aid. Perhaps we should not be so complacent, Roderick." The prince looked over at Galton. "Perhaps we should be about raising a force of our own?"

Galton nodded. "It would mean civil war, of course, but if the princess and Blackwater have the King, and have managed to delude Prince Wilam.... I agree with the Prince. We cannot afford to be made prisoners." Anything to get them away from the abbey. He was concerned about what the countess had said about Trevelyan, though. Was the baron's mind in danger? Or did she have some other purpose?

Palle reached a hand out beyond their shelter to gauge the severity of the rainfall. "Mud always slows armies. Real armies. But if there are reinforcements on the way, I am quite sure they are only a light mounted force. Speed is of the essence, here. Less than a hundred men, would be my guess. Soldiers, Your Highness. Men trained not to think for themselves." He looked over at the prince. "Confronted with the heir to the throne, I feel quite sure they would easily be convinced that they have, through no fault of their own, made a grave error."

"Well, that is a gamble you are suggesting! No doubt they have orders to arrest us, all three," the prince said, his voice rising just a little. "Why don't *you* confront them, Roderick? You are the King's Man and a regent, too. They are just as likely to listen to you."

Roderick stared impassively at the prince from the shadow of his greatcoat. "Shall I leave Your Highness here to deal with the situation? With the Duke of Blackwater and this unnatural countess? I saw her, Your Highness. I saw what she did. There can be no doubt that she has been following the arts of the mages."

This silenced the prince for a moment, and made Galton wonder again what Palle would do.

SEA WITHOUT A SHORE

"What will you do against such an adversary, Roderick?" the prince asked, voicing Galton's question.

Palle looked up at the ridge above them. "I am not sure, but there is something I find odd." He turned to Hawksmoor who stood just outside the shelter. "Bring me the baron," he said.

❦   ❦   ❦

Galton rode occasionally on Farrow, but there it was a pleasant occupation, done only in the best weather and over soft ground. The horse he rode this night had a terrible gait—though he had no doubt that it had speed bred into it like nothing else—and he jarred along the dark road in the continuing and worsening rain, cursing Roderick silently.

Palle was so sure the duke and his party were utterly determined to hold the abbey, and therefore would not venture out, that the King's Man had detailed almost all of their guards to support the prince and Galton. It was like Roderick to be so sure of himself—of his understanding of others—and Galton had to admit that Roderick was seldom wrong.

It had been decided that Galton would accompany the prince, the reasoning being that two members of the Regency Council would add legitimacy to their words, though Galton was almost sure Roderick had sent him to bolster the prince's resolve. The farther from the palace they went, the less confident the prince seemed, as though the source of his actual power really did lay in the physical symbols of it: the throne and crown, the great seal and staff.

No one spoke as they rode along in the darkness, the wind rushing past them, sweeping the chaotic sky with clouds. Occasionally the moon emerged, appearing itself to race as the clouds passed over it, and then the road would be illuminated for a moment. An empty road, filled with only the sounds of their horses, the voice of the wind, and the spattering of rain on their coats, and on the moving river.

Galton was not sure what he should do if they really did meet troops sent to reinforce the duke. If they outnumbered their own party at all, Galton might try to convince the prince to surrender; to cast Roderick adrift and swear allegiance to the King. The Prince could claim ignorance of what Rawdon and Palle had done to the King—keeping His Majesty in thrall to the seed, driving him into madness. Prince Kori might even retain his place in the succession—not an appealing prospect.

It was difficult to know what to do. Best to prepare himself to act, though; consider all possibilities, or at least all he could imagine.

He wondered if the prince actually could manage to sway any troops they might meet. Certainly Kori did not seem too confident of his place at the moment. Any guards sent north would, undoubtedly, be led by officers loyal to Princess Joelle, if not the King. But this far from the princess herself they may have begun to wonder about their choice, about what else went on in the kingdom in their absence. If the prince could regain his customary aplomb, he might well carry it off, and that would likely give Palle all the troops he would need to storm the abbey. Astonishing that matters of such import could be decided by a mere handful of armed men.

Better keep the prince from getting too confident, he decided.

"What if Rawdon has gone over?" Galton said suddenly, casting his voice over the sounds of wind and rain.

"What?" the prince said, clearly in bad humor.

"What if Rawdon has gone over to the princess? If they could produce a lucid King...." He let the statement hang in the air. For a moment the prince did not answer, and Galton began to think that he would not.

"I have thought the same thing," the prince said suddenly. "It is the greatest danger to our endeavors. And Rawdon ... well, he has been none too stable these past months."

"My thoughts exactly," Galton said, a bit relieved to hear the prince might be easily convinced this was true.

"But do not underestimate Roderick, Stedman," the

prince said suddenly. "He is the most formidable states-man in the Kingdom, and I include myself in this assessment. And we mustn't forget, if Rawdon really has gone over, and the King is found to be even reasonably lucid . . . well, what we are engaged in here will be even more important. We will never regain the throne but through this power that we seek. Have no doubt of that. We dare not fail, Stedman. We dare not fail."

A light appeared around the corner ahead, and then another. A large party was on the road—in this remote corner of the kingdom.

❦   ❦   ❦

The Entonne messenger was a small man, entirely be-grimed, and soaked to the very skin. He stood before Roderick and Wells, shivering uncontrollably, but no one offered him so much as a blanket, or even suggested he stand near to the fire. He had come out of the darkness and been snared by two of Roderick's guards. The King's Man was not convinced the man was actually a messenger to him from Massenet at all, but may have simply made that claim once he found himself a captive.

"You say Count Massenet has taken control of this chamber in the abbey?"

The man nodded. "Yes, sir. And I came out through a tunnel we found in a lower chamber."

"Convenient. So, what does the count want of me?"

"He says, sir, that it would be better that you and he form an alliance than to let the arts fall to your enemies. The duke and the countess: they are bent on taking this power for their own. But the count will not surrender the lower chamber, and he has Mr. Bertillon, whom the countess needs to gain her ends."

Roderick was alarmed now. Did Massenet really have the chamber and this man Bertillon? What was stopping him from gaining the power for himself? Roderick glanced at Wells, but he was not looking.

"But what does the count want of me?"

"I am to tell you that to achieve the countess' goal she

needs another with talent to perform the rites. That is what the countess told Bertillon. Under no circumstances should you allow Trevelyan to fall into her hands. Under no circumstances.

"At this moment no one has an advantage. The count controls the chamber. The countess and the Duke of Blackwater control the approach, and you, Sir Roderick, control access to the outside world. As things are, no one can win. Unless the duke can take the chamber from the Entonne, and there is another with talent, unknown to us. But time works against us. I can take you down to the chamber: yourself, and the baron, and a few others." The man looked quickly over at Wells, then back to Palle. "We each have a part of the text, and one with talent. The count believes we can bring this power to light, and share it equally. Neither with an advantage—as is the case now between our two nations." The man shifted from one foot to the other, shivering. "I will tell you something the count has learned. Your King comes. He cannot be far off. He comes in the company of an army, his intentions unclear. But why else would His Majesty journey so far but to have this power for his own, and to extend his already-long life? The duke need only wait. Time will win his campaign for him.

"Bring Trevelyan down to the chamber. With what you have learned, and what the Entonne know, the count believes we can succeed. Who knows what might be learned? A world of knowledge, Sir Roderick. The arts so long hidden."

Silence. The rain continued to drum on the tarpaulin and hiss in the fire. Roderick looked over at Wells, then back to the shivering messenger. "We shall discuss your proposal." Roderick nodded at the guard who took the messenger away.

"What do you make of this, Wells?"

The empiricist bent his head, looking down at the puddles forming around their feet. "I distrust Massenet in the extreme, but I suspect there is some truth buried in what he says. I agree that we should not allow Trevelyan to fall into their hands. The countess seemed all too interested in the baron for my liking. But I would not want the baron to fall into Massenet's hands either."

"Yes, I felt the countess' interest was odd as well, but Trevelyan claims he knows no reason for this. I spoke with him earlier. Do you think Massenet realizes that we have two who do our bidding?"

"No," Wells said quickly. "No, I'm quite sure he does not. I think we should find out how this messenger got in and out of the abbey, if indeed that is what happened. That would be useful to us." He looked up, trying to read Roderick's face in the darkness. "This news of the King? Do you think it is possible?"

Roderick shook his head. It was so implausible as to almost be true. "Only if Rawdon has betrayed us," he said with finality.

"If it is true. . . ." Wells did not finish.

"All the more reason that we must gain access to the chamber. Do you think this Entonne would know Trevelyan to see him?"

Wells shrugged. "I can't imagine why he would."

"Who shall play the baron, then? Noyes looks the part, don't you think?"

🥄 🥄 🥄

Moonlight glinted off helmets and lances, creating shadow armies on the narrow road. Both parties held their positions nervously. Banners were unfurled, though remained unrecognizable at a distance. Horses pranced nervously, sniffing the air and tossing their heads.

And then the colonel who had ridden out before the abbey and confronted the Duke of Blackwater went forward again. He stopped his horse in the center of the neutral ground between the two parties, and stared into the poor light with appropriate arrogance.

"The Regents of Farrland and His Royal Highness, Prince Kori, demand to know by whose orders you are on this road."

There was no answer while around the prince swords

were drawn and helmet straps tightened. And then a horseman rode out to meet their own.

"I know your voice, Hampton," the rider said, "but you are mistaken. The Regency Council is no more. It has been dissolved and the powers of the King restored. We are here on the orders of the King, and we shall bring all of those who conspired to usurp his powers to justice. Lay down your sword, Colonel, and tell your men to do likewise. You will have the King's mercy, for you have been misled and shall not be held responsible for what you have done."

"How many are there?" Prince Kori whispered to Galton. "Can you tell?"

Galton had no idea, fewer than he hoped was his fear. "It is difficult to tell, but their numbers are greater than our own, I think."

No one broke the silence for a moment, and then, having worked up his nerve, Prince Kori spurred his horse forward. He pulled up beside Colonel Hampton, and peered into the darkness.

"I am Prince Kori," he said with admirable calm. "Who is in command here? Bring him to me."

"I have been given the King's trust, Your Highness," the rider said.

The prince maintained the confidence in his voice. "The King is not well, and any who claim to represent his will are but opportunists attempting to seize power in the absence of the legally constituted council. It is you who have been misled. There are some within our Kingdom who would risk civil war so that they might seize power, and they are using you to achieve this end. Do not allow the peace of our nation to fall victim to such ambitions. Lay down your weapons and join with us. I am the heir to the throne, and a Regent of the council. I have no interests but the welfare of the people and the well-being of my father, the King. Do not bring my people to war, I beseech you. Join with us, and preserve the peace and the rule of law."

"It was a pretty speech, Your Highness," a voice came

out of the darkness. "As sweet a lie as I have heard in recent years, and I have heard many."

"Kent? Is that you?"

"Yes, it is Averil Kent. Do not waste more words for our benefit. We have seen the King with our own eyes. Spoken to His Majesty at length. Not just me, but these good officers whom you attempt to sway." The dark form of Kent appeared out of the gloom, sitting astride a horse. He rode forward where the moonlight fell upon him, and Galton could see the old-fashioned tricorn, and could not help but smile. If anyone could convince the prince to surrender it would be Kent. No one was more trusted.

"Rawdon has admitted what he and Palle did, Your Highness. The ministers of government know how these two plotted to keep the King in ignorance and near madness, but the King is returned to his senses, and to his rightful place. Tell these men to lay down their arms so that there will be no bloodshed. The King awaits your return, and we shall be most happy to make up your honor guard, Your Highness, for your return to Avonel. There is no question but that you have been the victim of the plotting of Roderick Palle, and the former King's Man shall pay the price."

Galton moved his horse forward slowly, trying to miss nothing, expecting the next conversation to take place between the prince and Kent alone. *Surrender,* Galton willed the prince. He spurred his horse forward to offer his council, but the prince wheeled his mount at that instant and set it to gallop, almost directly at Galton.

"Do not let them pass!" the prince shouted. "Galton!" he called as he thundered by.

Horses surged past Galton at that instant, and a guard grabbed his horse's bridle, pulling him quickly around and sending him off after the prince. Unwillingly, Galton retreated, then realized that battle had been engaged, and spurred his horse lest he be caught up in the midst of it, unarmed, and unrecognizable to either side.

Suddenly two guards came up beside him, hurrying him along, and any thoughts of defecting were put to rest. The sounds of fighting became more and more muffled as they galloped along the road, and after a moment the noise of their passing drowned out everything else. They came upon the prince and two guards in a moment.

"What has happened?" the prince asked, panting.

"We could not tell," Galton answered. "Let us wait here a moment, and send a man back to see." He wanted to stall, perhaps convince the prince that they were making a terrible mistake, but he was afraid that the prince's faith in Palle was unshakable.

One of the guards spurred his horse back along the road, and they all sat silently, straining to hear.

Suddenly the prince turned to him. Even in the dark Galton could see the despair written on the man's face. "Do you think it is possible?" he asked. "Have they managed to return that terrible old man to some semblance of sanity? Don't they realize that he would send them all to be hanged for a single draught of his physic?"

Galton did not know what to answer. But here it was: the prince would clearly take his chances as a rebel rather than submit to the will of the King. The tone in his voice suggested that he might rather face death. There was no chance that Galton could sway him now.

A horse galloped around the curve in the road, causing them to start. But the man called out as he came and they recognized him as one of their own.

"The fighting has broken off," he said, as he reined in his horse, "and the two sides face each other, waiting. We cannot be sure how large their party is, nor can they determine the size of ours. They'll wait for morning, I'm certain. Wait until they can judge the risk."

"But are their numbers great? Greater than ours?"

"We cannot be sure, Your Highness. We cannot be sure."

The prince turned to Galton, as though seeking council, but when Galton did not speak, he turned his attention back to the officer. "Send a rider to tell Sir Roderick what has happened. I cannot be sure if we should stand here and hope to delay these riders, or retreat back toward the abbey."

"If I may, Your Highness?" the officer said.

"Yes. Yes, of course. Speak up."

"If we retreat just beyond this point and fell trees over the road, we might delay even a much larger force for some time. The river is high and cannot be crossed, and there is no track up to the ridge above."

"That is what we will do. Tell the colonel to fall back as quietly as possible. We must delay Kent and his army. Even a day will make all the difference. Even half of the day."

🍂 🍂 🍂

Kent stood in the rain, staring into the dark interior of the King's carriage, waiting. Perhaps Rawdon had not managed to keep the King's lust for his physic under control—or worse, the physician had betrayed them. For some minutes now the painter had been waiting for the King to answer his question.

In the light of the coach lamp, the princess appeared, holding up the hems of her cape and gown. Lady Galton hurried along behind her. They stopped suddenly when they realized that Kent waited for the King to speak.

"Kent?" The terrible voice emanated from the dark carriage, though it was weak and unfocused.

"Your Majesty."

"We must find a way up. We must not be delayed."

"But it is a steep embankment, Your Majesty. I have seen it in the daylight. Perhaps young men might find a way up on foot, but there is no track for a carriage, or a horse either."

"There is always a track," the King said. "Find a shepherd or a huntsman. A good poacher would do. There will be a track up. But we cannot delay. My hour is near, Kent. My hour. Have you my portrait?"

"I–I have, sir." Kent said, answering the question for perhaps the dozenth time on this journey. He glanced over at the careworn face of the princess, who stood silently awaiting the King's words. A fine rain began to drizzle down again.

"Kent?"

"Sir?"

"Do you fear death?"

🐛 🐛 🐛

Kent was more than slightly in fear of his life. The path they followed was narrow, and though it was not properly a cliff they traversed, the drop to one side was steep enough that he was sure no horse could stop itself if it began to slide. Guards with lanterns were spaced evenly among the party, but these lights were not strong enough to matter. It was morning, or at least that is what Kent's timepiece claimed. But a fog had drifted in from the sea, and they made their slow way through this clinging haze. Kent thought the world seemed ominous, trees looming up almost like threats.

Ahead of him the King went, hunched over his mount's neck, immobile beneath his cape and hood. Kent had a memory of the King as a powerful man, and an excellent horsemen, yet this figure he could barely see in the gloom ahead seemed shrunken and fragile, not really human at all.

Somewhere up in the mist, a shepherd and his son led the way, picking their way along the path. The man kept flocks up on the abbey ridge in the summer months.

The dull thud of a horse's hoof striking a root came out of the gray and his own horse pricked up its ears. Kent patted the gelding's neck, and looked again down the steep bank to his left.

He wondered how Lady Galton and the princess were managing, though he seemed to remember that both had been keen riders in their youth. They were likely faring better than he.

Kent was forced to admit that the countess' spell of rejuvenation, or whatever it was called, was losing its power. He had begun to ache as he had before the miracle had been performed. His back was causing him some distress as they rode, and he did not expect it to stop until he could lie down on a proper bed—and he expected that to be some time off, if ever.

Bear up, he told himself. He wondered again how he had

refused Palle's offer. The memory of his tryst with Tenil came back to him. And it seemed impossible that this cell of pain in which he was imprisoned—his body—could have known such pleasure. If nothing else he had a memory recent enough that it might not fade so quickly. It still had . . . texture and substance, and evoked strong feeling. Something to take into the final infirmity of old age. Kent was like a man who felt an illness returning. Some dread disease that he had miraculously escaped, and then, without warning, the symptoms began to return. And this was an illness that, sooner or later, would see his end.

He looked up at the King on his horse, like a strange creature who guided him on a last journey.

Having come so far, Kent was unsure, now, of what use he would be. They simply didn't know what they would find when they reached the abbey, though somehow the King was not in doubt. His Majesty either did not believe that Palle held the abbey, or he simply did not care. They blundered on in the darkness, skirting Prince Kori's troops on the road, but perhaps riding into an even more hostile situation.

Several guards were at the head of the long line, and Kent had made certain that they would stop and reconnoiter the abbey. Whether they would be able to get the King to wait was another issue. His Majesty did not seem to care but kept saying that his hour was near and asking Kent if he had remembered his portrait.

And asking if Kent feared death.

Why does he ask only me, the painter wondered, overcome with a sudden wash of fear. Did the King have some premonition? Flames, but he wished he were still in Avonel.

Yet something drew him on. Somewhere ahead in the fog, he was sure the countess waited. He did not know exactly why he believed this, but he did. She waited, and there were things that must be resolved between them, once and for ever. Kent could not go on without a heart, and she had held it in her keeping long enough. Kept it in snow, perhaps, for it had not known warmth now for many a year. He simply could not go on like this.

THIRTY-FIVE

Noyes crawled out of the Farrelle-forsaken tunnel into a small damp chamber. Once he stood straight, he began to wipe at the dirt on his clothing but stopped, dismayed. Even in the poor light of the lamp he could see that it was futile. The wiry Entonne nodded to him and tried to smile encouragingly, and Noyes was sure he responded with a look of rage.

He wondered if the real Trevelyan would ever make it through such narrow openings. Noyes had barely done so himself. He hoped that Palle's men had managed to follow him to the entrance to this bloody hole.

"Shall we go on, Lord Trevelyan?" the Entonne asked.

"Yes, yes. Lead on." Noyes glanced around. It was a small room, the walls wet with seeping water but clear of any growth whatsoever, which meant no light found its way to this chamber, in any season.

He followed the ridiculously dim light from the tin lamp, up a few steps and through an arch, then left, he memorized. Through a larger room, then left again. He scuffed his shoe in the mud, marking the way in case Palle's men followed. Up a longer flight of stairs. The place was clearly a labyrinth. Through a door, and suddenly the man in front of him recoiled in fear, flailing with his arms so that the flame in the lantern sputtered. At the end of the chamber, just touched by the light, a woman in a dark gown disappeared around a corner, followed by her fleeing shadow.

The Entonne started to retreat, but Noyes grabbed hold of the man's jacket. "No. She ran from us. Take me on."

"But that is the countess," the man said nervously. "The mage countess."

"Yes, and I am a large baron with a dagger. Take me on." He pushed the man forward. In truth he was not so confident, but could not imagine going back to that twisting, narrow tunnel. He'd rather face the countess, whom he was sure was not really so formidable. She had managed to make a fire come to life and spread a thick smoke. Noyes had seen conjurers do much the same, and they were no more mages than he was.

The Entonne crept forward reluctantly, looking about a bit wildly. Noyes was not sure what the man expected, but then the tales of mages were part of the fabric of Entonne culture—and the Entonne were more apt to believe.

Noyes concentrated on memorizing the path. Finally they came to the bottom of a stair that circled up into the darkness.

"You must wait here, baron," the Entonne said, "I will go ahead to be sure that it is safe."

"I shall do no such thing," Noyes answered. Did this man really think he would be allowed to go ahead and alert Massenet? Noyes took the dagger out of his belt. "Go ahead. I hope there is no treachery planned, for your sake."

The man put his foot to the step, going even more slowly now. He swung the lantern before him, so that shadows wavered across the walls and steps. When they had gone up for a few minutes, he stopped and whistled softly. "It is Georg," he whispered. "I have brought the baron. Just the baron."

They heard a scraping sound, and then a whisper echoed down the stairwell. "Come up, but quickly."

The Entonne turned to Noyes. "There is a hole in the wall up ahead, to the left. We must pass through quickly. The duke's men are not far above." He turned and went up, holding the lantern before him so that Noyes could barely see his footing. The two raced up, and then the man passed his lantern into a hole in the stone. As he went through, hands took him and pulled him out of sight. Noyes sheathed his dagger and ducked through as the man's feet disappeared, and hands took hold of him, passing him inside to a dimly lit chamber.

He was helped to his feet, and there before him stood the Entonne Ambassador.

"Mr. Noyes," the count said, showing no surprise.

"Count," Noyes said, bobbing his head. His guide turned on him with a look of distress.

Massenet did not speak immediately, but stood staring as though wondering what he would do with this intruder.

"You have a message from Sir Roderick?" the count said at last.

"I am the ambassador of His Highness, Prince Kori, and the King's Man, yes."

"Can you tell me what goes on above? I have sent out men, but they have not yet returned."

"The countess is in the chambers below," Noyes' Entonne guide said quickly. "We saw her as we came."

"The countess, you say?"

The man nodded, but Massenet did not look overly impressed with this news. He turned his attention back to Noyes. "I assume Roderick will want some assurance of my intentions before he will bring the baron?"

"That is what we discussed before I came to you, but now that I have come through your tunnel, I am not sure that Trevelyan could follow. It is small, and the baron is old and weak, and far too large."

Massenet shook his head. "Fat old fool," he said almost beneath his breath. "Your King is coming, Noyes, and then there will be a reckoning. Unless you have an army racing to your rescue, your opportunity is about to be lost. I cannot hold this chamber forever. We are few, as you see, and poorly armed. Tell Roderick that we have no time to waste in negotiation. We must put aside our differences and seize what we may. We can retain the balance we have now, between Entonne and your own faction here in Farrland. But we must push Trevelyan down here even if we have to squeeze him like a stopper through a bottle."

"I have tried to tell the count that it will not work," a man said, and Noyes turned to find Bertillon, the Entonne virtuoso, sitting dejectedly on a stone. He wore a dressing torn from a shirt about his arm, as though he had been injured, and his look was tired and dejected. "He will not listen to me. All parts of the text are needed. But there is more. There is knowledge not contained in the writings. You would bring disaster upon yourself and more if you were to proceed with what you have now, and despite all threats, I will not cooperate. Only the countess can succeed. And she will ensure that no one comes to possess this knowledge."

Count Massenet rolled his eyes. "Charl has fallen victim to a woman's sorcery, but I'm still hoping he will come to his senses."

Noyes realized at that moment that Massenet was beaten—Bertillon would not do his bidding. The only card the count held was his control of the chamber, which he could not hold against a determined assault, Noyes was sure. Attempting to make a deal with Palle was a last, pathetic attempt to remain in the game. But the plans of Noyes' own group were in danger. Especially if the King really was near.

"Perhaps, Count Massenet, we can still manage without Mr. Bertillon's cooperation," Noyes said. "We know more, perhaps, than you realize."

"Count Massenet?" came a distant voice, echoing down the stairwell. Everyone in the chamber stopped where they stood.

"Count Massenet? It is Lady Chilton. We must speak. It is imperative."

The count motioned to Varese and moved toward the opening into the stairwell.

"What is it you want, Lady Chilton?" Massenet shouted.

"An end to this foolish struggle. Only I have all the pieces of the puzzle, Count Massenet. You gave the Lucklow fragment to Kent: you must realize what is at risk? The arts of the mages were never meant for the untrained. You cannot practice their arts, and master your enemies without terrible cost to the world at large. You would bring ruin upon yourself and your nation more quickly than you would gain mastery over others. It took fifty years to make a mage, Count Massenet. Half a century. And that was to allow them to practice their arts without bringing ruin to the world around them. And in the end even they failed, and realized that their arts must pass from knowledge. Consider what is at risk, Count Massenet. Give up your aspirations for the greater good."

Varese reached over and touched Massenet's arm. "I am not sure that she is not telling the truth, Count," he said, and then shook his head, obviously troubled. "The Lucklow fragment was ominous in the extreme."

Massenet considered for a moment, his face unreadable. "Why would I trust you, Lady Chilton? Once you have entrance to the chamber, how would I know your actions will do what you promise?"

Suddenly a figure shot through the opening, knocking the count back so that he slid down the pile of rock and dirt. Palace Guards began to pour into the chamber, with swords in their hands. Massenet was up immediately, tearing his rapier from its sheath, and Noyes took that opportunity to step forward and push the count from behind with all his strength. Noyes was not a swordsman of note, but he was large, and weight counted for a lot.

Massenet sprawled on the floor and one of the guards put a boot on the blade of the count's rapier, and the point of his own weapon to Massenet's throat. The fight was over in that instant.

A moment later Roderick Palle scrambled through the opening, followed by Prince Kori, and finally Baron Trevelyan, who whimpered and moaned like a man who had been beaten. He immediately collapsed on the floor, gasping for breath.

"Well, here we all are," Massenet said, shaking his head, "like rats in a trap. But you still have only one with talent, Palle, and that is one too few. You need me yet."

Palle looked around the chamber, and then back to the

count. "But we have two, Count Massenet. Two. And a third who does our bidding. Your part will be to witness," Palle said with some delight. "Yes, you can record the moment for history."

THIRTY-SIX

The moon continued to float heavenward, etching a brittle path across the sea. Tristam sat at the landing's edge looking out, thinking that he had sailed along that very path. Journeyed along it unknowingly, to this place: this very step.

It did not seem possible that he had come so far to suffer the fate of his shipmates below, but then it was he the Varuans distrusted. Tristam glanced down at his wrist in the dark, but the bird-viper had drawn back again to lurk somewhere in the vein—perhaps even in his heart.

For a moment he wondered if the crew of this expedition would suffer the same fate as Gregory's— disappearing mysteriously, so that no one would ever know their fate: no one in Farrland, at least.

Tristam turned his head, and found the viscount shrunk back into a tree's shadow, watching Tristam. The naturalist almost shuddered, and turned away. Everyone else was huddled close to the center of the landing, silent in their fear, but this macabre viscount could sense death. Could sense it below, where the mutineers had fallen, and perhaps sensed it coming, as well.

No one knew what the Varuans would do with them. The friendly islanders seemed suddenly unpredictable, capable of anything. Tristam was certain that the stories of human sacrifice had surfaced from everyone's memory.

"Captain Stern?" came a voice up the stair.

"Captain?" Tristam almost whispered, "it is Wallis."

Stern, who had been trying to reassure his people, came forward, crouching next to Tristam. "Mr. Wallis?"

The painter appeared out of a shadow, looking up, the moonlight turning his tanned face pale. "The Varuans are willing to let you go free, Captain, but they will only do so if you agree to cooperate."

Stern motioned to Wallis to come up. "I'm sure we can reach an agreement, Mr. Wallis," Stern said. "What is it they want?"

The duchess appeared at Stern's side. "Take care what you agree to, Captain," she cautioned, and Tristam saw Stern tense in anger.

"We are in no position to negotiate, Duchess," Stern said shortly. "Come up, Mr. Wallis. Tell us what the islanders want."

Wallis could be seen to turn and look down the stair, and suddenly a woman appeared. It was Anua, Tristam realized. Wallis followed obediently at her heels. Neither stepped up onto the landing but stopped some few steps down, so that they were eye-to-eye with the crouching Stern.

Anua looked at the Farrlanders, her manner not unfriendly but reserved. "You must agree to two things, Captain Stern," Anua said.

Stern nodded, but said nothing.

"You must depart as soon as you can ready your ship," Anua went on. "And Mr. Flattery and Dr. Llewellyn must agree to lend their skills to the King. If you will do these things, you will be given seed to take back to your King."

Tristam closed his eyes for a second, not believing what he heard. Better to leave this seed behind. He had seen Gregory and knew what desire for this seed would do.

"We will do as you ask," Stern said with finality, looking triumphantly at the duchess as he spoke. He turned back to Anua and Wallis. "What is it you want of my people?"

Wallis met Tristam's eye. "The ritual has not gone well. The King requires the help of Mr. Flattery and Dr. Llewellyn."

"No," Tristam said, "I will have nothing to do with it!" He rose from the step, starting to back away. He felt the duchess take his arm and shoulder, attempting to check his retreat.

"Tristam," she implored, "think what you say."

"No! Wallis was right; this seed is a curse. I will have nothing to do with it. They think I can perform necromancy." He thrust out his hand so that the scar could be seen. "They believe this means something. They will want me to take the physic again, but you can't understand what this would mean. I will become enslaved to it. Mad."

He tore his arm free of the duchess, and glared at Wallis and Anua, who stood silently watching. Anua spoke quickly to the painter in her own language, and then turned and began to descend the stair with great dignity, though her shoulders were stiff with anger.

"Mr. Flattery. . . ." Wallis said, "think what you do. The Varuan people ask your help, sir. And for this they will give you the seed you have journeyed halfway around the world to find. Though, in truth, it should be *you* offering to help them in their time of need. They have held back nothing from you; not food, not drink, not the favors of their women, not even this seed your King so desires." Wallis glanced down the stair. "Anua will return shortly to hear your answer. I will tell you honestly, Captain Stern, I don't know what the Varuans will do if you refuse to grant your assistance. Talk to Mr. Flattery." He looked back at Tristam. "There are more lives than his involved in this decision."

Tristam turned away, walking to the corner of the landing, separating himself from the others as much as possible. He saw Llewellyn talking to the duchess and Stern, glancing occasionally at Tristam. Out in the bay, Tristam could just make out the lamps of the *Swallow*. Did the men left aboard realize what had happened to their shipmates?

If we could only get to the ship, Tristam thought, though he could not imagine that there was any way down but the stair, and the Varuans waited at the foot.

Llewellyn appeared beside him, his lung affliction apparently vanished.

"Have things worked out as you planned, Dr. Llewellyn?" Tristam asked. Out of the corner of his eye, Tristam could see Llewellyn pull back a little to look at him in the poor light.

"Very closely, yes," the doctor admitted, surprising Tristam by not offering a denial. "We had not planned on the mutiny, but I soon realized we could not do without it."

Tristam met the man's gaze, which was cool and objective, bearing no animosity.

"Now you will have no choice," the doctor went on. "The safety of the ship's company depends on you, Tristam, and you are a compassionate man."

"And this will complete the transformation?" Tristam said. "Is that the plan? Did you foresee this?"

"More or less," Llewellyn said. "Your transformation will draw the power back. You are like a wick, Tristam, it will come up through you, as it has done to a degree for some time. Do not be downcast," he said, his tone almost consoling. "We will have no use for you after. You will have completed your part, and may live as you wish."

"But I do not get to choose who I will be? I will be transformed, a slave to the seed."

Llewellyn shook his head. "And you can live, perhaps two centuries, even if you choose not to explore this new world that will be opened up for you. But can you truly do that, Tristam? Will you not want to learn what you might do? To discover the secrets that have so long been hidden? You are a young man of great natural curiosity. Can you really resist?"

Tristam thought of Gregory threatening to spill the physic. "Yes," he said.

Llewellyn looked at him a moment longer, then turned to walk away.

"Dr. Llewellyn?"

The physician stopped.

"Do you fear death?" Tristam asked.

The man hesitated before answering, as though wondering if Tristam mocked him, as men were wont to do. "Every man fears death," he answered.

Tristam turned and stared at the doctor. "Well, death is here, on this island, waiting. He will take one of us before we leave. Mark this. I have dreamed it, and it will come true."

Llewellyn began to turn but stopped as though held by Tristam's vision. Finally, he forced himself away, though much shaken, Tristam was sure. It was small satisfaction—in return for the price he would have to pay.

Tristam sat down on the edge of the landing, staring out over Gregory Bay, watching the full moon rise up like a bubble through water, leaving a trail of luminescence across the surface of the sea.

"Tristam?" It was the duchess. She sat beside him, and for a moment said nothing.

There was a movement in the air before them, and a small owl landed on a branch not five feet away. It seemed to regard Tristam a little nervously.

"But this is not a falcon," the duchess said. "Is it drawn to you?"

"I created it," Tristam answered, his voice so devoid of emotion that it surprised him. "It is the symbol of my death."

"What are you saying, Tristam?" She put a hand on his arm, but he did not respond.

"The transformation. I will be gone," he whispered. "Like transmutation. I shall be something else entire. There will be little or nothing of Tristam left."

She put her cheek to his shoulder, apparently not caring what the others thought, and searched for his hand. "How do you know this?"

"I know. I felt the beginnings of it in the Lost City. Say good-bye to me, Elorin, for you shall not see me again."

She held his hand, almost desperately hard. As though she would not let go. But then the pressure eased.

The owl made a soft sound, as though in sympathy.

"Tell me why you have come, Elorin," Tristam said suddenly. "No more evasions. I must know."

She hesitated. "I was sent by the King to retrieve this

seed. That is the truth. And I hoped to save my place at court by bringing *regis* back. If that did not come to be, then it was my hope, Tristam, that I might find here a way to preserve my appearance, my youth—even for a few years—without suffering as the King suffers. It is vanity, Tristam, I know, but I could see the way my life was progressing—and I had the Countess of Chilton's example before me. That is the truth; I swear. I was sent by the King, and I was to bring Julian. The King would not say more." Silence slipped in between them. For a moment the tropical night seemed to be listening. "The King dreams," she said, her voice falling very low, "and some of these dreams he believes are visions. *I* believe they are visions. What we do here has, in some way, bearing on his visions. Or at least that is my guess. That is all I know, Tristam. His Majesty does not tell me all that is in his mind. . . ."

"Anua is here." It was Stern, standing back a few paces, as though he would not intrude on their privacy.

The duchess met Tristam's eye, clearly anxious, then she embraced him and rose, drawing him up by the hand.

"Will you help the islanders, Mr. Flattery?" Stern asked.

Tristam nodded, not meeting Stern's eye. Anua came up onto the stair with Wallis and several men who brought a captive Jack with them. *Kreel.*

Tristam stopped, staring at the man, who looked sullenly back. "What will be done with him?" Tristam asked.

Anua motioned for Tristam to go on. "That is for the King to decide," she said.

Tristam did not move but stood staring at the Jack. "I saved you twice, Kreel, I do not know if I can do it again."

The man said nothing, only continued to stare. "That is likely so, Mr. Flattery," he said slowly, "but I would still rather be me than you, for who is it will save you, that is what I wonder?"

Tristam shook his head, but it was not denial. He did not know who would save him.

He mounted the last flight of stairs that led to the Varuans' sacred city. Wallis and Anua behind him, followed by the Duchess and Stern, and then the others.

Ahead of him, perhaps ten feet above, the owl landed for a second, looked back, almost expectantly, and then disappeared up the stairs.

My course, Tristam thought. *Unavoidable, as I suspected.*

Burning Gregory's *regis* had not worked as he'd hoped. The Kingfoil was not the reason he was here. That was clear, if nothing else was.

Guards wearing elaborate feathered headdresses stood on the final stair, and they crossed their spears before Tristam, allowing him to go no further. Anua came up then, speaking to the two men, though what she said Tristam was sure was ritual, like requesting admittance to the palace to be knighted. They bowed to her and swept their lances back, inviting Tristam to proceed.

On the landing stood one of the Old Men Tristam had seen the night of the dance of transformation. Transformation from bird to man—a man who pursued a ghost, who gave him the *regis* blossom. Somewhere in the darkness Tristam heard the soft call of his owl, and it spoke to him so directly that he felt a chill, almost as though he understood.

The Old Man waved a talking stick around Tristam, chanting as he did so. A young girl delivered a half coconut to the Old Man, who formally presented it to Tristam, after Anua had instructed him to clap his hands loudly.

Tristam drank, emptying the kava, the metallic taste of root and soil seeming to cling to his teeth and causing a slight numbness in tongue and lips.

"You must remove your shirt, Mr. Flattery," Wallis whispered from behind, and Tristam did as instructed. A man came forward with a crude brush and a shell filled with dark liquid. Quickly, he began brushing a design across Tristam's torso and upper arms. Marks were added to his cheeks, and finally some small ornamentation was carefully applied to the center of his forehead.

Around his wrist a girl wove a bracelet of *regis* blossoms, covering the scar. Into his hand they put a polished, leafless branch, with one short limb projecting at right angles near the top. This, he was shown, should be carried upright.

The Old Man chanted over him again, and Tristam was brought forward to wait for the others to be purified so that they might enter the city. This took little time for they were not treated to such elaborate preparations.

Tristam looked out at the City of the Gods, lit dimly by moonlight and torches. He could see several large fales scattered about in no apparent pattern, and here and there man-high standing stones cast shadows in the moonlight. These were carved like the faces of Old Men, and faced east, looking out over the endless sea toward the rising moon and sun.

A jumble of stone rose from the center of the open area, and it was crowned with what might have been a platform—Tristam could not be sure. Palm trees and the sacred *aito* tree were planted here and there, as were the flowering shrubs most admired by the Varuans. The trade wind whispered languidly through their branches. Stern had been right; there was little here that resembled the Lost City, but even so Tristam found the mystery of the place unsettled him.

Some race had dwelt here before the present inhabitants, as had been the case on Farrow. A mysterious race; and just as it was clear that the race that had built the Lost City had some connection to the Ruin of Farrow, Tristam was certain that this site was associated with them as well. Associated with them—and to mages and their arts.

The Old Man finished his rites, and Wallis motioned for Tristam to follow, the others taking up the same positions as before.

They passed by a standing stone, the strange, elongated face staring empty-eyed, but its gaze somehow more penetrating for that. The jumble of broken stone in the center of the "city" loomed up, and Tristam could see that this was the ruin of a structure—the one building that had been left behind by the mysterious race who had once dwelt here. Some of the stones had been carved and carefully shaped, but now they lay in ruin, like the remains of his father's theater in Avonel. It made the entire moment doubly disquieting for Tristam, as though his father's ghost lurked even here half the globe distant from Avonel.

The Old Man led them on, the entire group passing from the ruddy light of one torch, into the cool moonlight, to torchlight again, as though they journeyed from one island of firelight to the next. Tristam glanced over his shoulder and found that everyone had been treated as he had, and were stripped to the waist: even the Duchess, and her maid, and Stern.

It was the custom of Varua that the islanders wore no clothing above the waist before their King, but Farrlanders had always been exempt from this practice.

The duchess did not seem embarrassed or concerned by her state of undress, though even the lowly Jacks could see parts of her body that, all her life, had barely been touched by a breeze.

A moment's walk brought them to the largest fale that Tristam had yet seen. This one had the most elaborately carved columns of stone supporting its corners and a magnificent and gracefully curving roof of thatch. A torch was thrust into the ground a few feet before either post, and these smoked in the small trade that blew, casting wavering shadows.

In the light of these torches, but standing respectfully back from the structure, Old Men had gathered. Seven in all, each wearing a headdress like the first, and an ancient and faded red-feathered cape. They stood silently, ignoring the Farrlanders, their attention fixed on the opening to the fale.

Tristam looked back at his own people again. They all appeared grim and frightened, but they were enduring in silence, hoping, no doubt, that it would be over soon, and they would be returned to their ship. Jacel sobbed suddenly, and Tristam saw the duchess take her softly by the shoulder, and hush her like a frightened child. The gesture touched him somehow, for it seemed so genuine. The heart was revealed when no one was thought to be watching.

But will I have a heart come morning, Tristam wondered.

Llewellyn was standing near the duchess, shifting the weight of the canvas bag on his shoulder. What had the doctor rescued from Tristam's cabin? Nothing of import to Tristam, the naturalist guessed. Things needed by Llewellyn, he was sure. And how was it that only Llewellyn had time to collect any belongings before the mutineers struck?

If Tristam could have felt anger in the state he was in, he realized he would have felt rage toward the doctor. Palle's minion. One of the group so casually using Tristam to further their interests. And Tristam was not sure there was anything he could do about it.

Suddenly the Old Men clapped their hands loudly in unison, and out of the fale emerged a man Tristam was certain must be the King. He was small by Varuan standards, shriveled and old, and he walked ever so slowly, as though each movement took concentrated effort. "Ancient" was what Tristam thought. The King paused before the building for a moment, the moonlight and wavering torchlight seeming to do battle over him, struggling across his crimson cape of feathers and his headdress, more grand than all the others. Tristam thought he was watching a battle between a light so ancient that it burned to coolness, and the brief, ambitious fire of man.

The King came forward and stepped into a small canoe that was set on the ground, taking a seat on red tapa cloth spread over a thwart. Around the King's feet, Tristam could see baskets, and small packages wrapped in leaves or tapa cloth, tools, and plants that had been carefully prepared for a journey.

Four young men came forward and lifted the canoe by two cross pieces that had been lashed to the gunnels, and laying these across their shoulders, walked forward following the procession of Old Men.

Tristam fell in behind the canoe, looking up occasionally at the man bent over beneath the weight of feathers.

In that light and from that angle he appeared almost bird-like. Some ancient flightless species, that had come down from the air to live on the land, its crest trembling with each step. And here was the last of the race, ravaged and ill, going quietly to its end in pathetic dignity.

They came to the edge of the City of the Gods and went in under the trees, shaded from moonlight, where the bloody glow of the torches seemed to grow brighter, casting wavering shadows around them. A wide sand path curved up the side of the mountain, turning occasionally, and cutting diagonally back, like the path of snake.

Tristam felt his wrist begin to itch under the bracelet of *regis* flowers, but he dared not touch it, afraid of what might be revealed.

They went up for almost an hour, their pace slow, almost stately. Finally the path leveled for a short distance. Tristam wondered if they were arriving at their destination when he realized that the Old Men had disappeared up into the trees, and the men bearing the King were preparing to follow.

Stairs, Tristam realized by the way the men moved. They had come to more stairs. Under the moonlight he found a broad flight of even stairs lifting up into the jungle. The stone was pale, almost white, and Tristam knew immediately that it was not indigenous rock. From what distance had it been carried?

He set a foot on the first tread and hesitated, staring up into the dark where two torches swayed beneath the trees, so that he appeared to be looking into a great columned hall.

"Don't falter, Mr. Flattery," Llewellyn whispered. "Think of the others." Whatever irony the doctor intended was buried beneath his tone of excitement. This was what the man had sailed halfway round the world for. He could barely contain himself.

Tristam thought about his dream of death. *Who will he chose,* Tristam wondered, more than a little disturbed at how much the question sounded like the ramblings of the viscount. Wind hissed in the trees, and Tristam closed his eyes for a second, feeling the distant pounding of the surf, beating always in the background.

He started up the steps, moving slowly in the wake of the King's canoe. The stairway passed up through the trees and into a deep ravine cut into the mountainside. The moon had lifted just high enough that its light flooded down on this section of the stair. *Like water,* Tristam thought. On the walls above, he could see ferns and flowering shrubs growing from every ledge and niche, and they, too, cast their moving shadows down the walls of stone. Tristam wondered if Beacham was experiencing similar feelings to his own. They had climbed such a stair before, led by an owl.

What awaited them atop this staircase? Would they be captured by dreams again? Tristam was reminded of his recurrent dream—the dream of being paralyzed in sleep, unable to wake. Helpless. That was what he felt now. As though he had been caught in a nightmare that would not let him free.

Above, the Old Men began a musical chant, their voices low though devoid of warmth. It seemed a song of sorrow, and then Tristam realized it was the same song he had heard Teiho Ruau sing before they set out on their journey. And then it had been sung by the Varuans who brought the bodies of Chilsey and Garvey down to the beach. What had Wallis said? It was sung at the outset of a journey, and for the dead, for death was thought to be a journey to an island—the Faraway Paradise. And here went the King before him, borne in a small boat, Tristam swept along in its wake.

The stair snaked up between the high cliffs, small gusts of wind accompanying them, like words almost forgotten, spoken just as one said farewell. *"Remember me,"* Tristam thought they were saying, the lament of ghosts and spirits.

Suddenly the owl fluttered soundlessly down and landed on the branch Tristam carried. It blinked at him with its yellow eyes, turning its head almost fully around.

Up they went until Llewellyn began to falter, and the stair ended at a high arched door, perfectly carved into the cliff. They stopped here, and the old men spoke and beat their staffs upon the stair. They chanted and Tristam smelled something being burned which gave a fair perfume to the air.

Ahead of him the Old Men passed in, and Tristam followed the King, wondering where they had brought him and what the Varuans kept hidden in this cave that they spoke of to no one.

The same white stone that had been used to build the stair made a short walkway in, and in the torchlight Tristam could see that it was laid over the natural rock. At first Tristam thought he had entered a passage cut into the cliff by the efforts of men, but as they went deeper, the cave became larger and less regular in shape, and Tristam realized it had once been a natural fissure in the volcano.

All of a piece, he thought.

They continued up a broad stair, perhaps a dozen steps, the torchlight glittering off the walls, then they passed along a landing and the cavern opened up before them. Tristam could see the stair curving down, perhaps half a hundred feet, and there against the end of the cavern, he saw seven pillars carved like the trunks of trees, set in a semicircle: the two outermost to either side were white, the next two were rose, the next pair were green marble, and the central column was black.

Water ran into a fount from the head of serpent, set upon the body of a raptor, and above, a small landing was borne upon the shoulders of a naked man and woman who hid their faces in shame.

Tristam lowered his weight heavily onto each stair, as stiffly as an automaton, unable to look away, or even to blink. *The race that had gone before,* he thought. A race that girdled the globe, seeking places to build their temples. Had the first mages been remnants of that race? Or had they somehow discovered their arts, for Tristam realized that the magic struggled to be reborn when the knowledge was lost.

The owl took to wing and circled once around the floor inside the columns, and then alighted on the lintel. A lintel scribed with characters that Tristam had seen before.

He glanced over at Llewellyn who stood rapt, his eyes

consuming the sight. *He does not understand what is happening here,* Tristam thought. *Llewellyn believes that he and his fellows arranged all of this, but it is not so. We play out some other's design, and cannot know if it is for good or ill.*

"Evil is done by those who mean only well," Lady Galton had said. Tristam looked back at the others, still standing awestruck on the stair. Would history say he had made a fool's bargain? That these few lives would have been better forfeit, and the arts kept from knowledge? Did he trust men like Palle and Llewellyn to act out of wisdom?

But it is I who will be a mage, or so Llewellyn inferred. What will I do with this power? Can I limit the harm these others might do? Will I be forced to learn the arts to stop these others? Or will it be me who is performing evil deeds, with the best of intentions?

"There is little time," Llewellyn said suddenly. "We must begin. In an hour you must learn your part, Tristam, though I shall be here to guide you."

Tristam half-hoped that the Old Men would wave Llewellyn aside and take control of what was to come, but they stood expectantly, waiting for the Farrlanders to lead.

Llewellyn set Tristam's bag down in the center of the design, and out of it took a portfolio of worn paper. He looked up at the naturalist. "Come, there is no time to be wasted. Much depends on you, Mr. Flattery. More than you know. Think of these good people." He waved a hand at the frightened Farrlanders. Tristam looked back at his shipmates—the duchess standing among them, her torso bared—and thought that he could do nothing but try to save them. *The best intentions.*

THIRTY-SEVEN

Jaimas and the prince emerged from the abbey floor not far behind the countess, who immediately began walking slowly across the expanse, staring down as though she could see through stone, right down into the heart of the earth. He stopped, letting the prince go on, and waited for her to notice him. After a moment he was forced to clear his throat. She did not look up.

"Is Massenet holding Lady Angeline and Bertillon?" he asked, chagrined that he had not been able to dislodge the Entonne from the chamber. But even more, he wished that he had been able to rescue the countess' niece—thinking of her gratitude.

The countess did not seem to hear the question. "It is part of the whole," she said, as though that was what they had been discussing, "but . . . it is hard to know where it fits."

Jaimy was taken aback by how unconcerned she seemed with her niece's safety. She continued to search the floor, as though it were the most important activity in the world.

It was quiet now; morning not far off. The moon had swung across the sky and floated above the eastern horizon. It cast long, indistinct shadows through the ruin that seemed somehow to evoke the past in Jaimy's mind. What had transpired here over the centuries? What secret history had Eldrich taken to his grave, or remained hidden away in the unread books of the Farrellite Church? It did not take much imagination to see mages at work here, and armies gathering to contest ownership of this sacred site.

A guard came up, bowing to the countess. "The duke has need of you, Lady Chilton."

She looked up, confused for a moment, as though she had been dwelling in that same past that Jaimy could see, and then she nodded. In the chamber where the hearth burned they found a small group standing around the table, while only one man sat, hunched over on a stool.

The countess immediately curtsied deeply.

"Your Majesty," she said.

"Lady Chilton?" the King responded in a voice that Jaimas could not believe came from the mouth of a man. "All is in readiness?"

"You intend to go through with this?" she said, surprising more people present than just Jaimy.

The King did not answer, but his head fell forward and then lifted slowly in a tired nod of ascent.

"There is something that must be done before we can proceed."

The King nodded again, his hood falling a little farther over his face.

The countess motioned to the duke, who stepped closer so that she might speak privately.

"Palle and the prince have gained control of the chamber," she whispered, surprising Jaimy again. They had reported odd sounds of men moving but had never made this claim.

"How?"

"We might ask Mr. Kent and Valary. There must be some entrance we knew nothing of."

Princess Joelle came into the circle of light, followed by Lady Galton who was supported by Alissa.

Jaimy's gaze found hers, and she tried to smile, but failed, and he thought in that instant that the decision had been reached. She would accept his release from her vow. He closed his eyes, and was swept by a wave of grief and guilt. He had allowed this to happen, through his foolish infatuation with Angeline Christophe. Why had he ever made such an offer? But it was impossible to retract it now.

His father, the duchess, and a few others went out of the chamber; rather than stay and hear Alissa's decision put into words, Jaimy attached himself to this group. Kent and Valary nodded to him as he joined them.

They stopped in the central hall of the old abbey, the walls and columns casting soft shadows in the moonlight, mist seeming to float through the windows.

"We will have to take the chamber by force," the duke said.

"No," the countess said firmly. "It is too late for that. They already have Trevelyan, and if they can press Mr. Bertillon into their service, great harm could be done here." The countess was looking over the chamber, gazing down at the uneven stones of the floor. "I shall have to chase them out on my own."

Two guards appeared, escorting a woman between them, and Jaimy felt a wash of hope, for it was Angeline, covered in mud, her dress torn. Then, as she was brought into the light of the lamp, Jaimy realized it was not Angeline at all but the Entonne singer he had seen at the palace!

He looked over quickly at the countess, her face hidden behind the veil.

"How in the world did you escape?" the countess said.

The woman looked frightened beyond measure and utterly exhausted. When the guards released her arms, she almost collapsed to the floor.

"I was not in the chamber when the count took it," she said in Entonne. "I had gone out into the stairwell and down—to obey the call of nature. I had a lantern, and hid in the cellars below. Eventually the oil was gone, and I was left in darkness, until one of Massenet's men came by with a lamp. I tried to follow him, but afraid of being heard, I stayed too far back and lost sight of him. What seemed like hours later he returned with another. And then more men came. Palle and others. I found the tunnel they had used and, in the darkness crawled up until I saw a tiny point of light—a star. And I came out on the surface in the wood behind the abbey."

The countess nodded. "Take her to Lady Galton, and ask that she treat her kindly," the countess said. She turned back to contemplating the floor, and though she passed by Jaimy, he could not tell if she met his gaze.

They are one and the same, Jaimy thought. She has chosen the path of the mages, and has hidden herself away, not because she is old and vain and has lost her beauty, but because she is *young.* Angeline was old enough to be his grandmother.

"I will need candles and ash from the hearth," she said suddenly. "Lord Jaimas, if you please? But bring no others here."

She slipped off her shoes and walked slowly across the stones as though searching them with the soles of her feet. Sensing vibrations, perhaps.

Jaimy rushed off to do her bidding and, when he returned, discovered that she stood facing the moon, her face buried in her hands, speaking softly.

"Put out the lamp," she said quietly, "and stand away. If you will stay, say nothing, and be still."

She took up a double handful of ash and began to sprinkle it in a line along the floor, muttering to herself as she did so. Jaimy crouched down near his father and Kent, all three in awed silence, fascinated, unsure of what they witnessed.

She scribed a ten-foot circle with the ash and then began careful lines of intersection. Jaimy counted them as she went. Seven. Taking up the largest candle, she began dripping wax along the pattern—evenly spaced drops— and then, in the center, she set the three candles, chanting over them for a moment.

Jaimy thought he felt a charge in the air, like a gathering lightning storm. He half expected his hair to stand on end.

But Angeline, he thought suddenly, she was not the woman who modeled for the portrait in their library. Oh, there were undeniable similarities, but they were not the same woman, there was no doubt of that. It made no sense.

The countess finished dripping wax on her pattern, and stood on the intersection of two lines. She began to chant now, in the language of the text. He glanced over at Valary, who was more alert than Jaimy had ever thought the scholar could be. Jaimy could see him memorizing every detail of what was done.

The countess raised her hands stiffly, twisting them strangely, as though they were not fully under her control. She seemed to be in a trance, unaware of what went on around her. Her voice changed, taking on the hollow sound of the King's; the alien words requiring an alien tone.

Three dark plumes of smoke rose from the candles, twisted about each other once, then joined into one. The smoke bent in a short arc and almost flowed like a stream of water, though inches above the stone, following one line from the center. It curved sharply along the outer line of the circle, and then suddenly turned down, to disappear through some fissure in the floor.

The duke rose slowly, and slipped back into the darkness. Jaimy heard him take several quiet steps, then break into a run.

For several minutes the smoke streamed from the candles and followed its unnatural course, then suddenly the candles began to gutter and then flickered madly, as though something were caught in the flames and struggling to escape. And then they went out, faint smoke now rising vertically in the moonlight.

The countess stood, embracing herself, fingers stroking her upper arms reflexively, and she rocked back and forth like some did who had lost their reason. No one dared approach her.

Jaimy saw the duke and a group of guards pass among the columns, their pace determined.

"Where does he go?" Jaimy asked.

"To intercept Prince Kori and the others when they are forced up from below," Valary whispered.

Jaimy rose, stepping back into the shadow of a column,

avoiding the others. He found a fallen stone in a dark corner, and sat there, overcome with remorse and sadness. "What a terrible betrayal," he whispered. "And it was all illusion."

The globe of the moon seemed, at that moment, as desolate as he felt. Alissa was gone and the woman who had caused him such confusion was not what she seemed. Not at all.

"What do you see in the face of the moon?"

Jaimy turned his head and found the countess perched on another stone a few feet away.

He turned back to his view. "A simple face, almost innocent in its beauty. And though it remains untouched by the years, feels no need to hide this."

"But even the moon changes, Jaimas: goes through its phases, disappears altogether at times, or is hidden by clouds."

"As you are hidden by a veil, Lady Angeline?"

"It is not the same, I think," she said softly.

Jaimy shook his head, he looked back at this woman, hidden by her mask. "No? Why do you hide your face from me? I've learned the truth now."

"No," she said. "You haven't begun to learn the truth."

Jaimy turned so that he was close enough to whisper. "What is the truth, then? You remain young. Is that not so?"

"I am ancient," she said harshly.

"But I have seen you, a beautiful woman, with all the excitement and yearning of youth."

"No. I am able to embody those things. That is all the difference between me and any other old woman. The old say that they are young in their hearts, though their bodies are aged. But I am old in my heart, and young in my form. I cannot see the world as I once did. It is impossible for another to understand, for it is unnatural and common only to those who practice the arts."

"You are a mage, then?"

She laughed bitterly. "I am not even an apprentice, as the mages reckoned such things. Even Eldrich was barely a mage at all. No, they have passed. Gone," she whispered. "*Gone*."

"Then what is it we do here? What do Palle and Massenet hope to accomplish? What will these texts do, and where did they come from?"

She sat silently, her hands around one knee, rocking back and forth, her manner giving lie to her claims of age. "They were hidden long ago. Before Lucklow and the others had made their pact. The mages could sometimes sense events in the future, as we see forms in the mist, perhaps. Hardly clear visions, but some were skilled in their interpretation. The texts were hidden so that they could not be located, even by a mage. It must have taken decades to accomplish this one act. Hidden away, to await certain events." She shifted her hands to the other knee and continued to rock. "Like the darkness calling forth the owl." She gestured down. "Their mark was above the door. The vale rose, and the falcon. It is their chamber."

"Whose mark?"

She shook her head. "The mages never spoke their names." She lowered her head, and was still for a long moment. In the moonlight Jaimas could almost see her silhouette beneath the veil. She seemed old at that moment. Old and in pain.

"But what do Palle and Massenet expect to find here?" Jaimas asked again, softly.

"Ascendancy, for themselves, for their countries. They fear others—that is why they sought positions of power. Their greatest dream is to have a King who dances when they move the threads: and for Massenet, to marry his child to the heir of Entonne, and sit his grandson upon the throne. The ordinary desires of those who rise to such positions. In their appetites, they are not men of great originality. Though they will do enormous harm in spite of that."

There was a scuffing noise and they both looked up to see Kent standing a few feet away, such a look of unhappiness on his face that Jaimy felt deep pity for the old man.

He has suffered so much longer than I, Jaimy thought.

"Will you leave us?" the countess asked softly.

Jaimy nodded and rose, but as he passed the countess reached out and pressed his hand as though she could not quite bear to let him go. "Tell the duke we must begin in one hour." And then she did let him go—Jaimy felt it—released him as much as she was able. It was up to him now.

Kent stood looking at the woman in the moonlight. He wanted to ask her to lift her veil, but it was far too late. He had made no demands on her all these years, and now the habit could not be broken.

"You have every right to feel as you do," the countess said suddenly.

"You know what I feel?"

"Resentment. Anger. Bitterness."

Kent shook his head. "No, that is not what I feel." He looked up at the moon. "*Loss*. That is what I feel. All the years we have lost. Why did you hide yourself away from me?"

She had clasped her hands in her lap, so tight Kent could see the veins stand out, even in the moonlight. "My heart belonged to another, Averil," she said, as though the words hurt her.

"Gone, how many years?" Kent said, before he thought, for he knew the futility of debating past decisions, or of attempting to change someone who could not change.

She took a long, deep breath of frustration.

"But then, I am old," Kent said, wistfully.

"And I am changed," she said. "Not as you remember me. The spell is gone."

Kent looked at her quizzically as though she had ceased to make sense or he was not understanding the allusion.

The countess began to pull back her veil, removing it altogether. She turned away from Kent as she did this, facing the setting moon.

"Come around, Averil," she said, her voice taking on a little warmth.

Kent moved slowly, keeping his distance, suddenly unsure of what might be revealed. And there, in the soft light of the moon, was the woman he had painted often from memory, yet it was not her—not quite.

"Am I as you remember?" her voice no longer flat.

Kent hesitated. "The light is poor."

"No. It is not the light," she said. "The form is little changed. But something is gone. Is that not so? I was bespelled, Averil. Or perhaps it was my mother or grandmother who was so unfortunate. But in the womb I was formed in no common way. And about me, all my days there was some unnatural attraction. Look at this face. I am still beautiful—and I say this without vanity. But would men I had not spoken a word to, duel over me? Would flocks of young gallants be reduced to fool's tears because I spurned them? You know the answer. The spell is gone, its purpose served.

"I was a trap for Eldrich, though I did not know it—nor did he. But he could not resist me, nor could the spell be detected, for it was wrought by men whose powers far exceeded Eldrich's own. He could not bear to see me age. And so he passed some knowledge on to me, against all his oaths and judgment, so that I should not lose my beauty. So that he would not lose it.

"And I have been the one keeping the magic alive in this world. I drew it, like a lodestone draws iron. And set in motion all that has come about. Though only slowly did I become aware of it. Me, Averil. I have caused all of this. Someone long ago, through augury, saw what might come, and set the stones in place. Laid the foundation of all that happens this night." She rose from her stone, and took Kent's hands in both of hers. They were so warm and soft, denying all that she said, for the flame of youth seemed strong in her. "And you were bespelled, Averil, like so many others. Bespelled, and I am sorry for it."

Kent's mind could not accept this. "There was more to it than that," he managed. "What of my feelings now? The spell is gone, you say?"

She raised one of his hands to her soft lips. "I cannot explain your feelings now, for I have not been kind to you. Decades of silence, and then I set you this impossible task. You should despise me. It is what I deserve." She looked up at him, searching his eyes. "But here we are, so many years later. Tell me honestly, Kent, do you think you love me? Love me a little?"

"I have loved you through all the years of silence," Kent said, almost robbed of his voice by emotion. "How could I stop now that I hear your beautiful voice again?"

She stood up on her toes and kissed the corner of his mouth. "Then if I live beyond this night, we will speak again. There might be a few years left to us. I have no skill at augury, but it is not impossible. Though I will tell you true, Averil, that it will be a miracle if I survive what is to come, and miracles have become rare in our age."

"Then I shall pray for a miracle."

She squeezed his hands, as though what he said had not pleased her. "I have need of you one last time. May I impose upon you again? I will warn you, there might be some danger, even to you."

Kent shook his head. "I have come this far. I could not shirk my duties now."

"Then come down with me," she said releasing his hands, her manner suddenly deeply serious. "I will ask a few others to accompany us."

She replaced her veil and then turned to go. "Kent?" she whispered.

"Yes?"

"I am afraid."

Knowing there was nothing he could say, Kent reached out his hand. She took it in her own and they set off in the last light of the moon.

A bird fluttered above, flitting from a window to the top of a column, and then to the head of the stairs that led to the rooms below.

They found Prince Kori, Stedman Galton, Palle, and Massenet gathered before the King, silent, as though judgment were being passed. The duke stood at the King's right hand, and Kent could not remember seeing the man so troubled.

"Why do you bother me with this?" the King asked peevishly. "Do you not see that my hour is here? I have no care for such trivialities! Let the succession fall where it will. Only a fool cannot see it is a curse! Let he that wants to, be cursed, and damn them for it." The King rose awkwardly. "Wil?" he called, looking around.

"I am here," the prince said, hurrying forward, clearly unsettled by what he had just witnessed.

"Take me down to this cellar."

Massenet took a step forward. "As the representative of His Holy Entonne Majesty, I demand to be present at this rite. Myself and Mr. Varese." Massenet did not quite know who to address with his demand, for clearly the King would not care, so he spoke to the larger group. "We want to be reassured that the countess keeps her word."

The King gestured impatiently as though giving permission.

"I will be present as well," Prince Kori said, "with Wells, and Sir Roderick. I will be sure that nothing goes amiss in my Kingdom." He looked over at the duke, something like triumph in his manner.

"He is a willful old man," Kent whispered to the countess.

"It does not matter," the countess said. "It is time, Your Majesty. Mr. Bertillon? Are you still prepared to carry this through?"

The musician stood as far from Massenet as the small room would allow. He nodded, though he could not hide his apprehension with silence.

"Lord Trevelyan?"

The baron had collapsed on a stool, where he leaned heavily on a cane. "Yes. Yes. Only let it be over. . . . No. Do not caution me. I understand the risk. But let us get on with it."

"I will need the help of others as well. The prince, Lord Jaimas, and Alissa. No. I meant Prince Kori," she said as Prince Wilam nodded his assent.

"I will have no part in this!" Kori said quickly.

The King paused, half-turning toward his son. "Of

course you will. Would I leave my throne to a coward? Bring him," he said to a guard. The prince looked over at Palle, who, for once, offered no counsel. A guard stepped forward, and the prince went on, his moment of triumph dimmed, and more frightened than angry.

They descended slowly by lamplight, no one but the countess aware of what they went to do. *"To seal off this knowledge,"* she had said.

Teiho Ruau began to sing in his native tongue, his fair voice lifting up above all the apprehension and fear. Jaimy found the music calmed him a little, though he had no idea what the words might mean.

Lady Galton caught up with him, leaving her husband behind for a moment.

"Did the King bring us here only to abandon us?" Jaimy said to her. "What will happen to us?"

Lady Galton shook her head, struggling a bit to breathe. "I do not know. But if the worst should occur, do not let silence be your final word." She moved her head indicating Alissa, who went before them.

"Alissa has chosen not to become a duchess," Jaimy said sadly.

"She told you this?"

"No, but I am quite sure."

"And I am quite sure you are having a misunderstanding common to youth. Be sure of nothing until you have heard it spoken. Spoken from her heart, mind you." She put a hand on his arm and pressed him gently forward.

At the bottom of a stair the party was held up while others made their way through some narrow opening, and Jaimy dared to whisper. "Alissa?"

She looked up quickly upon hearing his voice, a flash of desperate hope crossing her face.

"If it is possible, might we speak later?"

"Yes," she said. "Indeed, yes."

In the poor light he found her hand, and clasped it for a second. Despite their situation, he found his hopes rise. Alissa mouthed the words, *"Be careful,"* and then went on.

The entrance to the chamber had been cleared of stone

by guards, and the group struggled in. A large, damp cellar, Jaimy thought, half-expecting the place to have been transformed.

"There is no time for discussion," the countess announced, turning to address the gathering. "Please do as I say, and ask no questions." She waved a hand at the crowd. "All of you, back."

She went to the opening in the floor, farthest to the right, and nearest to the wall. "Mr. Bertillon, you will be here. You are confident of your part, I hope? Lord Trevelyan, you will take this next place. There was once a column here; stand as though it were at your back. Mr. Ruau?" she called, motioning the Varuan forward. "You know your place, I'm sure. To the right of the King. Your Majesty, please. You will have to leave him, Prince Wilam. Averil. You will be to the King's left."

"Have you my portrait?" the King asked, and Kent waved the role of paper.

"Give that to me, Kent," the countess said, taking the sketch from the painter. "Lord Jaimas. You will be here, next to Kent. And finally, Prince Kori." She addressed the last three to be placed on the pattern. "You have no part of your own in what is to come, but you represent others who are distant. You will feel them inhabit you, and you will lose control of your ability to move or speak. Do not struggle. They will not harm you. I cannot say, 'don't be afraid'; it is a frightening experience, but it will prove easier if you do not resist." She turned away, time too short now to offer reassurance.

"Lord Trevelyan, you have learned your part? Good. Lady Alissa?" she called, and Jaimy saw Alissa squeeze Lady Galton's hand, and come out onto the floor. The countess pulled back her veil enough that she could reach into the collar of her gown, and she drew out a glittering stone on a silver chain which she clasped around Alissa's neck.

"If this site had not been destroyed, your place would be on a small platform, here," the countess pointed to the wall that had been effaced. "But you will have to stand here, next to the font. When the ritual begins, you must put your hand upon this stone and fix its image in your mind. Imagine it a star burning bright in the sky above our heads. Then speak my name, over and over. Do not falter, no matter what occurs. This is of the utmost importance. I am trusting my life to you, my dear, because you are true of heart." She kissed Alissa on each cheek, and whispered something in her ear. "Where is my servant?" she asked, turning back to the others.

A manservant came forward with a leather bag, and from it the countess began to remove odd objects and small parcels. She glanced up at the servant. "You may extinguish the lanterns."

The chamber became darker as each lantern died, and finally it was entirely black, as only a cavern that sees no daylight can be black. Jaimy felt his heart pounding in the forced silence. All he could hear was the trickle of water and Alissa chanting softly, a name he could not catch. *Do not falter,* he thought, *and I will not falter again.*

The countess produced what appeared to be a glass jar filled with a pale, luminescent liquid. She set the jar on the floor where it cast a weak light around the room. Directly across from him, Jaimy could see Trevelyan, bent over, leaning with both hands on his cane. The baron appeared to be in pain. Jaimy hoped that not too much was to be asked of the old man, and that his own safety did not depend on the baron.

The countess removed her veil in one unconscious motion, as though all the years she had hidden her features were now of no consequence. Angeline Christophe stood before him—the woman in his father's portrait, but not quite. She went to the opening in the floor against the wall—the fount—and here she spoke quietly for several minutes, though to no one. Two feet away, Alissa chanted, her face determined, though a little pale.

The trickle of water increased, and the countess reached out and filled her cupped hands. She sipped some of the water, and then went to Bertillon, who tilted back his head and took a few drops on his tongue. She did this for each of them in turn, and Jaimy was surprised to find that it was only water, unremarkable in every way.

By some means that Jaimy could not see, the countess lit a short candle, and on this flame she cast some herbs that smelled sweet and fair when they burned. Jaimy almost felt a sense of calm inhabit him at that moment, as though nothing were amiss. He looked over at Alissa, but she was lost in her task, and did not notice him. *"Because you are true of heart,"* the countess had said. Unlike Jaimy, who had fallen to confusion the moment he had met this woman of beauty and mystery.

The countess took up her jar of luminescent fluid, and with great concentration, began sprinkling it over the floor, drawing lines, as earlier she had with ash. But each line glowed faintly, and here and there were little orbs of concentrated light that seemed to create a pattern across the floor; like constellations, Jaimy thought, though none that he knew.

From each person in the semicircle, lines were etched to the fount, and these the countess crossed with arcs. For a moment she studied her pattern, examining all the elements, and then nodded as though satisfied. Immediately she began to pour some seeds from a small bag into a mortar—*regis,* Jaimy realized, surprised at how benign they appeared, like peppercorns. She ground the seed methodically. A second bottle, though this one of darkened glass, was produced and she poured some inky liquid into the mortar, mixing as she did so, until a thick broth was made. She took this up, stepped to the center of the pattern, spoke a few foreign words, and drank the mortar dry, casting it into the opening that had once been a fount. She hung her head then, as though already exhausted, and Jaimy saw her waver and he almost stepped forward to catch her if she fell.

But she raised her head and stared at the fount for a moment, as though in prayer. She let out a long breath, and began to unfasten the cuffs of her sleeves. Though the light was poor, Jaimy was certain that she bore an ugly scar upon her right wrist.

She nodded to Ruau, who came forward, careful to step between the glowing lines, and coiled his belt of snakeskin around her right arm, so that the head of the snake

534

was at the back of her hand. He then retreated, and the countess looked up once more at the wall, held up her un-encumbered hand, and a small falcon, a kestrel, lit upon her wrist. Jaimy saw the bird dig its talons into the soft skin beneath her wrist, and tears of blood appeared, running slowly across the marble-white skin until a drop or two fell to the stone floor.

The countess stamped her foot, so that it echoed in the chamber. *"Curre d' Efeu!"* she said strongly, and let the words die. *"Curre d' Emone!"* Then in Farr. "Heart of flame! Heart of the world. *Vere viteur aupel e' loscure."*

"Your servant calls out in darkness," Jaimy heard Egar whisper to Valary.

"Vau d' Efeu. Ivanté!"

"Voice of flame. Come forth!"

"Par d' embou vere fant!"

"Speak from the mouth of your child."

Jaimy could not swallow, and his heart began a wild erratic pounding. Cold sweat dripped down his brow and stung his eyes. He felt himself gasping for breath, and speaking strange words.

❦ ❦ ❦

Only Tristam's skill with languages and trained memory allowed him to make use of Llewellyn's hurried instruction. As Tristam went over the text once again, Llewellyn began organizing the others. Before the first column on the right, he placed Beacham. Before the next pillar, to her utter surprise, the duchess was positioned. Then the viscount. The Varuans had placed the King in his canoe before the black column, and next came Wallis, standing before a column of green. An Old Man took up position before the rose column on the left, and the final position was left vacant.

"Are you ready, Tristam?" Llewellyn asked.

"Ready? As much as one can be with an hour to prepare. Do you know what will happen if I do not manage to do it right?"

"Once the ritual has begun, you will remember what is

needed. Do not fear." He gestured to gain the attention of
the Farrlanders. "Do not move from your place no matter
what happens. No flame can burn you, no thing can harm
you—if you stay in your appointed position. You shall
feel the will of another, do not resist, but let yourself relax. Breathe slowly, and concentrate on breathing. Everyone else ..." he said to the Farrlanders who remained on
the stair. "It would cost your life to set foot on the
septogram. Stay well clear. Look to your people, Stern."
Llewellyn glanced around the circle to see that everything
was in place, then took up his own position at the first
column on the left. "Mr. Wallis," he said, and the painter
crossed the few steps to the canoe and removed an object
wrapped in tapa cloth. Quickly he unwound the wrapping,
and unrolled the canvas within, revealing a portrait of the
Varuan King. He laid it at Tristam's feet.

Faairi crossed the floor to Tristam, and taking his hand,
placed it on her star tattoo. "Look for my star," she said,
then kissed him on both cheeks. She went to the fount
and climbed up quickly to the platform above, where she
sat, holding one hand to her star, and began to chant his
name, over and over.

It has come, Tristam thought, *as it does for every man.
The hour of my death.* He glanced around quickly at all
the others—the living. Those who would leave this chamber and resume their lives, while Tristam Flattery would
be gone. His horror was that he might still be within, conscious, but submerged, unable to move or speak, while
the *other* emerged into the world. Would that not be
worse than oblivion? He thought of Dandish, suddenly—
the kindly old don puttering in his garden—and he felt a
tear wash his eye and cling to the lid. Dandish had held
such hopes for Tristam, but in all his days the professor
could never have imagined this. Jaimy came to mind; no
doubt blissfully married by now, and Tristam felt a spark
of jealousy, though this was quickly overcome by love.
Let him live in happiness, he thought. *Let one of us live
so.*

He glanced at the duchess; unsure, even now, of his

feelings for her. Not even sure that he knew why she had come, despite all that had been said.

Beacham was staring at him, frightened, Tristam could see, wondering if he would be saved. Wondering if Tristam would suddenly refuse his part. *Young*, Tristam thought. *He is so young*.

The Farrlanders looked completely out of place and helpless, as though they were children. And like children, understood far less than they believed, yet blundered on with misplaced confidence. *It is the story of our race*, Tristam thought. *Their race*. But the mages, and the race that had gone before—the practitioners of magic—they had disappeared. Like species whose forms were preserved only in stone.

We built our most important city of such stone, Tristam thought, *built it out of their bodies*. All the species that had mysteriously vanished—as Tristam would vanish, to become something else. *Transmutation*.

"Mr. Flattery," Llewellyn's voice came. "It is time."

The torches were extinguished, and Tristam watched the light die, as though it were his last sunset; and then darkness. The earth sang its ancient song in moving water, and Faairi droned his name.

"Farewell," Tristam whispered, and then bent to begin his part.

He opened an earthenware jar which emitted a glow, like luminescence—the star-water that Faairi and he had collected. By this pale light Tristam went to the fount, and began to speak the strange words he had so hurriedly studied. At first they came awkwardly, but with each word he seemed to gain confidence, as though he could see the text in his mind and read the words. He filled his hands with water from the serpent's mouth, and drank, then went to Llewellyn and let a few drops escape onto the man's tongue, and then to each of the others in turn.

The most frightening thing was how natural it all felt, as though he had done it before, and Tristam had a nagging feeling that he had, or perhaps that he had done this in a dream. It was like a dance he had not performed in decades, but somehow his body remembered every step.

At one point he glanced over at the duchess, who kept her hands on her shoulders, so that her arms covered her breasts. She bit her lip in concentration, and Tristam saw her shiver, as though it were cool in the chamber. After that he had no thought of the others.

He sprinkled water carefully along the lines of the pattern on the marble floor, and they began to glow with a ghostly light. Overhead, on the dome of the ceiling, stars seemed to glitter.

From a bag of leather, Tristam poured seed into a stone mortar, and this he crushed to fine powder with a pestle made of bone. From the box he removed his uncle's wine—the blood of his ancestor—and mixed the fluid into the seed so that a thin paste was made. Standing to stare at the fount, Tristam closed his eyes and downed the bitter mixture, casting the bowl into the fount, where the water turned to crimson.

For a moment he was overcome, and felt the other move within him. He thought of Faairi's star, and then heard her voice, *"tamtristamtristamtris. . . ."* He raised his head and tried to focus but could not. The chamber had grown dark and was filled with shadows that moved and changed. Before him, the serpent tasted the air with its tongue.

Someone came forward and coiled the skin of the viper around Tristam's arm—the viper he had killed in the Archipelago. He held up his left hand and the owl dug its talons into his wrist, drawing tears of blood that fell to the center of the pattern.

Let us begin, Tristam thought, and opened his mouth to call out.

"Curre d' Efeu!" and then almost the same words he had heard Bertillon use that night at the house of the duchess. *"Curre d' Emonde! Vere viteur aupel e' loscure. Vau d' Efeu. Ivanté! Par d' embou vere fant!"*

There was a moment of stillness, and the air seemed to crackle with gathering lightning, and then a blossom of flame rose up from the water of the fount and consumed Faairi on her perch above.

🌿 🌿 🌿

Jaimy began to jump forward, but something checked his movement, and his arms and legs would not quite obey. The pillar of flame rolled across the ceiling with a strangled shriek, and then he heard the drone of Alissa chanting the name he could not quite hear. She was there in the fire, unharmed he prayed. But the flame did not subside. It boiled from the fount, rising up like molten liquid, but spreading no farther, and smoked not at all.

The countess began what Littel had described as a chant of warding, pushing her hands first before her, as though they were pressed against glass, and then behind. It almost seemed that the flame flattened somewhat against the wall.

"*Ivanté!*" she called out, spreading her arms.

Jaimy felt suddenly as though his vision swam. As though he had taken far too much wine. Stars appeared before him, and areas of spiraling darkness. For a second he thought the countess was a man, stripped to the waist, a white owl on his wrist. Vertigo took him, and he felt the floor tilting. Then his hands found something solid at his back. Stone. And he leaned back, grasping the rock.

He dared to open his eyes, and across the glowing pattern he saw others standing before pillars of stone; white, rose, and green. And there was a fount where flame boiled up from water, and above it, on a ledge that seemed to be supported by a column of fire, he saw Alissa, her right hand grasping something at her breast. And she was saying Tristam's name again and again, like a litany of love.

Voices seemed to speak in his mind, strange words he did not know, and they echoed and reverberated as though spoken by many at once.

Suddenly fire spread around the circle, burning in a thin line beyond the columns, casting shadows and strange patterns of light.

"*. . . loginé,*" voices were saying, and Jaimy realized that he was part of this chorus.

Jaimy tried to force his eyes to focus, but the form of the countess had become insubstantial. He turned his head and among the moving shadows, saw grim-faced men in tall headdresses, who wore capes of feathers. He was speaking again, chanting the language of the mages, and then he extended his hands and discovered they were covered in strange tattoos.

I am safe, he told himself. *I must not fear.* Desperately he listened for Alissa's voice, even though it was not his name she chanted, and again he heard a woman saying, *"Tristamtristamtristam."*

❦   ❦   ❦

Tristam finished the chant of warding, and felt something like exhilaration, like he had known after surviving his first action at sea.

Before he could consider what would come next, the flame before him rose up, hissing, and in response he felt the viper skin come suddenly to life, twisting quickly around his arm. The owl spread its wings as though it would take flight, and Tristam felt himself falling, slowly falling. And the snake and the falcon met in the air, striking, the viper twisting itself around its prey, and the talons of the falcon grasping. They fell, locked in battle. Fell through a lightless sky, through the net of stars.

Tristam felt the stab of the razor-sharp bill in his side, and writhed in agony. Then the hot fangs of the viper sank into his flank, and a burning poison spread. He fell. The scream of the falcon in his ears, the hiss of the viper.

"Tristamtristamtristam," someone said, and something inside him answered, *"Yes, I am Tristam."* And then they crashed to earth, pain overwhelming him, so that he screamed, the sound more like an animal than even the falcon's cry.

"I am Tristam," he said rising in the ruins of the darkened city. A small boy scuttled off into a hole, and Tristam followed. Someone whispered his name and he remembered, looking up until he found the star he sought.

He let the boy go his own way, to follow or not, and went seeking the bright star.

Once he stopped when he found his reflection staring back at him from a shallow slick of water on the stone, though it was the face of a woman, at once young and old. *"I am Tristam,"* he repeated and went on.

The sound of water splashing drew him, and when he found the source—water pouring, like a scream, from the mouth of a stone bust—he drank.

Then he felt himself swell with power and pride and anger, and the shriek of a bird filled his ears, and they fought again, high in the air. And fell again.

Seven times they struggled, and seven times they crashed to the earth. And some small part of Tristam crawled away from the death throes of the viper and raptor.

I cannot win, he thought, *I am Tristam. Yet I cannot master the other inside of me.*

🐚 🐚 🐚

"But what uneasy peace shall this be?" the countess sobbed, and Jaimy saw that she did not return to the fount to drink again, but lay writhing on the floor, her clothing torn, her hair in dark, wet ribbons across her face. Shadow swept over her, like the silhouettes of fleet birds. And she twisted as though in agony, as though she had fallen from a great height, to be broken upon the stone.

"You shall not master me!" Jaimy heard a voice call out, and he thought he should know that voice. Before him the countess rose, sobbing in rage, and defeat, and sorrow. A small bird fluttered past her, and then went skyward. She stood breathing as though she had not had air in uncounted time. Breathing like a beast in battle.

"Tandre vere viteur!" she called in her anger. "Hear me!" She wavered as she stood, as though she had lost what she would say. And then quietly, almost with resignation, she said, *"Ci's m'curre."* From the bodice of her gown she took a pale blossom and cast it toward the fire, but the kestrel swooped down and took it on the wing. It

circled the chamber twice, then with great speed, plunged into the flame, which vanished with the sound of a dying wave.

Darkness, and Jaimy felt himself spinning. He clung to the stone pillar until he felt the vertigo subside, and then opened his eyes. They seemed to be in very high place surrounded by stars. A faint, cool breeze moved in his hair and the feathers of his cape. It was silent, but for a distant tinkling, like chimes. Before him the countess lay in a heap of dark clothing.

"Where are you?" a terrible voice whispered.

"I am here," the countess answered, her voice small and devoid of all pretension. "Alone. With the alone. Among the stars."

"What do you hear?"

"The voices . . . of constellations."

"Then tell me your true name."

"Elaural," she breathed.

"Then you may scribe it here, among the stars."

Slowly, the countess rose, like a woman aged from a long struggle. When she got to her knees, she reached out and began to move her hand across the floor, and the pattern of light changed.

"Will you open the way, so that we may pass through?" the voice asked.

The countess nodded, raised her hands and began to speak. Jaimy felt the floor tilt, and his knees and hands strike hard stone. He moaned, and slipped into darkness.

"J?"

Jaimas felt that if he moved or spoke he would certainly retch.

"J? You're all right."

"Tristam?"

"Rise up, lad, you're not done yet. Come out of it now."

Jaimy lifted his head or, rather, felt that it was lifted for him, yet from within, somehow. The countess knelt before him, her arms outstretched, her head thrown back, and she chanted too rapidly for him to discern words.

They were back in the chamber now, though not quite the chamber he had first seen. The columns still rose around the circle, and the play of shadow and light was swift and confusing to the eye.

He managed to get to his feet.

On the floor, before the countess, Jaimy could see a portrait etched onto the stone. It appeared almost to ripple, as though it floated on the surface of some liquid. As he watched, the background of the picture changed, from the blue of a lagoon, to a sky filled with stars. She ran her finger around the edge of the canvas several times, and the last time, a thin line of red flame followed the gesture. And slowly the frame of fire began to advance, consuming the portrait.

The countess glanced over her right shoulder, and Jaimy saw the Varuan singer, Ruau, nod once, and then step carefully forward.

He crossed the few paces to the King, who was slumped down on the floor, unmoving beneath his cape and hood. Gently Ruau lifted the man in his arms, bore him up as though he were no greater burden than a child. Placing his feet as though he crossed a stream on stepping stones, the Varuan passed by the countess toward the flame.

Very gradually, as though it resisted, the column of flame began to part, almost trembling as it did so. Finally a passage opened in its center, beyond which Jaimy could not see stone, but only darkness. And then points of light. Unknown stars. A warm breeze touched him, and seemed to bear the scent of flowers and the sea. He heard a sound like distant waves. The portrait continued to burn, more quickly now, and the flame around the opening trembled. Ruau paused for a heartbeat, and then went quickly through. Jaimy saw him step into knee-deep water, and then heard his pure tenor lift in song. And though the words were in no language he knew, Jaimy understood them all the same.

> *"The mother wind carries us*
> *Into the distant west*

The great whale appears
With the sun's last rays.
And stars light to mark our way
Like islands cast upon the sea.

Suddenly the scene changed, the stars wavering like reflections in disturbed water, then they were gone. In their place Jaimy could see three curving structures, bridges he realized, that crossed over each other high in the air, supported so infrequently that they seemed to defy the forces of gravity. Behind them, painfully bright against the night sky, stood towers of brittle glass and light. As he drew in his breath in amazement, a noxious odor of unwholesome burning gagged him, and he saw that the air was an unnatural brown, and the stars had been blotted from the sky leaving only a stained moon, drifting in the pall.

Beneath the bridges men and women moved, but Jaimy could see that they were ragged and shuffled along with the slow pitiful steps of those utterly discouraged or ill beyond hope. A few stunted trees grew in the shadow of the great city, but their foliage was so sparse they seemed to be winter trees, despite the warmth Jaimy could feel in this filthy air.

It is the world that we build, a sudden intuition told him. *The world of empiricism and commerce—but not the world of men.*

A sallow boy darted across the opening behind the flame, and Jaimy saw lights moving, both on land and in the darkened sky. And then this scene changed as well.

They looked out through the branches of a forest, barren of leaves and blackened, as though it had been fired. On the horizon hung the slender crescent of a waning moon. For a moment it seemed that he looked into a world devoid of life, but then, on the darkened hillside beyond the wood, creatures moved. They were *men,* he realized, on a terrible field of battle. The stench of death was carried to him, and he felt bile rise in his throat. And then he saw the armies, or their ragged remains, drawn up upon opposing hills. About one hill lightning flickered from a cloudless sky, and the green sea-flame spread like a tide of light, while about the other he saw flames erupt while terrible explosions drove men screaming in terror. Faint cries of anguish reached him. Jaimy knew that this was the final battle of men: the forces of empiricism against the forces of magic. He felt all hope was lost, and then a cry went up from the gathered armies, like a note of grief and horror, and they charged once more across the field of the dead.

And, mercifully, the scene changed.

A moon floated over distant mountains. Peaks that rose out of calm water. From a mountainside, a single light flickered, and then the countess spoke out strongly in the tongue of the mages, and this flame guttered and died.

Jaimy was overwhelmed with distress by this sight, and then realized that these were the feelings of another within him. But was there only one? The flame within the chamber began to waver, and the countess spoke again, and then cried out. The other's distress turned to fear.

       ❧   ❧   ❧

Wallis could feel the others that were somehow with, rather than in him. Two, men, he thought, and one of his counterparts in this ceremony was a man of such kindness and refined sensibilities that his fear was assuaged. Like Wallis, this man had prepared the portrait of a King, and so was an artist. The castaway watched his portrait float within a burning frame, and somehow felt that he had some part in this magic.

"You must take him through," a voice said, its tone reasonable, but commanding all the same.

Wallis was not sure who this was speaking, and if it were here, or in the other locations where his counterparts dwelt. He saw Mr. Flattery, who slumped upon the floor, shake his head in denial, and the portal of flame wavered.

"You must! The lives of your people are dependent on you!"

Still Tristam refused, and Wallis felt a wash of fear. The speaker was right, the Varuans would be enraged if Tristam were to back out now.

"I will not," Tristam said. "I have scribed my name in the secret place, and now I will not conveniently disappear, Doctor. Take him through yourself."

There was a moment of silence. Wallis could feel the breeze touch him. He could smell the perfume of the Faraway Paradise. Almost he wanted to go through himself. To pass through without dying! Only gods had done this before. Only gods and now this half-mad King.

Wallis could see the King struggling in his canoe, where he slumped on the seat, his aged hands grasping the gunwales, the plumes of his crested hat moving as he sobbed. His moment was here, and no one would bear him through. Wallis turned to see what happened to his portrait and realized that it burned away quickly now. The moment would pass, pass utterly. Never to come again.

Out of the corner of his eye he saw someone move toward the King.

"Julian!" a voice called out in horror, but said only that one word.

Wallis watched the viscount bend, and with a show of strength lift the canoe, King and all, onto his shoulder. Stepping deliberately between the glowing lines, he crossed the pattern, speaking to Tristam as he passed, words Wallis could not hear.

As he went, the duchess reached out to touch him, but could not reach, and she dared not move from her place.

"No! This is wrong!" The voice of Llewellyn screamed. "It was not foreseen."

"Not by you, Doctor," Tristam said simply, his voice dry and sad.

The viscount bent to pass through the gate of fire, and stepped into knee-deep water. He lowered the canoe to the surface, and pulled it on, toward the distant shore. The Varuan song of farewell could be heard, far off, and then the gate wavered, and the King had passed from this world.

"Ju-li-an . . ." a voice whispered, though it was as close to a wail of sadness and loss as a whisper could be. The duchess buried her face in her hands and wept. And Wallis thought she wept, not from loss, but at what her

brother had become, and for the things he done in this world.

May he find peace in the next world, Wallis thought. *May we all.*

With great effort Tristam raised himself to his knees, every motion seeming to take minutes, as though he were exhausted beyond human endurance.

"What are you doing?"

"Searching, Doctor. And then we will seal the portal, seal it so that it cannot be opened until the stars align again."

"You cannot, Tristam! You do not know how." And then more desperately. "Think of the knowledge that will be lost!"

"Yes, far too much knowledge, and not nearly enough wisdom," Tristam said, his voice seeming to come from a man half-sunk in sleep.

With the cooperation of his other, for there seemed to be only one now, Wallis managed to turn his head to the left, to find Llewellyn, contorted in rage, shaking his small fists at the man in the center of the pattern.

A shadow flitted among the flames, and then Tristam began to chant, moving his hands in strange, intricate motions. The gate of flame wavered, and began to draw closed.

"Now is the time," Llewellyn said. "It must be done." And immediately he started toward Tristam, walking in odd jerky steps. He drew a blade from his coat, and raised it high.

"Tristam!" the Old Man beside Wallis called out, in a voice not his own, but the mage could not hear, caught in the midst of his labors.

Llewellyn cast a handful of white feathers before him and spoke in the tongue of the mages. The feathers caught fire, and floated, burning, to the floor—and still Tristam chanted and moved his hands, his eyes closed.

Llewellyn stopped, put both hands to the raised blade, and called out. *"Elé y'alin!"*

Wallis would have shut his eyes, but he could not. At that instant a Jack bounded onto the pattern, flames erupting at his feet so that he caught fire. The man's hands were tied at his back, but his speed and size were such that when he collided with Llewellyn, both were carried several feet, flailing—then into the flame.

There was no scream. Barely a hiss escaped, and Tristam continued as if unaware that death had brushed by him so closely that its breath had been upon him.

The gate turned to a column of writhing flame, and then subsided into the fount, which bubbled for a moment, and then was still.

Voices began to sing, the Varuan song of farewell. Tristam lay prostrate on the floor, unmoving, as though death had not missed him after all. Wallis wanted to move, but found he could not. He wanted to sleep, it seemed, for darkness called out to him. He let his eyes close and fell into dream.

THIRTY-EIGHT

"Auralelauralelauralel . . ." the voice droned on without pause. One star seemed, somehow, brighter than the others, brighter and more beautiful. Almost, it had a voice, like far off chimes sounding in the wind. *"Elaural,"* it rang in an unknown scale, and she followed.

Wind. She could hear wind in the branches of trees, and smell grass and blossoms.

"Lady Chilton?" a voice said with infinite tenderness.

That is not my name, she thought. But perhaps it was, in some odd way.

She opened her eyes and discovered that she lay upon grass, and a small, pale blossom was almost beneath her nose.

"Where?"

"I do not know," Kent said, his voice sounding terribly old. He laid his hand gently on her shoulder. "We are in a bower of seven trees, where a small spring bubbles up from the base of a short cliff, but whether we are in Locfal, or Farrland, or some other land or place, I cannot say. It is the morning of a fine day. The trees, the likes of which I have never seen, are in blossom, and even now rain their petals down upon us."

The countess rolled to her side with difficulty and lay still for a moment. Her head spun and she pressed a hand to her brow. When she took it away, she realized her skin was lined and spotted and was devoid of all its luster. For a moment she simply stared in shock.

"Yes," Kent said softly, "I'm afraid it's true, though I'm sure you need not remain so, now. You can be as young as any mage," he said a bit sadly.

"No," she said, her mouth almost too dry for words to flow. "I shall not be tempted again. This time I shall not weaken," she whispered. "I will wean myself of the seed, and grow old and pass on, as I should."

She saw Kent's shadow, on the grass beside her, nod in sad agreement.

"Are you injured?"

"Yes," she said, "but not in body." She felt pains, and stiffness, and aches, but they were nothing to her anguish. "Did you see, Kent? The vision? The vision of the mages?"

"I saw, but I did not understand. A great battle on a bleak landscape devoid of all trees, of all hope. And then a great darkened city, sinking in a pall of noxious fumes."

The countess nodded her head, and felt sharp pain in her neck. "Our two futures. The war between the forces of magic and the forces of reason. A war that would wound the world beyond recovery. I know now why the mages did not love men, though they bore a deep love of the earth right to the end."

"Is there no hope, then?" Kent asked.

"There is hope, but it is small. We have sealed the magic away again, so there shall be no final war. That was their choice. The mages knew that empiricism was understood by many, and the spread of it could not be stopped. But the arts—they were ever in the hands of a few, and therefore they believed it possible to avoid this war by bringing the knowledge of their arts to an end. That is my guess, at least." She paused, visions of what she had been through coming to the fore. "This world that empiricism will build, Kent—you read what Lucklow wrote. That was his vision, and it was hardly less dark than the alternative. But perhaps there is some hope there, though it is not great. If men were only as wise as they are clever. . . ."

She lay listening to the sound of the breeze, feeling entirely empty inside. Closing her eyes again, she tried to generate some response to the warmth of Kent's hand upon her—though the hand itself was not warm. Nothing. A tear streaked down her cheek. "The others?" she forced herself to ask.

"They sleep. But the prince, the King, Mr. Ruau, and Trevelyan are not here. Near the end Prince Kori came forward to strike you with a knife. I tried to move, to stop him . . . but I could not. And then, I don't know how, he stumbled and fell into the fire. Your doing, I think?"

She shook her head. "No," she said, but did not explain.

"What happened to him?"

"They are ghosts now," she managed.

This brought a moment's silence. She watched Kent's shadow move, as they surveyed their surroundings. "I have seen a small boy about; very furtive and quiet is he."

"Has he a shadow?"

"I believe he does."

She nodded. "Good. Kent?"

"Yes?"

"He is gone. . . . I believed with all my heart that I would find him, but he is gone. All these years . . . and he was truly gone."

The shadow put a hand to its face, and the hand bent a moment.

"Kent?" she tried to work some saliva into her mouth, to moisten the words, to soften them. *"I'm sorry. . . ."*

Kent did not answer, but she felt his hand almost tremble, and then be still.

"One of the lessons of age," he said softly. "Do not waste what time you have in regret." Kent brushed the hair away from her face—gray hair, and not so thick as it once had been.

With Kent's help, the countess sat up, then suffered a wave of nausea. Kent supported her, rubbing her back gently.

"I'm all right. We must collect the others, for we may have some distance to go."

"Do you know where we are?"

"Not exactly, though not far from the abbey, I think." She looked around at the bower of seven trees.

"Are you thirsty?" Kent asked.

"Yes. We must all drink from this fount," she said. "It will bring you luck, and health, and love, and. . . . Well, it is a long list, or so legends say." She waved a hand around the bower. "Look upon it, Averil, for you will not find it again, though you spend three lifetimes searching." She noticed Alissa lying on the grass, and crossed slowly to her, bending down too quickly.

The countess brushed the long tresses from Alissa's face, and found she clutched the diamond still. Softly she kissed the young woman's cheek, and gave her shoulder a gentle shake. "She was my star," the countess said to Kent. "I would not be here but for her. Alissa?"

Alissa opened her eyes to slits, wrinkling up her nose. "What has happened?"

"You have aided me, and all others immeasurably. And now you are safe and unharmed, and you shall soon be on your way home. Wherever that may be. But try to rise now, and quench your thirst at the spring. Then help me rouse the others.

Alissa sat up, staring at the countess for a moment, and then she looked away, realizing what she saw.

"Do not be embarrassed," the countess said to her. "I shall have to get used to people's stares."

Alissa put her hand to her throat quickly, found the diamond still there, and reached back for the clasp.

"No, no. It is yours, my dear, for guiding me home." Then she turned to Kent, thinking that he might be hurt by what she did, but he nodded.

"It is too small a fee, in fact," he agreed.

Alissa thanked them both, and went to the spring and washed her face, and drank. She realized that Jaimy lay unmoving against the bole of a tree, and she ran over to him, and found that he only slept, and it was a quiet untroubled sleep at that.

She shook him gently, and then kissed his brow. His eyes darted open.

"Have we survived?" he asked, and she nodded in answer. "Then will you, yet, marry me, Alissa Somers?"

She sat back, regarding him as though she would finally take his measure, now. "There is not another you love more?"

He shook his head.

"And there is no way to give up this title you will inherit?"

"Only through death, I understand."

"That seems a bit extreme. Then the answer, I suppose, is yes. Though you must swear that you will give up gallivanting across the country and visiting the homes of strange women."

"I swear."

"Then get up, you lazy thing, and see where we are. Not in the abbey at all."

Jaimy sat up and looked about, but he was clearly troubled. "Alissa, I thought Tristam spoke to me during the ritual. It was the strongest impression. Though it must have been a dream."

"Perhaps not. I heard another—or perhaps felt another who chanted his name, and called to him, as I called to the countess. We will ask her."

The countess and Kent roused Bertillon, who lay for a moment trying to gather his wits. Surprised to find this elderly woman with the youthful voice.

"Lady Chilton?" he said after a moment.

"Yes, Charl," she said, surprised at how much his shock hurt her. She turned away and went to the fount to drink.

Jaimas and Alissa stood back a little from her, perhaps frightened by how she had changed, or perhaps they merely sensed her pain.

The water was so cold it almost hurt to drink it, but she splashed some on her face, and shivered.

"Lady Chilton?" Jaimy asked tentatively. "I thought my cousin Tristam spoke to me in the midst of the ritual . . ."

"Perhaps he did. He survived the rite, Lord Jaimas, but I know no more than that." She could not in honesty offer more, though the look of disappointment and concern on the young man's face touched her.

Bertillon came up, looking around, still mystified. "But where are we?" he asked.

The countess shrugged. "It is a hidden place. . . ." She looked around hoping to find a clue to an answer. "Perhaps it is like the places reached through the gate of fire—very near, yet out of reach. The mages called this place the *fantime valone*. The 'phantom glen.' " She poked into her memory to find how it had been affected by the transformation. "These trees are the *valonemme*, called 'evermore' by the mages, for they are said to be always in flower." The countess realized that everyone was looking at her in wonder. "And that is all I shall tell you, for now," she said, oddly self-conscious.

Something caught her eye and she rose stiffly. "Drink from the spring and rest a little, but we must leave this place soon. Events go on without us, and I am concerned."

She turned away and beckoned Alissa and Jaimy. "We must coax a small boy to come out, but I have no sweets." She turned and stared into the surrounding wood. "Though perhaps it would be a mistake to pursue him. We will watch and see that he follows."

They gathered themselves together, and the countess led them reluctantly out of the bower, for no one wanted to rush from that place which felt so tranquil and removed from the worries of the world. They all felt that nothing evil could ever befall them while they stayed within that arbor.

Along a grassy path they walked, between beautiful trees that none could name, through a plain stone arch that stood alone without wall or structure, then down a stairway of flat stones set into the earth. When Kent thought to look back, he saw nothing but familiar trees—holyoaks and linden—but no archway or stair. A small boy darted between two trees, watching them as they went.

"We are back," Kent said, "and draw a small boy in our wake." And the countess nodded and took his arm.

❦ ❦ ❦

The sun had risen to the surface, and bobbed on the eastern horizon, the clouds that lay too close catching fire. Tristam sat with his back against the trunk of a tree and stared out over the endless ocean.

He had regained the world before the others and stumbled down the steps from the cavern, stopping here, somewhere above the Varuans' Sacred City.

He heard the steps of others coming down the pathway from the cave above. Varuans, he thought, by their pace.

"Tristam?" came a softly accented voice.

"Thank you for guiding me back, Faairi," Tristam said as she settled on the ground near him. "If you go down to your fale, I think you will find your sister returned from her journeys."

She put her hand to her mouth, and tears appeared on her cheeks. "How? Did you carry her with you?"

Tristam nodded.

She leaned forward to kiss his cheek but stopped, and then rose, backing away as though he were another forbidding Old Man, or perhaps a spirit that one did not trust.

I do not blame her, Tristam thought as he heard her steps on the pathway.

The sun lifted clear of the water, burning through thin cloud as it rose.

❦ ❦ ❦

The duchess roused to the sound of whispers and opened her eyes quickly. It was dark, though a thin light seemed to find its way into the chamber. People were moving about and speaking in hushed voices, both Varuan and Farr.

She sat up, realizing as she did that she was unclothed from the waist up, and quickly she began pulling her dress into order. And then, suddenly, she stopped as the memories of the night came back. She staggered to her feet, her eyes searching the room, and then she stared at the stone wall where the gate of fire had opened.

Julian was gone. He had taken Tristam's place, and gone into the fire—or whatever lay beyond.

May he pass out of torment, she thought. *For all that he has done, I cannot fault him or feel less for him. Poor Julian, he was born thus, just as Tristam was born with his talent.* And she lowered herself awkwardly to the floor behind the column, and there she wept. Wept silently and long, for what had come to pass, and for what might have been.

After a long while she realized Tristam was not in the chamber.

She looked again but could not find him. Beacham lay quite near her, unmoving yet, and she was sure those were Wallis' long limbs across the floor. That left only Llewellyn . . . and then she remembered that he had gone into the fire as well—pushed in by a Jack as he had tried to murder Tristam.

Upon the stairs and the sloping rock others stirred—Stern and the crew—but she did not want to speak with them now. She wanted to be alone with her grief. Alone to consider what had happened.

She rose and went quickly off the pattern and onto the stair. A Jack stood by his crewmates, as though guarding them while they slept. It was young Pim, she realized; the cabin boy.

"Mr. Flattery?" she whispered.

"Gone out, Your Grace, some moments ago," he said, his voice hushed with awe at what he had seen. "Is . . . is he all right, ma'am?"

"That is my hope," she said, and laid a hand upon his arm as she passed. She could not help it, the boy looked so frightened.

The light grew as the duchess climbed the stairs, and she realized, as she emerged from the cavern, that it was early morning. She had no idea how long she had been asleep, or how long the ritual had taken. It might not have even been the previous night.

She went slowly down the stairs, surprised at how fatigued she was, both in body and in mind. It seemed that her thoughts floated in a great hollow chamber in which there was an unnatural silence, and that it was from there that she looked out, vaguely distant from the world.

At the bottom of the stair she found Tristam, off the path on the edge of a high cliff, gazing out over the ocean.

As she approached, he glanced over his shoulder, and then turned away. She hesitated, not sure what this meant, but certain it did not bode well.

"Are you yourself?" she asked from three paces distant.

Tristam shook his head, but did not look up at her. Overcome with fatigue and loss, the duchess sank to the ground.

"Should I be frightened?"

He considered for a moment. "I am not sure."

She stared out at the ocean, trying to get her mind to work as it should. "This is never what I expected to happen," she said, almost to herself. "Where has he gone?"

"Julian? The Varuans call it the Faraway Paradise."

"Then he is alive?" she said hopefully.

"If you will never see or know of him again, is he then alive?"

"Yes," she said, "somehow I think he is, though I'm certain it is not reasonable." She looked at Tristam, his face in profile to her. He seemed much the same, though overcome with sadness, perhaps. "You do not care if he lives or dies," she said suddenly, not quite sure why.

Tristam shrugged.

"He took your place, Tristam. Grant him that."

"Yes, but I will not take his."

"I'm not sure what you're suggesting, Mr. Flattery."

"Beware, Elorin. I am now more powerful than you imagine, and less patient."

She almost moved back then, her fear ignited by how coldly he spoke. "Shall I go?"

He seemed almost to struggle within for a moment. "No. Stay." Neither spoke for some time. "I am sorry for your brother, Elorin," Tristam said. "Sorry for what he was, and what he did. But a man owes no debt to his shadow, and I cannot mourn his passing." Again he struggled, as though speaking had become difficult. "The Varuans believe regicide to be a crime that can never be erased. The family, the village, and the island of the murderer bear the stigma of it forever. It is an offense against the gods, and can never be atoned for. But an outsider . . . they have no concern for what befalls an outsider or his people. Passing into the Faraway Paradise, without first dying, has never been done by mortal man. Until last night. It is a sign that the gods' favor will return, they think, for the King and his servant will search for the gods. But no Varuan could take the King through into the other world, for that would be, to them, regicide."

"*That* is why we came halfway round the world?" the duchess asked.

"So the Varuans believe."

"And is it the truth?"

"A small part of it, perhaps. The design was infinitely complex, and I do not pretend to understand it all. Though perhaps I see more now." He stretched out his legs, such a common motion that it gave the duchess hope that Tristam was not completely gone. "The design was drawn long ago by men of enormous skill and patience. They sought to keep the arts from passing from this world. That was their intention. And you, and me, and Stern, and Averil Kent, and the Varuan King, and many others have taken part in this design. But I think it has been thwarted. Others perceived the intentions of these men, and worked against them. My uncle Erasmus, I believe, was one, for without him I could not have performed my part."

She watched him brush his fingers through his hair, pulling it back harshly from his face. He looked like a haunted man.

"But you, Tristam. You performed the ritual. Are you not one of them now? Are you not a mage, in fact?"

Tristam laughed, but joylessly. "By some miracle I survived—another came to my aid. . . . But I have not a thousandth the knowledge of a mage, nor do I have the least intention of exploring this *gift*. I saw the vision of the mages, Elorin. I know what they feared. I will take what I know to the grave. I swear. I will not be tempted."

"And the struggle between the viper and falcon. I saw it Tristam, saw you writhe upon the floor and cry out in strange tongues. It was a struggle inside of you, wasn't it? I sensed it."

Tristam covered his eyes for a moment, pressing the heels of his palms to his face as though he would keep something in. *"Yes,"* he whispered.

"The victory went to whom, Tristam?" she asked, afraid of the answer.

"There is no victory, only an uneasy peace. I have no words to explain it." He took his hands from his face and looked out over the sea. "I have been transformed, as though I aged half a century in one night, with all the unexpected changes that the years bring. I am not so different, and yet I am entirely changed. Do you see the waves crashing on the reef? They travel thousands of miles, and minute by minute they are transformed. The wave that dies here on the coral is the same wave that left the Archipelago so many leagues away, and yet it is unrecognizable. That is what has happened to me. I do not feel as though I have lost myself, only that I have changed, Elorin. Changed utterly."

Saying this he put his head on his knee and wept.

THIRTY-NINE

Although the sun in the phantom glade had indicated morning, it was afternoon in the world they returned to. They came out of a small wood up the ridge from the abbey and made their way across open pasture, then through the trees that surrounded the ruin.

Palace Guards were drawn up outside the abbey, looking tense and confused. Those who had supported the regents and those who supported the princess and the King were separated by open ground, watching each other warily.

As the countess and the others appeared, both groups fell silent, but no one moved to stop them from entering the abbey. Even before they found the others, they heard raised voices.

"I do not think my King will quickly recognize a regency led by Roderick Palle. Not after what I have seen," Count Massenet was saying.

Jaimy followed Kent and the countess into the chamber where the hearth stood and there found the others locked in heated argument.

"Where is the King?" Roderick said as soon as he saw the countess, as though he was not surprised to find her so changed. "Where is my prince, the rightful heir?"

The countess stopped and looked once around the group, giving a tight smile to Lady Galton. Then she turned her attention to Palle. "The King has passed through, as His Majesty chose to do. Prince Kori . . ." she looked sadly at Princess Joelle and the prince who stood by her side, "stumbled into the fire. He is gone, gone from this world."

"But you do not say the prince is dead," Palle said. "I demand you bring him back."

The countess stared at Palle as though he were a servant who had forgotten his place. "I regret to say that His Highness, Prince Kori is dead. I am sorry, Your Highness," she said to Princess Joelle, and then to the prince. "My heartfelt condolences, Your Majesty."

Others in the circle doffed hats and bowed to the prince, echoing the countess and her form of address.

"I will not accept it!" Palle shouted. "I demand this woman be taken before a court of law!"

"Have a care how you speak of Lady Chilton, Sir Roderick," the princess said, and then turned her attention to the countess and Kent. "We have been waiting anxiously for you. You have all returned unharmed?"

"Unharmed," the countess said, "if not unchanged."

But Roderick stepped forward, still not done, his usual demeanor subverted by anger. Jaimy thought the King's Man looked desperate at the thought that his power might slip away. "I might remind Your Highness that the countess murdered your husband."

"That is your claim, Roderick, but who here will support it but for your minions? Not I." She looked around the group, but none offered their support to Palle. He was alone, and realized it for the first time.

"Your Highness," Doctor Rawdon said. "Sir Averil is here. I think we should proceed."

Palle glared at Rawdon, not needing to speak the word: *"traitor."*

She nodded, then turned to Kent. "The King left a will with Sir Benjamin, with instructions that it was to be opened and read by you, Sir Averil."

Kent showed his surprise. "Me?"

"It seems you are the one His Majesty trusted."

Rawdon handed Kent a sealed envelope. "We have all examined the seal, Kent, but be sure of it yourself."

Kent located his spectacles and then turned the envelope over, finding a simple design pressed into sealing wax. "It is only the King's signet ring," he said, "not the Great Seal of Farrland."

Rawdon nodded. "His Majesty wrote the will in his own hand as we traveled. But it is witnessed, and properly so."

Kent broke the seal and opened the document. The writing was indeed that of the King, for it was a hand not soon forgotten; elongated and extremely old-fashioned. Jaimy watched the painter run his eye over the pages of the document. "But it is so brief!" he exclaimed. "Barely two pages. And who are these witnesses, Doctor? I don't know these names."

"The King's footmen, Sir Averil."

"Footmen!?" Palle exclaimed, for once speaking for everyone.

Kent shook his head. "His Majesty leaves all of his property and estate to his heir, Prince Wilam." Which surprised all present. Was this some mistake, Jaimy wondered or did the King have a premonition about Prince Kori's death.

Kent ran his finger down the page. "There are some special arrangements for servants and others—a house for Mr. Tumney, for instance. And His Majesty names the Duke of Blackwater to the Regency Council. Clearly he was not lucid," Kent said. "There is no council. It had been dissolved."

Palle looked at Wells, his face changing with the realization of what this might mean. "Was it dissolved in law?" he asked quickly.

The query was met with silence.

Palle's face suddenly lost its unaccustomed edge of desperation. "Then Sir Stedman and I are still Regents of Farrland." Then he looked over at Galton, who stood beside his wife, near to the Princess. "Though, perhaps, Sir Stedman will be returning to Farrow soon. . . ."

"No, Roderick," Galton said firmly. "Do not deceive yourself. Things have changed utterly. I shall stay for the course of the Regency. Two short years. If that is His Majesty's will?"

The prince looked over at Galton, his young face pale

with grief and shock. He nodded his assent, then turned to the duke. "And I would like to begin by having these two mysterious deaths in County Coombs investigated. Perhaps, Duke, you might take charge of this?"

The duke gave a small bow of acquiescence, and Palle fell silent.

"Then we can mourn our losses," the princess said softly, "and celebrate the new King."

"Long live King Wilam," an officer of the guard called out, and everyone present responded in kind, and then an echo came from beyond the walls as the message was relayed to the waiting guards. The prince glanced once at Alissa, standing near to Jaimy, and then he turned quickly away.

"I shall begin my reign by exonerating the Palace Guards of any wrongdoing, for all involved believed they supported the rightful government." Prince Wilam turned to the duke. "Do you agree, Duke? Sir Stedman?" And when each had nodded, he looked at Palle, who also nodded stiffly.

"But where is Trevelyan," Kent asked, suddenly aware that someone was missing.

"We have laid him here," the duke said, motioning through an archway.

Immediately Kent went through, and the others followed.

He found the body of Trevelyan lying on a window ledge beneath a deep crimson cover. It fluttered a little in the breeze. A fox darted out of a shadow, disappearing as the people approached, and the countess followed it with her eyes, almost starting to reach toward the beast.

"Look what ruin this seed brings," Kent said, his voice low and nearly breaking. He laid his hand on Trevelyan's breast. Jaimy had never seen Kent so affected. "One of the great minds of our time," he said, then turned to Palle, who hung back behind the others. "And what do you say now, Roderick? 'That he served his country well?' Have you brought enough evil among us?"

"You know me, Kent," Roderick said quickly. "My intentions were never to do harm. . . . I thought only of

Farrland. At all times I put my nation's interests above my own well-being."

Kent shook his head. "You believe what you say, that is the saddest part. Did Farrland ask you to bring our great Trevelyan to ruin? Did her people ask that you murder two innocent young men in County Coombs?"

"Kent," the princess cautioned, for the painter was making accusations that might never be proven.

Roderick did not look cowed by Kent's attack, nor did it seem that remorse touched him. Doubt, perhaps, crossed his mind—self-doubt—but it was not his way, and Roderick hardly knew what to do with such feelings. *Doubt?*

Wells tugged at Palle's sleeve, and though the former King's Man pulled his arm free, he reluctantly turned to follow, looking as though he felt he should not retreat—one should never retreat.

"We must be gone," the princess said. "We might make the next town before it is too late. And there is much to do elsewhere."

Carriages were drawn up, and the assorted parties began to climb aboard. Jaimy saw the prince turn and cast his gaze toward Alissa, almost in appeal, and then he nodded to both she and Jaimy, his face contorting as he attempted a smile. The carriage door swung closed, and the driver pulled away.

Alissa squeezed Jaimy's arm. "I am glad we are not going off alone," she said.

Jaimy turned and found her face very serious as she watched the carriage pass from view. "Yes," he said, squeezing her hand. "It is enough to one day be a duke—I am grateful I will never be a King. But at least I shall not be a duke alone." He turned and looked back at the ruined abbey. "I shall not soon forget what happened here."

Alissa smiled. "And I shall not soon forget the setting you chose to ask for my hand. Many claim that such a moment carries a little magic, but not so much as ours, I think."

SEA WITHOUT A SHORE

🐛 🐛 🐛

Tristam sat upon the bench Tobias Shuk had built for the pleasure of the duchess, and stared out over the bay toward the open sea. Stern and Osler were still examining the ship, as though during the twenty-four hours she was not under their command, something terrible had been done to her. The crew wandered about the deck, unable to keep their minds on their duties, for they had been witness to things that only happened in old tales, and their minds were not able to easily make peace with this.

Beacham roamed about the deck as aimlessly as any Jack, constantly distracted from his duties. Tristam kept noticing him staring off into the distance, though he knew that it was into his memory that Beacham stared.

I am little better off, myself, he thought. Pim came by to light the ship's lanterns as the sun disappeared, and Tristam thought that there was perhaps some truth to the old saw that the young were more resilient. Pim's step was light, and he sang quietly to himself as he passed, nodding to Tristam with a little bit of awe. The fact that the boy did not seem to be afraid of him was gratifying to Tristam. At least someone aboard could treat him as though he were not an object of fear and perhaps even horror. But they were now all polite in the extreme. Tristam had saved their lives, after all, and in the process had changed, becoming something they could not comprehend.

Stern came to inspect the shrouds of the mizzen mast, testing the tension of the lanyards, examining the dead–eyes. And then even Stern lost his focus, and stood for a moment like a man so aged that he had forgotten where he went, and why.

The captain turned slowly, noticed Tristam, and broke out in an embarrassed smile. "Ah, Mr. Flattery. She will carry us back," he pronounced, patting the rail. "I have no doubt of it, though we shall be desperately short of crew."

"I am at your disposal, Captain," Tristam said.

"And I shall have to take you up on your kind offer, Mr. Flattery. I think I shall have the duchess' maidservant standing tricks at the wheel before we are home." And then Stern's face became terribly serious, and a little of his usual confidence slipped away. "What you said last night ... about Gregory," his eyes narrowed. "Was it true?"

Tristam looked up at the face of poor Stern, a man whose illusions had suffered enough on this voyage. "No," Tristam said. "I hoped only to save the mutineers from what they would do. And save us as well. No, Captain Stern, it was a lie. I. . . . You may tell the crew it was a lie."

An islander had brought Tristam the dagger that morning, but Tristam did not think anyone knew.

Stern looked relieved, but still he stood there, something else on his mind. Something he did not quite know how to say. "Can you see a bit ahead, Mr. Flattery. Do you know what will become of us?"

Tristam shook his head. "I cannot, but even short of able seamen, I trust you will get us home, Captain Stern. I do not doubt it."

Wrinkles appeared at the corners of the captain's eyes, as though he tried to not grimace from some pain. "I was thinking of afterward, Mr. Flattery," he said, embarrassed by the admission.

Tristam realized what was meant. Poor Stern, he thought. "I have little influence myself, Captain Stern, but I shall certainly do everything I can on your behalf. I'm sure the duchess will do the same."

Stern nodded, not terribly reassured. He was certain that with all that had happened on the voyage—all the arcane occurrences—the Admiralty would want no word of it to get out. And with the King dead, as Tristam assured Stern he was, there would now be no recognition of his service from the palace. The mutiny would not be forgotten, though; he could count on that, at least. The already-stalled career of Josiah Stern did not look promising.

Osler sent a Jack from the bow to draw the captain's attention, and Stern went off to see to what he believed would be his last command. Stern, who had circled the globe with Gregory.

Jacel appeared to have been waiting in the companionway for the men to end their conversation, and she came quickly out now, curtsying to Tristam.

"I have some concern for the duchess," she said in Entonne.

"No one aboard is acting as you would expect, Jacel."

"But the duchess. . . . Well, it would be good for her to speak with someone, I think."

"You are suggesting me, I take it?" Tristam said.

She nodded.

"I will come along in a moment."

With a last look at the light dying across the bay, Tristam went below. He found the duchess sitting at the windows, staring out, apparently as unable to function as everyone else.

"I thought you might have a cup of tea left for a weary naturalist," Tristam said.

She looked up at him as though she had not registered the meaning of his words. "I think Jacel has some still hidden away. If it was not all consumed by mutineers."

Tristam took a seat near her, resting his elbow on the ledge of the open window. "You look lost in thought, Elorin." Terns called across the bay, diving desperately before the tropical day came to its abrupt end.

"Yes," she pulled at a loose thread on a cushion. "We will bury the mutineers at first light—bury them at sea that is—and I was thinking of Hobbes. I cannot help but feel pity for the man. Was he not driven to his actions by injustice? Was he not a victim of the greed in the Navy Board that sent him to sea in a rotten ship? And when he stood before us on the stair, did he not say many things that were true?—or at least partly so?"

"I thought he did, as well," Tristam said, surprised that 'fairness' was ever a concern of the duchess, who seemed much too self-interested. "One of the finest seamen in the navy, Stern called him, and he was ever kind to me when the Jacks were most hostile. I am not even sure that Llewellyn did not have something to do with the mutiny of Hobbes, though we shall never know now. It was a tragedy, the life of Mr. Hobbes, and I feel for him. But even so, he made his choices, and he was a man who would suffer the consequences. I don't think you saw, but in the end, when the islanders caught them on the stair, Hobbes went down last, as though he might shield his men from the stones.

"Odd, is it not? A mutineer. A man who would have faced hanging for his crime, yet he cared so for his Jacks that he let himself be battered to death by stones in a vain attempt to protect them. Not a simple man, our poor Hobbes, and I suspect that, at least in the eyes of the Jacks, his mutiny will not diminish him. There will be songs about him, and they will not be all lies."

The countess looked out the window again, thinking. "But perhaps he was only playing his part, as we all seem to have been on this voyage. Perhaps the mutiny of Hobbes was foreordained, just as the Duchess of Morland taking ship was fated—the duchess and her mad brother. . . ." she whispered. "I feel, Tristam, as though I have become lost among the endless reefs and islands of Oceana. Lost without charts or instruments. The King is dead, you tell me, so I no longer have a place at court. And what do I return to? Will the amusements of Avonel seem as bright now that I have sailed across the oceans and seen how people live on these beautiful islands?" she gestured out the window. "Will the splendor of the opera equal the beauties of a tropical lagoon in the day's last light? Will the theater even mimic the drama we have lived? I feel as though I have only recently come to life, for the first time since. . . . Well, for a very long time. And now I go back to my walking death in Avonel—the 'ghost duchess.' I will be dead soon enough, I have no desire to hurry it. And this. . . ." She raised her hands to her face and delicately traced her fingers down, across her lips and neck to her breasts. "My precious youth will be gone. Suitors will begin to seek me for my wealth." She almost wailed at the thought, and raised her hands to her face as though this were the greatest horror of all. "Have I wasted my years, do you think, Tristam? Will I squander the time that is left? The few years while I am still young? But how shall I use them wisely? If I renounce the games of courtiers, what shall I do? I cannot bear the thought that I will come to the end of my days and think I have wasted my short life. Wasted all that I was given. But what shall I do? How shall I choose to live my life, knowing what I know—having seen what I have seen—for the world of Farrland tolerates so very little.

"Think of poor Wallis. I do not blame him for what he did. What would he have returned to? The life of a little-known artist, struggling for recognition, for enough coins to rent a room in which he would not have even wanted to live." She stopped, as though suddenly realizing that Farrland was not her true home. She had no home. No place in which she could be herself and not cause whispers and odd looks of disapproval. "I have been transformed," she said quietly, as though it were both impossible to believe, and a tragedy of the greatest order—Elorin, the Duchess of Morland, could not be a victim of circumstances. Other people had things happen to them that were beyond their control, but not she. "And you, Tristam, have suffered this same fate—so much more than I. What will you do now?" She reached out and took his hand, and Tristam felt his breath catch—but she touched only his hand, not his heart.

He shrugged.

"But you can remain as you are, untouched by age, and Tristam, I could remain young as well. Could you not do that? We would, at least, have each other. And we could have love. Endless nights and years of love. I do not know what else remains, for it seems everything else has been taken from me. Everything but you. Could you not be happy with me?"

Tristam did not answer, but looked into her large, soft eyes, filled it seemed with desperation, and wondered what such a life would be. Filled with pleasure, no doubt, but desperate pleasure. He remembered his night at the duchess' home.

"I will not keep myself from aging. You saw the vision

of the war.... The arts must dissipate, disappear. I will not take such risks. I'm sorry, Elorin, but you must age as you will, though I do not think it will be so terrible for you. There is more to your beauty than smooth skin and lustrous hair, though you do not know it yet." Tristam looked out across the bay as the first stars began to appear. "But there is magic still. It is in the earth, and all the living things. I can feel it now, though perhaps I was aware of it before. That is the true magic and treasure of our world, Elorin. Greater than any work of man, magic enough for me, at least, if I can but learn to live simply in it. Perhaps I will try to take up residence on Farrow, and learn the art of growing grapes, perhaps even making wines. Though I do not know if I can live in the shadow of the Ruin. It has haunted me enough."

The duchess moved closer to him, nuzzling into the crook of his neck so that her hair tickled his face. "You are telling me that you will let me age, and become like every old crone?"

"Precisely."

"And my offer of endless pleasure does not tempt you at all?"

"More than I can say; but I shall engage all my will to resist."

"Small recompense." She was still for a moment. The darkness seemed to slip in and settle around them. "I do not know if I could live on Farrow," she said suddenly.

"Would an offer of nights of pleasure—though not endless—tempt you?"

"You know my particular weakness, Tristam," she whispered, "it is not fair." She pressed closer to him. "I cannot promise that I shall completely relent in my efforts to have you keep me young, if for no other reason than I do rather like getting my own way."

"I know." Quiet. Perhaps, far off, Tristam heard the call of an owl. "Elorin? I no longer know who I am. I ... I do not know if I am capable of happiness, of kindness even, let alone love."

"I make no promises either. We have been transformed, Tristam, suffered far more than a sea change. I do not know who we will become, but who else would even begin to understand what we have suffered?"

"Yes. Who, indeed."

❧ ❧ ❧

Tristam stood at the rail watching the distant shadows of dancers, as the Varuans began to celebrate the miracle of their King entering the Faraway Paradise without first passing through death in this life. And there was a new King as well—a boy of perhaps six years.

The night seemed very beautiful to him, almost imbued with enchantment. *It is inside me,* Tristam thought with some pleasure, *the night is no different.* At the same time he felt an ache. A sure knowledge that such beauty, and his experience of it, would be so brief.

There was a sound of some large fish in the water, or perhaps a dolphin.

"Tristam?" someone whispered from below.

"Faairi?" Tristam scrambled down the side of the ship into the yawl boat "Are you not afraid to be in the water at night? There are sharks and eels and barracuda."

"I am wearing a charm that protects me," she said.

Tristam felt her soft hands, dripping with water, take hold of his own. But she remained in the water. Starlight touched her, and he could just barely make her out, long hair floating on the surface of the water, and at the center of this darkness, her eyes. "I brought you a gift of parting, Tristam," she said, her voice sad. "Give to me your hand."

Tristam did as he was told, not having to ask which hand, and felt her fasten something over the scar on his wrist.

There, dangling from a woven leather thong, was a small carved head of stone. "It is a guardian," she said, "and will watch over you, keeping despair away. 'Despair,' is that right? The deepest sadness?"

"That is right."

"And it will help you in times of pain." She said nothing for a moment. "I thank you for finding my sister and guiding her back."

Tristam gripped her hand suddenly. "I have a message for Wallis. No. I know that he is alive. Tell him that if a Farr ship comes again they must never find out he is here. This is very important. Will you tell him?"

She pulled herself up so that she was half out of the water, and embraced him strongly. "Fare well, Tristam. May you find peace in your heart."

"And may you find peace in yours," Tristam whispered.

She slipped back into the water as though it were her natural element. It was all Tristam could do to release her hands.

"You need never worry for me," she said. "And if our child is a boy, I will name him Tristam."

Tristam was taken aback, and then realized it had been only days since they had had love—she could not know. "I think it is unlikely you shall bear a child of mine," he said.

"Oh, the Old Men do not agree. If she is a girl, I shall call her Elaural."

"Where did you hear that name?"

"When I was your star. I heard another, chanting a name: Elaural." She said something in Varuan that Tristam did not understand, and then set out for the shore. He stayed in the yawl boat a long time, hoping perhaps that she would come back, and even considering going after her, though he knew he should not. *I have done what I am to do here,* he thought. *The Varuans have no more need of me. Faairi has no more need of me.* He fingered the carving at his wrist, and the words of Averil Kent came back to him.

"*Isollae,*" he whispered to the night, but the night seemed not to hear.

FORTY

The survey vessel *Swallow* slipped into Avonel Harbor on a warm day near summer's end. It was early morning, just light, and the whitestone of the city seemed somehow faded and cool beneath the clinging vines and late flowers. Among the walls of stone and slate roofs, trees moved slowly in the breeze, some already burnishing to copper.

Tristam Flattery was aloft, furling sail with the topmen, but when the Jacks had finished their task and clambered down, eager to get ashore, Tristam remained, staring out over the city. He searched inside himself for a response to his return.

Is this a homecoming? he asked himself. But in truth, nothing inside of him said that it was.

"You are home," he whispered to see if the words would arouse the proper emotions, but they were only sounds, devoid of meaning.

Boats were being lifted clear of the deck and lowered over the side, but Tristam continued to sit in his aerie, staring out over the city. Below him on the deck even the Jacks were subdued, speaking in hushed tones. There was no laughter or song, no celebration of their arrival. It was a voyage all wished they had never made, and the events had left their mark on every memeber of the crew.

The young face of Pim appeared suddenly between the futtock shrouds. "Captain bids you come down, Mr. Flattery," the boy said with his usual exaggerated respect.

"Does he, indeed?" Tristam answered, making no move to comply with the captain's wishes.

"Yes, sir. There's been a signal from the tower," he said, pointing off toward a tall structure festooned with flags of various colors. "I don't know, Mr. Flattery, but it has the captain and Lieutenant Osler whispering, and looking none too happy."

"I'd better come down, then," Tristam said. He reached out and took hold of the backstay and slid down to the deck like a man with saltwater in his veins.

"We've been placed under quarantine, Mr. Flattery," Stern said quietly as Tristam arrived on the quarterdeck. The duchess stood nearby searching along the quay, then casting odd glances at Stern and Tristam. There was, Tristam realized, no one on the shore to meet her. Once the favorite of the King, now shunned. He thought she would slink below to hide her pain and humiliation. Tristam wanted to take her in his arms, but thought it would be little compensation. It was the admiration of the courtiers that she wanted, he was sure.

"We have no disease aboard," Tristam said, to Stern. "Is there some plague about that we know nothing of?"

He glanced around the harbor, and though there were ships of all nations he saw no quarantine flags flying, or any sign that men did not pass freely between shore and ship.

"A boat has put out toward us, captain," Osler said.

Beacham was standing by with a field glass, and examining the approaching cutter.

"It appears to be Admiral Gage, sir," he said, handing the glass to Stern.

"In a cutter? With no pennant flying?" Stern lifted the glass. "Flames! Prepare to pipe the admiral aboard." He looked around. "We are not ready for this," he said.

But before anything could be done, the cutter came alongside, and the old admiral clambered over the bulwark without even waiting for a proper boarding stair.

"No. No, stay your crew, Captain Burns," the admiral said, raising his hands. He bowed to the duchess, then looked around suddenly, aware of the men forming up on the deck. "This is not your entire crew, surely?" he said, turning to gaze at Stern as though to be sure he was the right man.

"All that's left," Stern said softly.

Gage looked around like a man disoriented. "But did you not have Hobbes aboard, and one of the King's physicians? And Viscount Elsworth?"

Stern nodded. "I have written a full report, Sir Jonathan."

"Well, don't deliver it to me," the admiral said, unable to hide his reaction. "Responsibility for the entire voyage has been taken from my hands. The palace will send a carriage for you at eight this evening. You, your officers and guests. No one else is to go ashore or have contact with anyone at all who is not a member of your crew. You'll shift your berth to the quarantine anchorage and fly the quarantine flag as well." He paused to look at Stern closely, obviously wanting to ask but knowing that he could not. "I don't know what in the world you've been up to, Burns, but you have the palace in a flap such as I have not seen since the last war. I hope you have done nothing that will reflect on the service...." It was almost a question, but not quite.

Stern did not respond. Not even the smallest shrug or shake of his head. "There's a bit of wind, Sir Jonathan," he said, "we should shift our berth while it holds. And Admiral? It's Stern. Lieutenant Stern."

Tristam was only halfheartedly working at packing his specimens. He had commandeered the 'tween decks mess and spread his hoard out there. Not so large a collection compared with other voyages, but not so small either. He sat on a stool and stared at the mementos of his journey—round the entire globe—having forgotten precisely what it was he had been doing.

"You look a bit distracted, my dear Tristam."

He looked up to find the duchess surveying the numerous vials and jars and boxes of skins and feathers and bones.

"Is it not utterly frustrating to be this close to the comforts of Avonel and forced to remain aboard?" she said. The duchess looked at Tristam, her gaze as penetrating as always.

"I seem to be in no hurry to go ashore," he said, a bit surprised by this statement.

The duchess' face softened suddenly, and she shook her head, coming to take a seat near him on a wooden box. "For almost four months we have had but one goal," she said, her manner earnest: "bring this great ship home with less than half a crew. That has taken up all of our energies both day and night. But we have been suspended between the things that occurred on Varua and our return to Farrland. During all this time, Tristam, we could both put off thinking about the future—what we would do when we reached Farrland. Who we would be. It has been like any journey, a respite, a time when no decisions need be made—as though time itself paused and would resume only when our feet touched the soil of Farrland. So we cling to this moment; or at least I do. Our cramped little *Swallow* suddenly seems a place of refuge, and I am loath to leave it, if you can believe that. My old life is past, Tristam, and I cannot imagine trying to build a new one. What effort it took to build the one I had!"

She took Tristam's hand. "So here we sit, among all your dead beetles and birds and dried leaves and plants, and we do not want the clock to begin measuring time again." She tried a weak smile. "But surely we will make some kind of life ashore, people such as ourselves. After all, we are not without resources."

"No, we will make some kind of life, I have no doubt of it," Tristam said. "I am just in mourning. Do you remember the boy who arrived in Avonel to answer the summons of the King?"

The duchess smiled at this memory.

"I am mourning his passing, I think," Tristam said, a bit self-consciously.

The duchess cocked her head to one side, regarding him with some affection, he thought. "We all grieve for the passing of our idealistic young selves, at some point or another. You are doing it sooner than most, and for good reason, but it is something we all must do." She paused for only a second, barely a hint of a smile appearing. "I have been doing it myself these last ten years or more."

> *"The frost lays its hand upon the bloom,*
> *For youth and beauty all must pass.*
> *Each child is lost and never found,*
> *And briefly wisdom's truce at last."*

Tristam tried to smile.

She leaned forward and kissed his cheek. "Wisdom's truce," she said, but no more.

❧   ❧   ❧

They were taken through a side gate to the palace and then in a small entrance. Ironically, this was the way that Roderick Palle had brought Tristam on his first trip to the palace. When they passed the spot where Tristam had first met the duchess, he looked over at her and saw that she remembered as well, which he found gratifying in some way.

As on that earlier trip, they were taken to the arboretum, though not to the place where *regis* grew. They passed through the transplanted jungle of Oceana, in single file, until they heard the sounds of water splashing into a pool. The smells of the place, and the sounds of the water tugged at Tristam's heart, and he remembered Faairi, and felt the languid tropical heat.

If only I could have done as Wallis did, Tristam found himself thinking.

They came out into the grotto and here they were greeted by familiar faces. Jaimy was there, with Alissa Somers—perhaps a Somers no more—the Duke of Blackwater, Averil Kent, Princess Joelle, Sir Stedman and Lady Galton, and Prince Wilam.

The Duke of Blackwater stood immediately. "King Wilam would like to bid you welcome, but first let me apologize for treating you so abysmally. Rumors are spreading of what happened at the abbey and on Varua, and the Farrellite Church as well as others are in a great panic. The nations around the Entide Sea fear that mages are among us again and that this power might be turned against them. We must have secrecy at all costs, as you will see when all has been told and all heard." He turned to the King, bowing, perhaps not realizing how surprised the *Swallow*'s officers and guests were to not find Prince Kori upon the throne.

Prince Wilam—King Wilam now—rose from his seat, smiling at the gathered voyagers. Tristam had only seen the young monarch once before, and he was surprised at what effect so few years had accomplished. Though he still had the youthful face of a scholar, his manner was that of one much older. Slower, more deliberate, more thoughtful of one's impact on the world around. "I am happy to see you returned safely," he began, "though saddened to hear of your losses. With all that could have befallen your ship and crew, Captain Stern, I am amazed that you were able to bring so many back, for you were sent off with so little knowledge of your voyage's true intent." He took three paces toward the pool, gathering his thoughts. "So much has happened in your absence. Much of it so extraordinary that if I had not been witness to the events myself, I would never have believed the reports of others." He shook his head as he said this, clearly not exaggerating. "But perhaps tonight we will make some sense of it, when all the stories have been recounted. There is a great deal that is still not clear to us." He looked over at Kent. "And Lady Chilton is not inclined to say more, for reasons of her own—which I feel we must respect." He paused, looking around the seated guests, holding each person's gaze for just a few seconds, and Tristam was touched by the warmth and concern in that look. "But I feel we must speak openly so that we might come to an understanding of what has happened, and form our future policy from knowledge not prejudice. We should speak of these matters, as well, for the peace of mind of those who have been involved, often against their will, in these strange matters." He gestured beyond the trees. "There will be a table set for all, but right now I think we are hungry for knowledge. Captain Stern, might I call upon you to begin, and others may add and fill in as needed? No, no. Sit. Be at your ease. It is a long tale, I imagine, and may need a glass of ale or two to help its telling."

Stern returned to his seat, more than a little self-conscious, and began his tale with being assigned the voyage of discovery, and the interview with Admiral Gage, the Sea Lord. By the time he had related the appearance of the falcon at sea, he had the full attention of his listeners.

It was, as the prince had guessed, a long tale, and occasionally it was interrupted by others. When Stern told of the Entonne ship, playing the part of a corsair, demanding Tristam be turned over to them, Kent was heard to curse the treachery of Count Massenet.

The escape into the Archipelago was overshadowed by the discovery of the Lost City, and here many questions were asked, and descriptions called for, astounding all those present. Tristam could see Jaimy looking at Alissa occasionally and raising his eyebrows in amazement, and the prince looked ready to take ship himself to see this wonder.

After this, servants brought food and drink to everyone, and Averil Kent, now the Earl of Sandhurst, took up the story, beginning with a letter from the Countess of Chilton, from whom he had not heard for many years. Tristam was surprised to learn that Kent had seen the locked room in Dandish's home where the plants had grown, and that he had suspected the death of Baron Ipsword had related to the baron's continual attacks on Dandish.

The duchess sat rigidly still during this, but Kent tactfully did not name the person Dandish had grown the seed for, nor did he describe in much detail the evening at the duchess' home when Tristam had set the rose aflame.

It was a complex story, with many players, and the

voyagers were as amazed by the revelations as the others had been by their exploits. The replica of the Ruin of Farrow in the cellar of Tremont Abbey was almost as much a surprise as the Lost City.

It was past the night's middle hour when the story was told and everyone sat in silence, still not quite able to believe that they had lived the story they had just heard, for it seemed too extraordinary to have involved real people.

A table was set there on the sand beside the speaking pool, and everyone found a place. Tristam beside Jaimy and Alissa, across from Kent and the duchess. Stern was seated to the King's left, and the princess to the right, and the captain was questioned carefully about all that he had said.

"You see now why all must be kept in confidence," the King said at one point. "And, Captain Stern, we must be absolutely sure your crew understand this, though I shall leave that to you and the duke to manage."

"But what was the purpose of this attack on our people in the Lost City?" the princess asked. She glanced at Tristam as she said this, but when he did not offer to answer, she looked quickly away.

"Like the Varuan King and Palle's group," Kent said, saving the moment, "this race in the Archipelago had some foreknowledge, and it was their hope to retrieve the arts that had been lost to them. That is what the countess believes. And they were part of the final ritual, adding their voices to our own, but Lady Chilton made sure their efforts bore no fruit. Sadly for these poor people, the knowledge was not regained. Sad for them, but better for the world at large, I think."

Tristam thought his uncle was unusually subdued, and there seemed to be some underlying sorrow in the Duke of Blackwater, though Tristam could not recognize its cause. He worried that it was the duchess, who had been so ill these past years. The man looked tired and deeply melancholy, though he struggled to be sure his manner and voice revealed none of this.

"Could you feel Trevelyan's presence, Duchess. Was he your counterpart here?" Kent asked.

She nodded, her manner solemn, and placed a hand on her heart. "I could. I felt his pain all through the ritual, and when his heart gave out, I knew his fear and then final resignation. At the last I felt him reach out toward death, as though he would embrace it and escape finally from life's suffering and sorrow. I felt him die, as though it were my own death, as indeed for a moment I thought it was." She looked very serious, as though it were her own death she spoke of. "I know now what that final moment is like; the utter horror one feels as the realization strikes, and then the resignation. It comes to us all—why struggle any more? And we slip our life off like a robe, and go into the darkness, like a swimmer diving into the sea." She shook her head, as though trying to forget what she had experienced, then looked up at the others. "It was peaceful for him in the end, almost his last thought was that he had been the great Trevelyan, and he was proud of that."

"As he should have been," Kent said in the silence that followed the duchess' words.

For a moment everyone turned to their food, but there was too much curiosity and the questions began again.

Jaimy wanted to know if Tristam had spoken to him during the ritual, and Tristam admitted that he had. The Phantom Glen was the subject of much speculation, as were the other worlds that they had seen.

Kent was questioned about these, hoping the countess had given him some insight. "I'm afraid I know little about this," the painter said. "The war between the forces of magic and the forces of reason—that seemed to be a vision, such as the mages were able to call up. The possible world we saw, filled with squares of light and astounding machines, and squalor and terrible crime. . . . I am not sure if that is a vision or another world, like the one entered by the King. 'A world near to ours, yet infinitely distant,' Lady Chilton said." He shrugged, gesturing with his hands to indicate it was speculation. He turned to Tristam. "But you saw the same visions, or very similar. Did you think them real?"

"I am no more sure than you, Lord Sandhurst. They

were real in the way that the future is real, or the past is real. We are separated from them utterly, but just because you cannot visit a land does not mean it does not exist. Two Kings chose to pass through the portal into one such world—the Faraway Paradise, the Varuans call it, so that, at least, seemed real. I could smell the flowers, and hear the sea. I saw Viscount Elsworth step into water, and I heard Ruau singing. But perhaps some of these worlds have substance in a different way." He smiled awkwardly. "Without the writings of the mages we cannot know. Perhaps even they did not know."

"Do you think then that the Varuan King sent Mr. Ruau here for that purpose?" the princess asked Tristam. "So the gate would be opened and they could pass from this life into this promised land?"

Tristam nodded. "That is what I think, though I don't believe that is the function all of this served. They were but players, performing their part, as were Mr. Ruau and the viscount. Somehow they were needed. They were almost sacrificial. But the countess knew that everything that had been planned by these others, whoever they really were, could be used to seal the way, though where she learned that part of the ritual I do not know. But I could hear it in my mind as though she spoke it to me, and together we were able to perform the rite. The rite that would avoid the war which would so gravely wound our world, as difficult as that is for us to imagine."

"Yes," the Duke of Blackwater said, "the world is so vast, and the strength and vigor of nature so ultimately powerful. Still . . . I do not doubt what was seen, nor what it meant."

Tristam was aware that people looked at him oddly, and when he met their eyes they would look away quickly—even Jaimy did this. And when Tristam spoke, other conversations would fall silent so that the speakers might listen. *They think I am a mage,* Tristam knew. *It is as though Eldrich had come to sit at their table.*

Tristam also noted that the new King did not look at Alissa unless she spoke, except once he glanced her way quickly, as though afraid he would be caught. There was another story there, Tristam was sure.

"May I make a toast to my cousin, Lord Jaimas, and his bride Lady Alissa?" Tristam asked suddenly, and his words produced smiles all around. "I know it is months late, but I could not be present at the wedding and missed my opportunity then." Tristam stood and raised his glass. "May life be kind, and friends loyal. Ventures profitable, children plentiful, and age like a slow turning of the leaves in autumn; grand, beautiful and tranquil."

Glasses were raised to the obviously happy couple and Tristam could not help but notice brief looks of pain on the face of the young King, and the Duchess of Morland.

Galton caught Tristam's eye. "I still do not understand how Llewellyn thought that he could attack you. Have I completely misunderstood things? Did you not perform a rite of warding?"

"I do not understand it myself, Sir Stedman," Tristam said, "nor was I aware of his attempt on my life."

"I think I have an answer there," Kent said. "The countess told me that, after the struggle with the emerging mage, there is a point in the ritual where the new mage can be slain. It was always thus, for some lost the struggle entire, and would have become something even the mages feared. But they had ways of knowing this at the time, and ways of dealing with it. This was in the text that Llewellyn and Wells had held back, even from some of their own people. They were afraid to show it to Sir Stedman or Dr. Rawdon—afraid they would alienate them—but I think they might have planned to use it all along to rid themselves of Tristam, once the portals were opened. This Jack who leaped onto the stage . . . He did not save just Tristam, I think."

The meal ended and the duke, as a member of the Council of Regents, swore everyone present to secrecy regarding certain aspects of the voyage, and a plausible story of the voyage was agreed upon by all present.

"I'm sure that word of this will get out to Massenet," Galton said, "even if we were to jail every Jack from the

Swallow for the rest of their natural lives. That cannot be helped, I'm afraid."

"Even more reason to send a ship back to this Lost City," the King said. "We must get there before the Entonne and make certain nothing remains that will lead them to these lost arts. Even with this portal sealed, it is yet possible that some of the arts might be recovered, perhaps not the power the mages once knew, but some part of it. No, we must send a ship to the Archipelago as early in the spring as we can manage to make contact with this secretive race, and to explore the Lost City." He turned to Stern. "Captain Stern, I would most like to see you in command of this voyage, if you can be ready for such an undertaking in so few months."

Stern nodded his head in deference. "I go where the Admiralty sends me, Your Majesty," the captain said evenly.

"And poorly they have rewarded you for it, Lieutenant," the duchess interjected. "Excuse me for bringing up this matter at such a time, Your Majesty, but an officer with such an exemplary career as Lieutenant Stern should have been made Post Captain long ago. The Admiralty have not repaid his service and loyalty in kind, that is certain."

Stern appeared mortified by the duchess' outburst, and the King turned to look at both Galton and the Duke of Blackwater, clearly irate. "It is a grave problem in the King's Navy," he said, as though he were not the king. "A man must have a patron to advance, no matter what his record of service. It shall be the ruin of Farrland, one day." He turned back to Stern. "But it shall be made up to you, Captain Stern. You shall have your post and more. In fact, you shall have a knighthood for your service to the crown, and the disservice you have suffered at the hands of my admirals."

Both Galton and the duke started forward as though they would protest, but a look from the young King stopped them. "A knighthood," he repeated. "And then the admirals can vie for your favor!" he said with more than a little glee. "The Sea Lord shall have you to dinner fortnightly, and the sons of peers will compete to serve under the great Stern, who sailed with Gregory!" The King exhibited a certain boyish delight at making waves in the Admiralty.

Galton glanced over at the duke and the two men smiled.

The duchess raised her glass, then motioned with it in the smallest way to Tristam; a toast to her still undiminished skills and timing, or so he thought.

The King rose at his place and lifted a glass. "And to you all for your efforts, those who journeyed to strange and distant lands, and those who entered the secret struggle here on our own shores. There will be rewards for all, and none shall be overlooked. Especially those who have crossed over—a saying that now has real meaning. The great Trevelyan, and even this poor officer, Hobbes, who was a victim of our corrupt service and the treachery of Dr. Llewellyn, I suspect. This mutineer Kreel who lost his life to save Mr. Flattery might have a family. All will be remembered. And some I have asked to name their reward must speak soon or I shall have to decide on my own." He looked pointedly at the Duke of Blackwater who would not meet his young sovereign's gaze.

"We must remember, Your Majesty," Stedman Galton said, "that if we are to keep so much secret, conspicuous rewards that cannot be justified in other ways will only start people asking questions."

The young King nodded, breaking into a smile. "Much can be attributed to the capriciousness of a young king, though I take your point, Sir Stedman."

The King retired then, asking for private audiences with a few of those present. Tristam went to him first.

The King had taken a seat in a glade filled with the flowers of Varua, and Tristam stood before him. He thought Wilam looked a serious young man, perhaps a little strained by his new responsibilities, for it was clear he was not sitting back and allowing the Council of Regents to run his nation. Knowing at least two of the regents, Tristam was certain they were not trying to marginalize this young ruler, but train him in his duties, and involve him in the running of his nation.

"I have been assured by your uncle, the duke," the King began, "that you will swear never to use these powers you have gained. Lady Chilton has said that the use of magic sustains it somehow, that it always remains a danger while even one practitioner lives. I do not know how the duke can presume to speak for you, Mr. Flattery, so I should like to hear what you have to say for yourself."

Tristam knew this moment would come, but he had long since made his decision. "Lady Chilton and the duke both spoke the truth. The arts cannot be practiced or all we have accomplished will be endangered. I will swear never to use these powers, and not to pass them on to another."

The young sovereign stared up at Tristam, his gaze filled with questions. "I know what price you will pay for this, Mr. Flattery," he said, "but I think it will ask even more of your uncle, the duke, and his fair wife. He had hoped to cure the duchess with the seed, for she lies wasting away from some mysterious ailment that no physician can even name, let alone cure. That is the price they will pay to see that the arts are not reborn, and I am deeply sorry for it."

Tristam nodded. He should have realized. Perhaps Llewellyn's story about Rawdon curing his wife had not been fabrication.

"Have you seed in your possession still?" the King asked.

"Some small amount that Dr. Llewellyn had. I have almost weaned myself of it now, though I am not quite done."

The King bit his lip for a second. "Well, keep it safe, Mr. Flattery. Let none of it escape, or it might find some way to propagate even at these latitudes. This seed is unnatural and strange; almost 'aware,' our own gardener claims."

"I will be sure it falls into no one's hands, sir," Tristam said, reminded of old Tumney by the King's words, and the day he had come to the palace for the first time. "No one has bothered to explain what happened to Sir Roderick Palle?"

The King blew out a long breath, looking down at the ground. "We have his man Hawksmoor and some others in prison, as we speak, but none will incriminate their master. He is, if you can believe it, still a Regent, clinging to power with a tenacity that can hardly be believed. And on top of that he has made himself enormously useful. The man has a cunning that one cannot help but admire—even if there is little else admirable about him. But it will not profit him in the end. The regency will end too soon, and I will not have forgotten what he did. Lord Jaimas told me the tale of how he and his companion were hunted up and down the length of County Coombs. Palle may not have ordered it, and I suspect he did not, but his flexible morality and ability to look away at just the right moment fostered it. I will see him end his life in such obscurity that he will begin to wonder if he was ever actually the King's Man at all." He looked up, impressing Tristam with his resolve. Palle's tenacity had met its match, Tristam thought.

The young King's gaze softened then. "And what can an inexperienced King do for you Mr. Flattery, for we are all in your debt—those who know what went on and the thousands who will never know? Few could resist what you will swear to renounce: long life, vitality, power, knowledge. I am not so sure I could deny myself these so easily."

"I saw the vision of the mages, Your Majesty. I am not so far removed from other men that I could allow that, nor could I allow the world to be brought to ruin. We have all given up something, sir," Tristam said, thinking of the look the King had given Alissa. "I deserve no more than any other."

"But what will you do now? Where does a near-mage make his life? You will suffer from want of this seed, I know. I saw what it did to my grandfather. It will be a torment, even to you. Is there nothing at all that I might do?"

"There is one thing," Tristam said, having already considered this possibility.

"Name it."

"I know this will be difficult because of the feelings of Princess Joelle, but if Your Majesty could bring the Duchess of Morland into the life of the court, I would be grateful."

The King looked up at him, a little surprised by this request. "I will do it if that is what you truly want."

Tristam nodded, suddenly unable to speak.

The King gazed at him a moment, eyes narrowing, perhaps feeling that this gesture bound them together. "The King left an envelope for the Duchess of Morland. I don't know what it contains, but Galton will give it to her. His Majesty cared for her, I know, and in her turn the Duchess protected him and brought him no small measure of joy—the daughter he never had, I think. I will do as you ask, for you and for the sake of my late grandfather. The princess will simply have to accept it. There is nothing I might do for Tristam Flattery?"

"Nothing, but I thank you for granting my request."

Tristam stood there, unable to retire until he had been given leave, but feeling the interview was over.

"This talisman on your wrist, Mr. Flattery . . . what is it?"

"It was given to me by the Varuans, to help me in times of pain."

The King took a long breath, absorbing the statement. "And does it?" he asked softly.

Tristam shrugged. "Perhaps."

The King considered for a moment, his young face so very serious. "Good fortune to you, Mr. Flattery," he said. "Call upon me if ever you have a need. You have not asked nearly enough of me and I will not forget it."

Alissa had retired to bed, leaving Jaimy and Tristam alone in the library of the newlyweds' Avonel home. It was near to morning. Tristam could hear the carriages of tradesmen passing already, though the light was still two hours off.

"I hope you will stay with us a while," Jaimy said, "though I'm sure you are anxious to see your home in Locfal again, after all that has happened. Though I will tell you, I wish you would find a place in Avonel so that you won't be so far away. After all, you might be an uncle one day, and one cannot perform one's avuncular duties from such a distance."

Tristam smiled. "I do want to make a trip to Locfal, though I am of a mind to spend the winter months on Farrow, perhaps even longer." Tristam could see Jaimy's disappointment at this news.

"Will you take after Uncle Erasmus and withdraw from friends and family? Become the recluse of our generation?"

"I find it difficult to be in society now, J. Oh, I do not include yourself or your bride in that, of course, but I am not as I once was, and the company of others seems only to succeed in making me feel even more odd, more isolated. I need to get away. I need to come to grips with what has happened, and with what I have become. And I need to rest. Perhaps it is a result of weaning myself from the seed, but I seem to be in desperate need of rest, of sleep, of time to contemplate. The duke has promised to give me Erasmus' journals and papers, and I would like to sit on the terrace, gaze out over the shoreless sea, and read. It is a chance to get to know this man who was my guardian, for he always kept himself a stranger."

"So I cannot manage a match for you with one of Alissa's sisters and convince you to buy a home nearby?" Jaimy said, a bit resignedly.

Tristam reached out and touched his cousin's arm. "There is nothing I would like more, but I'm not fit to be a husband to a young woman raised in the lovely world of Merton. I am haunted, Jaimas. I cannot begin to explain, but I am haunted. . . . I have not the words," he said, closing his eyes wearily.

Jaimy nodded, his look infinitely sad. "The countess told me that she was young in her form but ancient in her heart. I suspect this has happened to you, Tristam, and if there is anything at all that I can do to help, just tell me and I will do it."

Tristam was struck by what the countess had said, and touched by his cousin's concern. "You brought me into the fold when we attended Merton, Jaimy. Made me one of the gang. I would have been miserable there without you. But I don't think you can do that now. The problem is different. I knew immediately what the countess meant. In some inexplicable way, I feel ancient." Tristam shook his head, desperately wishing he could make his cousin understand, so that he might understand himself.

"I worry about you going off to Farrow, Tristam. I. . . ." He considered his next words. Tristam saw the skin around his eyes tighten, as though there were tears not far off. "I worry that you will slip into melancholia, and I will not know, for I am so far away."

"You need not worry, Jaimy. I think I will be all right. I don't think I am destined to follow my father's course. And I will write. There is monthly mail, even in winter. I will visit, I promise. And you might even visit me, and see the famous ruin."

Jaimy shook his head, almost a shudder. "I would be afraid to even glimpse it, Tristam. I have had enough of all that. I want to turn away from the visions I saw through the portal. I want to live in the world of the daylight and blue skies."

"And so do I, Jaimy," Tristam said softly. "And so do I."

Tristam sat alone in the library, unable to sleep. He clasped Faairi's talisman in his hand, rubbing it as though something might be absorbed through the skin—something that would dull pain.

"Tristam?"

He looked up to find Alissa standing in the doorway, wrapped in a warm robe, her hair in disarray.

"Can you not sleep?" she asked.

"I am not tired," he lied, and tried to smile. "This stone the countess gave you, Alissa; might I see it?"

She looked at him quizzically, clearly surprised by his

request. "Yes. Certainly." She half-turned in the door. "Shall I fetch it now?"

"Please."

A moment later she returned bearing a small silver box. She opened the clasp and took out a perfect stone, the size of which Tristam had never seen. He took it by the chain and held it up to the light, turning it slowly, and then he dropped it on his palm and closed his hand over it for a few seconds.

"You wore this during the ritual?" Tristam asked, and Alissa nodded. "And held it with which hand? May I see?"

She offered Tristam her hand, looking a little confused, but clearly showing her trust of him.

Tristam turned her hand over and seemed to stare at it, but then she realized that his eyes were pressed tightly closed. He released her hand, and sat back in his chair, his eyes opened but focused somewhere beyond the room. He still held the stone in his closed fist.

After a moment he looked up and smiled, opening his hand to reveal the glittering diamond. "This stone, Alissa, I am surprised the countess did not realize. It has some residue of the ritual in it still, for it was an instrument in what was done."

"You are saying it is magical?" Alissa asked, suddenly looking fully awake.

"More or less, yes. It has some residue of the power that was touched. Do you see? It will fade in time, I'm sure, but I can feel it strongly now. And your hand is the same, through to a lesser degree. You have some residue of the power there as well, though it will fade even more quickly. But while it lasts you will be able to perform some astonishing feats, I think."

"Such as?" Alissa said, raising her hand and looking at it.

"Has Jaimy not told you that I could flip a coin and have it land heads an impossible number of times?"

She nodded.

"Well, certainly you can do that, so you will be a terror at the gambling tables. But more important, you will be able to give people a blessing such as no priest of Farrelle ever managed."

"What are you saying?" she asked, suddenly a bit alarmed.

"Place your hand upon someone's brow and see what will happen in their lives. They will have good fortune in the extreme. And you will be able to heal. Oh, not terrible diseases, perhaps, but take away pain and heal minor hurts, I'm sure."

Alissa looked at him, suddenly wary, as though she wondered if he were practicing on her.

"I swear I am speaking true," Tristam said.

"Are you saying I might cure the duchess?"

Tristam shook his head. "No, you have not enough power or skill. But the diamond, Alissa. . . . Give it to the duchess. Have her wear it night and day, and I think you will see a difference. More than that perhaps."

"But Tristam, is this not dangerous? Did you not swear to never use the power you have gained?"

"I did, but I will not do it. This stone, its power cannot be taken away but by the arts. Perhaps the countess could do that, but she would have to use the arts. Do you see? The best thing is to let its power fade, as it will in time. But I think it will do no harm if it is kept safe around the neck of the duchess, for a while. Then have it delivered to me, and I will keep it safe. In a dozen years, perhaps, you shall have it back."

Tristam could see that the thought of a cure for the duchess brought Alissa close to tears. "But what of my hand? I cannot send that to you."

Tristam laughed. "No, but you shall do no ill, I'm certain. And it will fade soon. In a few months, I think. A year at the most. But tell no one, Alissa. Best even the duchess does not know. If word got out. . . ."

Alissa nodded, and touched her hand to her heart. "Do you know, Averil Kent once said he thought I had the power to heal in my hands. If he had only known."

"And perhaps he did. Never underestimate our good Kent," Tristam said offering the stone back to Alissa. She took it carefully, as though to drop it would be to condemn the duchess to a brief life of pain and suffering. Then she leaned forward, kissed Tristam on the cheek, and went silently out.

🥀 🥀 🥀

The stars were sinking beneath the surface of the morning sky when Kent arrived at the countess' Avonel home. She could not quite change the habit of the past decades and remained for the most part in seclusion within her own walls. Kent was not sure that would ever change— not within his lifetime anyway. But he stayed with her now most nights, and she accepted the occasional visitor.

Despite the hour Kent found the countess sitting on the terrace, a coffee serving on a small table at her side. She turned her face up to the growing light, as though the caress of the breeze gave her immeasurable pleasure. She had regained some of her youthful appearance since they had returned to Avonel, though as she slowly deprived herself of the physic, this was waning. He thought she had the appearance of a well preserved woman of perhaps sixty years. Her hair was very fine and pure white, lines drew a pattern across her once perfect skin, and her lips were bordered with the tiniest wrinkles. But Kent did not care, she was still beautiful to him. Just standing there looking at her he felt his heart swell. He was not sure what would become of them, but these last months he had felt a contentment like he had never known in all his life, and the countess seemed happier as well.

She smiled when she heard Kent arrive, but did not open her eyes. "Lord Sandhurst," she said, and the warmth and color in her voice caused a little surge of joy within him.

"Lady Chilton," he answered, equally formal.

"You have seen our voyagers?"

"Yes ... the few that returned," Kent said, his voice serious now.

She nodded, the look of pleasure disappearing. Her eyes opened, and she turned to Kent. "Come and sit by me," she said softly, "and tell me their tale." She poured coffee into a second cup as though she had been expecting his arrival, which she very likely had. Kent was quite sure she knew and could predict things in a way that was not natural.

"You spoke with Tristam Flattery?" she asked.

"Yes, and he seemed little changed. Oh, he has grown up a great deal and become more serious, if not a bit grim, but he did not seem utterly transformed as I expected." He looked over the countess, as though expecting an explanation.

She nodded. "Perhaps he has come through it better than I had hoped. And he swore never to use his new-gained knowledge?"

Kent nodded.

"I would like to meet this young man. Will you arrange that, Averil?"

"Gladly. And the Duchess of Morland would like to visit you as well."

"Good. I have a few words to say to her, too. Bring them both, but separately." She smiled at the painter and reached out and took his hand. "Do you need sleep? You have been up all night."

"No, I am surprisingly filled with energy these days." He saw the concern in her face, and it touched him. "Perhaps I will sleep a little later. But let me begin this tale, it is long and involved."

The countess settled back in her chair but did not release his hand. "Then let us begin, and then you shall sleep for a while and later this evening perhaps I would like to see the view from the high road to Brigham Head. Can one still walk there beneath the elms? It has not been spoiled?"

"No, there is a park there yet. Very pretty in the evening light." Kent sipped his coffee, and then began the tale as he had heard it from the voyagers. All the while he felt the warmth from the countess' hand in his, as though it gave him strength and more than that, happiness. As he spoke a small boy appeared in the shade of a tree, curling up against the bole to listen.

"Do you see, Kent?" the countess whispered, "he likes

you. Almost always he appears when you are here. And he takes food now when I leave it on the table, and does not always hide when I come into the garden. I have hope for him yet, poor thing. Imagine, lost in time, wandering in a dream all those years. How I want to learn how this happened, if the poor boy even knows. But your story first, my dear. And then we shall rest. Rest and take our leisure. We have no reason to hurry. No reason at all."

🥀 🥀 🥀

Autumn had come down off the northern hills and spread like a tide of copper and crimson and gold across the woods and meadows of Farrland. It flowed slowly, day by day, through gardens and along hedges until it came at last to the city of Avonel, where the reflections of the turning trees cast their dying colors on the waters of the harbor, where they looked like the wavering reflections of flames. And the tide turned and swept this fire silently out to sea.

Tristam stood at the rail of the mail ship, looking across the water to the city spread across the hill in the warm sunlight.

"I'm sure the duchess has been detained," Jaimy said, looking at his watch.

Tristam nodded. "Perhaps."

They stood in awkward silence, staring out toward the quay. An officer came up behind Tristam and cleared his throat quietly.

"The captain says we're going to lose the tide, sir," the man said.

Tristam nodded, then turned to Jaimy. "I guess you should be going, J," he said, masking all emotion in his voice.

Jaimy's look was filled with compassion. "You procured her a place at court," he said quietly. "I'm sure it's not that she doesn't have feelings for you. . . . But the duchess is a creature of the court, Tris, and well, Farrow. . . ." He did not finish.

Tristam nodded. "Your boat is about to leave."

Jaimy looked over the rail and then back at his cousin. "It seems so wrong, that you have sacrificed so much, and now I feel like you are going into exile. And going alone. But I cannot accompany you, Tristam."

"Your place is here, Jaimas. And don't forget, I have never had such a need for the company of others. My love to Alissa, and to you, J."

The two cousins embraced, and then Jaimy went quickly down the stair into the boat. He looked up at Tristam and tried to smile as they pulled away, and then took his place, and sat staring back at his cousin as the oarsmen pulled across the harbor.

Jacks began to labor at the capstan and the topmen scrambled aloft.

Tristam turned away as Jaimy's boat disappeared behind a ship. He looked out to sea, to the white clouds floating on the horizon, like clouds gathered above a distant island. He thought of Varua and Faairi, and closed his eyes, caressing her talisman between his fingers.

There was a shout from behind, and Tristam turned, searching for the source. Then he saw a boat making its way through the maze of ships, the oarsmen bent to their work. And there, among the Jacks, he saw the duchess. She raised a hand and waved, though not with enthusiasm.

She has come to bid me farewell, Tristam thought immediately. As the boat drew closer he was even more sure, for the duchess bore such a look of sadness—as though she were about to break his heart and did not know how to do it gently. A breeze caught a stray strand of her hair and it fluttered slowly in the wind and Tristam remembered the first time he had laid eyes on her. She had seemed so impossibly remote and beautiful to him then. But now he knew her face better than he did his own. Knew there was a tiny mole hidden in her hairline above her right ear. He could read her moods in her eyes and on her mouth. Knew that when she was truly joyous, her smile revealed too much of the upper gum— something she struggled never to do—but he loved to see it.

As the boat came alongside, he could see her perfect soft lips were pressed hard together, and she looked so filled with regret and unhappiness that Tristam thought his heart would break.

The duchess lifted up her skirts and came up the stair, watching every step so that Tristam could no longer see her face. When she reached the deck, she looked up and a smile that was forming dissolved.

"My dear Tristam, are you unwell?" she asked. "You look like a man lost in melancholia."

Tristam shrugged, not sure what to say.

She came up then and kissed his cheek, and took his arm, standing close beside him, and looking out at the city of Avonel. She sighed. "Well, have I passed your little test? Choosing you over the court?"

Tristam found her hand, and she squeezed his hand as though she were angry with him, but then this subsided and she caressed it gently. "I should never have doubted it," he said. "The countess predicted you would come."

"Did she?" the duchess said, genuinely interested. "She said something of it to me." She fell silent for a few seconds, lost in thought. "All she said to me, Tristam, was, 'be sure you have someone who can see past your beauty, otherwise you will find one day that you have become invisible.' You do care for me for what is in my mind and heart, don't you, Tristam?"

Tristam squeezed her hand. "Though your lovely lips and eyes have not lost their allure, to me at least."

The duchess was quiet again. The ship had begun to make way, heeling just slightly to the breeze, gathering way. "Did you see how she was with Kent?" the duchess asked suddenly. Tristam did not need to ask who "she" was.

"I saw."

"She does not expect to keep him with her for very long, does she?"

Tristam shook his head, thinking of how kind and generous Averil Kent was, and all that the artist had done in his years. "No," Tristam said, his voice almost a whisper. "I think we have seen the last painting from Averil Kent."

"Well, at least he shall have his heart's desire for a short time," the duchess said. "Not everyone can say that."

"Only a very few," Tristam said, squeezing her hand. He turned and met her gaze. For a second she seemed almost disoriented by the intensity of that look, but then her face lit in a mischievous smile.

"I must tell you, Tristam, the court is not what it once was. Everyone seems to possess half my years and a third of my wit." She shook her head. "It makes even Farrow sound enticing." But then, in the midst of her words, her mask of mocking good humor fell away, and she looked suddenly anguished. Tristam put his arm around her, and they did not speak for a while. When the duchess broke the silence, her voice was very small. "Do you remember setting out aboard the *Swallow?* You took your Fromme glass and showed me my home as we left the harbor?"

Tristam nodded.

"But where is my home now?" she whispered.

"I don't know," Tristam said, "but perhaps we will find it yet."

Jaimy appeared from behind a ship. He stood on the quay, and waved his hat, looking almost like a schoolboy at that distance.

Tristam lifted up his arm to wave in return, and a bird cried somewhere high overhead where it rose on a fair wind, at home among the clouds.